THE ATLAS COMPLEX

TOR BOOKS BY OLIVIE BLAKE

THE ATLAS SERIES
The Atlas Six
The Atlas Paradox
The Atlas Complex

Alone with You in the Ether
One for My Enemy
Masters of Death

THE
ATLAS
COMPLEX

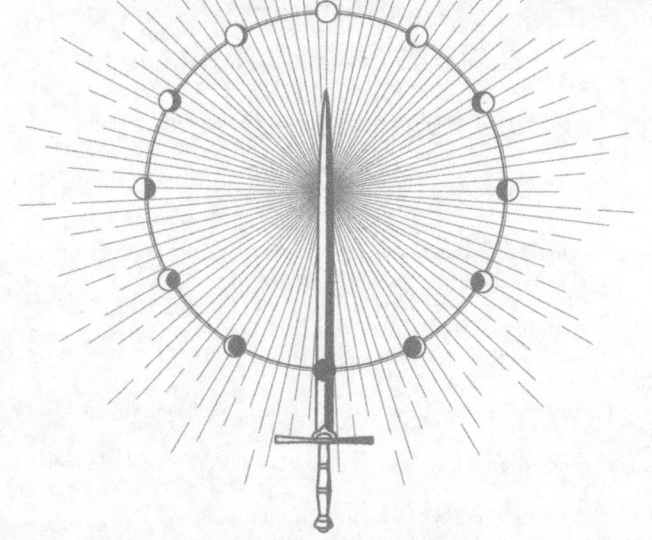

OLIVIE BLAKE

TOR
TOR PUBLISHING GROUP
NEW YORK

THE ATLAS COMPLEX

Copyright © 2023 by Alexene Farol Follmuth

Interior illustrations and endpaper art by Little Chmura

A Tor Book
Published by Tom Doherty Associates / Tor Publishing Group
120 Broadway
New York, NY 10271

www.tor-forge.com

Tor® is a registered trademark of Macmillan Publishing Group, LLC.

The Library of Congress Cataloging-in-Publication Data is available upon request.

ISBN 978-1-250-85513-8 (hardcover)
ISBN 978-1-250-33938-6 (signed)
ISBN 978-1-250-85515-2 (ebook)

Our books may be purchased in bulk for promotional, educational,
or business use. Please contact your local bookseller or the Macmillan Corporate
and Premium Sales Department at 1-800-221-7945, extension 5442,
or by email at MacmillanSpecialMarkets@macmillan.com.

First Edition: 2024

Printed in the United States of America

0 9 8 7 6 5 4 3 2 1

For Garrett, my muse.
Without you, none of this.

THE ATLAS COMPLEX

THE SIX

CAINE, TRISTAN

Tristan Caine is the son of Adrian Caine, head of a magical crime syndicate. Tristan would resent having his father as a point of introduction, but there is little Tristan does not resent. Born in London and educated at the London School of Magic, Tristan is a former venture capitalist for the Wessex Corporation, erstwhile protégé of billionaire James Wessex, as well as the estranged former fiancé of Eden Wessex. Trained in the school of illusion, Tristan's true specialty is physical; in addition to seeing through illusions, Tristan is a quantum physicist, meaning he can alter physical components on a quantum level (See also: *quantum theory*; *time*; *illusions—seeing through illusions*; *components—magical components*). Per the Alexandrian Society elimination terms, Tristan was tasked with killing Callum Nova. For reasons ostensibly related to his conscience, Tristan did not succeed. Whether this decision will come back to haunt him remains to be seen.

FERRER DE VARONA, NICOLÁS (may refer to DE VARONA, NICOLÁS or DE VARONA, NICO).

Nicolás Ferrer de Varona, commonly called Nico, was born in Havana, Cuba, and sent to the United States by his wealthy parents at an early age, where he would later graduate from the prestigious New York University of Magical Arts. Nico is uncommonly gifted as a physicist and possesses several capabilities outside his specialty (See also: *lithospheric proclivities*; *seismology—tectonics*; *shifting—human to animal*; *alchemy*; *draughts—alchemical*). Nico has a close friendship with fellow NYUMA graduates Gideon Drake and Maximilian Wolfe, and, despite a longstanding antagonism, an alliance with Elizabeth "Libby" Rhodes. Nico excels at hand-to-hand combat and is known to have died at least once (See also: *Alexandrian Archives—tracking*). His body is, while not entirely invulnerable, accustomed to the high demands of his personal survival.

KAMALI, PARISA

While much of Parisa Kamali's early life and true identity remains a matter of speculation, it is known that Parisa was born in Tehran, Iran, as the youngest of three siblings, and attended École Magique de Paris sometime after an estrangement from her husband, a marriage that took place under some duress in her teens. She is a telepath of great proficiency with a variety of known associations (See also: *Tristan Caine*; *Libby Rhodes*) and experiments (*time—mental chronometry*; *subconscious—dreams*; *Dalton Ellery*). In an astral plane simulation against another member of her cohort, Parisa stepped off the Society manor house roof to her demise, a decision that was either a tactical ploy or something more privately sinister (See also: *beauty, curse of—Callum Nova*).

MORI, REINA
Born in Tokyo, Japan, with astounding naturalism capabilities, Reina Mori is the illegitimate daughter of an unknown father and wealthy mortal mother. Her mother, who never claimed Reina as her own, was married before her early death to a man (referred to by Reina only as the Businessman) who made his fortune in medeian weapon technology (See also: *Wessex Corporation—perfect fusion patent, #31/298–396-May 1990*). Reina was raised in secret by her grandmother and attended the Osaka Institute of Magic, opting to study classics with a focus on mythology rather than pursuing a naturalist course of study. For Reina alone, the earth personally offers fruit, and to Reina alone, nature speaks. It is worth noting, though, that in Reina's opinion, she has other talents (See also: *mythology—generational*; *Anthropocene—divinity*).

NOVA, CALLUM
Callum Nova, of the South Africa–based Nova media conglomerate, is a billionaire manipulist whose powers extend to the metaphysical: that is, in layman's terms, an empath. Born in Cape Town, Callum studied very comfortably at the Hellenistic University in Athens before joining the family business in the profitable sale of medeian beauty products and illusions. Only one person on earth knows for sure what Callum actually looks like. Unfortunately for Callum, that person wanted him dead. Unfortunately for Tristan, he did not want it badly enough (See also: *betrayal, no fate so final as*). Atlas Blakely has previously condemned Callum's lack of inspiration, criticizing the ample power Callum has not made use of, but Callum has recently become very inspired (see also: *Reina Mori*).

RHODES, ELIZABETH (may refer to RHODES, LIBBY)
Elizabeth "Libby" Rhodes is a gifted physicist. Born in Pittsburgh, Pennsylvania, USA, Libby's early life was marked by the prolonged illness and eventual death of her older sister, Katherine. Libby attended the New York

University of Magical Arts, where she met her rival-turned-ally Nicolás "Nico" de Varona and her erstwhile boyfriend, Ezra Fowler. As a Society recruit, Libby conducted several notable experiments (See also: *time—fourth dimension*; *quantum theory—time*; *Tristan Caine*) and moral quandaries (*Parisa Kamali*; *Tristan Caine*) before disappearing, initially presumed by the remainder of her cohort to be deceased (*Ezra Fowler*). After discovering she had been deposited in the year 1989, Libby chose to harness the energy of a nuclear weapon to create a wormhole through time (See also: *Wessex Corporation—perfect fusion patent, #31/298–396-May 1990*), thus returning to her Alexandrian Society cohort with a prophetic warning.

FOR FURTHER READING

ALEXANDRIAN SOCIETY, THE
  Archives—lost knowledge
  Library (See also: *Alexandria*; *Babylon*; *Carthage*; *ancient libraries—
    Islamic*; *ancient libraries—Asian*)
  Rituals—initiation (See also: *magic—sacrifice*; *magic—death*)

BLAKELY, ATLAS
  Alexandrian Society, the (See also: *Alexandrian Society—initiates*;
    Alexandrian Society—Caretakers)
  Early life—London, England
  Telepathy

DRAKE, GIDEON
  Abilities—unknown (See also: *human mind—subconscious*)
  Creature—subspecies (See also: *taxonomy—creature*; *species—unknown*)
  Criminal affiliations (See also: *Eilif*)
  Early life—Cape Breton, Nova Scotia, Canada
  Education—New York University of Magical Arts
  Specialty—Traveler (See also: *dream realms—navigation*)

EILIF
  Alliances—unknown
  Children (See also: *Gideon Drake*)
  Creature—finfolk (See also: *taxonomy—creature*; *finfolk—mermaid*)

ELLERY, DALTON
  Alexandrian Society, the (See also: *Alexandrian Society—initiates*;
    Alexandrian Society—researchers)
  Animation
  Known affiliations (See also: *Parisa Kamali*)

FOWLER, EZRA
  Abilities (See also: *traveling—fourth dimension*; *physicist—quantum*)

Alexandrian Society, the (See also: *Alexandrian Society—uninitiated*; *Alexandrian Society—elimination*)
Early life—Los Angeles, CA
Education—New York University for Magical Arts
Known alliances (See also: *Atlas Blakely*)
Previous employment (See also: *NYUMA—resident advisors*)
Personal relationships (See also: *Libby Rhodes*)
Specialty—Traveler (See also: *time*)

HASSAN, SEF
Known alliances (See also: *Forum, the*; *Ezra Fowler*)
Specialty—Naturalist (mineral)

JIMÉNEZ, BELEN (may refer to ARAÑA, DR. J. BELEN)
Early life—Manila, Philippines
Education—Los Angeles Regional College of Medeian Arts
Known alliances (See also: *Forum, the*; *Nothazai*; *Ezra Fowler*)
Personal relationships (See also: *Libby Rhodes*)

LI
Identity (See also: *identity—unknown*)
Known alliances (See also: *Forum, the*; *Ezra Fowler*)

NOTHAZAI
Known alliances (See also: *Forum, the*)

PÉREZ, JULIAN RIVERA
Known alliances (See also: *Forum, the*; *Ezra Fowler*)
Specialty—Technomancer

PRINCE, THE
Animation—general
Identity (See also: *identity—unknown*)
Known affiliations (See also: *Ezra Fowler, Eilif*)

WESSEX, EDEN
Personal relationships (See also: *Tristan Caine*)
Known alliances (See also: *Wessex Corporation*)

WESSEX, JAMES
Known alliances (See also: *Forum, the*; *Ezra Fowler*)

A tlas Blakely was born as the earth was dying. This is a fact.

So is this: the first thing Atlas Blakely truly understood was pain. This, too: Atlas Blakely is a man who created weapons. A man who kept secrets.

And this: Atlas Blakely is a man willing to jeopardize the lives of everyone in his care, and to betray all those foolish or desperate enough to have the misfortune to trust him.

Atlas Blakely is a compendium of scars and flaws, a liar by trade and by birth. He is a man with the makings of a villain.

But above all else, Atlas Blakely is just a man.

· · ·

His story began where yours did. A little differently—no smarmy toff dolled up in tweed, no insufferable well-pressed suit—though it did begin with an invitation. This is the Alexandrian Society, after all, and everyone must be invited. Even Atlas.

Even you.

The invitation addressed to Atlas Blakely had developed a thin adhesive film from whatever misfortunate substance had been its neighbor, the invitation itself having been uneremoniously mislaid beside the bin in his mother's dilapidated flat. The monument to the misdeeds of an average Thursday (i.e., the bin and its rubbish contained within) lived inauspiciously above a square meter of scorched lino paneling and below a staggering tower of Nietzsche and de Beauvoir and Descartes. As usual, the refuse had mushroomed perilously from the constraints of the bin, old newspapers and takeaway containers and moldy, discarded turnip heads communing with untouched piles of literary journals, unfinished poetry, and a porcelain jar of paper napkins folded painstakingly into swans, so that beside it, a sticky square of posh ivory cardstock was almost entirely unnoticeable.

Almost, of course. But not quite.

Atlas Blakely, then twenty-three, plucked up the card from the floor between harrowing shifts at the local pub, a job for which he'd had to grovel despite his possession of a degree, two degrees, the potential for a third. He glanced at his name in elaborate calligraphic script and determined it had probably been carried there on the wings of a bottle. His mother would be asleep for several hours yet, so he pocketed it and stood, glancing up at the image of his father, or whatever the word was for the man whose portrait still sat upon the bookcase, gathering dust. About this or the other thing, he did not intend to ask.

Initially, the way that Atlas felt upon receipt of his Alexandrian summons could be put most plainly as repulsion. He was no stranger to medeians or academicians, being one of those himself and the progeny of the other, and knew by then to distrust both. He meant to throw it out, the card, only the adhesive of gin and what was probably the tamarind chutney his mother ordered by phone from the nearby Asian grocery ("It smells like Pa," his mother often said when she was lucid) soon glued it to the lining of Atlas's pocket.

His Alexandrian Caretaker, William Astor Huntington, was what Atlas would call overly fond of puzzles, to the severe detriment of things like sanity and time. It was later that evening, fiddling blindly with the card in his pocket—having just tossed out a man for the customary offense of having more whisky than sense—that Atlas determined the spellwork laced within its contents to be a cipher, which was likewise something he wouldn't have had the time or sanity for if not for being brutally wounded by love (or whatever it was that had mainly affected his penis) some twenty-four hours prior. In Atlas Blakely's later opinion, Huntington's scavenging methodology was a narcissistic faff. When it came to the Society, most people needed only five minutes to be convinced.

But that was later Atlas's opinion. At the time, Atlas was heartsick and overqualified. In the larger scheme of things, he was bored. He would come to understand over time that most people were bored, especially those in consideration for a place in the Society. It was a small, gentle cruelty of life that most people with a true sense of purpose lack the talent to achieve it. The people with talent are far more likely directionless, an odd but unavoidable irony. (In Atlas Blakely's experience, the best method for ruining someone's life is to give them exactly what they want and then politely get out of their way.)

The cipher led him to the toilet of a sixteenth-century chapel, which led him to the roof of a recently completed skyscraper, which led him to a field of sheep. Eventually he arrived at the Alexandrian Society's municipal quarters, an older version of the room in which he would later meet six of his own recruits—a forthcoming renovation which Atlas would not know until later was funded by someone who was not even in the Society, had never been initiated, had probably never killed someone, ever, which was very nice for the donor in question. Presumably they slept very well at night. But that is obviously not the point.

So what *is* the point? The point is a man, a genius named Dr. Blakely, had an affair with one of his first-year undergraduates in the late 1970s that resulted in a child. The point is there are inadequate resources for mental health. The point is schizophrenia is latent until it isn't, until it ripens and blooms, until you look down at the infant who ruined your life and understand both that you would willingly die for him and, also, that you will probably die for him whether the decision is left in your hands or not. The point is nobody will call it abuse because it is, by all accounts, consensual. The point is there is nothing to be done except to wonder if things might have been different had she not worn that skirt or looked at her professor that way. The point is a man's career is at stake, his livelihood, his family! The point is Atlas Blakely will be three years old when he first hears the voices in his own mother's head—the duality of her being, the way her genius splinters off somewhere, dovetailing into something darker than either of them understand. The point is the condom broke, or maybe there was no condom.

The point is there are no villains in this story, or maybe there are no heroes.

The point is: someone offers Atlas Blakely power and Atlas Blakely says, unequivocally, yes.

· · ·

He finds out later that another member of his recruitment cohort, Ezra Fowler, found his own cipher stuck to the bottom of his shoe. No fucking clue how it got there. Nearly threw it away, really didn't give a fuck, only didn't have any other plans, so, here we are.

Ivy Breton, NYUMA graduate who did a year at Madrid, finds hers inside an antique dollhouse, perched upon the replica of a Queen Anne chair that her great-aunt, a hobbyist, had varnished by hand.

Folade Ilori, Nigerian born, educated at Universitá Medeia, finds hers on the wing of a hummingbird in the vineyards of her uncle's estate.

Alexis Lai, from Hong Kong, educated at the National University of Magic in Singapore, finds hers tucked neatly into the excavated bones of what her team believed to be a Neolithic skeleton in Portugal. (It wasn't, but that was another darkness, for another time.)

Neel Mishra, the other Brit, who is actually Indian, finds his cipher in his telescope—*literally* written in the stars.

And then there's Atlas with the bins and Ezra with his shoe. They were destined to lock eyes, recognize the immensity of this revelation, and follow it up with some weed.

After Alexis dies and Atlas thinks a somberer version of well, fuck, better get on with it, he learns exactly how they were each selected. (This happens after Atlas discovers the existence of Dalton Ellery but before his Caretaker, Huntington, makes the "spontaneous" decision to retire.) Apparently, the Society can track the magical output of any person in the world. That's it. That's their main consideration and it's . . . underwhelming. Almost frustratingly simple. They look for whoever is doing a fuckton of magic and determine whether that magic comes with a price that someone else has already paid, and if not they say oi!, that looks promising. It's a little more refined than that, but that's the gist of it.

(This is not the long version of the story, because you're not interested in the long version. You already know what Atlas is, or have some idea of what's going on with him. You know this story doesn't end well. It's written on the wall—which, to be fair, means Atlas can see it, too. He's not an idiot. He's just pretty much fucked any way you look at it.)

The point is Ezra Fowler is really, really magical. So is anyone who steps through that door, but by the standards of pure output, Ezra tops the list.

"I can open wormholes," Ezra explains one night over indecency and small talk. (It takes him much longer to discuss the event that awoke his particular magical specialty, i.e., his mother's murder in what would later be called a hate crime, as if treating a virus as a coalition of separate, unrelated symptoms could possibly derive a cure.) "Little ones, but still."

"How little?" asks Atlas.

"Me-sized."

"Oh, I thought this was a shrinking down situation," Atlas exhales. "You know. Some *Alice in Wonderland* shit or something."

"No," Ezra says, "they're pretty normal sized. Like, if wormholes were normal."

"How do you know they're wormholes?"

"I don't know what else they'd be."

"Cool, cool." Drugs made this conversation easier. Then again, drugs made all of Atlas's conversations easier. It's actually kind of impossible to explain this to anyone, but hearing people's inner thoughts makes relationships approximately one million times harder. Atlas is an overthinker. He was a careful child, careful to conceal his origins, his bruises, his flat, his malnourishment, his expert forgery of his mother's signature, careful, so careful, quiet and unobtrusive, but . . . is he *too* quiet?, should we be worried?, should we speak to his parents?, no no, he's a pleasure to have in class, he's so helpful, perhaps he was just shy, is he *too* charming?, is it even natural to be *this charming* at five years old, six, seveneightnine?, he's just so well-behaved for his age, so mature, so worldly, doesn't ever act out, do we wonder . . . ?, should we see if . . . ? Ah, spoke too soon, there we go, a rebellious streak right on cue, a flaw, thank goodness.

Thank goodness. He's a normal child after all.

"What?" says Atlas, realizing that Ezra is still speaking.

"I've never told anyone that before. About the doors." He's staring at the bookcase in the painted room, at the layout that Future Atlas does not rearrange.

"Doors?" Atlas echoes meaninglessly.

"I call them doors," Ezra says.

In general, Atlas knows doors. Knows not to open them. Some doors are closed for a reason. "Where do your doors go?"

"Past. Future." Ezra picks at a flake of dry skin on his cuticle. "Wherever."

"Can you take anyone with you?" Atlas says, thinking: *I just want to see. I just want to see what happens.* (Does he ever get his comeuppance? Does she ever get well?) *I just want to know.* But he knows he wants it too much to ask it out loud, because Ezra's brain throws up a red flag that only Atlas is privy to. "I'm just curious," he clarifies through a smoke ring. "I've never heard of anyone who can make their own fucking wormholes."

Silence.

"You can read minds," comments Ezra after a moment, which is both an observation and a warning.

Atlas doesn't bother confirming this, since it's not technically true. Reading is very elementary and minds are illegible as a rule. He does something else with minds, something more complex than people understand, more invasive than people can empathize with. As a matter of self-preservation, Atlas leaves out the details. Still, there's a reason that if he wants someone to like him, they generally do, because meeting Atlas Blakely is a little like debugging your own personal code. Or it can be if you let it.

(One day, years later, after Neel has died several times but Folade only twice, when they're deciding whether or not to leave Ivy in her grave—if, perhaps, that might temporarily leave the archives satisfied . . . ?—Alexis will tell Atlas that she likes it, the mind reading. She not only doesn't mind it, she actively thinks it's ideal. They can go days without speaking to each other, which is perfect. She doesn't like to talk. In her words, children who see dead people don't like to talk. It's a thing, she assures him. Atlas asks if they have a support group, you know, for the children who see dead people who are now really, really quiet adults, and she laughs and flicks some bubbles at him from the bath. Stop talking, she says, and holds out a hand for him. He says okay and gets in.)

"What's it like?" Ezra says.

Atlas blows another perfect smoke ring and smiles the stupid smile of the truly overindulged. Somewhere else, for the first time in his life, his mother is doing something he has no idea about. He hasn't checked in. Doesn't plan to. Inevitably will, though, because that is the way of things. The tide always returns. "What, mind reading?"

"Knowing what to say," Ezra corrects him.

"Fucked," Atlas replies.

Intuitively, they both understand. Reading the mind of a person you cannot change is as powerless as time-traveling to an ending you can't rewrite.

·   ·   ·

The moral of the story is this: beware the man who faces you unarmed. But the moral of the story is also this: beware the shared moments of vulnerability between two grown men whose mothers are lost and gone. Whatever is forged between Ezra and Atlas, it is the foundation for everything rotten that follows. It's the landscape for every catastrophe that blooms. Call it an origin story, a superposition. A second chance at something like life, which is of course the beginning of the end, because existence is largely futile.

Which isn't to say the others in their Society cohort are unpleasant. Folade, Ade when she's feeling cheeky, is the oldest and she doesn't actually give a fuck about any of them, which is, honestly, fair. She fancies herself a poet, is deeply superstitious and the only one of them that's also religious, which isn't odd so much as impressive, because it means she gets moments of peace that the rest of them don't. She's a physicist, an atomist—the best Atlas has ever seen until he meets Nico de Varona and Libby Rhodes. Ivy is a sunny little rich girl who happens to be a viral biomancer capable of enacting mass extinction in something like five, six days. (Later, Atlas will think, oh. She's the one we should have killed. Which he does, in a way. But not the way he should have done it, or any way capable of meaningful change.)

Neel is the youngest, chipper and mouthy and deeply twenty-one. He was at the London school with Atlas, though they never spoke because Neel was busy with the stars and Atlas was busy cleaning vomit off his mum or covertly dismantling her thoughts. (There's a lot of physical junk in his mother's life too, not just the dregs of her psyche. At first Atlas tries rearranging things in her head, reassigning her anxieties about the unknown, because a well-organized mind seems moderately more helpful for a sanitized home, or possibly he has that backward. One such attempt successfully clears the produce drawer of unidentifiable nightmare rot for a week but then only makes it worse, makes the paranoia sharper—as if she can tell somehow that there's been a robber, that someone else has been inside. For half a second, things get so bad that Atlas thinks the end is nearer. But it isn't. And he's glad about that. But also, he's absolutely fucked.) Neel is a divinist and he's always saying things like don't touch the strawberries today, Blakely, they're off. It's annoying, but Atlas knows—can see very clearly—that Neel means it, that he's never had an impure thought in his life, except for maybe one or two about Ivy. Who is very pretty. Even if she is a walking harbinger of death.

Then there's Alexis. She's twenty-eight and fed up with the living.

"She scares me," Ezra admits over midnight shepherd's pie.

"Yeah," Atlas agrees and means it.

(Later, Alexis will hold his hand right before she goes and say that it isn't his fault even though it is, which Atlas will know because in her head she's thinking you absolute moron, you stupid little prick. There's no weight to it because Alexis really isn't one to dwell on things overlong, and aloud she'll say just don't waste it, Blakely, okay? You made your bed, fine, it is what it is, for fuck's sake just don't waste it. But he will, of course. Of course he will.)

"Is it just the necromancy thing? The bones?" Ezra is staring into space. "Are bones creepy? Tell me the truth."

"Souls are creepier than bones," Atlas confides. "Ghosts." He shudders.

"Do ghosts have thoughts?" Ezra asks, words slightly slurred with effort.

"Yes," Atlas confirms.

They're not that common, ghosts. Most things die and stay dead.

(For example, Alexis does.)

"What do they think about?" Ezra presses him.

"One thing usually. Over and over." Obsessive-compulsive disorder, that's one of the first diagnoses Atlas gets when he tries to see if someone can fix him. It's almost certainly wrong, he thinks. He understands that he's on the spectrum somewhere, everyone is—that's the point of a spectrum—but compulsion? That doesn't sound right. "The ones who stick around this world are usually in it for something specific."

"Yeah?" Ezra says. "Like what?"

Atlas chews on the corner of his thumb. His mother has seventeen bottles of the same hand cream and suddenly he wishes, desperately wishes, that he had some. For half a second he thinks he should go home.

It passes. He breathes out.

"Who cares what the dead want?" Atlas says.

He isn't stupid. If he were to die, he knows he'd stay gone.

· · ·

The Society doesn't usually choose its Caretaker from within. You don't know this yet because you haven't gotten to this point, but actually, the Society isn't operated by its own initiates at all. Its initiated members are too valuable, they're busy, and anyway, imagine the fucking cruelty of having killed someone, living with that, while you take an office job and man the phones. No, the Society is operated almost entirely by completely normal people who undergo completely normal job interviews and have completely normal CVs. They have access to almost nothing of consequence, so it really doesn't matter what they know.

William Astor Huntington was a classics professor at NYUMA before getting tapped for Caretaker. When the Society's council, which *is* made up of initiates, probed at Huntington's unconventional and slightly worrying choice of successor, they each heard a faint, insistent buzzing sound in their ears. It was distracting enough—and Atlas Blakely's smile so dazzling, his record so pristine—that they voted unanimously to end the meeting early and go home.

All of which is to say that Atlas being here, in this office, in this position, was no easy feat. Not that you have to admire him for that, but if you wanted to, you could. Caretaker is a political position and he politicked well, politicked beautifully, having had the entirety of his life for practice. Could you argue that Atlas Blakely has never let an honest word pass his lips? You could. Nobody would stop you, least of all him.

Anyway, of his cohort, Atlas is the first to realize the Society's initiation requirements. Their researcher is a Society initiate who can't stop thinking about it. An antique gun, close range, the trigger pull that goes off before he's ready, oh fuck oh fuck hands shaking, pull again, this time it's bad but not lethal, fuckfuckfuck you idiot, *someone help me*—

In the end it had taken four of them to get it done. Atlas, bearing witness to the memories secondhand, is like, holy fuck. Thanks but no thanks.

"But the books, though," argues Ezra. Atlas was already packing his things when Ezra came into his room, pestering him or perhaps merely reminding him. The skin of Atlas's hands was dry and he hadn't heard a word from the pub owner downstairs who was supposed to ring him if anything went wrong, but maybe the wards didn't allow for calls from neighbors . . . ? The house wanted him to kill someone, so honestly, who could say whether the phones worked or not.

"The damn books," Ezra sighed profoundly.

We haven't discussed yet how much Atlas loves books. How books saved his life. Not at *this* point in his life, because this was well on the road to ruin. But earlier. Books saved him.

(What he hadn't realized was that a *person* had saved him, because *people, they* wrote the books, the books themselves were just the tethers, the lifelines that dragged him back. But at the time he'd been working in a lousy pub and he thought he hated people. Which he did. Which everyone does from time to time. So anyway, this was a brief but critical error.)

At a time when Atlas was coming of age and learning how difficult his life was going to be—clinically speaking, these would be the spells of worthlessness and emptiness, the dull rage with its fuzzy, indiscriminate lack of concentration, the sharp spikes in antisocial activity, all the isolation and self-sabotage—Atlas was fortunate, at least, to be trapped in a palace of intellectual hoardery, surrounded by piles and piles of books that had once been formative to his mother's crumbling mind. He had only truly known her there, in the lines and passages she had underlined or dog-eared. The books were his only way of coming to know her as a person of bitter, prodigious craving, a woman who had expected to be eaten alive by love, who wanted desperately, more than anything, to be seen. The books where she still kept a letter, a note that proved it was never just in her mind—the labyrinthine place her mind would become—the convenient excuse for a man to one day decide his affair had been nothing more than her solitary delusion. The books she had taken comfort in, before and after her life had been cleaved in two by the birth of an unwanted son.

"You shouldn't have bothered," Atlas muttered to his mother once, thinking how it's a trap, really. The whole thing. Hitting go on an invisible timer for an ending you don't get to see. You don't know how it ends, so you just . . . you *do* and you *try* and inevitably you fail, invariably you suffer, and for what? Better she had stayed there, in school, where maybe her genius might have had somewhere to grow, some container to fill, something to become. Better that than this, him wiping drool from her cheek, her eyes listless and dark when they meet his.

"When an ecosystem dies, nature makes a new one," she said, which might have meant nothing. Maybe nothing at all.

Atlas didn't hear her at first. He said what, so she said it again, "When an ecosystem dies, nature makes a new one," and he thought what the absolute fuck are you on about, but then it came back to him later in that critical moment, the moment where he can't decide whose idea it really was. Ezra's, maybe, or maybe Atlas put it there. Maybe it had been both of them.

When an ecosystem dies, nature makes a new one. Don't you get it? The world doesn't end. Only we do.

But maybe . . . maybe we could be bigger than that. Maybe that's what she meant. Maybe we are meant to be bigger than that.

(Slowly, Atlas becomes sure. Yes, that must be what she meant.)

It doesn't matter where it started. Doesn't matter where it ends. We're part of the cycle whether we like it or not, so don't be the wasteland.

Be the locusts. Be the plague.

"Let's be gods," Atlas says aloud, and it's important to remember that he's on drugs, that he misses his mother, that he hates himself. It's critical to recall that at this very moment in time, Atlas Blakely is a scared, sad, lonely little speck of a being, a freckle on the arse of humanity's latest impending doom. Atlas Blakely doesn't care if he makes it to tomorrow, or tomorrow, or tomorrow. He doesn't care if he gets struck by lightning, dies tonight. Atlas Blakely is a neurotic, desperate-for-meaning twenty-something-year-old (twenty-five, then) under the influence of at least three mind-altering substances and in the presence of maybe his very first real friend, and at first, when he says it, he isn't thinking about the consequences. He doesn't *understand* consequences yet! He's a child, functionally an idiot, he's seen the tiniest sliver of the human experience and doesn't yet realize he's dust, he's a grain of sand, he's utter fucking maggots. He won't understand that until Alexis Lai knocks on his door and says hi, sorry to bother you but Neel is dead, he died and inside his telescope was a note that said you killed him.

Which is when, later, Atlas Blakely knows that he fucked up. It takes him at least two more of Neel's deaths to say it out loud, but he knows it right then, in that moment, even though he doesn't tell anyone what he's thinking, which is this: *I shouldn't have asked for power when what I really wanted was meaning.*

But now he has both, so. You can see how we're at an impasse.

· · ·

"Meaning?" says Libby Rhodes, whose hands are still smoldering. There are pale channels streaking her cheeks, salt mixing with grime by her temples. Her hair is thick with ash and Ezra Fowler is lying crumpled at her feet. Ezra's last breath was no more than ten, fifteen minutes ago, his last words some few seconds prior to that, and this part, too, will go unspoken: that although Atlas is angry, although he does not know what he expected to feel at the loss of a man that he once loved and currently hates, he still feels. He feels immensely.

But he made a choice long ago, because somewhere out there is a universe where he didn't have to. Somewhere, there's at least one world where Atlas Blakely committed a murder that saved four other lives, and now the only path forward is to find it. Or make it.

Either way, there is only one way this story can end.

"Meaning," replies Atlas, lifting his gaze from the floor, "what else are you willing to break, Miss Rhodes, and who will you betray to do it?"

THE COMPLEX
as an
Anecdote About Humanity

One side of the coin is a story you've heard before. Genocide. Slavery. Colonialism. War. Inequality. Poverty. Despotism. Murder, adultery, theft. Nasty, brutish, short. Left to their own devices, humans will inevitably resort to baser impulses, to self-eradicating violence. Within every human being is the power to see the world as it is and still be driven to destroy it.

The other side of the coin is Romito 2. Ten thousand years ago, when the rest of his kind survived only on their prowess as hunters, a male with a severe kind of dwarfism was cared for from infancy to adulthood without any—quote-unquote—conceivable benefit to the rest of his kind. Despite the threat of communal scarcity, he was provided an innate form of dignity: he was allowed to live because he was theirs, because he was alive. Left to their own devices, humans will inevitably care for one another at great detriment to themselves. Within every human being is the power to see the world as it is and still be compelled to save it.

It is not one side or the other. Both are true.

Flip the coin and see where it lands.

I

EXISTENTIALISM

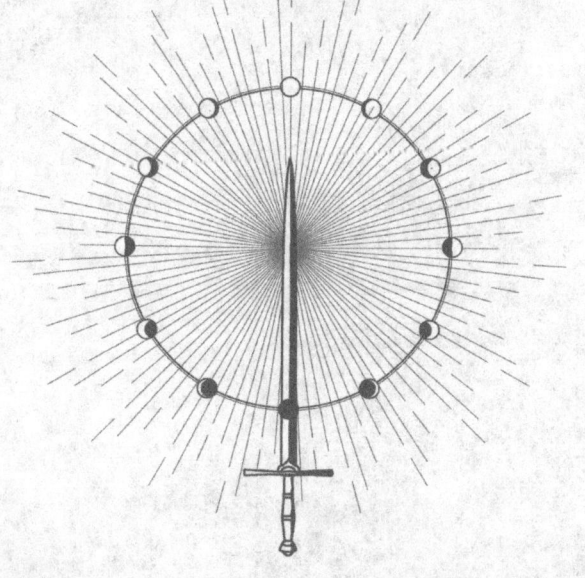

· EILIF ·

The blond man exiting the medeian transport at Grand Central Station wore a distinctive pair of sunglasses. Also, several layers of illusion charms. Some were recently applied, but most were years, perhaps even decades old. This, then, was no hasty disguise; more of a permanent cosmetic reconstruction. The sunglasses were aviators with a prismatic effect across the lenses, a gold that faded chromatically into silver on the arms. They reminded Eilif of a pearl encased in iridescence, treasure laid by an unfeeling ocean. Perhaps it was the sunglasses that drew her attention, or possibly it was the eerie sense that the man had unreadably met her eye.

He was not Nico de Varona, which was troubling; potentially disastrous. But Eilif knew enough to take what was very likely her final shot.

"There," she said urgently to the seal beside her, who was not the lovely barking kind, nor even a helpful selkie. In answer, he made a face like something had hurt his ears. She couldn't think what. "That one. He's got blood all over him." The lingering haze of the wards from the place he'd come from were unmistakably present, effusing from the blond man's skin in waves. Like an aura of toxic fumes or bad cologne. Though Eilif doubted this man's cologne was anything but expensive.

"That's Ferrer de Varona? Is he wearing some kind of illusion spell?" asked the seal—not of Eilif, but the small machine he wore in his ear. He wasn't even blue, much less navy. Eilif became concerned she'd unintentionally aligned herself with amateurs. "The brief says the target should be shorter, Latino, with dark hair—"

Eilif watched as the crowd parted graciously for the blond man. No. That did not happen in New York City. She tugged the sleeve of the seal beside her, which was one of a team of three but the closest within reach. "Him. Go."

He yanked his elbow free. "I think the tracker must have malfunctioned."

Again he was not talking to her, which was a pity. She would have told him that something magical had told him to say that; that this tracker of his would never function properly because he was a very ordinary human being, and such was the price of ordinariness. True, the seal had lots of muscle, presumably some adequate quickness, and therefore in the aggregate amounted to some preponderance of merit, albeit of an unremarkable variety. A very good killing machine, but Eilif had already known many of those. And none so far had impressed her.

She did not wait for the seal's median commander to inform him of the obvious. She took off in the ribbon of space left by the blond man's ostentatious exit, prompting a lurch of motion from the two other seals who lurked nearby. Good, they would follow her, she would find the blond man, and it would become very obvious very quickly that all was not well, that Nicolás Ferrer de Varona had bamboozled them yet again, and that in his place was this: a blond man who was also not usual, who had clearly come from the same house. The one with the blood in the wards.

There was a hiss from behind her, somewhere over her shoulder. Eilif followed the golden head through the low arches, bursting onto the street in his wake.

"She's running!"

"He said this might happen, just keep on her tail—"

She ignored them, chasing either her deliverance or her condemnation. *"Stop,"* Eilif called from the doors of the station, her voice leaving her in fumes. It felt good to use it again, this thing born in her chest that some might call her magic and that Eilif called herself. Survival meant concealing it, her *her*-ness, her *yes*-ness—the thing that made her feel there was a tomorrow. Not like the deals. Those made her feel there was a now, a someday, a today.

It curtained the street, the crowd of fortune hunters and bicycles and the simmering constancy of anger. A man in silver ear blockers did not notice, kept walking. Eilif briefly marveled at the efficiency of modern sailor's wax. Importantly though, the blond man had paused, his shoulders fallen still in their casing, a white linen shirt. At first he appeared unaffected by the morning's swampy threat of impending summer, but Eilif caught the magic evanescing from him in swarms. When he turned, she noticed the tiny bead of sweat on his brow just before it disappeared behind the pointed blankness of his metal frames.

"Hello," he said. His voice was caramel. "My condolences."

"For?" said Eilif, who had called him to a halt, and was not dead. Yet.

"I'm afraid you'll come to regret meeting me. Nearly everyone does." The blond man's magically altered mouth became a not-sorry crescent just as the two seals shook off the lingering effect of Eilif's command, flanking her in a way she hoped would soon become useful.

"Him," she said, with a nudge. Their chins snapped to the blond man, their hands simultaneously reaching for a pair of guns that would not miss.

The instructions were *apprehend*. The command, as per the terms of Eilif's deal, was *subdue*, as with an animal out of containment. She understood that in real life, outside the designs of strategists and theoreticians, many words took on different meanings. Meaningfully, so did hers. Her promise had been this: a key to the house with the blood in the wards. Alive or dead, her optimal target or not, the blond man was now her only salvation. Take him and cut him up in little stars, shove his broken body in a latch, it did not matter. Her promise of delivery was not contingent on the state in which her offering was delivered. After this many years, this many deals, she'd learned to be attentive to the nature of the finer print.

Magic was not required for evisceration. Eilif knew this. But on certain occasions it did not hurt, so she did what she could to hold him there. This blond man, she did not know him and could not hate him. She could, however, choose her life over his.

Unfortunately, things went wrong, almost at once. Eilif was attuned to quiet things, subtle motions, like the difference between a need and a wish. The hairline fracture of a gunman's hesitation. The seal to her left suffered a thought, or something very like one. More like a pulse of longing, or a pang of regret.

Someone, she realized, was curiously fighting back.

Another bead of sweat manifested and disappeared on the blond man's brow, hidden behind chromatic lenses. The seal to Eilif's right flickered, the motion of a candle flame. Rage, maybe, or desire. Eilif knew it well, the jolt of inspiration on which so much of her skill depended. The trick of the light that could, under certain circumstances, be read as a change of heart. Behind her, motion had slowed, no other seals remaining to follow. Whatever shift in atmosphere had launched the two beside her into perilous suspension, they were coalescing now, rejoining to some lighter, higher calling. Like cirro-form clouds to a blanketing cumulus, or a minor chord resolving to a major lift.

"The problem is you're desperate," said the blond man. Eilif realized only after the gunshots should have already sounded that he was speaking directly to her. Around them was an odd, performative silence that had spread from the seals to the crowd, creating a stillness like the hush before a standing ovation, the expectancy of unanimous applause. "You must understand it isn't personal," the blond man added, observing her belated calculation.

An entire city block reduced to silent paralysis. The seals designed to take down Nico de Varona would be no use after all. So maybe this was it, then. The ending.

No. Not today, not now.

"Neither is this," Eilif gamely replied, and tried to think only one thing: *You're mine.*

Dangerously, though, another element slipped through the intensity of her thoughts; not hesitation, but worse. Like the blond man's bead of sweat: a bit of pain, born from an ill-advised rush of feeling. The thrill of the chase. The high of a win. The flick of her tail. The spindly notches on her calf—the deals she made to remake her life, to reassemble her fate. And then, just at the end, like the crash of a wave. The particular glint of her son Gideon.

Unwise, to let that much of herself bleed through the effort of bending the blond man's will; cracks that would undoubtedly transfer to him, impurities like patches of corrosion, places from which a stray thought in opposition might inadvisably burst through. Still, she felt the blond man's mouth fill with an old, familiar yearning, the sour taste of want. Such was enough, usually, to earn her a window of opportunity, should she need it. In this case, enough that she could snatch the rifle from the hand of the nearest seal.

Enough that she could choose to hunt rather than be hunted, if only just this once.

She turned the barrel on the blond man, finger on the trigger, ancient curses ebbing and flowing through her mind. "Come with me," she said, sweet as siren song, the lilt of a new-old promise in her voice. She could feel enough of him to know he had the usual mortal wishes; expected pains of the unrequited and unfulfilled. All he had to do was what everyone did, and give in.

The blond man dropped his sunglasses lower. Low enough that she could meet his eyes. Blue like azure. Like the beryl waves of an inviting sea. In Eilif's periphery, one seal was weeping, tears streaming from his eyes with an odd, subjugating bliss of rapture. The other had fallen to his knees. The driver of a taxicab was singing something, possibly a hymn. Several pedestrians had dropped to kiss the ground. The blond man was resisting her and incapacitating them with impossible simultaneity; like holding two halves of the universe together, or stitching a wave onto the sand.

Eilif understood only after such an epiphany became imperative that the blond man's magic was not effusive out of waste. Many humans were wasteful with their magic out of relative ignorance of their constraints, bound to overuse a resource of which they believed they could never be robbed. The blond man, however, was accustomed to being emptied. He knew exactly how much of himself he could and couldn't be without.

"What are you doing to them?" asked Eilif, who couldn't resist the ill-fated moment of curiosity. One craftsman to another, she could not help but be awed.

"Oh, it's this great thing I recently learned," said the blond man, seemingly pleased by her attention. "Incapacitation via painlessness. Cool, right? Read it in a book last month. Anyway, no offense but I've got to go. I've got a vengeful library to reckon with, some retributive justice I'd like to settle. I'm sure you can relate."

He stepped toward her from the street, a tiny swagger in his gait. His eyes, upon closer inspection, were unexpectedly bloodshot, one of his irises now blown so wide it looked endless, almost black. So, not so effortless after all, his survival. Eilif reached toward him, touching the tips of her fingers to the clammy opacity of his cheek. One siren to another, she knew the call of an oncoming shipwreck. She knew the end would be a crash, a swirl of dark.

"That person you keep trying to protect," she heard him muse to himself, "why does he seem so familiar?" and Eilif knew, distantly, that the gun was on the ground, that her last chance was spent, that very soon the prayer would end, that the blond man had placed her directly into the hands of her fate, however unwittingly he'd done it. That he knew, somehow, who—but not what—Gideon was.

Beside her, the seals were stirring and the blond man's gaze cut away, though for half a second's lag, Eilif managed to drag him back. She understood that he'd be gone before the effects of his magic fully lifted, but there was something in him she had to see, to understand.

"Look at me," Eilif said. His eyes were blue, prophetic, sorry. Dark with anger, with purpose, with rage, like blood splashed artlessly across a set of ancient wards.

The pulse of a ticking clock; his end like hers materialized, waiting. "How long do you have?" she managed to ask.

He barked a laugh. "Six months, if I believe the story I've been told. Which, unluckily, I do."

The flash of a knife, his teeth in the dark,

"I love doom," the blond man said, his eyes gone wholly black. "Isn't it romantic?"

"Yes," she whispered.

Notch by notch, this life an anchor, freedom bartered for survival,
His eyes,
The dark,
His eyes,

. . .

"Eilif," said a new voice. Familiar and older. Less tired; less honeyed. "Your time is up."

The same redness blinked out from the endlessness of ocean depths. The same red ledger flashed impossibly from within the crevices of time and dreams.

She'd tried escaping, but no use. The Accountant had found her again.

For the first time, the mermaid had run out of gambles. She had nothing left to offer, no promises left with which to bargain, no beneficial lies with which to croon her siren song. The notches on her calf marking her debts flashed in the darkness like scales, anchoring her to her inevitable outcome. At last, she was meeting her end.

The Prince, the animator, was at large. Her son was missing. The blond man, her final attempt to clear her ledger, had gone horrifically awry. That place with the books, with the blood in the wards, the one she'd promised to the Accountant—it obviously bred monsters. Eilif of all creatures would know.

It didn't matter. Everything was over now, so she decided to enjoy what little she had left. Ample time for a curse or two, or possibly just a warning.

I love doom, Eilif thought. *Isn't it romantic?*

"You can have my debt," she offered generously to the Accountant, obliging him with a smile. "Enjoy it, it comes with a price. You have your own debt now. Someday your end will make itself known, and you will not have the benefit of ignorance. You will see it coming and be powerless to stop it."

Perhaps because she'd truly given up on fear, for the first time she detected a glint of something from the usual formless shadow of the Accountant—a flash of gold, some decorative sparkle. A tiny rune or a symbol on what looked like a pair of spectacles, the shape of it like birds coming home.

Ah, no, not a symbol—it was a letter. *W.*

Eilif felt her lips curl into a smile as the darkness began to maelstrom ever tighter around her shoulders, enveloping her like a wave and filling her lungs like a weight before she plummeted soundlessly into nothing.

The summons must have arrived during the night, having been slipped under the door of his New York apartment by the time Nico awoke—or rather arose, having slept not at all—in the wee hours of the morning. Very orderly, the summons. A distinct aura of tidiness to the white envelope, which was unceremoniously addressed to Nicolás Ferrer de Varona. There had been no weird wax seal, no ostentatious crest of arms, no obvious pretension to speak of. Apparently that sort of pageantry was reserved for the manor house Nico had left the day prior, and all that remained was a vaguely institutional call to arms.

(What exactly had he expected from the Alexandrian Society? Hard to say. It had recruited him in secret, asked him to kill someone, and offered him the answers to some of the greatest mysteries of the universe, all in service to something omniscient, ancient, and arcane. But it had also served a nightly supper via summons by a gong, so overall the aesthetic remained a bit muddled, truest somewhere between ideological purity and trial by fire.)

More curious, however, was the presence of a second summons, in that it was addressed somewhat more worryingly to Gideon no middle name Drake.

"So." The woman at the desk—forty-ish, Very British—clicked the mouse of her desktop computer and turned expectantly to Nico, who shifted twitchily in the leather office chair to which his thighs were currently adhered. "We have a variety of routine business to discuss, Mr. de Varona, as your Caretaker likely warned you to expect. Though I'm afraid we've had to call you in somewhat more . . . exigently," she remarked with a glance at Gideon beside him. "Under the circumstances, I assume you understand."

Below them, the floor rumbled. Luckily it was only Gideon seated beside Nico and not certain other parties who would chastise him for this tiniest of magical indiscretions, and therefore all that happened was a brief shared glance at the desk lamp to Nico's left.

"Well, you know what they say about assumptions," replied Nico.

Beside him, Gideon's head shifted just enough for Nico to become aware that he was being blessed with a rare (but never entirely out of the question) Drakean side-eye.

"Sorry," Nico said. "Go on."

"Well, Mr. de Varona, I think I can safely say this is a record," remarked Sharon, which was ostensibly her name. The nameplate neatly set upon the desk (in the same font that had once brandished the words ATLAS BLAKELY, CARETAKER) read SHARON WARD, LOGISTICS OFFICER, though the logistics officer in question had not bothered to introduce herself formally. She had said, in fact, very little between Nico's entry to the room and now.

"It's not the first time we've had any sort of legal trouble with an initiate," Sharon clarified. "It's just the first time it's occurred within twenty-four hours of leaving the archives, so—"

"Wait, sorry," Nico cut in, to which Gideon's brows knitted together ever so questioningly, in preemptive warning. "Legal trouble?"

Sharon clicked something on her desktop, scanning the screen before transferring a perfunctory glance to Nico. "Did you not destroy several million euros' worth of government property in full view of the public?"

"I . . ." Objectively true, but on a spiritual level Nico felt there was an underpinning of inaccuracy. "Well, I mean—"

"Did you not cause the deaths of three medeians," Sharon pressed, "two of which were CIA?"

"Okay," Nico obliged, "hypothetically I'll allow it, but was I the *direct* cause? Because they came for me first," he pointed out, "so if you think about it, everything really begins with a matter of personal—"

"Apologies." Sharon turned with a sense of loftiness to Gideon. "I believe you were responsible for one of those."

"What?" Nico felt the air in the room turn stale with a concern he hadn't had five minutes ago, but probably should have. "Gideon wasn't—"

"Yes," Gideon gamely confirmed. "One of those was me."

"You're Gideon Drake," said Sharon, the logistics officer whom Nico did not feel nearly so fondly toward now, purely on the basis of her tone. He had been willing to compliment her immaculate sweater set upon what he assumed would be an affable end to the conversation, probably over tea, but now he was reconsidering. "And," Sharon added, "you are not an Alexandrian initiate."

"Neither are you," commented Gideon.

"Yes, well." Sharon's lips thinned. "I should think one of those statements is a matter of relevance while the other is quite firmly not."

"Wait, you're not an initiate?" asked Nico, turning to Gideon in confu-

THE ATLAS COMPLEX ·

sion. "How did you know that? How did he know that?" he posed more firmly to Sharon, seeing as Gideon was doing one of his very Gideon things where he chose silence as a tactical matter. "Of course you're initiated—these *are* the offices of the Society, aren't they?"

There was a moment, absent any acknowledgment of Nico, wherein Sharon appeared to consider a wide variety of nastiness in answer to Gideon's look of slightly hostile tranquility. Normally Gideon was the height of politeness, which made this all the more bewildering.

"The Alexandrian Society is, of course, very uninterested in the legal complications that may arise from an event of this nature." Sharon was speaking exclusively to Gideon now, not Nico, which was unusual and vaguely alarming. "Its initiates are protected. Outsiders are not."

"Whoa, hang on," said Nico, leaning forward in his chair. Beneath him, the leather squeaked; underused or new, or not real leather. Which wasn't the point, though it was contributing to something—some sense that all of this was very uncool and fake. "You're aware that I was *attacked,* right?" Nico pointed out. "I was targeted and Gideon saved my life, which I would think counts for something—"

"Of course. We've noted that, or else he wouldn't be sitting here," said Sharon.

"Where else would he be sitting? Never mind, don't answer that," Nico amended hastily, as both Sharon and Gideon turned to him with an indication that he ought to be able to sort that out for himself. "I thought you called us in here to help!"

Sharon's green eyes met his blankly. They were nearly colorless, which wasn't an unflattering thing that Nico was only thinking now because he disliked her. (Probably.) "Mr. de Varona, are you by chance currently in a Parisian jail?"

"I—no, but—"

"Have you received a summons from the Metropolitan Police?"

"No, but still, I was—"

"Does any part of you feel presently endangered or otherwise at risk of either legal prosecution or impending peril?"

"That's not fair," Nico retorted, sensing the encounter had taken a turn for the passive-aggressive. "I'm constantly at risk for peril. Ask anyone!"

"So that's it, then," Gideon remarked without waiting for Sharon's answer, folding his arms over his chest. "Nico gets off with a warning, and I get . . . not arrested, which I suppose I should count as a victory," Gideon observed. He wasn't being impolite, Nico realized belatedly. He was just here doing business. He'd known he was walking into a negotiation, whereas Nico had thought this was an offering or at least a sympathetic heads-up.

Balls almighty, no wonder the rest of the world was constantly telling Nico he was a child.

"I'm guessing there will be some kind of memory impairment?" Gideon said.

Before Sharon could open her mouth, Nico swept in. "You're not fucking with my friend's brain. I'm sorry, you're just not."

Sharon looked taken aback by his language. "Mr. de Varona, I beg your pardon—"

"Look, if *you're* not initiated and *you* know the Society's business, then surely Gideon can have a pass of some sort." Nico didn't have to turn his head to see Gideon's look of extreme doubt, which Nico was nearly positive was being offered to him now as a means of shutting him up. But it had never worked before, and certainly wouldn't today. "Fine, not a *pass,* but . . . some kind of workaround. How about a job?" suggested Nico, straightening so firmly the base of the desk lamp chattered halfway over the edge of the wood. "In the archives. An archivist. Or something. Let me talk to Atlas," Nico added. "Or Tristan." Well, that would be pointless, probably, but maybe Tristan Caine would shock them both half to death and agree. (And speaking of shocking to death, Tristan *owed* him.) "I'm sure one of them could come up with something useful. Plus Gideon's got references from NYUMA, if you just reach out to the dean of—"

"Mr. de Varona." Sharon's eyes shifted to the desk lamp, which was teetering on the precipice of no longer being a lamp and being instead a pile of glass shards and ruin. "If you wouldn't mind—"

"Someone tried to *kill me,*" Nico reminded her, rocketing apprehensively to his feet. "And I don't know if you've noticed, Sharon" (unintentionally derisive) "but the Society didn't step in to protect me. I thought that was why we were here!" he growled, the lights above them flickering while the floor below them undulated once, then twice, upending the fastidious arrangement of books on a nearby shelf.

"You promised me wealth," Nico ranted. "You promised me power—you asked me to give everything up for it" (the titles fell from the shelf one by one, followed by a dangerous swing from the overhead light fixture) "and I do mean *everything,* and in the end only Gideon actually showed up to save my life, so at this point" (RIP the portrait hanging on the wall) "I think I've got a right to make one or two demands!"

The lamp finally fell to the floor with a clatter, the bulb splitting into three large shards amid a fine dusting of particles. One or two aftershocks from the fault lines of Nico's temper rattled the remaining structure of the desk.

For a moment after the ground settled, there was an eerie, unreadable silence. Then Sharon sucked her teeth with impatience and typed something on her keyboard, waiting.

"Fine," she said, and flicked a glance at Gideon. "Temporary placement. You'll be given no archive privileges aside from those the Caretaker requests. Which may very well be none."

Gideon didn't speak for a moment. Nico didn't either, being slightly stunned. He was used to getting his way to some extent, but even he felt this unlikely.

"Well?" prompted Sharon, whose neatly coiffed hair was lightly flecked with precipitating bits of ceiling.

"I assure you, I never expect any privileges," remarked Gideon with a faint hint of amusement, eyes marking the flurry of white paint.

"You'll be tracked." Sharon, unfazed, was staring at him. Glaring, Nico supposed. But in a very bureaucratic way that suggested she was very tired and wanted to go home more than she actually wanted him to suffer. "Every iota of magic you use. Every thought in your head."

"Oh, stop," said Nico, turning to Gideon with a scoff. "Nobody's tracking you. Or if they are, believe me, Atlas doesn't care."

"The Caretaker is not your friend," Sharon said. Or possibly warned. She was still speaking directly to Gideon until she turned with unimaginable glaciality to Nico. "And as for you," she began.

"Yes?" Nico couldn't believe how well this had gone. Well, not true. He'd thought he was coming in for a bunch of groveling—*their* groveling, that is, not his. Some pretty promises about how the Society would help him, how Atlas Blakely had spoken so highly of him, how bright his future was—all sorts of things he was accustomed to hearing and had come, at least partially, to expect. But for a moment there things were pretty touch and go, so after a fair amount of whiplash, Nico was now convinced that things had gone brilliantly. Even better than he'd hoped, which was saying something.

Are you insane, Varona? an insufferable voice in his head serenaded him familiarly. *They're not going to let Gideon move into the fucking Society like it's a goddamn slumber party. Did you even hear what I just said?*

"Try to stay out of trouble for at least the remainder of the week, Mr. de Varona." Sharon's eyes flitted to the floor and back up. "And for fuck's sake, fix my lamp."

Well, well, well, thought Nico smugly.

So he was a lucky bastard after all.

. . .

Yesterday. Was it only yesterday? He'd smelled smoke on the breeze before he saw her, but being out of practice at existing in a world where she also lived, he hadn't quite allowed himself to predict what might come next. For a year he'd been searching for her, questioning her absence, suffering some yawning internal void at the knowledge that maybe, possibly, if he were very unlucky and not, as she so irritatingly suspected, a person who had never encountered a hardship whose pants he could not charm off, then she might not return, and if she did not, then maybe, possibly, a part of him was gone also; a piece he did not yet know if it was possible to get back.

The would-be assassin—one of three would-be assassins who had attacked him upon emergence from the Society transport ward in Paris—lay freshly dead at his feet. Nico still tasted sweat and blood and the aftershocks of kissing his best friend. His pulse was still racing, blood still pumping to the tune of *Gideon, Gideon, Gideon,* and then he'd smelled smoke and it all came rushing back. The fear. The hope. The last year of his life like a pendulum swing in the making.

Varona, we need to talk.

It was Gideon who caught her when she fell; Gideon who'd leapt to put himself between Nico and danger once again; Gideon who'd given Nico easily one of the top five lines Nico had ever heard (and the other four were Nico's own, delivered successfully to other people) after giving him a top-five kiss. The number-one spot, quite possibly, and this assertion from a man who'd kissed Parisa Kamali was no small thing. Gideon had literally tasted like gummy vitamins and a cold sweat of panic and it was *still* a halcyon daydream, rhapsodic with birdsong, a dumbstruck haze. As far as capacity for meaningful thought went, Nico was absolutely fucking toast.

"Well, she's breathing," Gideon had said, ever the pragmatist, followed by, "This is a man's cardigan." In Nico's head things slowed, becoming pudding, becoming something with the viscosity of mud. Gideon's voice faded to a faint but unmistakable ringing sound as Nico once again cataloged the features of the Worst Person in the World: brown hair, bitten nails, clothes too large, much too large, clearly borrowed, also smelling faintly of sarcasm and daddy problems. And an English manor house.

"Also," Gideon said, "should we be concerned about . . . police?"

"Oh, fuckety balls" had been Nico's response, time warping around them as he blinked to cognizance. The Parisian pedestrian bridge had partially collapsed, cobbles dropping into the waters of the Seine below like cookie crumbs off the chin of a giant monster. "We should leave, right? We should leave." All the blood for passable sentience was somewhere else. Not very promising as far as impending performance.

"That feels correct," Gideon agreed, "but the unconscious girl and dead bodies . . . ?"

"Troubling, yes, good point." Nico was in possession of no more than two working brain cells, one of which was yelling about Libby while the other screamed loudly and pubescently about Gideon's very talented kiss. "Possibly we just . . . run?"

"Yes, good, fine by me," said Gideon with very little hesitation, twin spots of pink blooming in his cheeks when he looked again at Nico. God, when had Nico begun to feel this way? He couldn't remember, couldn't re-member anything ever changing, couldn't identify any chronological source for the flood of euphoria in his chest, which was matched only by the head rush of seeing Libby's wrist dangling from where Gideon had thrown her over his shoulder and begun, carefully but hastily, to walk.

Walk? They weren't mortals. His transport via the Society house was a one-way ticket, true, but that didn't mean he had to do something so pedes-trian as *walk*. "Hang on," Nico muttered, grabbing Gideon by the shoulder and heading sharply left. In retrospect it said a lot about Gideon's state of mind that he had allowed himself to plummet without warning off the side of a bridge. His judgment was impaired, he had kissed Nico, they were idi-ots. Nico, having adjusted the gravity beneath them to provide the cleverest escape he could conjure at the time, glanced over at Gideon and—god help him—grinned.

Libby awoke within minutes, just as they were nearing the Parisian public transports. A brief little faint, pure dramatics. Nico told her so the moment she came to, not even waiting for Gideon to set her fully on her feet. Literally, his first words to her—"You know, all of this could have been accomplished with about fifty percent fewer theatrics"—to which she responded with a narrowing of her slate eyes, a moment's pause, and then, just when she ought to have had a witty (witty-*ish*) comeback at the ready, an abrupt and thor-ough retching that resulted in a pool of vomit at Nico's feet.

"It really feels like you've had that coming for a while now," commented Gideon placidly, earning himself a backhand in the gut as Nico reeled back-ward into a lamppost.

"Are you okay?" Nico asked Libby, unsure what exactly to say to the woman whose unexpected resurgence in his life struck him like the sudden awakening of a third eye, or an additional singing octave. She was doubled over and clutching Gideon's left arm for balance. (Top two Gideon arms for sure.)

"Yeah. Yeah, fine." She looked incredibly not fine, though Nico was at least capable of keeping that sort of phrasing to himself. "We have to talk."

"So you mentioned. Can it wait, or should we do it now? Talk," Nico repeated. The immensity of the awkwardness was really something. He had about eight thousand questions and yet, somehow, the first thing that came to mind was "Is that Tristan's?"

"What?" She looked up at him, bleary-eyed, from where she'd been wiping her mouth on the sleeve of what Gideon had already observed to be a man's sweater.

"Nothing. You . . . you came from the Society. From the house." Yes, clearly she had, okay, excellent deduction by Nico. Slow, but he was tired. A modicum of logic. Brilliant. She gave him an odd look, her glance darting to Gideon and back. "Oh, he knows," Nico clarified for her, to which she replied with an all-knowing grimace. "What? Come on, Rhodes. Someone *did* just try to kill me, so I imagine I'm allowed t—"

"Who?" Her eyes became narrow slits of concentration.

Nico shrugged. "Impossible to tell at this juncture." Anyway. "The house," he reminded her. "Should—should we go back there, or . . . ?"

"No. Not yet." Libby shook her head, swallowing thickly and making a face. "Fuck," she muttered to the palm of her hand, into which Nico was sure she would once again hurl. "I need coffee."

Nico threw an arm into Gideon's chest, shoving him into a narrow side street just before a Metro police vehicle rounded the corner. "Rhodes," Nico said, gripping her by the elbow and pulling her after them, "I hardly think there's time for a café—"

"Shut up. Let's just go. Somewhere safe." Libby was off and running, or whatever running looked like for someone with severely cramped muscles and three or so decades of time travel under her belt. "New York. Your apartment."

"Did you pay the rent?" Nico asked Gideon as they charged off in her wake.

"Yes? I live there," said Gideon.

"You're a prince among men," Nico replied as they scuttled off through Paris, an odd little threesome floating along on a cloud of smoke. "Rhodes," he asked when they arrived, breathless, to camouflage themselves amid the tourists bustling around the transport near the Louvre. "Are you sure you're okay?"

It was a question he would repeat countless times throughout the process of returning to New York—something odd was happening at Grand Central; their usual exit point had been blocked off due to a security breach that Nico belatedly recalled might have had something to do with Callum, funneling them instead through a police checkpoint requiring minor illusion work and nearly all of Gideon's prowess at small talk—though it was clear there would be no meaningful reply until they could be sure no one had recognized one or all of them along the way.

In fact, it took them until they'd crossed the threshold into his former apartment (Nico took a deep, invigorating inhale of the aloo bhaja frying from downstairs and felt an overwhelming sense of rightness, as if the world could never again harm him despite the apparent governmental agencies out for his blood) for Libby to actually answer. Or rather, sort of answer.

After she'd asked twice if Max was home (he wasn't) and glared through the entirety of a hummus plate that Nico insisted she eat, Libby finally began to look interested in discussion. "Are there wards set up in here?"

So many he'd nearly killed himself making them, but neither she nor Gideon needed to hear that. "Yeah."

"You're sure they can hold?" There was a meaningful arch to her brow as a police siren wailed from the street, but this was Manhattan. Such things happened.

"Offense taken, Rhodes, but yes."

"We have a problem," she finally announced, giving Gideon a small frown before lowering her voice. "With the Society. With . . . the terms and conditions," she specified with a shroud of mystery, "that the six of us left unmet."

"First of all, Gideon can hear you," said Nico, which Gideon very accommodatingly pretended not to hear, "and second of all, what do you mean? Did Atlas say something to you?"

"Forget Atlas." She was chewing her thumbnail. "We should never have trusted him." She glanced again at Gideon, who strode to the kitchen, whistling loudly.

Obliging her sense of subterfuge, Nico leaned closer. "We should never have trusted him . . . because . . . ?"

"Because he's trying to end the world, for one thing," Libby snapped. "Which is apparently why he recruited us. Because he needs us to do something that's going to destroy everything. But that's not what I needed to talk to you about." She picked at her thumb again before giving it a sudden look of repulsion, turning her attention back to Nico. "We have two choices. We can kill one of the others before the archives kill us, which could conceivably happen at any moment, or we can go back to the Society house and stay there. Until, again, the archives decide to kill us. Unless Atlas destroys the world first," she muttered.

"I—" These were not entirely favorable options. Nico looked at Gideon, who was now humming aggressively to himself. "You're sure? About killing one of the others, I mean." He'd indulged himself the bliss of believing they'd gotten away with it until, well, now. As he considered the alternatives Libby had laid out, it did feel increasingly problematic that all six of them were simultaneously alive and existing in one universe. Their previous détente with the archives (one member of their cohort *had* been eliminated, though purely by circumstance) seemed worryingly nebulous in hindsight.

Acknowledged or not, Nico had definitely felt something draining him over the entirety of his year of independent study. Whether it was the library's customary treatment of its inhabitants or the result of a promise unfulfilled, exactly how much latitude had he expected to be allowed? He understood, in a purely theoretical way, that nothing the likes of which they had created could be achieved without something—many somethings—being destroyed.

There was a price for everything they'd gained as a result of their Society recruitment, and it did not escape Nico de Varona's notice that someone would ultimately have to pay it.

"Well, it might not be true," said Libby, with the air of repeating a bedtime story or an especially flagrant lie. "Atlas told me, and it's not like he can be trusted." She looked at Nico squarely. "But at this point, I don't know that I'm willing to chance it. Are you?"

Nico was lost in thought, his mind drifting to the pointless argument he thought he'd been having with Reina what now seemed like months ago. She must have already suspected this, he decided through a blow to his chest, like the kick of an engine failing. When she'd accused him of not being willing to kill one of the others to keep her—or himself—alive, she must have already known. "I mean, I guess not, but—"

"And speaking of Atlas. You don't seem all that concerned." Now Libby was looking at him with palpable exasperation. "You get that he *used* us, right? You did hear me say that he planned for us to do an experiment that would literally destroy the universe?"

"Yes, Rhodes, I heard you—" (Had she let him finish the sentence, he might have added a note or two about her characteristically dulcet tones.)

"And you're not the slightest bit concerned about the trivial issue of world-ending stakes?" She seemed infuriated with him, which, given the timetable on her return, felt noticeably expeditious. A mere handful of hours and already she seemed to wish he were dead.

"What do you want me to say, Rhodes? It's actively un-ideal." Nico considered it further, contemplating what exactly she wanted to hear. "Although," he began, unwisely enough that from the kitchen, Gideon's humming took a turn for the cautioningly frantic, "I don't know that it technically counts as using us. He would have had to recruit people to the Society regardless of whether he had a personal agenda, don't you think?"

"*Seriously?*" Libby was hissing at him. He felt nostalgic, almost fond.

"Well—" She hadn't yet listed the terms of destruction—if she even knew what they were, which quite possibly she didn't; out of anyone, Libby Rhodes seemed the most likely to enact a fully formed evacuation plan over the vague possibility of unspecified cataclysm—but Nico had a feeling he knew precisely what the world-ending stakes in question happened to be. Unless the last year of his life was a supremely unlikely series of coincidences, he was pretty sure he knew exactly what Atlas's research was about—the multiverse. The possibility of many worlds, which Nico himself had contributed to in private for the entirety of the previous year.

Did the existence of the multiverse, or any proof therein, necessarily mean the end of the world? Nico racked his admittedly altered code of morality and came up empty, suffering the unreasonable desire to spar with Tristan on the matter, or Parisa, or Reina. Even consulting Callum might not be wholly without its charms. "I think I know which experiment you mean. It has to do with many-worlds," Nico finally explained, watching Libby's brow knit with something closer to annoyance than confusion. "But Atlas just wants to find out if he can do it, right? It's an experiment, not a bloodthirsty quest for cosmic dominance."

For a moment, so fleeting it might have existed purely within his imagination, Nico could tell from Libby's eyes that she *did* know the finer details of Atlas's experiment; that perhaps she even had the same questions Atlas had, and that the same fundamental interest had been piqued. Nico knew her very well—knew her like he knew the fundamental laws of motion—and she was an academic at heart, compulsively curious, determined to have her many questions answered. It was a quality that Nico knew so well because he shared it. Because he, like her, was defined by the many things he wanted so instinctively to understand—a hunger that had come from somewhere ready-built, deep-seated.

In a moment that Nico would never be able to prove had actually existed, he understood one thing with absolute, purposeful certainty: that Libby Rhodes knew exactly what Atlas Blakely was so sinisterly desperate to accomplish, and that she wanted those answers, too.

But then she glared at him, and temporarily his suspicions were put to rest. "It's obviously more than an experiment if it has something to do with many-worlds, Varona. Nobody just casually opens the multiverse."

"Are you sure?" he countered. "Because as I recall, we very casually created a wormhole, and a black hole, and I spent the last year casually committing Tristan-related homicide—"

"Manslaughter," called Gideon from the kitchen.

"No, it was definitely premeditated," Nico replied before returning his attention to Libby. "Okay, so wait. You came all this way to tell me you think Atlas is the bad guy?"

"I don't *think*, Varona, I *know*," she hissed. "Because yes, now that you mention it, I *did* come all this way to tell you that. It's why I spent the last year of my life nearly killing myself to get back here, and it's the *entire reason* I was—" Her mouth tightened, gaze sliding impatiently elsewhere, and Nico saw her consider some darker, more vulnerable truth before backing hastily away from it. "Never mind."

No, unacceptable. She hadn't come this far just to back down from a *conversation*. (That, he thought with an undeniable smugness, was his move.) "That's the reason you were what?" Nico pressed her. "Is it why Ezra kidnapped you?"

Libby's eyes snapped back to his. "Who told you that?"

From a distance, Nico could see that Gideon had stopped moving.

"Um, Rhodes? I hate to be informing you of this now, of all times, but I'm not actually stupid," Nico replied with palpable irritation, firstly because she'd had to ask and secondly because he was now having to answer. "Or have you forgotten that I helped get you back here?"

He still had a lot of questions about that, actually. His questions—none of which had to do with world-ending stakes so much as the nature of *her* world, and therefore his—were mounting by the minute, especially with the way she so clearly did not want to answer them. She seemed fidgety, a bit feverish, and unquestionably in need of several weeks of fluids and sleep. But his mother had taught him not to interrogate a lady, especially given how battered she seemed by the aftermath of abduction-related time travel, and so he did not indulge the reflex to push her. Even if some internal voice with sandy hair and better judgment strongly suggested he should.

"Rhodes," Nico attempted instead, since it seemed important to mention whether he'd live it down or not. "I did miss you, you know."

Only then did she spare him an actual moment's attention. Their eyes locked, wariness melting gradually to something very nearly warmth, and it was companionable, honest. True.

Amid the reluctant lowering of defenses, Nico expectantly wondered which one of them would back down first. From somewhere across the third-floor landing, Señora Santana's hellish Chihuahua gave an existential bark.

"I think," said Libby, the motion of her swallow thick with something. Maybe longing. Maybe fear. "I think we should go with option two. If you're up for it."

"Option two?" He hadn't been paying attention, or maybe he had and then forgot.

"Yes. The one where we keep working for the archives instead of killing one of the others." She seemed suddenly tired, and a little lost. Nico noticed she no longer mentioned the possibility of her killing him, or of him killing her. Perhaps now, finally, their alliance was secure.

"Will that work?" asked Nico, who genuinely did not know the answer.

"Atlas stayed alive this long by sticking close to the archives, so . . . yes?" Libby shrugged. "It'll buy us some time, at least. We won't have to worry about anyone else taking over the world while we're the ones using the library. And it'll be safe there, I guess." Her attention drifted again to the window, to the signs of life and inevitable doom down below. "Safer than trying to make it out here."

There was something troubling underfoot, and Nico could sense it, whatever it was. There were many things Libby Rhodes was choosing to leave unspoken, and he doubted very much that they were all as mission-focused as her initial summons of him seemed to be.

Nico wondered what Libby's real plan was, or if it even mattered. He didn't exactly want to return to a house he already knew was actively killing him, but he also did not know where else to go, what else to do. He'd spent the last year desperate for release from his aristocratic cage, but outside of it he didn't know what he wanted at all. Maybe this was the trick to it, the reason he could not entirely hate Atlas Blakely; the reason he still felt curiosity instead of fear. Maybe Atlas had always known that Nico was incomplete without a project, without a mission. Absent the next step he had to take or theory he had to prove, Nico had never actually known what he wanted from life, or from work, or from purpose. He had all this power, fine, but for what? In the larger sense, it was Nico who had always been directionless, a little lost.

Well, aside from one thing.

The sun was setting then, finally. It seemed impossible that so much had changed in so little time. It had only been that morning that Nico had packed his things and said goodbye to Atlas Blakely, the mentor Nico had never acknowledged was someone he badly wanted to trust. But now Libby was back, some fundamental piece of Nico had been repaired, and soon he'd be yet another day older. Another day wiser, another day closer to the end.

The sun was setting then, impossibly. From the corner of his eye, Nico caught a glint of it.

Okay, he thought to the universe; to the many other worlds.

Okay, message received.

"Not without Gideon," he said.

. . .

The administrative offices of the Society to which Nico and Gideon had dutifully reported later that morning GMT (absent Libby, who after much coaxing and fussing had finally fallen asleep on their sofa, an ethical quandary over which Nico and Gideon had bickered capably in total silence before Nico's wilder protestations about the safety of his expert wards inevitably won out) were located in the very same building into which Nico had unsuspectingly walked two years prior at the behest of Atlas Blakely, mere hours after he'd graduated from NYUMA. Only now, upon return, did he recall the polished gleam of marble and its sense of institutional magnanimity, which was different from how the manor house and the archives had always struck him. This, the offices or whatever they were, seemed so clinical by comparison, with the sterility of a waiting room or the lobby of a bank.

Nico had forgotten about that sensation completely—the unidentifiable feeling of being lied to by someone—until now, following his and Gideon's fateful meeting with almighty logistics officer Sharon, who was not at all what Nico had expected to exist behind the Society's omniscient mask. True, Sharon had given him the sense that he'd been called a meddling kid and sent off to bed without dessert, much like NYUMA's Dean Breckenridge had always done, but witnessing the Society's administrative workings was like watching dystopian sausage get made.

So, this was what awaited him after the untenable had (presumably) been achieved; this was what had driven Gideon once to ask him who exactly paid the bills that footed his murdery lifestyle. To end the meeting, Sharon had asked Nico what he planned to do, like a career counselor for the chronically successful. "Do I have a choice?" Nico had asked exasperatedly, expecting to be told where to go, who to be.

"Yes," Sharon had replied with an ill-concealed look of contempt. "Yes, Mr. de Varona, that is precisely what comes of being an Alexandrian. That for the rest of your life, you will have this and every choice."

It was obvious an answer was required—that what came of being a so-called Alexandrian was not simply the freedom to achieve, but the necessity to make everyone else's time worthwhile. Which meant that Sharon's reply was . . . illuminating, to say the least. She did not care if Nico made a new world, destroying this one. She seemed only to care that he and his prodigious magic—the irreplaceable, unrivaled knowledge that he had done the unimaginable to claim—not step off a balcony somewhere in sweet surrender to the welcoming abyss, as it would be a poor return on the Society's investment. It would mean a great deal of paperwork, and an unforgivable, unprofitable waste.

So the meeting, then, was both a promise kept and an expectation rendered, which now seemed only to set off the creepy way the Society's fleet of marble vestibules sparkled from on high. Seeing it all through Gideon's more incisive eyes, Nico wondered if from the start he should have asked more questions. He wondered if he should have guessed that the Society, its archives, and Atlas Blakely might still turn out to be three separate entities, with three completely individual agendas. An institution, a sentient library, and a man, all sharing a wealth of resources with an underpinning of desire for something that was intrinsically Nico's.

Two years ago, had Nico erred irreparably by not pulling Atlas Blakely aside and saying be honest, tell me the truth—what do you actually want from me?

From us?

With a sigh, Nico jammed an elbow into the button to call the transport back to New York, thinking again about whether it was possible for one man to destroy the world. It didn't seem very realistic. Frankly, to his knowledge, a lot of men had already tried and failed. (Women, too, maybe. Equality and all that.) As Nico understood it, the world was actually very easy to destroy, at least in the metaphorical sense. With every election it seemed the fate of mankind was newly on the line. He felt certain martial law still existed somewhere, that plenty of people were still getting away with murder or worse. They had only just repaired the ozone, and even then, barely. So wasn't the world ending every day?

Not like this, Libby said tiredly in his brain. *We're different, you and I, and Atlas knows it. Surely you must know it, too.*

There was a rumble of arrogance beneath his feet, belying his actual answer. *If we're what's different, Rhodes, then maybe we can* be *different. We still get the right to choose.*

"Did it ever occur to you that I might not want to go with you?" Gideon asked him quietly, disrupting Nico's increasingly grandstanding inner monologue.

Nico blinked from his temporary reverie and glanced at him, wondering whether to be alarmed by the question. "Honestly? No."

Gideon laughed against his will. "Right. Of course."

"You'll be safer this way, too," Nico pointed out, which was conveniently true. "I did the creature wards at the manor house myself. You won't have to worry about your mother."

Gideon shrugged. Unclear what kind of shrug. "And what about Max?"

"True," Nico joked, "however will he afford the rent?" According to Gideon, Max had been summoned to his parents' summer estate, which was no dismissible summoning. Nico and Gideon tried not to mention it too often, but all three of them knew there were strings to being that rakish. (It involved massive amounts of institutional wealth.) "Anyway, we won't be there long."

"*You,*" Gideon corrected with a shake of his head. "You won't be there long. Because contractually speaking, you can still go back and forth if you want to. I'm the one who has to stay under house arrest, per your Society's terms."

It occurred to Nico to argue. To mention that, in fact, he might very well die himself if he left the manor house for very long, or at least Libby seemed to think he would, so how was that for employment contracts made under duress? But when the transport doors opened, Nico instead looked hard and searchingly at Gideon. He was looking for resentment or bitterness, which he didn't see, but he didn't find much to reassure him, either.

"You've got to stop following me into shenanigans," Nico determined eventually, stepping into the lift.

Gideon glanced down at the card in his hand, which he was still cradling in his palm like a tiny wounded bird. A very familiar thing, that card.

ATLAS BLAKELY, CARETAKER.

"Should I have let them brainwash you instead?" Nico asked casually as he once again hit the button for *Grand Central Station, New York, New York.* Gideon had been allowed twenty-four hours to collect his things before re-

porting to the manor house tomorrow, much like the instructions Nico himself had once been given. To be fair, though, what ostensibly awaited Nico as
an Alexandrian had always been knowledge, power, and glory. What awaited
Gideon now seemed distinctly more like witness protection with archival
duties, or being Atlas Blakely's underpaid TA.

"I'm not sure what you should have done instead," Gideon said with
apparent honesty. "But it does seem like whatever's happening now, Libby
needs you."

"Us," Nico corrected.

The doors dinged again with their arrival.

"You," repeated Gideon, a rush of passengers blurring the entrance to the
oyster bar.

Despite the sun setting and rising again on their unexpected change of
circumstance, Nico and Gideon still hadn't spoken about whatever had
passed between them the day prior. At first it was because of Libby, but after
Libby had fallen asleep, it was because neither of them seemed to feel discussion was required. From an optimistic standpoint there was an afterglow, a
tipsy haze of satisfaction, like ordering pizza when you know perfectly well
that pizza's what you want. The unspoken question they hadn't bothered to
bring up was more irrational—something like *okay, but do you want to eat
pizza every day?* which was, of course, impossible to answer.

For a normal person. "Look," Nico began once they emerged from the
station's exit doors. Yesterday's security risk had been cleared away, magically forgotten. "Last time, you disappeared on me because I didn't include
you in my antics. So this time I'm including you against your will, because
you're not allowed to disappear. Got it?"

"I'm thinking there ought to be a bit more nuance involved," remarked
Gideon, his attention flicking momentarily to the security cameras overhead before steering Nico along a less conspicuous path. "Like, for example,
do you plan to ask my opinion on the matter? Or will you be making decisions about what I do and where I go for the remainder of my uncertain
life span?"

"I never said I wasn't selfish." Nico hazarded a glance at Gideon as they
walked, fingers drumming at his thigh in a mix of assassin-related apprehension and unguarded personal conviction. "And for the record, you're the
one who decided to say it was *like that*. If I'm failing to properly understand
what that means, then honestly, that's on you."

It occurred to Nico to wonder if he was pushing it. If maybe he was doing
what Libby always accused him of doing and deciding on a reckless course

of action without concern for anyone else involved. Well, definitely he was doing that, yes, for sure, he wasn't totally absent the wherewithal to recognize the flawed and potentially troubling edges of his personality. Perhaps this choice of action—and the reality of its motivation—had been especially cruel, because it revolved around the particularities of his personal desires. When he'd first insisted on Gideon's inclusion to Libby in their plan for skirting archive-related demise, he'd told her Gideon could be necessary from a magical perspective—which, yes, was partially true. Her return was proof enough to him that Gideon was both exceedingly clever and reliably helpful. But the rest of it, the darker truth, was that for a year Nico had nursed a broken heart and now would rather trap Gideon against his will inside an English country house than repeat the experience.

They were silent until they reached their block.

"Well, it's my last day of freedom," Gideon observed. "What should we do?"

"Get darling Elizabeth to tell us what the fuck happened with Fowler," Nico said. "Maybe play a little Go Fish if we find the time."

He hoped his joking tone would be accepted as valuable currency. He didn't know the rules anymore, though, and wasn't sure. The rearranging of his feelings was probably akin to some kind of severe economic inflation.

"Okay," said Gideon.

Nico paused when they reached the door to their building, sidestepping the usual coven of youths outside the bodega and staring accusingly at Gideon.

"Do you hate me?" he demanded.

"No," said Gideon.

"You must have *some* feelings of negativity."

"One or two," Gideon agreed. "Here and there."

"So? Say it. *Te odio tanto. Je te déteste tellement.*" Unexpectedly, Nico swallowed hard. "Just say it."

Gideon looked at him with amusement.

"Say it, Gideon, I know you want to—"

"It's okay, you know," Gideon commented. "You can tell me. I don't mind."

Nico's chest strained. "Mind what?"

Gideon looked at him squarely, the insufferable mind-reader who was not and had never been a telepath, which meant it came from a place that Nico couldn't see but Gideon obviously did. "You actually *want* to go back there," Gideon pointed out, "to a place you've told me a thousand times that you hate."

"Did I say that, technically? I wouldn't say I *hate* it—"

"And it's not just the house." A quick, studious glance. "I know you want to do it, Nico. The experiment that neither of you want to say out loud. I know you've already started working on it in your mind—I can tell by the way you talk about it, and I know you don't just do things casually. You do them with your whole self or not at all."

There was a tiny siren going off in Nico's head, a blaring sense of caution that he ignored like all the warning signs and red flags he made it a custom to proceed through. He blinked away neon lights, forthcoming disaster, like sailing blindly into a storm on the basis of something he selfishly knew to be faith.

"Are you—" Nico cleared his throat. "Do you think I'm wrong to want to try?"

Gideon was silent for another several seconds as Nico ran the projections in his head. The many innumerable ways this could go poorly. Infinite, endless calculations that he simplified for purposes of statistical clarity. Ninety-eight out of a hundred, maybe even ninety-nine, they all ended badly.

For a normal person. "No, of course not," said Gideon. "And even if I did, if you want me, Nicolás—" A shrug. "*Je suis à toi*. Me and my ticking clock."

You and your ticking clock, Gideon, that's mine—"You're sure?"

"I know who you are. I know how you love. Manor houses, ideas. People. It doesn't matter." Another shrug. "Whatever you have for me is enough."

Nico's throat strained with the indecency of it. "But it's not like that. It's not like it's . . . it's not small. It's not some leftover piece, do you know what I mean? It's . . . it's more than that, deeper, like for you I'm—"

"I know, I told you, I know." Gideon laughed. "You think I could spend this long with you and not understand?"

"I don't know," protested Nico, "but it's not—with anyone else, it's not like—" He felt flustered, and aggressively perceived. "Gideon, you're—you're my reason," he tried to explain, and almost immediately gave up. "You're my . . . my talisman, I don't kn—"

Nico felt it then, the presence of another person's magic. The threat of Gideon living his life without knowing, without either of them saying the words had temporarily overruled the latest constancy of mortal peril, and Nico had spent too long not watching his back. He broke off with a growl to take hold of the sudden force around him, dragging a nearly unseen motion to a halt. Upon further inspection he identified the faintest flicker of it—of yet another assassin's finger on yet another trigger, this one an apparent sentry posted up outside his building. The latest threat to Nico's life, courtesy of the Forum or whoever else philanthropically wanted him dead, was costumed traitorously as a worker, loading and unloading crates of ramen noodles and hot chips into the cherished bodega downstairs.

Nico bit back a snarl of fury, mentally disarming the gun before it went off. (In theory, that is. In practice he merely turned it into an ice-cream cone before waving a hand to transport himself and Gideon up the stairs, into the apartment, on the safe side of the expertly warded door.)

So this is what life would be, Nico thought grimly, if he ignored Libby's warnings and chose to stay here, or tried to. Whether the archives came for him or not, it would still almost certainly be this. Jumping at his own shadow, looking over his shoulder to see what else might follow in his wake. What choice was that? It would be like living life *as Gideon,* as life had always been with Gideon's mother—which reminded Nico that the threat of Eilif was never to be discounted among all this, and she knew where to find them. If he couldn't trust the bodega guy downstairs, what point was there in doing anything at all?

Nico turned to say as much to Gideon, having lost track of what he'd been in the middle of explaining before. "What?"

Gideon's smile was radiant with fondness. "Hm? Nothing."

"Nothing?"

"Nothing."

Nico hazily recalled that he had been in the midst of a confession and decided this was Gideon's way of slipping reciprocation. Truly, a worse person had never lived.

Nor a better one.

"Idiot," said Nico desperately, taking hold of Gideon's jaw with one hand and punishing him with something. A kiss or whatever. Whatever. "You little motherfuck."

Gideon exhaled, a sigh that Nico coveted for the magnificence it was, and when Nico's eyes finally opened he felt elation so gruesome he nearly threw up.

Which reminded him. He turned away from the door, looking for the idiot princess herself. "Rhodes, as some of us aptly predicted, I've once again returned a hero," Nico announced, poking his head into the living room. "And you said it couldn't be—"

There was a vacancy on the sofa where Libby had been, a note left in her place.

"—done," Nico finished, storming over to the neatly folded blanket with a grumble and snatching up the scrawl she'd left in her absence.

I've already told you exactly what's going on. Come or don't come, I don't care.

"Fuckety balls," said Nico, whirling around to find Gideon shaking his head idly. "Well? Pack a bag, Sandman. I'll be so pissed if we miss the fucking gong."

· TRISTAN ·

He couldn't believe he'd never noticed that inside the office of Atlas Blakely, Caretaker of the Alexandrian Society's archives of lost knowledge for which thousands of people had been willing to kill, there was a motherfucking landline. But here it was, ringing; a fact so punishingly absurd it nearly functioned as an epiphany. *Remember when you thought you were capable of greatness? Remember when you agreed to open a portal to another world at the behest of someone who did little more than correctly observe that you were both kind of sad and pathetic for grown adult men? Wasn't that silly of you, bless your little heart. Take a seat, please, have a biscuit.*

Tristan raised the phone to his ear with a sense of entitlement he tried very hard (somewhat hard) to repress. "Hello?"

"Dr. Blakely," replied the crisp masculine voice on the other line, "it's Ford with Human Resources. Sorry to bother you but you've not yet replied to our most recent correspondence. Are you aware th—"

Tristan cut in, prickly with something. Maybe the idea of taking a call with Human Resources. Maybe the idea of a call. It had been a year, two years without much contact with the outside world, and the people he did speak to had all been largely willing to kill him. "Not Dr. Blakely."

(Also, *doctor*? Since fucking when? Unless they were all doctors now and nobody had bothered to tell him, which was entirely possible.)

Tristan cleared his throat and explained, "This is Tristan Caine, the new researcher."

There was a long pause. "Am I to understand Mr. Ellery is no longer in Dr. Blakely's employ?"

"No, Mr. Ellery is—" Mysteriously absconded. "He's fulfilled his obligation to the archives."

"Ah." A brief sound of irritation, to which Tristan could easily relate. "We'll have to note that in the file. We ought to have been informed immediately, but I suppose the Caretaker has much on his mind." Sarcasm! How refreshing that unlike Tristan, not everyone was so caught up in the cerebral, like whether they'd made a terrible error succumbing to the latest iteration of man's search for meaning. "Have you been given the appropriate paperwork, then?"

"Sorry, did you say this was Human Resources?" asked Tristan foggily. He remembered this, vaguely—the bureaucracy of employment forms and the general logistics of taxation—as if from a distant dream, or a former life. He hadn't yet considered that the Society might have a department that handled employment contracts, or that he himself was technically an employee.

"Yes," said Ford, as if he wished Tristan would do them both a favor and expire on the spot. (Also relatable.) "Is Dr. Blakely there?"

"Not at the moment," obviously. "Can I—" Tristan gritted his teeth at the indignity. "Take a message?"

Hopefully this was not what Dalton had done for Atlas Blakely on a daily basis, though Tristan supposed he ought to have asked in advance before mysteriously agreeing to take on the role of researcher for a man who tended not to leave a note.

"It's confidential." On the other end, Ford sounded bothered and then distracted. "You're sure he's not available?"

"Not at the moment. I'm unsure when exactly he'll be back." He was a mercurial thing, their Caretaker, which Tristan had known and long been suspicious of. But as far as human qualities went, he'd encountered far worse.

From his pocket, Tristan's mobile phone buzzed. He slipped it into the palm of his hand and glanced at the message, gritting his teeth. Then he shoved it back into his trouser pocket. "You may as well just tell me. I'm going to find out whatever it is anyway."

There was a brief moment as the HR representative warred Britishly with protocol. "There is a new hire," Ford conceded. Victory, Tristan's pulse glumly triumphed. "An archivist."

"Archivist? Here? In the . . ." (internal sigh at the redundancy) ". . . archives?"

"He will have about as much access to the archives themselves as any uninitiated member, Mr.—Apologies, what did you say your name was?"

"Caine. Tristan Caine. So he's not initiated?"

"I'll leave this for you to discuss with Dr. Blakely. Please contact the offices if he has any further questions."

"But—"

"Have a lovely evening, Mr. Caine." And then, like a disapproving purse of the lips, Ford with Human Resources was gone.

Tristan set down the phone, frowning, as the sound of lightly padding footsteps materialized from the doorway of Atlas's office.

"Who was it?"

Tristan turned to find Libby standing there, a mug of tea in her hands, thick woolen socks bunched at the ankles of her bare legs. She wore his jumper, a pair of his boxers. Tristan couldn't recall what had been done with her belongings or whether they still remained in her room. She hadn't been in there yet, didn't seem to want to. She seemed to feel she'd locked a prior version of herself inside it, perhaps didn't want to let it out.

"Human Resources," Tristan said, and she rolled her eyes.

"Very funny. Who was it actually?"

"I'm not joking, it was actually Human Resources. Apparently the Alexandrian Society is not exempt from the mundanities of a typical corporation." He turned to lean against Atlas's desk, waiting to see if she'd choose to venture any closer. She hadn't yet. There was a skittishness to her, or maybe something darker. He had the feeling that whatever it was, she didn't want him to guess.

"God, figures." She exhaled sharply, annoyed. A new texture for her. She carried around an agitation Tristan attributed most closely to himself. "Did you tell them about Atlas?"

"I didn't think you'd want me to."

She idled in the doorway a bit longer before taking a step toward him, her eyes flicking down to the empty space on the floor and back up. "Do you know where the others are?"

"I only know where they went when they left here yesterday." Tristan's phone felt heavy in his pocket. "If they're smart, they'll have disappeared from there by now."

"What about Dalton?"

"I'm guessing he went with Parisa."

Libby's attention shot up from the floor. "Have you told her I'm back?"

He could. Technically any of them could speak to any of the others at any time, including Reina, who had been reluctant to be included but hadn't exempted herself from being contacted. Tristan hadn't even known she owned a phone until she silently inputted her number.

It had been Nico, unsurprisingly, who'd insisted they create a fail-safe among the five of them. "We already know we're being hunted, so if we're also being tracked, we'll need a safer method to communicate," Nico had explained before expounding at length about the technomancy rabbit hole he'd spiraled down the previous night at 2:00 A.M. "Did you know that nearly all communications now take place across the same medeian signal?" (Parisa had chimed in then, ostensibly to needle Reina, who had mentally remarked that electromagnetic energy was Technomancy 101.) "Some medeian channels of communication are government owned, which is obviously problematic, and most of the privatized ones are owned by Wessex Corp or the Novas," Nico remarked with a glance at Callum, who toasted him with a breadstick, "so, you know. For obvious reasons I've set up our own."

Still, the possibility of communication with a person did not a willingness make. "Parisa and I are . . . not exactly on speaking terms." Tristan massaged the back of his neck, wondering how to explain the circumstances of their rift to Libby, or whether it was worth explaining something about how two people with little more than sex in common inevitably tended to drift apart. "Things changed a lot while you were gone."

Something dimmed in Libby's eyes at that.

"Yeah," she said, and turned away, retreating silently into the hallway as if she'd suddenly remembered she didn't want to be there at all.

Tristan stared after her, wondering if he ought to push the issue. Nico probably would, but Tristan wasn't Nico. It was one of his favorite things about himself, actually, that he wasn't Nico, or at least that's what he told himself most days. At times like these he rather resented the impulse to wonder what Nico would have done.

Tristan slid his mobile phone from his pocket again, glancing at the latest message. Another picture on the screen, this one an oversized doughnut held up against a backdrop of narrow cobbled stone. Tristan scrolled up to the first in this sadistic series of lifestyle microblogging, which he'd received yesterday.

A shock of golden hair stood out against foggy gray sky, a smirk alighting at the corner of an impossibly perfect mouth. There was a sign to the subject's left that read *Gallows Hill* in faded bronze, and beside that a blur of a black hoodie, like someone else had been walking by just as the picture was quickly and effortlessly snapped.

So this was what Callum Nova looked like standing in front of Tristan's father's pub.

Tristan stared hard at the selfie—of all things, *a fucking selfie*—with his thumb hovering over the option to reply. He sat there in silence, contemplating the best course of action. Delete and forget, never forgive. Definitely a solid choice. All his plausible replies would pale in comparison, though he had several at the ready.

So that's what your nose looks like to everyone else? Interesting.

Congratulations, you're clearly still obsessed with me.

I'm going to open up a world where you were never born and then I'm going to come back to this one and kill you. Lol.

Tristan exhaled sharply and stowed the phone back in his pocket before walking quickly out of the office. He shut the door carefully behind him and then took off up the stairs, hastening his pace as he went.

"Rhodes?"

As predicted he found the door ajar to his bedroom, a glimpse of Libby visible inside from where Tristan lingered on the threshold. It wasn't his old bedroom in the west wing, which wasn't where he lived anymore. That would be filled in eight years' time by the next round of potential Society initiates; the people who would inevitably stand where Tristan had stood and be told, as Tristan had been told, how very remarkable they were.

This was Dalton's old room, in the east wing of the house. It was a bit larger, with a drawing room that was mostly empty, which had once—or so Atlas told him—been filled with books, piles and piles of a decade's worth of research. It looked oddly skeletal now, and Tristan paused to consider the vacancy.

"I didn't actually expect him to stay," Atlas had said to Tristan the day before. "But certainly, if the books are gone, then so is Dalton."

There had been something in Atlas's voice. Exhaustion, maybe. He gave the impression of being many things, disappointed or possibly sad—after all, he had coexisted with Dalton in this house for over a decade—but Tristan had the feeling Atlas was not as conflicted as he pretended to be. Sometimes pain was easy, uncomplicated. Betrayal sucked. Time to eat pudding and dissolve into defeat, into self-serving melancholy. Surely even the great Atlas Blakely knew what it felt like to lose.

"I thought you needed him," Tristan had said, giving Atlas a sidelong glance. He wasn't used to it, the idea of trusting Atlas Blakely. He wasn't sure if he ever really could, though this—sympathy or whatever it was—certainly felt like it. If it wasn't trust, then it was certainly allyship of some critical and unavoidable kind.

He had put his fate in Atlas's hands. It was his duty not to let Atlas drop it.

Atlas seemed to know as much. "I do need him, yes. But I have his research, which is some of what I need," he clarified wearily. "Enough to know the answer to my question is yes, and thus perhaps Dalton will return, if my suspicions about his nature prove correct. I suppose it's optimistic of me, but I've yet to be wrong about him so far."

"You don't think Parisa might have her own intentions for Dalton's research?" It was difficult for Tristan to believe she'd ridden off into the sunset with Dalton for anything shy of global domination. She was not, as she'd made clear to Tristan many times, any sort of a romantic. If Parisa Kamali had an endgame in mind, it wasn't for Dalton the man. Perhaps Dalton the academic offered something more her style.

"I suppose I couldn't begrudge her the chance," said Atlas wryly. "She's far cleverer than I am, though unfortunately I may still know a thing or two more."

"Will you go after her?" Tristan asked.

The look Atlas gave Tristan then was remarkable for its hollowness. "I'm sorry," Atlas demurred, toying with something unspoken. Perhaps the thing they both knew would be Parisa's betrayal in the end. "If you take nothing else away from your time here, Tristan, let it be that. I never wanted it to come to this, with all of you torn apart. I did everything in my power to prevent it."

"What else did you expect to happen?" asked Tristan seriously. "Parisa is what she is. There's no changing that. And Callum is—" He broke off, considering that sentence better left unfinished. "I suppose it's only Reina who's been legitimately unpredictable, for all that predictability is worth."

To that Atlas inclined his head; posh affectation in lieu of a bitterer laugh. "I suppose I'd hoped that all of this could prove useful to you, one day. All the research, the discussions, the potency of your potential, living alongside the knowledge in these walls. The magic I believed each of you to be capable of creating. I thought it would be meaningful, the things you could accomplish among the six of you. That it might . . . change things, in the end." Atlas shook his head. "It's my fault," he finished with a quiet gravity. "It was all a terrible mistake."

"Which part?" Tristan had been joking when he said it, but Atlas clearly wasn't. It took a moment, several moments, for his gaze to settle with any clarity on Tristan's.

"I'm not sure," Atlas said. He didn't seem immediately self-pitying, though it was hard to rule it out. "I keep replaying everything, over and over. I said yes to a lot of things I shouldn't have. But then again, when could I have stopped?"

Tristan hadn't known what to say, and Atlas had laughed, guessing as much. "Don't burden yourself with my errors, Tristan. It's my mistake, but it's one I have every intention to fix." He opened his mouth, then stopped, shaking his head as if to casually dismiss his better judgment.

Then Atlas had given Tristan an empty, distracted smile and left the room to return to his office, departing as if there was nothing more to be said.

But there should have been more. Much more, in the form of everything that came after, in the time between Atlas being there and leaving, in the difference between Atlas being honest and being gone. Because Tristan would walk into Atlas's office only hours, minutes later to find that everything was different now, a sudden tilting of the axis of his world. But Tristan shook away the memory and stepped farther into the room to glance expectantly at Libby, who was still sitting on his bed with her back to him.

She stared into nothing for a few more seconds without looking at him.

"I think I killed people," she remarked in a toneless voice. "Maybe not that day. Maybe not in the blast. But people died, or they're dying now, or they will die. And at least some of that is because of me."

The blast that had taken her home, she meant. The pure fusion weapon, the nuclear explosion that had opened a wormhole through time, which only Libby Rhodes could have created on her own. The one that Wessex Corporation had been trying to re-create since 1990, the very year that an abducted Elizabeth Rhodes had found herself trapped in, which was information that Tristan—thanks to Parisa, and apparently to Reina—had framed specifically for purposes of convincing Libby Rhodes to do the one thing a former version of her would never have done. The blast that Tristan knew had led to a generation or more of medical ailments, radiation in the soil, genetic anomalies, shortened lifespans and higher mortality in a region where privatized healthcare meant that money alone decided who received the right to live. People died, and it was because of her, because of something that Tristan had told her. But the fallout, the possibility of death—that was only an idea. A concept without any proof.

The freckles by her eyes. The sound of her voice. They were real. They had been so real to Tristan even then that he had thought surely, whatever decision she made, it would be the right one. Rightness, goodness, it had a certain unambiguous quality to it.

Or at least it had once.

"Do you think I was a killer even before I walked into that office?" Libby asked in a low voice.

Tristan leaned against his door frame and pondered the possibility of comforting her. Unfortunately, neither of them were quite stupid enough for that kind of exercise. He wished he could have been just a little bit more ignorant, a touch more blithely daft. Maybe as stupid as he'd been the month or so ago when he'd first found her, before he'd reached through time to see her. Maybe the message he'd relayed to her should have been something else.

"Do you blame me?" Tristan asked instead.

She glanced at him and away so quickly it was near dismissal, as if he'd done the unthinkable just by making it even remotely about him. "I was the one who gave you a reason to do it," he explained, preemptively defensive. "If I hadn't put it to you in those terms, as a foregone conclusion—"

Libby lifted a hand to scratch the back of her neck, then finally turned to face him. "I would have done it either way. Eventually I would have run out of alternatives." She shook her head. "You just gave me the option of ignoring the consequences."

"I wanted you back," Tristan reminded her simply, striding forward to sit beside her on the bed. At first she froze, then shifted, gradually making room for him beside her. "And I didn't lie to you," he said quietly. More quietly.

He watched the motion of her throat as she swallowed and parted her lips. He wondered what it would be—whether it would be an apology next, or some confession of guilt. Whether she'd be sorry or sad, or if possibly, selfishly, the thing on her tongue was something that matched the flame still burning in his chest.

She'd come to him, after all. He'd been the one to murmur to her *It's all right, Rhodes, you're safe now. It's all right now, Rhodes, you're home.*

He'd also gotten rid of the body for her.

Things like that were easy now, thanks to Nico de Varona. Thanks to the last year of testing and stretching Tristan's every instinct, everything and everyone that had ever breathed or laughed or lied or betrayed was nothing now but meaningless quanta, some amalgam of particulate motion at Tristan's liberty to move. And after Libby had gone, rushing out to find whatever was out there for her to find, she'd come back here—to him. She had shown up that morning in the doorway of Tristan's bedroom where he'd lain awake, alone, and he'd made no demands of her, offered no promises. Merely poured her a cup of tea. Told her to have a nap, a shower. Whatever grime she had on her was now his by association, by the closeness for which he had given his total and unambiguous consent.

It should have been easy. Straightforward. Shouldn't it? He had missed her and now she was here. What in life had ever been more simple? Either his mistake was in failing to push her as Nico would have pushed her or his mistake was much, much earlier, but that was no longer an option. Atlas was right: Tristan, too, had made a terrible mistake, but one that was his now to own, to fix, or to live with. Conflict, hesitation, it was too late for the noncommittal cynicism that was Tristan Caine's personal brand. The miserly impulse to be right when others were wrong was no longer his isolated privilege. Tristan had handed her the instruction manual, written her the ending, lit the match, and walked away. For all that he'd joined his future with Atlas, his faith would have to be equally Libby's. Either way, doubt was no longer something Tristan had the luxury to feel.

He leaned closer, tucking Libby's hair behind her ear and watching the heat rise in her cheeks. An old tell. He stroked the bone of her jaw and she turned her head so her lips touched the tips of his fingers.

He felt the pulse of the room like the tick of a clock, counting down to something coming. Something looming. He brushed her cheek and she caught his hand, swift with sudden certainty. Their eyes met and he knew, he understood what was happening between them, what she wanted.

She didn't need to ask.

This time, dragging time to a halt was easy, like naming where in his chest his lungs were situated, where was the steady thrum of his heart. She couldn't see it, the way the room's new form took shape—she couldn't see the way he changed it, or they did, the energy between them now the only true reality left. They were like stars in the endless sky, like grains of distant sand, burning galaxies in some eternal funhouse mirror. No bigger than a glint of shine from the corner of his eye—and still, somehow, the only thing with meaning.

Still, somehow, the only thing.

She couldn't see it; everything he could see. The gleam of possibility like the auroras he'd once found her beneath. She could feel it, the way time dissolved under their tongues like spun sugar, like their shared lies of omission—but to her, the power itself was still unfathomable. Magic imaginable only as a sensation, or possibly a dream.

Maybe that was why he didn't know how to tell her. To convince her, Cassandra witnessing the fall of Troy, that somehow Atlas was right—that together they still meant something. That the magic they made was meaningful, and what they hadn't yet done still mattered. It was a fundamental truth that just by joining the Society—just by entering this house—they had all silently, collectively confessed.

Ends, beginnings, here it was all insubstantial nothingness; pointless, nonexistent pieces of an eternal answer, of eternalism itself. What was time without a place to start, a place to finish? It was nothing. Or it was everything, which was also nothing. It was a question that only Tristan could ever answer. It was a question that Tristan could now not help but ask.

Holding them there was like holding a pose, the flow of a sun salutation. Eventually time raced again; it slowed. It existed again, calling him back to the world, to the version of reality created by the sound of her breathing, in and out and impossible—impossible to fight. Not with the closeness of her. The way she had nearly been taken from him, but not yet, not really. Not quite.

"Do you worry much about your soul, Caine?" Libby's voice was heady with something. She was staring below her palms at the heart banging in his chest like she could see it. Like she knew the way it felt, could trace its motions.

The moment went on too long. He was supposed to say something, do something, but what might have been intended as a joke struck him square in the chest. "Not nearly as much as I should."

He tasted it again, the old tannins of craving, the way it left his mouth dry. He cradled her head in his hands, drawing her chin up to ghost a breath along the column of her throat. She let out a quiet sigh, lips softening around the shape of something he knew could be his name.

Tristan. Her stagnant eyes. Her ragged breaths. The stillness of the scene he'd encountered in Atlas Blakely's office, the conspicuous lack of motion from the body on the floor. The man he'd once known. The explanation he hadn't requested. The things he'd so dutifully ignored because she hadn't been ready, not then, but she'd have to tell someone eventually. She'd have to tell someone, and it would have to be him. Was she a killer even before she walked in the room?

Tristan, help me, please.

Below his lips he felt her hesitation, the tremors of her need warring with the presence of her fears. *You can trust me,* he channeled into his touch, and he could feel her softening. He could feel the capitulation, a little more with every breath. *I was yours then. I'm yours now.*

You can trust me.

She turned her head, brushing his mouth with hers. "Tristan," she said to the tension between them. He felt the possibilities crackling like static, the dissonance of a minor chord.

"Rhodes," he said in a rasp, "I need you to tell me why you came back to me."

He didn't bother asking why she ran. He understood that; had no need for clarity. There had been blood on her hands, now on his; the wounds were too fresh, too raw. They couldn't have spent last night together. There would have been too much guilt to share the bed.

But now—

She swallowed, her eyes on his lips. "You know why."

The words were sweet, gentle. Flimsy.

Inadequate. "Tell me."

"*Tristan.*" A sigh. "I want . . ."

"I know what you want. That's not what I asked." But it was exquisite, the torment living between them. This thing they'd pointlessly resisted, that they'd both so long and desperately denied.

"Rhodes," he whispered, so close he could taste her, temptation burning idly on his tongue. "Just say it."

"I wanted you," she murmured.

Excruciating, the waiting. "Because?"

"Because you know me. Because you see me." The words were rough, hard-won, the gasp that followed heavy with significance, with promises unfulfilled. "And because I . . ."

He tugged her chin up, fingers coiling tightly in her hair. "Yes?"

Her eyes searched his, hazy with something. "Because—" She broke off, spellbound, lost. "*Fuck,* Tristan, I—"

He heard it then, the unspoken admission. Tasted it, impossibly, somewhere on his tongue. Destabilizing, dizzying. Whatever was in his chest, it came alive, undone; the whole of it was swift and bruising. If either of them chose to bend, he knew it would be rapture. If either of them breathed, it would be agony, elation itself.

Only when the moment was strung tight like a bow, both of them aching, did Tristan finally give in.

Breathlessly, he touched her face. "Rhodes—"

He saw her again, alight this time with rage, particulates of ash afloat in the smoldering air to crown her. The sheen of her so bright, gone dark.

Atlas's face, in a blur. His unspoken parting, the weight of his sudden absence.

It's my mistake to fix—

"Rhodes—"

Tell me. Trust me.

The question Tristan couldn't yet ask.

What really happened in that room yesterday?

Her kiss, her touch. Molten, metamorphic. Perilous and waiting. He counted the breaths between them; the pulse of a waiting clock.

Tick—

Tick—

Tick—

"Tristan." Not a whisper. Not this time. Impossible to say what might come next. "Tristan, I—"

"OI," sounded abruptly from downstairs, "asshole! Daddy's home," was the unwelcome proclamation, followed absurdly by, "You're welcome."

The closeness, if it had ever existed, was gone. Dead. Erupted. Libby had shut down again, far enough away that no bend of time or space could reach her, and Tristan, swearing under his breath, pulled sharply out of reach. "You've got to be kidding me. Was that actually—?"

"Yes." Libby folded her arms tightly over her chest, the moment's plausibility lost. "Sounds like Varona's here."

· PARISA ·

P arisa Kamali entered the warm bronze lobby of her tasteful Manhattan hotel on a cloud of buoyancy and birdsong, and also, pigs were fluttering down Fifth Avenue and somewhere (surely Atlas Blakely knew where) hell was a balmy sixty-eight. Read: Parisa was in a mood, tediously hovering in the realm of malcontent most closely associated with hunger or men who do not arrive where they are meant to. In this case, a little bit of both.

It had been one month to the day since Parisa had stepped outside the walls of the Alexandrian Society's manor house. Somehow, despite this very reasonable timeframe, she had not yet been apologized to, groveled before, or otherwise in receipt of what she considered to be even marginally her due. Which was why, perhaps, upon sensing the presence of three to four greatly aspirational assassins folded within the hotel she'd selected on the basis of its exquisite styling, she felt a stirring in her veins most comparable to arousal.

She'd been very well-behaved, after all. Very good, very quiet, lurking politely in the shadows and hardly making anyone cry for purposes of sport—which was precisely the sort of subtlety she'd recently been accused of failing to possess.

"You'll be bored, you know" had been Atlas Blakely's parting attempt at psychological pugilism in the days before Parisa exited the Society's transport wards (destination: Osaka, per the Reina Mori terms of their cohort's strategic defense). Atlas had paused her as she'd been traversing the library to the gardens, biding her time with idleness until their contracted period of independent study ran its course. By then, two days before departure, her things had been packed for nearly a week.

"In case it has escaped your notice, outside this house is only more of the same," Atlas courteously reminded her. "The world is exactly the same series of disappointments as it was before I brought you here."

It was meaningful, most likely, the order in which he spoke his words; the implication that Parisa was one of his chosen flock and not, more flatteringly, a person of free will and/or meaningful institutional value. "I'm quite capable of keeping myself entertained," Parisa replied. "Or do you really think I'd go back into the world without a very, very interesting agenda?"

Atlas paused for a moment then, and Parisa wondered if he knew already which of his trinkets she planned to steal, like rifling through the house's silver. Would he have guessed that Dalton planned to join her despite her insistence to the contrary?

Perhaps he did. "You do know I am capable of finding you," Atlas murmured to her.

"How fascinating," she replied, adding a fashionably sardonic, "whereas I would *clearly* have great trouble finding you." She gestured around the walls of the house that they both understood him to be incapable of abandoning. If not for vocational reasons, then for personal ones.

"It isn't a threat," said Atlas. (Leave it to Atlas Blakely to make an obvious lie sound as mild-mannered as a breakfast order.)

"Certainly not," Parisa agreed, to which Atlas arched a brow. "You couldn't find Rhodes," she pointed out in clarification. "Or the source of your . . . little problem. Ezra, I believe his name is?" Atlas very cleverly didn't flinch. "So forgive me, then, if I do not tremble where I stand."

"You misunderstand me. It's not a threat, Miss Kamali, because it's an invitation." Atlas bent his head in as sly a motion as she had ever seen from him, concealing something so recreationally petty she couldn't quite name it at first. "After all, what will you do without me to rail against?" he asked. (Mirth, Parisa decided. It was definitely mirth.) "I give it six months before I find you at my door again."

There was a flash of images behind her eyes then, like a maelstrom of déjà vu. Someone else's sweets filling the cupboards; jewels she didn't even like; two sets of cups in the kitchen sink. The tedium of an old argument, a story relayed too many times, hollow apologies to keep the peace. She'd never be able to prove whether it came from Atlas's mind or her own.

"Now that," Parisa said, finding her heart in a sudden vise, "was a taunt."

"Or a promise," said Atlas, whose lips twisted up in a smile she'd never considered handsome because handsomeness, like most things, was nothing. "I'll see you very soon, Miss Kamali. Until then, I wish you every satisfaction." A parting benediction from Atlas Blakely was rather like a gauntlet thrown. "Unfortunately, I don't think you have any idea what that looks like."

"Atlas, are you suggesting I don't know how to have fun?" had been Parisa's feigned reply of shock at the time. "Now that's just insulting."

And it was. Though, perhaps fun was something Parisa had been woefully short on in recent weeks.

Now, standing in the hotel lobby with Sam Cooke crooning soulfully overhead, sublimely behaved and not-at-all-bored Parisa felt a sudden, pressing need to turn her day around.

Darling, you send me, sang Sam earnestly as Parisa allowed herself a long moment's perusal, taking stock of the scene with an eye to a bit of . . . what did Atlas call it?

Ah, yes. Satisfaction.

Parisa scanned the room, reconsidering the landscape of the lobby as if it were a battlefield. Oh, Parisa wasn't a physicist—she wasn't a fighter. She wasn't trained in much as far as combat went, though she wasn't without her talents for theater. And what a stage! The hotel was a beautiful conversion from its former life as a pre-medeian power plant, unnecessarily large, brutalism expressed in opulence. Gilded Age in splendor, if not in architectural devotion. The high ceiling was left exposed, naked beams framing its crown jewel: a bar that was exquisitely crafted from a single piece of wood and topped with a gleam of self-illuminating brass. A real centerpiece, and manned by a bartender so unapologetically trendy he seemed written for the part. Mahogany shelves lined the mirrored back wall, set back from draping black curtains; moody lighting glistened, jewel-like, off the laudable selection of spirits. The chandelier overhead was grand without being antiquated; a winding spiral of exposed bulbs that hung like suspended tears. The walls were cavernous, raw concrete swathed in velvet. It lent the whole place a sense of being deep underground, as if its guests descended the high street for hours instead of seconds.

A lovely tomb, as it were. For someone with less of Parisa's joie de vivre.

She sensed danger at her back, angling her head ever so beguilingly to catch a glimpse of her oncoming attacker. The first of her assassins wore a cloyingly old-fashioned bellhop uniform; he was withdrawing a pistol from the inner lining of his jacket. Two people were looking at her breasts. No, three. Fascinating. She pondered how long to let things go on; whether to ruin the dress, which was silk. Dry clean only, and who had the time?

Sam sang tenderly on from the lobby's speakers, momentarily distracting her. Parisa glanced to her left to lock eyes with the attendant behind the front desk (he, sweet thing, was looking at her legs).

"Be a doll," she requested graciously, hand snapping out to pause the murderous bellhop just as she felt his thoughts taking aim at the back of her head. "Speed this up, would you?" she asked, referencing the music playing overhead. "Oh," she added on second thought, sensing the intensity of a moment's calculation as the bellhop's finger gently stroked his trigger, "and kill the lights."

Darling, you s—

S-send—

Darling, you s-send—

The lobby went dark just as the shot rang out.

Then the bass dropped.

To Parisa's very great pleasure, Sam's crooning met up with a heavy, synthetic hip-hop beat, a fitting affair of soul and funk in tandem. The shift in atmosphere offset the sudden handful of panicked screams and became—to Parisa's *immense* satisfaction—something she could actually dance to.

The lights flickered back on just as Parisa had grooved her shoulders to the left, beckoning the bellhop to dance with a nod. He, uncooperatively, stood dazed at her back, staring with great bewilderment at the wild shot he'd taken courtesy of some expertly deployed telepathic subterfuge. Behind the bar, champagne now flowed freely from the bottle on the top shelf, collecting in a reflective pool atop the brass countertop. "Oh, come on," purred Parisa, hooking him with a finger from afar. "Don't make a lady dance alone."

The bellhop's eyes narrowed as his hips began to undulate against his will. His body rolled awkwardly to the beat while Parisa shimmied to the right, enjoying the feel of the song pulsing in her chest.

Only three figures had failed to move in the wake of the bellhop's shot, too professional to blink at the sound of a bullet. The other assassins, then, had revealed their exact positions in the room, however unintentionally. (Easy to tell that the very young woman who'd taken cover below her stool and the businessman who'd all but pissed himself beneath the flow of champagne were nothing more than a pair of unlucky onlookers. Cosmic punishment, Parisa thought, for conducting a sordid affair under a roof of such impressive workmanship.)

She'd just begun to really feel the bass when the second of her assassins— the bartender, whose mustache curled up at the tips for a somewhat cartoonish sartorial effect—leapt over the bar, pistol brandished in her direction. Parisa, tiring of her current dance partner's limitations (he seemed, for whatever reason, not to like her), swung in a graceful pirouette to stage left, the bullet grazing the place her cheek would have been had she not been so expertly choreographed. With an idle command—*drop it, there we go, good boy*—the pistol fell to the floor, sliding conveniently in her direction. She swept it up in a dazzling backbend just a breath before the bellhop wrenched himself out of his trance mid-shimmy and dove, leaving him to land, stunned, in a heap at her feet.

"Someone ought to enjoy this view," Parisa informed him, lifting her right foot to drive his cheek sideways into the polished concrete floors. Then she rolled her body to the steady hip-hop bass, swaying rhythmically beneath the arc of the bartender's oncoming knife.

She dug her heel deeper into the bellhop's cheek as she reached for the bartender's tie and beckoned to the concierge, who had recently finished compiling the various pieces of the rifle he'd been concealing behind the desk. *"Darling, you thrill me,"* Parisa sang, a little off-key, and then gave the bartender's tie a swift tug, yanking his hips flush against hers just as a quick buzz-roll of bullets drilled out like a parade band snare. Their tango now cut regretfully short, Parisa slipped under the bartender's flailing arm, grinding her heel until she felt the gravelly surrender of the bellhop's cheekbone giving way beneath her shoe. The bartender's chest, meanwhile, rattled with the impact of the bullets intended for her, dappling the bar's bronze sheen with a stain of freshly spilled blood.

The woman was no longer screaming, so presumably she'd put two and two together and left. The person at the front desk was frantically trying to evacuate what remained of the guests and staff. Five stars, thought Parisa, impressed. Proper hospitality could be so hard to find.

Another round of shots was fired, the bar's velvet curtains crashing perilously down as Parisa slipped behind one of the concrete pillars, sighing to herself about waste. It was such a shame, really, to damage such tastefully selected pieces. As the din of artless warfare continued to escalate within the lobby courtesy of the concierge's rifle, Parisa determined that a minor instance of telepathic discombobulation might not be breaking any ceremonial rules of combat. After all, what was an automatic weapon against one tiny, unarmed person? Unfair was what it was. So she gave the concierge something more useful to think about, such as the nature of perfect fusion and, as an added bonus, the task of solving the so-called homeless problem on whatever the city was calling a social service budget these days.

The concierge's mind now put to more nuanced use, obstacles yet remained. The bellhop, who had scrambled away on all fours beneath the hail of careless gunfire, was now imminently on deck. Parisa put a little sway in her hips as the bellhop stumbled to his feet, rushing her at the same time that her fourth assassin—a maintenance worker in full janitorial splendor, who had been wisely steering clear of his accomplices' more lethal shots—

withdrew a wrench from his toolkit and threw it wildly, without thought. Parisa, less mad than, say, disappointed, paused to pick up the knife that had long since plummeted from the bartender's hand (he was busy dying an ugly death) and turned, intending the blade to find a home between the eyes of the oncoming maintenance man. He, however, was somewhat quicker than the others. He dodged the knife and caught her wrist, spittle flying as he tackled her backward into the concrete pillar.

Parisa hissed in surprise and annoyance, her exposed back meeting cold stone. The knife had fallen from her hand from the force of the maintenance man's impact, the blade clattering to the floor just out of reach. To say the assassin had a few pounds of force on her was something of an understatement. She struggled to move, to breathe, the assassin's sudden wrenching of her arm augmenting the necessity for cooler heads. Parisa's combat style, after all, was theatrical but not stupid. Better not discover what a man in his position might do next.

Parisa spat in the maintenance worker's face and beckoned the bellhop with a little tug to his mind. His posture went rigid, first in opposition, then in submission to the force of her overriding command. With a grimace, the bellhop marched tightly forward and lifted a heavy boot, landing a hard stomp to the center of the maintenance man's hamstring and leaving him to collapse around Parisa's legs.

Parisa snapped the maintenance man's neck backward with a hard impact from her knee to his jaw, the sudden rush of blood in her ears joining up with the pulsing bass that still played over the hotel speakers. As the maintenance worker dropped, execution-style, to his knees, the knife skittered up from the floor into her hands, no less recalcitrant than the straining bellhop. Parisa grimaced; relieved, briefly, that Nico wasn't there to witness the limits of her physical magic. She discovered that she'd hate to lose any shine in his eyes, which was quite frankly disgusting.

Parisa drove the knife's blade under the maintenance worker's clavicle, repulsed with herself. He collapsed sideways on the art deco runner she'd so admired, convulsing once before falling still beside the beautiful, blood-sprayed bar.

The dress was ruined, too. Disappointing.

Two down, two to go. Behind the concierge desk, the most trigger-happy of her assassins was still sweating over municipal budgets, one hand clutched despairingly around the rifle like a child with a toy. The bellhop, meanwhile, shook off the effects of her telepathic command, one eye visibly obscured from the swelling of his cheek. She'd most definitely broken his face.

"Why should I let you heal?" she asked the bellhop. (Never let it be said she was a bully.)

"Fuck off," he spat in reply, or so Parisa was forced to assume, because it wasn't in English. She didn't recognize the language, which didn't really matter. Anyone could be bought. Regardless, the subsequent "bitch" was so obvious in intonation she didn't require translation, much less anything meriting debate.

"Well, it was fun while it lasted," she lamented with a sigh, bending to fetch the knife from the maintenance worker's gurgling neck. Overhead, Sam Cooke was fading gradually into tinny, uncertain silence. There was a slight ringing in Parisa's ears, some nausea. The beginnings of a migraine. She felt the bellhop's presence at her back as she bent to retrieve the knife, and for fuck's sake, the things that crossed his mind. As if it made a difference that she had the goddamn glutes of Aphrodite. To him she was nothing, nothing more than an object, something to be used or fucked or destroyed.

This was the world, she reminded herself. Atlas was right.

Suddenly, everything felt substantially less festive.

Parisa rose to her feet and flicked the blade across the bellhop's throat; a tight, efficient slash to his carotid. He staggered, then hit the ground with a thud. She stepped over him, panting, and swiped a slick lock of hair from her forehead with the back of her hand. Then she walked past the unmoving bartender to pause before the concierge.

He was still lost in thought—or, more aptly, trapped in it. He looked stricken as she withdrew the automatic rifle carefully, almost gingerly from his hands. Presumably he found the puzzle she'd given him to be very punishing indeed.

"Let me put you out of your misery," Parisa suggested, licking blood from the corner of her mouth.

The kick of the chamber discharging was really something. Then again, he should have known it wasn't a weapon meant for close range.

·　·　·

A few minutes later, the bell dinged with the elevator's arrival onto her floor. She paused for the requisite retina scan into the room (that, come to think of it, had been the probable source of her afternoon visitors in the lobby) and felt the latch give way beneath her hand. The door swung open, inviting her to step leisurely over the threshold into the tranquility of the room.

"You're back early," called a voice from the bathroom. "Am I to assume things went well at the consulate?"

The door shut behind Parisa as she drank in a calming breath. The rooms, much like the lobby downstairs, were the work of someone with excellent taste, though the teal chaise that had been so expertly chosen for the backdrop of mahogany paneling had been swallowed up by two days' worth of discarded clothes. From the handcrafted gold mirror on the wall, she could see the humidity had not been kind to her hair. Nor had the blood of four recently dispatched men.

"Define 'well,'" said Parisa, her stomach gurgling when she spotted the remains of that morning's pastries. A single pain au chocolat sat untouched beside an open page of scribbled notes on the desk. She reached for it, taking a wolfish bite just as Dalton emerged from the bathroom on an inviting wave of steam.

He wore a towel around his waist and nothing else. Pearls of water still clung to his chest; his dark hair was slicked back from his forehead, emphasizing the fineness of his princely cheeks.

It remained strange, Dalton being two people at once: the melding of his inner animation, the fraction of his ambition that had been forced back into his corporeal form, alongside the lofty version of him she'd initially pursued. His thoughts were the same as they usually were since she'd interfered with his consciousness last year; a mix of incomplete things, unintelligible and sometimes garbled, like radio static. The rest of him remained as pleasant a view as ever, though he'd begun to make small changes. Not so cleanly shaven. Less devotion to detail for his appearance generally. The notes on the desk were becoming increasingly illegible, disordered.

Wordlessly, his gaze traveled the length of her blood-splattered dress.

"Did you kill him?" Dalton finally asked with an undertone of amusement.

If only. But no, her intended afternoon had not remotely come to pass. "He wasn't there. I ran afoul of unpleasant company," she replied, licking chocolate from her thumb.

Dalton made a sound like *mm*, seemingly in admonishment. "I believe I mentioned I was available as an escort," he remarked.

"And as I believe I mentioned to you, I'm a very talented negotiator," Parisa replied. She flicked another glance at his notes, gesturing to them. "Discover anything new about the universe while I was away?"

A roil of his thoughts met hers. She parsed what she could and blocked out the rest. Latter stages of her headache were impending.

"Nothing that can't wait until later," Dalton replied, taking a step to finger the strap of her dress, implications featherlight and gossamer. "Will this be a problem?" he asked, gesturing tacitly to the bodies downstairs.

"I'll put a placard on the door," said Parisa. "In general I find the staff here to be incredibly fair-minded."

They would have to relocate momentarily, but Dalton seemed to grasp that there wasn't much point bringing it up. "Would you like to discuss it?"

"What more is there to say? Nothazai wasn't at the consulate and yet another group of men tried to kill me." Dalton's hands framed her hips in sympathy, palms gliding smoothly across silk as he leaned in to place a kiss in the hollow of her throat. "But I'm not bored in the least," Parisa added with a self-indulgent tone of brightness, "so there's that for the prophecies of Atlas Blakely."

Dalton chuckled into her neck as Parisa raised the pastry to her lips, indulging another bite. "Ah, that reminds me. Another summons came for you while you were away," Dalton informed her, disentangling for a moment to reach for a white card she hadn't noticed on the edge of the unmade bed.

Underwear had been flung beside the discarded duvet, a wrinkled shirt and a pair of mismatched trouser socks lingering in its wake like watchful shadows. Parisa was overcome with a sudden desire to tidy up, which was monumentally upsetting. So she ignored it, taking another bite of pastry to watch it crumble onto the floor.

The correspondence card that slipped itself before her face between the prongs of two dexterous academician's fingers was the third in a series of attempted correspondences, such that she did not need to know the details of the message contained within.

"He did say he'd be able to find me," Parisa murmured to herself, not reaching for the proffered card.

Dalton, taking the hint, withdrew it, though a look of boyish amusement remained. "This, I assure you, is not Atlas's work," he said. "And I take it you still do not intend to answer?"

"Does it require an answer?" Parisa arched a brow. "You led me to believe the logistics of the Society's institutional workings weren't a worthwhile concern."

"What I said," Dalton clarified, "was that the Society was as functionally tedious as any governing body. But that doesn't mean I think you ought to ignore them entirely, seeing as you'll need to gain access to the archives again."

Parisa's gaze strayed back to the open page of his notes, which were filled to the margins with his scribblings on worldmaking. "Do you think they've got any idea what we're up to?"

"No." He'd been sounding relatively himself until then, but then he laughed, an acerbic laugh, which was as new to his recent transformation as was that particular facial expression. "I assure you, Parisa, this summons is simply standard protocol. The Society doesn't possess the requisite imagination to guess you might choose anything but them."

"But it could be a trap by Atlas," she pointed out. "A method of luring me."

Dalton shrugged. "The Society tracks your magical footprint at will," he said plainly, confirming two years of Parisa's suspicions with the flutter of the summons in his hand. "But I highly doubt that Atlas would use any of the official Society channels to find you. That would require a paper trail, reports, administrative approval. Which," Dalton pointed out, "would counteract decades of calculated subterfuge to maintain his position without betraying the nature of his research. And I assure you, he's not that desperate yet."

"Yet," Parisa echoed, lifting her chin to meet his eye. It was there again, that indecipherable rush of chaos from his thoughts.

Eventually, though, it stilled, and Dalton's lips curled into a smile. "At some point, yes, it's possible Atlas may consider other means by which to interfere. Or he may simply try to be rid of you. You are, as he is well aware, a uniquely capable opponent."

"Not an opponent," Parisa corrected thoughtfully. "More of a nemesis. I wouldn't say we're playing the same game." The experiment was Atlas's driving force, his sense of purpose. He lived and breathed for the possibility of opening the multiverse. Parisa was notably more inventive.

"I think he came to believe otherwise over time." Dalton's hand stroked her shoulder, the tip of one finger slipping below the strap of her dress. "He isn't wrong, Parisa, that until one of you is rid of the other, neither of you is likely to succeed. And you could easily replace him as Caretaker," Dalton suggested, not for the first time. "The governing board meets routinely. What Atlas has done to win them over, you can replicate to greater effect. Then the archives and their contents can be yours, the others can be summoned, and the experiment can finally begin."

Dalton leaned forward, his lips brushing her cheek, and then her ear. "I can make a new world for you," he said to the edge of her jaw. "All you have to do is say the word, Parisa, and everything can be ours."

Everything. Men who stared at her breasts and shot at her heart.

Everything.

And all it would cost was the Caretaker who'd chosen to use her to help himself.

Parisa shivered as Dalton's touch grazed the flecks of dried blood on her arms. He smelled like hotel shampoo, gardenia lotion. The lingering haze of fresh coffee dovetailed the edge of his kiss. Her heart fluttered like the rounds of an AK, pulsing with adrenaline and hunger.

"Tempting." Her mouth was dry. She needed a shower, a glass of water. The headache would only get worse. Dalton peeled the dress from her body and she let him, the pastry falling to the floor as he kissed his way across her chest, down the planes of her abdomen, along the insubstantial panels of lace wrapped snugly around her hips.

He nudged her knees gently apart, eyes rising to meet hers slowly with his lips pressed to her thigh. Mysteriously, his towel had disappeared.

"You're set on villainy, then?" She meant it to be insouciant, but there was a definite edge of something less productive, more urgent.

"Yes," Dalton said with a princely smile. "I like you with a little carnage."

His thoughts roared with incongruity, power and softness, capitulation and control. The heat of it was daunting, increasingly perilous to stand beside.

Parisa was sore from overexertion, dehydrated, hunted, her stomach still growled. All the usual signs to cut and run were present and accounted for. Why had she felt Dalton Ellery a necessary constant after a decade of hard-earned solitude? Put it down to a mix of things: Vindication. Revenge. Desire. He was Atlas Blakely's favorite toy; Atlas's only chance at real, meaningful power. A maker, unmaker of worlds. The pure scale of it was enough to reorient her aptitude for company.

On the basis of power alone, Parisa could certainly commend Dalton's argument to give up her mundane attempts at survival in favor of total, world-dominating control—and with it, perhaps, finally, freedom. Actual freedom that looked a lot like a life.

Two problems. One: Parisa did not have the requisite pieces to complete the experiment as Dalton had postured. Dalton was necessary to call what needed to be called; Tristan was necessary to see what needed to be seen. For reasons any psychology undergraduate could guess, Tristan belonged to

Atlas as surely as Dalton belonged to Parisa, which at present left the players stagnant on the board. Libby, half their power source, was a question mark. Nico, the other half, was malleable, but still only half. Reina—fucking Reina—was an obstacle, at best; a generator who resented being what she was, and whose personal enmity was too irrational to be predicted. Winning the arms race to the multiverse against Atlas Blakely, then, would mean a tactical landscape of highly political, deeply personal warfare—for which, of course, Parisa was both uniquely challenged and particularly skilled.

The second problem was more pressing, and also more nuanced in that it was not technically a problem at all. Put simply: if Parisa won and Atlas lost, then the game would be over. The prospect of victory, however assured, had a hollowness to it that Parisa didn't like to question, for fear the answer would be Freudian. Or dull.

She would win. There was no question of it. But there was so very much with which to occupy her time until then; a checklist that could not reasonably be called irresponsible. Problems abounded, both in the form of organizations who targeted her cohort and assassins who bled on her silks. And, of course, there was the Society itself, which had promised her glory and so far fallen shy.

Business before pleasure, she recalled through a thud in her head, grasping the roots of Dalton's thick hair and giving it a gentle tug. "What happens if I don't answer?" she asked, gesturing to the correspondence card that had fluttered, forgotten, to the floor.

"What will the Society do to you, you mean?" Dalton brushed the curve of her thigh with his lips and despite her headache, Parisa felt more at ease with him today. He felt familiar to her at the moment, for the most part. The same could not be said for every day. (But she was not, she thought silently, bored.)

"They'll continue to follow protocol, I imagine. I expect I'll receive a summons shortly myself," he reminded her. "I got one ten years ago. As soon as they realize I'm no longer a researcher in the archives, they'll likely send me one again."

Parisa considered this, turning it over and over from every angle in her thoughts. "What do they want from us?"

"Exactly what they promised you. Wealth. Power. Prestige. Did you really think those things would only benefit you?" He looked up at her, mouth still hovering idly above the fabric of her underwear while his hands traveled the arcs of her calves. "They'll ask you your goals, put you in touch with other Society members, make for you whatever privilege they cannot steal or buy. And if you're not sure what you'd like to do as an Alexandrian, then they'll send you on to another department."

"Which one?"

He shrugged, slipping the underwear down her legs as she brushed a set of fingertips over the nape of his neck, tracing the patterns of his vertebrae. "I never went that far. By the time I got my summons, I already knew what I wanted."

That, or Atlas had already decided it for him, having sequestered enough of what Dalton was to ensure his compliance. A very different game indeed. "Mm." Parisa allowed him to nudge her backward toward the bed, collapsing onto the piled duvet and reaching for the errant sock below her hips before tossing it onto the floor where he knelt. "So then does it actually matter whether I reply?"

"Yes." Dalton laughed abruptly, though he didn't lift his head from the curve of her thigh. "The Society is only the Society if its members continue its legacy of prestige. You don't have the option," he reminded her, moistening his lips with the careful slip of his tongue, "of being average."

"You'd think with that sort of mindset they'd be more proactive about protecting their investment," Parisa muttered. Difficult to climb the entirety of her rage, obviously, what with Dalton's tongue being put to such productive use, but the events of the hotel lobby that afternoon hadn't been the first of such annoyances. When Parisa and Dalton first arrived in Osaka from the Society house a month ago, there had been medeians stationed at all the transports and secret police patrolling the trains, all thinking the name Reina Mori so hard that Parisa had felt personally insulted. Now, of course, *someone*—Nothazai, the de facto head of the Forum, being Parisa's best guess—had clearly formed the wherewithal to realize Reina would not have ventured far from her precious books, and certainly would not have returned to Osaka, a place to which she felt no connection. As the attacks began to increase in regularity, it was clear the hunt had really begun.

At which point it seemed fair to say that Parisa expected more than a correspondence card in assistance, or what had the past two years even been for?

"It's no different than what Atlas told your cohort at the installation," said Dalton, pausing his ministrations to meet her eye. "As far as the Society is concerned, people may be trying to kill you, but your lives are not in danger. You will always be more dangerous than anyone who could ever dream of hunting you. You will always be the most dangerous person in the room. They know it, and they will not protect you. The best they can do is use you, and hope that you'll be satisfied enough with the stupor they offer you that you'll resist the urge to become a danger to them. Because you, Miss Kamali," Dalton promised her with a flick of his tongue, "are the most dangerous thing in every world, including this one."

Parisa shivered unintentionally, groaning when Dalton slid her a knowing smile. "I've already run away with you, Dalton. Stop flirting with me and suck my clit."

Dalton chuckled and obliged, and Parisa came quickly, almost dizzily. Her hips cramped from the force of it and Dalton gave another low rasp of a laugh, massaging her with a look of amusement. "Do you want to—?"

"Later." She felt intensely aware of her headache now, the muscular fatigue beginning to take root like poison. "Dalton, I'm covered in blood."

"You wear it well," he said.

"Of course I do. But that doesn't mean I like the outfit." Her phone buzzed from where she'd set it on the dresser, a timely distraction. Parisa glanced over with a sigh before struggling upright, reaching it only after it had already stopped ringing.

"Anyone important?" Dalton called to her over his shoulder. He'd risen to his feet, striding naked to the wardrobe for a clean shirt. Admirable, Parisa thought, eyeing the edges of his glutes, the teardrop of his quads, the crevice of his hamstrings. Optically speaking, he must have been up to much more than reading during his sabbatical as a researcher. Even their customary recreation wouldn't account for that sort of obvious athleticism.

"Who'd be considered important?" Parisa asked with a snort. She'd had no contact with anyone for two years. There was rarely any purpose to her even carrying the phone around. For logistical purposes, though, she tapped the missed call icon.

Unknown number.

Parisa's skin pricked. Not just anyone had this number.

"Atlas," said Dalton immediately. "Or the naturalist. You did say you could talk her around."

A voicemail popped up on the screen. Her headache had worsened now that she was upright. Parisa fought the urge to jump to conclusions, only half-listening to Dalton. "Mm."

"The physicist sent a message while you were gone," Dalton said. "More speculation that the archives are trying to kill you, which you probably shouldn't ignore. I suggest the empath."

She considered hitting play on the voicemail, then reconsidered. If it was who she thought it was, maybe better to listen in private. She looked around for her clothes, suddenly overcome with annoyance at the mess. Dalton's towel was still in a heap on the floor. *Darling, you thrill me.*

Her head had begun to throb in earnest and she reached into the hotel mini-fridge, twisting off the cap and drinking directly from a glass bottle of water. "Okay," she said belatedly. It probably wasn't who she thought it was.

Though, Nico had promised the technomantic network he'd constructed to secure their devices was protected. And though Parisa hated to admit it, she did implicitly trust him when he did something stupid but impressive.

"Okay, you'll kill the empath?" echoed Dalton, sounding amused with her again. "It would solve a number of your problems, by my count. He seems to be the naturalist's comrade of choice purely on the basis of compliance, not magical aptitude. You're the better medeian, so perhaps there's something of a trade you could make to secure her for the experiment. Though I know you're not overly fond of compromise."

"I—" Parisa looked up from her screen, still lost in thought. Her heart was pounding somehow, like she'd run there from somewhere else. Like she'd been doing nothing but running and running all her life. "What?"

Dalton had sidled up to her, his breath warm on her shoulder. She tried reminding herself that Dalton could not actually see, hear, or feel the way her pulse had raced, or the places her mind had gone for as long as the voicemail remained unopened. That sort of telepathic infiltration was her expertise, not his, and she soothed herself with the fortunate recollection that she had never known anyone as good as she was.

Not counting Atlas Blakely. Or Callum Nova. Both of whom were not in this room and could therefore fuck off from her thoughts.

"So," Dalton remarked. "There is someone important to you after all."

Abruptly, Parisa determined she wanted to be alone. "I'm getting in the shower."

Dalton paused a moment like he would offer an argument, or worse, a taunt.

Then he shrugged. "Fine."

Parisa slipped into the bathroom and turned on the water, letting the shower run as she listened to two seconds of the voicemail. Then she hit call.

It rang once, twice. "Hello?"

"Nasser." She cleared her throat. "Hi."

"Hi, love. Give me a moment, it's loud—"

"Yes, that's fine." Parisa nudged the bathroom door open a crack, glancing into the hotel room. Dalton was lying on the bed now, flipping through channels on the television. He skipped through cartoons and sitcoms, then lingered for a moment on one of the twenty-four-hour news channels. Parisa recognized the outside of the Hague on the screen, scanning the closed captions for meaning. A human rights trial. Dalton would not understand the Farsi she was speaking, but he would know what it meant that she was speaking it at all.

"Parisa," said Nasser, his voice a quiet resurgence in her ear. "Sorry, I hadn't expected you to call back so quickly. It was silly of me," he added after a moment. "To call."

She didn't touch that. "What time is it there?" She hadn't yet adjusted to Eastern time; normally she was never more than two or so time zones from Tehran.

"Late, almost midnight. Just catching up with a few of the partners before the board meeting in the morning."

"I see. Business is good, I take it?" she asked, scanning the bathroom floor for something to make this less . . . whatever it was. It was a lovely tile choice, a rich magenta. Unusual and vibrant. Sanguine, like the flecks of blood still dotting her bare skin.

"You know me, business is always good." His voice was light, carefully restrained. She imagined hers probably sounded the same. "But you know I wouldn't call just to chat about money."

Parisa said nothing, realizing blood had stained her cuticles. She tucked her phone against her ear and turned on the sink, scrubbing the nail of her thumb.

Nasser audibly cleared his throat. "I haven't heard from you recently."

"You never hear from me, Nas. It's our thing." She tried to sound nonchalant and was alarmed by how easily she succeeded, as if this were truly just another phone call. Just a normal afternoon cleaning blood from the beds of her nails, admiring expensive tile. "Might as well get to the point."

"True." A brief pause. "Are you in trouble?" he finally asked her.

Parisa looked up at her reflection, noticing blood in her hair, on her scalp, wanting to laugh. How could he know? Deductive answers pressed in on her brain but she disliked them, ignored them. She considered a false answer, no answer, the truth. *Why do you ask? Did someone find you? Who was it?*

Was he wearing an unnatural amount of tweed?

"Nas, you know me," she said casually. "Never in more trouble than I can manage."

She glanced through the crack in the door again to observe the motion of Dalton's shoulders as he folded his arms below his chin. The trial on the screen was over the actions of a dictator, probably a mix of the truth with

Western opportunism, plus a dose of racism and hypocrisy to sweeten the deal. Parisa had a sudden craving for waffles; for a different world.

She also had a feeling that she knew where Nothazai, self-appointed champion of human rights, had gone that afternoon instead of his meeting at the Czech consulate.

"You're sure everything's okay?" Nasser asked, though he didn't wait for an answer before adding, "I'd like to see you if I can."

Parisa returned her attention to her reflection in the mirror, wondering what would happen if the bloodstains remained. Would she still be considered beautiful? Probably yes. "Are you planning to be in Paris?" she asked doubtfully, choosing to permit the assumption that she hadn't moved from where he'd left her.

"I can be wherever you are," Nasser said.

Parisa chewed the inside of her cheek, considering it as she peered through the doorway again. She had a new destination in mind given what she'd just gleaned from the news, but that didn't mean she couldn't make a quick side trip if necessary. She was done with captivity now, academic or otherwise. Free to do as she liked, to be who she liked, to go where she wished. A deeply hard-won freedom that, aside from this particular moment, she did everything in her power to take for granted and forget.

"I suppose I could come to you. You know, oddly enough," Parisa added, reaching for a coquettish tone that she found with alarming ease, "I've been craving bamieh since—"

"No," Nasser cut in, his tone firm before he gentled. "Not here. Sorry, sweetheart."

Parisa must have inhaled sharply at the unexpected admonishment, because Dalton had looked up from the news coverage (now just some idiot American talking about an election) to glance at her. She turned away, fighting the instinct to lower her voice, and shut the bathroom door, looking again at her reflection.

"Nas, are you worried about me or you?"

"Never me, always you." His tone remained sunny, unchanged. "You're still in Paris, then? I can meet you at the hotel you like. The fancy one."

She looked away from the logo on a discarded robe, an opulent pile of Turkish cotton. "No, not there."

"The café then? Same one I used to meet you?"

"That was years ago, Nas. I don't even know if it's still there."

"I remember it. I'll find it."

No, she thought about saying. It seemed easy for a moment.

"What time?"

"Maybe eight in the morning? Does that work?"

"I thought you had a meeting?"

"Yes, well, now I have one with you." He switched from Farsi to hush someone on the other side of the line, hurrying them off in rapid Arabic before returning his attention to Parisa. "*Eshgh*?"

Parisa swallowed around the term of endearment. "Yes?"

"I have to go. I'll see you in the morning, okay?"

"Nas." Parisa felt cold suddenly, folding her arms over her chest. She thought to ask a question, two questions, then chose very pointedly not to. "Can we make it later? Maybe eleven."

He was silent for a moment. "Okay, eleven. But promise me you'll be there."

She blinked. Once, twice. "Okay."

"Promise me."

"Yes, Nasser, I promise."

"I love you. Don't say it back, I'll know you're lying." He laughed, then, and hung up, leaving Parisa to stand silently in the center of the bathroom, not realizing she was staring blankly at her reflection until the door opened.

She set her phone on the counter as Dalton's arms came around her from behind.

"I didn't realize you were still in contact with your husband." Dalton's voice in her ear was the measured, patient one belonging to the version of him that Parisa already knew was capable of keeping a secret.

"Only occasionally." She looked over at the water still running from the shower. "I'm going to get cleaned up. And then we're going to Paris."

In answer, Dalton's face was shadowed with juvenilia again. Amusement, again, like he was laughing at her for something. "I thought we were hunting Nothazai," Dalton mused aloud. "Despite my ample protestations, I might add."

She felt a tremor of annoyance. "It's no loss to you, then, is it? If you think it's such a waste of my time."

Dalton shrugged. "I never said it was a waste. Just that Nothazai is no more likely to serve your interests than any other enemy. The Forum does not have what you actually need, which is the archives."

Parisa stepped into the shower and let the water soak her scalp, suddenly irritated with herself. The mess in the room, the blood on her hands, the length of time it would take to gather her things. Why had she ever been so careless? Two years away and already she'd forgotten she wasn't the kind of person who could afford to make a mess.

"Parisa." Dalton was still waiting for an answer. Parisa reached for the shampoo with a sigh.

"I don't have to find the Forum today, Dalton. I can find them anywhere, any time." Nothazai would be proselytizing in the Netherlands soon enough. If not, then he'd head back to Forum headquarters eventually, at which point back to London they would go. "And there's no point taking over the archives until we have the other pieces we need."

The fragrance of the shampoo was a temporary release until Dalton spoke again.

"You left him."

"What?" she called back distractedly.

"You left him," Dalton repeated. "But now you're at his beck and call?"

"Who, Nothazai?"

"No, your husband." He seemed to be needling her with his repetition of the phrase so she ignored him for a moment, rinsing the shampoo out of her hair. She felt nauseated; a little sick. Her head pounded again. Again. Again.

She lathered with conditioner, slicking it through her ends.

"Nasser and I don't talk," she said, with the implication obvious to her, if not to Dalton. Meaning: *He wouldn't ask me for this unless it was very, very important.*

She cleaned the blood of her would-be killers with a bar of French soap, scrubbing at her arms until the water at her feet had turned a rosy, feminine pink.

"He hurt you," Dalton observed, and Parisa felt vaguely aware of the tension in her jaw, the position of her teeth.

"I never said he—"

But the words stuck in her throat. She heard Callum's voice.

Who hurt you?

Everyone.

And Reina's.

You can't actually love anyone, can you?

And Dalton's.

I don't care who or what you love—

"It's complicated," Parisa muttered eventually, shutting off the water. She remained there in the steam, in the silence, for another minute. Another. The bathroom door opened, then shut.

By the time she stepped out of the shower, Dalton was gone. She exhaled something she told herself was not relief, then turned on the lights, the bright ones over the vanity.

Her phone wasn't on the counter where she'd left it. But she chose not to think about that right now.

She toweled herself dry, seeing herself in patches from the fogged-up mirror. What was she really? She wondered it again. She already knew what other people saw. What Dalton saw, what her assassins saw. Some kind of beautiful ratio, exquisite math, fortunate statistics, the indulgences she dutifully skipped (except for today—blood and pastries).

What had Atlas seen?

It didn't matter. Parisa shook out her hair, flipping it forward and then backward, leaving her cheeks flushed with effort as she raked her fingers through her damp waves, taming them, leaving them to fall where they naturally did, in some delicate, unintended perfection.

Why *had* Atlas chosen her?

Then, like cosmic punishment for irrational, pointless thinking, the voice in her head was suddenly her own.

Nas, how could I ever be happy here? I never wanted to be a wife, I don't want to be a mother, you want me to keep living my life in chains just because I was grateful to you for one thing, for one chance—

Parisa tousled her hair, switching her part from one side to the other. She didn't have a bad side.

—but I'm done being grateful! I'm done trying to make myself suitable for this family, for this God, for this life. I'm done being small, I've outgrown the person who needed you to save her, I don't even know who she is anymore—

She pouted at the mirror and started again, pinching her cheeks to see the color come and go.

—and I want more, so much more—

Lip balm. Mascara. Lips softer, eyes wider, be something different, something else.

—I just want to live, Nas! Just let me live!

What was the point of reliving the past? She was hunting her invisible nemeses, grappling for power, finding new methods of control. She should be busy, too busy being the most dangerous person in this or any world to think about why she'd been such an easy target for Atlas Blakely, a man in need of weapons just to make a universe that he could stand. But now—

Now she was thinking about Nasser, as if it mattered at all what kind of person she'd been over a decade ago.

Just an hour of your time, now and then. That's all I ask. I know, I know, I'm asking a lot more from you inside my head, but that's not fair—doesn't it matter what I choose to put in front of you? Someday maybe you'll understand that there's a difference between what a person thinks and who they choose to be—

A glint caught her eye from her reflection. A brief, unnatural sparkle in the placid lake of her appearance, the consistency of her beauty, the easy grace she always wore. She leaned forward, forgetting her internal monologue, letting it collapse.

Someday the view will be different, eshgh, *and I hope you see me in a softer light—*

"Parisa?"

Dalton leaned against the frame of the bathroom door. In his left hand was one of her dresses. In his right hand was her phone.

"I don't care if you want to see your husband. Sorry—Nasser. If you want me to call him that, I will. I suppose you're right, anyway, you'll need to see him, because if the Society could find evidence of him in your past then the Forum surely can as well, and so can Atlas. And so can anyone else who wants you dead." Another pause as Dalton set her phone back on the bathroom counter. "I replied to the physicist for you as well. I think you'll need to find out what he plans to do about the archives, or at least keep track of what Atlas is doing at the house. Atlas is going to win over both the physicists unless you can convince one of them to do it differently.

"What is it?" Dalton asked, frowning at her silence. His gaze traced the placement of her fingers, which had been parsing the thickness of her hair.

"I—" Parisa was caught somewhere between laughing and crying. "I found a gray hair."

"So?"

Laughter, definitely laughter. It escaped her in something of a rueful bray. Unattractive, like a selfish woman. Ugly, like an ambitious one. Like one who chose to punish a good man for not being the right man, who left because staying was too boring, too painful, too hard. Like a woman who had to be a weapon because she couldn't be anything else.

"Nothing." Only the future loss of her desirability, the collapse of her personhood. The first glimpse of an empire steadily falling to unseen ruin. The fate she already knew was coming, the punishment she'd always known she deserved. What timing!

"Sorry," she said, repeating, "nothing, it's nothing. What were you saying?"

—if the Society could find evidence of him in your past then the Forum surely can as well, and so can Atlas—

Confirmation of the thought she hadn't wanted to have. That if Nasser knew she was in trouble, it could only mean that he was in trouble, too.

Selfish. She had always been selfish.

I don't want to be a wife, I don't want to be a mother.

Reina again, unhelpful as always.

You can't love anyone, can you?

A younger Parisa, one without any signs of forthcoming decay, screamed, *I deserve the right to choose how I love!* while this Parisa, entering her crone era, whispered, *Maybe not, maybe you're right.*

Maybe I can't actually do it, maybe I don't know how.

(*The world is exactly the same series of disappointments as it was before I brought you here,* said the timely reappearance of Atlas Blakely in her thoughts.)

"Atlas," Dalton repeated impatiently. "And the other physicist—"

"You mean Rhodes?" Parisa reached out for the dress Dalton had brought for her, a simple knit fabric. She slipped it easily over her shoulders and turned to face him, telling herself nothing had changed.

So she had one gray hair, big deal. She also had assassins and a husband, a game still in the process of unfolding, a multitude of worlds and sins. She would die someday, either with regrets or without them. It would happen regardless of the color of her hair, or whether she was fuckable. Whether she could explain why or where it hurt. She was born with an ending built in, just like everyone else was. She had always known that desire was temporary, that life was fleeting, that love was a trap.

That her beauty was a curse.

"Yes, she's back, which means Atlas will have her running the experiment soon. Probably." Dalton was still frowning at her. "You look strange."

She shook her head. "It's fine. Just . . . just vanity." Just mortality, that's all. "Nothing lasts forever. The important thing is—"

Her head throbbed like a tribal drum. Something was whispering to her like a ghost.

(Eshgh. My life. *Run if you have to run.*)

(*I just want to live, Nas! Just let me live!*)

It was a small voice, but an unavoidable one. It asked a question she couldn't answer.

(Was this really the life she'd meant to chase, or was this just another way to run?)

But no, some voices had to be silenced. Some voices would never be quiet unless she was the one to shut them up. Because if Parisa was a person who'd learned to fight for herself, who'd chosen satisfaction over compromise and power over morality—if she was a person with blood on her hands—it was because she'd had to be. Because this world demanded it. Because she'd needed protection that no one but herself had ever been willing to provide. Because this was a world that would stare at her breasts and still count her for less if she let it; a world that would gladly tell her what she was worth and what she wasn't.

So what mattered about this world? Only that she remained the most dangerous thing in it.

"The important thing," Parisa repeated, louder, "is that we get to Rhodes before Atlas does." Yes, that was it. The game, the game still needed playing. "I can work with Rhodes. Rhodes will see the logic—that even if Atlas could somehow convince Reina, he still needs you." Yes, there it was. Parisa held the winning piece and always had. "You're the only one who can spontaneously create life, so—"

"There's no evidence showing it's spontaneous."

"What?" Dalton's thoughts were warping again, distracting Parisa's already frazzled mind. She heard the inside of his head in bursts, in newsreels and headlines, the mixed media of his disjointed thoughts. The American election, the Hague, apparently he could read Arabic well enough to guess at one or two of the things he'd heard her say, though not enough to understand Farsi. And not nearly enough to understand her.

"But if you really want to go—"

"Yes." She blinked. "Yes, let's go."

The transport at Grand Central was busy; crowded enough that Parisa could avoid the traps if she concentrated, if she focused hard enough. A small pool of effort at the small of her back, a gray streak in her flawless hair, all to remind her that not even perfection, not even the desire of a thousand commuting financiers would be enough to save her from death. She arrived at the café in Paris thirty minutes early, an unfashionable arrival time to pair unfashionably with her wrinkled dress, traces of blood still staining the tips of her fingers.

Not that it mattered.

Nasser never showed up.

THE EZRA SIX

ONE
Julian

Julian Rivera Pérez was *also* born as the earth was dying because everyone was, fuck you! Atlas Blakely wasn't special and frankly, neither are you. Neither was Julian. This was a sentiment, lightly paraphrased, that Julian's abuela used to express in a variety of ways, very often. A hard worker, Julian's abuela, and deeply religious from a place of faith, not fear. *Everything is hard, mijo, to live is a challenge. Eat your mofongo, it's getting cold.*

Julian's father was an American citizen, which was good, because although nobody ever said so, in all likelihood his Salvadoreña mother was not. She had a jitteriness, a jumpiness to her metaphysical existence that never quite left Julian, even though he executed this internal paranoia in such a way that prompted the white members of his wave of delinquents to refer to him mockingly (and incorrectly, but they were always mistaking him for someone else, usually Bryan Hernández who grew up to play in the big leagues) as the baddest bandito on the block. Julian was the oldest of three brothers, a real motherfucker, or so he thought until he met a girl with a terrifying father who successfully convinced Julian that he wasn't much at all.

"Anyone can throw a punch," Jenny Novak's father said to Julian, who at the time had a broken arm (but you should have seen the other guy). Big Nicky Novak took a drag from a cigar, something that later seemed ridiculous since it was the eighties, not the fifties. (Julian never found out whether the existence of Big Nicky implied a smaller one somewhere else.)

"You know what's a big deal, kid?" asked Big Nicky. "Shutting someone up when you walk in the room."

"How?" asked Julian, who wanted to be too cool to ask that question, but really, profoundly was not.

In answer, Big Nicky tossed a twenty at him. "Unload that crate," he said to Julian, gesturing to the box of soda in the corner of the store. "And don't ask questions."

Money was supposed to be the lesson, probably, and perhaps if Julian had had less religious zealotry in his blood he might have absorbed it that way. Instead, what Julian took from it was the sartorial tastes of an eccentric Bronxite gangster and the significance of *work*.

Because of Julian's upbringing and the nature of his neighborhood, it would take him a while to figure out his magical specialty, much less that he had any magic at all. He hadn't been around anything cryptography related, born too young for any kind of Enigma encryption, and the internet wasn't something he worried about until the Novaks got a computer, at which point Julian cared a lot more about what was under Jenny's shirt. But he did the Novak patriarch a favor or two, which led to the observation that things worked differently around Julian, and not solely because he was young. Someone, probably Jenny's father, paid for Julian to be discovered by a medeian scout, rerouting his future just as the world teetered on the brink of the technomancy age. (Presumably this was intended to establish some kind of perennial debt on Julian's part, until Big Nicky Novak got caught in the crossfires of some other world while idling on 163rd.)

That Julian found his way to the top of the CIA was, like most things, an idea that began as a tiny, insignificant seed. His family was pleased to know the unnamed government work Julian had fallen into would likely provide healthcare and a pension. He said he was a cryptographer and they believed him, because what else was there to believe? He got promotion after promotion, project manager roles into department heads into chairmanships into directorships into the head chair at the Pérez table, where the man of the family belonged. It seemed natural to the elder members of the clan, like the inheritance they'd all been waiting for since they left San Juan. After all, Abuela's generation still believed in the American Dream, even if Julian's brothers didn't. They didn't marvel at his government suits, his clean haircut, the way he slung his surname around his Americanized mouth with choppy hard lines, like Jones or Smith. They'd seen it, his brothers said, they'd seen what Julian was willing to do for an *attaboy*, they knew whose boots he was willing to lick.

Unsurprisingly, Julian's brothers amounted to nothing. And anyway, they didn't know about Jenny's abortion, the final nail in a star-crossed coffin, nor did they know what Julian had done in the name of freedom, the thing in which he and Abuela so fervently believed. (Or else why had they come here, anyway?)

But someone knew, of course. Ezra Fowler did, hence Julian taking the meeting at his request. But Julian would have come regardless, because who passes up the chance of breaking into the Alexandrian Society's archives? Julian may have been a suit now, but before that he'd been a technomancer for the United States government long enough to know that everything could eventually be stolen. That some secrets were meant to be hacked.

As for Ezra Fowler's convenient disappearance as of the past three or four weeks, whatever. Better he wasn't around. He already knew too much about Julian and anyway, they could do the rest of this without him. With everything unraveling from the botched capture of the initiates upon their return to the world, Ezra Fowler had already failed them substantially once.

"There, that one." Julian tapped the screen, freezing it on the appearance of a blond head in the crowd outside the Hague, the silent hunched silhouette of an Asian woman beside him. "He's tampering with the feed. You can see it here." He gestured to the program that Julian himself had developed once upon a time, a way to measure magical output in medeian airwaves, which were clearer, more expensive, like what could be accomplished in HD.

Nothazai leaned forward, as if that would help matters. As if he could understand Julian's life's work, which was an attempt that Julian ignored for now, because he understood the importance of hierarchy. He understood the concept of work. "Why wasn't he apprehended at the time?" Nothazai asked, dark eyes flicking to the man who could only be Callum Nova. (Who, by the way, was supposed to be dead, so put that down for strike two in the Ezra Fowler column. A third would not be tolerated even if Fowler had the decency to reappear.) "He's obviously using incredibly potent outputs of magic. Why not arrest him on the spot?"

"Two reasons. One, he's a fucking empath. He made a mess of Grand Central, and there was an entire Navy SEAL team and an actual goddamn mermaid involved. Two, the Novas are more than a beauty empire." The original Nova Corporation, incepting from their timely rollout of consumer-friendly illusions in the second half of the twentieth century, had expanded over time to dominate the so-called wellness industry in lifestyle e-commerce, digital streaming, and popular media. Eventually, they owned their own channels of communication. "It's legal if he's acting on behalf of a corporation," explained Julian with an expressionless glance at the Wessex daughter sitting beside Nothazai, who would know a thing or two about corporate privilege herself. "This trial was highly publicized—the Novas wouldn't be the only ones to see it as an opportunity to get a lot of eyes and ears. With a permit, it's no different than paying for sponsored content on the internet or tampering with the algorithm of a corporately owned newsfeed. This or similar footage aired on multiple feeds, including one owned and operated by the Nova conglomerate." Julian pulled up an article comparing the blond's profile to the unsmiling portrait of Dimis Nova's only son. "The empath could be selling lipstick right now for all we fucking know."

"But you do know." Nothazai looked placid. He did not seem to see the point in asking the obvious follow-up question, so Julian answered for him.

"You want to be seen questioning a Nova in full view of twenty major international networks? No, we have to be sure before we make a move like that in public. We only know he's influencing the crowd, the security, everyone. But there's no way to tell yet what his intended outcome is, just that he's using magic to do it. And—"

Julian looked down at his phone when it beeped. "Excuse me." He motioned apologetically to the others—Eden Wessex pursed her lips as if she had a manicure to get to—before he stepped away to take the call. "Well?"

"He got hostile." His agent's voice was grim. "Started making threats."

No. Not today, not when Julian was up to his ankles in shit already. "Don't tell me you—"

"Had no choice," Smith interrupted, which was obviously an excuse, albeit functionally an answer. "All due respect, sir, but there were four good men in that room. And it's not like the guy's an angel."

Julian bit back a growl. Anger wouldn't help things, though this was extremely unfortunate. Worse than unfortunate. This would either spook the telepath or drive her to vengeance, and so far, she had not proven herself reckless enough for that to work in their favor. Perhaps she and her husband were estranged enough that she would see it as a good thing, although Julian struggled to see how. Call records between Parisa Kamali and her husband went back years—Nasser Aslani was the only contact she'd ever had that exceeded a month or two in longevity. At least until she disappeared into the Society's network, when she went radio silent for two years and counting.

"Send me the tape," Julian said after a second to collect his thoughts. "Maybe there's a way to salvage this, make it work for us rather than against us." Maybe the husband had said her name in a derogatory way. Maybe he looked like he was about to cave, reveal her whereabouts. Maybe something, maybe something.

Silence on the other end of the call. Then, far too late: "Sir, there wasn't enough time t—"

No. "Fucking hell, Smith." Unbelievable. "No tape? How do you think this is going to look when that gets out?" Julian set his jaw, trying to think and failing to do so without at least *some* unproductive admonishment. "He's not some civilian off the street," Julian hissed into the phone, "he's Nasser *fucking* Aslani, he's the vice president of the biggest medeian energy corporation in the Middle East—"

"We'll handle it, sir."

"*You* will not handle it. *I* will handle it." Julian hung up the phone, inhaling several times deeply. His wife was a great believer in yoga and the power of positive affirmation. He tried to believe that things could be as simple for him as they were for a woman who shared a maiden name with two dead presidents and a sitting senator. Sometimes, very occasionally, it worked.

Breathe. Video could be altered. *Breathe.* Code malfunctioned all the time. Also, *Julian* was not the one currently influencing civilians over medeian airwaves, so it wasn't like he was the criminal in the room. This was all the Society's doing, and once that could be proven, it would also prove their doom. Nobody wanted to live inside a dystopian simulation, and anyway, it could have been much worse. Nasser Aslani's name could have been Nova or Wessex, a fact of life that was as much an atrocity as it was the honest fucking truth. Just like if anyone involved in this got caught, the second-gen Puerto Rican who'd so meticulously forged his mami's papers would take the fall while his subordinate, Idaho-born Paul Smith, graciously accepted his exigent promotion.

Julian was born to a shitty world but so was everyone, and what had they done about it? He was busy trying to make it better the only way that he knew how, so he re-entered the room and tapped the screen again, setting the surveillance video once again in motion.

They watched Callum Nova make eye contact with the camera, the corners of his mouth setting up in a smirk like the careless flick of a lighter.

"There's the proof we need that the Society's six candidates are tampering with international politics. What's next? Free and fair elections?" Julian said, his certainty ironclad. "And if *this* one's doing it in full view of the global public, who's to say what the others are up to behind the scenes? We could be talking about an outright attack on civil liberties here. Wouldn't MI6 be interested to know that, or even Li?" he said, forgetting at the last second that the Asian Alexandrian initiate standing beside the Nova was Japanese, not Chinese.

Julian noticed Nothazai watching him closely. *Too* closely. It reminded Julian to scramble the frequencies of the room, jamming any potential recording devices. Just in case they failed again, in which case Smith would be awarded Julian's position, Julian's office. In which case Julian would become a cautionary tale about diversity hires. A brown-skinned fucking blip.

If Nothazai diagnosed Julian's silence as malignant, he didn't say so. He merely shrugged, exchanging a pleasant glance with the Wessex daughter beside him.

"We can certainly let them know. As for the situation in Paris," Nothazai said, apparently forcing a change in topic, "do we have the name of the civilian yet?"

Right, that. Julian clicked on the FERRER DE VARONA file. "The other medeian is Gideon Drake," he said in answer, pulling up a picture from a NYUMA student-run newspaper, one of the few photographs of Gideon Drake that he could find. "He has juvenile records from Canada, which my agents are getting unsealed, but I had a hunch, so I distributed that photo to some of our informants. Apparently," Julian said, turning away from the laptop screen, "Gideon Drake is some kind of telepathic thief. He runs low-level jobs in the astral planes, or at least he used to. Good chance there's something in his NYUMA records, but the dean's not playing ball." He shrugged. "Yet."

Nothazai's brow twitched. "You're sure he's a telepath and not a traveler?"

Julian felt Eden Wessex's posture straighten with carefully concealed interest just as Julian's phone rang again, this time flashing with the name of his deputy director. Fucking fuck. "What's the difference?" Julian said, by which he meant *why the hell should I care*, though he would not get an answer that mattered. He had a mess to clean up, which would not be insignificant.

(Want to know what power feels like? Julian didn't know, had never really known, but he imagined it was the carelessness of "forgetting" a video recording. Or maybe it was Atlas Blakely greeting him at the door of a country manor house, sly as a fox, slippery as a ghost. If Julian's suspicions were right, the sentience of the archives would function like an algorithm by now, which meant that someone who spoke the right language could unpuzzle the answers to any imaginable question. Is there a heaven. How many nuclear weapons were Wessex—and his daughter—blatantly not telling them about. If Julian had just driven Jenny to the clinic like she'd asked instead of making her go alone, would his kids now have her smile?)

"Never mind," Julian said to the room. "Take five."

· GIDEON ·

There was always a time when it seemed appropriate to voice one's concerns, after which point doing so would only become increasingly unproductive. Naggy, in a sense. For Gideon, that particular moment had passed about a month ago, long enough for such concerns to lose potency.

Theoretically, that is.

"—so anyway, those are the archives, blah blah," Nico had said at the time, ending his tour of the Alexandrian manor house by pulling the reading room doors shut behind him. "I know they said no security clearance for you," he added, "but I can always pull anything you want. Or you can ask Tristan. Who is admittedly The Worst"—an eye roll, capital letters strongly implied—"but he owes you for getting Rhodes back and he's exceptionally transactional that way, so yeah. And you'll like Atlas, maybe. Probably. I think." A grimace. "I don't think there's any reason *not* to like Atlas—unless you, like Rhodes, think he's some kind of tyrant, in which case . . . Well, whatever, you don't have to marry him or work for him. Well, you're obviously working for him, but that's my fault, not his. Unless Rhodes is also right about his sinister plan for recruiting us specifically, but I don't know, she's not exactly at her best at the moment. Maybe you can talk to her? Every time I try to bring up"—and here, a drop in volume—"*Fowler,* she gets this look on her face like maybe I should have issued a trigger warning, and anyway, you're much more palatable to her in general, so . . ."

Nico finally took a sufficient pause for breath, glancing worriedly at Gideon.

"What do you think?" Nico asked, bracing himself.

What did Gideon think? Excellent question.

At the time, these were his thoughts, in order:

Something was off about Libby Rhodes. Not that Gideon wouldn't expect something to be off about her, given what he knew of her experience over the last year, but he had the distinct sensation that Nico either couldn't see exactly what it was or simply didn't want to. Nico chattered to Libby as he always had and met her barbs with his own as he'd always done, seemingly unfazed by the element of . . . something. Gideon had yet to put a finger on whatever it was. Libby was quieter than he remembered, but who wouldn't be quiet, given everything? There was something else wrong, though; something familiar but unplaceable. Gideon had been racking his brain for an answer, but it remained trapped on the tip of his tongue, unhelpful. Like a half-remembered dream.

Tristan Caine, the researcher, the one with whom Nico had an obviously charged history and half a meager rivalry, was another odd piece of the grand aristocratic puzzle. He was polite, or just British. Unclear which applied more closely. Nothing about him seemed obviously different from the way Nico had described him. Nothing he said was tellingly abnormal. There was tension between him and Libby, something obviously sexually unresolved (they both seemed overly conscious of the exact degree of distance between them at all times) but Nico had already clocked it and warned Gideon that was the case, so it wasn't necessarily that. Tristan didn't seem to have a problem with Gideon, perhaps because Libby didn't have a problem with Gideon, and people in general did not have problems with Gideon, except for—

Ah, *that's* what it was. The disconcerting element of Libby's new outward-facing persona—it reminded Gideon of his mother. Which didn't seem right, exactly, because Eilif was a criminal, a mermaid, and not in possession of any qualities that Gideon typically applied to his friends. He had always been wary of his mother, but not . . . not entirely *endangered*. It was Nico who found Eilif dangerous, not Gideon. Gideon was aware of Eilif's flaws—she was narcissistic, forgetful, generally a bit of a psychopath—but to him that was more like a pattern of scales than a weapon. Those characteristics were what made her, and he could no more hate her for that than he could a mirror. She was doing the best she could with what she had, which was . . . well, an addiction. Eilif was a compulsive gambler, and worse, she was equipped with a certain self-serving streak that meant every wager was a good one if there was even the slimmest chance for her to win. The last time Gideon had seen her she'd been more compulsive than usual, more certain, which also meant more desperate. The closer to ruin Eilif was, the more inspired she could be.

And not that Gideon would ever call Libby a gambler, but he could see something similar in her eyes. It wasn't dim in there, there wasn't loss, she wasn't visibly haunted by trauma any more than the average person. It was the spark that unnerved him. The sense that she had come for something, and now she would get it, no matter the cost.

Which reminded Gideon that his mother's recent absence felt . . . noticeable. No news was good news, sometimes, but sometimes no news was bad news, very bad news indeed. Impossible to tell the difference from where he stood. Impossible to tell what, under Gideon's usual circumstances, would even be considered good. He supposed he wouldn't hear from her anytime soon, if Nico was right about the creature wards, but unlike Nico, Gideon had a feeling the attacks orchestrated against Nico's Society cohort would eventually appeal to Eilif—if not originate with her, opportunistic as she was. He hoped that wasn't the case—that she would not actively endanger him or Nico purely out of self-interest—but perhaps if it wasn't her choice? She'd been in trouble, more trouble than usual, dropping stray mumbles about dreams and NFTs and debts. And again, Gideon did know her. Even if he didn't hate her for what she was, he was merely optimistic, not a fucking fool.

Speaking of optimism. Gideon wondered what to make of Atlas Blakely, whom Nico unwisely trusted and whom Tristan seemed to respect in a more dignified fashion. Libby was undemonstrative on the subject aside from repeatedly noting that Atlas could, quote, destroy the world. It felt like rhetoric to Gideon, the idea that the world could be destroyed. After all, what did that really mean?

But that wasn't technically the question on Gideon's mind. Actually, his question was much simpler. Not quite as simple as where *was* Atlas Blakely, although that was definitely a ponderance of significance. Nico found it normal that Atlas was absent from the house—which, true, was perhaps not suspicious enough on its own, and yes, fine, Gideon did not know what a Caretaker did or was supposed to do—but the Society on high had evidently not known either when they sent him here, which was an institutional carelessness that Gideon doubted very much was par for the course. This was not some underfunded municipality. He had been told, flat out, to his actual face, that he was being tracked and so were all the others. If he ran, they would find him. If Atlas Blakely had run, he'd certainly be apprehended soon. But Gideon did not take someone of Atlas Blakely's stature to be the running type, so it likely wasn't that. And more importantly, Tristan and Libby seemed to know something that Nico did not.

Other thoughts? If what it took to leave the Society wards via the dream realms was anything like the process of entering them, Gideon's periodic bouts of narcolepsy were about to become massively constrained and very, very dull. Would he be confined to the same prison cell in which he'd spoken to Nico every time his consciousness slipped? Also, he wondered if the house concerned itself much with dietary restrictions. He was slightly lactose intolerant—not enough to ignore cheese entirely, but enough that some internal decision trees were necessarily involved. He had been in houses like this one, of similar grandeur and size. Max lived in a house like this one. Something that Nico did not know (or perhaps did know but chose not to acknowledge) was that Max had nearly not received medeian status because his output as a shifter was minimal, squarely on the line between medeian qualification and mere witchery. This revelation had been part of an intoxicated "don't feel bad" speech from Max to Gideon sometime during their second year, wherein Max had disclosed that, actually, the Wolfe family had made a significant donation to the political office of the municipal medeian registry, because it was one thing to have a son without any corporate ambitions but another thing entirely to have one that was magically average.

Money, that was another thing Gideon worried over (as in, who controlled the Society's money? Because whoever it was, they controlled the Society and therefore—toppling gradually but surely, the last domino to fall—they controlled Nico himself) but Nico didn't think about that because he had it, was accustomed to having it. He didn't understand the way money made decisions, the way that on a looming, unavoidable scale, money determined what was wrong or right more critically than Sunday school or philosophical preponderance of thought. Money was a gift, a burden, one version of a cost. Gideon had had a dream recently about a man with red eyes, a red pen. An accountant asking questions about a prince. There was no escaping it, the threats, the greed. An accountant, because money was a weapon. An accountant, because to own someone's debt was to own *them,* full stop. His own mother had never been free. Not that Nico would need to worry about such things because he had Gideon to worry about them for him, but perhaps there was a reason the two things were so connected in Gideon's mind.

Nico didn't understand poverty the way that Gideon understood poverty, or hunger the way Gideon understood hunger, or fear the way Gideon knew fear. Not fear for his life—Nico understood that (just ignored it). Fear that his way of life was threatened. Fear that change would, for example, destroy the world that they had known, which was for all intents and purposes destroying the world itself. Nico knew but didn't *know* how simply (not easily, but simply) someone's soul could be bought, sold, or compromised, and while that wasn't necessarily something to worry about today, it would be someday.

It would be someday, and it might very well take place inside this house.

Atlas, and therefore Tristan or Libby, might already know something about that.

Something had happened to Atlas Blakely, that much was clear. Gideon heard hoofbeats and tried not to think zebras, tried to think horses instead. After all, Atlas Blakely's initiates were being hunted. One had already been abducted and Libby's loaded silence on the matter of Ezra Fowler was deafening, with implications very much implied. Atlas Blakely had made some kind of terrible mistake that he did not want the Society to know about, and whatever he was doing now, surely the only two people in the last place Atlas had been had every reason to cover it up. Wherever he was, it was relevant and unignorable, and something was very obviously wrong.

But critically, Gideon's final response in answer to Nico's question of what Gideon thought of the Society and the archives to which he was now contractually bound was simply that he'd been inside worse prisons for much longer. Prisons that had not included Nico pausing to pin him casually against the tactile Edwardian wallpaper of some privy chamber with inadequate ventilation—and if there was none of that, then there was no real reason for existing.

So yes, it was certainly possible the Society was fucked, and that Libby was right, and the world-ending stakes that Nico's curiosity (or arrogance, or ambition) seemed willing to overlook were very definitely on the line. But if life outside this house was just a matter of certain death and tireless capitulation to social norms regardless, then what difference did it make to Gideon if Atlas Blakely tried to break the world from somewhere inside it or not?

Which was why Gideon's ultimate answer was, "It's nice. Very quaint. Could potentially use a thorough dusting."

At the time, Nico's grin had broadened, satisfied. How easy it was to make him happy, both then and now. How unquestionably worth the effort, too. So Nico wanted to try some kind of nutty multiverse experiment that could only end in personal disaster, if not total annihilation? Very well, Gideon could be persuaded. It was already a miracle he'd been awake this long—a miracle that someone he loved could love him back with even a sliver of his urgency—so if this was where he died, if the line on his ledger was red, then it was just as fine as any other place to meet the reaper.

And anyway, the wormhole to the kitchen was funny, the end.

Of course, the more the days slid by, the more Gideon would wonder whether he'd been remiss in failing to mention the veritable buffet of potentially relevant problems. If a version of his future self was screaming, prophecy seemed as yet insignificant beside the singular pleasantness of his personal doom.

"What are the chances we can magic up some pie?" Gideon asked Nico aloud, having then decided not to worry about the other things over which to potentially worry. Because the end of the world would really be much better with some pie. He wasn't picky. Fruit pie. Savory pie. Cream pie would hurt his stomach, but it would be worth it.

"Oh, *avec plaisir,*" replied Nico happily. "I gotta text Reina again, which will probably end in tears. Mine, obviously. But give me five minutes?"

Five minutes, a lifetime. Potato, potato.

"*Con mucho gusto,* Nicolás," said Gideon, drowsily pondering the best place for a nap. "Take your time."

II

HEDONISM

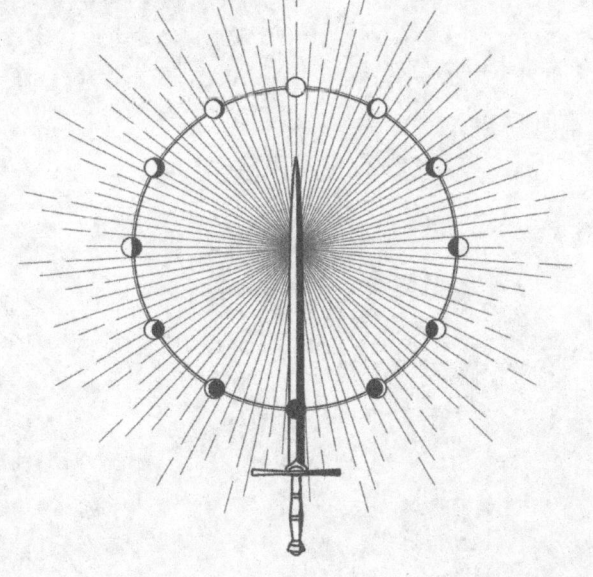

· REINA ·

S he woke from an unintentional nap with the distant smell of smoke in her nostrils, the vague image of a black dress disappearing into the periphery of her mind's eye. She choked on her tongue, jolting upright to realize the thing startling her awake was her own ringing phone.

She silenced the call from Nico—*"Reina! Me again, tag you're it, hey I never asked you, did you ever play tag? Real tag I mean, not phone tag, sorry for rambling I just keep running out of ways to ask you to call me back, to be honest I really thought the whole 'Atlas Blakely is maybe going to destroy the world' or at the very least 'the archives are trying to kill us' would pique your interest but anyway, once again I'm sorry for whatever I did, which Parisa refuses to explain to me—in, like, a hot way, obviously—oh, but speaking of Parisa she's also stopped answering her phone too, so, that's cool . . . Cool cool cool anyway I'll try again tomorrow love you bye"*—and checked the clock.

Nearly three in the afternoon. She rose to her feet, heading for the bathroom.

She splashed water on her face, then toweled it dry. Adjusted her nose ring. Stepped into her shoes. Then, observing her compatriot had made no apparent motion to proceed, she tapped her foot impatiently from the doorway.

"I hear you, Mori" was the only response from where Callum was draped over the hotel bed. (There were two beds, obviously, because Reina would rather die than share one with Callum, whose sexuality she did not understand. It was unclear whether he preferred men, women, both, or, more singularly, the hypothetical ire of Tristan Caine.)

"Which one of these do you like better?" Callum asked, beckoning her with a tilt of his chin.

Reina, worn to the bone by the thirty-first consecutive day with Callum Nova, turned her attention to the ceiling and sighed.

"Nobody's up there," Callum reminded her. "According to you, anyway."

Honestly. "For the last time, I'm not *the* god, I'm just—"

Callum smirked at her from the bed and Reina wondered yet again if she couldn't just do this alone. But he had unfortunately proven himself effective so far, so, "Fine." She stormed over to him and snatched the phone from his hand. "What is this? Is this a picture with Tristan's sister?"

"Half sister," Callum clarified unnecessarily, tapping the screen between one photo and the next. "And does my hair look better in this one or that one? I'm trying to go for, like, classically unkempt."

Reina swiped between the two pictures. "Has he responded to anything you've sent him so far?"

"Nope," said Callum. "Hence the need to really do it right. You know, with a very precise degree of spontaneity."

"You know that Rhodes is back." Nico had told her so in one of his rambling voicemails, and also at least seven of his daily text chains. (He'd also briefly attempted a group chat titled *Enemies to Lovers* until Tristan wisely advised him to please, for the love of god, stop.) "I don't think Tristan is thinking about you."

"Shows what you know," replied Callum, raising his arms to rest them beneath his head. "You're reading Varona's messages, aren't you?"

"Shut up." For whatever reason, Reina was taking this task absurdly seriously. She could feel the way her brain was melting, because she shouldn't have possibly cared less about Callum's unhinged plan for vengeance or whatever this was, but she was positive one of the pictures was better and she didn't want to be wrong about which. "Is it even a good idea to antagonize Adrian Caine?"

No, Reina thought silently. The answer was no. Aside from pointing a gun at them the first time they'd met, Adrian Caine had shown himself on multiple occasions to be the kind of man who extracted payment via pounds of flesh. Reina was quite sure his main business was in arms trafficking, a steady turnover of violence in and violence out, and she didn't think many people crossed him and lived to tell the tale—his own crew included. Some of this assertion Callum had deemed paranoia on her part (it was true that she couldn't *prove* it was a body in the freezer Adrian's goons were transporting, though one noticeably well-dressed witch had been missing for multiple weeks) but Reina had witnessed with her own eyes what happened when someone displeased the coven's leader. She'd been turning the corner from Gallows Hill pub in the middle of the day when she saw Adrian reaching for a visiting witch in what appeared to be a friendly greeting. Before she quite knew what was happening, Adrian had plunged a thin blade the size of his palm directly into the other witch's throat. The witch collapsed; a young beech tree screamed. Reina froze, coming to a halt so unexpectedly the sound of her boots on pavement was unmistakable. Adrian looked over and caught her eye, expressionless. Then he wiped the blade clean on the lapel of his compatriot's jacket before returning to the pub without a word, as if she'd merely caught him out for a midday stroll.

Callum, of course, seemed incapable of registering danger as a plausible consequence, or even a convincing atmospheric shift. To Reina, his willful embrace of chaos was both unsurprising and ridiculous. True, perhaps Callum's sense of safety lived, as he routinely claimed it did, in the comfort of his superior cleverness. Or maybe he'd always been rich, white, and male enough for the idea of danger to become laughably pretend. Maybe it was worse, really, that he was probably right about that.

In any case, Reina did not think today would be the day she convinced him, but it seemed irresponsible not to bring it up.

"It's just that Adrian seems to actually care about his daughters." The only times she'd ever seen Adrian without a weapon (the equivalent of smiling) were with his daughters and his dog, a medium-sized hunting breed that struck her as a theoretical dictionary entry for the word "dog." "And you're . . ." She looked up with a frown. "Not exactly unthreatening."

"I know, right?" said Callum.

"I mean that you're too old for them." Bella Caine was seventeen. The daughter in the picture, Alys, was only just nineteen. Callum was at least a decade older, probably more, and though he wasn't doing anything in the picture—they were making a salad together, which wasn't a euphemism, it was just . . . an actual salad—Alys was looking up at Callum and laughing, so to Reina it had an obvious, wafting element of *uh-oh*. Not to mention that if Reina found Callum's general air and behavior inadvisable, then Adrian Caine's muscle—the largest of which was a man unbelievably called Wyn Cockburn, whom Callum seemed intent on smarmying to death—openly considered him a punishable offense.

"You're just too . . ." Reina attempted to explain. "You know. *You.*"

"Rakish, you mean?" Callum suggested. "Narcissistic? Manipulative? Borderline sociopathic?"

"Yes," Reina confirmed. "And honestly just a terrible person in general."

"Noted," said Callum with no apparent loss of enthusiasm. "And if it eases your conscience, Mori, I have no plans to get involved with either of those girls. They're children, and not in the Varona way. In the actual way."

"I'm honestly pleased you grasp the line," muttered Reina, handing the phone back to him. She doubted any progeny of Adrian Caine's could be wholly innocent, but then again, Callum was living proof that at least one member of the Caine brood could not be counted on for ruthlessness even when it was the undisputed best course of action. "I prefer the first one. You look less devious."

"Oh." Callum frowned at it and Reina sighed heavily.

"Keep him guessing," she advised. "And also, get up. Let's go. The press conference starts in ten minutes."

"Ugh, fine." He sent the picture—no message, she observed, just a picture, which was now a string of wordless picture-messages to which Tristan had given no response—and slid the phone into the pocket of the blazer beside the bed before flinging it over his shoulder and giving her a swift, disapproving once-over. "That's what you think a member of the British press wears to cover an announcement from Downing Street?"

"It doesn't matter what I wear. Nobody's looking at me." Black jeans were unremarkable. It wasn't like she'd donned a kimono for the occasion. "And you can't blame me, by the way, for wondering if you've got some kind of revolting plan to seduce Tristan's sisters out of your misguided sense of revenge."

"Mori, I'm genuinely insulted. I may not have any morals, but I do have one or two scruples." Callum refreshed one of his illusion charms, the equivalent of pomading his hair, and Reina made a face. The Nova illusions all had a distinctly noticeable quality to them, like a signature scent, only more like the effervescence of glitter. A pearlescence, for lack of a better word. "I have absolutely no interest in seduction of any kind."

"But I thought you said being out in the world meant you'd pick up one of your other vices? You know, pay taxes, have sex, flirt with alcoholism, and die," she said, summarizing his post-Society plans and leaving out the bit about buying another yacht, which was for some reason unbearable to voice aloud.

"Tut, tut, Mori," said Callum, sliding a pair of loud, chromatic aviators onto his face that made him horrifyingly more attractive to someone who was into that sort of thing. "First of all, as far as I know the Nova Corporation has no plans to pay any taxes and I'm shocked you didn't already suspect that of them. Secondly," he added, throwing open the door and ushering her through it, "I thought you of all people would understand my position on carnalities."

"Me?" Reina asked as they made their way through the winding hotel corridors. (It was a nice hotel, but not *too* nice—not *Callum* nice, which was obscene. A compromise.)

"Yes, you," Callum confirmed, reaching to open the hallway door for her as it became obvious once again that chivalry was part of his sadistic self-entertaining power play. "You've made it very clear that other human beings are disgusting to you."

"Not disgusting." She beat him to calling the tiny lift—a small fuck-you on behalf of feminine activists everywhere—then regretted it when he stepped in first, taking advantage of the small space to position them face-to-face. "Just . . . not that interesting." She looked pointedly at the industry label on the door of the lift as it coughed its way into descent.

Still, it was unavoidable that he was smirking. "Right. Exactly."

"But you—" She frowned up at him, then immediately regretted it. He reveled openly in her discomfort. "You have sex."

"Do I?" She made a face, then caught a trace of laughter at the edges of his mouth. "Fine, yes, I do. Theoretically. But even in theory I don't do casual."

Every now and then Callum surprised her, which was when he was least terrible to be around. "You don't?"

The lift hit the ground floor. "I'm an empath," he said in the same tone he might have pointed out *it's a stop sign.*

"So?" Reina failed to see the relevance.

"So, vampires crave flesh."

"You mean blood?"

"I do love our little chats, Reina." Callum patted her shoulder and she shook him off, glaring. "Anyway, we're out in the world now, so let's try to focus, shall we? Lest you require my combat expertise yet again."

As if Callum had ever dirtied his hands, much less disturbed his hair. (A nearby vine snickered with agreement.) "Please. I needed your help *one time*—"

"By that logic, I only killed Parisa *one time*," Callum mused aloud, "and yet you're all so endlessly suspicious of me. When are my good deeds going to count for something, hm?"

Reina chose to ignore that response, opening her phone and scrolling through social media, a thing she had only begun doing because it was the quickest way to identify and undermine the villain of the day. She did not have an answer for Callum, both because she was aware that annoying her was something Callum was doing for fun (or possibly for sport) and because she did not want to think about Parisa, who had almost certainly set Reina up for assassination when divvying up their post-Society transport locations by conveniently forgetting to mention the gang of witches out for Tristan Caine's blood. True, Reina might have sorted that out on her own if she'd been paying any special attention to Tristan and Nico's hyperactive hunt for Libby, but Parisa would have already known she hadn't been. Choosing London as Reina's location for arrival was a cute little message, maybe, that Reina had pissed her off and Parisa was happy to play the long game, which Reina had no doubt was Parisa's version of a compliment. After all, Parisa was only three things: beautiful, an asshole, and sadistically unhinged.

But after a moment's lull, Reina tucked her phone into her pocket. Callum wasn't wrong that she needed to pay attention, because ever since they'd set up camp in London, the likelihood of apprehension by someone (though not Tristan's father's gang of witches now, thankfully) was never entirely off the table.

Reina and Callum had both received summonses of some kind from the Society, which they ignored. Well, Reina had ignored it. Callum went to the meeting as requested, apparently honoring his usual impulse of thinking it would be funny, or perhaps in an effort to ruin someone's day. Upon return, though, he'd shrugged and carried on living his life, adding that Reina wouldn't be interested in what he'd gleaned about the Society by uncharacteristically jumping when they presented him with a hoop.

"The real question isn't what the *Society* actually is, because we already know as much as we need to about them," Callum had said, pausing Reina before she could point out that, actually, she didn't know that, and would he stop being so pointlessly smug all the time. "Look, it's really simple," he explained in his usual infuriating way. "We know the Society tracks us somehow, maybe using the archives, maybe not. We can guess that they probably recruited us based on something that our assassins are now using to track us, so my guess is our magical output." He paused then, waiting to see if Reina would interject, which she was pointedly *not* doing just to needle him. "They produce important people by choosing people who are already bound to be important. It's a self-affirming cycle. So," he concluded, "the only real question left is which of us is going to kill which of the others."

"What?" had slipped out of Reina's mouth. She'd been doing so well at not rising to his taunts, but that one seemed especially unexpected.

"I told you." He seemed genuinely exasperated with her, not just performatively so. "I'm about ninety-nine percent positive that Atlas Blakely didn't kill the initiate he was supposed to kill, and then the rest of his cohort died. Hasn't Varona told you this already?"

Yes, but Reina had been trying very hard not to think of Nico, or of Atlas. She'd been especially desperate to ignore her disappointment that Atlas had done nothing to stop her leaving; nothing to even intimate his knowledge of her plans.

And anyway, if things were so doomed, then why hadn't Parisa returned to the house, either? If the so-called writing on the wall was read only by the anxiety of Libby Rhodes or the rich imaginings of Callum Nova, how real could the threat possibly be?

"So?"

"So, now that Rhodes is back—or perhaps even if she hadn't returned, which is a fun but pointless thought exercise—"

"Did you think there was a chance of that?" asked Reina, who despite her better judgment did tend to nurture a thought exercise, even one of Callum's warped design.

"What, Rhodes staying in the past? It was technically a viable option," Callum replied with a shrug. "You know what it cost to do otherwise. So did she."

"I wouldn't have stayed." Reina shuddered with the indecency of it—a trap that became a choice, and therefore a worse and more punishing trap. "I'd have brought myself home. No matter the cost."

"Oh?" Callum remarked, sounding overjoyed with the possibility of judging her response, and therefore her personhood. "I can't say I'd have bothered, truth be told. But then again, I can adapt to almost any situation." He twirled an imaginary mustache.

"Really? Including the one where Tristan is gone?" Reina prompted doubtfully.

Callum made a vague sort of gesture to the here and now. "Behold my adaptation," he announced, though before Reina could point out the many riddling holes in that statement, he added, "Besides, white men are always in fashion. I'd be just as well off then as I would in any other situation."

His tone was buoyant to the hilt, self-sabotage masquerading as actualized self-awareness, so Reina chose to let him flay himself as he pleased. "What about white women?" she asked, a flash of Libby in one of her numerous cardigans wafting guilelessly into her thoughts.

"You tell me," Callum replied. "Put yourself in Rhodes's godless fringe and tell me how threatened you are now. Better? Worse?"

It felt like manipulation, somehow. Reina frowned.

"The point," Callum continued, potentially too pleased, "is that we still have to kill someone. The archives are still owed their sacrifice. Either we all return to the archives to live in cloistered paranoia as we've always done, or someone has to die," he concluded to the tune of a jaunty singsong, like a deranged sailor shanty. "And it's not going to be me or you, so—"

"Who says it won't be you?" Reina muttered. "We picked you last time."

"Me, that's who says it won't be me," he replied. He no longer bothered to comment on her willingness to entertain the inevitability of his demise. "You guys already fucked it up once. Time for someone else to give it a try."

Reina recalled the significance of Callum's insistence on having some private plan for revenge. "Are you saying you're doing all of this"—*this* being the elusive messages, the deal with Adrian Caine, and the seemingly unproductive intimacy with Tristan's estranged family—"as part of your plan to kill Tristan?"

"Well, I don't have to be the one to do it, but sure, come to think of it, I wouldn't particularly mind that outcome." Callum had grinned at her, toothily, in a way that made a nearby oak do the equivalent of rolling its eyes. "Fine, fine, it doesn't have to be Tristan. I'm willing to consider Rhodes," Callum said with an air of solemnity.

"How generous of you," said Reina.

"I know, and to think you all routinely overlook it—"

"What about Parisa?" Reina interrupted with a frown, and Callum glanced at her.

"What about her?"

"Varona says she's with Dalton."

Thankfully he overlooked her very rare mention of Nico by name. "Yes, and?"

"And Dalton's got all the same pieces Atlas does. Plus, he's the only one who can, you know." She waved a hand. "*Summon the void.*" Or whatever Dalton could do that Reina had gathered from observing (interfering with) his research over her year of independent study. She knew that the aim of Dalton's research was to either create or awaken a portal of some kind from within the un-emptiness of dark matter—a task that Reina suspected couldn't be done without Tristan. Or Libby Rhodes. Both of whom had once been weapons wielded by Parisa and probably would be again, making Parisa the natural target, if murder as an ethical matter was anything of meritorious consideration.

"I truly can't pretend to have any interest in the void or any of its requisite accomplices," Callum had informed Reina at the time, which was borderline depressing, because Reina knew for a fact that Nico would. That Nico *did*. She could hear it in his voicemails, actually, how badly he wanted to do the experiment, the thing he kept referring to as the Atlas Blakely Sinister Plan. That he could make a joke of it was not unusual, per se, but Reina knew him well enough to know that he was curious, even eager to complete it, and now that he had Libby back, his limitations had dissolved enough for him to consider himself safe from Reina's ire. He wanted her mercy, at least in part because he needed her powers.

But she was busy with those.

She'd spent the last few weeks orchestrating a plan, something very simple. She wanted to effect change, so she was finding places to do it. The other day she (with, and here a heavy sigh, Callum) had managed to track down a prominent London-based manufacturer and change the building plans that would have disrupted a rainforest ecosystem in the Amazon. Just before that, they'd shown up to a workers' rights demonstration and persuaded a large corporation to allow its labor force to unionize. It was sort of uncomplicated work, figuring out what the right answer to any given situation was, except for the fact that—as Callum continually pointed out—changing one decision didn't entirely solve the larger issue. Reina didn't have all the time in the world, and speaking of, there were a lot of worthy problems. She thought she needed to start making some kind of bigger plan.

The situation at the Hague had been easy, possibly not even worth her time, but it had been the perfect testing ground to discover that Callum's power wasn't limited to the people in his immediate presence—with her help, his influence could be extended to anything that used a magical network of waves for transmission. It was Nico's technomancy research in application to their private communication that had given her the idea to try tampering with someone else's, and once that seemed promisingly effective, Reina decided it was time to think bigger, to try something internal. To detoxify the system from the inside out.

"That won't work," Callum had told her matter-of-factly when she told him of her vision for the next few months. To her, though, it was simple. Yes, there were the little bandages they could apply here and there—such as convincing a billionaire like James Wessex to solve world hunger, which would barely even scrape the surface of his annual wealth—but what she needed was something comprehensive, something that couldn't be undone. She needed to *actively* change people's minds—to make sure that when she was finished tinkering, the world could do the rest of the work on its own.

To which Callum said, "Don't be an idiot. Not that I care how you choose to waste the remaining months of your life until the archives inevitably come for us," he added perfunctorily, which she ignored, "but setting aside the despotism of your little god complex—"

"Ideologically beneficial progressivism," she corrected.

"God complex," Callum repeated, "but setting that aside, your whole plan is stupid, and also, it absolutely will not work."

Not that she needed his approval, but his dismissal was highly unwelcome. "Why not? If people just *understood* that—"

"Let me stop you for a second. You're not talking about a single generation's worth of fixing. Okay? There's no magic number of people to convince or some other quantitative value you can derive that would give your efforts any modellable or even lasting significance. Make all the plans you want, but it won't work. I'm only one influence, do you understand that? One of many." It wasn't like Callum to admit to weakness, and Reina had been about to tell him so when he interrupted again. "The way the world works, Mori, is that there are lots of influencers out there, even if mine is harder to deny because I'm using you to power it. The potency doesn't matter, because what I do isn't permanent. It can't be. By definition, people change." Callum looked hard at her, like he was disappointed she hadn't already come to that conclusion by herself. "It's one thing to draw on what people already want. I can't redesign a species, not at this scale. If you want an idea to stick, you need a telepath, not me. And even then, you couldn't guarantee the exact nature of the outcome."

Reina gave up on the conversation the moment it became implied that Parisa was the person for the job, because among other things, Reina didn't want to see or speak to or hear from Parisa Kamali ever again. Not for any particular reason, really. Just the regular ones of disliking her, which Reina always had. If Nico made it his business to keep tabs on what Parisa was up to, that was his pointless hill to die on. Reina had bigger plans.

She wanted to leave London soon, which would mean dragging Callum along with her, which she also knew he didn't want to do because he was busy haunting Tristan. But the UK's influence was old, it was waning, they were too enamored by their history of subjugation to understand that their time in the global sun had already come to an end. If the problem was structural, she'd have to break down the foundation.

If she was playing god, then so be it. Time to play god.

MotherMother, whispered a distant birch. There wasn't much near Downing Street, but as usual nature found a way. *Benevolent Mother, magnificent Being!*

"What is it you mean to achieve today?" Callum asked in his most infuriating drawl, glancing at Reina over the edge of his sunglasses. "Some little pipe dream of world peace, I'm guessing?"

Not today. Today was reproductive autonomy—the right to privacy that quietly underscored everything else. World peace wasn't entirely off the menu, but they had to start somewhere. And besides, Reina was just getting warmed up.

"Shut up," she said, placing a hand on Callum's shoulder. At the moment (sunglasses aside) he looked like a Parliamentary hopeful, which actually gave her an idea. Several ideas. She knew exactly what kind of person to look for the next time she got to her phone—a hero this time, not a villain.

There were, after all, plenty of the latter around. Her phone buzzed in her pocket, and later she would wonder if perhaps the timing was cosmically significant. If, somehow, the universe had known.

But that was a matter for later. "What's the easiest way in?" Reina asked then, observing the prime minister through narrowed eyes.

"Fear," said Callum. "Sometimes greed, sometimes shame, and on very rare but notable occasions, sometimes love. But always fear."

Reina felt herself latch onto Callum, her power pouring into his.

"Good," she said. Perfect. "Then turn it up."

S he was sitting alone in the reading room when Nico came bounding in, the chair beside hers at the table making a clatter when he dropped himself into it.

"So," he said. "I was thinking."

"Don't hurt yourself," she murmured.

"Tighten up, Rhodes, not your finest," Nico chirped, undeterred. "Anyway, listen—wait," he amended, immediately interrupting himself to glance around the room like somebody might unexpectedly pop out of it. "Atlas isn't here, is he?"

Libby reread the sentence she'd been trying to read for ten minutes. "Tristan said he was here yesterday afternoon. You could check the schedule."

"We have a schedule? Right, whatever. I had to check in with Max yesterday, so, you know, go figure. Anyway, about the sinister plot—"

"Stop calling it that." She kept her head down, trying fruitlessly to read, but Nico nudged her shoulder.

"Will you just listen to me? I know you're convinced the world will end or whatever—"

"I'm not convinced, Varona. I'm *sure*."

"Right, for reasons you won't explain," Nico blithely agreed, with obvious plans to dismiss said reasons entirely, to which Libby said nothing. "I know you're being very secretive about the whole thing, which is fine, albeit not the cutest look for you—"

Libby turned the page in her book as disruptively as it was possible to do with a thousand-year-old manuscript that pre-discovered Planck's constant.

"—but just so you know, I think I'm getting through to Reina."

Libby raised a hand to cover a yawn. "In what way?"

"In that I saw three dots come up the other day."

"Meaning?"

"Meaning she was obviously thinking about responding."

"Or," Libby sagely pointed out, "it was just an accident."

Nico made an alarming motion, like he'd considered high-fiving himself before choosing as a last-minute alternative to slap the table with an open palm. "She *opened the message,* Rhodes!" he trumpeted. "That's significant enough. I know her well enough to know she's thinking about it. Me. This," he clarified, as Libby gave him her most long-suffering look of impatience. "All we need is a few more dots and I'm ninety percent sure I can convince her to do the experiment."

"What exactly happened between the two of you last year?" Libby asked irritably, abandoning the pretense of reading. "Tristan and Callum I obviously understand. Even Tristan and Parisa to some degree. But you and Reina?"

Nico shrugged. "She contains multitudes. I deeply respect her labyrinthine mind."

"Whatever." Libby raised a hand to the throbbing pulse behind her eyes. "I told you, whether Reina might eventually feel up for ending the world with you won't matter if you only have months left to live. You really should be more worried about finishing off the ritual."

"The murder thing, you mean?" Nico said, ostensibly as a distinction between the other, more mundane sinister plot.

"Yes, the murder thing." How wonderful for him that he could joke about it. How *laudable,* really, that he would prove the better of them yet again by still being the dauntless one, the untouchable one, as if nothing else had changed.

But things were different now, even if Nico wasn't. It was noticeable, the distinction that now seemed to tear the fabric of reality between them, which Nico might be willing to ignore but that Libby lacked the luxury to overlook. They'd found synchronicity once, reflective sides of some cosmic mirror game, until she'd killed someone. Now, everything she did had to have a reason. She had altered the rules of her morality, rearranging herself down to the marrow, the basis of her code. Now, everything she did had to be in service to something purposeful. It had to have a meaning. It had to serve an end.

Lifeless eyes blurred before her vision, the stillness of familiar hands, disembodied prophecy still following her like a ghost. *He will destroy the world—*

(What else are you willing to break, Miss Rhodes, and who will you betray to do it?)

Abruptly, Libby shut the book and leaned back in her chair. "Look," she snapped at Nico, "I don't like it either, but it's looking more likely that we'll have to eventually complete the ritual. It's either that or we're going to be trapped here until we all die." Of all the things she'd gleaned from her return, that one seemed the most pressingly inescapable. That, and the fact that they'd been fucked the moment they accepted Atlas Blakely's card. Now, of course, it was too late, and there was only a limited amount of recourse; a narrow crevice of acceptability between sacrificial murder and world-altering apocalypse where Libby was meant to shepherd the others and try to live.

"But I thought we agreed on option two—you know, the one where we stay here and keep contributing to the archives," Nico pointed out. "That *is* what you're doing here, isn't it?" he said in a tone of voice she recognized. It was about as sly as Nico ever got, which meant he was on the unlikely edge of prudence.

"Yes," she said, meaning yes, but that had been before she realized the archives might not give her the materials she needed to save herself.

Or, alternatively, it meant *no, but go away.*

He ignored the subtext. "Well, then I hate to bring this unsavory detail to your attention, but I don't think just *living* here is enough." To that Libby spared him an iota of her attention. "Atlas has lived here the whole time, sure, but I'm sure the other members of his cohort must have thought of that, don't you think? *And* he's able to come and go as necessary, so it has to be more than just a matter of physical location. I mean come on, Rhodes, think about it, it's simple conservation of energy. What we get from the archives depends on what we contribute to them—which," Nico reminded her, "even living here, you technically have yet to do."

Ah yes, how she loved being reminded about her yearlong sabbatical, which was purely by choice and not at all against her will. "I'm researching, Varona." She raised the manuscript, and the book below it, which was a treatise on naturalism. "See? You'll recall that this is what it looks like, I'm sure."

"Yes, but be honest, Rhodes. Naturalism? Elements of quantum mechanics that we've already proven and defined? You're researching things that have already been done," Nico pointed out with an edge of fatality, "which is probably not reason enough for the library to keep you alive. By your own logic, anyway."

That Nico happened to be correct—or that Libby had already come to that conclusion herself—did not seem worth mentioning. Nor did the fact that it was all the archives would give her, refusing even the barest show of scholarly ambition with its familiar, amicable letdown of REQUEST DENIED. A proverbial *let's just be friends* to Libby's most heartfelt seduction.

A sudden image of Nico stroking the archive's walls, murmuring sensually for the library to be a good girl and produce some new phenomena for him drove Libby to a blink of temporary madness. "So you're the one making the rules now, Varona?"

"Technically no, since I'm not completely certain I believe your reasons for avoiding the experiment Atlas chose us for in the first place."

Libby could feel herself climbing the usual rungs of fury that seemed to only become accessible when Nico spoke. "So when I told you that I set off a nuclear bomb just to warn you that Atlas could destroy the world, you took that as—what, just a passing whim?" she demanded, cheeks heating with new-old rage.

"Did you?" asked Nico, temporarily destabilizing her.

"I . . . What?" she spluttered.

"Did you really set off a nuclear bomb just to deliver a warning?" he said, and Libby found herself so stunned by the question she didn't even produce a reply.

"See, I'm not entirely sure you actually believe that," Nico said plainly. "And I don't think you really believe some obscure doomsday foretelling, either. So as much as I love my ongoing servitude to a bunch of books that may or may not be tracking me, using me, or eventually plotting to kill me—which I do, Rhodes, I *love* it," Nico offered with gusto, "I also don't know what you want me to do about it. I've already killed Tristan loads of times, so." A shrug. "I'm pretty sure the archives are on board."

"I swear you're regressing," Libby murmured to herself, closing her eyes. She should have been pleased, probably, that he was finally summoning the capacity to be more than just a disrespecting rival. In practice, though, his change in temperament since her return was like being trapped on the weighted end of a seesaw. Without a balanced push and pull between them, she was just sitting on the ground.

"The point is," he continued, "either you're right that we need to kill someone or the archives are going to come for us individually to enact our brutal collective demise," Nico summarized, an obvious dramatization of the actual information she had relayed to him, "in which case you need to do something big—like, for example, opening a portal to another strand of the multiverse—"

"Which I won't be doing," she interrupted flatly.

"Okay, so then you're just living here and purposely doing nothing to save yourself because you're sad and you hate the world," said Nico. "*Or.*"

She chose very pointedly not to look at him.

"Or maybe, as a subset of misanthropy," he mused, "you do want it, everything we're capable of in here. Maybe, even though it's wrong, or immoral, or unethical, or just selfish—maybe you still want everything we can do *because* we came here. Maybe what you actually came back for was this—us. Everything we had yet to do, everything we had yet to make. Maybe you came back for the power we were promised. The power that, for better or worse, *we chose*." His voice was uncharacteristically raw with sincerity. "And don't you think I can understand that, Rhodes?"

She said nothing.

"Look, I get that you think it's wrong or whatever. I get that, I know you're always worried about the consequences. I know that part of this, the part you're not telling me about last year, and whatever happened with Fowler—"

Nico broke off. "I know you think the blood on your hands is unforgivable." His eyes were soft with sympathy, like he already understood it. "But maybe you can accept that what happened to you, the impossible situation you were in . . . it wasn't your fault. You did what you had to do to save yourself, so maybe you could let yourself move on from it. And maybe," he added, like he was about to deliver the hilarious punch line to an uproarious joke, "maybe you could actually, you know. Trust me."

Trust him. A quiet voice, prayerful knees. *Your secrets are safe with me, Libby Rhodes.*

Libby felt a shiver of recognition and turned away from him, then rose to her feet instead, prickly with something. Maybe it was the fact that Nico was being kind instead of obnoxious, which wasn't a texture of his personality she knew what to do with. Maybe it was the fact that he was giving her the benefit of the doubt; assuming, for once, that what lived in the unspoken was the best of her.

Or maybe it was because he was wrong.

"Can we talk about this later?" She reached for her books, turning away just as Nico caught her by the elbow. One hand wrapped tightly around the crook of her arm, sending an unintentional shiver up her spine.

"No, Rhodes. We're talking now."

The impact of his magic reaching out for hers was explosive, zero to sixty in one heartbeat flat. Libby felt it like a snare, the whiplash of a sudden noose, her breath catching in her throat fast enough to choke on.

She tried to pull herself away but it was too late, the building blocks of whatever they were already merging like an unlosable game of Jenga, pieces piling up on the shared foundation of power. She recalled again, unhappily, the sense that over the course of a year without him, she had known with hazy, fading certainty the necessity of Nico; the way that she would not have been trapped, not even for a moment, if Nico had been there. The fact that if, under very different circumstances, she had been lost *with Nico,* then she wouldn't have been lost at all.

There was a giddiness to their powers joining, a hyperactivity that Libby had already long associated with Nico himself. An energy that didn't pulse, not like it did with Tristan, but shot wildly outward, like fireworks—combustion that happened naturally, like stars colliding midair. The space between them was both necessary and insubstantial, like if they'd *actually* collided, neither of them would have noticed. It was, as it always was, pieces of her in pieces of him, the tangled web of it, and of them—the thing she both missed and had tried to deny.

Come on, just do it. She felt his magic lapping at hers with a feverish, childlike insistence. *Come on. Just give in.*

Unbearable. God, but she could feel herself stretching out again, filling the house, ready to swell beyond it, like outgrowing the bars of her container.

Fucking stupid. *Fine.*

Temperature was already high, pressure was already there, a path of circuitry was easily cleared. All that was required now—which Nico could take the helm and provide, but that he was waiting on her to do because, who knew, because he was bored, or trying to make a point, or just being himself, and annoying—was force. Something to convert the instability of his irresponsible burst of magic into kinetic energy that could be of some mutual use.

What did he want her to do, start a fire? Make another fucking bomb? No, but at least one thing had changed between them. Because now it wasn't about what he wanted her to do.

It was about what *she* wanted.

(And oh, here was the secret—she *wanted.* That was the trouble of it, the danger of having returned here. Of everything she'd sacrificed to be here, because now it didn't matter what she'd learned or who she'd been. The Libby Rhodes that Nico claimed to know was exactly, secretly, the problem. Her existence and Libby's own were fundamentally in opposition. They shared a body, a potential and a set of powers, but not a state of mind.

The old Libby was the one saying no. Yet another paradox: that Nico could look at Libby and still see her as she was—still believe her to be in desperate need of pushing—when she was indescribably, irreversibly different. Now, she was the Libby who'd burned through time and space, who concerned herself less and less with the ending Ezra had been willing to die for—to *kill* for—just to prevent, and that was exactly the problem. Because she had trusted Ezra once. Because she believed him, even if she hated him. Because who could be warned of the empire's fall and still carry on as before?

Only someone who'd paid the highest cost just to stand here. Someone who'd gone through hell itself just to belong here.

And now, when everything she wanted was so temptingly *in reach*—)

It was near-instantaneous, like the strike of a match, and when Libby's vision cleared—when the two of them disentangled, Nico's hand falling from her arm with the exultation of a prayer—she smelled the unmistakable presence of roses. Felt the brush of a dogwood overhead, like a congratulatory stroke of fondness. Libby still held traces of heat in her mouth, like the scorch of rubber on asphalt. A drop of Nico's sweat fell from his brow, meeting the blades of grass below with a delicate, whispered sizzle.

Outside the sun was high, the heat of July like a sudden conjoined incandescence. Magic rippled the grass in outward-spreading rings of consequence.

They'd managed to transport themselves from the reading room to the gardens. Not bad. Farther than the painted room to the kitchen, which two years ago they'd needed Reina to do.

Interesting.

Nico was watching her, waiting. Radiating, with so much unspoken triumph that Libby feared for the pastoral fault lines underfoot. (Not that London was known for earthquakes, but with this kind of incomprehensible magic tossed around at a madman's whim, who could ever really be sure?)

"Think about it," Nico said, and the look on his face, it was absolutely punchable. Libby tried very hard to hate him and it was easy, like breathing. Like convincing herself there was any substantial difference between coincidence and fate.

"Yes, Varona, I'm thinking about it." She left off on a growl and turned away, storming off from the line of dogwoods and taking a sharp turn from the gardens to the house.

Half of the truth was that Nico was right. The other half was that, more critically, Nico was wrong. She was worried, yes, and she was careful, as careful as she'd always been, but it wasn't fear of failure holding her back, it wasn't anxiety—it wasn't her customary paranoia about the consequences, not the way it used to be. It was Ezra who had told her the world would end, but Ezra was a liar and what he said no longer mattered. Ezra was over, his hold over her actions was gone. She had seen to it herself. What was left now was his prophecy, his warning, along with the sense that she had already come this far—already learned what it felt like to be truly in control—and it wasn't that she liked it. Of course she didn't *like* it.

It was another feeling, something closer to conviction. Like she was getting closer to reaching something, something she was chasing. Something she couldn't rest until she found.

She nearly walked into Gideon, who was crossing her path on his way to the reading room. At the sight of him, something inside her chest quickened with apprehension, which was ridiculous, because she was not afraid of Gideon. He was as mild-mannered as always, gently funny, a good housemate. He was clean and friendly and not a stranger, and not a threat, and yet—

"Something wrong?" asked Gideon, who was looking at her strangely. As if he'd seen the contents of her dreams and through her outward appearance to the moltenness at her core.

Lifeless eyes. The stillness of an outstretched hand.

(What else are you willing to break, Miss Rhodes—)

"No." Libby shook her head. "Just . . . Varona. Not in a bad way," she added quickly. "Just . . ."

"Ah." Gideon's smile was pleasant and understanding. "He's on his best behavior these days, so we're all a little unnerved."

"Right." She tucked a lock of hair behind her ear. "What's that?" she asked, gesturing to the papers in his hand.

"Hm?" Gideon glanced down as if he'd forgotten what he was holding. "Oh, well, you'll never believe this, but access to the archives is recorded with a paper file system." He gave her a pained look of helpless annoyance. "I'm aware that I was only assigned here to keep me out of your Society's way for a while," he mused, "but even so, the actual work involved is impressively mundane."

"It's not—" *It's not* my *Society,* Libby was about to say, but she did understand what he meant. She felt possessive over it, and as a result, Gideon's presence was slightly invasive—a pretty but foreign flora.

Like jacaranda trees in Los Angeles. Libby shuddered and said, "Sounds irritating. Did you have any sort of training?"

Gideon shook his head. "No, all this came from an internal memo. I'm starting to think I may have overestimated the insidious nature of the Illuminati."

"Hm?"

"Nothing, joking." He gave her another reassuring smile, and then hesitated before saying, "By the way, I don't know if you knew this, but, um. Your cell phone, it was . . . Someone was using it to communicate with your parents. I—" He stopped as Libby's mouth abruptly went dry. "I've been wanting to tell you for a while and it never felt like the right time, but it seems like if I let it go unsaid for too long . . ."

He trailed off and Libby realized it was her turn to speak. "No, I . . . thank you. Thanks, Gideon, that's—that's good to know. Do you have any idea where it is now?"

Lifeless eyes. A pair of feet fallen uncannily still on the office floor. Libby Rhodes, old and new, cleaved around the stiffness of a body. Gideon gave her a look like they both knew the answer.

"No," he said. "Anyway," he added, gesturing to the paperwork in his hand, "I should go, so—"

"Hey, Sandman, there you are," came Nico's voice from the other end of the corridor, and Libby quickly turned away to continue in the opposite direction, hurrying up the stairs.

She took the right turn she was becoming accustomed to, heart pounding as she reached the drawing room and shut the door quietly behind her.

"Rhodes, is that you?"

She exhaled slowly, pausing for a moment. A beat or two of time. "Yeah, it's me."

"Just give me a minute," Tristan called to her, and she nodded but didn't answer.

From where she stood in his drawing room, she caught the motion of Tristan's shadow moving around his bedroom, draping over the piles of books that had begun to take residence below the windowsill. Sun dripped into the room, the windows open, the smell of roses from the garden wafting up on the mid-morning breeze like a drowsy, intoxicating summons.

She stepped quietly into the room. Tristan was riffling through his wardrobe for a clean shirt, and when he saw her, something dimpled his forehead with concern until she stepped forward wordlessly, and then it morphed into something else. He turned to face her, and she kept walking until she reached him, the pulse in her chest loud and unambiguous—like asking, or possibly singing, *this-this-this*. She reached up to run the tips of her fingers over his chest, following the scar she already knew existed there. Like retracing her steps over long-familiar terrain.

She could feel his hands gently cupping her elbows, the smell of his aftershave sharp with tidiness, as if nothing had changed. As if every day for him still began the same way, even with all the distance that had come and gone between them.

What Nico didn't seem to grasp was that she wasn't the same. Not that it was fair to expect him to know her or understand her, and maybe it was unfair to accuse him of things inside her own head when he couldn't answer for his crimes. But Libby Rhodes was tired of fair, she was sick of it, of weighing the scales constantly, right and wrong. Every choice she'd made had come with crippling doubt, but she had still known it to be the right one. What Nico didn't understand was that Libby now knew something she hadn't before, which was that there was no right answer, no such thing as easy choices. Being good, or knowing what goodness even was—it was an old version of her that believed those things to be possible, and the new version of her was the one that understood the truth: that in the end, however simple a choice might feel, everything was complicated.

Doing the right thing, the necessary thing, would always come with pain.

Nico didn't understand that yet, but Tristan did. She could feel it in the way he leaned into her kiss, the way he'd been holding himself back until the very last moment, until he could finally give in. Capitulation. That was something Libby understood now; the dissonance that became inescapable clarity, just as the moment was right. She dug her nails into his chest and Tristan responded instantly, reflexively, moving with her easily until they both collapsed on his bed, the book in her hand long since tumbling to the ground. Tristan hooked his fingers around the waistband of the boxers she still wore, the ones she'd borrowed from him and hadn't returned, probably wouldn't. She exhaled sharply as he tugged them over her legs, pausing only to run a finger down the slickness between her thighs.

He knew what she was. She felt it between them: knowledge. Increasingly it had been difficult to ignore, the ways that he had seen her for what she was and still allowed her to transform—slowly but surely, like shedding scales. The person she had once been, he had wanted. The person she'd been forced to be, he had protected. The person she now was, unknown to them both, was being given permission to blossom, unfurling more and more each day until neither of them could stand to deny it. He stroked her and she bloomed under his touch.

She tipped her chin up to catch his kiss, gasping into it, muttering impatience at the loss of him while he divested himself of his trousers and returned, completing a sequence for which they'd been running the motions in silence, putting off the inevitable until it could no longer be denied. This, god, yes, she wanted it, she wanted this measure of satisfaction, of rightness. Of absolution, of absolute conviction. She wanted this, she wanted everything, she *wanted*.

This, all of this. This house and everything inside it. The possibilities. The carnalities, the kind of tragic ending she knew was in store for them all. Sacrifice, she understood it; nothing in this world came without its equal and opposite. Whatever had put this in motion, whether it was Atlas Blakely or human nature or Libby's own authoring of her fate, it had already begun, and what was put in motion did not stop. The origins of life. The possibility of the multiverse. The potency of power—*her* power. The way time stopped because she said so when Tristan was holding her, when he pinned her hands above her head.

It was fast and hard, rhythmic as a pulse, the build abrupt and the anguish exquisite. A sheen of sweat covered both their stomachs when Tristan fell beside her on the bed. The rise and fall of his chest, the pounding in her ears, again. Again. Again.

But first—"Hypothetically speaking. Do you really think the world could end?"

You couldn't fault me if you'd seen it, Ezra had told her once when she'd been groggy, half-awake, confessing his sins from a place of compulsion. *I don't know how to explain to you the way carnage looks. The way annihilation smells. That kind of darkness—and the bodies, the way they were . . . I don't have the physics for that kind of failure. The way it feels to stand in a place devoid of life, believe me, you'd find a way to stop it if you had to. If you saw what I saw, you'd choose betrayal, too.*

Tristan chuckled through ragged breaths, shaking his head. "Did I fail to capture your attention, Rhodes?"

"I just want to know." She let herself ragdoll out, limp in a wash of satisfaction.

"I don't—" He exhaled. "I don't know. I really don't."

"You've been thinking about it, too," she quietly observed, wondering whether to feel betrayed.

She didn't.

Tristan, to his credit, didn't seem to care. "Atlas said that Dalton would be the one to summon the void. I would be the one to see it, and you and Varona would be the key to the door I could conceivably unlock." A careful pause. "But to convince Dalton, we'd need Parisa." That, too, Tristan said like he'd considered it already. Like perhaps he'd already let his thoughts linger over Parisa's name. "And Reina, too, to handle the generation of that much output. Without Reina, a lot of other aspects could likely fail."

Libby shook her head. "Reina's just a battery. She's a crutch." She closed her eyes, then opened them. "If I have Varona, I could do it alone." She turned her head. "And you."

Tristan passed his tongue over his lips, still breathless. "By definition, Rhodes, that's not doing it alone."

"I'm just saying, the fewer things that could conceivably go wrong, the better. Reina being involved might mean Callum. And assuming Atlas hasn't already planted some telepathic bomb inside our heads, the most likely cause of apocalypse is Callum choosing to interfere."

Tristan made a low sound of agreement. "That, or Dalton's a closeted megalomaniac. A fun twist, I suppose, for the object of Parisa's affections to turn out seriously disturbed."

Dalton's pressed collars and stiffly academic lectures seemed a thing of the distant past, unimaginable as a bedtime story. "Callum," Libby continued musing to herself, "has always been a problem." The difference between theoretically peripheral and actively dangerous seemed starker from this side of the elimination clause. "And it's not as if he's favorably influencing Reina. We could always just—"

She broke off before she said it out loud.

Do you think I was a killer even before I walked into that office?

Maybe she had been one since the moment she first agreed on Callum to die.

Tristan shifted beside her. "Is that a change of heart, Rhodes? I thought righteous manor house confinement was your mortality stopgap of choice."

"Of course not. I didn't mean—" She stopped. "It doesn't matter. It's just a hypothetical. And anyway, the point is we couldn't possibly do the experiment *knowing* it's doomed to fail." She rolled onto her side to face him. "Right?"

He looked at her for a long time, his expression unreadable.

"It's just a door," he said eventually, to which Libby scoffed.

"That's like saying Pandora's box is just a box."

"It *is* just a box. Who's to say that Ezra even knows what he saw, or what happens sequentially to produce it?"

(*The world can end in two ways,* Ezra said to her back. *Fire or ice. Either the sun explodes or it extinguishes.* His knees were tucked into his chest; she knew it had been a bad day because she had known him, once. She had known him. *I saw both.*)

"Time is fluid," Tristan continued. "Reality is open to interpretation, or else what am I even for? There have to be several steps between discovering the presence of other worlds and blowing up everything in existence." Tristan hummed to himself in thought. "The experiment is just the box," he repeated. "It's what's inside the box that's the problem."

Inside the box, or inside the person desperate to open it.

Libby shifted with a sigh and Tristan opened one arm for her, tucking her securely into his side as she curled around to lay her head on his stomach. She counted the breaths between them, then lifted her gaze to rest her chin in the slats of his ribs.

His eyes were closed, one arm propping his head up against the headboard. She ran a finger over his scar again, wondering things.

They lay there so long in silence that the pace of his breathing slowed and deepened. Becoming restful. Almost sleep.

"Tristan." A swallow. "Do you trust me?"

She felt him tense, the vein beside his bicep jumping slightly from where his arm was bent below his head.

"You know the answer to that."

"I know. I'm just asking."

"You shouldn't have to ask."

"I know, I know, but—"

"It's done," he said. "You don't have to feel guilty anymore. You can put it behind you. Unless it's me you don't trust?"

"I never said that. I don't mean it like that, I just—"

The arm around her tightened and she realized she was bracing against him. Pulling away, or pushing. She wasn't sure, but either way she knew that he was anchoring her for a reason. As if he understood the things that kept her awake at night and would not reject her for the choices she already knew she'd have to make. The goodness she'd compromise for greatness if given the chance, because the unstained version of her was already gone.

She sensed that Tristan was watching her and took a long breath before meeting his eye.

He had beautiful eyes. Soulful. The expression on his face was carefully restrained and she thought again about what he'd said. *You can put it behind you.*

What he hadn't said. *I forgive you.*

"I'm sorry." So quiet it bled from her. He wrapped her in his arms, careful, and said the one thing that had brought her specifically to this room, to this bed.

The thing Belen Jiménez had already known; that Nico de Varona would never understand.

"No, you're not," Tristan said, and Libby closed her eyes.

No, she exhaled in silence.

She wasn't.

CALLUM

Tue, July 19 at 2:16 P.M.

Stay away from my sisters.

> Hark! He speaks!

> And do I sense an implied "or else"?

I don't have to imply it. You know what I mean.

> Indulge me anyway, as a treat.

Fine. Stay away from them or I'll kill you.

> Really? Over the half siblings you haven't spoken to in years?

> Given your track record it seems unlikely.

I barely need a reason, Nova. You've had it coming a long time.

Callum looked up from his phone screen for a luxurious drag of stale sweat and pub food, indulging a sip from his English pale ale with an air of revelation.

"Beautiful day, isn't it?" Callum called to one of Adrian Caine's little minions, who stood behind the bar glaring at him. ("Little" being an obvious misnomer, as Adrian Caine preferred his associates with more muscular bulk than sense. This one, who made a point of flashing his illegal handgun every time Callum came around the Gallows Hill pub, was called Wyn Cockburn. A witch—terribly full of himself for someone with cock in his name just sitting there, flaccid and unwrapped.)

"Oh, Callum." Alys Caine walked onto the pub floor from the kitchen, spotting him just as something rugby related happened on the television screen, resulting in a roar from a nearby table of witches. "I didn't realize you were back already. Are you looking for my father?" she asked, sidling up to the table in the corner where Callum sat alone.

"Just having a pint, Miss Caine, not to worry." Callum set his phone on the table and flashed her a grin, feeling particularly elated over his recent conversational success. "How's it going with the neighbor girl?" he asked, pointedly dropping his voice. (Their cock friend Wyn looked over with a flick of ownership, as if Callum had brazenly dared to play with one of his toys.)

"Despite your revolutionary advice to, quote, 'just be myself,' she still doesn't know I'm alive. So, you know. The usual." Alys sat down beside Callum with a sulky thud, teenagering with aplomb and speaking with precisely the accent that Tristan did everything in his power to conceal. (Funny that, as it was an unadulterated delight.)

"You probably shouldn't be here," Alys added, gesturing in Wyn's direction before reaching for a sip of Callum's beer. Callum chuckled, shifting his phone aside on the table and gamely nudging the glass her way. Alys was of age, obviously, but her father (or more accurately, her father's goons) had somewhat puritanical expectations for her behavior. Some that she'd been entirely too forthcoming with, too.

Alys's openness about her life suggested to Callum that her upbringing was starkly different from her elder half brother's. Unlike Tristan, Alys had an air of someone categorically unthreatened, who didn't need to keep things under lock and key. (Callum would guess she had conspicuously fewer bruises, too.)

"Wyn's not exactly a fan of yours," Alys cautioned, raising the glass to her lips as Callum reveled privately in the traumas of the only Caine son. "And I'm not sure Dad's as patient with you as he makes himself out to be."

Oh, Callum was aware. It was impossible not to be aware of Adrian Caine's feelings on the matter, as he was very much like someone else Callum knew, and therefore unable to conceal the perennial nature of his suspicion. Unfortunately, there were so few venues from which to adequately terrorize Adrian Caine's estranged adult children. Had Tristan felt more passionately about his former friends or fiancée, Callum would be engaging in different lifestyle choices entirely—but, as luck happened to have it, it was his familial past that Tristan had the most complex feelings toward, and let it never be said that Callum was incapable of meticulous research.

"I genuinely can't imagine why Brother Cockburn would be so opposed to my presence," Callum said, winking at Wyn and biting his lip lasciviously. An irresponsible taunt, but Callum reserved so little time for play these days. "After all, I'm doing your dad a favor by luring in the son he's been so adamantly tracking down."

"Yeah," Alys said, ignoring Wyn's wordless look of murdery rage and taking another unbothered sip from Callum's glass, "but Dad's got a way of compartmentalizing between people he personally dislikes and the ones doing him favors—right up until he doesn't feel the need for distinction anymore." She licked the beer from her lips and slid the glass back to Callum. "You don't think he actually means to kill Tris when he finds him, do you?"

People's interests were largely changeable, not unlike the bronze-colored liquid in his glass. Whether Tristan lived or died at his father's hands depended on who Tristan proved to be when Adrian "found" him. Callum, who had his own reasonably informed suspicions on the matter, shrugged. "You tell me. He's your father."

She grimaced. "He hasn't got much of a sense of humor, so it's probably not a joke. Still," she remarked with an air of opportunism, "he never says what exactly Tris did to cross him. Like, did he steal from him or something?" she asked, as if such a thing might be interesting and therefore befitting the mysterious estrangement from her brother.

She'd been asking variants of that question at increasing intervals over the past few weeks. "It's really between Tristan and your father," Callum said. "I'm not at liberty to say."

"Mm." Alys seemed to process that for a second, then kicked Callum's ankle. "Well, get out," she said. Across the room, Wyn had leaned over to one of the others, eyes never leaving the various places Callum might take a bullet. "And I say that as a friend."

There was a hint of cinnamon and clove behind her tone, a spice belying the warmth of the phrase, as if it pleased her very much that Callum should think she meant it. At her age they tended to be very secure in the quality of their duplicity, largely for undue reasons.

Still, he played along. "Don't tell your father we're friends," Callum advised. "I sense that would reflect poorly on you."

"Yeah, Bella's not a fan either," said Alys. "Thinks you're too pretty."

"She's absolutely correct," Callum confirmed.

"Right, well. Bye." Alys rose to her feet, giving him an anarchical look of suffering, and returned to the kitchen corridor, through which Callum imagined she would pass into the offices of Adrian Caine's operation and fulfill her daily destiny as Adrian's beloved daughter.

That, or pine silently over the neighbor girl, who Callum happened to be aware *did* know of Alys's existence, but telling her so seemed like ruining half the fun of adolescence.

Ah, youth.

"*There* you are." Conveniently, Reina had stormed into the pub, glaring around for emphasis. "Seriously, here again? Do you have a death wish?"

she asked, gesturing to Wyn with what was, for Reina, a mostly inoffensive scowl.

"You'd think so," Callum agreed as Reina filled the empty spot next to him where Alys had been. Something rugby related had happened in a negative way, Callum noted, which momentarily disrupted Wyn's telegraph of threats from the opposite side of the room. "So, what's wrong?"

"Nothing's wrong," Reina said, with another, more customized scowl.

"Right, obviously not, you're in a terrific mood." Callum drained the last of his pint, plucking his phone from the tabletop and returning it to his pocket. Inspiration had yet to strike for his reply. "What is it? Someone try to kill you again?"

"Yes, actually, another suit. Lost him a few blocks away." She glanced around with a look of unfiltered disdain. "We've really got to get out of London."

Callum shook his head. "Can't, though, can we? We're contractually obligated to Adrian Caine until I've fulfilled my part of the bargain."

"Which you're not even trying to do." She glared at him. "You promised him *Tristan,* which is essentially like offering to sell him something you no longer own. Which I'm pretty sure is also the foundation of what they do here," she added with a look of disapproval, almost as if she opposed it on a moral stance. A very Rhodesian school of thought.

"I know," Callum agreed. "I'm a genius." He rose to his feet, leaving a handful of mixed bills on the table. He'd never understood British currency and didn't plan to learn. "So," he continued, "what's on the docket today? Any other mobs that need straightening out?"

Reina wasn't listening, having noticed the resurgence of Wyn's tireless attention. Unfortunately, his looks did not kill, though Callum invited him to try. "Has Tristan even answered you?" Reina muttered, eyes flicking to the pocket where Callum had so cleverly hidden his phone. "I assume once you've pulled his pigtails for long enough, you'll once again find the energy for a more productive hostility."

"Of course not," Callum chided her. "As you know, there can be no end to the hostility until our oaths to the homicidal library have been adequately discharged."

"Right, so to recap the plan: you're going to anger him enough that he eventually comes after you just to kill you?" Reina prompted.

"No," Callum reminded her, "as this time, I'm going to be slightly less charitable and kill him first." And the answer to her actual question was no, Tristan hadn't answered him. Not sufficiently, anyway. Not yet. In the meantime, Callum was still mulling his response. "Have you answered your mysterious benefactor yet, by the way?"

Reina had been in receipt of a message from an unknown sender some days prior. She had not informed Callum of the message, but he was intimately privy to her emotions (and also, she had a tendency to leave her phone lying around). He'd let her have the secret for a while to keep the peace, but there was only so much entertainment to fill his time while he waited for Tristan to give in to temptation and play.

"I—" Reina glared at him again, with an air of violation this time. "How did you know about that?"

"I can't believe I have to be the one to tell you this, Mori, but—" Callum leaned closer as he angled himself toward the door. "I'm actually an elite member of a secret society."

She shoved him away, taking the lead. "I can't decide if I hate you more when you're depressed or when you're in a good mood," she muttered as they exited the pub.

"I love that for us." Callum waved to Wyn as they went, blowing him a kiss before donning his sunglasses and glancing again at Reina. She was feeling obstinate again, it seemed. "So, have you thought up a reply?"

Her mouth tightened. "There's no point. At first I thought it was—" She broke off, looking away as a mix of things that smelled paternal wafted generally around her aura; old leather books, mysterious offers, the unreachable nature of personal validation. The signature pathological fingerprint of Atlas Blakely. "But it wasn't."

Of course it wasn't. Callum already knew that, having actually saved Parisa's phone number to his contacts in the event of being elusively contacted by her, but as he was in such an obliging mood, he decided to overlook the basic protocols of personal communication.

"Shouldn't you be pleased?" he asked her, genuinely curious. "You wanted Varona to value you and now he does. You wanted Parisa to acknowledge you and now she has. Seems to me like everything's coming up Reina."

"I didn't say it was—" Reina gave him a spiteful look that was near perfect confirmation. "Look, I'm not interested in moving backward," she grumbled. "I'm not going back to the house. And as for Parisa—" Reina had a look, Callum was learning, that seemed specifically reserved for clenching her teeth around Parisa Kamali's name. "She didn't even say what she wanted. She's just expecting me to do her bidding, no questions asked."

Which was evidently tolerable, Callum observed, when Reina had thought the sender might be Atlas. But again, he very helpfully did not point that out.

"Seems unlike her," Callum mused.

"What? It's *exactly* like her—"

"No," he corrected, "I mean that it seems unlike her to attempt something she already knows would never work, like trying to get you to do what she wants. What did she say?" Beyond observing the existence of Reina's incoming messages, he gamely drew the line at reading them. (Also, he hadn't yet guessed her password.)

Reina, predictably, began to mumble in a lying way. "I'm perfectly capable of reading between the lines—"

"No, you're not," Callum corrected, holding out his hand. "Give me the phone."

"I told you," Reina argued, turning to face him. "Whatever she wants, it doesn't matter."

"Call it a matter of professional curiosity, then." He beckoned with his outstretched hand. "Give it."

Just as he said it, he sensed the presence of an inconvenience; a moment's distraction. A shift in the scenery, which had been occupied by the usual bland mix of human weakness until it became dominated by one particular thing. A tinny flavor, like the taste of blood.

"Why?" Reina growled. "Just so you can prove I'm—"

There it was, in uniform. Law enforcement again. What a convenient place to put an inferiority complex and a fondness for following orders. Callum pushed out his hand for what was unintentionally Reina's mouth, and she bit him.

"Ouch, for *fuck's* sake, Mori—"

Even with the sting from his palm, though, he gathered a little extra oomph. On his own it was sufficient to send the cop elsewhere, of course— even to convince him to come to Jesus or wherever Callum wanted to assign his salvation for the day—but lately, Callum had been enjoying the ability to override the fundamental nature he was so often having to use as a tool, or a mere jumping-off point. With Reina, in the same amount of time and with no substantial effort, he could rewrite a person's code from scratch. Suddenly, this particular cop was bereft of purpose, easily filled. Callum made one or two suggestions: take an interest in manual labor, commit to scrubbing toilets or laying brick for a change. And also, for fun, stop voting Tory, get off social media, and call your mum.

Callum had always been honest with Reina about the limitations of his powers. He had seen them in action, that whatever he put in motion wouldn't stop, necessarily, but *would* almost certainly warp. People were fundamentally in a constant state of self-correcting or self-affirming, changing or becoming more unchangeable depending on how pliable they had been to begin with. What Reina wanted was to force everyone to a single harmonious note of synchronicity; she wanted to make everyone care, and to both their credit, Callum could do it. He could do it on an enormous scale. He could override human nature for a time—to an extent. He could save lives or end them; he could raise the strings at will and make his puppets dance.

He *could* do it.

But he also knew something about the falseness of illusions, the thin veneer of compassion-seeming camouflage that could make a person *appear* to care. It wasn't the same thing as having the ability to actually do it. He could give someone a feeling, but how they acted on it was out of his control unless he stayed there, monitoring their every move.

For example, his mother. He could make her want to stay alive in the moment. He couldn't make her want to do it in *all* the moments plausibly preceding her natural death. That wasn't how emotion worked, or how people lived. Life was not a matter of saying yes once, on one significant but solitary occasion. Life was a series of difficult risings that followed impossible blows. To live was to experience a wide spectrum of terrible, destructive things, but only so often that the desire to make beneficial choices could still more frequently win out.

Reina might not understand the difference between those two things, but Callum did, just as he understood that changing the political affiliations of a man using a badge to obscure a homicidal nature was ultimately treating one small symptom of an incurable infection. No matter how Callum played this game, he would always lose it. If it wasn't this cop, it would be another. Someone would always want him dead for his magic or his personality, the latter of which was at least a very defendable reason. There were plenty of people others would happily kill just for the optics. Just to bend the world into a certain shape. Which wasn't to say Callum specifically felt anything beyond ambivalence about it—he'd benefitted from that kind of attitude for the entirety of his life and it wasn't up to him to question it, much less change it.

You didn't get to choose who hated you, who loved you. Nobody knew better than Callum how little a person could actually control.

"Give me the phone," he said once the cop was gone, having been adequately persuaded. Reina handed it to him, as sulky as Alys had been a few minutes prior despite being nearly a decade older.

Callum opened her messages, which were sparse, not even filling the screen. At the top was a conversation with an unnamed contact that was clearly Nico de Varona. Then another unknown contact, recognizable by the country code as Parisa, which Callum selected.

The first two messages were days old, from earlier in the week.

> Saw you on the news.
> I've got a better idea.

Then two more, hours old.

> Atlas will probably come for you soon. But trust me, the Society
> can go fuck itself and so can everyone else.
> We're down to five months at best. Use it or lose it, Mori. Come
> find me when you're ready to talk.

"Parisa's at the end of her rope," Callum judged, handing the phone back to Reina. "It's a peace offering. You know she wouldn't wave a white flag unless the situation was actually dire."

Predictably—if disappointingly—Reina didn't budge. "She could come crawling to me on her knees and it still wouldn't matter. I don't need her to tell me what she thinks I'm doing wrong." Reina tucked the phone back in her pocket and stared around at the thinness of the crowd. "Was that cop alone?"

"We're fine for now." Callum's good mood had evaporated somehow. Was it Parisa's message? He normally needed a person's physical presence in order to properly gauge their feelings, but somehow he felt it; some immensity of loss that was unavoidable inside her message. *The Society can go fuck itself and so can everyone else.*

Something had changed for Parisa Kamali.

Is there something specific you have in mind for me? Callum had asked the Society bureaucrat, Sharon something-or-other, the one who'd summoned him to the Alexandrian offices to chat about his prospects. It wasn't unlike the donation requests he still received from the Hellenistic University, who rang their alumni consistently for updates, collecting accolades for their proverbial shelf. In this case, the Society wanted to know: Did he have any interest in politics, or statecraft? Would he care to expand his family's empire? With everything he'd learned—the privilege of knowledge he'd been provided—what would he do next?

With your skill set, Mr. Nova, we do recommend public office, she'd said.

Fascinating. Worrisome. *Which office?*

She hadn't answered. *We can expedite your visa if you'd prefer to stay in the United Kingdom.*

You know what I can do, he replied. *You'd subject the general populace to it? Your own country?*

Callum had felt a lot of things in her answer. Responsibility. Bitterness. Everyone was mainly one important thing, and Sharon's important thing was so far removed from him, so distant, that she was one of the few people who'd ever looked at him and genuinely could not care less. *Mr. Nova, let me be very clear about one thing. I have a job. And your opinion of my performance is not relevant to my employment.*

A sick child was Callum's guess. The most important thing in the world to Sharon, whoever it was. He could tell it was expensive. It was bad enough to buy her the right to look at his file and dismiss the consequences out of hand. Probably this job of hers was lucrative for its requisite skill set—compared to similar positions, it likely had excellent benefits and a very good pension. Sharon had signed a nondisclosure agreement, most likely, and probably wore a permanent silencing charm. . . . He had focused for a moment and then found it; there was a tiny itch near the edge of her chemise, a small tattoo. She didn't hate it, keeping the Society's secrets. It was what allowed her to come home to a . . . daughter? Yes, a daughter who was still alive. For now.

The Society can go fuck itself and so can everyone else.

"Are you ready?" asked Reina impatiently.

A parliamentary special election. Their biggest attempt so far to rig the results and offer humanity a shot at doing something humane. Reina wanted to give it to the party who loved sick kids, probably, so that would be a win for Sharon. *You're welcome,* Callum thought.

"One second." He took out his own mobile phone, scrolling back to the messages from Tristan.

I barely need a reason, Nova. You've had it coming a long time.

That was from a few days ago. Callum had snapped a few selfies since, including one of himself in the pub, but he hadn't sent them. He didn't now. He typed very quickly and pressed send, though he would not receive a response for several hours. Maybe he *was* getting more powerful at a distance, because he was sure he could feel the tension. The times he knew that Tristan was opening his messages just to stare at Callum's name until finally, after at least a dozen rounds of sapiosexual edging, Tristan finally let himself give in.

Glad you're starting to get it

3:43 A.M.

Get what

That it was always meant to end with one of us.

· PARISA ·

There was a low buzzing in her ears, which she realized was coming from the bright white lights overhead. The thoughts in here were nothing outside the ordinary for a workplace. Someone had eaten Denise's salad and it was probably Frank. Evelyn was in a foul mood and Terrence desperately needed to get laid. Could Stephen believe that Maria's mother-in-law wasn't dead yet? Come watch this outrageously specific ad. (Medeian technomancy was such a marvel it might as well have been telepathy.)

"Miss Kamali?"

Parisa had heard the woman coming from where she sat in the waiting room, but politely looked up as if she'd only just been made aware of her presence. Because yes, she was capable of being polite. "Yes?"

"This way, please." The woman was terribly distracted and had her third straight migraine in a week. (Parisa could relate.) Her favorite was her oldest daughter, Maggie, and their problem child had kept her up all week. Rosie was prone to ear infections, Georgie had been misbehaving in school, Georgie was a biter. Still there was no point in wishing for more wishes, so the woman wished for Maggie's health and Maggie's health alone. "Sorry to keep you waiting. I'm glad you could find the time."

Parisa took a seat at the woman's desk. Sharon, her name was. Sharon's attention flicked warily from Parisa to the lamp at the edge of the desk, and Parisa calculated that Nico had been there weeks, possibly months before.

"Okay," said Sharon, opening a paper version of Parisa's file. "Now, as I mentioned, this is intended to be a collaborative process." This was not the first meeting Sharon had had with a member of Parisa's cohort. Callum had definitely been here. Reina and Tristan had not. "We understand that you likely have some career goals or personal ones to attend to, and the question is how we can help you elevate your—"

"I don't want career counseling," said Parisa. "You have a headache. Don't waste your breath. I'm only here because I want to know what happened to Nasser Aslani."

Sharon gave Parisa a dull look. "Who?"

Parisa felt her mouth tighten, then tried not to make it obvious. Making an enemy of Sharon wouldn't make any of this any easier. "Nasser Aslani. My—" She cleared her throat. "My husband."

Sharon's initial hum of disinterest was instantly drowned out by a sea of irritated thoughts, including but not limited to a vision of stabbing Parisa with her own stilettos. Fair. "This office does not handle domestic disputes, Miss Kamali. If you have an issue with your husband—"

"Two weeks ago, Nasser asked me to meet him. He was worried I was in trouble. He knew people were trying to hunt me down, which I assume you also know. Then he never showed up." Parisa crossed one leg over the other. "Nas doesn't not show up. Something happened to him, and I know it has to do with the hit put out on me by the Forum." Or worse, though Parisa wasn't going to mention Atlas by name. Not yet, when she might still need him to lose badly. Or win.

She could feel the thundering ache of Sharon's migraine like she was suffering it herself. "Miss Kamali—"

"You have a headache," Parisa repeated, her voice clipped. "Your daughter is dying. Let's not waste time you don't have."

Sharon stared at her.

"I know you track us," Parisa said plainly. "I'm fairly confident that tracking goes beyond your initiates. Nasser's a medeian; he was educated at the magical university in Amman. I know you know how to find him." Parisa could feel Sharon's brittle waves of spite, her disdain for Parisa's entitlement, for the perfection of her skin—but there was also a little respect in there, a kernel of it. Not enough to qualify for sympathy, obviously, but enough to acknowledge they were both the victims of a ticking clock.

This was the most Parisa had spoken about Nasser in years, and maybe it didn't take a mind reader to know it. "Just tell me where he is," Parisa said, "and I'll tell you whatever answer you need to hear to call your file closed. Job done."

Sharon was clearly underpaid. A consummate professional. She didn't sigh or even blink before turning to the desktop screen that wasn't even top of the line. She clicked a few things, frowned—she was initially denied access; even without reading her mind, Parisa could see the glare of red from Sharon's glasses—then she flicked a glance at Parisa before typing in her password (Maggie's birthday) and clicking something else.

Parisa saw it, her answer, before Sharon spoke anything aloud.

"Fuck," exhaled Parisa in the same moment Sharon said, "I'm sorry."

Parisa rose to her feet, wishing she were Nico de Varona. Wishing she could break something and laugh, walk away. "You knew where to look," she remarked after a second to collect her thoughts. Regret lived heavy in her chest, but it would have to wait. "You knew where to look when the database denied you access."

"We know about the threats against your lives," Sharon said to Parisa's tacit accusation. Sharon was thinking something else now, empathy maybe, the pity kind. She didn't dislike Parisa. How wonderful for them both. "We have active files open on your family members and known associates."

Parisa thought about Libby's family, her mother and father and ghost of a sister. Nico's mother who had taught him how to dance, his uncle who taught him how to fight. Callum's family could fend for themselves, they deserved an investigation, and anyone who knew anything knew that going after Tristan's family was a waste. Reina would probably stab her own parents if she hadn't already. "Has anyone else's—?"

Another click of Sharon's mouse. "There has been one possible breach involving a creature, which we are not capable of tracking. Tristan Caine's father and sisters are self-protected. The Ferrer de Varona family are friends of their government and private by nature. The Novas—"

Sharon's voice faded out, dissolving into the rush of blood in Parisa's ears. She didn't know what to do with this amount of sadness in her stomach, this ballooning up of anger in her chest. She didn't usually allow herself to feel it, this kind of bitterness, this mottling rage. It was purposeless, fruitless, pointless—she wasn't the kind of person who could afford to be wasteful. Every thought in Parisa's head was powerful, every moment of her time something that others would kill to have. What was anger except setting fire to the possibility of clarity? What would fury do aside from cloud her judgment?

But now, oh now. Parisa Kamali was fucking *mad*.

"How did they know? About me. About Nas." *It doesn't matter,* Parisa's brain said in a quiet, unhelpful voice. *It doesn't matter how.* "Was it the Forum?"

"Yes, we think so. A task force, probably, something privately arranged, but certainly the Forum at an operational level." Atlas, Parisa thought instantly. This was Atlas's fuckup. This was his fault, he'd said so himself. That motherfucker. Even if he didn't come after Dalton—even if he didn't come for Parisa himself—she'd absolutely kill him first. "This looks tactical," Sharon continued, "possibly an intelligence operation. I have to assume your husband chose not to cooperate."

Oh, of course. Something faded in Parisa's mind, or loomed. Never mind. It could never have been Atlas, he knew her too well, he would have known that harming Nasser wouldn't end with anything remotely beneficial to him. Of course it was someone infinitely dumber, for a reason that was laughable, nonsensical. Absurd. Because *of course* it was some American or British person single-handedly deciding that Nasser was dangerous—of course that's what it was.

Ironically the rage was too big to carry at that point, too cerebral. The tips of Parisa's fingers went numb.

"I always thought there would be time," she said, wanting to laugh. "I thought there'd be a time when I'd finally figure out how to tell him what he did to me. To explain it to him in a way that he could understand. I was so young, he had *no right*—"

She looked away, realizing she was still standing in the middle of the office.

She kept talking anyway, because once she'd started, she couldn't stop.

"I needed help and I knew he would help me, I needed him and I knew he'd say yes. But it wasn't right, what he wanted from me, what he made me feel I owed him. I know he was good, I know he was kind, but it still wasn't equal, it still wasn't right. It wasn't—it *couldn't* have been—love." She was breathing hard, like she'd been running. Or crying.

Sharon removed her glasses, staring at the lenses in her hand before beginning to polish one surface. Parisa wanted to thank her for the indignity of it. The necessary reminder that the world did not revolve around her personal pain.

"Anyway." Parisa carefully returned to the chair, smoothing down her dress. "Fair is fair. You gave me what I needed. What do you need from me?"

Sharon considered the pair of spectacles in her hand for another long moment before gradually raising the pads of her fingers to the lids of her eyes, pressing down on them. Right, yes, the headache. "Sorry," Parisa said, leaning forward. "Let me just—"

She reached out. Sharon balked, which Parisa disregarded. She pressed a clammy hand to the other woman's forehead and picked it like a lock. Pain receptors were easy to fool. It would come back if Sharon didn't get some sleep, which she wouldn't, but better that she didn't. She'd consider it a waste given how little time her daughter had left.

"Is it hopeless?" Parisa asked in a low voice. "For Maggie."

If Sharon was bothered by the invasion of her thoughts, she didn't show it. She merely shook her head. "There's a new magical trial," she replied with her eyes closed. "It's in the States. But they rejected her."

"It's probably very difficult to choose which patients can be helped." Parisa hadn't yet removed her hand. It felt good, being useful. Temporary, probably pointless, and yet oddly peaceful. It felt like having somewhere to put her anger down and rest. "Cancer is unpredictable. Biomancy isn't much of a science, it's more like an art. Mutations like that, they're—"

"Nothazai is a biomancer," Sharon said, taking Parisa by surprise. She supposed she hadn't been paying attention. She'd been using some unpracticed organ in her chest in place of her magic or her thoughts. "He's the chairman of the Forum's board of directors," Sharon added, though Parisa knew exactly who Nothazai was and did not initially see the relevance. "He was considered for Alexandrian recruitment but denied. They picked someone who could spread illness virally instead." Sharon's eyes opened.

Was that . . . bitterness? Against the Forum, or the Society? Parisa realized the precariousness of her own position, the plausible expectation for this shared moment of vulnerability. She was keenly aware of social transactions, the expectation of give that followed every take. This was what came of feelings, which had always been a waste.

"If you're thinking there's a cure in the archives somewhere—" Parisa paused. "The problem is institutional. It's greed," she said bluntly. "The inability to separate human existence from the necessity of profit. Even if a cure for Maggie existed in the library—"

"You think I blame the Society? Or you? I don't." Sharon pulled away to give Parisa a hard look of sudden hatred. "Do you think I'm angry about *capitalism*?" Sharon asked in a tone of condescension that Parisa was unable to parse, briefly short-circuiting. "You think I wouldn't willingly go into bankruptcy, sell my own organs, if it meant my daughter could have even one more day on this earth? It's not about what magic can't do for me, or what Nothazai won't. The point isn't even what *I'd* do that they wouldn't. It's not the injustice, Miss Kamali, or Aslani, or whoever the fuck you really are—it's the absurdity." The whole thing was crisp, like a well-articulated spell. "It's the privilege that I was given to be able to know her at all, which you'll never have. The fact that I'm going to be one of the very, very few witnesses to the sound of her laugh—it's criminal. And I feel sorry for all of you," Sharon concluded with an honesty so unfaltering, so absent its own agenda that Parisa wasn't sure how to feel except for small. "The way that none of you will ever know."

Parisa didn't understand the thoughts in Sharon's mind. She could see them, feel them, taste the hot tears burning a hole in Sharon's throat, but she couldn't make sense of them. It was too much; it was everything all at once.

The most dangerous person in the room. Hollowly, Parisa almost laughed.

"I'm putting in your file that you're going to consider an entrepreneurial venture," Sharon said abruptly, the din of her thoughts escalating to a sharpened stake of task-oriented lucidity. She typed quickly on her keyboard and then turned her attention back to Parisa, closing the file that bore Parisa's name. "We'll follow up with you in a year or so. Best of luck until then."

Parisa left the office shortly after. She walked to a café and sat down alone, phone still in her hand. She dialed a phone number and listened in silence while it rang and rang and rang.

"Who are you calling?" Eventually Dalton slid into the seat across from her.

"No one." Parisa put the phone away. "Nas is dead. The Forum killed him." She wondered how public that news would be, how they would spin it. Whether he would be considered a criminal by his association to her.

"Wasn't he a naturalist?" Dalton had ordered drinks for them, a cappuccino for her, tea for himself. It was so very picturesque, the two of them. A pair of clandestine lovers in bistro chairs, sitting close enough her ankles brushed the leg of his trousers. "What a waste."

What a waste. "Yes." Someone nearby was looking at her legs. Parisa took a sip of her cappuccino, then looked at Dalton. He was so refreshed, had slept in and showered. He faced the world with a sense of purpose. She envied that; needed it.

"What would Atlas do?" she asked.

If Dalton was surprised, he showed no evidence of it. He shrugged. "You know what he'd do."

Destroy the world.

No, but that wasn't it, was it? Not really. It was the world that was already dying, or maybe it was already dead. Maybe it was something like Maggie— the writing on the wall, pain and loss inevitable, and so what Atlas had done was much more proactive.

Gather all the pieces. Derive a plan. The answer wasn't to destroy the world.

It was to make a new one.

"What do you need?" asked Parisa.

"I told you. The two physicists, and the battery. And the other one to navigate."

"It's distinctly unsettling when you don't call them by their names," Parisa sighed.

"Fine, sorry." Dalton gave a small bark of a laugh. "Tristan Caine," he said clearly, "is unavoidable. He's the only one who can captain the ship, so to speak."

Parisa nodded, unsurprised. "You're sure you don't need Atlas?"

"Atlas needs you," Dalton said. "He doesn't trust himself."

Dalton had skirted the same point before, but as usual, Parisa didn't see anything alarming or cryptic in his maelstrom of thoughts. It felt as clinical as everything he usually did or said, more so than other things they'd recently discussed. "Doesn't trust himself to do what?"

"To . . . gauge the situation. To read it, understand it."

"What's to understand? I'm not a physicist."

"It's not that. He doesn't need you for the magic. He needs you for . . . for clarity, for—" Dalton frowned in sudden, warped frustration. Parisa recognized an older version of him inside the motion; a younger Dalton punching a castle wall. "Atlas Blakely designed the code," he said, straining for the right vocabulary. "He found the pieces and he built the computer. But he can't do it anymore, he's lost his objectivity. He's afraid the algorithm is wrong."

Dalton's thoughts blurred. It was a metaphor, clearly, but Parisa didn't entirely grasp its purpose. It wasn't a very good day for her, intellectually speaking. Nothing seemed to make any sense. "What?"

"He's running too many programs at once. He needs someone there who can test and debug. Someone to be the human."

Maybe it was the loss of her husband or the conversation with Sharon or the pointless shards of envy from seven tables away over Parisa's stupidly expensive shoes, which were pinching her feet. Maybe she'd always been this angry; maybe now that she'd become aware of it, she'd never be *unaware* again. Maybe now she'd be this stupid forever, which would frankly serve her right.

Parisa felt a wave of annoyance that made her brush aside her failure to grasp Dalton's argument and say, very brusquely, "So your point is we don't need Atlas. Is that it?"

"No, we don't need him." Dalton looked relieved to be putting his prior efforts aside. "No, if anything Atlas is the weakness in the whole design."

"Right. Okay." Parisa paused and typed a message on her phone, then a second one, then a third, trying to decide which one would ultimately be the longer project. (Nico was pleased to hear from her, of course he was—he was convalescing by the sea for the time being but would call her later, kisses. She hadn't expected a reply from Reina and four days later, still hadn't received one. But that was okay for now, she had time; it was Dalton who'd noticed Callum in the background of two separate press conferences alongside glimpses of the same black boots and hoodie, so it didn't take a genius to realize what Reina had been practicing over the last year to do. If Parisa knew one thing about people, it was that they were disappointing, and soon enough Reina would be disappointed. Parisa would know how to find her when she was.)

The reply from Tristan, however, had been instant and surprising.

Tristan's in the shower, this is Libby. Where do you want to meet?

To be perfectly clear, Atlas Blakely doesn't want to destroy the universe.

He just doesn't want to exist in this one.

· · ·

The question is not whether the world can end. There's no question that it can, that it does every day, in a multitude of highly individualized ways ranging from ordinary to biblical. The question is also not whether one man is capable of ending the world but whether it is *this* man, and whether such destruction is as inevitable as it may seem. What is the problem? The constancy of fate. The liquidity of prophecy. The problem is Einstein's theory of relativity. The problem is closed-loop time travel. The problem is Atlas Blakely. The problem is Ezra Fowler. The problem is the invariability of the particular strand of the multiverse in which Ezra and Atlas meet.

The problem is that Ezra Fowler had a sweet tooth, a snacking problem. A habit of humming the same insufferable pop songs while he thought. The problem is he left a thin film of peanut butter on every page of Atlas's incomprehensible notes. The problem is Ezra, who had an unusual mind because he did not submit to linear time, and often did not know what day it was. The problem is he chewed on Atlas's pens and occasionally fell asleep at the edge of Atlas's bed like a loyal hound and did not understand the purpose of knocking. The problem is that Ezra Fowler had night terrors, and hay fever. The problem is he read all the books on Atlas's shelves and left his own notes in the margins. The problem is Ezra was remarkable at backgammon; could have played table tennis professionally in another, less unusual life. He was addicted to filter coffee and often let his tea go cold. The problem is that Ezra was impossible to reason with before noon and occasionally after dinner. That he did not concern himself with the necessity of things like niceties of speech. That he was socially awkward and often brilliantly, bitingly angry. That he was bright and miserable and full of wonder, and such curiosity was infectious, and it struck a match in the lighter parts of Atlas Blakely's soul.

The problem is the latent human tendency to create an avatar of a person in our minds, reassembling them from the biases of our memories until the fragment of them in our heads becomes more simplified, and more and more inadequate over time.

The problem is that sometimes, when Atlas looked at Ezra Fowler, he saw himself, like facing down a mirror that showed him all of his best qualities and none of the ugly ones. The problem is that it was not romantic, not platonic, not fraternal.

The problem is that it was closest to alchemical—the feeling like you've met the person you want to make magic with for the rest of your life.

The problem is that sometimes, when Atlas looked at Ezra, he only saw an ending; someone to eventually, inevitably lose.

Because it is impossible to remove from the equation of the problem the fundamental nucleus of truth, which is that Atlas Blakely loved and was loved by Ezra Fowler, and that becoming mortal enemies is unfortunately one plausible strand of outcomes of loving and being loved this way.

. . .

It would be Ivy's idea first. From there Atlas would not know whether it was simultaneously occurring in the minds of the others or if it had spread virally, as Ivy had a tendency to do. She was very pragmatic, understandably so, being essentially the equivalent of walking, talking genocide. Her deduction had taken place quietly, almost forgettably, if such a thing could be forgettable. Atlas did not know who had clued her in that one of their cohort would have to die, or how she'd known (Atlas's theory was Neel, who did have a knack for seeing an illuminating part of the picture, if not the more comprehensible whole) or whether the impetus of the thought had been internally derived or external. Ownership of ideas was difficult to quantify under ordinary circumstances. The sudden materialization of *maybe the weird one should die instead of me* could have come from any number of places. But however it may have arrived there, the point is that it did.

The installation, wherein the Society's enemies were tipped off about the date of the new initiates' arrival, wasn't a personal practice of Atlas's. He and his cohort of Society recruits had had their own installation as well, which at the time similarly consisted of an early, crude attempt by James Wessex, various militaristic special operations, and a predictable handful of Forum goons. Atlas's cohort, which lacked the captaincy of two physicists companionable enough in their rivalry to serve as joint tacticians, split off individually. It was Atlas, standing alone in the drawing room, who alone felt the presence of Ezra Fowler disappear.

Eventually, there would be nothing that Atlas enjoyed more than crafting strategy with Ezra Fowler, who was clever and well-read and adequately trained in multiple specialties the way most medeians were not. Ezra called himself a physicist, and he was one, passably so, though he could also craft illusions well and had a keen mind for the theoretical and arcane. He was secretive, but not threateningly so. Closer to private, and deeply introverted. It was Ezra's gift in life to appear unremarkable, which in a house full of remarkability was more like a death sentence. Which, at the time, neither he nor Atlas had a reason yet to know.

So, on the night of their installation, Atlas would learn two things: that Ezra was opposed to loss of life, would do anything to avoid it; and that if he, Atlas, had not guessed or intuited that Ezra had slipped through time as well as space, then Ezra would not have told him. Ezra was easily spooked, preternaturally jumpy. Didn't like to disturb things—the quiet, the peace, the time-space paradox, any situation in which he allowed himself to become comfortable, which he did with a conscientious sense of doom.

"The way I see it," Ezra had told Atlas once, or at least as Atlas remembered it, "life has the capacity to be very long, and all the worst things are pretty much inevitable. So, you know, might as well rob the bank."

Shortly thereafter, Atlas and Ezra experimented with hallucinogens and began modeling the particle physics mechanism for cosmic inflation that would later be casually referred to as the Atlas Blakely Sinister Plot. They told no one, which at the time felt like the right thing to do. Right up until Atlas realized that Ivy suspected Ezra of possessing insufficient magic to tie his shoes.

(This, to be clear, was not her fault. Ivy Breton, as previously mentioned, was most at risk for group-determined elimination from a philanthropic, humanity-embracing standpoint, which is the one Atlas tended toward as a person of generally utilitarian belief. Her particular strand of biomancy— viral disease—was an explosive, unrivaled output of magic that was not so much useful as powerful. An interesting conversion of Reina Mori's gifts, but that is obviously not a matter for current contemplation. Just a sort of quietly tickling aside.)

After Ivy, Folade was next. She didn't like Ivy, but she also didn't like Atlas, and she liked Ezra even less. Neel, beloved idiot Neel, he sweated over it, but he had a tendency to leave things up to the divine, which in his case was a matter of the other five. Atlas would not discover until many years later what Alexis thought about all this, which by then would be too late to make a difference. But Atlas was a good enough friend and a better liar to conceal the entire nature of the truth, which was that Ezra had been marked by the others for one of two bad options: death, or more proactively, murder.

Or, for the dastardly clever and edgily punk, there was an additional opportunity to simply trick the powers that be, dazzling them right to their faces and gradually ousting them in favor of two slightly stoned near-men who both happened to think murder is bad.

Thus, from between a rock and a hard place appeared the option of time travel, a potential third.

(The problem, of course, is Atlas Blakely. The problem is his tendency to believe that he is smarter than the others, better, quicker, more prepared, when really what he happens to be is the universal answer key without properly listening to the questions. The problem is his lifelong necessity of being that way—of confusing telepathy with wisdom or worse, with understanding. The problem is also money, and most definitely capitalism. The problem is stolen knowledge! The problem is colonialism! The problem is institutional religion! The problem is corporate greed! The problem is entire populations forgoing equitable labor for the fleeting high of cheap consumer goods! The problem is generational! The problem is historical! The problem is the English! The problem is—)

"Cool," said Ezra.

("Did you actually kill him?" Alexis would ask later, in private, after the others had already accepted that the explanation Atlas gave was true. Easy enough to do, since there was no reason to question something they all desperately wanted to believe. No more murder, only books. A heady, collective relief, minus one necromancer's ambivalent qualms. "Wasn't he your best friend?"

"We didn't come here for friends" was Atlas's nuanced reply. "And what else might I have done if not kill him? Stash him in the cupboards?"

"Hm," said Alexis, who despite considerable telepathic evidence otherwise would later claim that she knew, or at very least suspected. She'd be dying at the time, so Atlas would give her the benefit of the doubt.

"What made you think it was a lie?" asked Atlas.

"Because," she said. "You didn't ask me to bring him back.")

So essentially, what started with Ivy had an irreversible tumble of consequence, one that Atlas would encounter again the next decade and learn from, choosing to use it to his advantage. It was unavoidable, that initial spark, born from a place of defensiveness as well as ambition, and a noble—if such a thing was possible—greed. Kill the weak one, kill the dangerous one, it doesn't matter your particular school of thought. You can always find a reason. Once the idea of death becomes necessary, even palatable, there is always someone the rest of the herd can stand to lose.

· · ·

The first time Ezra meets secretly with Atlas, five seconds from his exit that also happens to be five years on from his manufactured "death," Neel has already died three times, Folade twice, and as a method of experimentation, Atlas and Alexis are letting Ivy stay dead, just in case that happens to appease the archives for a time. What Ezra incorrectly reads in Atlas's posture as a continuation of his former swagger is a new-old coping mechanism built from panic, arrogance, and the final vestiges of youth. In that moment, minutes away from the decision they've both made to make the Society bow righteously to them, Ezra loves Atlas still, and Atlas loves Ezra enough to keep it from him. The storm brewing, which will eventually become a critical error, and an all-encompassing truth.

He knows you want to ask him. Go ahead, do it. Knowing what he knows—what *you* know—then surely by now Atlas understands the story he's been telling. You'll notice he hasn't yet made the claim that what Ezra Fowler predicted cannot possibly come to light. Thus, if Atlas already knows what Ezra was trying to stop—if he himself does nothing to deny it—then surely Atlas understands he is the villain.

Okay, so then Atlas is the villain. There, are you happy now? Of course not. Because in life there are no true villains. No real heroes. There is only Atlas Blakely left to settle his accounts.

· · ·

By the time Atlas Blakely meets Dalton Ellery, he already knows that everything in the universe has a cost. He has told you this himself, in justifying the price he has asked others to pay, which he himself did not. Because now he understands the meaning of sacrifice, and therefore he understands what comes for free, and what can be spontaneously created.

Which is to say: nothing.

Which is one way of saying that Atlas Blakely knows exactly how dangerous Dalton Ellery is, but by the time such a thought occurs to him, the debt of his life has already been acquired, and he is already much too late.

· DALTON ·

You are entering the cycle of your own destruction, the wheel
 Of your own fortune. Rome falls, everything
 Collapses. Limits, purpose, cages, fail-safes, walls,
Something put in motion does not
"Parisa?" looks smaller when she sleeps
Ashes of yourself the rubble from the fall We are such stuff / Dreams are made on / the past is prologue, Stop. This is my fault
Dalton are you listening? You have to be the one to live, Something put in motion does not
Viviana Absalon, forty-five-year-old female misclassified as a mortal
Stop now the past is
Prologue: something I learned long ago, not everything I bring to life stays alive
A portal of this magnitude, an output of this potency, it cannot come from nothing,
"Parisa, I need to tell you something—"
He can't always remember, it comes and goes, it's on the tip of his tongue, oh yesyes there it is
Can't promise there's no death inside the void, almost immediately another thought: What else is the Point
Do people blessed with longevity typically attract fatalities? (Does magic only give when it can take?) Is this some unspoken law of nature or is it proof of
The other half of his fate, a mirror-image of his soul, it isn't *not* romantic
If we don't try? An end to the hunger, a completion to the cycle, Rome falls, everything
Put in motion does not
Stop me, someone will have to, it will have to be
You don't understand, I want this too much, tell me the truth Dalton the truth is
DestroyDestroyDestroy!!!!!!
Listen Atlas when all the archives choose to give me is a university physics

textbook from 1975 I think we can safely say there's been a problem with the calculations

—such a thing as too much power? Yes oh god Dalton yes but it's too

Late, she stirs in her sleep but doesn't wake. "Parisa?"

Her eyes flutter open. She's cranky in the mornings, he's utterly turned on, what was he saying? Everything is so fragmented, impossible these days to hold on to

One single thought: *I want to build worlds with you.* Not love exactly but something very similar, symmetry, like finding a mirror-image of his soul, the other half of his fate. She seems worried, a little, but distracted, too distracted to see that he can't

Tell her, tell her now, neither created nor destroyed, *think about what that means—*

He finds a use for his mouth, a queen deserves a throne, yesyesyes there it is he thinks or possibly remembers,

Energy can neither be created nor destroyed; for any spontaneous process, the entropy of the universe increases; listen up you fuckhead I don't say these things for my health

How to ruin a man's life? Easy, give her anything she

Wants to tell her something, the caveat to this, have to remember something, something,

Have to remember, Dalton, that something put in motion will not

(Her sigh in his ear) Dalton please don't

Stop.

III

STOICISM

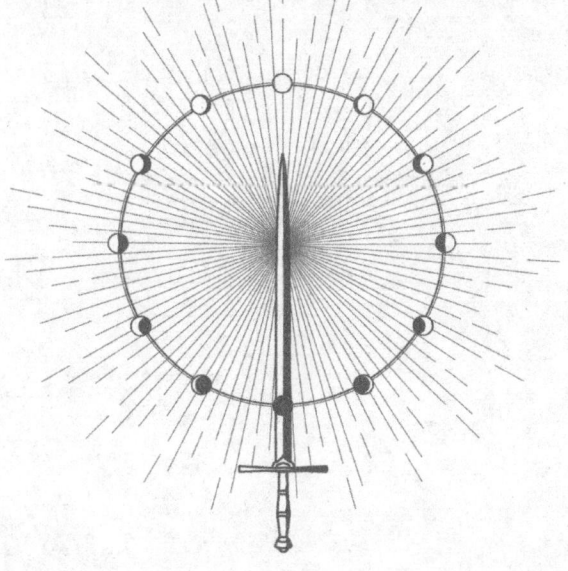

TWO
Li

Li was one of the most common Chinese surnames according to an English language database, which was why the Li in question (pronouns: they/them) had chosen to use it upon accepting the terms of inclusion for Ezra Fowler's plan.

Ezra had known a thing or two about the person called Li, including their actual family name, which was not technically as damning as the dossier of blackmailable sins that Ezra had on the other members he'd tapped for his anti–Alexandrian Society quest for global salvation. Li had very few sins, actually—a nearly shameful dearth of them aside from the usual faults of human nature, having been adopted by the state at the time of their birth, presumably due to the nature of their specialty or the poverty of their parents, whom they had never known. In Li's case, Ezra Fowler had offered more of a carrot than a stick, which Li had accepted despite knowing they would likely be pulled from the operation by their superiors at the first plausible hint of failure. Li occasionally wondered why Ezra Fowler had chosen them at all—they were of high middle rank but not exactly free to do as they wished—and determined it must have been the result of their particular talents. Ezra Fowler had likely watched Li for a substantial length of time to even discover said abilities, and that Li had not known . . .

Well, it was no different from the way Li had been watched from birth, technically.

For all intents and purposes Li was faceless, fingerprintless, invisible. To be both a shadow and perpetually observed by others was paradoxical in its way, and if Li had the kind of disposition prone to purposeless rumination, they might have asked things like, why? What was the reason for it, this existence so thin it could not be sliced in half, much less properly shared with another? What meaning could they possibly have, being so faint they would die and instantly disappear—that their superiors would make sure of it? Perhaps *that* was why Ezra Fowler had chosen them. Because Li had watched Ezra for a number of weeks and discovered a plethora of things about him, too. They'd observed mainly that Ezra was, not unlike Li, a shadow trying very hard to be a man.

"These two are the most active," the American CIA director was saying, sweat glistening above his brow as he gestured to the growing collection of instances wherein the naturalist and the empath appeared to be influencing events of an increasingly political nature. Interestingly, Pérez had not noticed that the empath's hand was nearly always outstretched toward the naturalist, a motion that might have looked like the tap of a shoulder or the brushing away of some invisible dust to someone not paying attention. "They've repeatedly dodged MI6 and appear to be ingratiated at least partially with some low-level thugs in London—probably the Caines," he clarified in answer to the Wessex daughter's scowl of apparent recognition, "so at this point I'd call their behavior an escalation. It's clearly a blatant taunt."

What was clear to Pérez seemed convenient. It was clear to Li, too, though in quite a different way.

"Bring the Nova in on corporate espionage charges," suggested Nothazai, who *did* seem to have noticed the significance of the naturalist, but appeared to have compartmentalized the observation, saving it for later. Perhaps a more relevant time, when what was clear to Nothazai—a third subjective form of clarity—was closer to fruition. "At this point any medeian statute violation will do, would it not?"

Pérez shook his head, flipping resentfully through slides. "We've tried, but the empath is too powerful for local law enforcement to apprehend on the spot. Whatever we bring against him has to be significant enough to merit public investigation. And it has to be specific, too, or the family will just protect him."

Li, who had already spent some time observing the Nova family, was about to disagree when Eden Wessex did it for him. "I know Arista Nova and I've met Selene," she said, naming the youngest Nova daughter first and then the eldest, who was over a decade the empath's senior. "The family won't cover for him unless it suits them, trust me. Not if giving him up proves to be the more profitable option."

"You're sure?" Pérez looked up with restrained impatience and Nothazai gave one of his sly smiles, the one intended to put people at ease, which did not serve to comfort Li. (It was a mouth smile that never reached his eyes.)

"Trust me," Eden repeated. "Bring the entire Nova Corporation under formal investigation. Give them a bigger problem and they'll turn on him in an instant."

It was something Eden Wessex could know because she believed it to be true for her own family. Li doubted she was wrong in this particular case, but Li also understood Pérez's hesitation. Pérez did not take the Wessex daughter seriously, and in some respects he shouldn't, because the actual Wessex patriarch's attention had been clearly and problematically elsewhere ever since Ezra Fowler had disappeared. In the absence of whatever motivating details Ezra had procured against him—and the absence of Ezra himself, their sole tie to the reality of the archives rather than the mythology in which they'd all profoundly, if delusionally, believed—James Wessex had chosen to pursue other avenues of interest. Within the limited capacity that Pérez deemed useful, then, Eden Wessex had her limitations as a tool.

But what had always been strictly business for James Wessex was obviously personal for his daughter, and a personal cause meant devotion of unbendable resolve. In Li's opinion, the sudden, prolonged absence of Ezra meant that now, only Eden could spur the fracturing group along. Already Nothazai's interests had diverged from the others. It wasn't clear yet how, but Li felt certain Nothazai would make different choices, cut different bargains if it suited him. In this instance, though, Nothazai gave a nod, tacitly approving Eden's tactics.

There was an unspoken vote remaining, not counting Li's. From their vantage point beside Nothazai, Li thought it clear that Sef Hassan, the Egyptian preservationist who seemed torn on the matter of the Nova family, already knew better than to get any deeper into bed with Pérez and the American government. Always an undue risk, even when the alternative was a thieving family of illusionists. (The lesser of two evils was rarely an Englishman or an American. That much any textbook could confirm.) When Hassan said nothing and Li merely shrugged, Pérez drew his own conclusion.

"Fine." Despite the tension, Pérez wisely acquiesced. "But the Novas aren't under our jurisdiction."

"The Forum will do it," Nothazai volunteered as Hassan's gaze remained on the projection screen, his concerns visible and yet methodically unvoiced. "An ideological media-driven crusade may pressure an institutional investigation."

Yes, Li thought. The power of the performatively virtuous mob would have its foot upon the governmental throat just enough to make the family hemorrhage legal fees for a month, perhaps enough to weaken one financial quarter. Which was enough to make them act expediently, if not compassionately. Publicly, but without any meaningful reparations as far as how they made their wealth.

Yes, the Nova family would certainly act to preserve the Nova fortune, which likely meant cutting the empath loose to save themselves—a fail-safe, if not a meaningful step forward. Forcing the empath to act by way of threatening his family would have been a tactical advance, if not for the unlikelihood that any of the Nova family could pressure the son into giving himself up on their behalf. The mother was a drunk, the father a bully, the sisters ruthless, and the older two with their own families now to protect. What love could the empath possibly have for them?

Besides, Callum Nova was supposed to be dead according to the information Ezra Fowler had given them. The fact that he was not—and that not a single member of his family seemed to know or even wonder about the threat against his life—suggested this was an idling attempt, one yielding little productivity.

Li said nothing, of course, on this matter, because Li's superiors had made it clear they were to find their way into the Alexandrian archives and do nothing else, commit nothing else, neither information nor unnecessary action. Li did have their own personal inclinations, which in this case were mainly to wonder what else Ezra Fowler might not have told them. What else Ezra Fowler might have gotten wrong.

Surreptitiously, Li had done their own research about the only member of the six Alexandrians for which Ezra Fowler had not meticulously gathered evidence—Elizabeth Rhodes, graduate of the New York University of Magical Arts, who Ezra had told them with ironclad certainty was not a method of assistance to their aims. An obvious matter of personal significance. "Handled" was his exact wording.

Li, the shadow chasing Ezra Fowler's shadow, vehemently disagreed.

Li had seen her face once before during the meticulous process of gathering their private (secret) dossier. She'd used a pseudonym then, a very poor one, but there was no doubt that the faded headshot of 1990 Wessex Corp employee Libby Blakely was, in fact, the Alexandrian physicist Elizabeth Rhodes.

She wasn't handled. She was neither in Ezra Fowler's control nor even under his purview, and if the circumstances of Ezra's sudden absence—believed by Nothazai, perhaps in the interest of fearmongering, to be the result of a recent run-in with the indomitable Atlas Blakely—were as Li suspected, then Elizabeth Rhodes was their primary threat.

She had chosen her pseudonym for a reason. Once a weapon, always a weapon.

Li did not fidget in their seat. Did not call attention to their impatience as the others often did. Let the others be the ones to chase the Nova Corporation's wealth, to advance the Forum's clout. The key to the Society wasn't money or influence, or else those things would have already opened the door.

It did not surprise Li that avarice was so intrinsically tangled in the aims of their piecemeal coalition, their monster of many parts, but Li knew that if anything could unlock the Alexandrian archives, it would not be greed.

It would be the furious young woman standing powerless at the door.

His initial interactions with Tristan after returning to the Society house had been strange, in that they were totally perfunctory and not at all as if they'd spent the previous year with no one but each other for company. Not that Nico considered himself and Tristan to be close, but there was something very intimate about murder, however temporary the result. It wasn't something to be followed up with routine cordial hellos, like ships in the night waving watercress sandwiches as they passed.

Something was very off with Tristan, in Nico's opinion. He was polite to Nico, even occasionally pleasant. Maybe having Libby back had put Tristan in a better mood, but that didn't necessarily explain it. Nico could tell something was going on between Tristan and Libby—it wasn't a very complicated *something*, either, considering Libby was always in Tristan's clothes and smelling vaguely of the grooming products Nico knew very well that Tristan used because he'd spent a year attacking him with them—but he didn't think that was the problem.

The tension between them; the way Tristan always seemed to kind of *hate* Nico, actually, at least a little bit; *that* was the part that was missing, and Nico couldn't figure out why. Lately when Tristan spoke to him it was as if Nico had feelings that Tristan was making a concerted effort not to hurt.

"You do realize that I don't care if you're sleeping with Rhodes," Nico decided to announce after several weeks of contemplation, startling Tristan where he sat reading alone in the painted room. "Wanting her back wasn't an issue of, like, seduction. I know that's probably hard to believe considering you all think I'm a child, but my relationships can be astonishingly complex. Besides, I have a—" Nico paused to consider the appropriate terminology for something that was the same as it had always been, only very slightly different. "A Gideon," he determined after a moment.

"I'd truly hate to witness whatever your version of seduction was," replied Tristan, who'd looked up in a way that was almost nostalgic—an old, ardent urgency for Nico to leave, which was a constant from the era of fragile alliance they'd entertained up until that point.

So maybe it had been the Rhodes thing after all, and now they could put it to rest and continue regarding each other as the forced proximity work associates they had always been. Nico pulled out the chair beside Tristan's, falling into it with relief. "I don't actually have any game, I don't think. Mostly I just ask nicely."

"Does that ever work?" said Tristan.

"You'd be surprised." Nico peered over Tristan's hand, eyeing the book he was reading until Tristan shot him a look of annoyance. "Has she talked to you yet?"

"About what?" Tristan hadn't denied anything, which was helpful. Nico couldn't imagine the trials of playing coy around someone he'd already strangled.

He shrugged. "Fowler? The past year of her life? Pick your poison."

Tristan shifted, and then the awkwardness was back. Nico didn't know how to quantify it. He just had a sense for it, like a truffle pig for unease. Maybe it was a physical thing, like body language or something. Tristan had shifted away, like he was concealing some part of his chest. "She doesn't have to explain anything."

Nico let out a heavy sigh. "Look, I know you're the king of emotional repression, but you're probably not doing her a favor by not letting her process everything that went wrong. Someone betrayed her—that's a big deal."

"You think I don't have any experience with betrayal?" That time Tristan's physical reflex was sharp, like the sting of a scorpion's tail.

"That's not what I meant, I just think—"

"If you want to play shrink, do that on your own time." Tristan flipped his book closed and Nico reached for it, peering at the cover with a giddy wave of delight.

"Whose notes are these?" Nico asked, because he could be an asshole, too. When the moment called for it.

Tristan glared at him. "Yours, fucker. Which you already know."

"So then you're thinking about doing it, aren't you?" Well, at least there was that. "Speaking of, where's Atlas been?"

"It's July," said Tristan. "This is England. He's on holiday."

So was Max's family, which accounted for Nico's personal comings and goings from the house—at very brief intervals, just in case Libby was right about physical proximity—but it wasn't like Atlas had ever been known for his leisurely summer hols. The Atlas of their fellowship era had still been a habitual fixture, if not a constant one. This version of him seemed vaguely Odyssean, though Nico supposed he had a right. No new initiates would be showing up for eight more years, so perhaps now was the appropriate time for recreational quests. "I still feel like he could at least stop by and say *hi*—"

"This . . . this theory of yours." Tristan turned the book toward Nico, opening the page to a diagram with what Nico realized were Tristan's own scribbled annotations. "Explain this."

Nico twisted around to squint at Tristan's tidy scrawl. "Why, you think it's wrong?"

"I think it's fucking incomprehensible, Varona. What the hell is this?"

"It's—" Fair, two-dimensionality wasn't Nico's strong point. "Hang on." Nico tore a page out of the book containing his notes, prompting Tristan to swallow a small squeak of opposition. "You've been hanging out with Rhodes too long. It's just a book, Tristan. Anyway, it's easier to explain this way." Nico folded the page in half, then folded the top half of the page back, accordioning it so that about an inch of the page had disappeared. "So, look at it this way," he said, placing the folded sheet of paper on the table and smoothing it down. "See? It's flat."

"Theoretically." Tristan flicked the side of the page that was already lifting up like the letter *Z* from the side.

"Right, well, this is very theoretical, is it not? Here." Nico forced down magically on the page of notes so that the distance between folds disappeared. "The missing inch is gone. When you look down at the page, it's flat."

"Right."

"But it's not flat." Nico released the force of gravity and allowed the folded part of the page to spring back up. "There's a pocket there, which is where ordinary matter can collapse. And if you did this several times throughout the single page, there would be multiple pockets, multiple collapses, reflective universes multiplying with every point where the density of one particular galaxy was disturbed. But if you lived on the top part of the page, you'd never see them. You'd be traversing over them, basically, and the whole landscape would look and feel perfectly flat."

Tristan's natural expression of concentration had a way of mimicking scorn. "You think the multiverse exists somewhere between the folds?"

"Yes and no," said Nico with a shrug. "I'm not making any suggestions about the multiverse—that's too far along in the experiment," he hedged, "and I'm starting with a hypothesis of what dark matter might actually be—what the *void* might actually be. As in, the presence of something that's actually the absence of it." That was something Reina had brought up to Nico about Dalton's abilities last year when she'd accidentally forgotten to hate him for a moment. "Which is something you'd be able to see," Nico added to Tristan, "theoretically, if I—or you, given that you're the one with ampler means of persuasion—could convince Rhodes to give Atlas's sinister plot a try."

"Stop calling it that," said Tristan, who was obviously too busy trying to process Nico's model of the universe to come up with a snappier reply. "So you agree with Atlas, then?" he asked with a Tristanly frown. "You think there's a way to draw an entrance to other worlds out of . . . dark matter? Some cosmic fold?"

"Sounds erotic, and yes," Nico confirmed. "Not that I know if Atlas agrees, because he didn't actually say anything about my notes, but theoretically yes. Ultimately," he concluded, "it's a question of producing enough energy to collapse a corner of this galaxy into its equal and opposite reflection, which Rhodes and I would have to do. But after that point, theoretically, you could see the shape of it and be the one to—"

"Fall in?" Tristan arched a brow.

"Open the door," Nico corrected. "You might also be the only person who could go between them, but that's a future concern. For now, I just need Rhodes to do the work with me, and Reina to generate whatever it is that Reina can generate. And to hold whatever Rhodes and I couldn't."

"And Dalton," muttered Tristan. "Who we won't get unless Parisa's feeling uncharacteristically benevolent."

"Right, but this is a hypothetical, anyway." Nico thought about it further. "And I suppose we'd also need Parisa, don't you think?" he added. "If only to ensure she doesn't die of archive-related vengeance. And to make sure Callum doesn't run off into some other world and start a war."

"No need. He's too busy trying to kill me personally to bother concerning himself with the whole world," muttered Tristan, who was still eyeing Nico's model of the universe.

"Could be worse," Nico said. "It's really kind of flattering, in a way. Want me to give him tips?"

"You're so fucked, Varona." Tristan looked over at him then, considering him for a long moment. "Would you do the experiment for Atlas? Hypothetically." The last bit was added on, Nico suspected, as a tactical matter.

"Hypothetically? Sure."

Tristan gave him another look of scrutiny. "Would you do it for Parisa?"

"She's already asked me. I told her the same thing."

"Which is?"

"That hypothetically, I'm seriously concerned I might leap into a crevasse if she asked me to. Which thankfully she hasn't yet."

Tristan rolled his eyes. "So then you think it's a good idea?"

"It's *an* idea," Nico corrected him with a shrug. "It's not inherently good or bad." Which, he did not add, was the point he'd been trying to make to Libby. "There's no decision-making involved. No ethics, just a moral dead zone. What you do if you *can* walk through that door, that's for a philosopher to decide. Or one of two very persuasive telepaths." Another shrug. "I'm just the physicist who can potentially help make the door appear."

"*Just* a physicist, he says." Tristan was being whimsical, it seemed. Talking to nothing. He looked back at Nico with a shake of his head. "Do you really think that's true? That there can be any decisions free from ethics?"

Like a proverbial state of nature, a stasis that had never existed without someone's agenda pressing in. "I guess technically no," Nico admitted, "not actually. But ethics are weird, they're tricky. I mean, I *can't* be ethical. I can't buy a T-shirt or eat a mango without harming a thousand people in the process. Right? I mean, clearly this is a discussion for Rhodes," Nico added. "She's the one with expertise on the moral high ground. I'm just here for my looks."

"Right, yes, of course." Tristan exhaled wearily, rubbing his temples.

"And anyway," Nico pointed out on a whim, "who says the doom *necessarily* lies with Atlas?"

"Rhodes," said Tristan.

"Well, yes. True. But the problem could easily be one of us. Who knows what the prospect of world domination might awaken in me? Think how pleased Rhodes would be to find out I've been the villain in the house all along."

Tristan seemed not to catch Nico's attempt at levity, choosing instead to frown moodily into nothing before broaching a change in subject. "Well, for the record, I didn't actually bother to wonder if you cared whether I was sleeping with Rhodes, as your position on the matter does not concern me."

"There he is, the Tristan Caine we know and love," Nico declared sunnily. "Glad we got past that, then."

"No, I'm saying—" Tristan rolled his eyes. "There's nothing weird between us," he clarified, gesturing between himself and Nico. "We're fine. I've devoted zero breaths to the subject of your feelings because yes, as you've said, you have 'a Gideon'—"

"Who actually seems to like you, so there's that for terrible judges of character." Nico paused to look around, having not really adjusted to the decrease in occupancy of the house. He still expected Parisa to pop in, Callum to show up, Reina to waltz in and render him inadequate with a glance.

Nico came and went from time to time now, at Max's behest, any time things felt too . . . claustrophobic. Too severe. If he spent too long in the house, Gideon or no Gideon, he felt himself start to go insane. The old jitteriness remained, the feeling that he was losing himself to something inside it, tapped like a maple tree for everything he contained. Now, though, it was worse.

Now, the longer he stood in this house, the more he longed to put himself to use. Now, Libby was back, and while that came with its own set of problems, it also meant something that was, for Nico, unavoidable, like being handed a new set of keys. It meant a chance to unlock something new; something he'd spent a year seeking.

A chance to see whether the universe might reveal its secrets if he seduced it right. If he asked it nicely enough.

"I really hope you're, like, happy," Nico said to Tristan, realizing he'd been lost in thought. "You're good together, you know? You and Rhodes. She doesn't seem so anxious."

Tristan made a noncommittal sound.

"I'm not just saying that," Nico added. "It's, I don't know. You're both—"

He stopped.

"It just makes sense," he admitted. "And she obviously trusts you." He wondered if he was making Tristan uncomfortable, or perhaps saying the wrong thing. "I just mean that you're—"

Another pause.

"Well, at the risk of being terribly gauche," said Nico, "I don't really mind being trapped in this house with you. I'd obviously prefer to leave," he added, "but as far as forced company goes, you're incredibly tolerable. Almost decent, really, to be around. So for Rhodes to feel the same way is—"

"I don't know where she is, Varona," Tristan said abruptly. At first Nico thought he'd said it to be obnoxious, but upon further inspection it became clear that, actually, it wasn't. He was telling Nico the truth.

"Oh." Nico turned away, processing it as Tristan's usual curt form of dismissal, when he realized it wasn't the end of the conversation.

It was the beginning of one. "Do you . . . ?"

He pivoted back slowly, facing Tristan as they both seemed to understand that the next question was of equal importance, if not more.

"Do you know where Atlas is?" Nico asked carefully.

He watched the muscle jump beside Tristan's jaw.

"Varona, I don't think—"

"There you both are." There was a clatter from the doorway behind them, Libby's footsteps followed by Gideon's, the latter of which was carrying a box of something that looked like leather-bound books. "What's that?" Libby asked, pointing to the accordioned piece of paper Nico had left on Tristan's section of the table.

"Ethical quandary," said Tristan at the same time Nico said, "Paper airplane."

"Not a very good plane, Nicky," said Gideon, setting the box of books down on the table beside Tristan's notes. There were four or five books in there, all enormous. Easily of a size to give a man a concussion or render him rapidly un-aroused.

"What's that, Sandman? Finally tricked the archives into giving you a little light reading?" Nico peered into the box and Gideon shrugged.

"Can't actually open the books, just have to send them in for new bindings. Huzzah," he added weakly to Libby, who Nico realized was wearing something that wasn't an article of Tristan's clothes.

"Did you leave the house?" Nico asked quizzically, though unless she'd gotten the wards of the Society's precious archives to make allowances for online delivery, she had obviously left the premises at some point that day. Which he'd been trying to get her to do for weeks now, either with him or without, but she had ostensibly leaned on their former traditions and customs of doing everything in their power not to be in the same place at the same time. Nico had thought it was because of Tristan, but apparently she'd procured something a bit more classic Rhodes (well, Rhodes *if* she'd met Parisa first, seeing as it was a dress and not the matching sweater set that seemed to be her shorthand for "a joy to have in the classroom") without even telling Tristan that she'd gone.

"Got a haircut," she said, which Nico realized belatedly was true. No bangs, thankfully. Her hair had gotten longer since she first arrived—long enough to be considered *long hair,* something Nico had never associated with Libby prior to this—but she'd cut it back to her shoulders. The whole thing was very reasonable, and yet he felt both accusatory and guilty at the same time.

"What've you two been up to?" Libby asked, looking at Nico.

Nico glanced at Tristan, who pointedly did not look back at him.

"Nothing sinister, I assure you," Nico attempted.

"Well done," Tristan sighed, now looking at Nico but not Libby. "Very smooth."

Gideon, meanwhile, looked very intently at the box of books. The whole thing was very awkward, Nico decided. And not the kind of clandestine awkwardness between people who slept together on a regular basis, either.

Actually, the energy had shifted substantially the moment Libby walked into the room, and Nico wasn't sure what to make of that. He supposed he was proud of her for growing a healthy sense of dominion (he'd been the one to tell her to do the equivalent of *have a spine,* which he supposed traveling through time would do) but there was a definite aura of something bigger in the room. Something unspoken and troubling.

"You can tell me the truth," Libby said to Tristan, possibly hitting the nail on the head, which wasn't something the old Libby would have done, so again Nico felt an odd sense of pride in her. "You don't have to lie about the experiment. I know exactly what *that,*" she clarified, dropping her gaze to the piece of paper on the table, "is supposed to model. I've read Varona's notes."

"Well, glad to hear someone could make sense of them," said Nico, at the same time Gideon said, "Notes about what?"

"A world-ending hypothetical." Libby gave Tristan a look of obvious significance, the two of them having a quick discussion in total silence the way people did when they'd seen each other naked.

Tristan hesitated a moment, then nodded. Libby turned away, glancing at Nico over her shoulder before fixing her attention more permanently on Tristan, who then left the room at her side.

Nico felt Gideon's presence enter his periphery like walking into a small patch of sun.

"How mad will you be," Gideon posed neutrally, "if I tell you that I think there's something wrong with Libby?"

"I've always known there's something wrong with her, *idiota.* I've been telling you this from day one." Nico stretched his arms overhead and filled Tristan's chair, kicking out the seat opposite his for Gideon to join him. "It's weird," he realized, having a moment's synchronicity, like déjà vu. Petal-pink toenails and telepathy, a crisis of conscience and Professor X—*just say it, Nicolás.* "You being here," he said to Gideon. "It's strange. Not bad strange, just strange."

Gideon slid into the chair, sinking down into it. "Thinking of something in particular?"

"Just realizing something I forgot to do." *Get a talisman.* A set of petal-pink toes in Nico's lap. *Then you'll never need to question what's real.*

He wondered what Parisa was up to now. She didn't ignore him, exactly. They spoke from time to time, briefly messaging back and forth about how cute he was and how hopeless; whether he'd still say how high if she asked him to jump. (Yes.) Truthfully, Nico wanted to ask more, or *say* more, but he didn't really know what to casually discuss with someone whose kiss he could still taste. He had a feeling she wouldn't approve of that kind of neediness—which was ironic, seeing as aside from Gideon, Parisa was the only person in this house who'd ever seemed to care about him at all. (*We're in my head, not yours.*)

Nico laughed to himself, turning back to Gideon. "Remember when I said we were supposed to get ourselves some talismans?"

"Vaguely." Gideon's smile was irreverent.

"Did you ever actually do it?"

"Get a talisman? No. Did you?"

"No. What for?" Nico shrugged. "I've always had you."

"True," Gideon said. Nico could warm his hands on that kind of fondness. "And anyway, there's still no evidence I've got sufficient mortality to get myself lost in an astral plane, so, you know. It's just another, slightly less world-ending hypothetical."

Gideon closed his eyes. For a moment Nico thought he was asleep, but then Gideon kicked his chair and Nico laughed.

"I'm still awake," Gideon said. "For now."

"Is it that bad? *Sois honnête.*"

"Would I lie to you?"

"Yes." Nico nudged him, knee to knee. "Of course you would. But don't."

"Fine, it's . . ." Gideon looked away. "It's not *not* happening."

He meant the episodes of what other people called narcolepsy, but that Gideon had simply called life until Nico interfered. For the past two years while Nico was away, Gideon had existed almost exclusively inside the dream realms. Belatedly, Nico realized he hadn't brewed a vial for Gideon the entire time he was gone.

"I can make more if you want—"

"You don't have the resources." Gideon waved it away, dismissing the offer entirely. "This isn't NYUMA where you can sweet-talk your way into Professor Breckenridge's private stash. Nobody here even has a private stash."

"It's a magic house," Nico insisted. "I'm pretty sure I can get it to conjure up some of the good stuff."

Gideon fixed him squarely with a look of supreme doubt. "Nicky, have you learned nothing? This house doesn't conjure up anything."

"What are you talking about? It's sentient, we all know that—"

"It's sentient, not a butler. Are you aware there's almost no food in the kitchen?"

"What?"

"There's almost no food, Nicky. I got an email from the catering company two days ago. Which," Gideon added, "Tristan said he would deal with, but—"

"Catering company?" Nico stopped for a moment to gauge whether Gideon was joking, which was very possible. Gideon was very charming and delightful that way, or tended to be, but he didn't seem to be teasing. "Wait, what?"

"The house doesn't cook your meals, Nicolás." Gideon rolled his eyes. "I know you're privileged, but yeesh." He was still smiling as he added, "Don't tell me Libby never once thought to mention it? Since I'm fairly sure she's the only one of you that didn't grow up having her meals prepared for her."

"Actually, Tristan isn't— Wait." Nico frowned. "So who cooks them?"

"You have a chef," Gideon said. "Or a few chefs, I think, who all work for the same company. The Caretaker or one of his underlings arranges for food to be delivered to the house, but according to someone named Ford in Human Resources who really doesn't care for me—and by the way, you have a Human Resources—those orders haven't been updated in over a month."

"What?"

"You've also had no visitors, as Ford decided to inform me. Apparently your Caretaker hasn't been letting people in, which is making Ford personally upset. He mentioned something about a vote of no confidence if this continues, whatever that means."

"Since when do we have chefs?" Nico only realized he was frowning when Gideon suddenly looked over at him and laughed.

"Oh, Nicky. Are you really so surprised? I told you to wonder where the money was."

"What money? And this was about you," Nico abruptly recalled, wondering if Gideon was fucking with him just to avoid discussing that his health was likely deteriorating. It struck Nico like an overly ostentatious gong that his reason for joining the Society had not been hypothetical at all—and yet somehow, amid two years' worth of mortal peril, he had managed to forget it.

"The money that keeps all of this going." Gideon made an ambiguous gesture to the house and everything inside it. "And I'm just saying, if the kitchen's run out of basic pantry essentials, I don't think you'll be doing any alchemy anytime soon."

"Was that Dalton's job?" Nico asked, frowning into nothing.

Gideon shook his head. "I don't think so. It's not technically my job, either, and Dalton was just a researcher. Isn't Atlas the house manager?"

"Caretaker," Nico corrected instantly.

"What's the difference?"

"I—" Nico didn't know, obviously, as he had never known what Atlas's job was. Scheduling? He supposed it had been Atlas who did things like plan the gala they'd had the year prior. Was it possible the man whose approval he'd begun to unwisely crave was some kind of . . . administrative official? He didn't know what to do with the image of Atlas taking inventory of the pantry beside the wormhole he'd given Nico the cosmic materials to create.

But all of this seemed part of a revelation Gideon had cleverly designed, so Nico decided he was better off saving these particular thoughts until later. Gideon already mistrusted the Society, and as marvelous as Gideon happened to be, he still had not met Atlas. It was very possible that Gideon had a right to his suspicions, but it was also a reminder that Nico had sorely needed. Because whatever larger mystery may or may not have been going on within the Society's walls, none of that was more important than what had brought Nico to accept the Society's offer to begin with.

If Gideon couldn't replicate Nico's sense of loyalty to what Atlas had done by choosing him, that was because Gideon was a consummate outsider, forced into objectivity because belonging had never been an option.

And also, he was still the one who needed help.

"I don't really know how we got so far off the point," Nico said slowly, "which is that if you're having problems, you should really tell me. I can always get things for you from outside the house."

Gideon gave him a thin smile. "What's a little collapsing of the realms here and there?"

Nico pondered whether to push the issue before deciding with great uncertainty, "Are you going to tell me who the Accountant is?"

Gideon blinked, then fastened a look of pure innocence. "Am I talking in my sleep again?"

"You are." A pause. "Have you heard from Eilif?"

Gideon drummed his fingers on the table.

"It's nothing," Gideon said eventually.

"Gideon." A shake of Nico's head. "Will we ever outgrow this?"

He hadn't meant it to sound so profound, so adult. It was a tone he hadn't realized his voice could even take. Something slightly sorrowful, like the last day of summer camp. Like maybe all this fun would have to eventually end.

But was that such a bad thing? Nico was inexperienced, but still. He felt assured that sometimes fun became something bigger, something deeper.

"You don't have to lie to protect me," Nico said. "And you don't have to keep any secrets just to keep me."

For the risk of spoiling everything, his undeniable reward: "Fine, you're right." Gideon gave him a look of reluctance. "There's someone looking for me," he confessed. "Someone must have consolidated my mother's debts. I think they're looking for me to pay what's left. They can't get through the telepathic wards here," he added, "but I haven't heard from my mother, so whether that's because I'm here, or because something happened to her—"

Nico had never understood Gideon's relationship with Eilif and didn't know whether this was guilt, concern, or something far stranger than both combined. "She's fine," said Nico urgently. "And whoever this Accountant is, you don't owe them anything."

"I know, but—" Gideon stopped. He shook his head, then shrugged. "The point is it's fine. I'm here to stay out of your Society's way—"

"To be *safe*," Nico argued.

"Safely out of their way," Gideon repeated. "So, if I happen to drift off unexpectedly, I don't think they'll mind. Even if I were to tumble out from between the balustrades, I'm fairly certain they have insurance."

Nico had the sudden, unavoidable urge to punish Gideon for his usual flippancy toward his own death, so he chose violence. He leaned over the table and kissed him square on the mouth.

"Shut up," Nico muttered with his eyes closed, unmoving, because everything between Nico and Gideon was exactly the same as it had always been, really.

With only the slightest degree of difference, in this case being that he could feel Gideon's smile like he had conjured it himself. "Nicolás. You're deflecting. This house is punishing you for something. Your Caretaker is missing. Your researcher is lying. Your many-worlds theory has you in a chokehold like some kind of academic siren song. And," Gideon added carefully, "I've been in enough of Libby's nightmares to know that her problems are bigger than any of you know how to solve—all of which you're ignoring because you've got an infernal gift for selective hearing." A pause, followed by a mutter. "Just because you make me happy doesn't mean you don't drive me absolutely insane."

Aptly, Nico only heard one thing. "Are you, Sandman? Happy."

"Oh my *god*," said Gideon.

But the rest was solvable, Nico thought. Whatever Atlas was doing, or Tristan, Nico felt certain Libby knew about it, and if there was one thing he could trust—aside from Gideon—it was Libby's moral compass. Yes, Tristan was clearly hiding something, but Nico had made a promise to Libby Rhodes once, and she'd made it back to him: if she needed something, she'd come to him. He would know when the moment came, and until then, he had fidgety hands in need of distraction.

Best to put them to good use.

The last part was a love story.

This one is a cautionary tale.

. . .

The first time Atlas Blakely sees his mother again is hours after the completion of his fellowship. Later he makes a habit of it, going to see her. A ritual performed on perhaps a monthly basis, so long as he never strays too long from the philosophical burden the archives have rendered his. At times, these instances hold little meaning for either of them, as she is incapable of carrying a conversation and he is unsure of his obligations beyond the filial.

Eventually, the visits start to blur.

"His name is Dalton," Atlas says, "and if I'm right, he can do something extraordinary. If I'm wrong—" He contemplates voicing it aloud. "Well, if I'm wrong, it's no less extraordinary. It just becomes slightly more dangerous, too."

His mother says nothing, silently chewing the steamed pudding Atlas is feeding her mindlessly with a silicone spoon, as if she were a toddler.

"Do you remember Clamence? Camus. *The Fall*?" No response. "He doesn't save a girl from drowning, remember? So as not to risk himself, and then everything that follows is the fall. 'Throw yourself into the water, that I might have a second chance to save the two of us'?" Nothing. "Never mind. I suppose that's an overestimation of myself anyway. Nobody technically called for me to save them.

"Still," Atlas goes on. "What is magic if not the chance to supersede the laws of nature? The rules of the universe do not have to contain us. Just because it has not yet been imagined doesn't have to make it less than real."

"You look the same," says his mother. (She isn't talking to Atlas. Later, an older, barely wiser version of Atlas will wish he had shared this part of himself with Parisa, if only because doing so might save her from replicating his flaws, repeating his mistakes. She is the only member of her cohort whose inclusion he cannot defend; she is not marked for elimination, nor, arguably, is she necessary for the enormity of his debt. She is, however, the single member of her cohort who might have even a sliver of a chance at understanding what it is to recognize yourself as nothing more than the symbol of something in someone else's mind. To realize that you are only the burden of another person's ghosts.)

Atlas nods, absently, and dabs gently at his mother's mouth. "The thing is," he continues to himself, albeit ostensibly to her, "I suppose I can't help thinking that all of this has to have been for something. Is it really a coincidence for this sort of magical capability to fall into my lap? Or does it mean something that only I can see what could be done with it?" (Atlas will ask himself the same question when Ezra discovers the existence of Nico and Libby; when later, he will have a similarly profitable hunch about Reina.) "It has to have been for something, the pieces falling into place this way. If it's not, then what was any of this for?"

His mother doesn't answer, and Atlas sighs.

"I was only trying to do the right thing," he says, feeling quite sorry for himself in that moment. "I really thought it was the right thing."

His mother lifts her tired eyes and stares at him. For a moment, it's nearly lucid, her thoughts a rosy blur of past and present things, and he thinks she might be about to touch his face. Something she hasn't done in years, perhaps decades.

But then, abruptly, she slaps him. Inadequately warned, Atlas feels his hands slip, and the pudding crashes to the floor. The bowl shatters at his mother's feet, jagged shards of porcelain haloing the lumps in her thick woolen socks. There's a hole in the toes. He wonders how long it's been since she last bathed.

"You made a liar of me," she says. "What am I supposed to tell Atlas?"

The moment extinguished, her attention drifts elsewhere, to the television in the corner. Atlas rises silently to his feet and thinks a sponge bath will do. He hired a nurse but she's on holiday. Other arrangements will have to be made, fail-safes of a certain kind. He'd like to go places, travel the world, be surgically extricated from his thoughts. He'd like to tell Ezra that if he ever steps off this path he'll almost certainly die. But wouldn't telling Ezra be placing the ethical dilemma in Ezra's hands? Wouldn't robbing Ezra of his freedom be its own kind of death sentence?

("You're not that French guy from your mum's book, okay?" Alexis says to Atlas. "You have a tendency to overly mythologize yourself. It's not your sexiest quality."

"What's my sexiest quality?" asks Atlas.

"Your moral turpitude," she says.)

Atlas fingers the spines on his mother's broken shelves. One of them is out of place, probably the nurse's doing. He pauses to trace the golden filigree on the pages of her King James Bible, glancing at the familiar photograph of a young man on the shelf. A man who so uncannily resembles him; like looking in a mirror, almost, including all the youthful capacity for pain.

"Mum," Atlas says without looking away. "If I do as Dalton asked and seal away the parts of himself he doesn't want the archives to see, then maybe he's right. Maybe the archives will give him what he wants, and then someday, with the right medeians, I can use his powers to find a way to save them." He pauses. "Or maybe I'll have ignored some very legitimate warnings and destroyed absolutely everything just to save five people's lives."

"Trolley problem," she mumbles, or at least he's pretty sure she does.

Regardless, Atlas smiles and turns away from the bookcase, leaving the photograph behind. As rituals go, he'll mark this one down as a victory. He'll tell Ezra their plan is working, and that his mum is doing fine. He'll find someone else to keep an eye on her, just in case. And suddenly, he thinks he knows just the person for the job.

"Yes, something like that." He stops again, contemplating everything. "You're the one with the philosophy background, Mum. Do you think there's such a thing as too much power?"

She doesn't answer.

She doesn't have to.

Atlas Blakely already knows.

· LIBBY ·

S o," Parisa had said, taking the vacant seat opposite Libby's at the Shoreditch café where they'd agreed to meet. "You found your way back after all."

Libby had slathered herself in illusions for the occasion, recognizable only by the paperback copy of *Jane Eyre* she'd set on the table for Parisa to see. Parisa, however, looked precisely as Libby remembered her, unchanged as a painting. She wore a knit dress in a brilliant cobalt blue that made Libby's new slip dress look drab and out of season.

Libby took a sip from her cup of coffee, glancing around to see if the two of them had an audience. It was a popular place, the casual atmosphere a shallow din to camouflage the nature of their conversation. Parisa had obviously not come to hide, but even so, it made sense to Libby to try and blend into a crowd.

"Did you doubt that I would?" Libby asked.

In answer, Parisa glanced over her shoulder, then raised a finger in the air. A motion so small it shouldn't have counted for anything, like the delicate fluttering of a handkerchief, and yet the bartender stepped instantly out from behind the bar to pause beside her at the table.

"Shall we have a drink?" she asked Libby, who fidgeted with her cup of coffee.

"I have one."

"Come on. We're celebrating." Parisa's voice had its usual touch of casual derision, like everything she did was at least 60 percent ironic.

Libby shrugged. It didn't matter to her what they drank, or pretended to drink. "Whatever you feel like, then."

"How about a bottle of—" Parisa paused to consider Libby for a moment as a server nudged the bartender aside, then another restaurant-goer stumbled apologetically into their table, obviously looking for the toilet. "Moscato?"

Libby managed a wan smile. "You're making fun of me, aren't you?"

"Nonsense, I like a little sweet." That was a definite *yes* to the teasing, but Parisa turned to the bartender in confirmation, dismissing him with a nod.

He disappeared, withdrawing a bottle from the small fridge behind the bar, taking the time to shine up two glasses before loyally returning to Parisa's side.

"Isn't it a bit early for wine?" Libby remarked after he'd poured a little into Parisa's glass.

"Probably." Parisa leaned forward. Methodically, she swirled the glass. Held it up to her nose. Held it up to the light. Took a sip so effortlessly sensual Libby half wondered if the bartender might be concealing an erection. "Lovely," Parisa determined. "Thank you."

He poured more into her glass, then some into Libby's, as if she hadn't just mentioned the fact that it was barely afternoon.

"If you need anything," the bartender began.

"I'm sure we'll let you know," Parisa assured him, flashing him a smile Libby could only call businesslike.

He retreated with a glow about him, as if she'd kissed him full on the mouth.

"Well," said Libby dryly, reaching for her glass. "I see not much has changed for you, then."

"Oh, look closer, Rhodes." It wasn't an actual invitation, as far as Libby could tell. Just a general admonishment. Parisa raised the glass to her lips and took a sip, letting it marinate on her tongue before setting the glass down with a renewed sense of purpose.

"So," Parisa said. "You set off a nuclear bomb."

Libby set her glass down on the table. "Thanks for not mincing words," she murmured, or possibly muttered. She had a feeling she'd possessed adequate levels of cool until she'd set foot within a square mile of Parisa.

"Oh, don't sulk, Rhodes," Parisa said with a laugh, "you and I both know I'm not known for my tact. And I think it's admirable of you, really."

"Is it?"

"Yes." Parisa was staring at her in her unnerving way, which to Libby felt somewhere between being undressed and flayed open. A subtle but important distinction. "To answer your question," Parisa finally said, "I knew you were going to be back, yes."

Libby arched a brow. "Even after you knew what it would take?"

"Especially then." Parisa crossed one leg over the other, reclining in her seat. Rather than making the restaurant look more cramped, the space only seemed to make way for her. "I'm wondering," Parisa added, reaching for her wine again, "whether it's rewritten you or not."

Libby eyed her own untouched glass with the distinct sense that she was still trying to get a good grade in the conversation, which was both impossible and infuriating. "You're the one who can read me. Do I seem rewritten?"

"Hard to say. You've been through a lot." It was delivered more factually than sympathetically. "So, listen," Parisa continued, leaning forward again and deciding, apparently, to do away with further pretense. "I imagine you've sorted out what Atlas wants with you."

"You could say that." In the end the Moscato was like pure honey, a golden drip.

"The sinister plot," Parisa said with a charmed laugh, as if Nico were sitting there in the chair beside them, eyes adoringly on her. "You think it can be done?"

Libby licked her lips. "It's possible."

"You think it *should* be done?"

Even she could tell that was the answer Parisa was waiting for. "Not necessarily. Maybe." Libby looked squarely at her, wondering when she'd feel like she'd earned a place in Parisa's esteem. Probably never.

"You set off a nuclear bomb, Rhodes." Parisa glanced away, distracted or otherwise uninterested. "I'd stop worrying about things like that."

Funny how Parisa could render a miracle of physics comparable to routine life achievement. *You set off a nuclear bomb* to the tune of *congratulations, it's a girl!* "Am I boring you?"

Parisa looked at her sharply. "I asked you to come here, didn't I?"

"Yes, because you want something from me. But I can still bore you even if you're trying to get what you want." Libby tried to sound direct, the way Parisa usually did, but she still came off like a whiny child. She was bored with herself, maybe. Maybe that was the problem.

"I met someone while I was gone," Libby added, eyeing the honey-colored glass. "Someone who reminded me a lot of you." The glare of a white screen in the dead of night rose to the forefront of her mind, keys typing out an old name. The fleeting glimpse of a bare shoulder on flannel sheets, the pad of one finger tracking the shape of a fine-line spider.

"I know. She's pretty," commented Parisa. "Or at least you think so."

"Yeah." Libby swallowed, then cleared her throat. "Anyway. What do you want?"

"Well, I asked you here because I want you to do the experiment. But not for Atlas," Parisa said, meeting Libby's carefully measured glance with an iron one of her own. "I'm done with Atlas. I just want to see what happens," Parisa said to the lip of her glass, "when you open up the multiverse, Libby Rhodes, and pluck out a whole new world."

Libby made a sound that was somewhere in the vicinity of a snort. "I don't think that's how it works."

"Yes, well. I really don't give a shit about the science." Parisa gave her a Mona Lisa half smile in reply, taking another sip of wine and holding it on her tongue. "But you have to admit, it would be impressive. Almost worth setting off a nuclear bomb to do."

Libby, who had been ready to counter with what was in it for Parisa, felt something in her throat go tight at the miserly accuracy of herself in summary. "Don't you think I'd deserve to do it, if I wanted to?" was the question she knew better than to ask.

So, instead, Libby picked up her own glass, turning the stem between her fingers. Considering responses. *I'm not doing it.* She'd said that to Nico enough times, and even he barely believed her. *Hypothetically speaking,* as she'd put it so often to Tristan. She doubted Parisa would let her get away with that. "I've considered it, if I'm being honest."

Parisa's eyes flicked over her. "And?"

"And nothing, I've considered it, that's all." Libby set the glass down again without drinking it. This, she abruptly recalled, was her negotiation, not Parisa's.

Libby alone had nothing to lose. It was Parisa who needed her. Not the other way around. If anyone was going to answer for something, it would not be Libby, who'd already paid the highest price just to be sitting there. Alive. Unharmed. And more powerful than ever.

(*Do you think I was a killer even before I walked into that office?*)

(*What else are you willing to break, Miss Rhodes—*)

"Why should I do it for you, if I even do it at all?" Libby asked. "It's not your experiment. Not your research." It wasn't Libby's, either, but if one of them deserved ownership, it certainly wasn't Parisa. She wasn't the one who'd suffered for the bare fact of its existence. As far as Libby could tell, Parisa hadn't changed at all over the year Libby had been gone.

Parisa and Tristan may not have been on speaking terms, but Libby could still feel her between them, opaquely present. As if Parisa's absence still controlled them both just as much as if she'd lain between them on the bed, one hand on each of their necks.

"You need Reina," Parisa said without expression. She seemed to know they'd entered the business portion of the meeting. The energy around them shifted, tightening like a cyclone. "She won't do it for Atlas. But she'll do it for me."

"I doubt that," Libby said warily.

"Oh, by all means, Rhodes, doubt me," Parisa invited with a gamine laugh into her wineglass. "Try it and see what happens."

"It doesn't matter." Libby put the wineglass aside with a small rankle of agitation, picking up the coffee she'd ordered for herself instead. "I don't need Reina. Put it your way: I set off a nuclear bomb," she reminded Parisa, who paused for the first time, the glass hovering on its pathway to her lips. "I don't need a battery. Or a crutch."

Parisa's dark eyes narrowed. "That's not what Reina is."

Something had shifted, Libby realized with a tiny thrill. At the mention of Reina, the expression on Parisa's face had become something new, something more . . . frustrated. "I thought you didn't care about the science?"

"I'm not talking about the science." Parisa set the glass down, disregarded. Libby did the same, sliding her cup of coffee away so that nothing stood between them. "You think you can do this without Reina?" Parisa asked, something unidentifiable in her voice.

Was it fear? "I know I can do it without Reina." There, Libby thought. Now Parisa was seeing it. "You wanted me to know my own power, Parisa? Congratulations. Now I do."

She met Parisa's eye with her first truly unflinching glance.

She wasn't sure what she expected to happen. Not that Parisa would suddenly fall to her knees, but when Parisa's mouth twisted, what came out of it was like a slap to the face. "Oh, I see. You fucked over your girlfriend and murdered your ex, and now you think you know how to be the bad guy? Cute."

It took everything in Libby's power not to feel slighted, but she managed it. "I thought we were in agreement that the nuclear bomb thing wasn't insignificant."

"It's not," Parisa said. "But you can't tell me you've forgotten about the rest."

The rest. Nico using *Rhodes* to mean weakness; Tristan dismissing her with a glance; Reina telling her they had no reason to be friendly; Callum's effortlessly mocking face. To the forefront of Libby's thoughts rose an erstwhile guilt, an ever-present anxiety. Against her will, she regressed to the old version of herself that she couldn't entirely cast off—the eternal whisper in the back of her mind, the feeling of being dwarfed by a better model with bigger potential. The institutional lights of a hospital room.

For a moment she was speechless with it, her own perilous smallness, until her newer voice slipped back in. The angrier one.

Libby Rhodes, the good girl. Wasn't that what Parisa had always mocked her for?

Her virtue? Her *goodness*?

"Isn't that your whole thing? Not giving a fuck about people?" Libby said as coldly as she could manage, which was surprisingly cold. Even she was nearly taken aback by it—the way that all of a sudden, Parisa seemed like a decorative paperweight in a nice dress.

She felt her mind being rearranged, like Parisa was hunting around for something in the back of it. So Libby shut down hard, like a guillotine.

"I don't need you," Libby said flatly. "Not your approval, and certainly not your magic. Whether I do this or not, I'm not the one that's expendable. The only difference between you and Atlas is that you're more selfish and have less to lose."

"You think you've got a winning team with Tristan?" Parisa asked, arching a single brow. "He's the match I struck to save you. Now you think he's your answer?"

"I don't need an answer. *I'm* the answer." Libby considered storming away, only she didn't feel like it. She was fine right where she fucking was. She was drinking the cup of coffee she'd chosen, and she wasn't running away from a fight.

"I'm back, Parisa," Libby said flatly, "and you know exactly what it took to get me here, so maybe now's the time to remember that I'm not yours to play with anymore."

She felt a loose corner somewhere in her thoughts, hazy images floating to the surface. Lifeless eyes. A hand unfurled. A pair of unmoving feet.

A weak edge being lifted. *What else are you willing to break, Miss Rhodes—*

She smoothed it over. Parisa's expression remained unchanged.

"You're the bug," Parisa murmured, more to herself than to Libby.

It caught Libby off guard. "What?"

It took a moment, but then Parisa shook her head, picking up her wineglass and draining it. After the barest moment's pause, she said, "You're compromised. Don't do this."

Compromised? Was that how Parisa chose to characterize Libby's abduction, or was it just the year of being stalked like prey? "What's that supposed to mean?" Libby snapped.

"You think you're in control," Parisa observed, unnervingly stoic. "But I can see the guilt, Rhodes. It isn't clarity. All you learned how to do was justify a higher price."

Telepathy or not, it stung. "You think you have any right to talk to me about price?" Libby hissed through her teeth. "You have *no idea* what I did to get here—"

"No. *You* have no idea what *I* did to get here." Parisa set the glass down empty, her mouth a thin line. "You think validation comes from painful choices, Rhodes? It doesn't. People do terrible things every day and all it does is make more pain." She lifted her dark eyes to Libby's with something close to condemnation. "Didn't your girlfriend teach you that?"

"Aren't you the one who told me to take what I wanted?" demanded Libby, flaring so precipitously at the mention of Belen she nearly singed a hole in the tablecloth. "What makes *your* ambitions so fucking moral?"

"They're not." Parisa paused, stilling for a moment as if she'd suddenly malfunctioned. "They never were."

She seemed agitated for a second, then shook it off. "But I'm just the villain, Rhodes. It's my job to lose." Parisa smiled grimly, then uncrossed her legs to stand. "You think you're okay," she said with an air of finality, "but you're not. And believe me when I tell you you'll regret whatever you do next."

Oh, so that was how Parisa wanted to play it? Libby had been warned about the end of the world before. She was no longer taking such things under advisement.

"Stay out of my way," Libby said, making sure Parisa understood that she meant it. That whatever Parisa thought to gain from her, she wouldn't get it. Libby Rhodes wasn't a gun for hire. She wasn't one of Atlas Blakely's toys, and she wasn't Parisa Kamali's, either.

"Oh, Rhodes." Parisa shook her head, rising coolly to her feet. "I'm not interested in your way. I want nothing to do with it."

Right. Like Libby had never heard her use that exact same tone on Callum. "You really think that's going to work?" Libby scoffed, wondering how she had ever been so easily manipulated. It seemed so obvious now, so blatant, like finally recognizing a well-concealed tell. "Even if you walk away, Parisa, you're walking away with nothing. You called me here because you need me."

"I thought I did, yes. But I was wrong, and so are you." Parisa looked quizzically at her, and for a moment before Parisa reached for her sunglasses, Libby could see that she was considering something, a show of her hand. A confession, probably. The real reason Parisa had wanted to have this little chat.

It would be a power play, of course, because everything with Parisa was a power play, but it didn't matter. Libby understood her now. She understood that Parisa's purpose in the world was to destabilize people because she couldn't find her own footing. Because no matter where Parisa went, bartenders would fall over themselves to serve her, but nobody would ever give her what she actually wanted. Nobody would ever see her for what she actually was.

But Libby knew. Parisa Kamali had been left on her own to survive, and there was nothing Libby understood more fully. If the two of them were defined by nothing more than the ways they'd been wronged then there would be nothing left to say about it, but Parisa was at the end of her rope. Libby's was just beginning.

The difference between them was obvious, and maybe it was cruel to say it aloud, but Libby had recently learned a thing or two about cruelty.

"I can make new worlds," Libby said. "But all you have is this one."

That was it, really. All there was to be said. Libby looked up from her cup of coffee while Parisa slid her sunglasses onto her face, and they both knew that this would be the end.

"Whatever happens," Parisa said, eyes unreadable. "Live with it."

Then she walked out of the restaurant and was gone.

· · ·

In an ideal world, nothing Parisa said carried any further weight.

Instead, though, Libby lived in an antiquated manor house where the moral indictments of snide ex-lovers followed her around like grim hallucinations. That afternoon, Belen's face blurred with Parisa's, accusations punctuating mental images of lifeless eyes, archival taunts.

REQUEST DENIED.

She'd thought it would make her feel better to do something productive, to read something new and worthwhile. Instead, it was as if the house had joined the mockery, taunting her like a beating heart beneath the floorboards.

"If it helps," remarked Gideon over her shoulder, startling her out of her momentary reverie from where he'd been fitting books into a box, "I can barely summon an airport paperback."

That's because you're not an initiate, Libby wanted to say, before the obvious reply hit her as if it had been said in a silk dress, swirled around in a sweet honeyed wine:

Neither are you.

She lay awake in bed for hours, cursed with sleeplessness. Not that she was the only insomniac. Tristan tossed beside Libby in the dark, his phone screen lighting up against the black. He reached over for it, the glow reflecting on his features as he scowled, then typed something back.

"Who was it?"

He looked at her, startled to find her awake, then leaned over and kissed her shoulder.

"Varona. Apparently we're out of hummus." He set the phone on his nightstand again, turning to face her. "I told him to bring it up with our new archivist, since I'm pretty sure he doesn't have an actual job. And besides, they're in the same room."

"Mm." Libby exhaled slowly, staring up at the ceiling. "I don't really like Gideon being here," she admitted after a second.

She felt Tristan position himself on his side, tracing light patterns over her forearm. "I thought he was your friend?"

"He was. Is." She shook her head. "It's . . . I don't know, complicated. I feel like he's watching me or something. Like he—"

Like he knows.

Lifeless eyes. The stillness of an unfurled hand. *Was I a killer even before I walked into that office?*

(*What else are you willing to break, Miss Rhodes—?*)

Tristan was quiet for a few moments longer.

"I told you," he said. "It wasn't your fault."

"It was my fault. I did what I did. You don't get to absolve me by rewriting it." She regretted the choice of phrasing almost instantly. Parisa's face in her mind was dismissive and pitying, or maybe she only remembered it that way. *You've been rewritten.*

"I'm not rewriting it. He was going to kill you, kill all of us. I'm not downplaying it, I'm saying it wasn't your fault. *He* made the choices that put him in that room. Not you."

"I still made a choice." That mattered. Lately, that was the only thing that mattered. "I'm not saying I regret it. I'm just—" She shrugged. "Owning it."

"You're carrying it around," Tristan said.

"Isn't that the same thing?"

"I don't know, is it?"

They were both quiet for a while.

Tristan rolled onto his back, sighing. "I made a choice, too."

She nodded though she knew he couldn't see it. "I know."

"I chose you."

"I know." She reached blindly for his hand, drawing it up to her mouth. She buried a kiss in his palm, closing his fingers lightly around it.

"Will it always be between us?" Libby said to the dark.

The house was so quiet—no sound but the low tick of a nearby clock. From the window came a rustle of leaves, the haze of crickets. The sighs of summer unfurling like a lifeless hand toward fall.

Tristan snaked an arm beneath her, rolling her over until she was pressed against his chest, arranging the two of them face-to-face. She could see a thousand projections of tomorrows that all played out like this.

"I know what I chose," Tristan said.

She shook her head. "That's not what I asked."

"I'm just saying, I know what I chose."

She rested her head against his chest, listening to the sound of his heart-beat. "Why do you want to do it? The experiment." *The sinister plot.* No matter what she did, Nico was there, insufferably dimpled.

Tristan's fingers traced her spine. "Why do you?"

Because if I have come this far, it has to have been for a reason. Because if I choose now to settle for ordinary, I'm spitting in the face of every life I traded for my own. Because I paid an impossible price to be here, and now I have to answer for my choices.

Because if I was given this much power, I have to let the fucker burn.

Because it wasn't just this particular experiment. It was everything she'd be after she finally said yes. Life was a choice, a series of choices, destiny was saying *yes, yes, yes* until eventually, something happened. Something would have to happen. If nothing happened, then there was no meaning, no purpose. If nothing happened, then life was just a dead sister and some cheap high; five seconds of being valedictorian. It was just fucking over your girlfriend and setting off a pointless bomb and seeing yourself reflected, in all your spineless glory, in the mirrored sunglasses of a woman you'll never speak to again.

"Because I can," Libby finally said.

"Because I can," Tristan replied, like a sung refrain. A common chorus. And then he kissed her, and Libby waited for his breath to steady in peaceful slumber before she made her way downstairs.

·   ·   ·

In retrospect it might have been too simple. Too easy. How many times over the course of her residence had Libby sunk proverbially to her knees before the almighty archives, debasing herself in supplication, only to be met with an almost hostile indifference?

Only one other time in her life had Libby desired something so basely, so carnally, that careless acquiescence seemed borderline cruel. (It was no wonder, she thought, that she'd begun to personify the archives in her head as Parisa Kamali, mentally rendering them effortless, tactile, and cold.)

So. She had not expected an answer, and yet there it was. It took the form of a page of careless, fractionally legible notes, in handwriting she recognized at first glance; two spindly initials she'd glimpsed on very spare occasions. Like an answer from a ghost or a breathless rush of time travel, two letters seemed to leap from the page, catching her eye:

AB.

If only she could say she mistrusted the circumstances more instead of less. If only she'd properly schooled herself to associate Atlas Blakely with danger instead of relief. *This is all your fault,* Libby thought in practiced repetition, running her fingers gently over the page of his voice; trying—or so her internal narrative would craftily amend itself to read—to remind herself that everything currently in her hands was rightfully, deservedly hers.

The initiation ritual was ceremoniously underlined partway down the page in Atlas's academician's scrawl. He must have written it years ago, perhaps when he was a researcher in the position that was once Dalton's, now Tristan's. Libby shivered briefly with the realization that Tristan would later hold this in his hands, consult it.

Not a shiver of fear. One of possession. Of envy.

Rhodes, Nico taunted in her head, *either you're enough or you never will be—*

She read the page uncarefully, as if the faster she read, the more convincingly she could deny having ever read it. Like skimming the dirty bits of a bodice ripper smuggled home from the library; the feeling she'd soon be caught in a compromised position, the doorknob sharply turning as she hovered breathless, on the edge.

Bad news for horny teens: an inattentive read wasn't enough to secure plausible deniability. Atlas's lethargic cursive may have sprawled rhapsodically across the page, but the contents of the ritual were remarkably, even worryingly, uncomplicated. Like telling every conveniently braless blond girl in a horror film to run.

Equally as pointless, too. After her first read, when it became clear it was not a set of instructions, but a letter—then Libby scanned the page twice, hungrily, and a third time. Then, with a flutter low in her belly, a fourth. She glanced at the door to the reading room, pondered it, and then thought, wildly and hormonally: let them catch me if they want.

If there was more to the beginning of the letter, that was not for her to know. It began somewhere in the middle of a thought, perhaps even the middle of a sentence.

purpose of the ritual not technically known but guessable by certain nuanced intellectuals (me). It's not the original ritual, can't be, given that nobody mentions it in any text until the eighteenth century. (I want to be surprised by this information but am obviously not—this sort of philosophical transition from craftsmanship to manufacturing can only be industrial in nature. Not to be overimaginatively halcyonic but the flying shuttle—is that what it's called, the thing that automated weaving?—can progressively suck my dick, end quote.)

WHAT IS KNOWN—the archives have no body: they want our blood. As far as rituals go, remedial, elementary, slightly complimentary (ha), carnivorous. Equally known, this—the archives have no soul: they want ours. Why? To re-create us is my guess. Or torture us. Not mutually exclusive. Is the ritual a matter of showcasing thought, or pain, or magical capability? Yes and yes, probably, and also yes. Or maybe it doesn't care what we think or feel, it's very possible I'm projecting, but why should we be deconstructed by the archives if not for them to witness our materials, to see the viscera of which we're made? The trick to all of this, as you and I have so cleverly sorted out, is very simple: there is no genius behind any of this. No magic. This is the Society, haven't you been paying attention! It is only ever about ownership and control. Close your eyes and pretend you see none of it. Bow when they ask you to bow, break when they tell you to break. If only I could continue my conspiratorial tones of antiestablishment magniloquence but even I have to admit that sitting here with a sentient library—a brain almost the entirety of human history in the making—it is not without its reward.

Shut up, Ezra, I can hear you mocking me from here and it's not funny. Anyway, here's the entire logistical form of the initiation ritual—are you sitting down? Ask the archives to let you in and they will answer. We gave them a brain (not you and me we, we as in the metaphorical thousands who've shed their blood and taken their oaths) (so technically not us at all, which I say with admiration and my usual panache) (yes I've been smoking, what of it?) and as some fraction of the specialties already know, the archives are always listening. Somewhere there's the usual leather-bound tome (a la Medici grimoire) detailing exceptional holiness etc etc but that's the gist of it. By the way, did you know I faced you in the ritual? I killed you this time because it wasn't real and anyway I couldn't very well let the archives know the truth about your doors or what would be the point? What is the point, indeed. Possibly that I am a frankly marvellous pretender.

Hm. Better left unsent I think. I'll tell you some version of this when I see you next as it is so easily summarized. Why am I still writing, then? Good question, Ezra, perhaps because it's day 57 alone in a very creepy house and shy of spoon-feeding my mother I'm left with little else. In what has become a mad exercise in isolation I bid myself adieu.

In the story Libby would later tell if she had to, her legs collapsed under her in shock. In shock! Certainly there were no witnesses to say she summoned a glass of water (no need to be stupid) or rearranged the tables of the reading room to leave an open space. Nobody could attest to her sneaking fears that it would be Callum she faced, or more likely Parisa. Or even, perhaps in a fit of poetic justice, Atlas himself.

Nobody would hear her say to the house, "I want to do the ritual," and then, when it did not answer, nobody would hear her add, "You gave me the letter." And also, "You can't say I haven't earned it. You can't say I don't deserve the right to try."

Then, finally, after five more ticks of silence, nobody would witness Libby Rhodes saying to the Alexandrian Society's palatial manor house: "Just let me in, you fucking *fuck*."

The lights went out. The reading room was always less illuminated than the rest of the house for the sake of the archives' contents, but even so. There was a difference between dim and darkness, tantamount to being swallowed up.

Libby scrambled to her feet, listening for something. A long-legged stride or the tap of a thin stiletto heel. Her eyes gradually adjusted to the darkness—identifying the hazy outlines of a sofa, a mantel, a chair—before she remembered she wasn't an idiot and turned on the lights.

She didn't hear her opponent. She felt him out of instinct, like the throbbing presence of a bruise.

The painted room at night. Without looking, she knew a lone figure stood smirking at her from the doorway.

"Rhodes, don't hurt yourself."

She spun with a whirl of force, aiming a blind—but not uninformed—wave of energy in his direction. Nico dismantled it like a toy, swatting it lazily down. What information would the ritual take from her, then? That Nico had always been better, faster, more natural?

Or that she still believed as much of him?

"I earned my place here," she reminded him, before striking him from afar. He parried or something with a laugh, as if he were merely sparring with Reina. In real life, Nico was asleep, or possibly gone again with Max, she never listened when he offered explanations of his absences. (Yes, she did. He now explained it, his whereabouts, with painstaking detail and a not-insignificant measure of kindness, as if she'd once been lost to time and space and thus he did not want her to worry, did not want her to feel alone, an unsolicited reassurance that he was always safely within reach.)

"Five members were already initiated, Rhodes." His eyes were different. The usual gleam of boyish wrongdoing felt malicious, or maybe that was just the archives taunting her with qualities that Libby herself had falsely ascribed. (Was the ritual a game, a dream, an exercise in torment, what?) She walked briskly up to Nico with half-considered aims of slapping him and he caught her hand before she raised it, or maybe she had placed it deliberately within his reach.

"Five," he repeated, "were *already initiated*. Which means you," he added with a salacious wink, "are redundancy in its dullest, most pointless form."

She yanked her wrist from his hand. "You don't actually believe that." Oh, but this was her brain, not his. She fed the simulation, not him; hadn't Atlas said as much? "*I* don't believe that," she corrected herself. "I've earned my right to initiation." She pivoted sharply, addressing the bones of the house, the apse beside the painted room window, the ash in the hearth. "It's Callum we decided to kill. Intention means something." Lethal arrows, luck and unluck. "The sacrifice was already made the moment we picked him."

Magical significance. Atlas's voice in her head, then Ezra's. *You're his weapon.* (Who is the arrow, who the archer?) *Was I a killer even before I walked into that office?*

(*What else are you willing to break, Miss Rhodes—?*)

It mounted in her head, pressing inward, tender and excruciating, erupting like entrails. Heartsick and ashen with rage, Libby snarled at the house's faceless walls. "Don't tell me I didn't bleed for you!"

"Ah, but alas—a philosophical divergence," interrupted Nico's simulation, prompting Libby to spin back toward him. "You didn't do any of that for the archives."

She swallowed around the presence of something bitter. "Of course I did—"

Nico lifted a finger, silencing her with a roll of his eyes. "The *archives* never needed you to return, Rhodes. Why would they, when they already have me?

You only came back to prove something to yourself. Something you're still trying to prove."

Libby could feel her secrets being robbed from her then. An unsophisticated pain, like a charley horse in her gut, and she responded with a blow to Nico's face, which he dissipated with a blink.

"Honestly, Rhodes? Congratulations," Nico said with a laugh. "So, you're finally willing to burn this world down, but only to prove that *you personally* matter—"

"I'm *not* burning it down," she hissed through gritted teeth, reminded again that this was all a trick of her own mind. (*The world can end in two ways,* Ezra whispered into nothing, *fire or ice*—) "I'm *obviously* not, seeing as that's the one thing I'm very purposely *not doing*—"

"And the sad thing, Rhodes, is that even if you did, you still wouldn't believe it." Nico inspected his nails, the whisper of smoke around their heads the only evidence she'd tried to disintegrate him with a homemade flamethrower.

"Believe *what*?" she snapped at him, realizing with a tiresome jolt how handsome he was, an added sting to salt the wound. A thing she'd always known and resented, how naturally, how unfailingly he pleased the eye, a trick no amount of mascara or illusion charms had ever accomplished.

He looked, for a moment, almost like Callum—

Until, with a gleam so bright she forcibly turned away, he was.

"Oh, Rhodes. You're still chasing a finish line you'll never get to see." Callum looked smug and beautiful, just like he'd been in her dreams. As if he'd been personally tutored in condescension by Parisa while Libby had been lost, and alone, and away. "You thought once you were recruited, you'd feel valuable. You thought once you brought yourself back home, you'd feel powerful. You thought once you got initiated, you'd finally feel worthy. Now you think sure, if you can open a door to a new fucking world, *then* you'll—"

"I'm not going to do it," Libby hissed. (Belen's face warped in her mind: *You're going to do it, aren't you?*) "Why would I do something I already know to have catastrophic results?"

To her dismay, Callum smiled.

(*I can see it there, on your stupid fucking face!*)

And then, all of a sudden, he was Nico again.

"Because Ezra's a liar and an idiot and you don't believe him," Nico informed her gaily, as if nothing had ever brought him so much pleasure to say aloud. "A thing I've told you many times, by the way, and something you've always secretly half believed, because ironically"—quick pause for laughter, as if to charmingly debauch a society toast or outshine her at her own birthday party—"if I had liked or even *marginally respected* him, you probably wouldn't have dated him, because everything in your life has always been about proving something to me."

"That's not even remotely true—that's—I can't believe you'd even—" Faintly, she felt aware there was a very real, very reachable possibility of argument, and yet somehow, it seemed to dissipate the closer she got.

"It gets worse, doesn't it?" Nico leaned toward her, stepping in close enough to reach her. Or kiss her. He morphed, then, and was Callum. Morphed again, and was Tristan.

Then Parisa. "You love me, fine, terrible but manageable."

Nico again. She could feel his breath in the air between them. "Somewhere in that moralizing, catastrophizing brain of yours you already know this warped somewhere between us along the way, but that's not the thing that kills you after all. That's not the real fatality here, because part of you knows I could love you back—I *could* do it. But you're not as good a person as I think you are, are you?" His stupid eyes were framed by lashes so long they nearly brushed his cheek.

"Because the real banger of a truth," said Nico, his voice dropping just above a whisper, "is that if you were actually a good person, you would have just stayed lost."

Shock cantered painfully across her chest when his eyes slipped to her lips. "What?"

"Admit it." He danced back with a grin, flicking a wave of force so abruptly in her direction that she staggered over it, like snagging her toe in the carpet. "You've already done the math, Rhodes. You already know the cost to bring you here was indefensible. It was one life for possible thousands. Maybe generational. Maybe worse. With how incessantly you worry, there's no way you didn't know."

"That's—" Libby felt dazed. "That's purely theoretical, and—"

"Oh, sure, so it already happened," Nico said with a dismissive wave. "Time is a closed loop, so arguably the damage was already done. But that wasn't the question, was it? The question was *what is the right thing to do,* and you chose—ding ding ding!" He was Callum again, so briefly it stung her eyes, like looking directly into the sun. "The wrong answer."

Nico returned. Libby felt herself lifting from the floor before hastily rerouting the force of gravity, her feet meeting the floorboards with a sudden, painful crash.

"Which is how I know you're going to do the experiment," Nico added, reentering the span of her reach to brush a kiss to her cheek, knocking her reeling to the floor. "Because you burned the world down once and walked away unscathed, and you're dumb enough to think that means something."

She scrambled to her feet, eyes on his, and set fire to his pant leg. He let it burn, like it didn't hurt. Like she could never truly, actually hurt him.

"Because simply knowing the experiment exists already means that nothing else you live to accomplish will ever be enough," Nico said, this time with a softer look. A look she knew, because she had seen him give it to Gideon. Because it was a look he gave Gideon all the time. "Because it's another finish line you have to cross, or you will always be a failure."

Flames rose from the floor at her bidding, licking devotedly at his T-shirt. He raised the material from his skin and watched the flesh of his stomach redden in welts, then gradually blacken.

Nico leaned closer to speak in her ear, sweat dripping from his cheeks to her shoulders like carefully unshed tears. "Because successfully completing that experiment is the only thing you have left to prove that anxious, annoying, unlovable you is worth the price you forced everyone else to pay," Nico whispered, "all so you could believe for one fucking second that you matter at all."

He stepped away, finished, and it occurred to Libby that she had ample evidence in contradiction. That if her jaw dropped, it was only circumstantial; because it was hard to breathe through so much smoke, and the Nico her mind had made for her would burn if she allowed it.

Understandably, she chose a less admirable path.

"Shut *the fuck* up," replied Libby, punching him in the face.

Parrying the impact of the blow, if she'd ever had a chance at landing one, was so squarely within his talents he barely blinked. Then, abruptly, he was Reina.

"Oh, Rhodes," Reina offered, with the utterly psychotic look of indifference she seemed to reserve for Libby alone.

A tendril of something reached out, a jolt of force or nature sending Libby flying backward. She crashed through the bookcase to land on her back, hissing through the pain. She felt exhausted, broken, spent; a vine reached tenderly around her throat, stroking her jaw.

Then a shadow crossed her face, blocking the light like a sudden eclipse.

Dizzied, Libby blinked.

Standing over her was herself, her hands dripping with blood.

"What else are you willing to break, Miss Rhodes?" Libby asked in a whisper.

There was a flash of pain, a blinding light. Then Libby calmly woke to the dim light of the reading room, understanding two things: that this had been the ritual, and she had failed.

IV

NIHILISM

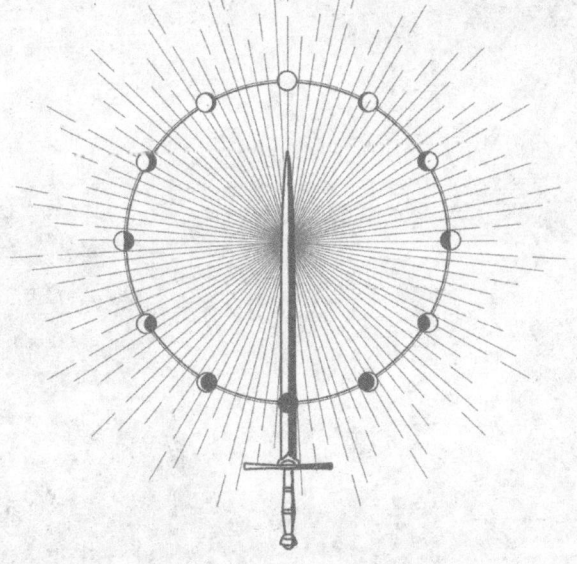

TRISTAN

So, Tristan, how do you think you'll kill me?

> Slowly.

We know a knife is out. Unless you want to try it again.

> I have no interest in being that close to you.

You wouldn't technically have to be, but I see your point, it's
very intimate. A very sexy death.

> And therefore inappropriate for you.

Lol

If only you meant that.

TUESDAY, AUGUST 23

You know, now that I've met him, I can see that I was wrong
about your father. I thought it was simpler than it was, more
easily defined. All those little traumas you're so desperate
to block out from your past. At first it seemed so unoriginal,
straightforward. But it's quite complicated between you, isn't it?
Love can be so deeply twisted.

I mean, I was right, technically, in about 99 different ways,
particularly as to the nature of your victimhood. But I was also a
bit wrong, so this is me being sorry about that.

> I doubt you've ever been genuinely sorry about anything.

Not true. I'm sorry I killed Parisa.

> You mean you're sorry you let her trick you into killing her.

That too, but no, I'm actually sorry I did it. Well, I didn't kill her,
that's not fair. She made that choice, I didn't influence her into
doing it.

> Semantics.

Yeah, but semantics are kind of important here, right? Like,
they're relevant to this specific conversation. I want you to know

I didn't convince her to do it. I just . . . peeled away her reasons
for not doing it.

> Semantics. And bad ones at that.

Right, well, the point is I'm sorry. Don't tell anyone but I miss her
a little bit.

> . . .

What? I like Parisa. She's fun.

> She's literally a sadist.

Tristan, please. Don't act like that's not your EXACT idea of fun.

THURSDAY, SEPTEMBER 1

Did you hear the news?

> You're still alive, apparently. Bummer.

LINK: EDEN WESSEX FINDS LOVE WITH DANISH ROYAL.

> Is this supposed to make me . . . jealous?

Of course not. I know for a fact that guy's too short for you.

> What is the point of sending me this? Obviously Eden wasn't
> going to sit around pining for me.

Strange jump, don't you think? From you to royalty
Unless it's an issue of class solidarity and all that, in which case
hello? I'm clearly available

> Fuck you etc

Right, so on and so forth, go on

> Eden's progressivism was always performative. Obviously,
> seeing as she's apparently trying to kill me now that I can't
> make Uncle Louis uncomfortable at the dinner table.

Is she trying to kill you? Oh Eden, where is your dignity.
Obsession is not a cute look

> Says the guy still texting me

How did you know she's trying to kill you? I mean I obviously
knew that, but I wasn't aware you did.

> I asked the Society who was behind all the attacks. Not
> surprising there's Wessex money involved.

Does that necessarily mean Eden?

> Almost certainly.

Do you intentionally look for homicidal streaks in your partners?
Or is it just, like, a fun bonus
Wait, nevermind, I hear you're with Rhodes now. Though she's
not NOT a murderer, so . . . I think I've made my point

SATURDAY, SEPTEMBER 10

Don't tell me that actually bothered you. I told you there'd be a
bomb involved.

You can't have it both ways, Tristan. Either Rhodes is a saint
who's still trapped in time or she's back because she's just as
fucked up as the rest of us

> You're really saying there's no difference between you and
> Rhodes?

Oh, hello! Funny seeing you here. No romantic Saturday plans,
I take it?

SUNDAY, SEPTEMBER 11

Does she know you're still thinking about me?

> Yes. She knows I haven't decided on a murder weapon yet.

Did she suggest a nuclear bomb?

10:10 P.M.

OH COME ON THAT WAS FUNNY

WEDNESDAY, SEPTEMBER 21

> Varona has a theory that you're using Reina to influence people
> over airwaves

Sorry, who is this?

3:45 P.M.

I'm allowed to joke, Caine. And for the record, I'm not using
Reina. She's using me.

6:15 P.M.

> Ha. I doubt that.

8:21 P.M.

Why would I lie to you?

> . . .

Fine, why would I lie to you about this, specifically? I have
no interest in world domination. Reina's the one with the god
complex.

> You're really just going along with whatever she wants?

My desires are unfulfillable and tiny. Hers have scope. I admire her, in a sense.

One (1) sense?

Well, she's going to fail. But that's going to happen whether I help her or not, and it's not like I have anything more pressing to attend to.

There's the matter of your death, of course, but I'm in no hurry for that.

Is there anyone you actually believe in?

I can tell there's a ring of cynicism to that question, Tristan, but I'm being perfectly sincere when I tell you that you have everything all wrong. I believe in Reina. I believe in you. I even believe in Rhodes, in my own silly way, or I wouldn't have given you the information I gave you in order to help bring her back. But believing in someone doesn't change who they are. No matter how many times you run the simulation, the odds remain the same.

You said there was no chance Rhodes would come into her power and you were wrong.

No, the LIBRARY said that, Tristan. But in fairness it has the sentience of a machine.

What does that mean?

It means the archives are "alive" the same way artificial intelligence is "alive." It tracks us. It maybe (probably) thinks in some rudimentary way. But its information about the world doesn't come from its own intrinsic existence—it comes from data that we supply.

And?

And that information is imperfect but it's still not as imperfect as humanity. In nature, things that don't fit the pattern die. Evolution is a code, it determines that the life cycle of any species is a matter of pattern recognition. But humans don't let other humans die even when they should—even when it means disproportionate resources to keep them alive. Or they kill each other off in direct opposition to the codes of survival, based on something as irrelevant as skin color or which thing they speak to in the sky. Whether a person lives or dies is almost completely arbitrary.

I've got a theory.

Yeah? Hit me.

You just spin nonsense out of thin air to distract people from the fact that you've got absolutely no idea what you're talking about.

Oh Tristan, none of us have any idea what we're talking about, the whole thing is a fool's errand. In any case, the point I'm trying to make is that of course the archives can still be wrong. Of course there's one chance out of a million where you actually manage to kill me or that Rhodes does something impressive all on her own. There's at least one universe out there where Atlas Blakely killed someone to save four other lives and that's precisely why he's looking for it.

But does it matter?

Does anything matter?

See? Now you get it.

You're so full of shit.

2:37 A.M.

Do you think the library dreams?

Something keeping you up, Caine?

4:13 A.M.

I don't know.

I think that's the first time I've ever heard you say that.

Oh, your memories of me are clouded with silly things like how you think I'm a murderer or whatever your problem with me is.

Of course there are things I don't know.

My main problem with you is that you're too arrogant to function

Just arrogant ENOUGH to function, actually

Every now and then I suddenly remember you're a youngest child and it starts to make a lot more sense

Oh, don't equate me with Bella. That's just rude.

I'm not joking when I tell you to stay the fuck away from my sisters

No <3

7:44 A.M.

Jesus, I'm joking. What do you think I'm going to do with them?

They're CHILDREN, Tristan. They're INFANTS.

I'm glad you've noticed.

It's very interesting, actually, seeing you through their eyes.
Are you aware that on some level they think you've abandoned
them?

It's only natural that they'd think that. I left a long time ago. They
were actual children then.
You knew what your father was like and you still left them?

Tristan, I'm baiting you. It's our love language. The truth is: you
don't have to feel guilty. And come on. Be honest. You don't.
Why should you feel guilty? You knew they'd be safe. He's
different with them than he is with you. And they still have
their mother. The nonsense you let yourself carry around, I
didn't realize it was so richly imagined. They're fine, Tristan.
They're more than fine. They're certainly better off than
you.
Why the fuck would you even say that then?
Because I'm a sadist, Tristan, what do you want from me?
And in case it bears repeating. You don't have to feel bad that
you left a situation that was killing you.
It wasn't killing me.
Tristan. I've felt what you feel. You do not need to lie to me.

I think I made a mistake.
Probably. Probably several. But who among us can't say that?
Which part would you undo if you could?
Which strand of the multiverse would I follow, you mean?
Fine, if you prefer that thought experiment.
I don't believe in the multiverse
Not even if I could prove it existed?
Okay, I believe in it as a theoretical possibility, but I don't
BELIEVE in it. We don't get to undo our mistakes. We just make
new ones and try to make the next ones more interesting
Indulge me anyway. Which moment do you change?

I know which answer you want me to give, but I still think the
whole thing is pointless
>Which answer do you think I want you to give?

Oh, I don't know. Influencing your choice of beverage. Killing
Parisa. It really doesn't matter now
>I could make it matter.

Oh, right, because you and Rhodes are making your own
universes, I forgot
>Is it really so hard for you to believe that I didn't choose her over
you? I just chose NOT YOU, which is extremely distinct. And
frankly a matter of self-preservation

Is it?
Or did you make a mistake?

TUESDAY, OCTOBER 11

1:15 A.M.

>What if I did Atlas's experiment?

Shoot for the moon. Even if you miss you'll land among the
stars
>I truly, deeply, fucking hate you

I know right!!! lmao same
>Answer the question.

Since when do you care what I think? According to you I'll be
dead soon
>I think we both know you can't resist a chance to wax poetic
about why I'm wrong and you're right and humanity is terrible
and this is all just the universe's latest episode in its series of
forthcoming doom

Humanity isn't terrible, it's just not worth trying to fix or
change, which is honestly the second time I've had this exact
conversation today, but I can see that this is just as pointless.
What's the question?
>Scroll up, fuckwit.

Right, should you do it, should you not . . . I don't care, Tristan,
this whole thing is exhausting
>Wow.

You're going to do the experiment! I know it! You know it! Atlas
Blakely knows it! Rhodes knows it! And on a more relevant
note, even Her Divinity knows it, because Varona left yet

another voicemail trying to persuade her to join the fun. So I
think YOU can see how this is all a very silly exercise of moral
hypotheticals.

> Why is morality so silly? It's only the basis for society, give or
> take some innate human dignity or whatever it is we all seem to
> care about that you can't figure out

Oh, you're so grumpy. It's so cute.

> You're right. I'm a total masochist. What's wrong with me? Why
> am I here?

It's a mystery!!! I love it!! I can't wait to see how you decide to
kill me
Anyway, I know what you're telling yourself, which is that the
experiment isn't inherently bad, and you're right.

> So you think I should do it.

I think you're going to do it, which is extremely well-established,
but of course I don't think you SHOULD. What does Parisa
think?

> Right, because I definitely asked for her opinion.

If you haven't you should. Either she thinks you should do it, in
which case you should absolutely not do it, or she thinks it's a
terrible idea, in which case she's right

> I believe you may have inadvertently revealed your stance on
> the issue, Socrates

Oh 100000% my answer is don't do it. But you're going to! So
you can see how this is a waste of my international minutes.

> How is your plan for world domination going?

Pointlessly once you open up another strand of the multiverse,
but try telling the Goddess that. She simply won't hear it, so off
to the Americas I go

> Why American politics?

Why coffee and not tea? Why is the sky blue?

> I can't wait to kill you.

Have you come up with the weapon yet? Or will you simply
transport yourself to a world where I was never born? I imagine
there are a few of those hanging around somewhere under the
multiverse's sofa cushions

> Why do you think I shouldn't do it?

Let me count the ways.

. . .

That was meant to be poetic. I'm not going to literally count the
ways. I'd be here all day

> What else do you have to do?

Fair point. Fine. My main reason is that you're always someone
else's weapon. You're Atlas Blakely's. You're your father's.
You're Eden Wessex's. You're Parisa's. The list goes on. I think
the main reason you want so badly to be in love with Rhodes is
because you think she'd never use you

> By that logic, can you blame me for preferring anyone but you?

Tristan I am so exhausted by this argument, can we skip it for
now? You can always recount it later when you're strangling me
or whatever it is you plan to do. Pushing me off a cliff sounds
easy. And I have it on good authority (Reina's, so maybe not
THAT good) that I'm incredibly easy to lure.

> You're magic. Too many ways you'd survive that fall

I just got chills!!! Talk murder to me you cheeky minx

> You know what's honestly ironic?

TELL me. I'm dying to hear it. x

> You won't kill me, Callum. You can't. Someday I'm going to kill
> you and you're going to be completely shocked because no
> matter how powerful you are, you can't actually DO anything.
> Varona's figured it out, you know. You're using technomantic
> transmitters to influence the actual mob. You're fixing an entire
> country's election, and not just one candidate, but every single
> one. You're going to overturn an entire system of government
> and yet, SOMEHOW, you're too afraid to find out if the universe
> might be a little bit bigger than you think it is.

> You're too scared to be disappointed. You're afraid to be
> dwarfed, to be wrong.

> And you're terrified of a world without me because you know
> that once I'm gone you'll be alone.

I think you made a lot of points there, Caine. Some of them
really quite valid.

> Of course that's all you have to say.

What do you want me to tell you? Of course the universe is
bigger than I am. I don't make decisions about the universe.

> Right, Reina does.

Yes, Reina does, and I go along with them because I grasp that
to every action there's an equal and opposite blah blah blah

and it'll come back and smack her in the face because the only
thing I actually understand is equilibrium and a general cosmic
comings-around
But what do YOU want to hear? I genuinely have no idea

      Can you influence me over text messaging?

Why, do you feel influenced? No, you're right, let's not go
down that rabbit hole. I don't know the answer but I don't
think so. This is Varona's network and strange as it is to say it
feels unsportsmanlike to fuck with it. Plus I can't do the same
thing over webcasts that I can over television, Reina and I've
already tried. Presumably the magical infrastructure is weaker
or something, or maybe it's stronger, I don't know. Even if she
figures it out it doesn't matter.

      Right, because nothing matters.

Right! You get it!

      What if I refuse to believe that's true?

Well what does it mean to matter, Caine? What does that look
like?

      Mattering?

Yes, mattering. Purpose. Meaning. What about the world
suggests to you that those things can actually be met? There
are no happy billionaires. I should know, considering my father's
one of them. People who claim to be happy get forgotten within
one generation, maybe two. So what are you actually aiming
for, here, Tristan, because to me it seems not only pointless but
impossible

      Isn't this what it is to be human? To want to matter? To have a
      purpose?

Let me ask you something. If your purpose was to open the
multiverse, what would happen afterward?

      What does that mean?

Assuming I don't beat you to the punch and kill you before you
kill me, you're going to live another . . . what, fifty years or so?
Say you open a portal to the multiverse tomorrow, or next week,
or whenever it is your little team of physicists decides to give it a
go. Then what?

      Then I'll have opened a portal to the multiverse.

Right. But will your father love you? Will your sisters miss you?
Will the archives stop trying to kill you? Will you be able to

stop thinking about me? Will you finally have the answer to the questions you've always wanted to ask? Will you understand why you had to go through so much pain just to be here today, just to exist? If you can prove that you matter in some concrete, un-theoretical way, will you finally believe it's true?

THURSDAY, OCTOBER 13

12:32 A.M.

No

But I'm going to do it anyway.

. . .

The odd thing about the reading room was how dark it was; the significance of time always seemed to vanish, hours passing like minutes or breaths. Tristan looked at the time stamp on his last message and realized he'd been sitting there for ages. Despite Nico and Gideon's comings and goings throughout the evening, neither he nor Libby had moved.

"Who are you texting?" Libby murmured through a yawn. She lifted her head from her page of notes and looked impossibly familiar, like herself from a lifetime or two ago. Like this was a moment from a warped sense of retrospect, in a time and place that never actually existed, or simply hadn't yet.

"Hm? No one." Tristan put his phone aside, rubbing his eyes beneath the lenses of his glasses. He needed a new prescription. Everything was starting to make his eyes hurt. It felt strange and also somehow apt to be succumbing to decay while quietly planning something of this magnitude.

"You're sure," he said slowly. "We could do it without Reina?" Libby slid him a glance and he added pointedly, "Hypothetically speaking."

"Hypothetically yes, I'm sure. And anyway, I don't really think we can trust her. Especially now, given what she's up to." Libby tossed him a rueful smile. "If I'd had to put money on which of us would try to take over the world, I really wouldn't have picked Reina."

"I would have," said Nico, abruptly dropping a pile of books on the table. "And as for hypotheticals," he said. "I'm done with that. Let's say, *realistically speaking,* that we know what we're doing—"

"Brief interjection: no, you don't," said Gideon from where he was carefully returning books to the shelves of the painted room.

"Right, correction, we don't. But that's why it's an *experiment,*" Nico insisted, plopping into the chair beside Libby. "And if you're right about the vengeful archives, we're already nearly five months into a possible six. So, either we kill someone tonight—Gideon exempted," he offered genially, to which Gideon tipped an invisible hat, "or we do the experiment. And if it doesn't work, then it doesn't work."

Libby shifted instantly away. "If it doesn't work we only unleash the power of the sun," she muttered. "Very casual, Varona, you're right."

"Please, we've got more control than that." He beckoned to Gideon, who stood just beyond the table as if uncertain whether he should enter the sacred space of their eternal hypothetical. "Have a sit, Sandman, you're making everyone nervous."

Tristan's screen lit up with a message. He flipped it below the table, glancing down to see the response to his first real voicing of his intentions. *I'm going to do it anyway,* he'd confessed to Callum, and his pulse skittered across his chest as he surreptitiously read Callum's reply.

I know. And I genuinely wish you omnipotence.

Tristan looked up again to find that Gideon had noticed him checking his phone, though Gideon had glanced hastily elsewhere. Tristan slid the phone back into his pocket, wondering why his heart was thudding so profoundly in his chest. As if he'd been caught.

(Tristan already knew what he would do when the time came. Not a knife, not a gun, not a weapon. He didn't need one. Wasn't that the point of it all, discovering that he could break something on his own, change it into something else? He'd simply dismantle the thing in Callum's chest pumping blood to his brain, which Tristan hesitated to call a heart. He would flip it like a light switch, on to off, easy, simple, no pause for doubt, no mess, no guilt. He had the feeling that Callum would laugh, or maybe even thank him.)

"I think," Nico continued, "we're overthinking this."

"Impossible," said Gideon, who'd stepped closer, hovering beside Tristan's chair.

"He's right," said Tristan, who realized he hadn't spoken in a while.

"Fine. *Rhodes* is overthinking this." Nico patted her hair as she swatted him away, missing by an inch. "So let's just, I don't know, stop."

"Engrave it on my headstone," Libby muttered. "*Let's just, I don't know, stop.*"

"I'm putting 'brb' on my headstone," Nico said, then snapped his fingers. "Gideon, you're in charge of that."

"I'm aware." Gideon sounded wry, too close. Tristan had the sense that Libby was right, that Gideon knew something, knew many things. He didn't *seem* like a threat, but that was somehow worse. The idea that he would see everything and not try to intervene. Tristan felt unmoored by it. Destabilized.

"We should do it soon," Nico said. "Tomorrow, even."

"Even if I agreed with you, we'd need rest," Libby said. "Food."

"Dalton," Tristan pointed out.

"The point is the *intention*," Nico argued. "If, say, Dalton could be convinced by Parisa, or possibly, I don't know, via Tristan's seductive wiles—"

"Right," said Tristan, noticing Libby's disgruntled shift in her chair. "Very plausible."

"—then we'd bacchanal tomorrow, sleep for forty-eight hours, and make a new fucking world." Nico punched the air in a way that Tristan found hugely inappropriate for the time of night it happened to be. "The point is the arrow. We need to decide." He paused for a moment, almost pleading. "We need to just *do* it."

Libby pushed the book away from her, locking eyes with Tristan. "Please," she said. "Tell him again, because I really can't."

He felt Gideon shifting behind him. Unclear what Gideon was seeing, or thought he saw.

Do you trust me? Libby had asked him that. But exactly how far did trust go?

("Mr. Caine, this is Ford again, sorry to bother you but have you heard from Dr. Blakely? We've yet to receive any reports about the new archivist. The board of governors has reserved their right to a call for a vote of no confidence for now, but it's only a matter of—")

Tristan's phone felt heavy in his pocket. He thought about texting Callum, just for an element of absurd, something to loosen the apprehension in his chest that was so obviously misplaced, so pointless. A vestige of a prior lifetime, one riddled with fear.

What if I fail, to which Callum's response would surely be *Oh darling, but what if you fly?*

"Hypothetically," said Tristan. "I might agree with Varona."

Either there was more to this world or there was nothing, in which case Libby would stop looking at him like that, and eventually the pain would pass. Eventually.

The table shook as Nico slammed down a hand.

"Boom," he said euphorically, or prophetically. "Yes. Done."

· REINA ·

Reina scrolled through the news app on her phone while the crowd around them shuffled this way and that, heat wafting maliciously above the pavement as they walked. Paris was unexpectedly muggy and dense in late October, summer increasingly overstaying its welcome until shades of umber and forthcoming rot were forced to crowd into its torrid space. The streets seemed eternally flooded with tourists, ambling beside locals who dressed disconcertingly like Parisa. Topically, Callum looked like pure evil beside Reina in his crisp white shirt—too shiny to burn, too cool to melt, wearing those outrageous chromatic aviators. If he weren't currently busy texting his ex she'd hate him for his unimpeachable nonchalance, but he obviously had bigger (dumber) problems.

A message floated onto Reina's screen. We've got pretty much all the preliminary research done, so. Just keeping u updated! Party hat. Three popping champagne bottles. A red flashing siren. Feeling V BUMMED that u have not accepted my zillion apologies. Not quitting tho love u besos

"My god," said Callum, leaning over Reina's shoulder and dropping his sunglasses to eye her screen. "How have you not blocked his number? Just throw the whole phone away."

"You're one to talk." She glared at him for good measure. "I take it Tristan's already told you about the progress with the sinister plot?"

"It's cute that you're even using Varona's pet name for it." Callum's reflective lenses were glaring on his face, dazzling Reina with the vision of her own scowl before he gestured to her phone screen with his chin. Nico's message alert had disappeared, leaving only the browser window she'd been scrolling through. "What are you looking for?"

"New candidates." She showed him the article from the Texas newspaper about the young potential congresswoman whose numbers were on the rise. "We could check this one out. Or skip to her opposition, if that's easier." By that point, Reina could tell based on how much power was pumping through her to Callum that it required less energy to make a crowd hate someone than it did to reroute a mob, or even simply temper one to moderation.

In response, though, Callum made a face, gracefully circumnavigating a group of tourists pausing for a selfie. "No. I don't like Texas."

"Why not? It's not all zealots." Their stop there last week had been to dismantle a potential bill filing in the state senate that Reina had uncovered as part of a social media call to action. The senator authoring the bill had a change of heart (thanks to Callum and Reina, obviously) but that hadn't really done much to block progress. One of the other US congressmen simply rallied another party leader in the state senator's place, and at that point, even swaying public opinion hadn't changed as much as Reina had expected—for reasons probably related to her unfamiliarity with the American political landscape. Hard to believe, given the predominance of American politics that had led her there in the first place, but Callum explained it as a matter of translation. Governments were like people, and speaking the precise language of any systemic corruption was a necessity. In the United States, influence was a combination of money (expected) and geographical districts (unexpected, annoying, irrational).

The point was that knowing the bill was wildly unpopular with the public didn't appear to be any sort of threat to the politicians involved. Ultimately, Reina and Callum had been forced to stay overlong, making at least four or five additional drop-ins to really make a mess of things and fully kill the bill. She could tell—he had made it inescapably clear—that Callum hadn't been happy about it. She understood in a distantly sympathetic way that what Callum took from her (or what nature took when she allowed it) could be replenished faster and more easily than whatever Callum channeled within himself upon Reina's request.

"It wouldn't have to be like last time," she said gamely. He'd been sore and sick for a while afterward and had concealed it, or tried to, with a series of antics—mainly the antagonizing of the Caines, father and son, through the perennial nature of his presence. It was almost believable as a distraction, because Callum's singular drive to be obnoxious was insuppressible and frankly, a preternatural gift. Still, Callum with a ten-hour nosebleed wasn't an image Reina was prepared to forget.

He gave her a look of contempt, like he could sense her concern. It was the same face he made whenever they came into contact with the Parisian sewers. "I don't care for the ants in Texas," he said, adjusting his collar. "They're too big and they bite."

Sure.

They paused at a traffic light, waiting to cross the street. In the spare moments of stillness, Reina looked back at her phone and scrolled again, kept scrolling. Something about the Hong Kong election; she'd have to turn her attention to that as soon as the American campaigns were done, assuming she made it that long. (The alleged six-month deadline approached but it seemed impossible, at least to Reina, that the archives would not consider the work she was doing to be an undertaking on their behalf; if anyone died first for the crime of being undeserving, she guessed it would be Parisa.) A military strike, fuck, she thought she'd already successfully railroaded defense spending, but war was limitless, she supposed. (For now.) Something about internet privacy, medeian statutes on tracking being violated, motherfuckers. Add that to her list. A listicle called "Ways You Can Help the Victims of the Southern California Wildfires" followed by an article called "Why Nobody Is Talking About the Floods in Bangladesh."

"What's that?"

"Hm?" Reina looked up to find Callum eyeing the headlines on her screen.

"That." He pointed with the edge of a pinkie finger, his pale brow furrowed. "I know that face."

It was a middle-aged woman, unremarkable. Southeast Asian, maybe Filipino or Vietnamese, but it was an American headline. "University lab to close pending investigation over misused public funds." "This?"

The crowd was moving again. Callum reached blindly for the phone and Reina gave it to him, the two of them pausing below the awning of a nearby brasserie. He read in silence, no more than a paragraph or two, then opened a new tab, searching for something in her browser.

"Something interesting about the lab?" Reina asked, wondering what she could have possibly overlooked.

"No, not the lab. Well, maybe the lab, but—" Callum stopped, apparently lost in thought as he scrolled through a list of academic articles.

Reina craned her neck to read the search inquiry he'd typed in: *Dr. J. Araña.* "I've never heard of her."

"I met her last year. Well, not really." Callum's usual faultless appearance looked no more disturbed than ever, but she thought she caught a thin trickle of sweat from behind his ear, disappearing into the sharpness of his collar. "She was at the gala last year. Atlas spoke to her." He tapped a link to her Wikipedia page, skimming it.

"And? Is she of any use to us?"

"Hm? Of course not, Mori, she's being investigated for fraud. And treason, by the looks of it." He handed the phone back to her, the tab now closed and the browser returned to Reina's original search. "Oops," he added, and continued walking, moving to cross the street as Reina hurried to catch up.

"*Oops*?" she echoed in disbelief. "What does *oops* mean?"

He didn't slow down. "We have an errand to run, Mori. Did you not say this was the only Forum event for the month on Nothazai's public calendar?"

Only about seven hundred times, the first six hundred and ninety-nine of which had been like pointlessly singing an aria. Dragging Callum away from London was like pulling teeth, as if the farther he got from Tristan the more he lost a sense of purpose. Reina had only gotten her way this time by assuring him that surprising Nothazai for purposes of retribution and/or extortion was very much up his alley, and potentially quite fun. "Oh, so now you conveniently care about Nothazai?"

"Of course I care. I've always cared." He was prickly, agitated. Interesting. This was a side of him she rarely saw but knew immediately was worth unraveling.

"What did you do to that woman?" she asked, intrigued. "And don't say nothing."

He grunted something in response.

"What?"

"I said, how much longer before you give up and reply to Varona?" he asked loudly. "I know you're starting to cave."

Yeah, like that was going to work. "*Assuming* Parisa lets Dalton off his leash, which she won't," said Reina, "then Varona's going to do his little experiment, fail, and realize he needs my help, end of story. Answer the question."

"Ah, so you *do* require groveling." Callum looked pleased. "I've always suspected that about you."

"Who is she?" Reina pressed again. "If she was at the gala last year, she's obviously someone important. Is she in the Society?"

"No."

"The Forum?"

He was silent.

"Callum," Reina growled, and he came to a sudden stop.

"Remember when I told you that my magic doesn't have rules?"

Reina paused in a combination of pure surprise and a near run-in with a pedestrian. "What?"

"My magic." He looked different than usual, even with the characteristic effervescence of illusion. Reina racked her brain for what this particular expression was and couldn't think of anything. "It doesn't . . ." Callum hesitated. Intriguing. Very un-Callum. "I can't control the outcome," he finally said. "I can push something, or pull it, but I can't always determine which way it'll go after I interfere."

"Wait." *Remorse,* that's what it was. Fascinating. "Are you saying you did something to her?"

"I think so." He grimaced and looked away, glancing at the building they'd paused beside. It looked like all the other buildings on the high street. "We're here, by the way."

Ah, but as far as stealthily plotted ambushes went, this errand could wait five minutes. "What do you mean you *think* you did something to her? Shouldn't you know?"

"I was a little compromised," he said testily.

"You mean drunk?"

He dropped his chin to glare at her. "Fine. Yes. I was drunk. She'd shown up to kill Atlas and decided not to. I could feel her giving up, so I turned the dial up." He looked away.

Reina stared at him. "What dial?"

"Does everything have to have a name, Mori? It's fucking magic, I don't know. Her purpose, her . . . *joie de vivre,*" he said in a sardonic tone. "It was fading, so I turned it back up."

Reina felt a sharp stab of annoyance at the outcome of this obviously poor decision. "Is she one of the people hunting us now?"

"Obviously not." Callum gestured to her phone with an irritated flick of his wrist. "She's under federal investigation. If she's not currently in jail, she will be soon."

"Because you put her there," Reina realized. "You . . . you made her do things?"

"No, I made her *want* to *continue* to do things," Callum corrected. "How was I supposed to know what those things would be? I didn't tell her to go out and do crime," he muttered gruffly. "That was entirely her decision."

Reina arched a brow. "You really think it's defensible? You essentially drove her insane."

"I didn't drive her *insane.* She got reckless and stopped being careful. That's just, I don't know, a natural feature of her personality regardless of my intervention. She used to be an activist," he added. "She has a public record."

"None of which you knew about at the time." Reina wondered what was happening to her. She felt a stirring of something she couldn't name. A sensation in her chest that felt a lot like weeds growing higher, bursting up from the cracks in the ground.

"Are you scolding me? You're the one using those exact powers now. You have been for months. I warned you things wouldn't always go as planned—"

"Let's just go inside." Reina's heart was hammering in her chest at the prospect of something. Consequences, possibly.

But Callum had been intoxicated when he did that, whatever he'd done to the professor. He had acted alone and impulsively. Reina, however, had a plan. She had many plans. She didn't run around lighting people on fire without calculating the risk of what went up in flames.

The man at the front desk said something in French, probably asking for their credentials, but he quieted at a glance from Callum, who hadn't even removed his sunglasses. Reina's pulse was still a little fast, just enough to make her throat dry. She cleared it and looked at Callum—a long look, for something she wasn't sure she'd find—until they stepped into the lift side by side.

"I told you," he said again. Less angrily this time.

The lift rose with a quiet whir, dinging when they reached their intended floor.

Reina let out a reluctant sigh.

"Yeah," she finally said. "I know."

They stepped out of the lift in near synchronicity, reaching the landscape of an open-plan floor below a series of glass panes, skylights. The shadows fell over a sea of empty desks in sharp lines, like paper cranes.

"Hello. Welcome to the French offices of the Forum." A woman at the reception desk greeted them in English, her accent softening the consonants. "Nothazai's in a meeting. He'll be with you shortly."

Nobody was supposed to notice them, much less be aware they intended to speak to Nothazai. Reina balked, glancing at Callum for confirmation that he'd done this. He looked back at her with a tiny shake of his head.

"Have a seat," the receptionist said warmly. "I'll bring you some coffee. Unless you prefer tea?"

"No." Reina would have been more polite if she felt the receptionist was acting of her own volition. Nobody should have known they were coming. This reminded her of Callum's work, though they'd come at least far enough as a unit that Reina believed him when he said he hadn't done something.

"Very well, some lemonade instead," the receptionist said, stepping out from behind the desk to disappear behind an unmarked door.

Reina turned to Callum, eyeing the evidence of confusion furrowed between his brows. "Is she dangerous?"

"Her? No. She's on autopilot." Precisely as Reina had guessed. "As far as I can tell she doesn't even know she's awake."

"What about—"

"Nothazai? If he's a threat, I'd say we're well-equipped to handle it." Callum glanced around, then took a seat in one of the leather armchairs. "She said to wait, so let's wait."

"Are you sure we shouldn't—"

"Why spoil the surprise, Mori?" He sounded disgruntled, perhaps because it was the second surprise of the day. "Just sit down. If we have to kill someone, then we kill someone. It's just another fucking Tuesday." His voice was dull, more perfunctory than wry.

"It's Monday." Reina sat warily and he glared at her. "Fine. Point taken."

He pulled his phone out of his pocket, clearly planning to ignore her and bother Tristan, or maybe just search for the best sushi nearby, who could say. Reina did the same, reopening the browser tab of news.

"Wessex Corporation acquires latest disruptor in consumer healthcare market."

"The Forum wins landslide victory in international human rights case."

"They really think they're the good guys," she murmured.

"Everyone does, Mori," Callum muttered beside her. "Everyone does."

Annoyed, Reina gave up on the news, instead choosing to open her social media app of choice. She had zero followers and followed only a dozen accounts herself, mostly news outlets, but right away there was a picture that reassured her. A dog and a baby curled up together, both wearing matching bonnets. The caption was the snoozing face, with the zzzz.

"Bae again?" asked Callum.

Reina looked up to find that he was watching her. "What?"

"Nothing." He was smiling faintly.

She sighed internally. How easily he could transition from fear and despair to suddenly possessing the upper hand. "His name is Baek, not Bae."

"Right, well, you'll forgive me for forgetting."

The account belonged to Congressman Charlie Baek-Maeda, an American politician up for reelection. He was young and beloved, handsome and well-spoken and the son of immigrant parents of modest means rather than the usual product of nepotism like the incumbent he'd ousted to win his district's congressional seat. Baek-Maeda's daughter Nora was ten months old, his rescue dog Mochi a constant fixture on the campaign trail. His social media followers—including Reina—numbered in the hundred thousands as a direct result of both.

"His puppy *and* his baby." Callum peered over admiringly. "Is that him playing guitar?"

Below the top three photos was a video from the campaign trail, in which Baek-Maeda played guitar while baby Nora, wearing headphones, was perched facing out in the harness he wore across his chest. "Is there a woman alive whose ovaries haven't exploded at this point?" Callum mused. "Minus yours, I suppose."

"Please don't discuss my ovaries," Reina muttered, scrolling.

"Do you have a crush on him? Tell me the truth." Callum sounded gleeful.

"I'm keeping an eye on him for political reasons. He's on the money committee."

"Appropriations committee," Callum corrected. "They're all money committees."

"Whatever. It's vocational."

"You like him." Callum's voice had taken on a wretched element of whimsy.

"I can *use* him."

"Both can be true."

Fine, Reina thought internally. Callum wasn't wrong. Baek-Maeda's supporters were idealistic enough to succumb to occasional glimmers of hope—truthfully, most people watching his press conferences could be convinced even without Callum and Reina's help—but she had a streak of benevolence toward Baek-Maeda himself. Possibly because his baby was cute, but more likely because his values aligned so beautifully with hers.

"He's your chosen one," Callum said sympathetically.

"Stop it."

"The gods all have favorites," Callum noted. "Why shouldn't you?"

She sighed heavily. "You're mocking me again."

"Yes, Mori, always. But am I wrong?"

No. Callum was right—she *did* have favorites. Baek-Maeda had come so far on his own, with no help from Reina or anyone. And it wasn't like she was asking him to slaughter his firstborn or build an ark. "Is it so bad for me to want to help him?"

"Of course not."

She glanced at Callum again, checking for a smirk. "It's not the same as you interfering with some war criminal," she warned.

"She wasn't a war criminal *until* I interfered," Callum said.

Reina frowned. "I assume you know that's not a defense."

"I," Callum said, "am generally undefendable. You already know that."

The office was eerily quiet. No plants, Reina realized, glancing at the floor beside her. There was a ring of something that must have at one point been a potted tree. It had obviously been removed recently—she could see traces of dirt.

In the resounding silence, Reina looked around, spotting more evidence of plants that had been removed. A decorative watering can on the receptionist's desk. Empty spaces on empty desks where sun would be most advantageous. "Are we in danger?"

"Nothing I can sense." Callum kicked one leg out, crossing it over the other.

"Could someone have tipped him off, somehow?"

"You haven't made a secret of your movements, Mori, but I doubt Nothazai could follow the threads just from watching. Just relax," Callum advised. "Don't waste your energy. You might need it later."

Fine. True. Reina sat back with a sigh. "Maybe I should start carrying around a small succulent."

"Don't they annoy you?"

"*You* annoy me."

Callum's phone buzzed in his pocket. He took it out, glanced at it, then returned it. Obvious who it was, as Callum only had one real correspondent.

"Are you going to reply?" Reina asked.

"Later." He looked at her. "Are you?"

He meant to Nico, possibly, or more generally to Parisa. Not that Reina had heard from her since the last message, which had been months ago.

Still, she kept asking herself the same thing. "Me? I'm busy."

"That's not an answer."

Agreed, it wasn't. "I don't owe you an answer."

"And yet I've been so generous with answers today, have I not?"

Reina turned to face him. "Why was she there to kill Atlas?" she asked tangentially. "The war criminal doctor."

"She's a professor. And he's the head of a secret society guarding an infamous magic library, so." Callum flicked a glance at her. "Kind of a nobrainer, Mori."

She frowned. "What would killing him have done?"

"I don't owe you an answer," Callum replied. She glared at him, and he laughed. "I don't know," he admitted. "Nothing, I guess. It felt personal."

"In what way?"

He didn't answer. She was about to push him, to prod him along like the stubborn cow he was, when the unmarked door opened again and Reina jumped.

"Miss Mori? Mr. Nova?" said the receptionist, holding a glass of sparkling lemonade in each hand. She shouldn't have known who they were, as they were both more illusioned than usual for the task of entering the serpent's den, but by then it was obvious something had interfered with their best laid plans. How nefarious that interference would ultimately be remained to be seen, though, as none of their previous assassins had offered them refreshments. "Right this way, please."

Reina glanced at Callum again, wondering if she should be more concerned. He stood with a shrug, taking the glass of lemonade, then gestured for Reina to go first. "No," she hissed at him, pointedly refusing the proffered glass, because no one practical consumed food from one's enemies, or the Underworld.

"Fine." Callum strode forward, following the receptionist, whose high heels clacked against the marble floor. "If it's booby-trapped, I'll scream 'ahhhhh.' That can be the signal."

"Shut up." The receptionist gave no indication of hearing them, leading them first through a corridor at the end of the bright, airy lobby, then taking a left to pause before an office door that had been left ajar.

She didn't enter, merely gesturing them in. "Nothazai will see you now," she said with a smile, before turning around and retreating the way she'd come, Reina's lemonade still clutched in one hand.

When the receptionist had disappeared around the corner, Callum pushed the door farther open, revealing another sun-filled room. An office, glass panes, elegant leather furniture, a desk.

"Oh," Callum said, pausing so abruptly Reina nearly crashed into his back.

"Oh indeed," came a voice behind the desk, and Reina groaned aloud.

"You." The figure behind the desk wasn't the man who'd once tried recruiting Reina to the Forum.

It was a woman.

A *specific* woman.

"Surprise," said Parisa Kamali, lifting a pair of gold high heels onto the desk one by one, propping one delicate ankle atop the other. Her dark hair was pushed back by a pair of sunglasses remarkably similar to the ones resting in Callum's breast pocket, and her dress, a blue so pale it might have been gray, was as immaculate as ever.

She looked unchanged. Reina could think of no reason for the thud in her chest aside from some belated pulse of fear, or a renewed one of loathing.

"Where's Nothazai?" asked Reina with a growl. Callum set down his glass and pulled out a chair, falling into it. Reina did not do the same. She had no plans to make herself comfortable, something she hadn't been for months and certainly wouldn't be now, even though she struggled to imagine somewhere safer than wherever Parisa Kamali was. She struggled, in fact, to imagine Parisa Kamali nervous or scared or even properly threatened by anyone who wasn't Reina herself, who'd once stabbed her in a projection that felt like a dream. Still, Reina's pulse had yet to slow.

"Oh, for fuck's sake, sit down," said Parisa, glancing at Reina.

She hadn't realized that she could forget how beautiful Parisa actually was until the surprise of it landed like a blow. "Fuck you," said Reina.

"Ladies, please," said Callum.

"Fuck you," said Reina and Parisa in unison, to Callum's apparent delight.

"Works every time," he chuckled to himself, earning a glare.

"Sit," said Parisa.

Reina, much to her displeasure, sat. "Where is he?"

"Nothazai? He cleared out a few hours ago, not long after we had some words. Pâté?" Parisa offered, sliding a plate across the desk. Callum sat up for a bite, which Reina obviously ignored.

"Did you really make us wait in the lobby for no reason?" she growled.

"No," Parisa corrected. "I made you wait in the lobby for one very important reason, which was my amusement."

"Don't antagonize her, Parisa, you'll only make her more difficult to persuade," Callum warned, sampling a spot of liver from the edge of his thumb.

"Fuck you," Parisa assured him once again, cordially nudging a plate of frites his way. "Anyway, you really should learn your lesson from this. You're incredibly easy to predict and even easier to follow." She zeroed in on Reina. "What exactly was your plan here?"

"He's trying to kill us," Reina said bluntly. "My plan was to ask him—" Callum snickered, and Reina glared at him. "—to stop."

"Ah. Well, you don't have to worry about Nothazai anymore," Parisa said with a shrug. "I have a feeling he's seen the light."

Absurdly, Parisa killing one of Reina's would-be assassins on Reina's behalf made Reina want to have killed Parisa's first. Or potentially Parisa herself. The balance of power was all amok again. Was Reina supposed to now grovel in thanks? She considered what would make Parisa angriest and decided it was choosing not to play. So, Parisa had taken the time to meet them here? That could only mean she wanted something.

Whatever it was, she wouldn't get it.

"Fine. Enjoy." Reina rose to her feet. "We're leaving."

Callum, unfortunately, did not take the cue. He raised a small handful of frites, examining them. "You don't happen to have any—?"

"Here." Parisa pushed a small saucer of aioli toward him. "Reina, sit down."

"Whatever you want, I'm not interested," Reina said.

"That's an outright lie. You're so interested you can barely think. Sit." Parisa's dark eyes met Reina's expressionlessly. "I need to talk to you about Rhodes."

"I'm offended you're not including me in this conversation," remarked an idly chewing Callum.

"Only because I already know your stance on the matter. We need to kill her," Parisa continued to Reina, tonally unchanged. "I don't like it, but it has to be done."

"Oh, fine," said Callum, as Reina let a beat of confusion pass.

"I'm sorry, what?" Reina felt herself sit down again. "I thought this was about something else."

When she'd first read Parisa's messages—the ones she had not bothered to respond to and had not thought about—had not thought about *that much,* anyway—Reina had assumed Parisa's game centered around the experiment Dalton had been researching, Nico's so-called Sinister Plot. The one about cosmic inflation, creating new worlds, the spark of life that Reina had already proven she could make. At first, Reina had foolishly allowed herself to believe it might have been Atlas reaching out to her, admitting at last the nature of his ambitions for which Reina had been carefully selected, and she had been fully prepared to say no. Or, in moments of total fantasy, to be gently and luridly flattered in a way that would still—probably—end with no.

But now, knowing it was Parisa, even the fantasy was out of the question. Creating worlds for someone so fundamentally uninterested in the contents of this one did not feel wise, nor particularly responsible. Parisa had not accepted the Society's invitation to save the world or even fix it; like Callum, Parisa did not believe it could be fixed. *Unlike* Callum, however, Parisa was motivated, competent, and angry.

Not a chance that Parisa's endgame was anything short of personal tyranny.

"Says the woman who is actively manipulating public elections," remarked Parisa.

"I have my reasons," Reina muttered.

"So do I." Parisa considered her for another long moment. "Look, I changed my mind," she said in a tone Reina might have called honest if she believed that to be within the realm of possibility. From Parisa, honesty could only ever be tactical. "The experiment is a bad idea. And regardless, we have more pressing concerns."

"We?" Unbelievable.

"Has Atlas tried contacting you yet?" Parisa asked, sitting upright and folding her hands beneath her chin.

Reina knew Parisa already knew the answer and loathed her powerfully, anew. Reina resented that in arranging this meeting, Parisa had intentionally placed them like this, hierarchically, as if only her opinion mattered. As if only her voice had a right to be heard. "Why should Atlas contact me? Our time at the archives is finished. I have other plans, none of which include him. And if you're trying to dissuade me from the sinister plot" (damn it, Nico) "there's no need to worry about it. The pieces are incomplete whether Rhodes suddenly becomes amenable to it or not. They still need me, and they definitely need Dalton. Atlas will never convince me. The others will never convince you to let Dalton do it for anyone but you. As far as I can tell, we're at an impasse," Reina concluded, "so the experiment is already dead."

"So to summarize, your answer is 'no,' which I find very troubling," Parisa observed aloud, turning to Callum. "Don't you think so?"

He shrugged in tacit agreement. "I had my suspicions we'd be subjected to further philosophical posturing from Atlas by now, but Reina's still doing well on her own, so maybe not."

This again. Callum had already warned Reina that Atlas would come to persuade her to his side—to be a weapon deployed at his bidding, just as everyone had always expected of Reina, who could do so little on her own without the (usually shrill, plant-speaking) demands of someone else—only at the moment she'd lost all hope. Parisa had made the same offer, and come to think of it, so had Nothazai, once.

Maybe the mistake everyone else had made was in assuming that Reina would ultimately fail, which she had not. She would not, and *of course* she wouldn't. She had gone so far as to align herself with Callum Nova just to make sure that apparent destiny would never come to pass.

Nico she would forgive when the time was right; someday, when thinking of the year without him hurt her less. Eventually, her disappointment in his underestimation of her friendship would no longer be relevant, and it would pass. But she had already made good on everything Atlas had promised her the day he walked into her Osaka café, and if he had not found her worthy of confiding in before now, then she had no plans to reroute her design for his benefit. Her powers may not have always felt like hers to use, but they were hers to ally if and when she chose to.

She had already taken what she needed from Atlas. There was no further value to being his choice.

"The merit of Reina's success or failure is a theoretical exercise for another day. Presently, we all have a very real problem. I talked to Rhodes," Parisa continued, turning her attention to Reina again. "She's back."

"I know." Reina could feel herself muttering again.

"She's not the same," Parisa said, before reconsidering. "Or maybe she's exactly the same and that simply wasn't a problem before. Moral inflexibility can look like virtue in certain lights. But it is very much a problem now."

"What changed your mind?" Callum asked, ostensibly pleased by the turn of events. "You're the one who went out of your way to make sure your little lamb stayed out of trouble when the requisite murder-plotting was afoot. If you hadn't, she'd be dead already."

Arguably false, even in Reina's mind. Perhaps for that reason Parisa was still looking at Reina when she answered Callum's question. "Maybe Rhodes changed my mind. Maybe the fact that you're still alive and of apparent use to society changed my mind. Does it matter? I'm complex, Callum, it happens. I'm capable of changing my path when circumstances are no longer applicable. Rhodes, however, is not." Parisa reached daintily for a fry. "She knows something, something bad, and even Varona knows that someone has to die," she said quietly, as if Reina might have forgotten. "It's either one of them or one of us."

"We're not an us," Reina said at the same time Callum said, "I had a thought I might kill Tristan. You know, for fun."

"Please don't waste my time," Parisa said to Callum before turning back to Reina, saying, "We're an 'us' insofar as we're the people most at risk. The other three went back to the Society for a reason. The archives can still use them; the house can still drain them. They might have longer before our collective breach of contract strikes, but the farther we travel from the archives, the more danger we're in. Not to mention the very many other threats that are tracking us everywhere we go."

"I thought you solved the Nothazai problem?" Reina said dryly, being intentionally difficult, which unfortunately Parisa already knew, because it no longer seemed to land.

"We already know that Atlas didn't fulfill his ritual and it killed everyone else in his cohort," Parisa said. "All six of us are alive. The archives are owed a body."

"I can kill you right now," suggested Reina. "Save us a lot of mess."

"Yes, you could," Parisa agreed. "It'd be a waste of this dress, but fine."

Their momentary standoff was disrupted by Callum, who had returned his attention to the plate of frites.

"What changed?" he asked again. "Why Rhodes?"

"I always told you she was dangerous." Parisa drummed her fingers on the desk. "Of course, previously I meant it in the sense that she ought to live and you shouldn't, because she had potential she hadn't yet reached and yours had a ceiling we already knew. I can see now that I was wrong to trust the scale of that potential. And clearly," she said with pointed deliberation, "if someone should die for the crime of being dangerous, you were always the absolute worst choice."

"Insult taken," Callum said. "And I'm telling you, I'm going to kill Tristan."

"When?" Parisa asked with obvious exasperation.

He doused a fry in aioli. "I'm getting around to it."

"Murder threats," Parisa said tartly, "are not an appropriate seduction."

"Have you tried?" Callum said through a mouthful of food.

"Yes, Nova, I'm not an amateur—"

Something else was bothering Reina. Something flimsy, but something nonetheless.

"Why are you asking me?" she cut in, interrupting Callum and Parisa's argument.

She felt Parisa in her thoughts, probably moving things around in her brain. "I asked you a question," Reina said irritably. "Just answer it, and maybe I'll answer yours."

Parisa's glare was impatient. "I don't understand the relevance of your question."

"The relevance? No relevance. It's just a question. You put in all this effort to find me, to contact me—to *convince* me—when you're the only one of us who's actually seen Rhodes, and therefore you could have killed her on the spot. Unless you didn't because you couldn't," Reina realized, "in which case there *is* someone less dangerous than Callum, and it's you."

"Zing," said Callum in an appreciative whisper.

"Shut up," said Reina and Parisa in unison, at which point Parisa rose to her feet.

Her mouth was tight with something. Annoyance, probably, that Reina had made a salient point—which Reina was *always* doing, for anyone properly keeping score. It was everyone else who didn't make any sense.

"The ritual is arcane, not merely contractual," said Parisa tightly. "There's a reason we studied intent. The purpose of the elimination is to derive a sacrifice worthy of the knowledge provided to us." Her lovely mouth was uncharacteristically thin. "We all chose Callum. That choice was significant. We should all choose Rhodes. The arrow is most deadly only when it's most righteous. If that sacrifice is going to save the rest of us this late in the game, then it has to be done right."

Interesting. Very interesting. The analysis was sound—Parisa wasn't an idiot, nor was she inadequate as a medeian or a scholar—but that wasn't the interesting part.

"You're lying," Reina deduced with a sense of triumph, and when Callum did not contradict her—he didn't agree with her, either, but Reina was going to take her wins where she could get them—she felt a smile cross her face. "You can't do it, can you? Because you're afraid of Rhodes."

Parisa's face went motionless.

"Maybe I am. Maybe you should be." Reina understood from experience that Parisa would leave soon. She would leave because Reina had gotten close, too close to the truth for comfort. Reina knew something now that she shouldn't, which was that Parisa wasn't capable of taking care of this on her own. Because Reina was supposed to be the useless one, the pointless one, the one who wasn't in control of her own magic—but in the end, it was Parisa who had come out of the Society house more powerless than she had been before.

She had walked in capable of murder. She had walked out full of softness and regret.

"You came to *beseech* me. To petition me like an *actual god*." Reina couldn't keep laughter out of her voice. "You tried to make me think I was crazy for even trying to change things, but I wasn't. I'm not. I can make this world different. I *chose* to change this world, but you can't do that. You aren't capable. You never were."

It all seemed so ridiculous now. Reina's rivalry with Parisa, or whatever it was that had made her care so much for so long about what Parisa felt, what Parisa thought. It was a game that Reina had been playing for over two years, but now she understood that she had always been winning it. She had already won.

Parisa's face was drawn. Callum was silent.

"Is that what you think?" Parisa asked.

"You know what I think," Reina replied.

There was a moment when the pulse in her chest fumbled. When there should have been some sardonic reply, some cutting remark, and there wasn't one. Parisa was silent for a long time, too long, and eventually Callum rose to his feet.

"Come on, Mori." He nudged Reina with his shoulder.

No, Reina thought, staring at Parisa. *Say something. Have the last word, I know you want it. Try to take it from me.*

Fight back.

Parisa didn't answer. She looked tired.

She looked—

"Mori." Callum beckoned her with another motion of his chin. "We're done here. Let's go."

Parisa didn't stop him. She said nothing. Victory was Reina's, or something like that, but it wasn't satisfying. It felt more like a forfeit.

No, it felt like an ending—that was the word. Everything was over now, finished, the end. There had been no latent threats, no promise of danger, no warnings to dog her around, no further games to be played. No *fear me, Reina* to keep her company in the dark. The last look on Parisa Kamali's face had been one that Reina had seen her wear only once, just before stepping off a manor house roof.

And now Reina would never have to see her again.

Reina ambled after Callum warily, nearly pausing twice, a third time, to leave some final comment, to win the game more, to make it harder, escalate it. To uncover a new level, something else to fight for. Not that Reina didn't have enough on her plate as it was. Injustice would take a lifetime to fight. This world would take far more than six months to fix. Reina had a to-do list the length of which could span the full diameter of the globe, and she did not need Parisa Kamali to give her a reason to stay in this room.

But she waited for one, just in case.

Still, the office was a finite space. It had limits, and eventually Reina crossed the threshold, leaving Parisa motionless behind her. Reina's footsteps echoed beside Callum's as they exited the lobby. Parted ways with the receptionist, sweat glistening now on Reina's forgone glass of lemonade.

"I'm not wrong," Reina said, stepping into the lift. She meant, of course, that nothing she'd said had been inaccurate, and it wasn't. Parisa *was* afraid of Libby Rhodes. She *had* come to Reina only because she had no other options. Reina's criticisms of Parisa's motivations were tactile, definable, real, and Reina had not been mistaken.

Callum's sunglasses were already on, his shrug nearly imperceptible beside her.

"To err is human," he commented ambiguously as the lift doors shut, eclipsing the brightness of the office and swallowing them up.

· INTERLUDE ·

A Book Club Guide to
Atlas Blakely's Rise to Power

1. After Atlas discovers the Alexandrian Society's terms of initiation (i.e., the elimination clause), he and Ezra decide to fake Ezra's death in order to avoid committing murder. Atlas claims the point of this deceit is to overthrow and eventually revolutionize the Alexandrian Society. Do you think Atlas Blakely is telling the truth?

2. As researcher, Atlas lives alone in the Society manor house for an extended period of time. During this time in isolation, Atlas's resentment for the Society grows and his clinical depression worsens. Do you think this is why he allows his fellow cohort to die repeatedly in ignorance rather than confess to them the truth? Do you agree with Atlas that he is essentially a murderer?

3. When Atlas discovers that his failure to fulfill the terms of initiation has begun killing the members of his cohort, his personal motivation undergoes a dramatic shift. The possibility of a parallel universe and respective alternative outcomes (i.e., his own personal redemption) begins to override his philosophical opposition to the Society. Is this a healthy emotional way to process his sense of loss?

4. After Dalton Ellery determines that the Society's archives will not give him the information he needs in order to produce the quantum fluctuations that summon alternate universes, he asks Atlas to attempt a form of telepathic surgery that obscures his true ambitions from the rest of his conscious mind. Despite Atlas's private certainty that such a thing will 1) hurt, 2) cause irreparable damage to Dalton's consciousness, and 3) be a potential danger to the world at large, he agrees. Should someone have killed Atlas as a baby?

5. Before Atlas performs significant, irreversible damage to Dalton's consciousness, he decides to test it on someone he cares less about. He chooses his father. Rather than isolate a portion of his father's consciousness as he later does for Dalton, however, Atlas instead creates a loop inside his father's thought processes, like a hamster wheel that overrides his natural thoughts. Every month, like clockwork, his father has the sudden, undeniable compulsion to visit a dilapidated flat in

London with groceries and a vase of fresh flowers, and thus he is forced to remember on an unresolvable loop that the destruction of a woman's mind is entirely his fault. Does the fact that this is true and richly deserved justify Atlas's decision to punish his father telepathically? He knows what this will do to his father's mind; he has already seen it happen naturally to his mother's. Is permanently damaging his father's brain a healthy emotional way for Atlas to process his rage?

6. When Atlas performs the necessary telepathy to sequester part of Dalton's consciousness, he can tell it is physically painful to Dalton. In fact, Dalton screams "stop, stop, you have to stop" no fewer than five times throughout the process. Even when the troublingly powerful animation of Dalton's ambition taunts to Atlas "you fucking idiot don't you understand there's no such thing as spontaneous creation do you have any idea what you've done," Atlas continues. At what point did Atlas Blakely relinquish his soul in exchange for cosmic omnipotence?

7. In order to become the next Caretaker, Atlas Blakely telepathically overpowers his own Caretaker, corrupting his cognitive process and damaging his brain for the remainder of his life. Does Atlas's justification that William Astor Huntington was born to a life of leisure and would certainly retire to a convalescence of leisure actually mean anything to William Astor Huntington's family members? Does it matter? Does anything actually matter at all?

8. Do you think Atlas Blakely is a bad person?

9. Do you think the fact that Atlas Blakely is definitely a bad person means that he should suffer?

10. Do you think the only defensible moral outcome to this story is Atlas Blakely's death?

11. Is that a joke?

12. Is *that* a joke?

13. When Atlas Blakely opens the house's wards to allow Ezra Fowler's final entry, he does so on the gamble that Ezra, who is morally opposed to killing and unwisely allied with several people with arguably more detestable motives than Atlas's, can be persuaded back to Atlas's side. Is Atlas the asshole?

14. Although Atlas has no way of knowing that Libby Rhodes will overhear Ezra admitting that logically he has no choice but to kill her now, Atlas's provocation in that moment is consistent with the petty bullying of Ezra that has worsened over the course of twenty miserable, secretive years. Objectively speaking: Atlas believed that Libby would return;

he could have predicted, then, that her return *could* have happened at any moment, including that one. Thus, while Atlas cannot have known with certainty that he created the circumstances leading to Ezra's murder, he cannot have reasonably ruled it out. Does this mean his actions definitively killed Ezra, bringing his murders up to five?

15. How many lives has Atlas destroyed in pursuit of power? If more than one (and it is definitely more than one) does that make him a worse person than his father? Does it make him worse than Ezra Fowler?

16. Is there such a thing as too much power?

17. Or is power just a body count after all?

V

RATIONALISM

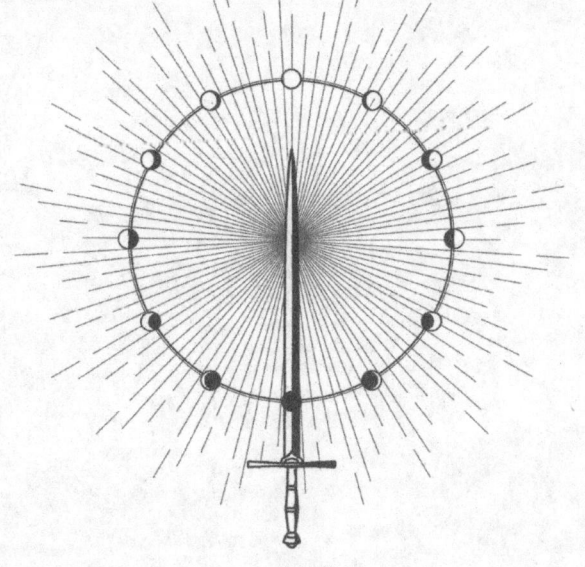

· PARISA ·

"Where were you?"

Dalton's voice startled her from the corner of the rented flat she still wasn't accustomed to. Part of her had been practical, determined to find a place for her things, for the remnants of herself she kept mislaying on the floor. Impractical lingerie, expensive shoes. She'd resumed her life as it was before, with one exception: the obligation to another human being, who apparently chose to haunt her like a ghost, sitting in the dark beside the open window.

"I told you, I was dealing with Nothazai." It was a simple matter, simpler even than whatever Reina had planned, which was the equivalent of forced entry. Reina was going to bulldoze her way in, break down the door, put Nothazai's only option to him like a gun to his head: fuck off or die trying. Parisa preferred a smoother opening than that. "I'm tired of knowing there's so many people out there who want me dead," she said, bending to unstrap one shoe. "I had a hunch that taking the Forum off the board would resolve a significant portion of my daily inconveniences, and I was right. Now I'll only have to sort out the reprisal of the archives and Atlas Blakely, assuming I make it long enough to try."

Dalton rose from the chair and came toward her, shirt unbuttoned, barefoot. He lived like a poet or an artist these days, always distracted, always in motion. Half-drunk cups of espresso littered the balcony, piles of books towering beside the hearth.

It was all very French between them now. Pastries and sex in the mornings, red wine and maniacal ramblings at night.

"Anything else?" he said expressionlessly. Parisa's impulse to lie snagged on her supreme ambivalence, the place where her passion used to be.

"Yes." She stepped down, one shoe off. "I spoke to Reina and Callum."

Dalton's expression was stony as she bent for the other shoe. "And were they any help?"

Again, she contemplated lying. Not that there was a better lie.

"No," she said, pausing to straighten. Her head hurt. It was constantly hurting now, which she blamed—at least in part—on Dalton. Parisa had always been subjected to the thoughts of other people, which had mostly been background noise, annoyances, like elevator music but usually no worse than the buzzing of a fly inside her ear. Dalton's thoughts weren't like that.

She hadn't realized that what she'd liked so much about him before had been the silence, the quietness inside her head whenever he was around. Now it was increasingly variable, loud and soft, shrieks and blasts of things, memories or ideas, she couldn't tell which.

"You don't need them," Dalton said.

You know where to find me if you need me, Callum had said in her head before he and Reina had departed the Forum's French offices.

I don't need you, Parisa had replied.

Fine. Suit yourself.

She was a sore loser, it turned out. And there was no doubt she was losing, two steps back for each step forward. Somewhere, Atlas was being tweedily mirthful.

"I know," said Parisa, but Dalton shook his head.

"No, I mean for the ritual," he explained, which gave her pause. "You don't need them," he repeated. "It's not a team effort—just choose someone. I didn't consult the rest of my cohort before I picked up the knife."

Parisa remembered the feel of the blade under Dalton's palm. The memory he'd subjected her to, the palace he built to lure her in.

Her specifically? Maybe not. But if not her, then someone. Possibly anyone.

(Which wasn't any more devastating a thought tonight than it would have been if she'd had it this morning. Or so she told herself, for now.)

"You won't like it," Dalton said. His thoughts were muddled and prickly with disappointment, something she suspected had to do with her. Seeing herself through his eyes was no worse, technically, than with anyone else. To him she was still beautiful, still the object of formidable desire, but she was also something that wouldn't obey, a problem in need of fixing.

A bug in the code, she thought grimly.

"You won't enjoy it," Dalton continued, "but it will have to be done, and the sooner you get it over with—"

"I can kill Rhodes." She might need to, though practicality suggested one of the others might be easier, less protected. Less paranoid, and therefore more likely to be caught. "I can kill any one of them." Nico would be easy, Parisa thought with some perversity of fondness. She'd open the door and he'd scurry right in, wagging his tail, saying *thank you, I love you, bye.*

"Can you? You couldn't kill the dreamer," Dalton pointed out, referring to Nico's beloved Gideon. "And you considered him a risk at the time."

"That was different. I didn't need him to die." She finally took off the other shoe, rubbing at the indentation of the strap that had dug into her ankle. "This time I do."

You'll have to kill them to keep yourself alive. She'd been warned from the start, and yet how different things seemed to her now. How much she'd been willing to do before, which now felt vaguely exhausting and perfunctory, like a Pap smear. Something invasive for the benefit of her long-term health.

"You're not giving up, are you?" said Dalton, and Parisa looked up, seeing another little blur of herself from his eyes. This one not so lovely.

"Giving up?"

"The empath helped you kill yourself once," Dalton observed. Parisa shuddered at the snub of it, the wording. The others had always referred to it as a murder, as if Callum had been the one holding the weapon, but ultimately Dalton was more right.

Of course, Dalton was only right because Parisa had told him that, using those words herself. She'd put that knowledge in his hand, lighting it like a match. If it burned her now, that was her own fault. Such was the nature of intimacy. Of honesty, which she had never bothered with before.

"I don't want to die," she told him irritably. "I just want to be left alone."

Another whorl of things, a fraction of lucidity. "That's what he wanted, too."

"I'm not—" Parisa felt herself snap, then forced herself down, quieting the sensation inside her chest that she already knew to be unwise. "I'm not the same as Atlas Blakely," she said through gritted teeth. "I don't need my own multiverse just to feel virtuous about making an exit door. I don't want to give up. I just want—"

To live my life, she thought to say, but even she could hear how empty that sounded. Ten years, more than ten, and she kept saying the same thing, as if there was a finish line of happiness she still couldn't touch. An ending that kept shifting out of reach.

Dalton seemed sympathetic. He came up behind her with a gentler sense of welcome, like maybe he'd rather be nuzzling her shoulder and feeding her sugar cubes from his hand than arguing with her just then. She leaned back against his chest, allowing a moment of complacency, something to preempt an episode of calculation.

A plan. She always, always had a plan.

"I can't do it without the physicists," Dalton said in her ear, and Parisa sighed, turning to face him.

"Why *this* experiment?" she said in a grumble. Fine, so she was a sore loser, but she was a pragmatist, too. Someone, somewhere, had to come to their senses, to choose a different path when the one they were on left their husbands for dead.

"Won't there be other experiments? Better plans? The Forum is ripe for the taking," Parisa pointed out. "We could do it tomorrow. We could do it right now and I guarantee you, Nothazai wouldn't bat an eye—"

"This experiment is my birthright," Dalton said. "It's what I was born for."

Internally, Parisa sighed. Men and their greatness—their *callings*. Why was any of it her burden? Exhausting. "You can find a new purpose, Dalton, people do it every day—"

"No," he corrected brusquely. "It is *why I was born*."

Parisa fell silent, wondering if she ought to be paying attention. If perhaps it might be worth returning to an old reflex; feeling around in his mind like pouring herself into the cracks she knew lived in the foundation, the many weaknesses in the frame.

"Watch," he said.

Dalton sat down on the floor, cross-legged, like a small boy in a grown man's body, the muscle of his chest and torso outlined by the flickering of an invisible flame. It was still mostly dark in the flat, illuminated only by the twinkles of iconic streetlamps down below the open window. Only those and whatever Dalton was making. Whatever Dalton could do.

There was no explanation for what she saw, what she could see. It was like the glitching pixelation she'd once seen inside the castle Dalton had built into his brain, the princely cage he'd once been trapped in. But unlike then, Parisa knew this to be real life. She understood this to be real, and it was like a child's magic, something wonderfully alive, the way he made the darkness bend. He coaxed it, played with it, life from proverbial clay.

The way his hands moved looked familiar, the shape of them. She'd seen them that way before, sensual like that, passing over the curves she'd so long known and disregarded. He was molding the light, shaping it like a sculptor at the kiln.

It was only after his hands stopped moving—twitching from exertion, or maybe cramping with pain—that Parisa realized it wasn't just her imagination. He wasn't just re-creating the shapes of her curves. He was producing them from nothing.

She stepped toward him cautiously, tiptoeing forward to see what he'd made.

Her hair. Her mouth. Her hips.

"How did you—?"

Then the version of her lying on the floor suddenly opened its eyes, staring blankly up at Parisa, who scrambled backward in alarm. "Is that—?"

"She's alive," Dalton confirmed, rising to his feet and lowering a hand to the animation of Parisa, who accepted. It pulled itself up and stood, tilting its head to look blankly at the real Parisa, who suddenly needed a drink. Four drinks.

She stepped backward and the animation of her stepped forward. She walked in a slow circle around the flat, the animation of herself following her motions, turning with excruciating patience to keep a measured gaze on wherever Parisa was. She now understood what Dalton had meant over a year ago, how sure he'd been that only he could have created the animation of a grisly death that had been left behind in Libby Rhodes's place. Parisa had never seen anything like this—except for when she'd seen it then. The only difference was that the previous animation had been a corpse, and this one . . .

Telepathically speaking, there were sparks of something, maybe curiosity, probably something more like awareness. Synapses firing, maybe, if that were possible to do from thin air.

"Dalton," Parisa said in a low voice. "It doesn't have any thoughts." Not real ones. It wasn't like the voices in Reina's head, the plants who called her Mother. This thing didn't have a mother; didn't try to look for one.

"It's life," Dalton agreed. "Not brain."

"But you can't—" Parisa felt herself struggling to find the words for it, for her sudden need to vomit. "You can't produce life from nothing. No one can."

"I'm not," he said with a shrug. "I'm producing it from something. Atlas knew that. The archives knew it. That was the whole point of me staying on."

"But I thought your research was about the multiverse. A portal." Parisa's animation had lost interest in her. It was testing the use of its fingers and lips, practicing sultry poses. "I thought you wanted to make a new world."

"That was the *application* of my research," Dalton corrected. "That's what we intended to do with what I already know is out there." He seemed amused by her hesitation. "You don't light a match just to watch a matchstick burn, Parisa." A childish taunt, like a schoolyard bully.

"So then where do you get it from? Life." Parisa watched her animation begin to pout, then smile. Then widen its eyes with wonder. Then carefully test the arches of its feet, pointing its toes like a ballerina before taking a cautious step.

"That's the point of doing the experiment," Dalton said.

"So you don't actually know?" The animation took two steps, then locked its knees to push out its hips. A runway step, like the models from the noughties.

"I'm drawing it from somewhere. From something. There's a chance it's coming from something else out there—dark matter, the void, whatever you want to call it. The energy inside a vacuum is still energy, it still exists, and maybe I'm doing something with it. Or maybe I just killed something to bring this to life. Creation is entropy—cause enough chaos and maybe the sun will implode. Who knows."

Dalton shrugged again as Parisa finally tore her attention away from the animation, which was cycling through a sun salutation, framing its naked body around the absence of the sun.

"What?" she said. Her animation found her left shoe, picking it up by one strap.

"It's possible that opening one portal destroys another one," said Dalton. "There's no way to tell. We have to try it to find out. But the answer is out there, and I exist to find it. I exist because I'm the key. The bridge between whatever we are and something we can't yet see."

He looked at her hungrily, with an ache of guilelessness, with wonder. A small boy with a shiny new toy. Parisa had thought that so often when he looked at her, but now it was unnerving, because it implied something worse than innocence. It was undeveloped, empty of everything maturity was supposed to bring. Disappointment, yes. Disillusionment, yes, and pain, but also empathy. Compassion.

Self-control.

"I deserve an answer," Dalton said. "I let him cage me for ten years. I kept myself locked up, I behaved, I was good." *I was good.* Hadn't she said that once? Dalton was growling it while Parisa's animation suddenly stopped moving. It had donned both her shoes and fallen perfectly still, watching. Listening.

"The experiment has to be done properly." Dalton ticked them off on his artist's hands, his dexterous fingers: "Both the physicists. The naturalist. The seer. And me."

"Atlas needs me," Parisa realized suddenly. Dalton had said it before—used those exact words—but she understood why now.

She thought she'd understood when she saw the things that Libby had tried to hide from her, but Parisa was wrong, or half-wrong. Yes, Libby was the bug, but only now did Parisa understand why. She had seen glimpses of Libby's guilt, her need for validation, and presumed them to come from a place of self-defense, even selfishness—but that was Parisa's own bias. Parisa's own pain.

Parisa knew the constancy of self-destruction that came from selfish choices. Parisa, who had chosen herself over someone else's love, over living by the rules of so-called "moral" men—she understood that her selfishness was ugly. That however right she had been in her choices, they would still haunt her for the rest of her life, because they had necessarily come with pain. She had thought Libby's pain was similar, that Libby was hiding the things she didn't want the world to see, because Parisa knew what it was to be judged a selfish woman. Libby had asked what made Parisa's ambition purer, and Parisa had known the truth: it wasn't. But Parisa also knew what it was to be told she was too corrupt, too sinful, too impure to live, and she had chosen to do so anyway, because life was not something she had to be told she deserved.

But it hadn't been pain in Libby's mind. Parisa had seen the sense of something unresolved in Libby and presumed it to be guilt, but now she understood it was surety, absolution. It wasn't doubt. It was certainty, too much of it. The bright-shining conviction in her own rightness, blazing like zealotry to light the path ahead.

It was all too much; the shine of it hurt Parisa's head. It was too similar to the very certainty that Parisa now felt cleaving from herself, shucked from her like scales by the smallest of events—the loss of a man she hadn't loved enough.

But hadn't that always been the source of her danger? Not her magic, not her power, but her rootlessness—her willingness to light a match because she loved nothing on this earth too much to watch it burn? Certainty meant security of judgment. Certainty was polarity, as self-appointed judge. It wasn't unlike Reina's delusional sense of sureness, and yet it was totally different. Libby wanted to be a hero; Reina wanted to carry a hero's burden. On Reina, that kind of world-making purpose was more like a beacon of light. It was pointless, of course, it would never work, but it still might drive others to follow her—Callum already had. By contrast, what could possibly grow on the path that Libby Rhodes would raze?

In answer to her suffering, Libby Rhodes had conferred upon herself the right to be virtuous. To be, without question, right. And that was perilous. It was worth fearing. The most dangerous person in the room wasn't just whoever could still see where they were going—it was the person who couldn't be stopped.

And now, Parisa understood that it was exactly what Atlas believed of himself.

So, Atlas needed her. Parisa knew it now—she understood how simple it actually was. Atlas *did* need her, because he was at least wise enough to recognize his own weakness. Atlas wanted it too badly, and trusted her to do what was right.

Specifically, he had trusted her to realize that this experiment was extremely fucked up from every possible angle and yet she had missed it, missed every single sign, because as much as Atlas had known the sins he was committing, he had also wanted to get away with it. He had wanted to do something horrifically irresponsible and as an act of ineffectual self-sabotage, he'd chosen Parisa—someone who had the power to stop him but wouldn't. Someone far too selfish to actually say no.

Atlas had trusted her, and what had she done with that trust? He must have known she would misuse it. No wonder he hadn't bothered to hunt her. He didn't need to. His faith in her was pitted and flawed for a reason.

He must have known she'd let them both down.

She didn't realize that she was staring blankly at the animation of herself until she saw herself suddenly convulse. Dalton had reached over for the corkscrew, the one left beside an empty bottle of wine, and casually punctured the animation in the navel, almost comically. Like someone sticking a pin in a balloon. Parisa watched herself bleed out and turn blue and felt, suddenly, frozen. Libby had realized Parisa was nothing, Reina had known it all along, and now it was finally Parisa's turn. Finally, Parisa understood.

All this talk of worlds. Libby could try to make a new one. Reina could try to fix this one. They'd both be wrong, and they'd both come to the same conclusion she did now—that she was nothing and *so were they*—and still, Parisa could outlast them both until every hair on her head had turned gray, but for what?

For what?

"It's not real," Dalton said flatly, with something just shy of a laugh, like Parisa had been silly enough to believe in Santa Claus; like Dalton had caught her wishing on a star. The animation of Parisa had staggered to her knees and fallen forward, not even bracing for the impact. Her hair fell over her face, a pool of something that couldn't have been blood spreading thinly across the floor, molten like gold in the darkness until all that remained were the shoes.

Heart thundering in her chest, Parisa took a step backward. Another.

"Don't run," Dalton said.

She took a third step and Dalton shook his head.

"Stop." A warning. A fourth step. "Parisa. Listen to me. Whatever you think I might do—"

It wasn't what she thought he *might* do. It was what she could see very plainly he was *willing* to do, which was a vast unknown bracketed only by extremes that warped and flickered in his head. She supposed that by some definition telepathy was failing her for the first time in her life, because she couldn't say for certain what his next move would be. She felt, for the first time, a helplessness she hadn't known before, witnessing the presence of a danger sign with no specific instructions. Would Dalton kill her? No, probably not, he seemed opposed to death, but who better than Parisa could project the many creative outcomes that could be—would be—worse?

She had always known Dalton was dangerous. It wasn't that she'd been wrong about him but that she'd been right. She wanted to be dangerous, but she wasn't. Reina was right about her. She was good at having the last word but that was it, and that was nothing.

The only thing Parisa truly was was angry. She couldn't remember a time when she hadn't been; when things had seemed normal or fine. It was like she'd been born with a window to the world that nobody else could see, or that everyone else ignored, and it was a horror that she alone had lived with, like Cassandra and the fall of Troy. If Dalton had recognized something in her, or she in him, it was this—this feeling that she was put here, made this way, for something. It had to be for something, because otherwise it was just a fucking curse.

Her brother Amin was fine. Wealthy and fine. Her sister Mehr was married, three babies, she didn't appear to think about Parisa at all. The only person who had ever really been kind to Parisa had been Nasser, and he had always had an agenda. It wasn't different just because he called it love. Parisa had been grateful to him, first, and then repressed by him, and then guilty for what she'd taken from him; by the fact that she had accepted his kindness only to cut and run. But all along she knew what she really was, which was angry at him.

Everyone wanted to own her. Everyone wanted to control her. She was beautiful on the outside, designed to be looked at, but on the inside was a blackened mess of spite and jealousy and rage that she alone had known was ugly underneath it all. Maybe Reina had seen it. Parisa had thought at times that maybe Reina could, because Reina didn't look for beauty, didn't look for desire at all—but even if Reina *did* see her, that didn't make her truth less grisly. There were people capable of being seen and then there was Parisa, who would only ever be looked at. She'd thought Dalton was different, that she had found a partner in him, but he was still an arrow set in motion by Atlas Blakely, and she had never been the archer. She was just the fucking bow.

And Dalton was coming toward her now and Parisa understood very calmly that the magic she used against other people wouldn't work for her this time. There were too many severed pieces in his head, like he'd lit a pipe bomb inside his former self. Had he always been that way? Maybe he had—Atlas had certainly implied it, and maybe she'd always been wrong about Atlas Blakely being a liar. Maybe the only thing Atlas Blakely had ever really done was tell a despicable truth.

"Stop," Dalton said again, but Parisa heard *run*.

She turned to the flat's only door, hearing Dalton's blood rushing in his own ears, the way his senses were primed for a chase. Adrenaline, familiar as a pulse. She made as if to sprint through the door and instead pivoted, dropped to one knee, and punched him hard in the fucking ballsack with the full strength of her disappointment. She waited for him to fall to the ground before taking off toward the open window, thoughtless. Flying through it, wingless and barefoot, her skirt fluttering madly on the stillness of Parisian autumn air.

Physical magic wasn't her strong suit, but survival was. Parisa pulled back on the force of the night like a set of reins, which in turn yielded like an obedient steed, allowing her to drop to the ground as if she'd jumped a few feet instead of three stories. Then she took off running, hair clinging to the sweat on her neck, deciding to make a few changes in her life. No more dresses designed to be braless. Her life had been a constant series of escapes and she had to grow up and accept it, to live like it, like a person on the run.

Because this was the truth: she had killed herself once with Callum's help, and what she had told no one about that day was that she still remembered what it felt like. She remembered the fall, the teetering sense of oncoming relief—but it hadn't actually happened that way. It wasn't blissful, it wasn't ecstasy, there wasn't a climax. It was only a fall, and at the bottom of that leap was nothing. Maybe she had no purpose, and maybe that was fine. Maybe all Parisa had was rage and fear and maybe those things *were* ugly, maybe when the rest of her hair turned gray she'd be nothing but a shriveled-up ball of disappointment and pain, but that didn't have to cheapen her.

Maybe her only purpose was to survive, which was fucking difficult, and so maybe that was enough.

She'd left without her phone, without a wallet, without the motherfucking shoes. She stumbled and the blisters on her feet were raised and raw, and the hurt of it was temporarily blinding. She realized it was tears only belatedly, when she discovered that she had nowhere to run, nowhere to go. She didn't think Dalton would bother to go after her. He only wanted one thing, and Parisa was struggling to find the energy to stop him just to save the world right now. *Could* it end, really? No. The world would go on. Life as they knew it ended every day, little pieces of it at a time. Hope was robbed, peace was stolen, the world still turned regardless. They could all drop dead tomorrow and the planet's orbit would go on unchanged. Take it from any single one of Reina's plants.

Where the fuck was Atlas Blakely now? Parisa coasted to a stop, the flame in her chest burning and burning as she felt the presence of a threat, the constancy of it. Always someone these days, following her like a shadow. This one wasn't law enforcement; a medeian, she felt sure of it, listening to the drone of telepathic defenses. The would-be assassin shifted his jacket aside and Parisa clocked something she hadn't before—the logo on something she hesitated to call a handgun. This wasn't a normal mind, and therefore likely not a normal weapon. Was the insignia a *W*?

Didn't matter. Always someone, always something. She sent him away from her direction with what little of her energy remained.

You were supposed to give me more, she thought at Atlas angrily. She was supposed to have been able to stop running, to stop lying—two years with all the arcane knowledge in the world and she still didn't know how to live. *You promised me more than this, and me, I'm the idiot, I believed you when you said there was something else waiting for me. You didn't ask me if I needed meaning because you already knew, you should have known that my answer was yes.*

She wiped her eyes and laughed at the smear of black across her palm. Around her people were wondering if she'd gone insane, if they should call the police, if she needed help or if she was crazy, and she realized with a little spark of hysteria that despite all of that, despite it all, at least four people were still staring at her breasts. This was humanity! Why should she care anymore, why had she ever cared, what had the world ever done for her?

Why should it matter if Dalton swallowed them up and used their remains to remake the universe for his own twisted sense of purpose, why did it matter if Reina still believed in bending the whole thing to her will, what was the point of even trying, where should she go, what should she do, who should she become with the time she had left, which was ticking by, *ticktick-tick* like the clock in Tristan's heart, like the countdown to destruction that Parisa had caught a glimpse of inside Libby Rhodes's mind. There it went, another second, another, her feet on the pavement in aching, unsteady steps, just keep going, go. Go. Go.

Go.

Would anyone listen to her? No, yes, maybe. Maybe that was the part that was different, because she wasn't alone, not actually. At least one person had thrown her at least one life vest, so okay then. Okay. It would hurt, it would be shameful, someone would probably hold it against her for the duration of whatever obscurity she had left, but swallowing her pride would sting at first and then, eventually, it would fade.

This was it, the chronic condition—the only meaning Parisa had left in life. It wasn't a secret society, it wasn't an ancient library, it wasn't an experiment that had taken two decades to design, it was waking up every fucking morning and deciding to keep going. The tiny, unceremonious, incomparable miracle of making it through another goddamn day. The knowledge that life was mean and it was exacting. It was cruel and it was cursed; it was recalcitrant and precious. It was always ending. But it did not have to be earned.

Parisa shivered and tried to remember the thing in Libby's mind amid the wreckage; the specific thing that Libby hadn't wanted Parisa to see. Blood on the office floor, okay, so Libby had killed someone, that wasn't unexpected. Parisa had killed someone too, more than one someone, but there was something else, something more concrete in the realm of Libby's thoughts of Atlas Blakely. Something recent, knowledge she hadn't shared.

Of course—Atlas Blakely. Even the Caretaker had a history, a point of origin, some place with which to begin. If he wouldn't chase her, then Parisa would chase him. There, some velocity. A destination, or at very least a direction. A next step to take, if she chose to keep going.

Okay, Parisa thought, orienting herself. Okay.

Then she took off into the night.

· CALLUM ·

T

So, how goes the experiment preparation?

IN THE BEGINNING, THERE WAS ONLY DARKNESS.

AND THEN THERE WAS TRISTAN CAINE.

Don't tell me you're suddenly interested in the foundations of the universe.

Of course not. But unless my count is mistaken, you're currently surrounded by three idiots in their early twenties.

Mid-twenties.

Right, critical distinction. Now they're old enough to be aware of how stupid they are.

Isn't that all maturity is in the end? The gradual acceptance of personal idiocy?

You're feeling whimsical, I see. How many drinks have you had?

Two

Interesting. Rhodes isn't making you rest up for your impending miracle of cosmology?

We needed an outlet. Tension's been strange lately.

Between you and Rhodes?

You're so desperate to hear something. I wonder what it might be

It's all going into the Tristan Caine murder file

Right. So, tell me the truth, would you? Since I'm feeling whimsical. Join me in spontaneity. You met up with my dad and told him you could kill me for him, right? That's what all the pictures of my family are for?

Yes. Not my best work as far as subtlety but sometimes the obvious is obvious

What did he say when you showed up? Tell me he at least called you a toff

I'm not a toff

Right, so that's a yes. What else did he say?

> You're sure you want to do this now? You're not normally a proponent of being truthful. From my recollection when it comes to acknowledging your amplitude of shit, honesty hurts

Whimsy, Nova, whimsy. Tickle my fancy. I'm at the full scope of my power, lend me some trauma to combat the hubris. Nothing can hurt me, I'm two drinks in

> Categorically false

Don't pretend you're not fucking RELISHING the opportunity to subject me to untold degrees of humiliation and despair. You're desperate to talk to me and even I know it, so come on, Callum. Talk.

What did he say?

> Fine, he pointed a pistol at my balls. Not a man of many words, your father

No, I'm serious. What did he say?

> I'm serious too. Though I suppose I did do a little forced entry so fair enough

Callum. Can you answer the question, please?

> Do you really think just asking nicely is going to do the trick?

Yes.

> Fine.

. . .

> I told him I would find you for him, bring you to him. Said I knew where you were and how to bring you in.

So you lied to him. Bad call. Historically he doesn't care for that.

> I didn't lie. I'm going to bring you to him. I simply didn't specify when

You really think you can snap your fingers and I'll come running? You just told me outright that you're in league with my homicidal father. And more importantly, I hate you.

> Yes, all of this has been taken under advisement. But there's one thing you can't resist

Which is?

> Have you forgotten? You have to kill me, Tristan Caine. Or I have to kill you. I'm losing track of which is more pressing at the moment but the point is there's a sense of inevitability looming
>
> Call it an actionable item. Or what the hell, call it fate

Are you romanticizing murder?

> It's not NOT hot, Tristan. It's not my fault we make the game of
> cat and mouse look so damn cute

You've told me exactly what your trap is and you still think I'm
going to fall into it? You're the worst supervillain in the entire
world.

> That ruling is hugely TBD. And you're the one following through
> with the sinister plot

I don't think Atlas is as sinister as you think he is

> Hope he is, more accurately, and I know. It's one of my life's big
> disappointments

[typing]

> You've been typing for an Age, Caine. What's going on over
> there

> Are you curious what I'm wearing? You need only ask

I thought about saying something and then changed my mind.
It's not worth it

> What's not worth what? Try me

It's not worth the effort. You'll only spew some horseshit and
honestly who has the time

> You, Tristan. I'm the one that's a sitting duck for a dozen
> assassins and a bloodthirsty library. You literally have so much
> time.

See? That is exactly the kind of pleasantry I can look forward to,
so why bother?

> Oh, I see. Were you going to ask me if I'm in love with you?

> Yes, Tristan, I love you. I NEED you. I CRAVE you. X

Wow, fine
I was going to say that I wish you had just been honest with me,
even once. You gave me pieces, you let me see the outlines
of everything, but if you'd just told me that your life was a
fucking disaster and frankly it's done a number on your ability
to function in society . . . I don't know. If you'd just said that then
maybe I could have understood. Or if you'd just asked me a
fucking question instead of trying to tell me who I was and how I
felt. If you hadn't made me into your personal soliloquy. If you'd
let me stay open-ended instead of knowable and finite it could
have been difficult, but simple. We could have at least been
friends.

Yes, well. Pour one out for our lost friendship I suppose.

Yeah. Guess so. Night.

12:32 A.M.

My life is a fucking disaster. And frankly it's done a number on my ability to function in society. Or make friends.

A little late for that, Nova

Is it? You're here. I'm here. Define "too late"

I have to kill you. Or you have to kill me.

So easy to lose track, right?? lol

The point is we don't get to undo it. We don't get to pick up where we left off. Or start over

I'm not doing either of those things. I'm telling you, my life is a fucking disaster

Tell me about yours

You already know about mine.

Yes, but as someone recently told me, I should have "fucking asked" instead of trying to tell you who you are or how you feel

Fine. I'm a sad adult boy with daddy problems

You don't have to use Parisa's words for it

Not inaccurate, though.

I do miss my sisters a bit, or maybe I just like the idea of missing them. I do hope they're happy. I hope I didn't fuck them over by leaving. I just couldn't stay.

My sisters protected me. Kind of. In their way. They don't like me, but they at least act like I belong to them

How do you know they don't like you?

Nobody likes me, Caine. That's kind of my thing?

I'm just saying, maybe my sisters think I don't like them. Everyone has their own shit, their own problems, their own lens. Maybe even empaths can be wrong.

I'm not wrong, but thanks for playing

You were wrong about me.

In what way? I've predicted everything you've done.

No, you haven't, and that's what hurt you so much, wasn't it? Being wrong about me. Being surprised. But again, if you had just asked me what I wanted to drink . . .

Will pettily reliving the past ever grow old, I wonder?

I think the point is to be surprised by people. It's not to know

them completely. It's to see them in a new way all the time,
always turning them over and finding something different, some
new fascinating thing. I know I'm mostly a cynic but when I'm
three and a half glasses deep in whimsy and the window is
open and I look at the stars I start to remember that all the best
feelings come from a place of being fucking
I don't know
Startled

MOSTLY a cynic???

That's why I want to do this, actually. I'm tired of worry. I'm tired
of anxiety. I want to be scared. I want to feel awe, I want to be
shocked to my core. I want to remember what it feels like to feel
something close to wonder

Being shackled with Rhodes is really doing a number on you

This is not about Rhodes, Callum, that's why I'm saying it to
you. I'm telling you that this is not about Atlas Blakely and it's
not about the universe.
What if I come face to face with God, Callum?

God's asleep in the next bed, Tristan. She's wearing an eye
mask and ear plugs because apparently I snore

You do, and more importantly I know you're listening to me.
I know you listen to me. I know what you actually look like
and I know that you're not a psychopath because frankly a
psychopath would make more rational choices

Thank you?

I don't want to live like you, Callum. I just don't. I didn't stay in
this house to hide from something, I stayed to FIND something.
To discover something. I don't know what it is. I don't know what
it will be. But I know it's out there. I know you want me to be the
person you like, which is a person as closed off to excitement
as you are, because this kind of eagerness and enthusiasm is
embarrassing and it's childlike and yes the idiots in this house
are idiots but Varona has something that you and I will never
have, and so does his weird little friend and so did Rhodes, and
it matters. It's allowed to matter. I'm allowed to want more for
myself and if you had told me you wanted more I would have
helped you find it.

Don't think I'll miss that use of past tense there, Caine.

God, you're impossible. Never mind. Go to bed. Tell God I say "just return Varona's calls for fuck's sake I'm getting tired of his energy"

Do you want to talk?

We're talking, idiot.

No. I mean it. Do you want to talk?

Yes, you absolute imbecile. Yes. I want to fucking talk.

. . .

Callum tiptoed into the hotel bathroom, contemplating turning on the lights before deciding no, that wasn't necessary. He perched on the lid of the toilet, then paused to open the small shower window, shivering gladly at the late-autumn draft. Winter lurked; his time would be up soon, and whatever remained would be greedily earned. Or merrily won. The mystery thrilled him, a cheap, fleeting high.

"Where are you?" he said, stepping over the edge of the bathtub when his screen lit up.

"That's how you answer the phone? I take back what I said about you not being a psychopath."

Callum rolled his eyes. "Would you answer the question?"

"I'm upstairs. In bed."

"Alone?"

"Yes. Rhodes and Varona are downstairs and Gideon's passed out in the archives. Are you trying to make this dirty? That's not at all what I meant when I said I wanted to talk."

Another eye roll. "Gideon meaning Varona's little dreamer friend?"

"He's not actually that little, and yes. He got roped into being an archivist or something, which is not a real job as far as I'm aware. But apparently it's the Society's version of a witness protection program."

"How is he?"

"Extremely unnerving. Very quiet. He's given me at least seven jumpscares because he walks so quietly. It's like having a cat that startles you while you're reading."

"You said you wanted to be startled."

"Not like that, which you know. Are you only going to be difficult?" Callum heard the rustle of sheets, the motion of Tristan turning over in bed. "I could simply hang up and go to sleep if that's the case."

"I'm probably going to be difficult, yes." Callum paused, another chilly breeze going by before he decided to sit down, possibly even get comfortable. As much as that was likely to happen on the lid of a toilet. "I wanted to tell you that your sisters don't have any bad feelings about you."

A pulse or two of silence. "Oh?"

"They're confused, a bit, but it's not . . . it's nothing you need to feel badly about. They know your father wants them to hate you but they can't reconcile it with their memories of you."

"They told you that much?"

"Alys likes me a bit more than Bella, or at least doesn't actively hate me, but either way they don't have to tell me. Alys knows I'm going to murder you and yet she still asked me questions about you. Because she knows I'm the only one who can give her answers, even if they're bad."

Tristan said nothing for a moment. "And what did you decide to tell them?"

Callum, likewise, was silent for a while. "I told them you're still fairly grumpy."

"That's it?"

"And that you don't like soup and you've got too many turtlenecks."

"Just the basics then."

"I did tell them that you can stop time." A pause. "That the main reason everyone wants you dead is because you're so powerful. Because you can make a whole new world and it's dangerous."

Another pause.

"Did they believe you?"

"Yes."

"Though surely my father told them something very different."

"Yes, almost certainly. But they believed me anyway."

"Because you're very convincing?"

"Because the idea of you being special is actually very easy to believe."

He could practically hear the sound of Tristan thinking.

"Is this part of your plan?" Tristan said eventually. "Influence me over the phone? Get my guard down? Convince me to meet you somewhere and then hand me over to my dad?"

"Of course that's my plan. But it'll never work, will it? Since you're going to be the one to kill me first."

"It's only fair."

"*Is* it? You already had your try. Technically I think it's my turn."

"You had a whole year to murder me and instead you spent it getting pissed and doing maths."

"I know, right?" Callum laughed. "Anyway, that's what the kids call a slow burn."

"No it isn't."

"No, it isn't." Callum felt the laughter stick in his throat. "Anyway, I just wanted to tell you that, obviously because it's part of my plan to soften you up for my eventual assassination."

"Worst supervillain in the world," Tristan muttered.

"But you clearly need your rest, so I'll just—"

"I can't decide if it would be better or worse," Tristan interjected, "if I could have felt my father's feelings."

Callum said nothing.

"On the one hand, perhaps there might have been some complexity I'm missing? Or some kind of . . . reasoning? Maybe I could have understood the triggers, the things that got him so angry, maybe I could have stopped them before they happened. Or maybe that would have just been exhausting. Watching where I stepped, making myself responsible for him. Maybe I would have felt like I needed to stay behind, just to make sure nothing bad happened in my absence."

Callum scratched idly at the thinning paint beside the bathroom vanity. "Is that meant to be a metaphor?"

"It's an attempt at empathy, actually. So I can understand why you'd find it so difficult."

"Hilarious," Callum said dryly, "and for the record, my situation is quite different."

"Is it?"

"Of course. It wasn't like I stayed where I was purely because I had to."

"Oh, Callum." Tristan gave a long-suffering sigh. "You do see how that's worse, don't you? Wanting to stay with someone you already know doesn't love you."

"Ouch," said Callum. He felt it somewhere small and sharp, like resting his heart or his entire sense of worth on the prick of a needle.

"That's not what you're doing now," Tristan said.

"No, I know that. I'm either talking to my future murder victim or my future murderer, depending on who gets there first."

"It's hard," Tristan said. "There is nothing harder than loving someone who can't love you back. It is very fucked up, Callum, and nobody blames you for that part." A pause. "They blame you for everything else, which as you know is intensely earned."

Callum snorted a laugh. "Being with Rhodes has made you disgustingly zen."

"No, it's the whiskey. Being with Rhodes is actually incredibly suffocating."

Callum blinked. "Well, that's—"

"Don't be too delighted. It's not that I don't have feelings for her, because I do, and that's exactly the problem. It's just—" Tristan paused. "There's more to it now, more shit she doesn't want to share with me but has to. Which is why," he added, "I can finally put into words how annoying it was that you tried to take every burden off my shoulders but couldn't fucking ask me what I actually wanted from you."

"I'm gathering that there were some flaws in my management style," Callum said after a moment. "Which should make it all the easier to kill me, I imagine."

"Actually, yes," said Tristan. "This sort of thing makes it very easy to want you dead."

"You're welcome." Callum shifted from where he was sitting on the toilet lid, facing away from the vanity and toward the shower, reclining a bit in the space. "For what it's worth, I hope you do see God. Or whoever's out there."

"Assuming Rhodes finally admits she wants to do it, yeah, and assuming Parisa lets Dalton off his leash for long enough to try. Though, for the record, I'm hoping it's more of a construct than a deity."

"It's all the same," Callum said. "It'll always be something bigger than we can understand."

"Maybe bigger than *you* can understand," said Tristan.

Callum chuckled. "You've taken well to the prospect of omnipotence. How many god complexes does it take to change a lightbulb?"

"Six. Five to agree on one to die," said Tristan.

"Speaking of Parisa, I saw her recently." Tristan was silent. "She wants to kill Rhodes."

"Does she? Quite a change of heart."

"Parisa doesn't do changes of heart." Actually, her heart was as consistent as it had always been. Callum had already seen her pain and recognized it for what it was: constant. (He'd mentioned that already several times, not that anyone ever believed him.) "Though I suppose a change of mind isn't entirely off-brand."

Tristan hummed in equivocation. "I take it you're in agreement?"

"It's irrelevant. You're going to kill me, or I'll kill you. At this point I've forgotten which, so long as it happens before the archives feel so moved."

"I don't think Rhodes is in a position to be killed," Tristan commented. "In fact, I really don't advise it. Also, I need her."

"Is that your affection talking? Because the Rhodes we knew was very killable. Probably her main feature."

"You know that's not true."

"Yes," Callum exhaled deeply, "fine, I know that's not true—"

"Did Parisa say why?" Tristan's voice had changed. Callum couldn't identify the texture, but it was different, more alert.

"She seems to think something's wrong with Rhodes. Possibly that something's interfering with that moral compass you admire so much." Callum waited for a response, then decided to test the waters with "But you already know that."

From the other line Callum heard nothing but silence. He tried to imagine the room Tristan was lying in, the way the house used to sound at night. The crickets and the stillness, like being lost to time and space.

"Did you know this house has a hired staff?" asked Tristan suddenly, and Callum choked on a laugh.

"Who did you think made the salads you enjoyed so much?"

"Have you ever spoken to the chef?"

"Of course not, Tristan, but still the house is sentient, not alive. It doesn't know how to julienne a carrot."

"Are there groundskeepers? Why did we never see them?"

"Maybe there are tiny little elves that push up the grass at night."

"Do you think everyone chooses this? The power and prestige, all that jazz."

"I think they do, yes. The murder clause is fairly specific."

"It's different now, though." Tristan was quiet. "I don't want to kill you for the books. Maybe I never did, but in the moment . . ." Another pause. "Now I want to kill you because you've pissed me off royally, and apparently someone's got to."

"I warned you," Callum said. "I told you that the moment Rhodes came back we'd all be sitting ducks."

"I'm still contributing to the archives," Tristan said. "So it's you who's got to watch out, or Reina. Or Parisa. You'll be the ones to die first." Any minute, perhaps.

"Beat the library to it, then," Callum suggested invitingly. "It'd be such a shame to die of something dull, like typhoid."

"The plague."

"Drowning in the bath."

"Cardiac arrest."

"High cholesterol."

"You're right, a steak knife to the carotid sounds much better," Tristan said.

"Carotid? Jesus. Femoral would have worked just as well."

"Noted," Tristan said. "For next time."

Callum felt himself nod, but said nothing.

"Well." Tristan cleared his throat. "I don't remember why the fuck I called you but I think I got whatever I was supposed to get out of it."

"Homicidal fantasies," Callum supplied.

"Right, that. And stay away from my sisters."

"No."

There was a low growl from Tristan's end. "Motherfucker."

"Same to you." A pause. "Good luck, then."

"I know you don't mean that, but thanks—"

"If you see a white light, stop walking."

"Jesus. Are you done?"

"If there's something wrong with Rhodes, Tristan, then for god's sake ignore your impulses for theater. It doesn't have to be a faff. The femoral is incredibly easy to reach."

"Wow, again, thank you—"

"Just a small incision, really. She won't even notice. It'll be like a love bite, only with a letter opener, maybe—"

"I know this is difficult for you to understand, Callum, but I do love her. I'm really not interested in killing her."

"Are those things mutually exclusive, though? You love me," Callum observed, "and yet murder's almost incessantly on the mind."

There was a click as the line went dead. Callum pulled the phone from his ear, looking at the smear of sweat across the screen from where it had been pressed against his cheek.

"Are you done?"

Callum jumped, looking up to find Reina waiting sourly in the doorway. Another terrible instance of his usual senses being overpowered by something else. Something gruesomely private and internal, like agony or constipation.

"Sorry." He shot to his feet, waving her obligingly toward the toilet. "All yours."

He sidled past her to their separate hotel beds, Reina's farther from the street-facing window (there was a vine outside with what she called a tendency for voyeurism). She turned to look at him as he went, the outline of her face glowing against the bathroom light.

"You might as well tell Adrian Caine and his cock-faced goons that you're not going to be following through on your offer," she said. She sounded grumpy, as she nearly always did, though there were gradations to her tonalities that Callum had learned to listen for. He did not care for the implications of this one.

"If I sound," he began, opting to finish with, "*attached*—"

"*If?*" she echoed, repulsed.

"If I sound attached," he repeated, "that's not necessarily a bad thing." Callum fell into his unmade bed and shrugged. "The sacrifice has to mean something, does it not?"

"So you admit Tristan means something to you."

He opened his phone, refreshing the page of recent headlines. "Nova Corporation under investigation for antitrust violations." "What exactly is going on with everyone's favorite illusions company?" "Nova shares dipped 3 percent in extended trading." "Everything you need to know about the allegations against Dimitris Nova."

"Would you stop acting like you've tricked me into something? Of course he means something, that was never a secret. You've been mocking me for it for over a year."

"No," Reina said emphatically enough for Callum to look up. "I haven't been mocking you for having feelings. I've been mocking you for having possibly the dumbest revenge plot I've ever personally witnessed."

Callum heaved an irritable sigh, tossing his phone away. "If we want this to actually *work* and save the rest of our skins, it can't be nothing. I can't kill Rhodes because I dislike her, and neither can you, because you have no opinions about her. Parisa's right, the arrow's most deadly only when it's most righteous, and that means—"

"I'm done listening to Parisa." Reina shut the bathroom door, dousing what remained of the light.

Callum was aware that Reina had yet to put words to the feeling she'd walked away with when they left Parisa behind in Nothazai's office. The taste in her mouth, the mix of acridness and bile, and the worst of it, the sweetness. Like sugar to hide the medicine, only in reverse.

Easy to name it hatred. Much, much harder to call it what it was.

Callum knew that feeling well. He rolled onto his side, picking up his phone again like an addict, contemplating something else. Teetering on the edge of giving up some of his power if it meant another line or two with Tristan's initial at the top. The toilet flushed and Callum changed his mind, shoving his phone back under his pillow.

"You're sure you don't want to help Varona?" he said, mostly to annoy her, but also because he was feeling vulnerable and it was gross.

"I'm sure." Reina fell into her bed, reaching for her earplugs.

"What if their experiment fails?" Assuming that such failure would not be instantaneously catastrophic, of course. Easily done, as Callum rarely assumed apocalypses could befall him. He couldn't imagine where people found the time for such impractical neuroses.

It seemed that Reina agreed, or had elected to disagree privately, like a lady. "Then he can grovel again when it's over. Life goes on."

There was something potentially ominous to the flippancy of her tone (inauthentic such as it was, and unfittingly heavy, like claggy bread), but as hubris was one of Callum's particular strengths, he did not investigate it further. "Stone cold, Mori."

"I wish." Grudgingly she flashed Callum a view of her phone screen, which consisted of a daily bubble of conversation (and then some) from Varona, followed by a single line in reply.

> If you do it in the painted room don't forget to move the potted fig it doesn't like big magic. Reina.

"Oh my *god*," said Callum. "You don't have to sign your messages, Mori, they're not emails. Are you actually eighty years old—?"

"Can't hear you," said Reina, pointedly putting her earplugs back in, and Callum rolled his eyes, flopping onto his back and thinking again of the headlines he'd just scrolled through.

"Who exactly is Callum Nova and what does he have to do with the Forum investigation for medeian corporate fraud?"

Regrettably, he might have to do something about that soon.

"Growth," Callum remarked into the darkness.

"Shut up," said Reina sleepily.

With a laugh, Callum closed his eyes.

· DALTON ·

> Dalton's decided to come join you. He knows how important the experiment is to Atlas. :)

this is the creepiest thing u have ever said to me
but ok !!!!!!
miss u ur royal softness

· · ·

> Dalton's decided to come join you. He knows how important the experiment is to Atlas. :)

Jesus Christ Parisa you sound fucking deranged
Like you're going to put pieces of my dismembered body in a
stew
Not to mention this is an incredibly unexpected change of heart,
which even Callum knows you don't do.
. . . Nothing? No taking the piss over me still talking to Callum?
I know you think paranoia is my defining feature but are you
dying or did someone steal your phone

· · ·

> Dalton's decided to come join you. He knows how important the experiment is to Atlas. :)

I thought you said I was wrong.
Now suddenly you've changed your mind?

Nico had forgotten things about the world outside of the Society. The pungency of New York City in the summer, which autumnal foliage temporarily relieved before the cautionary sogginess of winter began. How often he was supposed to get haircuts. How frequently people would ask about his prospects. "Don't tell me you're going to waste away in academia," things like that, though Nico wasn't entirely sure what the alternative to wasting away in academia was supposed to be. Wasting away in bureaucracy? In heterosexuality? In his brunch khakis?

"What you need to do is find a corner of the industry that's primed for disruption" was the unsolicited take from Max's father, the elder Maximilian Wolfe, with whom Nico had been trapped in conversation at the Wolfe second home in the Berkshires. "And remember, a solid valuation is everything. Put in the time, with the right investors, and you can really build a portfolio from there."

"Did he say that to you, really?" Max asked Nico in the getaway car later, sounding a bit awed by Nico's retelling of the story (only loosely paraphrased) as they meandered glacially through city traffic with the top down. (It was chilly for such an endeavor, but what was life if not a series of irresponsible choices in pursuit of shrieking joy?) "Just what does he think you're going to disrupt? The mouse pad industry?"

"I think more along the lines of the economy," Nico guessed, "which is admittedly a figment of everyone's imagination."

"Well, sorry you had to deal with that." From the driver's seat, Max slid him a grimace. "But you know the deal."

"Yes, I do." Once a year since they'd first met at the NYUMA dorms—Nico's Society initiation years excepted—Nico had accompanied Max to his family's country home to perform a spectacular double act involving the pretense of something-something entrepreneurship, thus securing Max another year's income from the inscrutable elder Max Wolfe. It was ultimately a small price to pay (usually a lot of golf, at which Nico prodigiously cheated, with many Oscar-nominated peals of laughter) but draining all the same.

"Perhaps," Nico suggested, "next year you might consider abject poverty, as an alternative?"

Beneath Max's sunglasses was almost certainly the presence of an admonishing glance. "Nicky, I'm not above getting a job, as you well know—"

"Do I?" Nico said doubtfully.

"Fine, I'm barely employable, point taken. But how am I supposed to keep an eye on Gideon, hm? This is merely a brief sabbatical from my full-time calling as our beloved Sandman's au pair." Max, still in costume as tremendous go-getter and prodigal son, nudged his Wayfarers down to grimace at Nico. "How is he doing, by the way?"

"This'll help," Nico said, referencing the vial Max had procured, which Nico had tucked away in the pocket of the attaboy navy blazer he reserved specifically for these occasions (currently framing the poshest of his kicky cable-knits). "And I think he's mostly fine. Well, no, he's almost certainly lying to me about his state of mind," Nico corrected himself cheerily, deciding not to mention Gideon's ongoing nightmares about some realm-dwelling accountant—or perhaps they were simply accountancy nightmares; unclear whether Gideon had a thriving stock portfolio, and Nico knew better than to underestimate him—"but he doesn't seem worse than usual. Just . . . more reserved." Nico riffled a hand through his hair. "Have you seen him recently?"

Max nodded. "Slipped me a note by dreamscape carrier pigeon while I was napping the other day. Says he's fine."

"Ah yes," Nico said with a sigh, "I believe I, too, know all the words to that refrain. The hit single off his platinum album, *Everything Is Pie*—"

"You do know," Max interjected, "that he's been in love with you for six years? Just checking that that information has passed between the two of you in recent months." Again, he paused to face Nico from the driver side of his new car, which was smart enough to know when the light would change and also, somehow, a tax write-off. "Which I say not to express the indignity of an *I told you so*—"

"You've expressed that particular indignity several times this week despite *not*, in fact, telling me so," said Nico. "Despite deliberately *concealing* it from me, in fact—"

"—which I bring up merely to say: don't rob him of this." Max wagged a finger. "It's a mixed bag, I understand that. It's not ideal and you're a fusser, et cetera and so on. But he's happy in whatever way Gideon understands happiness to be despite being held hostage by the Illuminati, so, you know," Max concluded. "Don't ruin it."

"Not the Illuminati," said Nico. "Just some pals I happen to know."

"Whatever. Don't ruin it for *me,* either." Max clapped Nico on the shoulder as they finally reached the passenger bay at Grand Central. "All right. Get the fuck out of here. And try not to think about me while you and Gideon make out," he advised.

"Not once have I ever thought of you," Nico said, clambering out of the car, "and yet now I'm decently concerned that I might."

"Be honest, Nicolás," Max yelled after him. "Not even once?"

Nico flipped him off over his shoulder and made his way through the station as usual; bypassing the crowd of sleepy passengers and oysters; flummoxing the surveillance wards specifically marking him for ambush; generally performing the song and dance as he had done what now felt like a thousand times before. He felt a routine mix of things throughout this process of leaving the real world and reentering the dimension of the Alexandrian archives. Like walking through a portal to a fantasy world, except it instantly made his lips chap and his muscles ache.

"I'm back," Nico yelled when he entered the house, making his way through the foyer to the staircase. He heard something in response, a lackluster greeting that probably belonged to Tristan, and raced up the stairs to drop off his bag in his room. It was the same room as it had been over the last two years, except for little details here and there—Gideon's T-shirt hooked on the bathroom door, pairs of Nico's socks rolled up neatly in the drawer because they "didn't belong on the floor all mismatched and lonely, Nicky, it's sad." Nico smiled faintly and then made his way down the stairs, colliding with someone unexpectedly on the landing.

"Hello," said Dalton Ellery stiffly, as Nico blinked. Their former researcher seemed different somehow, not merely because he no longer lived there. Nico found himself a bit startled by something. Perhaps the lack of spectacles, or the addition of a leather jacket that Nico suspected (despite all evidence to the contrary) might have been extremely cool.

"Dalton?" Parisa had texted him that Dalton was coming, but still. "You look—"

"I see that my former room is now occupied. I was just moving my things." Dalton referenced a bag that was slung over his shoulder.

"Did—" Nico frowned, determining firstly how to ask whether Dalton was alone and secondly whether that answer had the potential to devastate him (for three to five minutes, probably yes). "Did Parisa convince you to come?"

"She told me you were planning to attempt the experiment."

"Well, sort of." Assuming they could get Libby on board in reality as well as in theory, which was thus far proving uncertain, though if anyone could manage it, it was likely Parisa. Nico resisted the urge to peer around Dalton's shoulder. "Did she come with you?"

"It appears she's lost interest in my scholarly pursuits. As is her nature, she's busied herself with other things." Something like impatience flashed in Dalton's eyes. "So I suppose I'll just take her former room."

"Oh . . . right, yeah." Nico tried not to mentally draw a diagram of who in the house had occupied which variety of bedrooms. "Right, well. See you around, I suppose."

Dalton nodded and walked quickly past Nico, a strange new lean to his posture. Was it . . . swagger? Nico was alarmed to realize it might have been, though he supposed one did not get to be the object of Parisa Kamali's affections without adopting a sort of strut. (Ah yes, there it was, the momentary pull that was really more asynchronously nostalgic than actually devastated. Other lives, other worlds.)

Nico didn't think it sounded like the Parisa he knew to suddenly lose interest in anything, much less a scholarly pursuit, but he felt it slightly arrogant to presume he'd ever been allowed to truly know her. He shrugged and continued down the stairs, noticing the light on in the reading room.

He stepped inside warily, uncertain who he might be disturbing, and felt a wave of relief upon sight of its occupancy. A wayward glint of sandy hair rested above a mahogany table, a single lamp illuminating an outstretched arm, the steady motion of slumber. Nico paused in the doorway, framing the moment like a photograph before gingerly creeping forward with intent to shift Gideon from the chair and up to bed.

As he came closer, he noticed something below Gideon's cheek. A book, he realized with a pang of fondness. So, even the archives could be convinced to let Gideon have a treat. Nico slid away the copy of *The Tempest* and touched Gideon's cheek, gently. Gideon bent his head, nuzzling into Nico's palm in his sleep.

"Ah, I was just coming to wake him." Nico turned to find Tristan in the doorway. He noticed the empty glass in Tristan's hand, the book under his arm. Tristan was on his phone, typing something quickly before looking up.

A mix of guilt and worry skittered across Nico's chest at the implication that waking Gideon might have become part of Tristan's nightly routine. "Does this happen often?"

Tristan gave him a sympathetic look. "Rhodes told me about the narcolepsy."

Something in Tristan's voice suggested he had used that word to avoid awakening something more vulnerable in Nico.

"Thanks," Nico said, which felt appropriate for the significance of the offering, if not the specifics of their conversation. He lifted Gideon off the ground, tilting him slightly. "Hey," he added tangentially to Tristan, "did you know Dalton's here?"

Tristan nodded. "I suppose we're meant to gather that it's Parisa's attempt at being helpful? Explaining herself would obviously be a step too far."

Nico eased his shoulder carefully under Gideon's arm, then glanced back at Tristan. "She's a nice person, Caine. But obviously don't tell her I said that or she'll kill me." Tristan laughed, and Nico felt a small wave of something. Contentment, he supposed. "Heading upstairs, then?"

Tristan nodded, lingering in the door frame until Nico joined him. "Did you notice anything weird about him?" Nico asked, shouldering Gideon's weight more comfortably as they walked.

"Who, Gideon?" Tristan asked with a glance. "He's been in there all afternoon. Only dozed off a bit ago, maybe an hour or so before you arrived."

"No, Dalton." Tristan looked over at Nico with a distracted frown, like his mind was elsewhere. "Never mind. How's—" Nico hesitated. "How's Rhodes?" To Tristan's arched brow, he clarified, "I, uh. I don't think she's too happy with me at the moment." She hadn't been, anyway, the last time they spoke.

"Is she ever?" Tristan asked dryly.

"Valid. Unhelpful, but valid." They walked in silence for a few moments up the stairs.

"No change since you left last," Tristan remarked without elaboration, which Nico took to mean several things—that she still hadn't budged on the sinister plot and she still wasn't completely looking Tristan in the eye since he'd sided with Nico and admitted his intentions to do it. Neither of which felt worth mentioning.

They parted ways on the landing, Tristan still mentally elsewhere. Nico brought Gideon into their room, toying a bit with gravity to soften the landing.

"*Hey, Mr. Sandman,*" Nico sang under his breath. "*Bring me a dream, make him the dumbest that I've ever seen—*"

No motion. Gideon was fully out. Nico laughed quietly, then paused, touching his thumb softly to Gideon's forehead with one word forming idly in his mind.

Precioso.

Nico wasn't quite tired himself, what with the time zone change, so he decided against climbing into bed and instead faced the door with a sigh, contemplating his alternatives. He supposed there was still a conversation to be had.

When he made his way to the painted room, Libby was tucked into the corner of the sofa. She was frowning into the flames of the hearth, gripping what Nico realized with surprise was a glass of wine. "Are you drinking?" Not that she never did, but he'd only seen it in a social context. Drinking alone was something Nico associated most closely with Callum.

The glare she turned on him was so familiar he nearly whooped with relief.

"I've recently been advised to relax," said Libby dryly.

"Oh. Right." That had been him just before he'd left, which was over a week ago now, though it wasn't in her nature to forget. She was like an elephant, but specifically for the ways that he had personally wronged her.

He'd been trying to coax her into something, a game. A reminder, some form of combustion that could conceivably, who could say, make new worlds and such. It was strange doing magic with her now. Her magical signature was different, like she'd switched hands or learned a few new words in a different language, or something. It was hard to explain. Or maybe it felt like when you sleep with someone new and then the old kiss, it's not the same. She kept pulling back, cutting him off too quickly. It was throwing them both off balance until finally he'd let her carry the brunt of the error, shoving the pain away instead of sharing it equally between them, just enough so that she'd feel it—not a *dangerous* amount of pain, of course. Nothing lethal. More like her leg had fallen asleep, or like he'd kicked her hard in the thigh.

He sought her out later, finding her in the chapel where he always seemed to be delivering bad news. "Sorry," he'd said, expecting the usual glare— *Varona, you idiot, you could have killed me*—but everything was off between them; strange. He'd thought the magic was the worst of it, but maybe not.

"This is stupid." Her eyes were elsewhere, staring out over the empty pews from where she sat in the glow of the stained-glass triptych.

"Yes, it is." He tried to find the words to soften that, but came up empty. "You know that we can do it. I know that you want to. The only thing I don't understand is why you're still trying to hold us back."

"I told you, Varona, the consequences—"

"Stop trying to stay small, Rhodes," he snapped at her, feeling himself lash out over something, over nothing. "You can't stay in this house forever just because you're scared that if you actually make a choice the world will end—"

"You think I'm worried about being too *small*?" Her expression in response was a troubling stillness, bathed in the luster of knowledge's torch. "You wanted me to let it burn, Varona, and I did. You don't get to talk to me about my choices." From the stained incandescence of enlightenment or arson, he could see the set of her jaw. The tiny fissure between her brows. "If I'm going to set myself on fire again, I won't be doing it just to prove something to you."

There was an insult there, something worse than usual. An accusation that held weight, like maybe this was somehow his fault. Like she had changed and he would always be stuck, always a waste of her time, always an idiot. Like she had outgrown him when all he had done was try to shrink down for her. All those months treading carefully, being kind, being considerate.

Apparently that meant nothing to her, so fine. So be it, he'd thought.

Time for a different tactic now.

"Okay fine, fine." He felt his teeth gritting in something, anger or disappointment, because he didn't understand this, didn't understand her anymore. "I just think you need to relax a little bit, Rhodes—"

"Relax?" Exactly the wrong word, but he pressed her anyway.

"This experiment, this . . . this *magic,* it's what we came here to do!" he said, too angrily. Too much. "It's why we came here—to prove that we're *the best,* that we're the *only ones* who can do this, and the fact that you can't even see that—" He broke off in frustration. "Why did you even bother coming back if you're just going to let everything we are go to waste?"

He'd known it was the wrong thing to say even before he saw her face. Afterward, though, there was no way to properly apologize—no way to eulogize the people they'd been before the words left his mouth.

That night, a week ago, she'd walked away, and he'd gone to the Berkshires with Max. And now they were here again, and she was looking at Nico with something he thought might have been a white flag, or her version of it, which wasn't actually conciliatory. More like *we need to talk.*

By the time he ventured in from the threshold, Libby had poured a second glass, which she'd set on top of a coaster. Nico sat on the floor in front of the fireplace and she hesitated, then slid down from the sofa to join him, handing him the glass. "I have no idea if it's supposed to be good," she admitted. "Tristan picked it out."

"Oh, then it's excellent," Nico assured her. "Didn't you know he's the house purveyor of quality wines and sarcastic comments?"

"What does that make you?" she countered.

"I," Nico replied, "am mostly here to piss everyone off. Cheers," he added, clinking his glass against hers before taking a sip.

She mirrored him, her eyes warily on his above the glass.

"Listen, I was thinking—"

"Look, I'm sorry," he said in the same moment. They both paused, and since he figured he was more in the wrong, he continued, "I know better than to tell you to relax. But in fairness to me, I have no idea what our rhythm is anymore."

"I—" She cut off like he'd taken the wind out of her sails. "I didn't expect you to put it so un-obnoxiously, but yeah. That's—" She fiddled with the stem of her glass. "That's pretty much what I was thinking, too."

"You got mad," Nico said. "Like, actually mad, not fake mad."

"I'm never *fake* mad," she muttered with annoyance. "You're a constant disaster."

"Thank you—"

"But I know what you mean. I reacted badly." She took a sip and he frowned.

"I wouldn't say *badly,*" he said. "Just . . . like you've forgotten something."

"Something?"

"Like you've forgotten I'm not your enemy." Ah, there it was. "Like you've forgotten I'm supposed to be your ally. I'm on your team."

Her glass had been partway to her lips when she paused. "Are you still?"

"What?" He blinked at her, a stab of something crossing his mind at the distant imagination that he could be otherwise. "Of course."

"Are you actually wounded or just being theatrical?"

"I'm—" He stopped. "Well, wounded is a theatrical word, first of all, but yes, actually, now that you mention it, I *am* wounded. I mean, we already went through this," he reminded her, thinking of the day she'd saved him, almost two years ago now, when he'd been trying to reinforce the house's wards on his own. The state of exhaustion he'd been in, which he would never have admitted. The help he never would have requested from anyone, which she'd offered without a single string, just because she'd known him. Because she'd known.

He had made a promise to her then, that he would turn to her for help, and she had promised she would do the same. "It's like you've completely forgotten that I already gave you my word."

"Oh, silly me," she said bluntly. "I wonder if anything *remotely traumatic* might have happened to me between two years ago and now—"

"But that's what I mean." He set the glass aside. "You need me right now, more than you've ever needed—" He stopped. "You need *someone*," he clarified, because the expression on her face had become something he didn't fully understand, and he suspected that maybe he was assuming too much. "You obviously need help. You need to talk to someone, and it doesn't have to be me, but—"

He looked away, glancing at his discarded wineglass and deciding never mind, he did need it after all, and then brought it up to his lips, taking a long pull. "Fuck," he said, eyeing the glass when it was empty. "That is actually delicious."

"I really wouldn't know," she said, though she stretched up toward the side table for the bottle, pouring more into his glass. "The only wine I've had in the last year came from a box."

Aside from her cataclysmic reminders about the apocalypse destined to befall the earth, that was more information than she'd revealed so far about her time away from him. Nico was hesitant to spoil the mood. Instead, he leaned against the couch, settling into a more comfortable position on the floor and inviting her to mirror him.

She did.

"It's not—" She paused, hesitating. "It's not that I don't want to tell you about it. It's just—" She stared into the fire, and so did he, recognizing that eye contact would be far too vulnerable a thing to ask from her. "I don't even know where to start."

"Was anything good?" he asked.

He saw her blink with surprise. "I . . . yeah. Yes, actually."

"Any good meals?"

She laughed, seeming to have surprised herself with it. "Seriously?"

"Completely serious. Even when there's nothing to live for, there's always your next meal," he joked, and she laughed again.

"Wow. That's so . . ."

"Hedonistic of me?"

"I . . . guess?"

"There's also revenge," he added. "The two most important things in life."

"Food and vengeance?"

"Yes." He hazarded a glance at her and saw that she was smiling. Naturally his instinct was to spoil it, so he did. "And also," he mused, "the chance to come back and tell me that I was right about Fowler all along."

He waited for her to clam up again, shoving all her pain into some box she didn't want anyone else to see, but instead her mouth thinned with something he could have sworn was a smirk.

"You know, don't let this go to your head," she said, "but I actually had that exact thought several times last year."

"What, that I was right?"

"No, that you'd somehow realize telepathically that you were right from thirty years away and still manage to annoy me with it." She glanced at him, and the unexpected eye contact sent his pulse cantering somewhere out of reach.

He raised the newly topped-off glass to his lips, taking another long sip. "Is it weird to be sitting here drinking expensive wine and talking about your ex-boyfriend?"

She laughed again, caught off guard a second time. "Yes."

"I feel like we're in a pretentious film about tortured geniuses."

"Yes."

"But actually we're just babies with expensive glassware."

"I actually think these are crystal." She tilted her head, eyeing the glass in the light. It caught the flickering heat of the flames in the hearth, sending the colors dancing. Nico watched for a second, living on the precipice of the moment. Bracing for the fall and whatever could no longer be left unsaid.

"I did think about you, you know." He took another swallow of whatever Tristan picked out for them. "I think the technical verbiage is I missed you."

Libby said nothing.

"When I thought you were—" Nico stopped, feeling a strain in his throat. "For a second I thought you were gone, and I was . . . It was like I lost a piece of me."

She tucked her hair behind her ear, burying her nose in her glass.

"And I don't mean that like—" He hesitated. "I know we've always been . . . us," he determined for lack of a better word. "But I don't know, there's just something about you, about knowing that you exist. It's like without you, I'm just push, you know? Just push with no pull, but then you were gone and I just fell over." God, he sounded like an idiot. "Sorry, I don't know what I'm saying, I guess I just wanted to tell you that it wasn't nothing to me, you know? I know I make it seem like everything is nothing to me, but it's not."

This was only getting more incoherent. "I just want you to know it matters. You, I mean. Us." He motioned awkwardly between them. "I got a taste of what life is like without you, and . . ." He sighed, expelling a breath and leaning back to rest his head against the sofa. "I just want you to know, officially, that what you said to me at graduation, about us being done with each other—that's not what I want. If I ever meant it before, I definitely don't mean it now. I don't actually want to never see you again."

The fire crackled and danced, the clock on the mantel ticking.

Then Nico snorted into his glass, taking another long pull. "Wow. Really good speech, Varona," he mimicked in Libby's voice.

To his relief, Libby laughed, a hiccup of a giggle, and turned to him with wine-flushed cheeks, a dance of amusement in her slate-colored eyes. "*I don't actually want to never see you again,* as the poets say," she mocked.

He rolled his eyes. "Yeah, yeah—"

"Without you," she said with feigned solemnity, "I would simply . . . fall over."

Ah, fuckety balls. "Okay, we get it, Rhodes, you're hysterical—"

"It's not *not* cute," she said, reaching over to riffle his hair as he ducked out of reach, straining not to spill on the rug he did not know how to clean.

"Rhodes, come on, I know you're a heartless monster but please, I'm just a human man—"

"I always thought—" She stopped, and he slowly swayed back to sitting, arching a brow in prompting as she looked over at him and hesitated. "No, never mind."

"Oh, come on." He nudged her with his shoulder. "I undressed in front of you. You know, metaphorically."

One brow shot upward. "Are you telling me to strip?"

"Metaphorically," he repeated with emphasis, "yes, I am. Here," he said, reaching over for the bottle and moving to pour more wine into her glass. "You're empty, maybe this'll help—"

"Right, help me *relax*. If only you knew," she muttered to herself, taking the bottle from him.

"What's that supposed to mean? Don't tell me you spent your year on the run starting a boxed wine club without me."

"No, but I definitely thought you being right about Ezra was some kind of cruel cosmic joke." She sighed and abandoned the tyranny of a glass, lifting the bottle for a sip instead. "Promise me you'll let me get through this without interrupting?" she said through a mouthful of old-world vintage.

"I promise. It'll crush me inside, but I'll be quiet, I swear." He saluted her with his glass, and she offered him the bottle. "Fine, when in Rome—"

He took a swig, and she took advantage of his distraction. "You weren't *right* about Ezra, you know. You just weren't wrong enough, which is somehow equally annoying."

"Too true," he said giddily.

"You said you'd be quiet," she grumbled, taking the bottle back from him. With a glare, she continued, "I don't want to joke about it. I don't want to *talk* about it," she clarified, "but I guess I just . . . I guess—" A sigh. "Some part of me kept thinking that if I'd had you, things would have been better. Or that without you, I was more lost than I'd ever been."

She took another sip, contemplatively that time, and Nico, who was not completely without nuance, remained very silent, even though he could tell something had shifted. Some form of resistance had begun to give.

In the silence between them, Nico's mind wandered a little to the bedroom upstairs, to the way Gideon looked when he slept; to his sense that Gideon would approve of this conversation in some way, and of what Nico had tried to say, even if another part of Gideon would be pained by it. Not wounded, exactly, but pained. Nico thought he understood the difference, which was also to understand the complexity of everything that existed between him and the dreamer upstairs.

"Do you ever—?" Libby began, her voice rough, but not uncertain. Nico didn't move, didn't breathe. "If we're right," she said. "If the experiment works—if Atlas's theory is right, and there really are other versions of our world out there, and we've met in them, do you think—?"

She turned to him, the bottle forgotten.

The flames danced. The clock ticked.

She spoke first.

"Do you ever wonder if maybe it's supposed to be us?"

It felt inevitable, that moment. That question. Like every alternate path still led them here. Like somewhere innate, they both knew they'd spent lifetimes dancing around the gravitational pull of the obvious.

"Yes," Nico said. "I do."

THREE
Eden

Her father was meditating again. That's what he called it, "meditating," as if Eden couldn't possibly comprehend the scope of what it actually was. As if staring blankly into space was somehow important when he did it.

He'd been "meditating" for most of her life; nearly all of her childhood and most of what felt significant of her adulthood. He had been "meditating" when she told him about Tristan Caine, thinking finally something would awaken the great James Wessex from his pickling, pointless sleep and force him to see what he was missing. The inadequacy of Tristan—who had apparently also been "meditating" throughout most of their relationship—choosing not to see what Eden did (or whom) when his back was turned. Choosing, then, not to see *Eden*, which was often challenging in a fun way, like constructing a careful mirage. It was fun for a while, being good enough for someone with tastes so discerning he spent most of his time staring moodily at everything offensive within his line of sight.

But then Eden realized that she was trying to impress someone so clearly beneath her, and it hadn't mattered anyway. The sex was rousingly good and they got on like a house on fire when they chose to, when they were both feeling up for a laugh or a spirited debate, and if she had to spend twelve hours locked in a room with someone she'd want it to be Tristan, only Tristan.

None of which could change the fact that all he'd ever wanted from her was her name.

She backed out of her father's study and returned to the video call she'd left open in the living room. "He's busy," she said crisply, though she could tell by the unchanged expression on Nothazai's face that this was the answer he'd expected—and worse, that this answer was the nail in an unspoken coffin. Another reminder, after all, that Eden Wessex was no substitute for her father. Selene Nova could breezily wander the streets of London putting stockholders at ease while her father's corporation underwent global investigation for fraud, but Eden was only James Wessex's messenger. Not the inheritor to his crown.

"There's still no sign of Tristan Caine," Nothazai said, which was not the first time Eden had heard it. "And until he steps out from the premises of the Society's archives, he is unlikely to be a worthwhile target. In the meantime, as we said, it's best to focus on the empath."

"You can't just stop looking for Tristan. You know how my father feels about this." Eden worked very hard to keep her voice free of feminine hysterics. "And what about the telepath?"

Parisa Kamali looked like the type of woman Tristan might be fucking. Like Selene Nova, chic as all hell while the world burned at her feet. If Parisa Kamali wasn't currently employing some diabolical form of subterfuge against all of them, Eden would eat her hat.

"We're doing everything in our power to apprehend Miss Kamali, same as all the others," Nothazai said with unfathomable patience, hitting Eden's sensibilities like the dulcet tones of a nursery school teacher trying to defuse a tantrum. "But based on her actions thus far, we do not consider her to be our primary concern."

"Is that a joke?" Eden did everything in her power not to gape at him. "None of your people have ever been able to lay a hand on her despite her obviously going about her life as normal, and you think that's a coincidence because . . . why? Because she's a woman? Because she looks blatantly fuckable every time she leaves the house?"

Almost immediately, Eden had the sense that Parisa had found her way in and was watching Eden at that very moment, laughing to herself. Eden didn't know exactly what it was she found so infuriating about Parisa, but it seemed . . . familiar, as if all the men who considered Eden a lovely little bauble with no thoughts in her head would be equally incapable of registering Parisa as a threat. (Also, Parisa had been photographed wearing a dress that Eden herself owned, and Eden could not stop seeing Tristan fuck her in it.)

"Miss Wessex, please." Now Nothazai's tone had transitioned to openly patronizing. "Tell your father that if he wishes to alter the course of our investigation, he is welcome to speak with me at any time. In the meantime, I don't want you to be late," he added, with a pointed glance at Eden's ascot-related sartorial effects, which included a hat she'd found charming in the salon but now considered a complete humiliation.

Sit down, little girl. Enjoy your feathers and jewels, fuck your father's secretary and see if he notices, if he even cares. Oh, so a man broke your stupid self-sabotaging heart by lacking the decency to be fussed about the knowledge that you'd cheated? Darling, that's because he never loved you, are you really such a hopeless fool? Anyway, he's very important and you're not at all, go play with your ponies now with the other silly girls in stupid hats. Run along then, sweetheart, go on.

"Have you considered," Eden seethed, "that the empath's agenda seems unrelated to the Novas' corporate gains? That the politics he appears to be influencing have to do with personal autonomy and human rights"—things that he, as a man, already had—"rather than anything remotely profitable to him or his family? So perhaps it's the *naturalist* you need to be looking at," Eden spat, "unless you really think the empath aspires to some dystopian world domination that he could more easily achieve from inside the Nova boardroom?"

She had lost him, she knew that much. Nothazai was smiling without any indication of having followed her train of thought. "We'll continue monitoring the naturalist, of course. Local authorities do have files on all six potential initiates. Oh, and by the way, I understand congratulations are in order," Nothazai added, his eyes drifting down to her hand.

Fucking Christ. "I'm not *engaged*," Eden snapped. "It's just a fucking tabloid!" Which, like any tabloid, saw only what she wanted it to see. A rich heiress about town, cavorting with a handsome man and pretending that was power.

What *was* power, really, if nobody would listen to her? If they'd pay a fee to take her picture, to make her into a fantasy that she could curate but never actually own, then did it matter how sharp her teeth were, or how invisibly her heart could break?

The telepath was the dangerous one. Eden knew it, could read it on the wall, interpreting it with the same perfect clarity with which she had manipulated headlines ever since her breasts came in early at twelve. She and Parisa Kamali almost certainly drew from the same skillset, which meant forget Callum Nova, forget Atlas Blakely, forget the presence of powerful men who all shared the same weakness. What had Parisa Kamali done to compromise Nothazai, Eden wondered, knowing it was something. Eden had had enough affairs of her own to understand how cheaply men like him could be bought.

Her own father had his vices. Eternal life, like every other rich man. Unoriginal hubris for which he'd pay any price. What might the equivalent have been for Nothazai, who seemed to want nothing more or less than whatever Atlas Blakely currently had . . . ?

Not that it mattered. The world was not—*could* not be—as unfair as it seemed. A person could only have so many wins. Tristan would encounter a rupture somewhere, would feel his heart blister in his chest the same way Eden had felt such pain in hers. Let the men play out their doomed fantasies.

When they finally asked for too much, let them discover the myriad ways the world could say no. Engagements broken. Eyes closed while meditating.

Fuck it.

Eden Wessex would solve this one on her own.

· LIBBY ·

A bottle of red wine, two glasses on the painted room's side table, Tristan's face looking so brutally impassive she thought she might actively hate him. *I don't know if this is fixable.*
Do you mean us? Or do you mean me?
(Not an ambush, he'd said at the start. Just a thought.)
Doesn't something feel . . . wrong?

· · ·

Libby's heart hammered in her throat as Nico looked at her.

Wasn't it always this way? Leaving and returning, always in each other's orbit. Maybe that meant something. Maybe her gut had been right the first time. Maybe *Varona, we need to talk* had been the right move all along. Maybe she'd suspected this and tried to fight it; maybe she'd thought it was something she could outrun. It was uncreative, a classic story, the wrong one turning out to be right. Maybe it was okay to figure that out now, right now, when both their cheeks were flushed with hope and humiliation. Twin flames of maybe yes, maybe you, maybe me. Maybe she'd been looking for signs, missing the obvious right in front of her the whole time.

She swallowed and contemplated how to move forward. How to close the distance. She hated his mouth, how strangely sensual it was. That tendency to chew on the pens he borrowed from her, his arrogant smile, the dimples she loathed with a heat she could have easily mistaken for something else. Had it been this all along? Maybe she'd known it. He had pushed her, always, he was at the center of her every accomplishment, standing beside everything she'd ever achieved. Every goal she'd ever reached. He was there in her orbit, and maybe that meant something.

Maybe it was this. Maybe it was now.

Maybe—

"I think there are a solid three universes where we're together, Rhodes," Nico said, his mouth moving again just as she felt herself tipping forward, trying invisibly to connect the dots and join them up between her lips and his. "Maybe half of all the parallel worlds, if I'm feeling optimistic."

He turned to the side and picked up the bottle of wine, and Libby blinked at the sudden disruption of things.

Blinked again, wondering if she'd misheard. "And in the other half?"

"Oh, we've killed each other." He smiled at her, shrugging, inviting her to laugh, though she didn't. Wanted to, kind of, but at the moment it seemed like it might hurt too much, might rupture an organ. "But we're definitely both there in all of them," he said with certainty. "It's hard to imagine that there's a world where either of us exists alone."

She fought the urge to reel backward, to pinch herself awake. "So that's your multiverse hypothesis—fifty-fifty odds, death or marriage?"

He laughed into the bottle, taking a swig and then toasting her with it. "Maybe forty-nine-forty-nine, with some wiggle room for academic rivals that occasionally split a bottle of wine."

She waited for her pulse to slow, wondered if he could feel how big and loud it had gotten. She doubted he could miss it, attuned as he was to her every move, her every flaw. She could no longer determine the atmosphere in the room, which she'd thought she understood with perfect clarity five minutes ago, or maybe less. Allies, he'd said. What was that supposed to feel like? "Those odds could be worse."

"Sure." He shrugged. "Sometimes I think I'd take that gamble."

"Sometimes?"

He lowered the bottle. Took a long look at her. She felt an inward plummeting even before he opened his mouth.

"You want me to be your answer, Rhodes," he said eventually, "but I can't be. I'm not an answer. Granted, I'm a lot of things," he qualified with a smirk, "but what you want—absolution or whatever—that's bigger than me."

She hated him again. Just like that, it was back. "So is Gideon your answer, then?"

He looked away, and she wondered if he would deny it. She felt certain that if he lied, she would know. He'd told a lot of truths in the past few minutes. She knew enough about him to know that whatever they'd been doing here, she hadn't been *that* wrong.

He cleared his throat. "My mother does this thing," he explained. "She touches my forehead, right here." He pointed to the spot above his brows. "She blesses me. And I've always found it annoying, I don't really share her beliefs. But then—"

He broke off.

"Now I understand the desire to bless something," he said eventually. "I don't know. I don't know how to explain it. I just understand the impulse, that need to acknowledge something precious, to treat it with reverence, to call it things like "beloved" and "cherished" and "dear." And—" He shrugged, the moment fatally collapsing. "The point is no, Gideon is not an answer, Gideon is Gideon. But I'm not the one asking a question." His eyes met hers. "*You* are, Rhodes, and neither Tristan nor I can answer it for you."

"You're doing it again." She could hear her heart beating in her ears, somewhere behind her temples. "You're telling me how to feel."

"Right, sorry, I don't mean to do that. I don't mean to . . . I obviously don't understand." He shifted away from her, and with a sudden strike of panic and rage, Libby understood that he intended to leave. "Sorry, I think . . . I think this got weird, it's my fault, I didn't mean t—"

"To what? Lead me on? Lie to me?" She tasted bile, wondering if it was heartbreak or the undrinkable red wine that Nico found so delicious. As if they'd been existing in two very different worlds the whole time.

Nico looked at her squarely. "Do you have feelings for me, Rhodes?"

"I—" She had traveled through time. She'd defied the principles of physics. She didn't have to back down from a stupid little question like *do you have feelings for me* from someone who'd been pulling her pigtails since day one. "Maybe I fucking do, Varona. Are you saying you don't?"

"Of course I'm not saying that. This, we both know it's . . . it's complicated, it's weird, it's not the same as anything we have with anyone else—"

"And those aren't feelings?"

"I'm saying right now that they're feelings, of course they're feelings, but I just—I have *a lot* of feelings, okay?" Nico looked irritated, which made Libby want to strangle him with her bare hands. "I'm in love with Gideon, I'm in love with you, I'm probably a little in love with Parisa and Tristan and, god, maybe Reina. And honestly," he added with a look of strain, "if Callum asked me to get a drink with him, I can't even promise I'd say no—"

Helplessly, Libby tasted smoke on the tip of her tongue. "What are you even saying right now?"

"I'm saying that I have feelings and I also make choices, and right now my choice is to go to bed," Nico muttered, rubbing his neck as he clambered to his feet. "I'm saying that—*yes, okay?* Yes, obviously I wonder sometimes, Rhodes, because you push me and I need that, and I need you. I want you in my life in a way that fucking *bleeds* significance, but it isn't . . ." He grimaced again. "Maybe it's not the kind of significance you want it to have."

"I never said that." Oh, it was definitely potent, the hatred, the thing she felt for him that was so far off the charts. "I never said I wanted anything from you."

"Okay, good, great, fantastic." He sat back down, apparently recognizing the instability he'd created. "So we love each other, Rhodes, so what?"

"So what?" She felt hysterical. "Are you really asking me that?"

"Look," he sighed, "all I want to do is go to bed, wake up, make a new fucking world with you, maybe have some nachos when we're finished." When he looked at her, she could only see a teenager, a child. Like he was offering to hunt the monsters under her bed. "I would love it if you could tell me what's different, what's changed about you. What you clearly feel so awful about that you don't want me to know. But that's just it—don't you get it?"

He was staring pleadingly at her.

"Maybe there's a version where we end up together, Rhodes, but it isn't this one," he said. "Maybe that just means not yet, but it definitely means not now. How could it be now?" he pointed out, his voice absent any of its usual playfulness—any of its eviscerating arrogance—though Libby found she could just as easily hate it nonetheless. "You can't even tell me the truth!"

"You want the truth?" She leapt to her feet then, agitated. "I trusted someone who betrayed me, Varona, who trapped me and forced me to make an untenable choice, so it's not completely out of the realm of understandable that I don't want to talk about it, don't you think?"

"You're angry at me? Really?" He was standing now, too. "How can you be this angry when I've done nothing but tell you how much you matter to me?" His eyes narrowed scornfully. "And don't act like you've been pining for me when you know you went to Tristan for help. Not me."

Libby was fuming, pushed over the edge by a flood of anger and bitterness and guilt. "Do you even realize how childish you sound—"

"Go ahead and call me a child." His tone had darkened. "Everyone does. Do you understand that? Everyone *but Gideon* does," he said with a layer of warning, "and so maybe that means something to me. Maybe that means more to me than some twisted mirror game we've spent six years playing," he snapped, "chasing each other's tails over and over only to realize that all we're ever doing is *running away*—"

"What do you want me to be? You want me to be perfect Saint Gideon so that you can feel good about loving me instead of trapped? I *killed* someone, Varona." The words fell out of her mouth unbidden. "I'm not sorry, I'm not even sad—" She felt like she was wringing the words out of her, cracking every vertebra to let the truth fall out. "I'm not the same person I was, and could you still have loved me, knowing that? Knowing the whole truth of what I am?"

"*Yes.*" His hands were up now, combatively. "Yes, you fucking idiot. Do you think that's what I love about you, your morals?" The look on his face was pure exasperation. "Did you really think I could only love you if your hands were clean?"

She blinked.

Blinked again.

Nico's chest sagged, and he scraped a hand through his hair in frustration.

"I will spend my life orbiting yours," Nico said, and the exhaustion in his voice, she knew it. She understood it. "I consider it a privilege. Does that mean less if we never sleep together? If we never have babies and hold hands, does that have to mean less? You're in every world I exist in, your fate is my fate, either you follow me or I follow you, it doesn't matter which and I don't care. If that's not love then maybe I don't understand love, and that's fine with me—it doesn't make me angry to know I'm actually an idiot after all. And if it's not enough for you, then okay, it's not enough. That doesn't change the fact that I'm willing to give it. What you're willing to accept doesn't change what I'm willing to give."

He took a step back. Two steps. He walked to the door and she didn't stop him.

Then he paused on the threshold, looking back at her where she faced the flames in the hearth, cooling herself on the shapes of them.

"Rhodes," he said. A question, or a plea.

She closed her eyes, sighing.

"Fine. You're right," she said. "I know you're right. It's just . . ." She waved a hand. "Wine."

He hesitated. "Are you sure you—"

"—even *like* red wine?" she finished for him. "No." She shook her head. "That stuff tastes like Jesus."

Nico managed a laugh, and she almost did. Almost.

"This," he said, voice cracking with sincerity. "You and me. You can't escape it. You don't get an out."

"Is that a threat?"

"Yes. It's a promise, but menacing." He lingered a moment longer. "I mean it, Rhodes, I don't think I'm the answer you're looking for. You wouldn't be any more fulfilled with me. You'd just have this, exactly what you feel right now, but with someone who can dance much better than Tristan."

Nico looked smug, of course he did, but to her benefit—to her great relief—Libby knew he was right. She realized it like engaging a reflex she'd been afraid to test—like finally putting weight on a muscle she'd been routinely, chronically babying. The thing his simulation had said to her—that everything in her life revolved around him, or eventually led back to him—had never been real. Nothing more than Libby offering herself another invisible finish line, another weak and insubstantial solution. Because if that were true, then admitting her feelings for Nico might have given her closure, completing a very simple, very solvable feedback loop—but it didn't, because it wasn't the problem. It wasn't about him at all.

She understood that now, the reason she failed the ritual. Well, presumably she would never have been initiated because there were rules, but the reason she'd lost so spectacularly—the actual, much sharper truth obscured by the convenient romantic one—was that everything in her life *was* about proving something, but that had begun long before Nico de Varona had entered it. She hadn't met him and *then* felt starved, insatiable, unwanted. She had met him already feeling those things—already believing them, building herself unsteadily on top of them—and Nico's presence as some living embodiment of her shortcomings had gladly stoked the flames.

So she did manage a laugh, albeit a hoarse one. "Stop telling me how I feel, Varona. You don't get to tell me what I want."

"No, but I can ask you." He shrugged. "What do you want?"

She looked back at the flames.

What did she want?

An answer. Fuck it, he was right. That's what all of this was—had been—for.

She wanted an answer, but not to this.

"I want to do the experiment," she said. "Tomorrow."

She wanted to believe it was her decision. That it was rational because it had come from her, and not from half a lifetime's well of loneliness.

Not that it mattered.

"Okay," Nico said. "Okay."

. . .

"You always have this dream," said Gideon.

She didn't know when he'd gotten there, or how. There was smoke coming from somewhere over the hills, just out of sight. At first she thought it was the neighbors barbecuing, the sizzle of burgers, her father's silly apron that Libby had made at school in fifth grade. Katherine with the eye roll. Dad, you look stupid. Normal things. Normal life.

But now Gideon was here, and Libby understood that for whatever reason, she now connected him with this, the intersection of dream and nightmare.

She glimpsed something, a blemish on what had been her nostalgic suburban idyll. A familiar pair of shoes sticking out from underneath the neighbor's chaise lounge. An unmoving pair of legs. A pool of blood seeping into the cracks in the pavement.

Lifeless eyes. A hand unfurled.

She shaded her eyes from the red-burning sun, saying nothing.

"I can't find him," Gideon remarked mildly, not looking at her, and Libby closed her eyes.

The world can end one of two ways, Ezra reminded her with his legs folded into his chest, next to the heart he used to say beat for her. *Fire or ice. I saw both.*

He used to say a lot of things. *I love you. I can kill her.*

Lifeless eyes. A hand unfurled.

Wake up, she thought. *Wake up.*

. . .

She had forgotten the particulars of this bedroom. The way that, for a year, the sun had poured in too early from the east side of the house unless she pulled the drapes tightly shut.

She was supposed to be sleeping—resting. She turned on her side and the door opened behind her, then fell gently shut.

She felt him climb into bed with her, curving around her with his usual grace.

"Maybe it'll be different," said Tristan's voice in her ear. "After we do this. Maybe it's something about the house, or the archives, or maybe we just have to shake something loose. I don't know." Then again, quietly, "I don't know."

She reached behind her to take his hand, toying with his knuckles.

"Maybe," she agreed, which had the flavor of an apology. Top notes of a wish.

. . .

When they made their way down to the painted room, Nico was levitating a large planter outside through one of the windows surrounding the apse. Tristan glanced out the window, observing the small garden Nico seemed to be constructing of potted houseplants, then looked questioningly at Gideon, who shrugged.

"Neither of us know which one the fig plant is," he explained.

Tristan and Libby exchanged a glance of mutual bemusement, but were interrupted by the sound of entry behind them before either could reply.

"This would be easier," came Dalton's voice, "if we had the naturalist."

Tristan didn't turn, but Libby did, surveying Dalton with a glance. He was less poised than usual, or perhaps needed a haircut, or a shave. She and Tristan had not exchanged much more than a few words with Dalton in greeting upon his arrival the previous day, though for obvious reasons Libby had worried whether his presence might represent an unknown variable of Parisa's agenda. (Not as related to the experiment, necessarily, but some other, more furtive motivation Libby would not understand until she woke up hungover, divested of her scruples and clothes.) Then again, maybe when Parisa had warned Libby to leave the experiment alone, what she meant was that she was washing her hands of all of it. Or maybe she just wanted Dalton gone. Neither would have surprised Libby, who was coming to think of Parisa in retrospect as an insignificant piece of the equation.

"Believe me, I tried," came Nico's chipper voice, absent any emotional damage or fraught psychological torment from the previous night's discussion. He emerged through the window with an easy sweep of the room's occupants, Libby included, as if nothing of concern had recently been done or said. Probably true. Probably reasonable. "Reina's not having it. But I think she's hoping I'll fail and then she can gloat a bit and call me an idiot. No harm, no foul," he added, and if that was meant for Libby in any way, she decided to simply accept it.

"I don't expect to fail." Dalton glanced sideways at Gideon, who was frowning at him with a sense of unease, possibly recognition. "What are you contributing to the experiment?"

Gideon opened his mouth warily, then closed it. "Just the audience."

Dalton's gaze narrowed. "We don't need an audience."

"Emotional support," Nico offered quickly, manifesting again at Libby's elbow. "Fetcher of snacks, master of hydration. You don't mind, do you?" he asked in a murmured aside to Libby as Tristan turned away, conspicuously fixing his attention on his coffee cup. "It just seemed weird to make Gideon wait outside."

Dalton appeared to have disregarded this as a matter of concern, instead signaling Tristan over. Libby watched as Tristan braced, irritated at being summoned, but gave in, wandering over while Dalton produced a thick notebook full of maniacally scribbled notes.

Libby and Nico were alone in the corner. Gideon pointedly busied himself with the readjustment of the books on a shelf across the room.

"Gideon can do something in dreams, can't he?" Libby said in an undertone as Nico looked at her with surprise.

"Of course. Didn't you realize that last year? He's the one who found you."

"I know that, but we never actually talked about what that meant." She realized her voice sounded guarded when Nico's forehead creased with apparent concern.

"You're not mad, are you? I guess it feels invasive at first," he acknowledged in a troubled voice, "but we needed him if we were ever going to find you—and anyway, he's not going to interfere with the experiment, so don't worry about that," he added hastily. "If anything, I'm a little—"

Nico stopped, his mouth still forming words.

"Just say it, Varona," Libby murmured, and he turned to her with a look of something not quite apologetic enough. This, she reminded herself. This was the Varona she knew and did not love. He was right, he was the same, and maybe she craved that sameness, or needed it or clung to it or something. Before him had been grief and after him had come guilt.

It was not rejection, she told herself.

"Do we think it's odd?" Nico said. "The messages we got from Parisa. Dalton being here without her."

"It's his research, not hers." Libby didn't want to call it a relief. That was too strong a word. She knew what she was capable of alone; knew, too, what she was capable of doing with Nico. Wasn't that the trouble, knowing what she'd always known? She resented it, being tied to him, but the real weight to carry around was the irony, the unassailable significance, the ease of picking up where the other left off.

The horror of knowing what it meant to be a soulmate. Not quite as romantic as the stories made it seem.

"I know, I know, I just—I've never seen him do any magic before, not really. And it's . . . another variable," Nico said. His hair was askew and he seemed about to explain something to Libby that she already knew, like the definition of a variable.

"We've all conjured together before," she pointed out.

"Not without Reina. Not *with* Dalton." Nico was speaking quickly and quietly now, like he worried Dalton might overhear.

"Aren't you the one insisting we should do this?" Libby glanced at him with more admonishment than she intended.

"Well, right, the circumstances are just—" He shook his head. "But you're right, we need him. It's fine."

She hadn't technically said it was fine, just that he'd been in a rush. Before she could point it out, though, he assured her, "I trust you, Rhodes."

At that precise moment, Tristan looked over.

Do you trust me?

Libby shook herself, annoyed, counting the signs and then choosing to discard them. That was an old reflex, looking for things that could go wrong. Searching for evidence of failure. She was tired of it, she was no longer that person, she wanted this. Cosmic significance could go and hang.

Gideon's eyes met hers across the room and she felt a flare of something. Certainty. Envy. If anyone didn't belong in the room—if anyone had not made adequately humbling choices to exist within these walls—it was Gideon, and Libby tried not to call that feeling rage. Callum wasn't here, so she didn't have to put a name to it. She knew what she did *not* feel, which was doubt.

She'd forfeited the right to doubt a long time ago now. Not that it didn't linger now and then. In her dreams. In her mind. In her search history. The redundancy of typing *Belen Jiménez* only to produce exactly what Libby had expected and no more than that. No less.

She didn't have to sit around and wait for meaning. Significance was heavy, like the weight of the stars on her back. No amount of questioning it would lighten the burden. No grief had ever brought the dead back to life.

What Belen had believed of Libby couldn't diminish her now. What Tristan had seen of her couldn't compromise her. Nico trusted her, and Nico was right, had always been right. Either she was enough or she never would be. Either this choice was hers, too, or nothing was, and who could ever be satisfied with that—with having power only to waste it? Belen Jiménez had all but disappeared into the annals of time. All that was left was clarity, and that voice, the one Libby had chosen, had never been Belen's.

What else are you willing to break, Miss Rhodes—

"Make sure to stretch," Libby told Nico. "It's time to make a new fucking world."

—and who will you betray to do it?

There is a sob story here, obviously. In Atlas's defense, he won't burden you much longer with the rest of it. The fundamental questions have been answered; the important details have been shared. What else is left to ask? What can be made of nature or nurture? There is only choice. There are only ends. This is what Atlas Blakely believes and we are in his story now, so this is all you need to know.

It isn't sad right away, the series of events that follows Alexis Lai proverbially knocking on Atlas's door. She's thirty when she does it, or maybe thirty-one—time has dulled that particular significance, but Atlas knows it was mere months after their exit from the Society manor house, no more than half a year. Atlas was twenty-six then, a researcher, learning the ins and outs of the Caretaker job; studying the Society like an exam he's soon to take, and planning—but not yet meeting—with Ezra Fowler, his accomplice in time.

As you have likely gathered by now, Atlas is not exactly what one might call a *good person*. There's a lot to be said about what *the system* produces—a lot to be said about systems in general—so, in some ways, Atlas is a product of a maths equation, the parameters for which are so predictable they form the basis of any political platform by the left. There are the virtuous poor, the good immigrants, the martyrs and saints of an underfed class, and Atlas is not one of those. He's not without his tools or choices. A person with Atlas Blakely's propensity for magic is not exactly helpless and, likewise, a person with his ambitions and desires is not completely heaven-sent. If he hadn't grown up running jobs as a telepath for hire then maybe he wouldn't see everything that way, like an endgame with a clever workaround. In another world, Atlas Blakely does something with much smaller consequences, like becoming very rich and living a life of unethically derived capital investment that ends in the occasional bloodshed rather than outright societal collapse.

(In terms of Atlas's early life, there are the years he spends with his mother before she begins to experience an uptick in bad thoughts, thoughts that Atlas can hear but not make sense of, which go away when she drinks—a form of self-medication that can also swallow her good voices up. Like building a wall that shrinks her smaller and smaller until not even Atlas can get in. Bolstering his mother's crumbling mind requires keeping them both alive, which, simply put, requires money. It also requires sympathy, kindness, and love, things that no one but Atlas seems to have for her, but money is the easiest of those things to procure, even if the others are a lot more valuable. Too valuable, and in worryingly short supply.

So, simply put: until Atlas is recruited by the Society, Atlas agrees to stand there and hold things and not look too closely at any of the thoughts involved when people assign him directives. He simply turns the money into groceries and rent and doesn't trouble himself with whatever comes next. Anyway—)

"Neel's dead," Alexis says, explaining apologetically that Neel *also* believes Atlas has killed him, does Atlas know anything about this? Atlas, plausible denier that he is, says that's ridiculous, he has an alibi which is that he was several countries away and not a murderer, to which Alexis says—with a faint flush in her cheeks that suggests she really isn't a fan of confrontation by the living—that she figured as much but, well, anyway, here's Neel.

She steps aside and in the doorway there he is, Neel Mishra, telescope in hand, perfectly fine. Well, sort of. Atlas is uniquely positioned to know that Neel's not as fine as he looks—that there are . . . things missing, or perhaps new things where the old ones were, the equivalent of oxidation over the place where his instincts or sense of self should be, or maybe, optimistically, his depth perception has merely worsened, or he's lost a few centimeters here and there; can no longer see the world from the same position, instead just a little bit below it?—but as we know, Atlas is not and has never been the paragon of virtue we all want him to be. Instead, Atlas points out to Alexis that it's rude to openly accuse someone of murder when one is a necromancer who can clearly ask the victim about the alleged murder. In reply, Alexis waves a hand, impatiently stomping off while Neel is sheepish but adamant. He saw it in the stars. Atlas Blakely will kill them all.

Yikes, says Atlas, or something of that equivalent, and he plays it off like he doesn't know exactly what it means, even though he does, because he is not an idiot and he knows, as Neel has not thought to ask the cosmos, that the man that Atlas Blakely supposedly murdered to honor the Society's initiation terms is very much alive—in fact, they have an appointment looming. In lieu of divulging such obviously problematic details, Atlas asks Neel how he died. Alexis returns with chips, says aneurysm. He seems fine now, observes Atlas. Yes, he was hardly even dead, basically just sleeping. They laugh about it. Atlas puts them both at ease, dismantles the bomb in Neel's head, which is something that can be done with brains that are resurrected and mostly lucid but not the ones besieged by voices and left behind by their lovers to care for their illegitimate sons. (Ironic, isn't it? The powers we have and the ones we don't. The people we can save and the ones we can't.)

"You're probably right, oh well, I guess even though I'm the most powerful divinist in the world it remains slimly possible that the stars might have lied," says Neel. This is lightly paraphrased on Atlas's part.

Neel returns to his telescope and the woman he loves, which the stars have unfortunately determined he will not live long enough to marry. Alexis, however, stays behind with Atlas, or rather, she stays behind. The "with Atlas" part is an afterthought. She tells him that she'd just come from a meeting with someone in the offices of the Society. They asked her career aspirations and she said, well, pretty much exactly what she was doing before, except with more government clearance. It's granted. Just like that.

"What did you tell them?" she asks Atlas suspiciously, and he sees something in her mind that's very unnerving. Neel trusted him, but Alexis doesn't, and Atlas considers changing her opinion. A little tweak, small but structural, which is something he does with everyone else in the Society, because what they think of him is critical to the plan that he and Ezra have made to one day have the Society and its archives under their command. Criminals who leave signatures are always caught, though, so Atlas doesn't go so far as to make people *like* him. He repairs any doubt they might have, plants their opinions on a faultless platform of rationality. What is there to fear from Atlas Blakely? Nothing at all, especially then, at twenty-six, when he has yet to know the full extent of what the archives contain, or what kind of moral necessity can drive a man to betray his only friend.

But Atlas has inherited something from his mother. Illness, mostly, but also exhaustion. A misfiring in the very brain that can overpower other thoughts; an alteration in the very mind that can alter others however Atlas wishes, whenever Atlas wishes to, which Atlas does not do to Alexis at that moment, because he's feeling tired and guilty and a bit like perhaps things would be better for everyone had he not been born. He feels this a lot. In recent years he's given himself an answer, obviously, which is the part of the story you already know, because you can clearly see that he has a goal in mind and a plan in motion. He's going to find a way out of this world, the one where the Society hoards its own shit and only doles it out to the rich and classically powerful for the price of a ritual slaughter. Even at twenty-six,

Atlas Blakely knows he's going to make a new world. He just doesn't mean it literally yet.

So anyway, in the moment when Alexis Lai asks Atlas what his future is, he's angry and tired of burning, unable to concentrate, missing the very same mother he resents while craving some falseness to dull the noise. (At times like these, Atlas still hears everything the same way he always does, but his interpretations of what he hears changes, not unlike the weather. Magic is not the same thing as clarity. Knowledge is not the same as wisdom. That is the duality of man, in a way. A person can see everything and nothing all at once.)

"I told them I just want to be happy," Atlas says.

"Ah," says Alexis. "What'd they say?"

(*Consider a change in vocation, Mr. Blakely. See what the archives have to say about that.* On a whim, he'd written "happiness" on a slip of parchment, then watched the pneumatic tubes deliver his response. It had come from a place of sarcasm, so he probably shouldn't have been surprised by the reply. REQUEST DENIED.)

"They said they'll get back to me in four to six business days," Atlas replies.

Later, Alexis comes back to the Society manor house (where, for the record, Atlas now lives alone, their Caretaker Huntington choosing to remain in his country house in Norfolk whenever there are no fresh minds present to train or corrupt) with Folade, who was recently poisoned. When Folade insists on consulting the archives and Alexis, staring hard at Atlas, says nothing, Atlas wonders if he should have been a bit more proactive. Alexis's doubt in him has now grown roots, which is a difficult condition to remove. Not impossible—very doable, in fact—but he doesn't, and at the time he thinks this is his great error, the grave mistake that will be his undoing. Folade is clever, a physicist, very science-minded. She spends the evening trying a variety of different requests to the archives while Alexis and Atlas quietly eat a bowl of noodles in the kitchen. Eventually, Folade stomps back in and tells Atlas she thinks it's a curse. Not the most scientific of conclusions and even Folade seems disappointed by it. She asks Alexis if she's heard anything more from Neel, so Alexis calls, no answer. She wipes sesame oil from the edge of the bowl and says with a heavy sigh: *Fuck.*

After Alexis brings Neel back the second time, the doubt is flowering. She says, "Has anyone heard from Ivy?" and when Atlas says no, Alexis gives a similar sigh and storms out.

By the third time Neel is revived from a lethal bout of pneumonia, Alexis no longer has any doubt. Now it's just barrels of accusation. "At least don't sit there denying it anymore. Either take the thought away from me—I know you can do that, don't lie—or tell me what the hell is going on!"

How many times can a woman look you dead in the eye and dare you to change her mind before you finally realize you're kind of in love with her? Three, it turns out. But this isn't the part of the story you're interested in, so we'll go right ahead and move on.

At what point does Atlas Blakely, idiot with a past, become Caretaker of the Alexandrian Society, and thus a man capable of destroying the world? Arguably he was born with that power, because if there are blueprints for our lives, then this was always one of the outcomes. This was always a possibility for Atlas, or perhaps it's a possibility, period, because if one tiny grain of sand in the ocean of human history can be capable of such a thing, then can't any one of them be in danger of causing it? If life is just a system of dominos falling that then leads to the collapse of the world as we know it, then who's to say where it really begins? Perhaps it's his mother's fault, or his father's, or it goes back even further than that, or perhaps something set in motion cannot be stopped. Perhaps the only way to stop something is to cancel reality altogether; to pull the rug out from beneath it so that reality is not reality at all.

This is the problem with knowledge: its inexhaustible craving. The madness inherent in knowing there is only more to know. It's a problem of mortality, of seeing the invariable end from the immovable beginning, of determining that the more you try to fix it, the more beginnings there are to discover, the more ways to reach the same unavoidable end. What version of Atlas Blakely does what he's told and simply pulls the trigger he's been given? He runs it in his head, the calculations, the projections where things go differently, and yet they never do. Neel could see the future—he warned Atlas this would happen—but did that change anything? Cassandra can't save Troy and Atlas can't save Alexis.

All that matters are the ends—and where can any of this end, apart from death?

VI

DETERMINISM

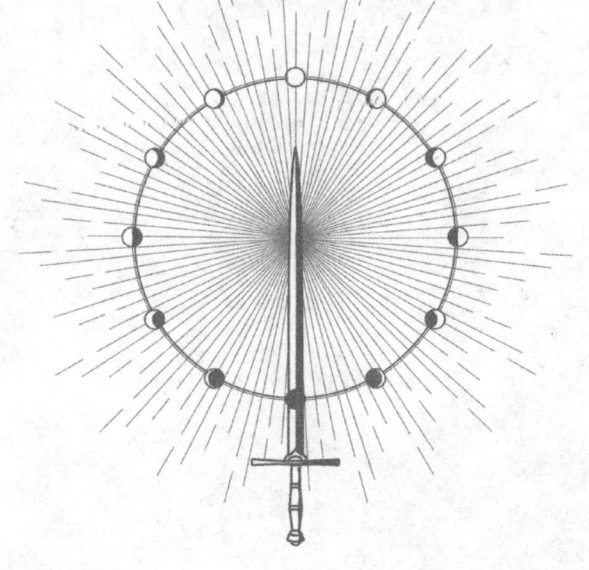

· REINA ·

SHE LIIIIIIIIVES!

Fireworks. Three red hearts. More fireworks. Party hat. Party hat. Kiss face. Party hat. Margarita. Clinking champagne glasses. Inexplicably, some kind of goblin face. A sneeze. Three crying faces. Party hat. Was he having a stroke? Probably. A birthday cake.

Ok I moved all the plants just for u lol, followed by photographic evidence. At least ten potted plants sat in a circle in the garden, near the roses.

PROBABLY NOTHING WILL GO WRONG! Ten more party hats. A thumbs-up. Two salsa dancers. Love u mean it

Reina shook her head. You should be arrested. Bye

She put her phone away and sighed, yawning a little from beneath the thinned-out canopy of an adolescent oak. It was November. This kind of warmth was absurd. True, she'd recently spent too much time on an island known for fog, but the heat of the sprawling Maryland park was inexplicably unbearable by anyone's standards. The weekend prior had been near-glacial with storms, and yet now the forecasted high far exceeded the region's most optimistic seasonal averages, to the point where the sparsity of remaining foliage made little difference. The lawn beneath Reina's feet thirsted loudly, tickling her ankles like tongues lapping roughly at her skin.

"I'm going to need to run an errand for the empire," Callum had told her that morning, presumably referring to the Forum's report of the Nova Corporation's wrongdoings (many of which Callum cheerfully confessed with stunning, unsolicited frequency). "Can you keep the divinity running without me in the meantime, or should we just put you on ice?"

"I'll be fine." Reina *had* wondered if he'd been feeling some heightening measure of responsibility as the investigation progressed. She was alarmed to discover she'd gotten used to Callum's presence, but did manage to recall that she hadn't always relied upon his magic (or his sarcasm) to get herself through the day. "Is going back to London something related to your family," she prompted, temporarily concerned he might shock them both with the truth, "or just your revenge project?"

"Oh, always," he said in an unhelpfully distracted tone. He'd been comparing two identical white shirts before throwing one in an overnight bag.

She wondered what drove him to his version of filial piety. Perhaps whatever it was that drove her to the opposite of such things. It was really for the best they'd never discuss it.

"Great." She lingered insouciantly near the door, allowing him to prolong the lie in what she considered a charitable endeavor. "Bring back Tristan's ear for safekeeping."

"Sure," he said, before looking up with a frown. "Mori, do you expect me to *dismember* him?" he asked, and to her shrug of obvious ambivalence, he made a face of repulsion. "And for the record, his ears are hardly anything of note."

"So true," she agreed. "Bring back his pectorals."

"I can't believe I'm saying this, but you're disgusting," Callum informed her admiringly, and then was gone, both of them fully aware that Tristan would be alive and well and completely unharmed and Callum would never admit that this particular matter was his version of philanthropy. Once or twice over the last hour Reina had considered reaching out to him to ask if his field trip was going well, but then narrowly managed to remember at the last second that 1) it didn't matter and 2) she didn't care.

It was true that without Callum there were fewer actionable items to cross off her list, which wasn't ideal, but not all the elements of her plan required him. She chose to pay a visit to Charlie Baek-Maeda's reelection celebration in Maryland, figuring she did not need to *influence* the crowd so much as observe them. Quietly check in.

She glanced at the time, which was what she'd brought her phone out of her pocket for (and not to check Nico's text again, though she did feel grudgingly amused by the picture. For fuck's sake. She had missed that damned fig). There were still a few more minutes before the event was scheduled to begin. Several people hovered nearby, trying to find some semblance of shade amid increasingly skeletal vegetation. They were mostly young, obviously liberal. Baek-Maeda's campaign slogan was splashed across their chests in rainbows, bright and cheery. *BE THE REVOLUTION!* in the entire spectrum of Roy G. Biv.

Beside Reina, a young Japanese American girl was standing with her white boyfriend, stickers with Baek-Maeda's face on them dotting her cropped tank top. "Oh my god, babe, look," she gasped, a thrill running through the crowd at the very same moment that Charlie Baek-Maeda appeared, his dog's leash in one hand, his baby daughter Nora bouncing on his hip. Reina followed his motion through the crowd, realizing that she was straining to see him.

Briefly, she smothered Callum's voice in her head. *You loooooove him.*

She didn't. Not the way Callum suggested, anyway, a fact he understood perfectly well or he wouldn't bother haranguing her with it. If anything, Charlie's wife, Jenni Baek-Maeda—a pediatric surgeon, because Charlie Baek-Maeda could not *be* more perfect—was considerably more aligned with Reina's interests, but it was this that Reina loved: the atmosphere that Charlie Baek-Maeda created. The crowd that his politics drew. The girl with her boyfriend. The baby. The undeniably adorable dog. Even if the whole thing was curated—even if the parasocial nature of an audience feeding off one man's convictions and loving his progeny was problematic and alarming—something about their tiny glimpses into Charlie Baek-Maeda's world made everything else feel . . . less pointless. It made everything seem, at least for the moment, right. Or at least a world that was capable of being fixed, and Reina needed that, the reminder that all this effort was for something. That a generation existed somewhere that authentically clung to something good, to the creation of something meaningful.

All gods had their chosen ones. Reina's just happened to be—according to both Callum and *The Washington Post*—conventionally hot.

Speaking of heat—the late-autumn sun, or what should have been fall but was still punishingly summer, was indomitable, borderline profane. Bare branches of the oak tree nearby swayed overhead, fanning her with an upbeat teenage whine of *Mother hot hot aeeeeeee!*, and Reina realized she'd drawn a few glances here and there as a result of it.

"Stop it," she muttered to the tree, which angstily huffed its irritation. Reina took a few steps away, moving closer to the stage.

There was a local band on stage playing a mix of original songs and covers, and Charlie Baek-Maeda—having handed his daughter off to his wife—took the stage, accepting the lead singer's proffered guitar and strapping himself in with a laugh. He played a few chords, joining in, a song that everyone around Reina seemed to know. She thought of Callum again: *I wonder how many women just spontaneously ovulated.* Inwardly, she rolled her eyes. The song was infectious, like a disease. She was overcome with a sudden desire for lemonade. But other than that, she felt centered, and fine.

She looked over at Jenni Baek-Maeda, at the chubby baby in her arms, a pair of tiny headphones fixed around Nora's tiny ears to block out the ceaseless din of adoration for her father. Reina didn't even like babies. Jenni was wearing a red dress and she reminded Reina of someone. Long black hair, an irrationally perfect figure; the sense that, if challenged, she could easily outsmart everyone in the room. Someone handed baby Nora a petite bouquet of flowers and Reina thought of standing beside the manor house's garden, staring into a set of ice-cold eyes and reading something in them. Something desperate. Something true.

But then the song ended, Charlie Baek-Maeda took the mic, and Reina pushed all thoughts of Parisa Kamali aside.

Or tried to. She wondered what it was Callum had seen in Parisa that he refused to explain to Reina, probably because he assumed she wouldn't understand. Whereas what *he* didn't understand was that if Parisa wasn't a rival, then Reina was just a bully—a role reversal that didn't make sense—so he should really tell her the truth and spare them both the trauma of her having to worry, or worse, to care.

Maybe that was really the worst of it. That if Reina couldn't hate Parisa then she'd have to acknowledge something else she felt about her, something far more complicated, like the fact that Reina wanting to win didn't work out so comfortably if it meant Parisa had to lose. So maybe Callum was doing her a favor in the end?

But that didn't seem likely. This was Callum, after all.

Mother, let us fix it. A patch of dandelions were restless. *Mother let us grow, let us goooooooooo—*

Charlie Baek-Maeda's speech was punctuated every now and then by applause, some cheers, some fervent nods and whoops. Reina's mind drifted as she listened, growing drowsy beneath the morning sun. Nearly everyone had thin patches of moisture spreading over their Baek-Maeda T-shirts, hands alternately framing their brows from the glare. There was motion in the crowd, like a breeze that riffled the grass, parting a path that nobody resisted. They were all equally melting, Reina supposed.

It was strange, though. The quickness. It was disruptive. Reina wasn't the only one who looked away from Baek-Maeda and into the crowd, from which a ripple of motion suddenly bloomed. A gasp. A scream.

MOTHERMOTHER, something shrieked. *MOTHER AIIIIEEEEEE EEEEEE!*

A sound went off, explosive, ringing in Reina's ears by the time she finally clocked it. The thin wail in warning had come from the bouquet of cut flowers clutched in Nora Baek-Maeda's chubby hands. Reina felt herself turning to find safety, her pulse racing, but before she could decide where to turn, another shot went off. She was jolted apart from the girl's boyfriend beside her, a shock of her own power surging so abruptly at the suddenness of the sound that a root had burst forth from the asphalt, tearing through the crowd and leaving the ground below them to heave like tectonic plates in a wave of rippling aftershocks. Reina fell unsteadily backward onto the undulating ground, knees buckling as she tried to keep her balance and failed.

A high-pitched whine of static screeched in Reina's ear as she struggled from her back to her knees, heart thudding with the sudden recollection of a similar scene. A set of familiar balustrades, gunmen emerging like toy soldiers from the dark. Nico's laugh, ringing from somewhere just out of sight. Reina blinked, vision obscuring as she lifted her head, a rush of blood loud in her ears. The crowd had blurred into a sea of colors and shapes. There was a woman screaming, a dog barking, someone was shouting, shoving Reina aside just as she'd finally pushed up to her feet.

MOTHERMOTHERMOTHER WAKEUPWAKEUP—

Yes, wake up. Focus. Charlie Baek-Maeda had dropped out of sight, his body flung backward and now sprawled, lifeless, on the stage. The everyman pair of jeans, the revolution pin, the sunny rainbow insignia were drenched now by a pool of dark red, like a shadow. People had swarmed around him, everyone was yelling. An ambulance, Reina thought. Someone should call an ambulance. She looked, bizarrely, for the baby. Where was the baby? Someone cover her eyes. She shouldn't have to see this. She shouldn't have to hear her mother scream.

Reina took a step, she didn't know where, her blood was pumping in her ears, she was going the wrong direction. She thought she heard Callum's voice—Callum, was he okay? Where was Callum? When had Callum's welfare begun to matter to her? Would Callum have known this was going to happen and had he seen the baby, was she safe?—and turned, *Mother are you listening, Mother pay attention—*

MOTHER THE TIME HAS COME TO OPEN YOUR EYES!

Reina felt an arm grab her around her waist, followed by a hand that came over her mouth. She bit down and threw an elbow blindly, with a burst of something crude. She heard a masculine voice cry out in pain and turned, ready to strike again, when she realized her attacker was in uniform. His expression of fury from the blow she'd landed to his nose morphed rapidly to a knowing smile; a blatant invitation to try it again and see how that went.

What would happen to her if she attacked an American police officer in plain sight? Reina's breath came haltingly and she took a hasty step back, colliding with yet another fleeing member of Baek-Maeda's swarming crowd.

The officer came toward her, signaling to someone out of Reina's range of sight while her heart hammered in her chest. *Breathe. Think.* The police officer who'd grabbed her had a partner, at least one. She could see out of the corner of her eye another blur in her periphery, another oncoming attack. The lawn below her was screaming and she nearly tripped over the root of the oak that had burst up from beneath the stampeding crowd, stumbling long enough to reward her attackers with an opening. They were coming for her, no question about it, she'd forgotten to pay attention to her surroundings, or maybe this much unintentional magic on her part had been what set them off. Either way, someone now had a hand on her arm, wrenching it back as she tried again to pull away. Nobody would notice if someone took her, of course nobody would notice, everyone else was equally running for their lives. What a fucking country. Two sets of assassins and now a baby would grow up without a father, and as for Reina . . .

Fuck, what loss was Reina to anyone? Fuck, fuck, fuck. At least if nobody was paying attention they couldn't stop her from fighting back. She wrestled out of the grip of the second attacker, striking blindly at the face of the first. Her chosen one was still on stage bleeding to death; she was going to be taken—arrested, maybe, or killed—and had this been the whole point? Her whole life? *This* was what she had fought for—her agency, her right to exist independently of anyone or anything—just so she could go down somewhere in a foreign country where no one would even see her, a tree brought down in the forest as if she'd never existed at all? Some mother she was. Some person, some daughter. Some friend. The cop she'd punched had reeled back like a pendulum while the other had thrown an arm around her neck from behind, an artless chokehold. Reina scrabbled blindly at the hand around her neck, kicking at the other, but she was tiring quickly, exhausted and hot, straining so hard it ached in her lungs, a breath she couldn't quite catch. She heard Parisa's laugh in her ear, the mockery of Parisa's little smirk. Parisa, who never found herself cornered. Parisa, who always found a way out. *Oh, Reina. Are you a naturalist or aren't you?*

Her vision smeared, airpipe faltering. She felt the impact of her own kicks landing, but not nearly forceful enough. Everything was diminishing, everything was fading.

Help, Reina thought desperately. *Help!*

For a moment she thought she'd been swallowed up by rage. She thought she'd disappeared inside it. The earth was trembling and she thought, *Fuck, Varona, I'm sorry, the whole thing was so stupid, I just honestly thought I had more time. I thought it could wait, that we could talk about it later, when I was over it, when I felt nothing anymore, when I felt nothing at all. But here we are, I could die at any moment, and that day still hasn't come. I don't know why you intentionally seek this feeling out, Nico, why you love to put yourself at risk, you're not meant to face this down and thrive, it's counterintuitive, it's bad for the species. I'm sorry I didn't just tell you that even though you're an idiot, it's still a hell of a lot easier to miss you than to hate you. I'm sorry I wasted a whole year trying to live a stupid lie.*

Everything went black. Reina was braced for disaster, twisting with less and less proficiency out of her attackers' reach, when a sudden shift in momentum sent her plummeting to the grass beneath her. The officer who'd grabbed her from behind had abruptly released her, and Reina twisted around to prepare for another attack, her vision still dangerously compromised. It was dark all around her, pitch black like a sodden, heady midnight. After a moment, she realized it wasn't just exhaustion that had blurred her vision. Color had gone away because the lawn, the ground itself, had opened up.

The charge she'd been expecting still hadn't come. Blearily, as if from a dream, Reina's eyes adjusted to the darkness and she caught sight of a set of vines that had materialized from somewhere, stretching and twisting until they'd braided themselves across the flayed open ground, forming a set of restraints. The cop who'd held her in a chokehold was now screaming obscenities, thrashing, disappearing slowly into the molten blackness of raw, unopened earth while the other, visibly purpling from Reina's kick to his face, aimed his gun at the teenage oak tree, which was reaching out for Reina with its spindly branching arms.

Mother help! wailed the tree, younger now, no longer filled with juvenile tedium. Frightened and lost, like brand-new innocence. Tiny headphones, cut flowers, the kind of world no baby deserved. The kind of violence no child should have to see. The fragile voice grew distant, smaller and smaller, shrinking and fading, like departing through annals of time.

The gun went off, deafening, a ringing left in Reina's ears where the sound of nature's voice should have been. She felt her equilibrium topple and fail yet again, knocking her dizzily prostrate onto the earth, unable to discern which way was upright, which path was forward. She forced herself to her knees, her view of the park still a bloodstained darkness punctuated only by occasional blurs of motion. The cop's silhouette swam again before her as dirt cycloned up from the ground, obscuring her view of his hand wrapped tight around his pistol. The smell of gunpowder burned familiarly like smoke in Reina's lungs. She retched up bile, spitting out of the side of her mouth, and for the first time that Reina could remember, she understood that nothing was coming to her rescue. She could hear nothing but the sound of her own pulse.

A wave of momentary stillness brought her clarity. The thick cloud of dirt—or ash—cleared from her eyes for the brevity of an instant, and she saw, seemingly in slow motion, the truth of her distance from the cop. A few short but painful steps. His head was turned and his arm was raised in the direction of the teenage oak, his finger resting on the trigger for a second, more lethal shot.

The world resumed its frantic pace, momentum spiraling through her.

"No," said Reina, launching to her feet and clawing at the officer's arm, scrabbling blindly, recklessly for the gun. "No, you don't get to touch her—!"

He threw an elbow into her nose, breaking it. Reina bit her tongue, tasting blood, and crumpled limply to the ground.

· CALLUM ·

I t wasn't a courtroom. That was their first mistake. The blond woman under interrogation inside the university chambers looked more like a bust on a pedestal than a criminal on trial. Obviously nobody had asked Callum his opinion, but even he could have warned them she'd arrive radiant, pristine—not too smug, not too guilty. Surely they had expected someone different and were realizing their error now—the way the woman glowing angelically beneath warm, academically softened light had conjured up some innate, sacrosanct goodness that only she could project while a row of balding men faced her down, unsmiling. She looked like she was being bullied and Callum already knew it, that no caption from the coverage of this trial could remove the impression that Selene Nova was the victim of a weaponless, self-indulgent witch hunt. It didn't matter her actual sins, nor the sins of the father.

Or, more aptly, the son.

Callum crossed one leg over the other from his vantage point in the audience, realizing that his presence hadn't been necessary to do a damn thing. His sister was fully capable of handling this, and the moment her eyes fell on his, blankly, and with pointedly withheld recognition, he felt a familiar wave of the exhaustion she had always felt for him. Ownership, a responsibility of care, the way some people fostered sick pets. *Well, the poor thing needs a home,* so on and so forth, but that didn't necessarily halt all repulsion. It didn't necessarily equate to love.

The trouble was that Selene was not a bad person, or not a bad enough person. Presumably the Forum thought they'd be dealing with Callum's father, who would have appeared guilty—racist, classist, bigoted, a product of a foregone era—even before opening his mouth. Selene was different; she was careful enough as managing partner to defend as necessary the various business practices the Nova conglomerate had been brought under fire for. Nobody could prove something as unquantifiable as *influence.* That was the nature of it, was it not? Nobody could *prove* that government officials had been persuaded or that audits had been altered or that any of the Novas actually disliked Callum aside from a slight niggling in the corner of their minds; a sense that surely no logic could defend an outcome of this nature.

Some things you simply had to take at face value. *I can't speak to the nature of my brother's political involvement except to say it is of no relation to any corporate dealings.* The best arguments were the simplest, especially when they weren't even lies.

Where is my brother now? An incredible feat for Selene not to let her gaze stray into the audience, though it was one of many performances in which Selene Nova had been trained from birth. *I wish I knew. But as to the matter of our business practices, I assure you we have always maintained the most rigorous standards.*

Only ten minutes in and Callum could not be more aware that his presence was wholly unnecessary. Now that he thought about it, Selene probably had more to do with the errors the Forum had made than the Forum itself. Who had chosen this venue, who had determined the members of the adjudication committee, who had made sure to invite the press?

On second thought, magical influence was only one way to go about things. Money was more than enough. Or, as Selene put it: *Our success speaks for itself.*

Which, in its way, was true. So the Novas were more successful than any other conglomerate of their ilk. Did wealth *always* necessitate corruption? Yes, obviously—*obviously,* Callum thought with an inward scoff, profit was made off the backs of someone else's labor, that was the part widely considered genius—and thus, inevitably, some viewers would walk away from this sham of a trial radicalized by the obvious; by the uncompromisable paradox of an ethical billionaire, no matter how sweetly she spoke or how prettily she made false promises.

But as Callum had told Reina countless times, this wasn't a world where knowing that something was wrong did anything at all to prevent the ongoing nature of its wrongness. This was a world where stolen knowledge could stay stolen, because plenty of knowledge that came freely remained unscrutinized every day.

He rose to his feet with his usual feline elegance and nodded invisibly to his sister before leaving the room, choosing not to acknowledge the weight in his chest that might have been a reckoning. Probably Selene would take over now as CEO. Clearly the Novas would let Callum take the fall in some way, perhaps by mentioning that he'd been ousted from the company on account of oh, who could say, perhaps his history of routine tardiness or his unexplained two-year absconsion.

He was already out of sight, so the best he could do was stay there. Every oligarchy masquerading as a family had some generational black sheep. Look at any one of the sitting royals.

Callum emerged from the university library into a prodigious gasp of unseasonable heat, feeling parched, slightly sore, a bit annoyed by the need to redirect the eyes of every Forum trap that had so obviously been set for him. Disappointing, really, that this was the best they could do. He tried to make a game of it, sending this one off on a craving for biltong they'd clearly struggle to find while distracting that one with a daydream of heaving, pillowy breasts, but it was all starting to feel so monotonous, so undeniably silly. Callum already understood himself to be the threat the Forum had targeted most intensely, a fact that had been hysterical until this morning. Now it was merely infuriating, because he was so obviously useless in the end.

His sister did not want him. What Callum had helped build over the last two decades—ever since his father had come to the sinisterly critical realization that Callum's nannies were exclusively purchasing the snacks Callum preferred, or possibly that Callum's mother was more or less a caricature of happiness depending on whether or not Callum was in the room—was no longer necessary. Callum's contributions could stand on their own now, a billion that generated other billions just by interest alone, just by existing. The world was already dependent on Nova products, the market was already disrupted by Nova corporate practices, so what now? Callum could drop dead and frankly, it would make Selene look lovelier. She would only glow ethereally in black.

So what did that leave, exactly? He could help Reina with her silly little American congressional campaign, her schoolgirl crush on the physical embodiment of optimism. God, that would come crashing down on her head, either because the handsome congressman would inevitably disappoint her or because the adorable pink-cheeked baby would grow up to be a woman who made choices that her government did not like. Still, Callum supposed he should be getting back to Reina, on the off chance that someone had finally noticed she was far more dangerous than Callum, purely because she still cared what happened next.

What next, indeed. Only one person ever came to mind when Callum asked himself that. His hand twitched a moment as if to find his phone, but no, not yet. Not now. Chances were too high that he might say something counterproductive, such as I miss you or forgive me. Or tell me you love me, even once.

Though, it wasn't *not* inspiration. Tristan, and therefore Tristan's impending murder! What a bolstering thought. Callum adjusted his sunglasses, figuring Reina would ask him about his revenge plot regardless. Why not preempt the conversation's inevitability by tending to it like the nurturer he so obviously was? Besides, the pub was not so far away.

The walk did him good. It was peaceful, even refreshing, though the typically rowdy establishment was unnaturally quiet when he walked in. Unusual. Over the course of his walk he'd heard chanting from the other pubs and shops nearby, the grunts and whoops that usually meant one sportsman annihilating another. He thought he'd seen one of Adrian Caine's witches at one of the pubs along the way, though Callum had never bothered to commit their faces to memory. They all, for the most part, hulked.

Now, though, the quiet unnerved him. The pub's dining room was empty, without even a bartender standing by. Callum wandered over to the door separating the pub from Adrian's office, shoving it open to call into the hull of Gallows Hill.

"Alys?" he called, waiting for a response. Reina, he was sure, would have Words about his insistence on what she called poking the bear, but was it so wrong to check in, say hello? Obviously Callum would continue to return to Adrian Caine's pub for as long as such things remained interesting. Purposes of vengeance, et cetera, which did not technically require checking on a teenage girl he barely knew, and yet he felt ignoring her would be far less productive. (Not because she belonged in some way to Tristan, of course. Though arguably she did, and if Callum could not be close to Tristan—for, again, purposes of vengeance—then Alys Caine was the next best thing.)

Step one of the revenge plan: infiltrate the family. Step two was a little up in the air, but somewhere down the line Callum felt it would resolve itself neatly, mission accomplished, or something vaguely like that.

In any case, the pub was unusually quiet. Odd. Callum reached around for distress and did not feel it, though there was something else. A little flicker of it: the sulfury mouthfeel of sabotage. It was somewhere nearby, and Callum turned, searching the shadows for motion.

"You really must have a death wish," remarked the adolescent voice of Tristan Caine's half sister, and if Callum had been himself in the moment, he probably would have clocked it, the hint of warning that lined the silhouette of her half-concealed face.

But he didn't feel fear. He didn't taste danger. It was relief at first—good, she was fine, nothing to worry about here. Bland relief was often flavorless,

like a cool glass of water, so at first he didn't recognize the particular powerlessness of silence. For Callum, everything was tasteless beyond the presence
of spilled beer and old wood. Quiet.

All the better to hear the sound of a gun cocking pointedly at his back.

· PARISA ·

The apartment had an overwhelming smell of something. A mix of cleaning solution and something else, something that struck her as bodily. Vomit, maybe, or urine. Something animalistic, like there had always been a herd of cats living here alone.

It hadn't been emptied yet, not entirely. There were two large piles of books that looked both unreadable and unsellable; if there were valuables here at any point, they'd already been removed. The unit itself had been paid for, said the chatty real estate agent (made chattier, of course, at Parisa's behest), by an unknown source, in cash, every month without fail.

Until recently.

Parisa walked through the living room, noticing the broken blinds, the dust from an attempted renovation on the sills. The windows looked sealed shut. The grime on the walls looked like someone had tried to remove it and then given up, deciding to strip the wallpaper before getting called away to some other task—the kitchen, most likely. Parisa meandered through trash bags full of unknowable contents. Not food, but when she nudged one with her foot, she heard glass. Bottles. Dozens of them.

"Bit of a lush, the old tenant," said the agent's harried voice behind her, an attempted humor to the sound of his panic. "But the property's lovely and the floors are original Victorian, just in need of a little shine, that's all—"

Architecturally, the building was almost unnoticeable; residential flats above a series of little one-stall ethnic markets, a pawn shop, a pharmacy, a new and effortfully trendy gastropub. There were older townhouses nearby, the area not completely outside the realm of desirable; not too busy, with the walk from the closest Tube stop nothing too oppressive. If it had been cheap in the 1970s, it probably wasn't now, or wouldn't be for long. The building had been bought in recent years by a property management company with several other holdings scattered north of the Thames.

"How long ago did the tenant vacate?" asked Parisa, using the agent's choice of words. He looked flushed and grateful when she turned over her shoulder.

"About a month ago now, maybe two. It—" His complexion went rosier still. "It took a bit for us to . . . to know that she'd, you know." He looked flustered.

"A month?" Parisa echoed. The last time Tristan had willingly spoken to her, he'd explained Atlas Blakely's absence with some sardonic triteness about summer holidays. November—or October, as it would have been then—was well beyond any reasonable summer holiday, even if Atlas Blakely were the leisurely type. Libby, meanwhile, had not explained Atlas's absence at all, though perhaps that was Parisa's blunder, in failing to ask. Perhaps not.

The agent mistook her tone of surprise for concern about how little had been done. "We had to wait, you know, for next of kin," he rushed to assure her, "so we did as much as we could, but when the bloke finally got here he only took the good stuff, the old books and whatnot, one or two valuables. The rest is—"

"Bloke?"

"Yeah, big guy, bald." Parisa's ears told her one thing, her magic another. It was not Atlas Blakely in the estate agent's head, but someone much older. Old enough, in fact, to be Atlas's father. "Rich by the looks of it. Sad, when you think of it. Only came to pick over her things."

Parisa returned her attention to the cabinets, opening one and half expecting something to crawl out of it while the estate agent went on about what the man had taken—family heirlooms, a picture. He hadn't given his name, but there was a prestigious university logo on his briefcase, nice shoes on his feet, an air of gentility, and (this a bit of telepathic skullduggery on Parisa's part) the picture had clearly been a younger version of himself. Thus, Parisa's agile mind became acquainted with Atlas Blakely's nonmagical father, which, while privately intriguing, did not sound as if it did anything to help her find him.

Hitting a dead end, she chose to expedite things. *Tell me about the woman's family,* she instructed the estate agent, leaning into the command with slightly more force than necessary—something she hoped she wouldn't come to regret in her state of increasingly depleting exigency.

Helpfully, though, the agent explained that the previous pub owner from downstairs (before it had been trendy and been, instead, old) had reached out after hearing the news and informed them that the woman had a son. A posh professor-type as well, but a good lad, who tipped generously and always stopped by for a cup of tea, like it was some kind of personal ritual. The pub owner had wanted to pay his respects, as he'd said on the phone, but there had been no news of a funeral. The pub owner seemed astonished to discover that there hadn't been one. Such a good lad, he insisted, a good lad, messed up a bit here and there when he was younger but he'd done well, he'd tried, he wouldn't just leave her like that, alone like that, he wasn't that kind of man, he must not know, had they reached out to him?

"But we can't seem to find him either," concluded the real estate agent, before frowning at Parisa like he hadn't been aware he was talking. "Sorry, what was the question? I seem to have lost my train of thought—"

"Price per square meter," Parisa prompted.

"For this neighborhood? Abysmal," the real estate agent supplied, a bit too cheerfully in the wake of Parisa's alterations to his capacity for truth.

So, there was Atlas Blakely's life, Parisa thought in silence as the agent babbled on about the exorbitant nature of London's rent. Sick mother wasting away, absent hypocrite of a father. Had Parisa known any of that for certain while they'd both still lived in the same house she would have had a field day with it, and it occurred to her that Callum's exuberance over knowing what made their Caretaker who he was must have been well-founded in the monotony of it all; the textbookery of his psychological trauma.

Libby Rhodes wouldn't have laughed of course, or at least not the Libby Rhodes that had once existed. Though, perhaps the newer model of Libby Rhodes was the more relevant concern? She was, after all, one of only two people still aware of Atlas's comings and goings, the other of which was Tristan, who did not seem adequately informed. Something was definitely off with Libby, which continued to be troubling.

Or—if Parisa stopped looking at who Libby Rhodes had once been and started understanding who she'd become—then troublingly helpful, perhaps.

· · ·

A week ago, Parisa had sat in a blinding white office in Paris, fixing her attention on the view outside the window when the door finally opened.

She registered thoughts of surprise at her presence, which were to be expected, followed by the precipice of a decision that she trusted to reveal how the rest of the meeting would go. Either the owner of the office would call for assistance in dispatching the wanted medeian currently sitting in his chair, or he would weigh his options, gauging the possibility of advantage. If he was calculating enough to consider her value, then she could certainly work with that. Barring such convenience, she could kill him. Considering that she had already avoided one such threat to her life that morning (as she had nearly every morning since she'd left the Society manor house, like a new step in her beauty routine), she was in the mood to bargain. But not to play.

"Parisa Kamali," said the man at the door.

"Nothazai," she replied. "Is that a first name? Surname?"

"Neither." He shut the door quietly behind him. "To what do I owe the pleasure?"

He was a little older than Atlas and significantly easier to read.

"Let me put this to you simply," Parisa replied, letting her head fall back against the office chair and its respective lumbar charms. "I'm growing tired of running for my life. Truthfully, I'm finding your part in that to be something of an inconvenience."

His gaze flicked to the distance between them. "I'm not under the impression that your survival has been much of an effort," Nothazai said. He lingered near the door as if to say *I'm listening, but not indefinitely.*

"Just because I make it look easy doesn't mean it is," replied Parisa. She gestured to his desktop computer, watching a spark of apprehension alight in his eyes. "It seems that your computer network has been hit with a security threat. You'll be unable to access your company server for a while."

She felt Nothazai scanning her for something. Defect, most likely. Something he could leverage, which was a calculation that by necessity she understood. "Some of the best technomancers work for us," he said. "The network will be restored shortly."

"A week, probably," Parisa agreed. "But still, call it an even trade."

He smiled thinly, good-humoredly. "An inconvenience for an inconvenience?"

"I felt it appropriate, to say the least." Parisa sat upright, resting her elbows on his desk and peering at him for a moment.

"Has Atlas Blakely sent you?" Nothazai asked with a sense of wariness.

Interesting. Parisa noted his unease before filing it away, choosing not to deny the presence of an assumption that was so obviously advantageous to her cause.

"So," she demurred instead. "What will it take, then?"

He considered her for a moment. A respectable amount of time before saying, as she'd known he would, "You belong to a tyrannical organization." Nothazai folded his arms across his chest. "Your archives contain knowledge that was—and continues to be—stolen. The Forum wishes only to distribute that which belongs t—"

"I said," she repeated with a sigh. "What will it take?"

He quieted.

Then, "We will begin by publishing the truth about the Society's recruitment practices. The blood that we know you and your cohort of initiates have spilled. We will release the names of all those members who have benefitted, economically or politically, from the database of confidential tracking systems which the Society has failed to disclose. Should the dismantling of your members' influence prove insufficiently persuasive, we will disseminate the contents of the archives of your library ourselves, beginning with those civilizations most grievously defiled throughout the annals of time. Tell Atlas Blakely," Nothazai invited with a tight smile, "that we shall have to see if that does not drive the rest of the world to mutiny, and whether that kind of revolution is the sort your Society is prepared to survive."

Parisa wasn't listening. She had heard all she needed to hear, none of which Nothazai had the indignity to confess aloud.

Good. The more certain he appeared in his agenda, the better this would work out for her.

Rising to her feet, she advised, "Counteroffer. None of that comes to pass." She waited for him to argue, but he was at least clever enough to wait for the other shoe to drop. "You call off the hits on myself and my associates. In return, I arrange for you to take over as Caretaker of the Alexandrian Society's archives."

"Did you not hear me?" Nothazai said, and to his credit, he spluttered only slightly. "The purpose of the Forum and its aims are perfectly clear. We are defenders of the forum *of humanity,* the free exchange of ideas without submission t—"

"You," Parisa corrected, "are not a we. *You,*" she informed him, "are a man hiding a lifetime's worth of envy behind a shield of performative morality, but luckily for you, I have neither the time nor the interest to judge the quality of your personal ethics. You've made your offer, I've made mine, and I think you understand that we should not discuss this particular 'exchange of ideas' with anyone outside this room." She sat back down, adjusting the charms on the chair. Making herself comfortable. "After all," she said. "Think of the headache when the rest of your office discovers the server is down."

By the time he left the room again, vacating his people from the offices entirely—upon her directive; she was expecting Reina, after all, and had a penchant for theatrical entrances, relishing the idea of Reina being both outsmarted and made to wait—Parisa had observed two things from Nothazai's mind.

One: Nothazai's biomancy clearly extended beyond diagnostics. If he had wanted her dead or comatose or degenerative in some way, he could have made it happen the moment he walked in the door, unlike most of the subpar assassins he'd sent thus far to do his dirty work for him.

Two: he had seen her body and thought of it just like that, a body. Not the way a surgeon looks at a gaping wound. More like how a mortician would look at a corpse. He hid it well, even admirably, but she knew—as Atlas Blakely would have known—that to Nothazai, Parisa was neither a danger nor a threat, not even a person. To him, she was merely a future death.

Which was, ironically, a philosophy she knew immediately she could work with.

·   ·   ·

If Atlas was gone—absconded, perhaps, or hunting down the person who'd initially taken Libby Rhodes—a person that Atlas was very likely intent on apprehending, considering the pathological savior complex that made a great deal of sense to Parisa now that she knew the truth about his origins—then all of this would be much easier. It wasn't very difficult to rile up a mob. Parisa was lost in rumination as she left the estate agent behind to recollect his thoughts, having been forcefully persuaded to part with details better left unsaid. (Not her wisest of attempts, using more magic than she'd needed to use, considering some people turned out to be leaky faucets. The whole thing had been set to blow with one clever wrench, but control was a skill like any other, and she was tired. She hadn't slept well since she'd left Paris, or perhaps even earlier than that.)

She stepped into the street, contemplating her options. Where to next? Rhodes perhaps, to answer a few questions, though that was likely pointless. Possibly a phone call to Sharon—yes, that was certainly an option, Parisa realized with a moment of epiphany. If some people were leaky faucets, others were ticking clocks. It wouldn't take much to determine how far some people were willing to go.

Unfortunately, Dalton had her phone along with everything else she'd left behind in their Paris flat, and none of her communications would be safe now. She certainly didn't have Nico's energy (or hyperactivity) to craft a new technomancy network all on her own. Parisa was about to step into the pub below Atlas's mother's apartment instead, determining that the quickest way to a secure phone call would be to find any idiot boy with a phone, when something chilled her slightly. Not the weather, of course, because it was infernally hot, even worse here than in Paris. There was something else, something missing, and she paused to listen.

Which was when she realized that she could hear nothing at all.

She felt something jam in the small of her back. A hint of fragrance reached her nose. She knew that perfume.

She wore it.

"Parisa Kamali," came a feminine voice. "I so hoped you'd set foot in London soon."

With a flick of a glance over her shoulder, Parisa clocked long blond hair, designer dress. A distant familiarity.

"Eden Wessex," Parisa guessed aloud.

The heiress in the Louboutins slid a hand familiarly around Parisa's waist, the pistol snaking up Parisa's spine and below her hair to press itself into the base of her scalp. To any passersby they would have looked like girlfriends, or perhaps lovers. A pretty set of trinkets of no consequential use to anyone walking by.

Everywhere Parisa looked was blankness. Deadness. No thoughts but her own raced by.

"Funny," remarked Eden. "I thought you'd be taller."

Parisa had never had to search around for power. Telepathy came more than naturally, it came oppressively, like a punishment she couldn't avoid. Eden may have blocked her thoughts from Parisa, but this was different, this was absence, hollowness. Emptiness. A void where her magic should have been.

She tried to summon anger and felt nothing beyond the usual. It was always there, actually. The razor-edge of a precipice she routinely walked. The one that was both a chasm and a question. The one that looked and felt like the ledge of a manor house roof.

She remembered her gray hair, her impending invisibility. How much mortality was she capable of, exactly? How many times and how silently could a woman actually die? Girlhood was shot down early, followed inevitably by credibility and relevance and desire. She'd always thought beauty would go last, but maybe it was power. Or maybe, in what was Parisa's only true unspoken fear, beauty and power were synonymous for her. Or worse, symbiotic.

But then she remembered the archives, their collective broken promise. *We are beholden to the archives as they are beholden to us.* It had been exactly six months to the day from the moment she left the house.

Right, thought Parisa grimly. So my time's up, then.

Fuck.

"Are we taking a walk?" she asked her captor calmly. The barrel of Eden's weapon secured itself in the nape of Parisa's graceful neck, the placement sensual with promise.

"Do you think I'm stupid? No," said Eden Wessex with a girlish laugh, which Parisa couldn't help but admire, or at the very least respect. "Believe me, we're ending this here and now."

· NICO ·

The painted room looked empty, sparser than usual without its furniture configuration (moved to the outer corridor, someone else's problem) or the plants. It reminded him of the initiation ritual, the person he'd been a year ago, thinking there was no such thing as a loss he couldn't swallow or a problem he couldn't fix. Had it been a lesson he hadn't learned quickly enough? Something that should have warded off his recklessness sooner, to remake his personality somehow into something more subdued, a little wiser? The distance traveled between then and now covered a mix of melancholia and contentment, a push and pull of loss and love. He felt more aware of his limits now, even as he prepared to stretch them farther than they'd gone before. It felt different, bravery that was tinged with wonder, like explorers diving into the wild deep. Facing off against the lure of the horizon, chasing the perennial unknown.

He was customarily optimistic that his exuberance on the matter had appropriately affected Libby's state of mind, which seemed outwardly unchanged but also, importantly, did not prove the last-minute obstacle Nico suspected it might have been. She seemed . . . subdued, a mettle slightly more iron than complacent, but even if she'd been hesitant, it wouldn't be the first time Nico had dragged her into something that had proven worthwhile in the end. If he had any real significance in her life, it was to be the constant drive, the momentum to force her forward. She was the same thing for him, whether she recognized it or not. If to others they seemed inseverable, like a single object to the naked eye, there was no point feeling resentful about it now.

Nico chose not to feel resentful, actually, about anything. Not when Parisa chose to exempt herself from their lives (disappointing but unsurprising, the way she apparently had nothing more to say to him) or when Dalton usurped captainship of the experiment. Not when Reina ended her replies with an impressively geriatric "bye." Nico had woken that morning to Gideon playfully criticizing the stars in his eyes and now he was completing a journey he'd begun two years ago, maybe more. Yes, definitely longer ago than that. Somewhere in the back of his head Nico had been building this ship ever since the moment he saw what Libby Rhodes could do—since the moment he'd recognized the presence of a worthy adversary, who would become an invaluable ally—and now, finally, it was time to set sail.

"Ready?" Dalton seemed more alive than usual. He was tremulous with anticipation, or maybe that was just Nico's energy infecting everyone else. "If I'm going to be able to do this"—*this* being the animation of the void at the proper rate of not-so-spontaneous cosmic inflation—"I'm going to need you to hold a fair amount of heat."

Roughly ten billion degrees, so yeah, a fair amount. "We've just got to casually handle a supernova, we know. No worries, Dalton, we've got it covered." Nico waltzed to the center of the room and stood across from Libby, holding out both hands. "Just another Tuesday, right, Rhodes?"

"It's Wednesday." But she sighed and placed her hands in his, warily. No more warily than normal, of course, but still, Nico surmised that she could have been a little more upbeat given that it was her who'd brought up the obvious. At long last, they were doing the unfathomable, succumbing to their magnetic pull, which had always been ineffable. It had always been so bright, so glaring, the impossibility of the horizon. The *potential* they'd always known they had.

What had they been born for if not for this?

What had they been orbiting for so long, if not the inevitability of what they could be?

"Have a little perspective, would you? I know we're not mentioning time travel by name, but that's an accomplishment you can hold over me, at least." To that, Nico thought he caught the presence of a tiny smirk. "What's a little stellar energy between lifelong nemeses, eh, Rhodes?"

"Varona—" She hesitated for a second, like she was about to say something, and his heart flipped in his chest at the possibility of being overrun.

"Rhodes. Come on. I spent a year training Tristan for this," he said, which Tristan (standing beside Dalton near the apse, looking broody in contemplation as opposed to his usual resting broody face) either didn't hear or chose not to. Which was gratifying, as Nico had a feeling he was pleading a little, trading dignity for ardency. But he hadn't woken up that morning prepared to make worlds only to settle for making dinner. Or small talk. Or sarcastic comments, though they were hard to avoid. "Come on, what have I always told you? Either you're enough or—"

"Stop, there's only so many Varona aphorisms I can take." Her palms felt small and weightless in his.

"Rhodes." He lowered his voice, leaning in. "If you're worried about whether we can do this, believe me, we can. You get that, right?" He searched her slate eyes for understanding, or acknowledgment, or merely the indication that she was listening. "We didn't get here by accident."

As soon as the words left his mouth, he understood that this was happening. From where Nico and Libby faced each other, Dalton stood coiled and ready on Nico's left, like a hurdler next in line for the baton. From Nico's right, Tristan stood at the opposing point of their conjuring diamond, looking characteristically grim. But Nico had never seen Tristan defeated, and he already knew this would not end in defeat.

"We," Nico said again, his gaze flicking to where Gideon sat respectfully outside the perimeter of their experiment, head tilted absently amid the sun streaming in below the apse. "We are not an accident."

This was happening, whether Libby had hesitation left to voice or not. If he dragged her, kicking and screaming, then so be it. He dragged her.

Enough talking.

Time to go.

Power was easy to find. In this house it was always just below the surface, always just within reach, his foot constantly hovering atop the gas pedal. Since Libby had left, since she'd returned, all Nico had done was coast. Her absence, that was paralysis, the ongoing sensation of a hoax. But she was back now—she was here, with her hands in his, and she was strong, stronger than she had ever been, and he was intent on proving that to her. It was a rev of the engine, the wave of a flag, the chatter of a light fixture, Edwardian lamps trembling atop Victorian tables.

His signal, waiting for her reply.

Her power caught onto his instantly, reflexively. Nico felt a half second's drag and then whiplash, taking off like a gunshot. The blast of it was deafening at first, like a ringing in his ears, and for a moment he faltered. Tristan and Dalton disappeared from either side of his periphery; Gideon had been swallowed up by a brightness he couldn't name. The impact of the blast was everywhere, inside his chest and out, inside his pulse, inside his veins, exploding behind his eyes like the bottom dropping out, the engine failing—powerlessness. A beat of it. A pulse.

For a moment Nico felt weightless and insubstantial, suspended in nothing. He felt the motion of his chest cease, the air in his lungs contracting, a loss of feeling in his arms and legs, his feet, his hands. All but the knowledge, the counterbalancing thought of Libby's presence fell away. Power overwhelmed him like rapture, suffocation. Aneurysm, embolism, and seizure, all at once. A thud of his heart, and then nothing.

Nothing.

And then.

And then—

· TRISTAN ·

Eternity stretched before him from the bend of reality that had once been the painted room hearth, and it looked like a lot of things. Like space. Like the night sky from his bedroom window. Like a twinkle half remembered in his mother's eye. Like the shine of a diamond, the halting way he'd made and broken a promise. Like the dots of a message still typing, an answer yet to come.

Whatever Dalton was coaxing from the emptiness of space looked precisely like Nico's diagram, too, which annoyed Tristan, ignited him, made him furious. The kind of fury that felt like elation. The kind of fury that made him suddenly ravenous. As if he'd waited his whole life to swallow it whole.

He saw stars and he saw planets. He saw emptiness, and it was full of space. He saw the many endless doors of his imaginings, he felt fear that tasted like sunrise, he understood what he was born for.

This. Exultant with it. He was born for this.

He reached and he was weightless, too heavy to fall, too lovely to burn. For the first time in his life Tristan Caine felt no hatred, no regrets. He understood something important, which was that he did not matter, and it was freeing because, in that moment, he was free. He didn't matter! He didn't *have* to matter! Nico was right, the whole world was an accordion of secrets, nobody mattered after all. Not Tristan, not his pain, not his pleasure. He would feel this moment of bliss and eventually it would pass. It would live and die and in the meantime, he would bear witness.

He saw it all, he was a witness, he existed, *he was there!*

.   .   .

Only for a moment did he falter. An error, something short-circuiting, a spark in a flurry of static while Tristan reached out to part the curtain of reality, to finally see behind the cosmic veil.

Amid all this glory, all this triumph, a split second of weakness. A hair's breadth of shame.

What else are you willing to break, Miss Rhodes, and who will you betray to do it?

Tristan's heart hammered in his chest. Dull thuds of consecration.

Libby's voice. The same and different.

I don't know, she said, *and I don't care.*

.   .   .

As Tristan Caine's fingers grazed the fabric of impossibility, past and present chased each other's tails, catching up with him at last.

He saw it all because he was a witness.

He saw it all because he was there.

· DALTON ·

This was what Parisa had once seen in Dalton Ellery's mind:
"Mama, look." Seven or eight, opening his dirt-covered hands. A seedling cupped inside it. Energy still flowing through him. Power he didn't yet know how to name. "Mama, look, I saved it."

"My sweet boy, my clever boy."

A warp, a loss, a wilting. His own stricken face when it died anyway, because things always die. It's the crux of it all, beginnings and endings. There are some things you simply can't save.

·   ·   ·

That was what Parisa had seen in Dalton's mind because it was how Dalton remembered it. Certain memories made for stronger walls, more impenetrable foundations in the mind, and so they stuck.

Even when they happened to be lies.

·   ·   ·

"Mama, look." In his mind he always turned her head, forcing her to see it. "Mama, look, I saved it."

But now she wasn't looking. She was too busy crying, and he was frustrated, jealous. Annoyed.

"Mama," Dalton said again, but she still wasn't listening.

"My sweet boy, my clever boy—"

Dalton had brought the sapling back on the same day his brother had died.

Coincidence?

Probably.

Maybe.

Statistically speaking, it was likely. One event did not necessitate the other.

Either Dalton forgot because to wonder was too painful.

Or he forgot because he knew better, and chose to bury it alive.

· GIDEON ·

He had opened his eyes that morning to the low bleed of early sun, the way the waves of Nico's hair had spread across his pillow, knees curled into his bare chest, one hand below his cheek. He was facing Gideon, his eyes closed, his breathing steady. Gideon didn't move, didn't breathe. He had never had a very good handle on the line between dream and reality, but it was especially thin in moments like this, tinged with unexpected sweetness. He felt a heaviness in his chest, a longing for something. Nostalgia for a moment that hadn't yet passed.

To Gideon, time felt especially theoretical. Like something he would always chase and never really have. He wished he could say that the feeling was a portent, that it was knowledge of significance, but it was something terrible, something worse. Dread. Hope. Two sides of the same desperation. Belief that if a moment was perfect, it was surely undeserved; it wasn't meant to last. Cosmic significance dictated that light would fade; that something gold could never stay.

"Stop staring, Sandman, it's weird," said Nico without opening his eyes.

Gideon felt himself laugh, and the moment, the possibility that he might have correctly intuited it and done something differently—might have chained Nico to the bed, maybe, or dared him to do something truly unpredictable, like stay inside and read a book—evaporated. Time moved forward. It was what it was. "You stole my pillow again."

"You say stole, I say gentlemanly borrowed." Nico was fully awake then, looking at him. "You seem restless."

"I'm trapped in a haunted house, Nicky. Not too many ways to fill a day."

"Not haunted. No ghosts." Nico's hair had gotten lighter from his week on holiday with Max. He took to luxury so beautifully, wearing it like a summer tan. It was no wonder Libby tried her best to hate him. Also no wonder that she failed.

"What is it? *Dites-moi.*" Nico was peering at him now, perhaps because Gideon had taken too long to answer. Too distracted, he supposed, by the spoiled man in his bed. Well, this was Nico's bed, though Gideon occupied it more often. Like a strange captive at Nico's idea of camp.

Maybe if Nico hadn't looked at him so . . . plainly. So openly. Perhaps if Nico had not looked at him like that—like Gideon's next words had the ability to ruin his day—he might have told Nico the truth. Maybe if everything hadn't been so fresh and painfully, terrifyingly pleasant, Gideon would have said to hell with it, things are bad, Nicolás, I told you this whole thing was a mess, I told you this was a disaster waiting to happen.

But you know what Nico de Varona did not like? *I told you so.* And also, things were beautiful, and Gideon did not know what to do with this ability, this new tool he seemed to have picked up somewhere without noticing, where Nico's entire mood seemed to hinge on the degree of happiness that Gideon outwardly expressed. Nico had always said that, obviously, that Gideon was his problem, that Gideon was his, but that was before Gideon had understood himself to be a plausible outcome for Nico, not simply a possession. They had always been built on a platform of shared omission, but now it was different, the highs higher, the potential for lows more distressing.

It was both security and vulnerability, this new shape their relationship had taken. There was so much joy. There was also so much fear.

"I just want you to know," Nico began at the same time Gideon said, "Nico, I think—"

They both stopped.

"Yes?" said Gideon, because they both knew Nico would want to talk first.

Nico took Gideon's face in his hands. "I think you should probably know that I can be much better at devotion than you think I can. I'm generally unpracticed," he acknowledged with a shrug, "but I feel, on a very deep spiritual level, that I will eventually become unbeatable at it, and when the day arrives that I have once again exceeded all expectations, I hope you will consider ample praise."

There was a moment of silence for both of them to process what had just been said.

Several moments, as it was layered, and insane.

"My god," said Gideon eventually, with very real astonishment, "*the ego—*"

And Nico had kissed him and he had laughed, and so what Gideon had not relayed was this:

"We meet again, Mr. Drake." The strange, masculine voice from somewhere just outside the jail cell of the Society's telepathic wards. Gideon dreamed as frequently as he always did, but not as freely. With very rare, very critical exception—the excruciating effort, for example, he took moments after that particular visit to the subconscious of Libby Rhodes—Gideon's wanderings were limited to what he could accomplish from the space inside the telepathic jail cell. "You should know that I never expected someone so young."

Gideon, who knew very well what it took to enter the Society's wards, did not take this greeting to be anything less than the threat it so obviously was. "Are you going to tell me who you really are this time?"

The Accountant, Nico had said, or perhaps Gideon had said it first, muttering it in his sleep. Unclear and unimportant now.

The voice stayed conspicuously out of sight. "On the subject of our mutual friend. Perhaps you've heard."

Knowingly, Gideon's heart sank. "I take it my mother wasn't able to pay her debt."

Money, he prayed. Please be money.

"Eilif never mentioned you were her son." The voice took on a note of amusement. "Well. Then I suppose she had a soul after all."

Had. The past tense put Gideon's heart in double-time.

"You're aware that it has not been difficult to find you," the voice continued. "Not without its challenges, of course, but you do understand that your face and name are known. You are known, Gideon Drake."

Known was not the same as caught, but Gideon understood the line was growing thinner.

Gideon had not asked what that particular visit was about, because he already knew. He'd been in hiding for two years and now there were no significant options, nothing to come to mind aside from the only thing he'd recently done. Or not done, as it were. The job Eilif had recruited him for. Breaking someone out of their own conscious mind. The significance of that particular person had never been an issue for Gideon, who had learned long ago not to ask too many questions about who or what Eilif came by. But according to Parisa Kamali, Gideon had failed to deliver the Prince from his captivity, and it appeared that Eilif had paid the price for that.

Or rather, the price remained unpaid with a job unfinished. A task left undone.

"Let me see her," Gideon attempted, and the silence in reply was deafening.

"No" eventually sufficed.

Gideon felt a strange sadness, one that was tinged with relief. He had lost a defining piece of his life. A bad one, but a defining one nonetheless, and he supposed that in his mind Eilif had always been unkillable, unbeatable.

Perhaps one always looks upon one's parents that way, and in Gideon's case, his sorrow was in part a disillusioned one. If Eilif could lose this gamble, then the world was so vulnerable, so at risk for being robbed of its magic. The more Eilif's absence became reality, the more human it became—tone, as Nico would say, derogatory.

"You can't reach me here," Gideon pointed out. "Not in any way that matters. You already know that, or you wouldn't keep coming here just to talk."

"Perhaps not," replied the voice. "But someday, Mr. Drake, you will no longer be behind the safety of those wards, and believe me when I tell you that I have the time to lie in wait."

Great. Grand. So it was written on the wall, then, or in some kind of invisible ledger. Gideon's mother's debt had passed to him, and now there was no escaping it. He could spend his life in servitude or he could spend it on the run—in which case, what life?

So Gideon did not need to know who this was or what they wanted. "Fine. What do you want me to do about it?" was what he asked instead, not knowing the answer would present itself so coincidentally. Without Gideon even leaving the house.

Because Gideon had recognized him immediately. The hair, the punchable face.

The Prince.

Here he was in the flesh, and surely he'd recognized Gideon, too—impossible he hadn't. Gideon wasn't a genius physicist, he wasn't a cynic and he was barely even an archivist, but he was very much someone who knew a problem when he saw it. He hadn't been born to a mother like Eilif just to not realize when trouble had walked in the door.

So the telepath had lied to him about his success in retrieving the Prince's trapped consciousness. No surprise there, Gideon supposed, but what to do with that information? That here was the Prince, perfectly whole, his consciousness repaired, or at very least reunited. Was that normal? Was that safe?

He thought Dalton Ellery would be the problem.

He was very, very wrong.

· NICO ·

*T*his. This was what he'd been waiting for—this feeling, this moment of harmony, the thing he'd been fighting that he had also been seeking. This thing between them that was coming to life, bright with impossible certainty, absent the usual risk of burning out. It sped through him, energy and magic, power and heat, waves like a furnace stretching out from him in beams, in blinding waves. He wondered what Tristan could see; if looking at them together felt like staring into the sun; if it was obvious now that this was what they had always been. Varona and Rhodes, duality and synchronicity.

Beginnings and endings, stardust and stars.

· LIBBY ·

Atlas's experiment was not inherently evil. Yes, the ethics of such a thing were questionable, but what about existence was not? Libby understood this now, that to be alive and to have this kind of power in her blood was to be indeterminately responsible for making or unmaking worlds, whatever she chose to do. Whether she acted or failed to act, it would invariably cause a rift. What was right, what was wrong, who was good and who was bad? These were unanswerable questions about ineffable concepts. What Ezra Fowler had seen or what he knew was less important than how he had acted, and whether she ultimately believed him. She didn't.

And even if she had once, the materials were already at her disposal.

She had the tools to circumvent the threat, and so she did. She already had.

. . .

What happened between Libby Rhodes and Atlas Blakely in his office wasn't personal. It wasn't even—as Ezra's death had been—a personal matter, a coin-flip of vengeance or self-defense. This was a simple question, simpler at least, than the one the Society had asked of her. It was straightforward, can you save the world? And her answer had been yes. Yes, I can.

Six months ago now. Six months ago, precisely. She had struck Ezra down with the force of her rage, using his chest for a target. A wild, uncontrolled blast to the heart he'd once promised was hers before she fully understood she'd taken aim.

I can kill her, Ezra had said with the same lips that had kissed her. In the end, it left her more like a sob than a strike.

She had not yet recovered full sensation in her hands when Atlas began talking—incessantly talking, on and on without stopping, eternally and without end. She remembered most of it like a dream she'd once had, absent chronology or meaning. None of it seemed important or even relevant at the time.

"What else are you willing to break, Miss Rhodes, and who will you betray to do it?"

There was a ringing in her ears from the moment Ezra's body hit the floor. It had been growing louder, steadily, unbearably, until all of a sudden, it broke. Gone, just like that. It gave way, and in its place: clarity. A way forward. A next step.

Not personal. Just a job to be done. He's going to destroy the world, Ezra had said so, and was she really willing to risk it? Suddenly, the answer seemed obvious.

Not just obvious. It was the only thing. There was nothing else.

"I don't know," Libby said, "and I don't care."

. . .

The combustion, the explosion of pure fusion, was difficult to hold from the beginning. Almost immediately, she felt the distance between herself and Nico blur. They had always been like stars in orbit, chasing each other, faster and faster until sometimes they got caught, becoming one with the orbit itself. The line where he ended or she began, it inevitably became irrelevant. Her magic responded to his like it had been born in his body. His joined up with hers like it had finally found its way home.

It was beautiful—it really was. The moment of pure synchronicity was like meeting up with fate. Like the kiss at the end of the movie, two souls becoming one. She could feel it, the way it was different this time, because they both accepted it. There was no use fighting anymore. No use lying about it. The constraints of their respective powers evaporated the moment they resigned themselves to the inevitable; the unexplainable and inarguable. The moment they both finally said yes was the one that opened the door.

Difficult to hold was not the same as difficult to see. Libby saw the bliss on Tristan's face, the orientation of his destiny. The tips of his fingers outstretched like Adam reaching tenderly for God. She saw the sweat on Nico's brow, the glimpse of a smile on his face, the triumph of something, peace and acceptance. From now on he could be satisfied, maybe even happy. He had seen his purpose through to fulfillment. He was vindicated and whole, and she told herself she felt no bitterness. No envy.

She saw Dalton. The flickers of him. The flash of something in his eyes. She saw Gideon. But Dalton's eyes, there was something about them. They reminded her of something lifeless, unnaturally still. She saw Gideon. Tristan's hand outstretched, the surge of mania on Dalton's face—had he even asked her about Atlas?

She saw Gideon. *I can't find him.*

Nico's reassurance. *I trust you, Rhodes.*

Tristan and the wine, is it over? Is it broken?

She saw Gideon. *I can't find him.*

He knows, she realized. He's known it all along.

She saw Gideon clearly now. He wasn't the nightmare. The nightmare was hers. There was something wrong with Dalton and something was pulling at her, unraveling like a thread. Was it possible that Ezra was mistaken? He said Atlas was the dangerous one. *His plan is already set in motion.* But Atlas was not the weapon. She was. Everyone in this room was an arrow, which had always meant Dalton, too.

She saw Gideon, she saw Nico's look of serenity, she saw Tristan's look of wonder, she understood that nothing in the universe was purely ugly without something beautiful; nothing wholly good without the shadow of something bad.

Where did Dalton get his energy from? She saw Gideon. She saw the thing she should have questioned, the inconsistency she should have fought with from the start. *Miss Rhodes, nothing in the universe can come from nothing.* Not even life. Especially not life. She saw Gideon. She saw Nico. Either she was enough or she never would be.

But what did it mean to be enough?

Something was wrong with Dalton. Something was wrong with all of them—they would never have enough. This Society was a sickness, a poison. She had always known it. She had always been right. She had always been wrong. She saw Nico, saw that he could convince her again, could convince her of anything, she listened to him, she always had. She saw Gideon. Something twisted inside her now, something solely hers, something only she could bear. A burden that only she could carry.

I trust you, Rhodes. A choice that only she could make.

She saw Gideon, the things he had not done, the things he had not seen, the price he hadn't paid. The consequences he could never understand. She saw Tristan. Saw Nico. Saw that only she could do it. *Listen to me, Libby, you're a weapon, I saw to it myself.* No, the strain in her chest, pieces of her brokenness like shrapnel. No, Ezra, I am not a weapon. Belen's face reappeared in her mind, twisted with accusation. *He said that nobody was killed, that's very specific phrasing—!*

No one else could have made that decision. This would be the same. It could not come from a place of nothing. No one else could possibly understand the intricacy of it; the *why* of it that would look like nothing but ultimately mean everything. Sacrifice. Lethal arrows. Salvation could only be made from the rib of Adam. Sacrifice from carving out a piece of her own heart.

I am not a weapon.

She saw Gideon just as Tristan's hand met something. A new reality. An alternate world.

See your path, Miss Rhodes, and change it.

No one was the hero. So she would have to be the villain.

She saw Gideon.

What else are you willing to break, Miss Rhodes, and who will you betray to do it?

I don't know. I don't care.

But that was only half the answer. The rest of it was the truth.

It doesn't matter, because I am my own weapon now.

They couldn't move forward. She understood that now. The other side of the door was not the problem. The existence of the door was not the problem. The problem was what it took to turn the latch. Which meant the stakes were not just high, they were precisely as Ezra had said they were: annihilatory, apocalyptic. Only she knew it. Which meant that only she could save them all.

She was desensitized now, anesthetized. The right thing, the necessary thing, it came with pain that only she could bear. If this was going to end, if it could be salvaged, then only she could do it. Only she loved deeply enough. Only she had ever been strong enough to make this choice.

She saw Gideon. She saw him mouth one word.

NO—

· CALLUM ·

"You think this is a game, Nova?" The voice of Adrian Caine's favorite goon in Callum's ear was a thin stream of muttered distaste. "You think you can come and go as you like? I've known men like you," hissed Wyn, "and I assure you, whatever the big man's willing to let slide on your behalf, I won't be so generous. I do not enjoy being played."

Callum turned slowly to face the weapon Wyn Cockburn had pointed at him. So, someone had tipped off Wyn about Callum's approach. Perhaps Alys had even taken part in setting the trap for him, judging by the look of apparent nothingness on her face. One of these days, Callum thought, he would have to stop assuming the Caine progeny were all equally incapable of sabotage.

"Where's Tristan Caine?" snarled Wyn. "Because if you still can't answer that question, pretty boy, there's no need for you at all."

Well, Callum was very pretty, so there was that. And what kind of man grew so infuriated that his own son wasn't dead yet? Trick question, a bad one, which wasn't exactly news, but Callum had always known that Tristan's life or death was not the point of this degree of violence. He did not require magic to understand Adrian's intentions, nor did he need it to undermine Wyn's.

But suddenly he tasted the presence of something crisp and tart, like the bite of a freshly plucked apple. So he used it anyway.

Just for fun.

"Put the gun down," Callum said firstly, "because it's rude, and take a seat, because it's about time we had this conversation." He had not needed to be warned not to mess with Adrian Caine or his variety of underlings, which was precisely the point of the mess-about. Some men needed to snap before their true colors came vibrantly through.

There was some resistance on the witch's part, which was to be expected. Wyn was unwilling to listen to Callum, perhaps even more vehemently than people normally were. He assumed it was on the basis of something stupid like hatred of Callum's pretty face or envy of Callum's position in Adrian's ear. But although Callum was normally very hospitable, he was officially in a motherfucking mood, and whatever lapse in judgment had caused this unnecessary brush with danger, the window of paralysis to his magic (or to some other aspect of his emotions that he did not want to acknowledge, like the possibility of disappointment in a person he'd foolishly seen in an optimistic light) seemed, thankfully, to have passed.

After a breath of obligatory contrariness, Wyn slumped into a seat.

"Here's the deal," said Callum, glancing up at a little flicker of motion to see that Alys Caine remained in the doorway of the kitchen, observing them both. "Tell your boss that putting a hit out on his own son is a terrible way to get him back."

There was some strain beneath Callum's control, so he eased it a little, enough to permit casual conversation. Wyn's smile bared his teeth as usual. "James Wessex will not be killing that good-for-nothing fuckwit," he muttered. "And neither will some puffed-up toff like you."

Callum was not a toff, as he had already corrected Tristan. Callum was an asshole and a prick and very wealthy, but toff seemed a stretch. He chose to discard the finer details of that assessment in favor of the obvious, which was Wyn Cockburn's unmistakable longing to kill Tristan himself.

"So that's what this is, hm? Jealousy? And here I thought it was a mercy kill for the sake of your little cult's reputation." The sense of entitlement here was absurd, well outside the scope of reasonable. Not that Callum hadn't known that already—he'd expected a double-cross to come along at some point from Adrian Caine or his merry men—but hearing it like that, stripped of its complexity, was almost embarrassing for them both. *A rich man won't kill Adrian Caine's shitbag son! I'll do it for him, he'll love it, it'll be grand.*

Right, well, easy enough to sort out. "Listen to me. Tristan is not an extension of Adrian Caine. His fate is not yours, nor your boss's, to determine." Callum leaned closer, just to be sure that Wyn Cockburn was paying attention. "Never was," Callum murmured, lips barely parting. "Never will be."

Wyn wanted to say something in return, of course. Understandably, they disagreed on the matter of Tristan's autonomy as well as Wyn's own. He couldn't speak at the moment, though, so Callum continued. "You won't be killing him. In fact," Callum determined, finding whatever reserves of usefulness he could and shaking loose the spare change left inside it, "if you do encounter him, you'll have no choice but to tell him the truth: that he's the better man. The man Adrian ought to have been if only he'd been able."

Wyn's mouth was slick with spite, maybe a little unhinged spittle. Oh, so he didn't like Callum? Oh no! Whatever would Callum do about it? Perhaps leave him with something to contemplate, like how it was terribly poor form to harass someone's grown son on the basis of pseudo-sibling rivalry.

"Here's what you're going to do," Callum said without looking up at Alys's unmoving silhouette. "You're going to tell your fellow thugs that Tristan Caine is not to be harmed. Not a hair on his head. Not a wrinkle on his shirts. In fact, if you even mildly distress him, there'll be hell to pay for it. I've decided that someone with better reasoning should kill him," Callum added whimsically, "like, say, me, and if anyone else tries, you'll be the first to warn me. Call it meaningful reparations for fouling up my already shit-filled day.

"So," Callum finished, "are we clear?"

It had been a while since Callum had done this without Reina. Something felt a little crackly, like improper wiring, but Wyn was sweating against the waves of Callum's influence, teeth chattering beneath the effort of fighting his restraints.

"That'll settle in after a beat," Callum advised, straightening. "In a few minutes you'll find that the whole thing was your idea, actually. Call it a change of heart."

He strode to the door, pausing just before he walked through it to lock eyes with Alys Caine, who looked a modicum of sorry. But that was life in this household, wasn't it? Being sorry for things and doing them anyway. A terrible way to live.

Callum was about to send some parting message her way, perhaps some advice for cunnilingus since she seemed genuinely eager enough to learn, but then his phone buzzed in his pocket. Wouldn't it be a nice coincidence, a full family reunion, if it was who he thought it was? Though, apparently Alys Caine was very much her father's daughter, which made Tristan all the more singular. No less killable, but still.

So much for a sexual awakening. Alys's loss. Callum chose instead to push through the door of the pub, feeling . . . well, satiated.

If a bit murderous now.

Think, Parisa thought. Emotions were for losers.

"Is that a gun?" she asked leisurely, twisting around as much as she could without setting off a bullet for noncompliance. "Seems off-brand for you, Eden."

"It's enough of one," Eden Wessex replied in her ear. "Top-of-the-line Wessex model, actually."

Like a blaster then, pew pew. What an uncivilized death. Suddenly it seemed unacceptable, the possibility of being shot by a woman wearing a pair of shoes that Parisa didn't even like. It surged up in her like an epiphany, an idea. A spark of thought.

Think.

No, wait. Don't think. Parisa flexed her fingers, magic reigniting in her veins. Okay, so it wasn't her time, then. Not yet. If the archives were still owed a body, it hadn't decided yet on hers. No point dwelling on how or why.

Don't think, Parisa.

Act.

Turn the gun around. Eden's wrist snapped so hard from the intensity of Parisa's command that Parisa wondered if she'd broken it. Perhaps that was overdoing it a little, or maybe not. Parisa whipped around to take hold of Eden's throat, backing her against the wall of the gastropub and digging in with perfectly manicured fingers.

Give it to me.

The effort of raising her arm looked painful. Parisa felt a little sorry for Eden Wessex, though ultimately not sorry enough. "Thank you," Parisa said, reaching for the gun—it was pistol-shaped, if not an actual pistol—and tucking it into her purse. "Does that thing have a safety? Never mind, I'm sure I'll sort it out." She tightened her grip on Eden, who was looking dangerously contrarian now. Never good to underestimate someone whose magic Parisa didn't know. She searched Eden's thoughts, wondering where they'd travel; where the other woman kept the reserves of her strength. Nothing. "Who else is hunting us?"

"Fuck you," spat Eden.

Fine. Eden winced as Parisa asked, ever so politely, *Who else is hunting us?*

Well, Eden was strong-willed, but had no telepathic defenses to speak of. Parisa caught the tail ends of names and faces, some of which she recognized, most she didn't. Nothazai was only the de facto captain of a much larger team, its members recruited by the same man Parisa already knew to be Atlas Blakely's six-foot problem. "That's quite a task force."

"You're dead." Eden wasn't snarling anymore. Most likely she'd realized it was a waste of her energy, and now she was making an effort to calm herself down, to slow her breathing. A much better tactic. Despite herself, Parisa approved. "All of you, you're dead. Kill me and someone will still come for you. Someone will find you. They'll come after you," she said flatly, "and they won't stop."

That sounded like the truth, unfortunately. Not that Parisa felt the situation had escalated to hopeless, but it certainly wasn't ideal. Also, Eden was taller, and Parisa's arm was starting to strain from holding her like this.

Fine. Parisa released her, taking a step back, and Eden's eyes went wary, flicking from Parisa's face to her purse, calculating how hard it would be to grab the gun. Idiot. Not exactly the kind of thought you let a telepath be privy to.

Unless, Parisa realized, you have no choice.

"You're not a medeian," Parisa realized aloud, and nearly started laughing when Eden flinched, her cheeks instantly flushed with Nova-tinted humiliation. "You don't have any magic at all." Embarrassing, not to mention dangerous. "How'd you cover that up? With Daddy's money, I suppose?"

It didn't matter what Eden's answer was because Eden Wessex's significance in Parisa Kamali's life had already been eclipsed by something else, something more troubling. Parisa had somewhere else to be, so she turned and began to walk.

Eden Wessex called after her, the trot of expensive footwear echoing in Parisa's wake. "Where do you think you're going? You can't run from this—"

No, she couldn't. That was precisely the problem, that Parisa had always known that. It would never end, the running.

Nasser had said that to her once. *If you run, Parisa, you'll only be running for the rest of your life.*

She turned and locked eyes with Eden. "I'd tell you to go fuck yourself, but I'm worried you'd have too good a time."

Eden's eyes narrowed. If she had backups on the way, they'd been too slow. God, the hubris. Had she thought Parisa was just another hot girl in expensive shoes? Parisa could take one look at her and rearrange her brain, scramble her thoughts before serving Eden Wessex her own sanity over easy.

Stay, she told Eden, who was then affixed to the spot on the pavement. It would take some considerable effort to undo, but that wasn't Parisa's problem.

She walked away, returning to the question of where to procure a phone. She had, most pressingly, a question, and then after that she had an errand.

The archives were still owed a body.

If no one else was willing to take care of it, she would.

· REINA ·

She could tell she was bleeding profusely from where the cop had thrown her on the undulating ground, deep in the chasm of earth that her bleeding need had opened and too far from the oak tree to even make her broken body any use. Her head was pounding, her vision compromised, a thousand problems rolling into one. She had no proficiency for healing. No proficiency at all. She'd only had one thing her entire life and she'd resented it, she'd cared nothing for it. She had not cared for it at all.

Fuck this. Fuck all of it. She still felt a buzz of nothingness in her limbs, her empty hands, but chose to ignore it. *Have it, whatever you need,* she thought to the adolescent oak tree, the one that had tried to save her for no goddamn reason at all. *Take it, you need it more than I do—if I have anything left in me then take it, have it all!*

The silence that followed dropped like a guillotine. Game over.

Just another wasted life.

Then, belatedly, it burst from her like spring.

Like music. A crescendo into dazedness, into song. Like the darkness had been, the sudden efflorescent bloom was equally blinding. Something landed with a thud near Reina's feet, and though her vision had not yet cleared, she could sense the presence of petrichor—the air was suddenly rich with it; from old deadness, new life. She closed her fingers around the object that had been thrown to her: the policeman's handgun. Realizing what it was, Reina kicked it away, as far as she could, tilting her chin upward. Looking up through slitted eyes toward a blur of sanguinary sky.

Blink. Another blink.

It swam in front of her, gradually clearing. *Mother, open your eyes.*

A canopy hung above her head, not sky. Shading her from the battering sun. A circular grove of trees stood in newly fertilized ground, petals the color of freshly spilled blood.

The cops were gone. The park was empty. The heat was gone, a cool breeze ghosting gently by. Fruit hung heavy from the branches of the newborn trees and Reina struggled to her feet, sore and bruised, to gently pull one down. The tips of her fingers brushed the skin, glossy and smooth.

Pomegranates.

Staggering with exhaustion, Reina sank to her knees and she cried.

· GIDEON ·

No. No.
No, no, no.
"NO—"

· SHARON ·

Her phone buzzed from its usual spot in her drawer. She dug it out, thinking it might be Maggie, that maybe a doctor needed something, or her husband, who could never keep track of which snacks Maggie particularly liked. An unknown number. The internal judgment was always the same: Probably a sales call. But possibly a new clinic. A new trial. Probably bad news, but possibly good.

Sharon brought the phone to her ear. "Hello?"

"Sharon, it's Parisa Kamali. I need you to look up someone in the Society's tracking database for me."

"Miss Kamali." Sharon rubbed her eyes and sighed aloud. She hadn't disliked the telepath, exactly, but even so, there were limits. There were rules. "As I told you once before, the Society does not—"

"I can save your daughter, Sharon."

Sharon was quiet for a moment. "That's not funny."

"I'm not joking. I just need one answer. I can save her without it," Parisa added tonelessly, over the sound of a bus, the low din of a pub as she must have walked by. "But it'll be easier if we do it this way."

Sharon weighed her options.

No she didn't. Fuck that. She said, "Who are you looking for?" and Parisa, predictably unsurprised, didn't hesitate either.

"Atlas Blakely," she said.

That sort of information was protected by miles of protocol, by forms upon forms of approvals that, as logistics officer, Sharon would have to responsibly seek. Ford had already threatened to do it several times, but Ford was up to his ears in spoiled Alexandrian outrage and Society board requests. Bureaucracy, as Sharon well knew, could so easily be a nightmare.

But it could also be a weapon. Or a gift. Sharon Ward may not have had the keys to the kingdom, but she had the administrative password. For the right door, that was close enough.

"Very well, Miss Kamali. Please hold."

It happens slowly over the course of the decade, Alexis trying to save the others until gradually, she can't. Cancer. It happens to medeians too, a mutation that can't be predicted, that could probably be stopped or slowed, only she doesn't catch it quickly enough—she assumes the fatigue to be something related to necromancy itself, or the house, which is draining Atlas, too, albeit not as quickly. Not as thoroughly. Alexis's magic goes first, and after that she's just a soul inside of a failing body, so Atlas runs her baths and reads her books and tries all over again to love someone he can't save.

She was always fed up with living. Not really a fan of dying, either, though. "Just don't waste it," Alexis says. Atlas knows she means his life, that he should go out and do something beautiful with it. He knows this—he can read her fucking mind—but he willfully misinterprets her last words, betrays her most cruelly right there at the end. Because when she says *don't waste it* what he hears is *fix it*. He tells himself he can save her, he promises to do it over, to make a new world, a better one. (Maybe one where he never existed at all, which is the worst thing because it's selfish. It's wish fulfillment, the fantasy of a broken mind.) It's technically the same plan he promised for Ezra, but no longer a rosy-tinted quest for societal betterment. Now the burden is different, because it's Atlas's alone.

By then Atlas has discovered Dalton Ellery, chosen by the Society, and because Atlas understands some things implicitly about the world, he knows that what Dalton can do is something deeply and violently disturbing. But also, by then Atlas has achieved enough success—he is just arrogant *enough*—to believe that certain minds and futures can be altered. There is a life cycle to power, the rise that comes before the fall, and when Atlas is at his lowest, he mistakenly thinks he sees a peak. He sees a chance and he takes it.

Ezra Fowler, who has missed all of the baths and noodles and accusations, dismisses the danger in the obvious signs: the way Atlas remakes himself, changes everything about his clothes, his voice, his perception. Ezra doesn't see the way that Atlas quietly blames him—not for what Atlas has done, but for what Ezra has unknowingly failed to do by not killing Atlas himself. Ezra misses the way that Atlas now believes the right outcome is the one everyone else failed to organize: that Atlas Blakely himself is the one who ought to have died. (Many friendships end on invisible slights so really, none of this is a stretch. Besides, unfortunately for telepathic friends of time travelers, the loop is already closed. Even if Ezra amicably came to his senses much sooner, some futures are already too late to stop.)

It isn't hard to plant ideas. Manipulating a mind takes work but it isn't actually *hard,* not the way grief is hard, or the way living slowly becomes impossible. The most difficult thing in the world there is to do is to wake up in the morning and keep going, and the only way Atlas manages it is by manifesting his life into a single outcome—a single defining goal.

Let's be gods. You understand what it means, don't you? It's not some child-ish request for glory or riches, because wouldn't omniscience mean knowing everything—knowing every kind of sadness, every kind of pain?

Atlas Blakely does not do blessings; he doesn't care for benedictions. What he wants is control. The ability to rewrite the ending—and surely you of all people must understand that compulsion. You, of all people, must under-stand.

Weren't they all gods in some way because they were unnatural—because they were *preternatural*—and didn't that give Atlas Blakely a responsibility, a purpose, a reason to go on? You'll forgive him his blasphemy—they're the words of a man born to a dying world, a man who thought having knowledge was the same thing as having answers. But you've come this far, you've listened this long, so you already know, of course, that Atlas Blakely is nothing special after all.

You have your own pain, your own regrets, many of which are impossible and futile, most of which engulf you whenever you're most vulnerable—resilient only for another opportunity to bring you low. You can close your eyes right now and destroy yourself with them if you want to, and because you can do that—you, and everyone else who has ever been born—none of this is the moral of the story, nor is it even the story. People live and people die, and the why of it is never enough to make a difference.

You already know that your loss is an ocean, Atlas Blakely a speck in the sand.

VII

RELATIVISM

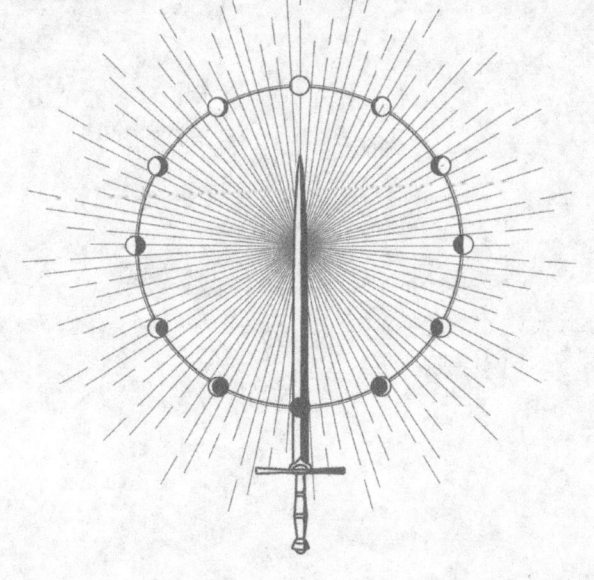

Six months ago, it went like this:

"What else are you willing to break, Miss Rhodes, and who will you betray to do it?"

In that moment, as the static in her ears reached a climax, or perhaps an end, Libby knew only one thing. She had her own pain. Her own regrets, many of which were impossible and futile, most of which engulfed her whenever she was most vulnerable, waiting for every opportunity to bring her low. She could close her eyes at any moment and destroy herself with them if she wanted to, and because she could do that, she knew that nothing Atlas Blakely had to say to her could be the moral of the story, nor was it even the story. People lived and people died, and the why of it was not enough to make a difference.

Her loss was an ocean, Atlas Blakely a speck in the sand.

Which was why it had been so easy to end it there, to let him be precisely what he said he was. Just a man. They lived and they died. He was the problem, okay, so be it.

She wondered if he knew what she decided in the moment it became clear to her. She felt confident he did—not because he said or did anything, but because he was a fucking telepath. That was the crux of it, really. There would be no strike of reckoning, no sudden bolt of epiphany. No tremors beneath her feet, no realignment in destiny or coagulation of fate, because Atlas Blakely was not a god. He was not a villain, fine, but he certainly wasn't a hero. Neither was she. He was a telepath, she was a physicist, and they were all just doing their jobs the best they knew how. She had explained all this to Tristan and he had agreed at the time, or seemed to agree, though the rift between them had deepened as the weeks slid by, perhaps because unlike Libby, Tristan was incapable of actually acting on the choices he was given.

He had not killed Callum. Now, because of him, they no longer had the luxury of time.

So after Atlas Blakely told her of the horrors he'd unleashed over the course of a cursed telepathic lifetime, Libby Rhodes understood the only thing his story did not have. An end.

She looked him in the eye and realized it would not have to be gory. It would not have to be violent. It would not require passion. The sacrifice she'd made to put herself in that room meant that every choice after would be difficult, but at least this one could be rational.

This decision could at least be hers.

He was standing behind his desk. Caretaker. Two years ago he'd held out his hand for hers and offered her a future if only she were dauntless enough to take it. If only she were brave enough to try. He hadn't mentioned the other things—the price, the way power was not something waiting to be called on like a lover but something to be stolen like a right. Power came at someone else's loss, and she knew this about Atlas Blakely: he had to lose.

He had to, because if he didn't, she would let him offer her power all over again, and this time—if she allowed him a *this time*—she knew it would be different. It would be different because she would not mind the blood.

She had walked into this house unwilling to kill one person. She walked out with a massacre staining her hands. What was one more body?

She watched herself reach out, the motion between her hand and his breath a perfect, unfaltering calculation. It was sudden enough that he could not stop her, or he just didn't bother to try. She reached out, touched his chest, and felt his pulse fail beneath her palm. Bodies were so faulty already, just moments away from total collapse. The shapes we take—the things housing our souls that we resent and mistreat and yet trust so implicitly— they were just objects of force, constantly acted upon. She was not numb with disbelief, not frozen with shock. She knew what she was doing. She understood the life she was taking.

Afterward, she looked at his lifeless eyes, the way his hand unfurled, and grasped, finally, what power truly cost.

"Why?" Tristan had asked her later, and Libby had told him the obvious answer. The world was capable of ending. If it did, it would be Atlas Blakely's fault. Tristan himself had subjected her to the trolley problem once—a question of ethics, killing one to save five lives—and so she posed it back to him: kill one to save everything. Was it actually that simple? No, but was it actually that *hard*? She had come this far and bloodied her hands this much, and now nothing could ever restore her. Nothing could turn things back the way they'd been. Ezra had told her Atlas was the problem, but now, thanks to her, that was impossible.

Atlas Blakely was not a problem. He was a man.

A dead one, now.

.　.　.

But she'd miscalculated badly. Just because she killed the man did not mean she had disarmed his weapons.

Libby no longer troubled herself with questions of regret, though if she had one, it would have been this: her quiet desperation to carry out Atlas's experiment. To let her own search for meaning twine irretrievably with Atlas's influence, his plans. Atlas had warned her of it long ago, and again when she stood in his office. *The trouble with knowledge, Miss Rhodes, is its inexhaustible craving. The problem is your need to know something because, after everything you've seen, the pain of not knowing would drive you mad.* The madness had started years ago, before she'd ever set foot in this room, when she had named her worth by her power, by the immensity of what she could do. She had been primed for use by Atlas Blakely by her own compulsion to be the best, to be the smartest, the most capable person in the room. The perils of a small existence would be to wonder what she might have done, who she might have been, but she did that—suffered it—every day already. She had tried and failed to explain it to Belen, failed again to explain it to Tristan. That her sister Katherine hadn't lived long enough to know who she might have been; whether she would have been a hero or a villain, whether she would have lived long and happily or wasted away in obscurity, neither she nor Libby would ever know.

If Libby was granted longevity and chose to ignore it, then her curse would be worse than blindness. It would be the unforgivable crime of living her life with her eyes shut tight.

Which was why the signs piled up and she ignored them. Tristan and the wine, Nico and his demurral, Gideon and his presence in her dreams. Parisa and her warnings. The appearance of Dalton Ellery. Two years had gone by with no thought to who he was or what he studied. How had Libby never wondered? She had trusted him, and that was her problem. When she trusted other people, things always went awry.

She looked at the scope of magic in the room and understood that Atlas Blakely was still alive in her, in everyone in this room, and knew that he could never die, not really. Not until she destroyed the framework of his grand design.

In the moment when Dalton's eyes went wild with expectation, Tristan's face euphoric with joy, Libby wrenched them back in the opposite direction. From where she stood on the precipice of creation, she slammed on the brakes, taking everything with her, extinguishing the pressure, reversing the order, allowing the chaos they'd opened to catastrophically collapse.

That much energy, that degree of entropy, it had to go somewhere. Just as it could not come from nothing, it could not simply disappear. This was the calculation she had not done, that Tristan and Nico had ignored, because they had not anticipated a reason to move backward; to let a moment of greatness—of monstrousness—fail.

Unlike her, they still believed in what magic could do without knowing what it could cost. How many lives had she destroyed just to come here, just to stand in this room and play god? Her mistake was letting any of it happen, or maybe her mistake was coming back at all, but Atlas was right, he was right, it wasn't too late to change her path. To change all of their paths. There was only one way to rewrite Ezra's ending, and it wasn't the safeguard of Atlas's death. Whatever world they might have found, whoever controlled the experiment, whichever personal ethics took the wheel—it still would have cost them this one, and Libby understood, finally, that the price of knowledge was too high.

There was such a thing as too much power. Such a thing as too much knowledge. Atlas Blakely was a speck in the universe, a single grain of sand, but his failure meant a ripple of consequence. The edges of his control stretched out to the precipice of this moment. Only Libby could see it. They weren't gods. Just specks in the universe. This wasn't their door to open.

Only she could change their fate.

She knew what the cost would be to make it stop. If Reina had been there . . . Parisa was right, and Libby hadn't listened. There was no spare battery, no external generator to help absorb the reversing charge. (If Parisa had been there, a voice in Libby's head whispered, maybe she would have stopped the whole thing sooner. Even Callum might have known they'd all been compromised, that certain things should not be done.)

Too late for what-ifs, for would'ves and could'ves. All that mattered now were ends. The rest of the story was simple: they couldn't move forward. Everything they'd conjured so far would have to come to a screeching halt. But physics had rules, and so did magic: something set in motion would not stop. If she pulled them back now, all of this power would have to go somewhere. Like stars in the sky, they would have to find somewhere to die.

There were only two options for who or what could be the vessel for that much power—its two conjurers. Only one of which knew enough about what was coming to be adequately prepared.

Once again, Libby Rhodes faced down the barrel of the unthinkable. She locked eyes with the unbearable. If this would finally be the thing to prove unendurable, so be it.

She had lived through the unlivable before.

So there they were again. Same problem. Same so-called solution. Kill one to save everything. Life was nothing but giving pieces of yourself away, little crumbs of joy to anesthetize the constancy of pain. Would it always be this, loving things only to lose them? She felt two hearts in her chest, twin pulses. Two souls in one orbit.

One beginning. One end.

It's an alliance, Rhodes, I promise—

I've got you, Rhodes, from here on, I swear—

I trust you, Rhodes—

I trust you—

Gideon's scream was piercing.

Then, finally, the dust settled, and for a moment, everything went still.

Libby closed her eyes.

Inhaled.

Exhaled.

Her hands shook. Her teeth chattered. Without warning, her knees collapsed.

"What have you done?" Dalton's voice was snarling in her ear, his true colors finally showing. "You realize you're pointless without him, we need him, *I need him*—"

Her cheek was pressed to the floor, her vision blurry when her eyes finally opened. It took her several blinks. She counted them. One. Two. Gideon hunched over. Tristan wrestling Dalton away from the uncanny stillness on the ground.

She'd never seen him not fidgeting.

Three. Four.

I trust you, Rhodes.

She closed her eyes again. The world cleaved open and she succumbed to it gladly, willing the darkness to swallow her up until finally, the earth fell still.

· NICO ·

What did it mean to be a soulmate? To know someone in every world, in every universe? To slip effortlessly between where they ended and you began?

He'd meant what he said, that he believed Libby Rhodes to be present in every theoretical universe of his existence; to be a person of great significance in every single one. It was too familiar, too traceable. Too many places their lives would have collided, a web of unavoidable consequences where coincidence dressed up like fate. Within it, Nico truly believed all their other outcomes ricocheted, but eventually returned. Other lives, other existences, it didn't matter. They were polarities, and wherever they went, his half would always find hers.

But this world, this life, it wasn't theoretical. This was their universe, and their universe had laws, where in addition to the constancy of polarities, there were limitless variables, too. Newness. Wonder. Love. There was a world where the sky was purple, one where the Earth fell off its axis, one where Gideon was born with hooves, all the ones where something went awry in Gideon's hellhole of a past. The ones where he and Nico never met.

A variable could mean a rarity—a shooting star, a singular event. The chance for the birth of the universe itself. So maybe it wasn't every eventuality. Maybe it was just one sliver of an outcome because it had only required one chance to get it right.

So it wouldn't be forever. Did that make any of this less precious, less beautiful?

No. If anything, the opposite.

He hoped Gideon would understand.

· CALLUM ·

The buzzing on his phone as he'd walked out of Gallows Hill had not been, as he'd hoped it might be, a sarcastic comment or tantalizing threat from Tristan. Instead, for unknown reasons and without his noticing, Callum had become the kind of person that other people came to for help. Was this any sign of improvement on the state of the world? Surely not. But he was game for anything, really, so maybe that was all anyone needed to know. And conveniently, he was already in London.

Mere hours after he'd left a slightly traumatized Wyn Cockburn in the belly of Adrian Caine's pub, Callum arrived in another, more forgettable establishment of near identical styling. Only this time, someone familiar was waiting for him by the bar in a pair of black jeans, her silk top draping beneath the hard lines of a dark gray blazer.

"This," Callum said as he sidled up to her stool, "is borderline butch for you, Parisa."

He leaned one elbow onto the counter as she slid a glance at him, a glass still clutched in her hand. "Yes, well. I recently had to go shopping."

"So it appears." She seemed in no particular hurry to move and did not invite him to take a seat. "Are you going to explain this any further?"

He had received the message from an unknown number, alerting him as to time and place with no mention of why. When he'd rung the number back just to see, a masculine voice delivered the message that Pierre was unavailable, or something to that effect. Callum's French was not so good.

Parisa shrugged, finishing her glass of something clear, which caught the light. He arched a brow and she rolled her eyes. *Water, dipshit.*

Callum smirked, and Parisa nodded to the bartender, a young woman in a low-cut top, who flicked a glance at Callum. "This guy bothering you?"

"Yes," said Parisa. (Callum smiled beatifically back.) "But unfortunately, I asked him to." She left money on the bar alongside her bill and rose to her feet, gesturing for Callum to follow. "Well? Dazzle me, empath. How am I doing?"

Ha. Well, context clues aside. "Poor," Callum judged. "Very poor indeed."

"Mm." She seemed to be chuckling under her breath. "And you? Very convenient that you happen to be in London."

"Is it?" said Callum.

She shrugged. "I hope Reina's crusade for divinity isn't terribly inconvenienced by my call."

They were delivered into fading London sun from the cool intestines of the pub; the sun was setting earlier and earlier, eradicating daylight in favor of festive garlands and twinkling lights. Still, Callum reached for his sunglasses while Parisa donned hers.

"You know," he remarked, "I do slightly resent being treated as an accessory."

"Why? I take very good care of my accessories." True, her lenses were spotless.

"You're feeling very purposeful," he observed aloud. "But don't think that conceals all the other things you've got floating around in there."

"Shall we compare notes?" Parisa came to a sudden pause, turning to face him as two pedestrians went around them on the sidewalk. "Nobody else is listening. We can be what we are."

"Fine." He observed her as closely as he typically pretended not to. "You don't actually need me."

One brow arched.

"You want my help," he said. "Though you're not nearly as cross about it as you should be. I can't think why."

"Of course not. You're too busy thinking about Tristan." Now she was smirking. He wondered if that was how he usually looked and deduced that it was. No wonder people generally couldn't stand his presence.

There was something else, though. Something autumnal, deep-rooted. Earthy.

"You're grieving," Callum realized aloud.

Beneath the lenses of her sunglasses her dark eyes left his, floating temporarily to something over his shoulder before returning. A liar's tell. "You're misinterpreting," she said in a clipped voice. "It's not grief."

"Isn't it?" He did occasionally misinterpret. Emotions had their inaccuracies, their misleading fingerprints. He wasn't mistaken here, but there was no point arguing that.

She shook her head, perhaps witnessing his skepticism.

"Doesn't matter," she said. "But I messaged you because Atlas is dead."

The news took a moment to settle. Callum had suspected death, obviously, but these were not the feelings he associated with Atlas Blakely. There were no hollow corners of mistrust, no sticky feelings of misuse. This was something closer to longing, not quite regret, not entirely remorse. More like inhaling the unfamiliar, the feeling of being far from home.

Callum straightened, choosing not to indulge his own thoughts on the matter, whatever they were. "What are we doing about it? Don't tell me you're going to take over the Society."

"Of course I'm going to take over the Society." She tossed her hair over one shoulder. "In a sense." She gestured with her chin for him to follow. "Come on. We've got an appointment."

"You were really that certain I'd show?" He slipped through the crowd in her wake, catching up to her in two long strides. "And be careful," he added with a glance around at the figures lingering in doorways. "There are quite a lot of people who want us dead, and I'm not even counting the other four people in our cohort."

"Not anymore. Well," Parisa amended. "Not if we do this neatly."

"Do what?"

She stopped in front of a colonial building; Dutch Baroque in style, if Callum had to guess. Sober and restrained, with Palladian windows supported by classical columns, a triumphal arch. There were no labels on the glass doors, no numbers on the building. Marble floors winked at them from the glossy interior.

He recognized the soul of the building instantly, as Parisa must have known.

"You and I," she offered in explanation, "are attending a meeting of the Alexandrian Society Board of Governors."

Callum craned his neck to look upward, quirking a brow. Yes, this was the same building they'd been in once before. A mix of old and new, with the taller contemporary addition masked by re-creations of the original Venetian-influenced design up front. "Our objective being what? To seat you at the head of it? Crown you High Empress or something of the sort?"

"You've spent too much time around Reina. I have no interest whatsoever in ruling anything." Parisa waved a badge in front of a sensor, the door creaking open for her.

"You're right, it's more complex than that." He could feel the gravity, the organization. A sequence of dominos falling, one thing that led to the next.

"Of course it is," she told him, making her way through the lobby.

No heads turned their way.

"Of course it is," Callum echoed under his breath.

Parisa walked as if she'd been there before, familiar with the territory. He sensed no apprehension, though there was plenty of doubt. He felt the tick in a ledger, her steps like the tapping of an abacus. Not a victory, not quite. Her loss was calculated but still substantial. "This is a compromise."

"Yes." She stepped into the lift, hitting a button for the top floor. "Any other observations?"

He flexed a hand, realizing this was recreational. Like children on the playground. It wasn't *not* fun. "You made a deal with someone?"

"Obviously." She glanced at him with disapproval.

Fair enough. He'd been around amateurs too long. "It's not personal," he added with interest.

In response, she snorted derisively. "Of course it's personal. Haven't you heard? I'm not capable of selflessness."

"Ah, I see Reina hit a nerve." Parisa removed her sunglasses and glared at him. He did the same and laughed. "Fine, maybe it benefits you, but it isn't *for* you," he corrected himself. "I know what you look like when you're winning."

"I don't see a win. This is close enough." The lift reached her chosen floor and dinged. Parisa stepped out, and Callum reached out to take hold of her arm.

"You mean that." It was disconcerting, the sincerity. It was not unlike the thing he'd felt before from the professor he'd impulsively fucked with at the Society gala last winter. Heaviness that was also emptiness. Parisa didn't just not see a win—she was no longer looking for one.

"Of course I mean it," Parisa said irritably. "What would be the point of saying otherwise? We'll do this thing and then tomorrow I'll do another thing. And eventually I'll get old and nothing will have changed and I'll die and so will you, and it'll be over." He had the distinct taste of something acidic in his mouth. Balsamic vinegar and a paper cut. "I don't see a win," she repeated. "So maybe I'm done with winning."

"But then—" Callum realized he was frowning when Parisa's glance flicked laughingly to his forehead.

"Careful," she said. "Time to check on those fine lines."

"Don't weaponize my vanity just to get out of talking about yours." He searched her for something else, something that used to be there or something that had changed. Existing just to exist, he'd said that about her before. Surviving just to survive, out of a pure instinctual meanness. It was still there, though, everything he'd seen in her before. Was it the lack of change that was so disconcerting?

She laughed aloud. "You're missing the obvious, aren't you? I'm the same as I always was. You were just wrong about me the whole time."

"No." No, he wasn't wrong. He occasionally misinterpreted, but he had always known Parisa to be dangerous, to have the constancy of a threat.

"Here's what you're missing, you beautiful idiot. *I* didn't change," she informed him. "*You* did."

If he was staring blankly at her, it was only because he was trying to concentrate.

She looked amused. "Atlas Blakely's dead," she reminded him, "and what was your first thought?"

"Good?" he guessed.

Her expression in response was familiar, at least. "Wow." She turned and continued walking. "Come on, we're going to be late."

"Wait." He chased her down with another long stride. "What was my first thought?"

She ignored him, pushing open a conference room door and waltzing through it without waiting.

"Parisa," Callum hissed. "I'm—"

He stopped, realizing the room was already occupied by the wafting stench of boredom and a uniformly catered lunch. Gluten-free sandwiches. At least two bankers. Bacon. Two women aside from Parisa. Oh, wait, one was Sharon, the woman who worked in administrative services. The other was older, quite a bit older. She did not care for the dimensions of Parisa's neckline. Callum sensed egg salad and envy, watercress and distaste.

One not-Sharon woman. Five men—no, six. Several were indeterminately European or American, one was brown-skinned, South Asian or Middle Eastern—and slightly familiar, Callum thought, tucking hazy recollection away—and another more of an olive, Italian or Greek. Two men were arguing in Dutch (only one was a native speaker) until Parisa cleared her throat, gesturing for Callum to join her. She'd pulled two chairs for them, away from the table.

"They don't seem to be wondering what we're doing here," Callum observed, sitting in the chair she'd offered him.

"They wouldn't, would they?" Parisa agreed, which was enough, he supposed, of an answer.

"Shall we begin?" called the woman primly. French, maybe Swiss.

"We're still waiting on—"

The door opened again, a much younger Asian woman stepping through it. She bowed her head in apology, clocking Callum and Parisa and then appearing to ignore them.

"Ah," said one of the Dutch-speaking men. "Miss Sato."

Parisa shifted in her chair. Without being prompted, Sharon—Callum jumped, having forgotten Sharon for a moment—leaned forward to answer the unspoken question in Parisa's ear. "Aiya Sato. She's been selected for nomination to the board of governors."

Parisa nodded, thinking. Callum could hear the tumble of consequence again. "Young," she observed. "Japanese?"

"Yes." Sharon, Callum could see, was proving a very useful resource, though he couldn't imagine what possessed her to serve as Parisa's personal assistant.

"Did someone die?" Parisa asked Sharon casually.

"Yes, and another stepped down. There are two vacancies needing to be filled. Nine total governors."

"Only one vacancy, then," Callum said with a frown. "There are eight people present."

Parisa glanced at him from her periphery. "When you're needed, I'll let you know."

The other members had begun taking their seats at the table. One, Callum realized—the South Asian gentleman—took a seat opposite the others, who took their place in a line. Aiya Sato had not been offered a seat, which had not surprised her. She pulled one from the end, glancing briefly at Callum.

Iron. She was used to this.

"So," the French or Swiss woman said, before the Italian man began speaking over her.

"Can we be quick about this? Some of us have business to attend to."

There was an instant wave of agreement with one or two pricks of annoyance. Someone was Portuguese, Callum guessed, looking more closely at things like designers, details of importance, loyalties. Three total Brits.

"Fine, does everyone have the minutes?" One of the Englishmen rose to his feet. "It's early still, but we should keep an eye on the latest recruitment profiles."

"That could easily be an email." Ah, Callum had been wrong, one of the Brits was actually Canadian. "I thought this meeting was called to take a vote?"

"Right, a vote of no confidence in Atlas Blakely—which should be very simple," the Swiss (Callum sensed neutrality) woman said, "seeing as he has not bothered to appear."

Callum glanced at Parisa, who shot him a warning look. *They think a dead man has simply absconded his post?*

You know what you forgot to ask? she informed him in reply, turning her attention back to the members at the table. *Who killed him.*

"All in favor?" called the Italian.

"Aye," said the remainder of the room. The South Asian gentleman hadn't spoken yet, but Callum could feel a smugness wafting from him, a sense of satisfaction. Lavender and bergamot with milky condensation, like a floral cup of London Fog. He looked terribly familiar, like someone Reina had pointed out to him before. (Which naturally he had not committed to memory—whatever for?)

"Done," said the Swiss woman. Aiya Sato, on probation, sat quietly in the corner, frowning.

Parisa leaned toward Callum. "Turn her suspicion down."

Callum frowned questioningly, but shrugged. It was easy to find, easier still to tinker with. Aiya's shoulders relaxed. She stopped toying with the cuticle of one finger. Odd that only one person carried any suspicion, Callum thought, but at least he wasn't having to strain.

Are you going to tell me why?

No, said Parisa.

Couldn't you have taken care of this alone?

Yes. Something pulled at the corner of her lips. *But it's hot and I am le tired.*

The South Asian man's sense of entitlement was gently suffocating Callum, who slumped down further in his seat, leaning into Parisa's shoulder. *This is the man you chose to replace Atlas Blakely? He doesn't seem your type.*

What exactly do you think my type is?

True, I have no idea what you saw in Dalton, Callum replied with a shrug. *Nor, I suppose, in Tristan.*

Ah yes, you have no idea what could possibly be attractive about Tristan.

Sarcasm via telepathy was somehow more grating. *Those weren't my words.*

One of the Dutch men was speaking. *In this particular instance I like my men obedient,* Parisa informed Callum over the drone of some perfunctory introduction, *and useful.*

Should I be insulted? he replied, and she drew a finger to her lips, shushing him.

"This is unorthodox, to say the least," the Swiss woman was arguing with the Italian. "It's not as if we've never recruited from the Forum before—"

Callum shot a look at Parisa, who shook her head, silencing him again.

"—but can you honestly say this speaks to any particular integrity? Or—"

"If I may," the South Asian man cut in smoothly. "I understand your reservations. My mission as part of the Forum has always been to prioritize access. But I do believe there is some value in building bridges across high-minded philosophies, and my position on the Alexandrian Society has always been one of utmost respect."

It struck Callum far too belatedly. This was Nothazai, the Forum's de facto head. *Respect? This man has tried to kill us several times.* Callum wasn't unfamiliar with delusion, especially not shared delusions among powerful men, but that was impressively misguided.

It's cute, isn't it, Parisa replied. *Wait and see how many people nod.*

Callum counted. Three. Four. *Is this your doing?*

Parisa shrugged. *I planted the idea in that one.* She nodded in the direction of the Canadian. *He did the rest.*

Why him?

It didn't really matter which one. They don't have many adequate choices. The other candidates that Sharon provided to them were all . . . Parisa's mouth pursed with derisive laughter, something both condemning and unamused. *Unsuitable.*

Callum wondered which weapons she'd chosen to use. Unsavory background? Sexual orientation? Place of education? Quality of birth? Presence of vagina? The members of the Society's governing board weren't opposed to *all* women, obviously, given the presence of two. Optics suggested their voices could be handily ignored, but even bigots had their favorites.

Yes, Parisa confirmed.

Fun, Callum replied. *Shall I nominate myself for this board?*

Only if you want to subscribe to their weekly email.

Noted, Callum said with a shudder, and quietly, Parisa laughed.

So I take it you want me to persuade them to vote in favor of Nothazai? Callum pressed her.

She made a noncommittal sound and he could taste it, the disappointment, when she said, *If you like. I don't think you'll need to, but it would end the meeting sooner.*

He thought he'd understood why she brought him when they walked into the room, but upon further consideration he hadn't the faintest clue. *All this to avoid breaking a sweat?*

No answer.

He pushed her again. *What did Nothazai do to convince you?*

She looked at him. *What makes you think he had anything to do with this?*

Callum scoured the room another time, looking for the piece he must have missed. He didn't see it. Whatever weapon Parisa intended to use was unclear, as was whatever she might have needed a weapon for. *You could have easily chosen yourself. You could have taken over if you really wanted to.*

Callum. She looked at him tiredly. *What was your first thought when you learned Atlas Blakely was dead?*

He opened his mouth to answer but was interrupted by the sound of scattered applause.

"—the ayes have it," confirmed the Canadian man, rising to his feet to extend a hand to Nothazai across the table. "Congratulations, Edwin."

Edwin? Callum made a face, but Parisa wasn't listening.

"Thank you," Parisa said over her shoulder to Sharon, whom Callum had once again forgotten, before rising to her feet, gesturing for him to follow.

Wait, where are we going?

When Parisa pushed open the conference room door, no heads turned this time. She moved more quickly than Callum anticipated, as if she had somewhere else urgent to be.

"Wait, Parisa—" Callum jogged after her again. "What am I really doing here? You didn't need me for that meeting." Nobody in that room had needed his help to do something infernally dumb, not that anyone had asked for his opinion.

She pushed through another unmarked door and Callum followed, bewildered. He felt the pulse of her stride in his ears, loud and ringing.

No, wait, that wasn't her stride he could feel, it was—

"Parisa. Where are we going?"

Not her footsteps. Her heart. The sound in his ear, it was the rush of her blood.

She hit a button to call the lift. "We're going back."

"Back?" There was only one place to go *back* to, though he couldn't imagine what the point would be. She'd wanted out and so had he. "Why?"

She shoved something into his hand and he blinked, closing his fingers around it.

"Parisa, what the—"

"I'll tell you when we get there," she confirmed as the lift doors opened, leaving Callum to bear the burden of the pistol in his hands.

· TRISTAN ·

It was a bit like drowning. Like being swallowed up by quicksand. His recognition had been lightning, the strike of realization like an epiphany or a thunderclap of fear, but the effects hadn't happened fast, not instantaneously. More like bath water slowly being drained.

Which meant he'd had several seconds to realize what was happening. Something had failed in the experiment, that was obvious. He had seen them, other worlds, and they didn't look like doors. Not like particles. It looked like time stretching out over a curvature of vastness, a fun-time mirror warping Tristan's own image of himself. Like he could yawn outside himself and slowly return in a different form, melting from one world to the next like butter.

Wait, he thought when he felt it; sensed it, the drain starting to come undone. Like a sneeze that wouldn't come or the seconds before an orgasm. *Wait, I've almost got it, I'm almost there!*

It was true! They had proven it! There were other worlds living on the backs of this one, burrowed into the notches of its spine! Maybe in one of them Tristan was married to Eden, maybe his mother was alive, maybe his father had actually killed him that time over the Thames, whoopsie, though at least in that one nobody needed to coddle his daddy problems.

Maybe in one of the worlds Tristan was happy.

Maybe there was a reason the archives didn't want him to find out.

The first person in his head wasn't Libby. He had already known that in a way, that things between them could never be the same, that even if he loved her he also hated her a bit, for giving him yet another reason to hate himself. Because he'd spent a lifetime wondering what am I, who am I, do I matter, am I useful? only to watch himself stand paralyzed in the corridor, tucked out of sight while she reached over and stopped a man's heartbeat. Tristan had neither offered to help her nor stepped in to make it stop.

The decision, whether someone lived or died, that wasn't his concern—yes, ultimately this was who Tristan Caine was, a man so morally repugnant that the murder itself was not the issue—but rather, it was his reaction to it that continued to plague him. The impulse to freeze in place, to do nothing. Insert something here about a reservation in the hottest circle in hell (he was familiar with that proverbial outcome), but he wasn't a good man and he'd already known it. He'd *known* that. If he were a good man, he wouldn't still be talking to Callum Nova. He wouldn't be desperate like this, devastated by the loss of potential omnipotence, because he would care about other things. He didn't know what, exactly, but maybe there was some other Tristan in some other world who did! Maybe there was a Tristan who enjoyed hobbies and practiced daily meditation, but now he'd never know, and *that was what bothered him.* That six months ago, Libby Rhodes had proved him to be the kind of man who stood by and did nothing. And now, finally, he had been about to do something. And she took that from him all the same.

But he didn't think about Libby, not really. He thought, first, of Atlas Blakely, the man who'd stood in Tristan's office two years ago and told him he was born for something more. At the time, Tristan understood it to be a cheap ploy, a tool of rhetoric. A man had stood there and told him he was special and he had not looked for signs, hadn't checked for weapons, hadn't realized the weapon was *him.* But this feeling, too, was not resentment. Tristan had seen the possibility of other worlds and was now at least in awe enough to feel some form of wonder. To feel the presence of great significance—*eureka!* He was met with elation and abject stubbornness. It was nobody else's right to drain the bath.

Because Atlas Blakely was right, they were similar, they were *the same.* They were dreamers! Not the productive kind, the kind with goals, but sad, empty dreamers. Half-broken men who made plans because they could not make terror—the awestruck kind, like glimpsing an angel with flaming torches for eyes. They were men who made terrible decisions because it was the only way to feel at all. *I understand now!* Tristan wanted to shout. *I understand why you made yourself god, because it was the only way to honor your sadness!* The loneliness was so fragile, so human, so pitiful it was almost cute, nearly forgivable. A belief like that, a purpose like that, it could not be shakable. It could not be silenced. You could build castles on certainty like that. You could use it to build brave new worlds.

They'd made a mistake, the Society, choosing a man like Atlas who would in turn choose a man like Tristan. The Alexandrians should have stuck to what they were good at—breeding aristocrats who would not argue, who'd have no trouble with secrecy, who'd kill and kill and kill and never question what would come of that spilled blood. Crusades, the Age of Exploration, the world was built on men knowing how to keep a secret, how to restore order, how to sentence others to ignorance just to keep themselves on top. The Alexandrian Society, what a laugh. Someday someone really would burn it down, destroy it, because eventually the right blood would *no longer exist,* the right birth would *no longer matter*—somewhere, someday, not in a parallel world but in this one, there would be a revolution. The comeuppance this world deserved was coming, and then all that would be left were Tristans and Atlases who were born *already knowing* that this world was broken. Who knew that this library and all its contents had never belonged to the ones who'd been willing to kill to keep themselves alive.

At that moment, Tristan knew: someday this world would end, and in its place would rise a new one. Someday, in a world that did not make its inhabitants this hungry, someone would use this library to read a book and take a goddamn nap.

Tristan knew all of this, puzzling it out as he watched particulates of magic, motions and flurries that danced and ricocheted and sought a target, and he knew—like a book he was reading, a plot twist he was expecting, some narrative device he'd already witnessed ten times over—what was coming. He braced himself, waiting for where all that power would land. Not him. He was small and embarrassing, he was nothing, a speck in the sand, and he knew he was never capable of holding it. Morally speaking, ethically speaking, perhaps even in terms of metaphysical intangibles like substance or soul, Tristan was paltry, transparent, riddled with vacancy—if *he* jumped on a grenade, it would still destroy everything in its path. So then there were only two choices.

No, only one.

He was surprised how much the realization hurt, although he shouldn't have been. If someone had asked Tristan before he walked into that room to choose one person to carry the weight of the world, he would have said Nico de Varona. He would have said it without hesitation. It would have been in a sardonic tone but he couldn't help it, that was just his voice. He would have said that Nico de Varona was the only one who could save anyone. He'd already seen him do it. Tristan himself was living proof.

Like a drain, it went faster toward the end. Implosion, that was the word. The reverse of inflation. Tristan felt gravity return to his chest like a gunshot. He stared and stared and it was only a split second, the dance of things, the aurora of life that hovered for a moment before flickering out.

No, he thought. No, this isn't right.

Someone was screaming, and Tristan wondered if it was him. If he'd stood by once again, helpless as always, or if he never moved because he was never the archer, he was always the arrow. He was someone else's weapon yet again.

They were all thrown backward by the impact. Dalton was first on his feet, the first to see through the effects of the blow, which had jarred Tristan so hard his vision danced with fluorescence, bright spots of color where Nico had been.

"—ou know what you've done, do you have any idea?"

Dalton's voice came and went, alternating with a piercing shriek in Tristan's ear.

"—ve to fix it, get out of the way, someone move him—"

Tristan sat up. The room spun this way and that. He turned his head and vomited, vision clearing just enough to see that Libby's face, pressed to the wooden beams of the floor, was ashen. A small gash on her forehead, tears on her cheeks. She didn't make a sound, like she had no idea she was crying.

He didn't *not* love her. Tristan rolled to his hands and knees, reaching for her, stumbling over a body on the floor.

"—eed to do it quickly, then we can do it again. Out of the way, get out of the way!"

Tristan had never heard Dalton sound like that. It was more than anger, more like childish frustration. A tantrum. "You stupid girl, do you have any idea what you've done, what it'll take to restore him? That's *if* he has any magic left in his body that you haven't killed!"

Tristan shoved Dalton away, wrenching him back until he was mildly sure Dalton wouldn't compromise the body. Then, sluggishly, he finished the effort of reaching Libby's side.

Time and circumstance contorted again as Libby shrank away from him, shaking her head. "No," she was saying to herself, too calmly, like maybe she hadn't realized she hadn't simply woken from a dream. "No, no, this is . . . This isn't— Gideon," she pleaded, pulling away from Tristan to reach for him. Gideon, fuck, Tristan hadn't even thought about him, had forgotten him entirely. "Gideon, I'm sorry, I can . . . Somewhere in the archives must be something, a book or something, we can fix it—"

"We?" Gideon snarled at her. Tristan had never heard that tone of voice from Gideon, either. "*We* can't fix this, Libby!"

"Atlas can do it," Dalton was saying in a studious voice. He was warping in and out of rage, reverting to scholarly certainty. "I can bring the physicist back for long enough to reserve whatever's not broken, and then Atlas can put it in a box like he did before. Or else the archives can—"

"Will you shut the fuck up?" Gideon's voice again. Tristan was distracted by the feeling in his own mouth, rubbery and thick like paste. "You're not putting him in a box. You *cannot* put him in a box, he's not some science experiment for you to Frankenstein back together—"

"Gideon." Libby's voice again. It was still a little chilly, a little numb. "You don't understand, we couldn't let it happen. The experiment, it was—"

"Stop saying *we*." The words were ice cold. Even Tristan suffered the effects of them like a sudden, dousing migraine. "Don't tell me you're sorry, Libby. You made a choice. Fucking own it."

"I had to." She was reaching for Nico's unmoving hand and Tristan's stomach turned again, bile coating his tongue. "I know what I did and believe me, Gideon, this wasn't easy for me—"

"I don't care how hard it was!" There was an expulsion from Gideon, a thin blast of heat that threatened to scorch Libby's fingertips. She recoiled like a child, stung. "Do you understand that? Do you understand that there is no world where I forgive you for this?"

"We were going too far," she repeated. "We'd gone too far, all of this was too far, you have no idea what I've already seen, Gideon, what I've already done just t—"

She stopped when she saw his face. Tristan wiped his mouth, looked up. He knew that face. It wasn't rage. Not anger.

It was anguish. Something deeper than pain, more silencing than fury.

It was grief.

"You don't get to stand on his death and call yourself a hero," Gideon said. His eyes were dull, lifeless. "Leave." And then, more firmly, "Now."

Libby's mouth tightened. "You weren't the only one who loved him. You're not the only one who's lost him. Don't be selfish, Gideon, please." Gideon flinched at the word *selfish,* and even Tristan wondered if she hadn't struck too low. "Listen to me, you don't understand what's in these archives. What kind of knowledge is in these walls." Her eyes flicked to the door of the painted room, to what Tristan understood belatedly was Dalton's absence. The reading room, Tristan realized. Dalton must have gone to the archives. "Gideon, this isn't over. If Dalton can just find a way t—"

"He's not doing this. He's not touching him." Gideon had curled into Nico's side, his head on Nico's unmoving chest. "Whatever mutant you want to bring him back to be, I'm not letting you do it. You have to live with what you've done."

The words were muttered, quiet as a prayer. Devastating as a curse. Tristan felt the waves of consequence and he knew it was over. It was over.

"Gideon." To her credit, Libby was too righteous to tremble. Good, Tristan thought absurdly. Nico wouldn't have been pleased to die for anything less than absolute certainty. He could practically hear Nico's voice—*Rhodes, if you're going to murder me at least be sure about it, second-guessing is just so juvenile, you might as well re-grow your fringe.*

"You know what's funny?" Gideon said in a small voice.

Libby didn't answer. Tristan didn't move.

"I never wanted the answers he was looking for. Who I was. *What* I was." Gideon sat up from Nico's body, dazed. "I never needed to know because I was satisfied just being his problem. However long I got, it was enough just being his sidekick, being his friend. Being his shadow, fuck, being his left shoe." A swallow. "That was always enough for me."

Libby wet her lips, eyeing her hands. "Gideon, if I could do it over—"

"Yes. Yes, answer that question." He turned his head to Libby with a sudden feverishness. "Would you do it over?"

Libby paused. She hesitated. Opened her mouth.

"You have to understand, this was—"

"Good. Own that." Gideon dismissed her with a shake of his head. "Get your redemption somewhere else. Live with this."

He curled back into Nico's side and closed his eyes, and Tristan, who was not a religious man nor a sentimental one, understood that there were rites to be performed and this was one of them. He rose to his feet and took Libby by the elbow, guiding her slowly out of the room.

"He wasn't the only one who loved him." Her teeth were chattering, her legs shaking. Tristan guessed she was severely dehydrated and probably needed to sleep. "He doesn't get to make this decision. We can fix it."

A few hours ago it would have been a blow. Now it was just an insult. "We?"

"We just have to make sure Dalton doesn't try that experiment again. But he can bring Nico back," Libby said, "I'm nearly positive he can, or the archives can, and once he's done that—"

Tristan didn't realize he'd stopped walking until after she turned to look at him.

"What?" she said, though her tone was flat. She must have known precisely what.

"Why did you do it?" he said.

"What?"

"Atlas." Tristan was breathing hard. "Why?"

"Tristan. You know why." She sounded tired, exasperated, like he was wasting her time. "Everything I've done has only been to try to save—"

"Why is it only your choice?"

She blinked. Hardened. "Don't tell me you blame me for this, too."

"Why wouldn't I blame you? You did it. I don't recall you asking for my opinion." He could feel his pulse speeding near his ears, whizzing like nausea.

"Tristan." She stared at him. "Are you going to help me or not?"

He wasn't sure what his problem was, only that he was rapidly approaching it. There was a buzzing in his head, a fly or something, or maybe it was Callum's voice, or Parisa's, or maybe it was Atlas saying *Tristan, you are more than rare.*

Maybe it was the fact that he couldn't find his own voice in the midst of all that fucking noise. "Help you?" he echoed.

Tristan, help me—

He had already seen what death was. What a body could become. Particulates, granules. Meaningless components that combined could be a miracle. The coexistence of meaning and imperfection. The universe was an accident, a series of accidents, an unknown variable that replicated over and over at astronomical speed. This world was a fucking miracle and she treated it like a maths equation, like a problem to be solved. *Her* problem. *Her* solution.

And Tristan, of course. To clean up the mess.

"Did you really think you were so different?" he asked her in disbelief, wanting suddenly to laugh.

"Different from what?" Her eyes had narrowed and god, she had never looked so young.

"From Atlas. From Ezra. From anyone. Did you really think you were doing something different, making a different choice?"

She reeled backward, lurching away from him like he'd struck her. "Are you joking?"

"The irony is that I don't think Atlas could see it. That after everything he tried to do, he was never making a new world. He was only re-creating himself." So much for playing god! Imagine a god who did nothing but make smaller, worse gods. Well, that was mythology, Tristan supposed. Maybe Atlas thought he was Yahweh or Allah when he was actually just Cronus eating rocks, missing the evidence of his progeny as his own unavoidable doom. "If you keep going like this, Rhodes, you're just going to dig yourself deeper. You're just going to mutate along the way." That's what Gideon was

talking about. Nothing comes back the same. Libby Rhodes was not the same, she could never be the same, and whatever Nico de Varona had been, they had already lost him. They had lost him.

Nico was dead. It settled like a stone in Tristan's chest.

Grief, oh god, the weight of it. Depression was hollow, sadness was vacant. Neither was anything like this.

"Just tell me one thing," he managed to say, as if one right answer might still salvage everything. "Could it have been you instead?"

He understood the betrayal he'd committed by asking, but surely she had to know. Surely she knew he had to ask.

She looked stunned for a moment. Only one.

"*Should* it have been me?" she snarled in lieu of confessing the obvious. That Tristan had asked her to choose herself last time, and now how could he blame her for doing it again? He couldn't, of course. Not fairly.

But what about any of this had been fair?

By then, Libby had set her jaw, determined. Even in anger, in frustration, Tristan didn't belittle her pain; he knew she was feeling it, that she would have to live with it and that was her curse, whether Gideon levied it or not, and Tristan didn't have to wish suffering upon her to know that it was coming. He cared enough about her to understand that the outcome of her choice had damaged her irreparably. He loved her enough to know that she was hurting unimaginably.

He just didn't want to help her do it anymore.

"From day one we knew there'd be a sacrifice," she said, lifting her chin. "This was the only one that would have saved us all."

Oh, so she thought she loved Nico more than Tristan loved anyone? Interesting. Salt in the wound. This much salt, though, and he could fill an ocean.

"We all wanted to be the best," he said eventually. "Congratulations, Rhodes. Now you are."

He kept walking until he passed her. She followed him, footsteps quickening to keep up with him as he went.

"Tristan." Her voice was worried at first. "Where are you going?"

"Upstairs."

"Tristan, we have t—"

"*We* do not have to do anything. *We* are done now, Rhodes. We've been dead for a long time." He continued up the stairs, faster, her anger magnifying in peals of smoke as he went.

"So what was any of this, then? You're saying it doesn't matter?"

He ignored her. He could hear the panic rising in her voice and he wanted to say something, anything, but he didn't think she'd understand. He didn't think either of them were in a place to understand what she'd done wrong, which was either everything or nothing.

"I listened to you," she reminded him, stopping in the doorway when he reached his room. He glanced around, looking for a bag, a clean shirt. This one had vomit and stardust on it. He picked one up, half listening to her rant. "You're the one who told me how to get back. What did you think was going to happen?"

She was still standing there when he returned, having swapped his previous shirt for a new one, having decided the trousers could stay. What else did he need?

For what?

"Where are you going?"

Away, his brain said. *Anywhere, just not here.*

He took the stairs quickly, but not hastily. He wasn't fleeing. He was leaving.

There was a difference.

"Don't worry, Rhodes. I'm not going to tell anyone."

"I—" She sounded shaken. "You said yes to this, Tristan. You knew blood was the price. You knew it just as much as I did, and if you think—"

He turned. Took her face in both hands and kissed her.

"It mattered," he said. "All of it."

From her stricken face he knew she'd heard the unspoken goodbye.

"Tristan," she croaked. Unclear whether it was *stay* or *go.*

Whatever it was, it didn't matter.

Just as Tristan turned to leave, he heard a scream from somewhere down the corridor. The reading room. The archives. The light in the corner was red, signaling a problem in the wards, and he and Libby both glanced at it, frozen. Both of them registering the threat.

But Tristan wasn't the archives' Caretaker. He was a researcher whose paperwork hadn't even been filed, who had done nothing in his capacity beyond covering up another man's death, and frankly, enough was enough. He'd said yes to all of this once, true, but that yes was no longer applicable. What good had anything inside this damned house actually done?

Tristan turned and kept walking. Libby disappeared from sight, a shrinking image in his mind. He finally stepped outside the wards of the house, the setting sun meeting his eye at an angle.

He inhaled deeply. Exhaled.

He thought it would feel . . . different.

"Oi, now, *now*!" came a voice behind him, followed by the sudden black-ness of absolutely no thoughts at all.

I
n Aiya Sato's village—some years before her Alexandrian Society re-cruitment; shortly after Dalton Ellery problematically resurrected a sap-ling, but before Atlas Blakely discovered his future among the detritus of his mother's bin—there was a cat that was believed to be lucky. It did not belong to Aiya or her family. It belonged to a neighbor girl, having found her after slithering out from the wreckage of an earthquake and a storm, and later in life, that neighbor had the very great fortune of marrying well, bear-ing several healthy children. Of course, the neighbor was also the prosperous daughter of the village doctor. So, who knew if the cat had really chosen her, or if it had simply gone to the house where the heat was already on?

Aiya Sato did not like cats, she thought, eyes drifting to her ankles, where one was currently rubbing its head in a mewling sort of way, desirous and impertinent. She withheld the urge to make a face and instead looked up with the smile of the elegant Tokyoite she had painstakingly become.

"Yours?" she asked.

"Oh god, no. My daughter's." Selene Nova fell onto the sofa beside Aiya, crossing her ankles daintily and brushing away a nonexistent stray gold hair. "She begged and begged. Ultimately it was easier this way, kept everyone much quieter, and at least it was not a dog. Coffee?" Selene asked with a gesture that summoned someone from nowhere.

Aiya did not keep servants. Somehow they all reminded her of her mother. She could have hired a man, of course, but keeping men in the house felt similar to housing stray cats, however lucky they happened to be. "No, thank you."

Selene mouthed something to the woman, who nodded before disap-pearing and returned with a glass of sparkling water. "Thank you," Selene said with the look of slavish adoration given to someone underpaid without whom she could not live. "Anyway," she continued, sipping her water, "as I was saying. About this little—" A flick of her wrist. "Forum issue. Obvi-ously it's going away."

"Obviously," Aiya agreed. The fact that it was the Forum at the helm of the investigation of the Nova Corporation was like bringing it before the

United Nations. Public condemnation was well and good, but then who would conduct the tax audit? That was the crux of it. There would be no prison time no matter how self-righteous the Forum chose to get.

This was the thing, the only important thing worth knowing about the world. If you could not properly demolish a Nova's wallet then you could not hurt a Nova, which was a law that exceeded the limitations of any government or well-meaning philanthropic cult.

"But still," Selene continued, "I thought maybe you'd have some ideas. You know, woman to woman." A faint, sly smile. "Or at very least, CEO to CEO."

"Oh really? Congratulations," said Aiya with genuine pleasure. Selene had her moments of inauthenticity but she was not an idiot, not a monster. She could not help the fortune she was born to. No worse and no better than the owner of the lucky cat, and anyway, Selene had been managing partner for almost a decade. Not a chance Dimitris Nova had done any substantial work since his daughter took the helm. "When did your father officially step down?"

Selene waved a hand. "Recently. Very recently, maybe a week or so ago, it hasn't even been announced. I thought the board was going to have to pry it from his cold dead hands," she added, exchanging a knowing glance with Aiya, "but in the end, he knew it was for the best."

Aiya knew a little of what Selene must have endured in order to inherit her father's kingdom. It did not matter that Selene was blood, that she was competent, that she'd grown up with more wealth than any member of her board could possibly earn in seven lifetimes. A man who did not want to listen to the voice of reason (or a woman) was a man cursed to deafness, to blindness, though unfortunately never to silence. Only the threat of losing money—or the favorable chance to pass the mantle of failure to a woman—was ever enough to shut him up.

"It's good business." Aiya wanted a cup of tea, but it was never as good outside of home. Though, she had recently bought a very expensive kettle for her new London flat on a whim, a cheery red that had matched her outfit, which didn't make tea the way her mother did.

Because it made the tea much better, of course. Technology was really something, and Aiya had exquisite taste.

"Anyway, I'm thinking some philanthropy will be in order. A distraction, you know, from all the bad press." Selene took another sip of water, looking momentarily glum. "I should have asked Mimi for something to eat. Are you hungry?"

"A little," Aiya admitted. "Something light, like last time?" She had liked her mother's omurice. She loved Selene's caviar.

"Good idea." Selene motioned again, Mimi reappearing. "A little of the osetra, with cream? And . . . do you prefer blini?" Selene asked in an aside to Aiya, who nodded. "Blini, please," Selene continued, "and obviously some of the Pouilly-Fuissé? Unless you prefer vodka." This, again, to Aiya, who made a small motion with her head to indicate it was Selene's choice. (There was no wrong choice.)

"Right, wonderful. Thank you!" Selene sang to her household help, the cat mewling again at Aiya's ankles. "Sorry, I can have her taken to the nursery—"

"No, it's no problem." Aiya, who did not kick animals or hold grudges, tickled the cat's chin lightly with a finger. "And yes, perhaps it might be worth it to appeal to one of the Forum's pet projects," she added, calling back to the original subject. "They're very concerned with poverty. It would put all of them in quite a frenzy if you simply made it disappear."

Selene laughed the way Selene often did, with an effect that crinkled her eyes adorably, without disrupting her illusions. She was very tasteful, only a little augmentation here and there, never too perfect. She looked somewhere in her thirties, which was respectable for a woman nearing middle-age. "Oh, my father would be furious. *Furious.*" Selene shook her head. "Maybe something smaller, like oh, I don't know. The Global Children's Fund?"

Aiya made a slight gesture with her chin, a quiet contradiction. "Your demographic skews younger and younger, does it not? The little ones like a promise here and there that we won't let the world go to shit. Think of it as a small hit for a larger gain." Like killing one to save five, for example. Impossible in the moment. Unimaginable.

Easily forgotten in the rearview.

"The board will have one big heart attack. They'll say it's bad business, no capital return. But the board is a bunch of idiots." Selene hummed to herself, still smiling, so Aiya knew she was considering it. "I like it," Selene confirmed. "It's bold."

It was also very likely a dollar amount Selene Nova made in interest per annum, purely for being alive, for being born. For breathing. Enough to sting, perhaps, or merely singe. A little pain for a great deal of pleasure, and Selene didn't have her father's outlandish tastes. She had no interest in yachts and was much too beautiful to pay for sex. Her board would not see that as a benefit, of course, being only less successful carbon copies of the Nova patriarch, but if Selene acted decisively enough, they would not be able to stop what was already set in motion. If she announced it, even hinted at it publicly so that a word from her went instantaneously viral, the crusty board of governors would have no choice but to bend.

A woman's power looked different than a man's. It had to have the right hair, the right face, but Selene Nova had all of that and more. Crowned in gold as she was, she had something even Aiya did not.

"I suppose I'll have to do something as well, to show support," suggested Aiya, as the caviar arrived in tiny plates over crushed ice, delicate iridescence gleaming from the mother-of-pearl spoons. Someone else aside from Mimi arrived with a glass in hand, perfectly chilled. Aiya made herself small in gratitude, glancing demurely through her lashes at Selene. "What do you think, shall I host something? A charity event? A silent auction to celebrate the birth of our new world?"

Selene laughed again, spooning a tiny amount of caviar onto the stretch of skin between her finger and thumb. "Can you imagine? I think possibly it will help me enjoy the world more. New York without the vagrants might actually make it palatable."

Selene slid the caviar into her mouth, savoring it with a look of bliss before reaching for her wine. Aiya did the same, enjoying the texture of the caviar meeting her tongue. She liked it with the little pancakes and cream, but this method of consumption was slightly erotic, like licking sea salt from bare skin.

"Perhaps we should simply fix America," Aiya suggested in jest. "The traffic there is terrible. Possibly we should gift them a train or two for our own convenience, maybe one from New York to Los Angeles? It would vastly improve Fashion Week, I suspect."

Selene chuckled into her wineglass. "Quite a stretch, don't you think? From one coast to another?"

Aiya began compiling a decadent bite's worth of caviar and crème fraîche atop a blini. "Are they not neighbors? I can never remember."

"Either way it would be silly. Talk about no capital gain," said Selene, the two of them laughing prettily in unison. "But yes, let's do a party!" Selene added with a toast. "If we're going to remake the world, we might as well do it in style."

"So it's settled, then," Aiya said. "You'll come to Tokyo in the spring? For the cherry blossoms? Your board will love it. And mine will be horrified by everything they do." She could see it now. Soy sauce poured carelessly over rice. Chopsticks funereally upright. Confusion between what was Chinese or Japanese or maybe even Korean. "It will benefit us both."

"I do love the way your mind works," said Selene admiringly.

The wine mulled in Aiya's mouth. It was all so sensual, the silks of Selene's blouse, the tartness, the little sighs of pleasure. Expensive caviar always reminded Aiya of good lovemaking. Nice furniture was always softer, fancy glassware much shinier, beautiful lingerie containing a type of magic that even a Nova's illusions could not provide. It was a pity that so much of power was theater, a play put on for a thousand empty seats. A pity that Aiya could not simply lean forward and suggest Selene follow her to the bedroom, where everything could be even simpler. Just a little sweetness for the palate. A little friction to relax them both.

Alas, no lucky cats for Aiya. Just the luck she made for herself, which had its limits. Regardless, she had a vibrator for every mood, even the smallest of which (a pearly-pink clamshell the size of a compact, which currently sat in her purse) was more effective than the lips or fingers of any actual person. And was anything more delicious than good champagne? Everything else—happiness or purpose or goodness for the sake of goodness, the ability to love or even fuck without judgment—the ability to not be talked over by a room full of white men—all of that was just insubstantial glitter. Just noise.

If Aiya could not have luck, then at least she had the patience, the fortitude to know that real power was very simple. It was not compromisable. It was the ability to forget an empty house, an empty life, because it meant not being buried in an unmarked grave after a lifetime of servitude. It was the freedom to make choices that did not end in destitution or death.

Anyone who thought otherwise had not tasted hunger, or Selene Nova's caviar.

"Here's to our new world," said Selene, raising her glass to Aiya's.

Aiya smiled beatifically in reply. (Had Atlas Blakely chosen to confide in Aiya Sato rather than Dalton Ellery, she would have told him this: When an ecosystem dies, nature does not stop to mourn it. Why accept the terms of the Society for any reason but to live?)

"To our new world," she agreed, meeting Selene's toast with the tenderness of a kiss.

W e have unfinished business," she said after handing Callum the pistol with the gleaming *W* logo that she'd taken from Eden Wessex, leading him into the transport when the doors obligingly opened. "You're going to help me take care of it."

Callum followed warily, glancing over his shoulder like he was sure they were being watched. "You want my help killing Rhodes, then? I doubt I'm the right person to do it," he hissed, preparing to shove the gun into his waistband like some kind of idiotic cowboy.

"Careful with that thing, which I can see that you do not know how to use. And correct." As in yes, correct, Callum wasn't *at all* the right person to kill Libby Rhodes. Also correct were the variety of doubts floating around in his head about whether Parisa even needed his help given that she'd just single-handedly orchestrated a coup.

If Parisa wanted anyone dead, it really wasn't a matter of difficulty to achieve it alone. She could probably plant the idea in anyone, even him. *Especially* him, whether he wanted to acknowledge that or not. As for the matter of the sacrifice, anyone else would have made that particular death more valuable. It would cost Callum nothing to see Libby Rhodes disappear.

Parisa needlessly donned her sunglasses again, listening to his thoughts as he frowned down at the pistol. They were ordinary Callum thoughts for the most part, largely about himself and his own questionable nature. He sidled into the lift beside Parisa with a sigh, wondering internally about when he'd begun to differentiate between her heartbeats.

"Is this thing magical?" he muttered, giving up on stowing the pistol away. Instead he opened her purse beneath her arm, shoving it back in.

"Yes. Some kind of Wessex prototype. And no to killing Rhodes," she told him, adding a somewhat unenthusiastic "Sorry."

"Well, I certainly hope you don't mean Tristan." Callum folded his arms over his chest, glancing sideways at her. "That's my thing, which would make this extremely rude."

"No, not Tristan." Not that he was getting any closer to accomplishing that.

"Varona, really?" Callum frowned at her. "Didn't see that one coming."

"Not Varona." Callum glanced at her, and Parisa shrugged. "He's too cute."

"He's a normal amount of cute. And if not him—" Callum frowned, having run his process of elimination and come up short. "Then who?"

She tried to consider how to explain her answer and almost instantly gave up. She could entertain his narcissism, at least, so she let it play from the vault of her memories: his own voice. The real reason she'd called him.

You have only one true choice in this life. The only thing no one else can take from you.

"Whether we like it or not, the archives are owed a body," she reminded him as the lift doors shut, leaving him to hear the unspoken.

It might as well be mine.

If she'd wanted to be taken seriously, she should have chosen someone else. "That's the dumbest thing I've ever heard" was Callum's immediate assessment, announced with a scoff even before the transport delivered them just outside the wards of the Society's manor house. "And yes, I'm aware of the irony of me saying that." He followed her out of the transport lift before catching her arm, pulling her back and frowning up at the manor house's ostentatious facade. The sun had slipped out of sight just moments prior, lending the house's face a blend of rosy pinks. "Are we going to be able to get in? I imagine someone should've changed the wards by now."

"Maybe if the Caretaker wasn't currently dead," Parisa confirmed. "Or if I hadn't already arranged to make sure they weren't."

"Sharon again?" Callum guessed, so at least he'd been paying attention. "What'd you do to her? She seems abnormally grateful. And not, you know." He shrugged. "Telepathically undead."

"Unlike you, I don't have to rely on turning everyone into zombies. I cured her daughter's cancer." Technically Nothazai had, as a stipulation for Parisa's assistance in seating him at the head of the very Society he claimed to hate.

Interesting who people were willing to side with when it got them what they wanted. Or rather, not interesting at all, because it was such lethal fucking confirmation of everything Parisa already believed about mankind.

"Which you did to be . . . nice?" Callum asked with visible confusion.

"For obvious purposes of leverage," Parisa corrected him, making a face. "I think we both know I'm not nice. It is actually very easy to make one person happy," she pointed out to Callum. "At least until her daughter reaches her teenage years and hates her, and then she realizes her other two children resent her, and they all completely waste and take for granted the time they have together that they otherwise would have treasured. And lost."

She hadn't meant to sound so bitter about it, but there wasn't anything for it. The world simply was what it was.

"Parisa." Back to the original subject, then. She saw Callum's mind turning, wrestling with something she knew to be unhelpful to the cause. "You can't seriously be thinking of killing yourself."

"Why not? Someone has to die." A shrug. "You're the one who realized exactly what happened to Atlas's class. If I'm going to die anyway because the rest of you've decided to be precious about a condition we've known about for over a *year*—"

"I'm going to kill Tristan," announced Callum idiotically.

"Oh, right, sure," Parisa replied. "And when will you be doing that, pray tell?"

"Now, if you want." He was staring at her. "I had a different outfit in mind but believe me, I'm not attached to these trousers."

"Don't be an idiot." She turned to continue walking, though Callum followed doggedly, right on her heels.

"That's my line. *Parisa*." This time he caught her by the tips of her fingers. "Look at me. Listen to me closely. I'm not going to help you with this."

"Why not? You already killed me once." She remembered the feeling well. Presumably he did too, as it had been the beginning of his personal disaster.

"That was different. That was—" He broke off, looking frustrated. "I was trying to prove I was better than you."

"Okay? So do it again."

"No, this is—is this even a sacrifice?" he countered, golden brow furrowing neatly as he stared. "You can't just give up on life and call it a day."

"Callum. Believe me when I tell you this. I *love* me," Parisa informed him.

"Okay, but—"

"It's not life I have a problem with. I'm not choosing to die because death feels *better*. It's just that—" She sighed, doubtful he'd understand. "It's that running is exhausting and my hair is turning gray and all the rest of you have something to live for, but I don't. All I have is me, and I don't mind that. I never have. But if someone's going to lose something, then maybe I want it to be on my terms."

She wondered if he'd been toying with something, fiddling with the dials inside her chest. Reina was right about at least one thing—Parisa had forgotten what it felt like to be honest. She was a composite of lies, of terrible things and selfish motives, and really, she didn't resent that about herself. She was a survivor, and surviving was something she was greatly, uncompromisingly proud of in the end. She'd have done it forever if she really felt it was worth it, but she wasn't an idiot. Reina would do good for this world until it killed her. Nico would make out with his roommate or whatever he would do, which either way he deserved. Callum was never going to kill Tristan and Tristan was never going to kill Callum, and as for Libby Rhodes . . .

Let Libby take on the burden of survival for a change.

"I'm not sad," Parisa said. "If I had more time, then yeah, I'd probably take over the Forum. But then what? New shoes? I've seen this season's Manolos." She'd meant to sound droll but it came out a little bit worse. Not wobbly, of course. Just slightly bitter. "What for, Callum? The world's full of assholes and monsters." Reina could fix them. Parisa could gut them and leave them for dead. Did it matter either way? No, not really. The world simply was what it was.

"Parisa." Callum stared at her. "Before you do this. I really, really—"

"Yes?"

He let out a deep sigh. "—think you should reconsider killing Rhodes."

Parisa rolled her eyes, turning to the house. "Come on."

"Wait—" He stopped her with an outstretched hand. "The wards feel different."

She realized it too, in a similar moment, just a hair too late. "Barely."

"Barely isn't the same as *not*."

"Shut up." She pressed a hand to the wards, feeling them greet her in that uncanny way, analyzing her touch. Not like a computer. More like a puppy sniffing her hand. "You're right. Something's wrong."

Callum and Parisa exchanged a glance.

"There's something off about the fingerprint," Callum said, which wasn't a technically accurate term for the house's sentience, but she agreed there seemed no better way to describe it. There was a massive injection of something, like a foreign substance, or drugs. It felt like it had two years ago— back when the six of them still conjured up various cosmic phenomena just to prove their right to belong—but this degree of output was . . . less stable. More dangerous, and slightly burnt. "Do you recognize it? That magic in the wards?"

Yes. She did. She knew it well. Intimately, in fact.

Troubling.

"I felt that," Callum said as gooseflesh rose on Parisa's arms, his gaze straying warily to hers. "Something I should know?"

No. Well, not fair. Once she'd died, she took that information with her. Which seemed . . . problematic, to say the least.

"If you can influence Dalton, you should really try," she said. "It'll be different this time from the last one. Harder, I expect."

"Had a bad breakup, then?" asked Callum with a smirk. "So sad."

No point explaining. Parisa stroked the wards until they purred beneath her touch. "Yeah," she said, and stepped inside.

It was obvious almost instantly that something was amiss. The house was trembling beneath her, but also, something sinister was missing. The sense she'd had for a year that the walls were draining her, that the brain of the archives was watching her . . . it was gone. Evaporated. In its place was a low rumble, like oncoming thunder. Storm clouds closing in. Teeth chattering, something on the edge of collapse.

Parisa rested a hand on the threshold of the entry hall.

"Something's wrong," she said again, surer of it now. She felt the presence of something fractured, something familiar. Something she should've known she'd eventually have to answer for. "In the reading room."

Callum paused. "Are you sure it's the reading room? There are multiple people in the house." His brow creased with what might have been concern. Fair enough, but a multiplicity of threats did not render them equally dangerous. Parisa knew exactly who the problem was.

And she knew she was to blame.

"Don't do that. Wrinkles." She walked quickly to the reading room, leaving Callum to follow in her wake.

"Didn't you hear me? There's at least one person in the— Oh," Callum said, as he must have caught wind of the same slightly harrowing instability she'd clocked wafting in from the direction of the archives. "Right, this is more pressing. Fine."

She could see the familiar flickering light of animation well before they entered the room. Even from the corridor, the reading room, which ought to have been dark as it usually was, looked fluorescent with activity. The pneumatic tube that delivered manuscript requests to and from the archives had been wrenched from the wall. The tables had been overturned, sparks flashing from the outlets torn apart beneath them.

"By influence, did you mean tell him to calm down?" Callum murmured to Parisa.

She pushed the door open wider, catching the familiar silhouette and breathing out. "Dalton."

Dalton turned with a manic pivot in her direction, something crackling as he moved. "Parisa," he snapped, striding over to her like she was late for an engagement they'd previously discussed. "I need something from the archives."

In his head was something; something uncertain. "What is it?"

"He knows." Dalton jutted his chin toward Callum. "Ask him. I know it's in there," he shouted in the direction of the archives. "I know you have it!"

"Dalton." It seemed a waste of their time to criticize the energy in the room. "What do you need from the archives?"

"She killed him, she fucking killed him. I can't do this without him, it can't be done—"

Dalton's thoughts were their usual mass of fractures and Parisa felt Callum stiffen beside her, looking at the mess. Looking at, feeling, sensing, whatever Callum did, surely it was just as difficult to interpret—Parisa would have done it herself, something to fix for posterity's sake, but as usual, she couldn't make sense of Dalton's mind. It was too illogical, the seeds of lucidity, the humanity it took a lifespan to create, those were too hard to plant in someone so badly severed. She needed something less precise than neurosurgery, less tangible, less machine.

What Callum could see, what he had done to her once, she understood that it was not a science. Goodness, worthiness, morality, right and wrong, those things were fluid and dynamic, they still took root in poor soil. Could pure evil exist? Maybe, but then what was Parisa in a world of polarities? The meaning of life was either unimportant or unknowable, the why of it all a matter of constant change from day to day. Life itself would always be mutable, entropic. It would always be imperfect. But the one thing it was not was absolute.

Which meant that fixing Dalton did not require a surgeon. It needed an artist. Even if that meant asking an artist who cared nothing for the canvas, the medium, or the art.

What does he want? Parisa asked Callum, but Dalton had rounded on her again.

"You know what the library tracks us for, don't you? It's modeling us, predicting us, so that we can be re-created. That's what the rituals are for. Atlas knows, Atlas can explain—I kept your secrets!" Dalton shouted again, raging against the impassive sentience of the house. "I kept them, and now you owe me! I gave you everything—now *give me the physicist back!*"

"Dalton—"

Callum pulled Parisa aside, speaking in a low voice to her. "What he wants, I've pulled it before. I know what he's looking for, what it is."

"And?" She scanned Callum's hesitation for meaning. She couldn't parse it, not really. Not that Callum's thoughts were anywhere near the incomprehensiveness of Dalton's, but he was running through a file in his head. Statistics or something, like gambling odds.

"And I'm not normally one to comment on the shoulds of any given situation, but this one feels troubling," Callum said with a look of something Parisa might have called disdain had she not already been aware that his range of facial expressions was limited.

"Oh, so *now* you grow a conscience," Parisa muttered as Dalton stormed up to her in a rage, seizing her by the hand.

"I need his magic," Dalton said. "I don't need his body."

"Whose body?" Callum asked, and Parisa saw it in Dalton's mind.

She saw it lying still.

"No." She reeled back, temporarily legless. "No, not—" Her stomach turned. "Tell me you didn't, Dalton—"

"Of course I didn't. *I need him!*" He was shouting at her now, and she flinched in spite of herself. She had known too many men like this, and it was always ugly, this place of no return. This anger, the kind that Parisa herself was not allowed to have, and certainly not allowed to show. "I *need* him," Dalton snarled, shifting to grip her tightly by the shoulders, "and either I will revive him or I will *remake* him, and the traveler will simply have t—"

There was a sudden blare of red light from the corner that caught her attention from behind Dalton's head. It was like a flashback to another crisis, many worlds and lives away. For the second time that Parisa had witnessed, the wards of the house had been breached by something unknown.

"What now?" Callum hissed in her ear as Dalton whipped around without releasing her, registering the presence of the threat only half a beat after she had.

Parisa, torn between the mess she'd helped make of Dalton and the forthcoming necessity of violence, blistered with sudden impatience. "For fuck's sake, you know what that light means, Callum—"

"There's someone in the house," came a ragged voice behind them, startling all three of them into sudden silence.

The doors had banged open, a staggering set of footprints reaching them from the hall. In the same moment, Dalton let out a scream, nails biting into Parisa's skin from a jolt of something.

Pain. She felt it too, gritting her teeth through the sudden roll of thunder in her mind.

Yes, there was someone—many someones—in the house, but not via the physical grounds. It was the telepathic wards that had been breached. *Her* wards.

And unless she was very much mistaken, they had broken into their secrets the same way she once had—via Dalton Ellery's subconscious.

"What *is* that?" Callum had turned toward the reading room door as if the threat to them were corporeal. As if the problem were the young man stumbling half-dead into the reading room behind them.

Parisa recognized him immediately, even through the muddiness of her vision, the abstractness of the telepathic pain. It was like someone slowly flaying her thoughts, peeling away her lucidity like layers of skin, gradually traversing the cerebral down to the animal, the primordial; down to the spark in her mind that told her to live. Which yes, she did possess, thank you very much to Callum. It was there at the core of her, the reflex to continue without actually knowing how or why. Because that was survival, one step in front of the other—leave the burning building, struggle to the surface, take the hard-fought breath. It was difficult and it was worthy. At the core of her, she knew that, knew it above all else. That pain was not a symptom of existence, not a condition, but a fundamental particle, an unavoidable component of the design. Without it there could be no love, which Parisa avoided not because it was meaningless, but because the cost was too high. She understood it one way and one way alone: that to love was to feel another's pain as if it were your own.

Dalton collapsed against her with a roar clenched between his teeth, spittle flying as he went down. She stumbled blindly, nearly taken down with him, when someone reached her side, fumbling to prop her up by the arm. Callum was still there, then, still incorrectly assessing the wrong threat, and Parisa leaned against him with one hand, the other pressed to her temple. The pain was increasingly searing, like staring too long into the sun.

"What's going on?" Callum's voice grew faint, and ever fainter. The louder the pain in Parisa's head, the farther away Callum sounded, like he was calling to her through sinking miles of ocean depths. She closed her eyes, the pressure of his hand beneath her elbow slowly falling away, the echo of his voice increasingly distant.

When she opened her eyes, the reading room was gone. In its place was the wreckage of a castle, piles of broken stone beyond miles of brushfire cypress. She pivoted swiftly, looking for Callum, or Dalton.

"Your telepathic wards have been breached," came a low voice beside her.

She turned to find Gideon Drake standing there. Waiting. She wondered if she should have been surprised. He handed something to her, something heavy. She closed her fingers around the familiar weight.

"Telepath," Gideon greeted her tonelessly.

Parisa lifted the sword in her hand. The one she'd nearly killed him with. Fine, so she wouldn't be dying today. Not this way.

"Dreamer," she replied.

· GIDEON ·

What had once been a fairy-tale castle looked more like antebellum ruins now. The trees were overgrown in clusters, blanketing what might have been a sky. The labyrinth of thorns was smoking, overgrown like moss at their feet. The air was thick with choking fog, a noxious gloom that clung to them like perspiration.

Beside Gideon, Parisa Kamali looked more like death than ever. Her expression was gruesome with loveliness, exquisite as always, eyes flat and emotionless as she surveyed the landscape in silence.

"You let them in," she said without looking at him.

She wasn't wearing her usual armor. Also, technically, that wasn't the same sword she'd once conjured for herself. Their powers weren't identical, so it couldn't have been. Her magic was theoretical, Gideon's was imaginary. Funny, then, how the ends were functionally the same.

Funny, yes. Very funny. All Gideon could do now was laugh and laugh.

"Yes," he confirmed, and she sighed, adjusting her grip around the sword. "And you lied to me about the Prince."

The smoke coming from the castle was a lure in its way. There were only two things to do with fire: run from it or put it out. He wondered which she would choose. They were *her* wards, after all, and this particular consciousness—this realm or astral plane or whatever it was—it was hers in some way, if Gideon's previous contact with her was any indication.

She looked at him sideways. "Whose side are you on?"

"I didn't set a trap for you, if that's what you're asking." He was too exhausted for that, hadn't known or guessed that she would come. It wasn't as if the world had ended, but certainly a large part of what mattered was gone.

Where would he go now, who could he be without the evidence of Nico de Varona? What was left to run from if his mother was gone? Gideon felt suspended, nothing to push him forward, even less to hold him back.

Though, perhaps there was an element of personal responsibility. "I didn't actually want them to get in," Gideon clarified to Parisa's silence. (He didn't hate Dalton Ellery, didn't hate the Society, didn't hate anything. Was not, ultimately, capable of hating something that Nico de Varona had loved.) "I don't want to destroy the archives, but they were going to force me to let them in either way, and I just wanted—"

To stop. To rest. To grieve.

"Yeah," Parisa said as if she understood, the sword suddenly blazing in her hand. "Well, come on, then. Let's go."

She stepped forward as if she'd always known he'd follow, and possibly that was obvious. He was, after all, just standing there. He'd handed her a weapon, which was basically like saying he'd specifically come to help her hunt the thing he'd brought down on their heads.

The Accountant who'd visited Gideon again the night prior had been lying in wait near Gideon's subconscious, just as he had threatened to do for the rest of Gideon's unnatural life. Waiting, expectantly, as the Accountant had promised to be, until Gideon's mother's debt was paid, the Prince relinquished, and—because Gideon was not an idiot—the archives and their contents ultimately stolen. Gideon, who was still flimsy by nature, always one foot outside this realm, knew that it had always been more work to stay awake than it had ever been to fall asleep. He had only ever tried so hard for one specific person, who was no longer breathing, no longer laughing. No longer capable of dreaming.

So, in the wake of Nico's loss, with nothing but rage and emptiness inside him, Gideon had come to a very simple decision: *Fuck this house. Just let it burn.*

At the first glimpse of haziness between consciousness and dreaming—in the usual pulse between asleep and awake—Gideon had thought simply *the Prince you've been looking for is here,* and then something had materialized for him. The telepathic ward, the one he'd once plucked like a guitar string for Nico, to show Nico the kind of prison he'd chosen, the opulence of security that Nico lived within.

Gideon found it then, again, and tiredly he'd thought okay, gigantic fucking scissors, and then he'd cut it like a cartoon mayor at some political charity event. He hadn't even seen the Accountant materialize. Hadn't seen the sound of the Accountant's voice take shape. It was more like a slither, a poison slowly seeping through the vents. The door to his telepathic jail cell swung open, and then Gideon could have walked through it. He could have left it all behind. He saw his window of opportunity to go, and thought with a sigh: Nico will be so disappointed.

Then, after the house's wards had been breached, he'd heard the distant screaming from the archives and forced himself awake.

But now Gideon was back in the realms, trudging silently behind Parisa, ambling in her wake while she surveyed the broken landscape of the erst-while Prince's castle grounds, mouth growing tighter with disquiet the farther in she went. The thorns made no indication of giving way, the trees largely apathetic to her presence. She stopped for a second to let out what seemed a long-suffering sigh of annoyance.

"Why am I doing this?" she asked the empty air, or possibly Gideon.

"Dunno," Gideon replied dully. Then, because he might as well have an answer for himself, "What is he? The Prince. Dalton. Is he a necromancer?"

"An animator." There was another scream. "I don't know the difference."

Gideon did. He had studied theoretical magic, after all, since there was no opportunity to major in Probably Not Human Studies or whatever Nico would have joked. Gideon was not as quick as Nico, not as funny, not as anything, except potentially more informed in this one (1) specific area. "A necromancer is a naturalist for dead things. An animator is more like a manufacturer of alive things."

He could feel Parisa looking at him but didn't meet her glance. "Meaning?"

"Naturalists take from nature. Animators don't take anything, they make it." Something like the difference between a ghost and a zombie, or the definition of pornography. Easy to point to while it was happening but hard to legally define.

There was an explosion from somewhere in the distance. Another scream. It was obvious there was a battle taking place somewhere, which Gideon realized now they were simply witnessing, not partaking in. As if Parisa had yet to decide.

Reading his mind (probably), Parisa shaded her eyes. "When you let the Prince out of his cage, you changed him."

"From what to what?"

"From a lockbox to a bomb."

"Sounds dangerous."

She nodded but didn't move. "I imagine Rhodes must have thought so."

Gideon's head swam with residual badness at the mention of Libby. Not hatred. Nico had not hated her and Gideon wouldn't, either. Still, an element of bitterness was there.

"You agree with her," Gideon observed, sensing that Parisa was not in a rush to save Dalton, nor to rescue the Society. They were both simply watching the fall of Rome. He pondered whether he should make popcorn. Nico liked his the same way he liked his elote, which was neither relevant information nor any longer a useful thing to know.

"The world," Parisa commented factually, "is full of dangerous people. I struggle to rob Dalton of his right to be destructive when so much of what's out there is so worthy of being destroyed."

"Still," Gideon noted. "Probably a bad idea to let him become someone else's weapon."

Parisa grimaced, and Gideon realized that she was thinking. Planning, more like.

"We could try to put him back inside the castle," she said aloud, testing the theory. Gideon realized they were meant to be brainstorming, which was, again, quite funny. Overhead the storm was growing increasingly real, with what little they could see through the canopy of trees streaking with lightning from time to time, thunder groaning from afar.

"You want to put the contents back inside Pandora's box?" Gideon asked doubtfully.

"Just because it's futile doesn't mean it's not worth a try. Life is futile. By definition, its only outcome is failure. Invariably it ends." She looked at him. "Does that make it less worthwhile?"

"Grim," said Gideon.

"And as for the archives . . ." Parisa was wrestling with herself now. "I don't know if the Society deserves them."

"Pretty safe conclusion," Gideon confirmed. He had trouble unseeing what he had already seen of the Society's reality, perhaps because he had never been offered what Nico had been offered. Greatness, glory, that had never been on the table for him. Just the micromanagement of an unpaid internship by a bunch of faceless people under hoods.

"But whoever this is is probably worse," Parisa sighed.

"Also a valid point."

Parisa looked at him with an obvious grimace of resignation. "Do you know who it is? Whoever you let inside?"

"Best guess is some associates of the person my mother called the Accountant," Gideon said. "He bought her gambling debts and consolidated them into one impossible price."

"Oh, cute," said Parisa. "Like a metaphor for poverty."

"Yeah."

"So probably not a good idea to let his friends into the house."

"No." He paused before adding, "Sorry."

"You're good at this, though, aren't you?" She inspected him for a second, hand tightening around the sword. "Better than Nico led me to believe."

The mention of him hurt, but Gideon had known pain before. "I'm . . . proficient to a certain degree. With significant limitations."

"Meaning?"

"Meaning . . ." He shrugged. "This, my magic, it's not real."

The tiny quirk of her brow was like a chorus of disdainful accusation. "Does it work?"

"To some extent."

"Then what about it isn't real?"

Gideon opened his mouth to say *everything*, then considered altering his response to *nothing*, and then he simply stood there.

If he had known the answer to that question, would Nico have joined the Society?

Would they, either of them, be standing there now?

"Well." Parisa correctly read the insignificance of Gideon's knowledge on the subject and sighed again, stepping forward with a sense of reluctant acquiescence. "I can't say I'm suited to heroism but my head fucking hurts, so let's give it a try."

She lifted the sword to the thorns, slicing through them, or trying to. It wasn't working very well, probably because swords were not made to cut through thorns. They were made for slicing down humans, and thorns were apparently made of stronger stuff. Well, this was Gideon's fault, technically. Parisa had initially produced a sword because she was a telepath who had thought-magic, but thoughts were only made of things that people had borne witness to before. There were other *kinds* of thoughts, obviously, like ideas and creation, and certainly she could create something different if she really tried, but this was Gideon's expertise.

What was designed to get through thorns? Probably a thorn-specific chainsaw.

It materialized in Gideon's hand. He looked down at it, then set it on the ground, engaging the trigger switch to start the motor. It roared to life, chomping eagerly at the bed of thorns before them, and Gideon looked up at a waiting Parisa.

"Well, it's not aesthetically appropriate, but it'll do," she said amiably, motioning for him to go ahead.

Right. Well, walking would be slow. Gideon dreamed up a convertible, the kind Nico had told him that Max's father had just bought. (Max, Gideon thought with a sudden warmth. The world still had Max in it, so it wasn't over. It wasn't ending. It hadn't yet been destroyed.) Parisa slid into the driver's seat and Gideon, still holding the active chainsaw, jumped into the passenger side as she revved the engine, expectantly holding out a hand.

"What?" Gideon asked her over the roar of the chainsaw before dreaming it into a quieter model.

"Sunglasses, please," she said. "If we're going to do this, we might as well make it look hot."

He shrugged and handed her a pair, dreaming up another for himself. Hers were aviators, his were the fifties-inspired model that Nico had loved and subsequently lost. He'd thought they made him look dapper and he was right.

Parisa took off as Gideon leaned out the side of the convertible, slicing through the thorns and overgrown branches that swung from the trees. Bigger chainsaw, he thought. Two chainsaws. Chainsaw hands.

"Looks dangerous," commented Parisa with a sidelong glance. "Better swap those out before you have any weird fantasies."

"Just drive," sighed Gideon, realizing that Nico had probably liked her a great deal and deciding that, actually, he did, too, even if she had nearly killed him once. Especially for that, in fact.

She was a very good driver, or Gideon had dreamed a very good car. Excellent suspension. Her control over it was magnificent, and he realized she was using a gear shift. He had made her a manual car?

"No," she answered his thoughts. Then, after a moment, "Someone taught me this way."

"Who?"

She circumvented a tangle of trees. "My husband. He's dead now."

Gideon swiped madly at a particularly dense thicket, accidentally toppling a tree that fell into their path. (Convertible maybe a bad idea. Bulldozer with racecar engine.) They shot upright, their imaginary scenario rearranging itself, and then Gideon swapped the chainsaw hands for his regular ones, nudging the sunglasses up on his nose.

"Did you love him?" Gideon asked. "Your husband."

"Yes," said Parisa. "But life goes on."

In that moment, Gideon abruptly recalled his suspicion that the telepath who had crafted the Society's wards was a sadist, and realized that perhaps people who underwent the most pain probably knew it most skillfully. He felt a piece of his old self come back to him, a piece that wasn't broken even if Nico was gone. It was the piece that knew the hardest thing about existence was having a talent for causing suffering and declining to use it because it was bad. The piece that understood that success was not quantifiable by any form of capital. That it was most admirable to walk around in the world and choose not to break things just because you can.

"Yeah," Gideon said, because if he knew only one thing about life, it was that. "Life goes on."

They made it through the woods of the castle grounds, coming upon the rubble at the base of the castle itself. This was a dreamt bulldozer and thus it was very effective, but there were other things now to contend with; glimpses of spectral things, half-human. "There's Dalton," Parisa said, slipping out of the driver's seat and pointing. She glinted as a bolt of lightning struck; clad again in armor, the sword back in her hand. Gideon hadn't realized she'd brought it with them. He leapt down from the passenger side, circumventing the bulldozer's blade to join her on the left side of the push frame. Then, for fun, he conjured himself a bow and arrow, which Parisa looked at with a wrinkle of her nose.

"Be practical, Drake," she said, and he sighed. He was actually very competent with a bow, but she made a good point.

"Fine. But I'm not happy about it." He dreamt up an automatic crossbow with an enhanced scope. Practically driverless, on the off chance he had to go up against a telepath who was anywhere near her skill level.

"Better," she said approvingly, hefting the sword upright and forging ahead.

Dalton, the Prince, stood in what might have been a central courtyard, the remains of his castle splayed on either side like the graveyard of his personal cage. There were three—no, four—other men present, all converging uniformly on Dalton. If they were telepaths, their time here was limited before their corporeal limits failed and their magic ran out. In these numbers, though, telepathic combat would be easy.

A puzzle, however, was not.

"Keep them inside the courtyard," Gideon said to Parisa, who looked at him quizzically for a moment, then nodded. "All of them," Gideon clarified, including Dalton that time in his assertion of who their enemies were, and she nodded again, more certain that time, as if she understood his plan. Which she likely did, though he wondered if she was pleased taking orders from Gideon, or anyone. Didn't matter. He knew how to do some things, which included solving a problem without any more damage than necessary. Gideon had lived a hunter-gatherer kind of existence, one that looked starved to others, but it had kept him alive this long. It had given him Nico, so whatever anyone else thought of his survival was irrelevant. It was a life of abundance. He had had more than anyone strictly needed—so much so that he could give it away now and still have plenty to spare.

Which was not to say magic was wholly unlimited. It was a good thing he was no longer the subject of Parisa Kamali's ire, because she had not grown less talented over the course of their brief acquaintance. She dropped into the center of the courtyard, resplendent in black armor, and Gideon understood at least enough to know that what she was doing—the game she was playing—had slightly different rules. For her, just being here was an effort. Lucid dreaming, astral projecting, they were diametrically different even if they felt precisely the same. Gideon could be trapped here forever whereas Parisa could disappear, disintegrate at any time.

It was an issue of time, as everything always was. A question of mortality. The thing that made them fallible, the only true separation from the divine—for them, there would always be an ending.

Gideon wasn't here to be a hero. He was here to be a foreman, to oversee the construction of a simple but impenetrable thing, which was realistic and impossible at the same time. Luckily the others, the intruders, whoever they were, were no better off than Parisa—worse off, probably, for not having her natural skills. Gideon wondered, in fact, how it was possible they were doing this, breaking into a telepathic fortress that even he had not been able to successfully penetrate, until he noticed something about each of the attackers. They were all wearing glasses.

Not *just* glasses, obviously. Glints of something flashed from the temples, the place where a fashion brand's logo might have been. A small *W.* The equivalent of wearing their team's sponsor across their chests.

Well, Gideon thought with a mix of resignation and disgust, which was what he mostly felt toward epiphanies about humanity. So. This was what James Wessex—the Accountant—had done with a billion dollars. Feed the hungry? Preserve the earth's resources? No, why would anyone do that, who would it help besides, um, everyone? Developing impossible telepathic weapons, on the other hand—something that surely cost as much as a space program to fund—was *clearly* the better choice. How else to stick one's flag in something and call it theirs?

Focus. What would help the situation? Nico, probably. Nico always knew what to do. Nico was the kind of person who looked at something and saw it differently than everyone else. He saw what things *could* be. It was his problem with the things he had problems with, what he loved about the things he loved. What had Nico seen in Gideon? His potential? Something to fix? No point dwelling on that now, but the lens was significant, because

Nico would look down and not see a broken courtyard or a morally questionable telepath fighting alongside an animator with the power to destroy the world—he would see a solvable puzzle. A winnable game. He would see the broken pieces of the simulation and make them whole. He would look at the problem and fix it. He would do it with a blink, but Gideon wasn't a physicist, so he would have to see it differently.

Parisa had taken Dalton's side, correctly recognizing that the easiest way to keep him within the scope of Gideon's plan would be to face the library's intruders all at once. The four attackers were using weapons the equivalent of sci-fi blasters, no doubt also of Wessex Corporation funding and design. Hm, how to gauge the danger level of a weapon whose parameters Gideon did not know? Presumably they could be used on just about anything, walls of a ruined castle included. What kind of fortress could be strong enough to withstand any amount of telepathic prowess, previously imaginable or not? Almost everything in nature eventually broke down. No shape was wholly impenetrable. Boxes got opened—it was what they were for.

But why make a box when he could make a dream?

This was his expertise, the types of dreaming. Searching for something impossible to find. In that sense, Libby was his inspiration—the constancy of her searching, the painful labyrinth that was her subconscious mind. At the reminder of Libby and her nightmares, Gideon understood two things.

One, that he would forgive her. It would take a long time and it would be difficult, but it would happen all the same.

Two, that everyone had something from which to run.

Gideon sighed. Time to make a monster, then.

The creature of Gideon's worst imaginings would not be clawed. It would not have sharp teeth. It would have charisma, the warmth of the sun, but also the sense that his entire significance would be erased if that affection was ever dimmed or withdrawn. Gideon's monster was part obligation. It was unearned, helpless loyalty to someone finned and flawed. Gideon's monster had hunger, it had fear, the primal ones of survival and pain, but it also had a sense of rightness. It had the fear of wrongdoing, fear of harm, fear of some inner fatality, some internal corruption. It contained Gideon's sense that he was not, and would never be, completely whole.

Gideon's monster was not without some goodness. It had enough sadness to suffer, but not enough that it could give up. It had tenderness that was wasted, love that was selfish, love entirely unlike his own because it was rationed and conditional, transactional, tit-for-tat. Gideon's monster had no home, no reason for existence. It was lonely but tireless, cursed to know the exact shape of its vacancy, to perennially seek its other half. It had only one driving quality, which was a desperate need for validation that would never come.

Gideon's monster was shapeless and changeable, identifiable when it stood within the shadows of his periphery but unable to be faced head on. Gideon's monster was tiny and unavoidable, like a bee sting or an embolism, a bubble trapped inside a vein. Gideon's monster was enormous and indefatigable, like bigotry or climate change. Gideon's monster looked like the barrenness of the realms he would never be able to map and the horizon of the ending he would never be able to reach. He made his monster out of familiar things, bits and bobs that he could find, an eyeball made of his pointless virtues, the tendons of his reigning vice. Gideon took the sorrow he would never escape and tied it to the monster for a shadow, something to follow it around. It was filled with the feeling of crisp autumn air, the first bite of an apple, a startled kiss on a Parisian bridge. It wore the unbreakable chains of the fleeting joy that Gideon had won and lost.

When he opened his eyes, his monster was already moving. It was ambling through the courtyard, swallowing everything up like an eclipse. The gray sky that had been raining was dark now, dark enough to see glints of unreachable starlight—comedy with a tragic ending, peace that wouldn't last. He saw Parisa pause, sweat slicked along her hairline, her eyes softening with understanding that was also fear. She spotted him from afar, eyes wild, nearly swallowed up, and so Gideon changed her weapon. Instead of a sword in her hand, she now saw an object of Gideon's imagining: a Magic 8 Ball, which, when shaken, would give her the answer she needed to whatever question lived tirelessly inside her soul. A thought to keep her alive, to keep her armed and fighting. Whatever thought she needed that to be.

It was enough to clear a path for her, a mad scramble up the side of the castle's broken walls. She was bleeding, her armor was oxidizing, the castle was disappearing. The dream was swallowing itself up, an inescapable, infinite trap. She was struggling to pull herself out, the Magic 8 Ball clutched in one tight fist, and Gideon thrust out his hand for her free one just as he heard a sharp scream of rage that pierced the oncoming night.

Something had caught onto Parisa's ankle—a hand. A hand that became an arm. Out of the disappearing castle came something, someone—

Parisa kicked at Dalton Ellery's hand, her grip on Gideon's weakening. Gideon gritted his teeth and dreamed himself an anchor to keep him steady, but Parisa Kamali was not an object of his dreaming, so whatever she did next wasn't his to control. Dalton's head emerged, gasping, swearing, something spectral and equally nightmarish rearing up from the dissolving nature of Gideon's dream like a noble steed, a set of open jaws. Parisa's grip slackened again, her resolve tiring, or perhaps her corporeal self was fading. The Wessex intruders were gone now, swallowed up and powerless in this realm and the next. Parisa and Dalton, and whatever hold they had on each other, were all that was left. If Gideon pulled her up, he also pulled up Dalton. And then all of this would be for naught.

It struck Gideon with bruising force: he wasn't going to be able to save her. At the thought, it dazzled him slightly that he still had it, more sadness left to feel, even after he'd used it to make his monster. Even after Nico had been lost. The reserves of his pain were an ocean, rising higher and higher, into which poured the melting ice caps of regret and frustration and shame. Gideon's pain was eternal, a time loop, back and forth between meeting Nico and meeting Nico's fate, and he wanted to save Parisa—he wanted to save *someone*; he wanted, for once in his fucking life, to be of some use, not just to someone but to *her*—to be what he couldn't be for Nico.

But wanting things was not enough. Loving someone was not enough. You gave and you gave and you gave and sometimes, as was the way of things, that love did not come back, or even if it did, it died young. Sometimes you couldn't save things, and the knowledge of it, the finality—the odd, horrifying satisfaction of the conclusion that nothing was in Gideon's control except himself—was like a falling blade of certainty. Yet another heartbreak. Another goodbye.

Parisa's fingers were gradually unclenching from his, one by one. Dalton had one hand in the tangles of her hair, dragging her backward, pulling himself forward, and Gideon realized that letting go would be the sacrifice; the thing it would take to end the apocalypse that Libby Rhodes had been trying to prevent. The thing that Nico had unwittingly died for was now ironically Gideon's to prevent.

He realized it, locking eyes with Parisa, who nodded. *Yes, do it. Let go.* She tossed the Magic 8 Ball at him, her free hand hanging loose, and—

Gideon grabbed on to her, pulling her up with both hands.

Dalton, too.

"What are you doing?" Parisa gasped, Dalton spitting triumphantly into the circling drain of his kingdom of consciousness. Gideon opened his mouth to answer when Dalton lunged forward, hand outstretched, and then—

Then Gideon woke on the floor of an unfamiliar room.

Blink.

Blink.

Above him, the air hung heavy with smoke.

A circle of gold hovered overhead, the barrel of a pistol smoking. A vaguely human shape cocked its head, peering at Gideon, before a hand lowered the pistol carefully, letting it rest in the center of Gideon's forehead.

Gideon closed his eyes, exhausted. A voice spoke from the back of his mind, like something half-remembered from a dream.

It is decidedly so.

VIII

NATURALISM

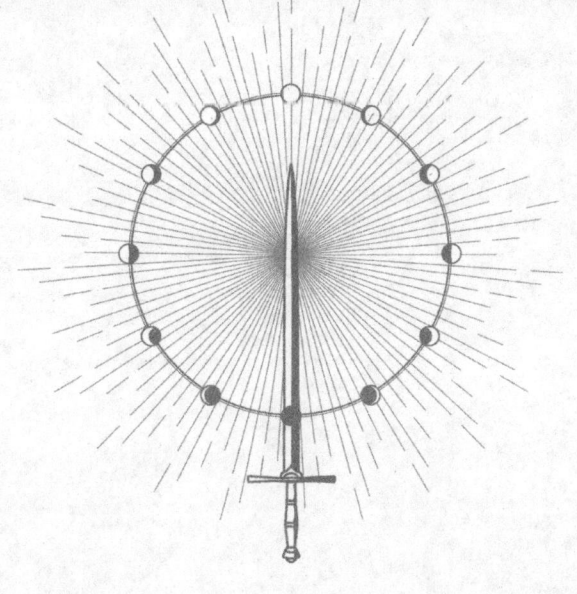

· LIBBY ·

The scream that had torn her attention briefly away from Tristan as he was leaving was enough to awaken her to urgency again.

So Tristan wanted to go. So what? She had known from the beginning that he wasn't capable of her brand of loyalty, her kind of moral conviction. For a moment she hated him more than she had ever hated anyone, with the glaring exception of herself. It was a long and serious enough moment that she had no trouble letting him leave, especially when she saw his face. The nothingness he wore, the look of relief at passing the buck to someone else. His obligation to her was at an end—and maybe that was actually reassuring, Libby realized, because up until then, everything between them had been a consequence of guilt. If he washed his hands of her then good, she no longer owed him the pretense of apology.

She wasn't sorry she killed Ezra. Wasn't sorry she killed Atlas. Wasn't sorry she killed Nico, either, because everything else she felt about that was so far beyond remorse it could not be calibrated. Could not be measured.

She had killed another piece of her heart, the piece containing everything Nico de Varona had meant to her—every moment of incapacitating inadequacy, every glimpse of impossible, unavoidable admiration, every ounce that every universe contained of something that had to be, could only ever have been love—and the complexity of it, the impossibility of it, it dwarfed whatever longing she currently felt for Tristan. She had been a smaller person when she'd chosen him, someone capable of smaller feelings, so when he turned away from her for the last time, she let him go without a word. She followed the scream instead, because that was who she was. She was the kind of person who had done everything in her power to protect the life she'd chosen, and unlike Tristan Caine, that included the contents of this house. Whatever else she had done to endanger it.

She whirled and took off toward the reading room, following the sounds of struggle. The inarguable presence of a threat, coming from the archives. She half imagined it might have been Nico—*just kidding, Rhodes, as if I'd let something as inconsequential as my death stop me from making your life immeasurably worse!*—but she knew who it was when she caught a glimpse of him from behind. The judgment she'd been both waiting for and dreading.

"Callum," Libby realized tightly, entering the room to see Dalton on the floor, foaming at the mouth, with Parisa seizing, unconscious, beside him. Gideon had reached out a hand for Parisa's shoulder before falling into the gulf between her and an overturned table, a placid look on his face. As if he were merely asleep.

"Oh, fucking great," Callum said when he clocked Libby's presence in the doorway, an expression of disgust contorting his features. "Just what the doctor ordered. Haven't you made enough of a mess yet, Rhodes?"

Yes, she thought. I fucked it all up. You were always right about me, Callum. I'm not capable of power. I'm too weak to bear it gracefully. I exist in this world purely to break everything good I ever touch.

But instead she took a step. Another step. Another, faster and faster, and watched with a sickening pleasure as the look on his face transformed, blanching at the delayed recognition of an oncoming missile, an incoming threat. By the time she reached him he was too surprised to move, and the impact of her fist meeting the bone of his cheek was blissfully shattering. Like hitting the center target with an arrow on her first try.

He went down hard, with almost no resistance. She couldn't tell right away if it had been a normal punch in the face or if she had used any magic. Something had come loose from Callum's hands—something metal that crashed to the floor, landing at her feet.

She looked down at the shape of it and wanted to scream with laughter, to shake with tearless sobs. A gun—a fucking *gun*. Like Chekhov descending from the ceiling. How ridiculous that Atlas had once sat within these walls reading *The Tempest* when it had been *Hamlet* all along! Nothing but vengeance to haunt her, tomorrow and tomorrow and tomorrow. A tale told by an idiot, with no reason to stop now that she'd already come this far.

Libby bent down and picked up the gun, the little pistol, weighing it in her hands. *Be careful with strong emotions,* Nico had warned her once, but she no longer worried about Callum's ability to control her. She no longer worried about Callum at all.

The gun was cold in her hands. Lifeless. Callum was sitting up, one hand pressed to his face, a pair of chromatic sunglasses thrown from the gaping of his now-bloodied shirt. She'd broken his nose, probably cracked his skull. His face was growing more inflamed by the minute, warping his illusion spells so that she could see him, parts of him, at last. She half expected to find cobwebs living beneath false cheekbones, dishwater eyes encased in bloodshot rims. She thought about the fact that she was assigning him, mentally, her own hair color, her own eyes, her own patent unremarkability, and finding they had suited him all along. As if somewhere, she'd quietly known her same inadequacies lived in him.

She considered, again, the same thing that she had once considered within these very walls, which was that some specialties should not exist. Some *people* should not exist. She had already raised the gun in her hand before she knew what she was doing, before she had fully decided what she wanted to do next. Her pulse rushed in her ears. Parisa was convulsing off the floor. Dalton's eyelids were fluttering. Gideon looked as if he would never wake again.

She had started this two years ago and she would finish it.

"Go ahead," croaked Callum with a thin smile, and Libby felt a quick trigger-pull of hesitation from somewhere in her chest.

"You're influencing me."

"Why? You want me dead all on your own. You don't need my help with that." He was smiling at her now, garishly. His face had never been beautiful to her, but now it was an almost sympathetic ugliness, like staring at her own reflection and clocking all the blemishes that everyone else could surely see. "Rhodes, honestly, I respect you as much as I hate you right now, and that's just a fact."

"I don't need your respect." She had never needed it, never wanted it. Callum was the physical embodiment of everything wrong with the world. Apathy, falseness, privilege—for fuck's sake, he was the literal product of colonialism and genocide. The equivalent of a bomb.

She waited for him to argue or lure her, persuade her, to do that slippery thing Callum did and had always done, but he only laughed again, laid his head back. Reached for his sunglasses. Closed his eyes. "Rhodes," he said, "you realize I've always known your emotions, don't you? You've always been dangerous."

"Don't lie to me right now," she scoffed, finger lightly testing the weight of the trigger. "You've always thought I was useless—"

"Of course. Because danger and power aren't the same thing." He cracked one eye to look at her, and already his face was ballooning up from the impact of her fist, disfiguring him entirely. "You have always been capable of destruction. You have always been capable of horrifying things. Forgive me for not considering that alone to be impressive." He closed his eyes again, folding his hands over his chest like fucking Count Dracula holding a pair of aviators. "Killing me will be the least of it, as long as you realize it will also be of completely no help."

Libby begged to differ. She felt that the absence of Callum Nova would be of significant and noteworthy help. For one thing, it would mean no longer seeing his too-perfect face in all her moments of insignificance. No longer imagining his smirk from the periphery of her helplessness. She would be able to live her life knowing that he had built their relationship on the falsity of his belief that he was superior to her, that he was stronger, when in actuality he would crumble in the palm of her hand like nothing. Like the immateriality of an illusion. The inconsequence of a single grain of sand.

But he did not look beautiful now. This house, this room, it no longer felt sacred. She remembered the red light in the corner, the violation of everything she'd fought so hard to protect. The things she had allowed to give her meaning. The person she had allowed so many times to make her feel small.

How easily a puncture gave way to fatality. The moment she saw it, she couldn't unsee it. Callum's death would change nothing. Atlas's death, arguably bigger, grander in the scheme of Libby's design, had also changed nothing. Nico—

She felt overcome by a wave of her own triviality. By the childlike desperation that had taken residency in her chest since it had followed her home from her sister's hospital room, half a lifetime ago. She lowered the gun, then let it fall from her hand and drop to the floor with a hollow thud.

Callum's face was unrecognizable. Blood had stained the crevices of his lips, beginning to dry in patches beneath his nose. If he tried to smirk at her now it would hurt him, and she took only that. A small selfish pleasure to carry out the door with her as she turned and fled.

The leaves on the trees were almost gone now. The flowers had long since dropped their petals and drifted away. A season of rot was approaching, and with it the unavoidable sense that life would go on unhindered. The world would not be destroyed, and it would not change. Not for Libby. She could power the stars, unmake universes, leave a trail of destruction in her wake—and still, she would be nothing more than a speck in the universe. A single grain of sand.

She didn't know where she was going until she arrived there, numbly passing through the transport lifts, away from the oyster bar, through the turnstile, across the street, past the lobby and beyond a set of unmarked doors. One more lie, this time to an orderly, to finally bring herself to tell the truth.

The woman in the hospital bed turned her head at Libby's entry. Blinked. Stared blankly for a moment. Then turned away.

"Took you long enough," said the woman Belen Jiménez had become.

· CALLUM ·

When Libby left the room, Callum raised a hand daintily to his face, which he was aware had swelled well beyond its usual constraints by then. From somewhere behind the engorgement of his left eye he surveyed the landscape of bodies in the room, the red light in the corner. A messy tangle of emotions, all hopelessness and despair. Granted, some of that had been Libby's, and part of Callum was disappointed she had chosen the high road yet again. It might have been fun to try and stop a bullet. But whatever, there were other errands here to run.

Callum leaned over the young man's body, the one who looked placidly asleep. Did not seem threatening. No knowing for sure, of course, but the vibes were very much cinnamon rolls and puppy dog tails alongside rarity and abstract power. Something priceless and unknown all at once. (This, Callum recalled hazily. This had been the precise impression he'd sensed once before, felt from the center of another doomed siren's heart as if it had been born inside his chest. Interesting.) Then he shifted to Parisa, who was clearly worse for wear. Suffering—he'd tasted it from her once, exquisite, and it was honeyed again now. The drip-drip-drip of a tropical sunset, golden dregs of a buttery Chardonnay.

Dalton. What a fucking mess. Callum tucked his sunglasses into his shirt pocket and crouched down beside Dalton's body to watch it twitch with interior warfare; tension that Callum could see but not read. Desperation, definitely. He put a hand on Dalton's tremorous shoulder and thought calm thoughts, serenity, dull academician things that Callum had associated with the person he'd always believed Dalton to be. The singular delight of reading for pleasure, with no thoughts as to world domination. A warm bath. A scented candle. A nice cup of herbal tea.

Nope. No such luck. Whatever emotions were battling in Dalton, they were unrecognizable and incomplete. It would be like trying to piece together a mosaic from individual grains of sand. Maybe not impossible, but by the look of Parisa's increasingly waxy pallor, Callum didn't have all day.

Callum straightened with a sigh, or rather, an intended sigh that was more of a gasp of pain, because Libby Rhodes had really clocked him. Good for her, or something. She had other problems and so did he. Could he join the astral circus, pay a little visit to Parisa's telepathic realms? He *could,* but he doubted that was worth doing. The wards seemed to be resolving themselves, the garishness of the red light in the corner growing fainter. Pulsing gently, like watching something disappear into the rearview.

The sleeper, the other man, whimpered a little. Callum leaned over him, then straightened when he spotted something from afar. The pistol, glinting at him from where Libby had dropped it. He bent over to pick it up, then returned to the sleeper's body, peering at him. Listening to the sound of resolution, like a newly tuned violin. The strum of a minor chord—a perfect answer to an unanswerable question. Darkness hidden behind beauty, discord that lived inside a sigh.

From his periphery, Callum caught sight of Dalton jerking himself awake. Then Dalton abruptly sat up, eyes wild when they met Callum's. Instantly, a rush met Callum's tongue. (Smoke on the horizon, a river of blood, top notes of apocalypse. If annihilatory rage could have a flavor.)

Callum raised the pistol in his hand and pulled the trigger quickly once. The sound was deafening, but only briefly.

Then the sleeper opened his eyes and Callum, with a healthy sense of caution, shifted the barrel of the pistol back to him. The sleeper locked eyes with him, wordless.

"Callum, you smarmy idiot. Don't."

He turned over his shoulder toward the sound of Parisa's voice. She had lifted her head, still dazed, to take in the scene, which Callum realized was likely problematic. After all, a smarmy idiot—Callum—stood over a total stranger with his finger on the trigger amid the wreckage Dalton had left of the reading room. Beside Parisa, Dalton himself lay faceup on the ground, eyes open. Perfectly still.

With a gaping wound where his heart should have been.

"Callum," Parisa began, her eyes finding and then leaving Dalton's blood-soaked chest. "You look like shit. And what the fuck did you do?"

Callum glanced at the sleeper, who still said nothing. Not a threat, as Callum had already known. So he tossed the pistol away, turning back to Parisa.

"I," Callum began, wondering how to phrase it. Nothing very impressive came to mind. "Sorry" was what he offered insincerely. "But you don't get to die today."

Parisa stared at him for a long time.

And then, abruptly, she laughed.

Laughed, hysterically, until she choked. And then it was clear it wasn't laughter anymore.

Gingerly, Callum sank to his knees beside her. He didn't move to hold her. She didn't push him away. Behind him, he heard motion but didn't turn, noticing only that Parisa had locked eyes with the sleeper over Callum's shoulder and said nothing. Then the slight limp of fading footsteps and the man, the sleeper, was gone.

Parisa raised her chin to look at Callum. "He won't be back," she said, mostly to herself, but Callum didn't know who he was and didn't care, so he said nothing. Parisa's eyes flicked over Callum's face, a little wave of repulsion warping over it. "Rhodes did that?"

"You should see the trauma I left on her," Callum said dryly.

"Callum. We've *all* seen that." Parisa lurched to her feet, avoiding Callum's hand when he offered it to her. From his pocket, his phone buzzed. She glanced at it, mouth pursing. "How long were we out?"

"A few minutes?"

"Felt like hours." She seemed to force herself to look at Dalton again before looking away. "I really didn't want it to come to this."

"I know." He did.

She sighed aloud, then grudgingly looked up at Callum. "For what it's worth, I would have done the same."

"What, kill my boyfriend?" Callum asked doubtfully.

"Oh, so we're calling him what he is now? No. I meant I would have saved you." She dusted herself off, reaching a hand up to her sodden hairline and making a face. "Gross."

"You'd have chosen me over Dalton, really? You hate me," Callum mused as she sought out the nearest reflective surface, opting to tie her hair in a knot atop her head in the gleam of a gutted pneumatic tube.

"First of all, we're dealing in hypotheticals, so all of this is meaningless." Parisa cleared the vestiges of struggle from her throat. "But you really should have just let me die. It's what I brought you here to do." She didn't sound as if she'd ever really believed it. Callum chose, quite admirably in his opinion, to let that go unmentioned.

"Please. I'm not winning on a forfeit." His phone buzzed again. Parisa's gaze dropped to it before rising back up to his.

"Jesus." She shook her head. "You look monstrous."

It wasn't pity, so there was that. It was more of an observation. No disgust, which was how she'd often looked at him previously. Just a simple, unaltered fact. "I'm choosing to accept the compliment," Callum replied.

"What compliment?"

He arched a brow, and she rolled her eyes.

"Fine," she said. "So I might actually like you after all."

"Don't worry," Callum assured her. "It'll pass."

His phone buzzed a third time and Parisa made a sound of incoherent agitation. "Just get that, would you?" she said. "Get out of here. I need to—"

"Wash your hair," Callum advised, reaching for a loose tendril. She slapped his hand away.

"Take a nap. Do away with some bodies." A brief shudder, which he felt but did not comment on.

"Do you think someone's coming after us for any of this?" he wondered aloud, meaning any of it. The dead researcher. The dead Caretaker. The telepathic threat he could tell Parisa had successfully negated, either with brain damage or its functional equivalent. The fugitive sleeper who, come to think of it, might have been the fugitive archivist.

Varona.

Callum suddenly wondered whether they'd see Libby Rhodes imprisoned any time soon for her part in whatever this was. He found the thought amusing, but not nearly as funny as he'd have liked.

"You think anyone's coming after us in a house where someone dies every ten years? I imagine not," Parisa scoffed.

Callum shrugged and tried to slip the phone surreptitiously from his pocket. Parisa, with obvious annoyance, yanked it out for him, slapping it into his hand.

"Go," she said, and walked out the door of the reading room. Or tried to, until Callum called after her, pausing her in the threshold.

"What was it?" he asked. "My first thought after you told me Atlas died."

She stood perfectly still for a moment, and he understood that her answer would be a lie intended to spare him.

"Doesn't matter," she said. "It wasn't true."

Then she walked away, leaving him behind.

With a *dead body,* Callum realized with a shudder, taking off like a shot the moment he recalled. Parisa had gone into the garden, staring blankly at a small circle of potted plants. His dismissal was probably for both their sakes, so Callum obliged her solitude, looking at his phone, which had a missed call from Reina, no voicemail. Two messages from an unknown number.

We've got Caine.

The pulse in Callum's chest beat double-time, a wave of nausea coming over him.

PS—fuck off and die.

Well, fair enough. He'd only influenced Wyn to warn him, not to like him. It was helpful, really, if a bit worrying. Not that Callum knew what Adrian would do; not exactly. Whether Adrian Caine genuinely wanted his son dead was an emotional matter, not a logical one, and therefore mostly fluid. Whatever Wyn thought would happen, whatever the other witches had been told about Adrian's intentions, Callum knew better. Adrian's mercy or condemnation would almost certainly amount to a split-second decision, one based more on what Tristan said or did than anything pre-conceived.

Regardless, this was not ideal. Not ideal in the slightest. Callum fumbled for his contacts, dialing as he sprinted to the transport lifts on the house's west side.

"You really shouldn't be calling."

"Alys." Teenagers. Why any man would want anything from a girl her age was beyond all comprehension. "I know Adrian's thugs have Tristan. Just tell me if they've brought him back to your dad's pub."

"Why, so you can kill him yourself?"

"Alys." Callum felt himself growl with frustration. "I think we both know I was never going to harm a fucking hair on his goddamn head."

The line was silent as the transport doors closed, the wards left unre-paired behind him. He assumed that would be Parisa's to fix, or someone's. Not his, in any case.

"He's here," Alys confirmed, followed by the click of the line going dead.

Callum stormed from the transport doors into the delivery point at King's Cross, shoving his way through the crowds of travelers, throwing himself into a cab.

"I'm going—"

"Mate," said the driver, looking troubled. "Don't you need to go to hos-pital?"

Oh, right. His broken face. He fumbled for his sunglasses, shoving them on to the extent he still could. "It looks worse than it is. Just drive," Callum said, adding, "break any traffic laws necessary," and with a little push of per-suasion the taxi was in motion, speeding through the nearest intersection and narrowly missing a pedestrian as they went.

This, Callum thought, would be very simple so long as it was well-timed.

It would be hard to save face afterward, he realized, given both the state of his literal face and his obvious attempts at heroism, which would be difficult to defend as any conceivable form of vengeance. So much for the revenge plan. Not that he felt he was fooling anyone, or ever had been. Adrian Caine and his cocks were right—Callum was never going to deliver Tristan to them, and even pretending so at this point was idiotically transparent. Instead, Callum would simply have to look Tristan in the eye and say, as un-pathetically as possible, you don't have to choose me. Just know that it won't stop me from choosing you.

Oh, that was actually kind of brilliant, Callum thought, wondering if he should write it down as the taxi screamed down a narrow lane, forcing a man with a suitcase to drift shoutily over to the sidewalk. Which was where he belonged! Callum felt nothing but heat in his cheeks and lowered his window, letting the evening wind whip into the sting of his gaping wounds. He couldn't wait to tell Tristan that Libby Rhodes had punched him. God, what a fucking tale that would be. And he'd shot their former researcher. Fucking hell, where would Callum even start? All of it, the whole story, life and death and everything, it was shaken up inside him like some depraved martini, all these things, these sentiments and feelings. He wanted a drink, but not the way he'd wanted one last year, like trying to drown it all and find some silence. He wanted a drink the way he used to get a drink. Taken by firelight, with Tristan sat nearby.

Callum felt his heartbeat counting the miles of proximity, ticking in his chest like a clock. He wouldn't kill Tristan with a knife, he'd kill him with such cherishing. He'd offer to take Tristan to the movies, he'd feed him grapes, he'd brush his hair. He'd make a meal for him, the kind his mother had always insisted on when she was in a good mood, food that was meant to be eaten with leisure. He'd peel an orange for Tristan, share the slices of a clementine, drizzle him with honey. It would be embarrassing and he wouldn't die of humiliation. He would simply live with the providence of it—the sacred proffering of shame.

Yes, Callum thought, I understand it now, Tristan, the meaning of life, it all makes sense. We are given exactly as much time as we need to be as human as we are, and that's it. That's the entirety of the magic. We're not gods, or maybe you are, or Reina is, but I'm not a god, Tristan, I'm just very very sad and stupid! I have been looking for inspiration and it turns out I'm not inspired, I'm lazy! I only want to hold your hand! I don't want to rule the world, I don't want to control it, I don't even want to influence it. I want to sit beside you in a little garden, I want to put your needs before mine,

I want to fetch you a glass of water when you're thirsty. I want to laugh at your jokes, even the bad ones, and bury my head in proverbial sand.

The taxi pulled up to the pub and Callum burst out of the door, tossing his entire wallet over his shoulder, his license to be a carelessly rich man. He slipped through the crowd and walked straight through the kitchen, aiming himself into the back office until he finally hit the closed door housing Adrian Caine. Callum slammed a jolt of bliss through it and walked inside, and right there, in the chair where Callum himself had once sat, was a familiar set of shoulders. An unforgivably attractive head.

Tristan turned in his seat and Callum felt his own heart leap into his throat, a mission of utter fatality. Here, he thought, yanking the sunglasses from his misshapen face—see me. See all of me for what I really am. You're the only one who ever has.

He didn't see Tristan's expression become one of horror, which was good, really. For the best. Callum's last glimpse was of the ceiling when his head snapped back, which would not make sense to him until it was too late for any sense to be made.

But before that, importantly, it had been Tristan.

It was perfect, and it was honest.

And it was also over now.

In his final moments, Callum Nova understood this one last piece of everything: that this was what inspiration felt like. If fate was an answer, if destiny had a flavor, if Tristan loved him back, if peace was attainable even if—especially if—it was wholly undeserved . . . these were details that no longer mattered.

He could feel it anyway, and that meant all of it was real.

FOUR

Sef

Sef Hassan had not always made his money honestly; he may have occasionally strayed from the path he intended to take; he may have loved too imperiously or punished too harshly; he may not have been the academic his father had been so much as a revolutionary in academic's clothing; but he was not a liar. Not like this.

"Trust me," said Nothazai in an undertone, pulling Sef away from the rest of the room where the dwindling members of Ezra Fowler's team sat plotting. "Where I'm going will be better for all of us. For everyone who shares our values, our goals. *Unlike* the others," he added in a softly disdainful voice, "who came here seeking power they have not earned."

Nothazai placed a hand on Sef's shoulder in a way that was meant to be conspiratorial, positioning Sef away from the Chinese secret service medeian, the Wessex daughter, and the American CIA director, none of whom Sef truly liked. His disdain was not a secret. Sef already knew that Pérez had had something to do with the death of Nasser Aslani, who had been a younger student at university with Sef. They had not exactly been close, but they had been aware of each other, and congenial. Aslani had been friends with other medeian scholars that Sef had known, the quiet counterpart to an ideologically progressive group of eldest sons from wealthy families—which Sef was not. Wealthy, that is. Ideologically, Sef was a survivalist.

Which was why he suddenly realized that while he had never been able to place the origin of Nothazai's accent, he could not unhear the Oxbridge vowels now.

Sef nodded politely at Nothazai in a way that meant *don't worry, I trust you,* because it was what the moment demanded. Sef had not submitted to this coalition under false pretenses, zealously willing to trust anyone who claimed to share the virtues of his lifelong task.

Sef had not liked Ezra Fowler and did not mourn his loss. He did not like Atlas Blakely either, and to that end, whatever had happened to the Society's former Caretaker was probably well-deserved. As far as Nothazai, the ends would have justified the means had the Forum's resources proven successful, but Sef knew better than to blindly follow him when their motivations had clearly diverged.

Let the others be the snake eating its tail, the Hydra destined to fall. The Society promised power and to others it delivered, but power was still in the eye of the beholder.

Power did nothing to soften a grave. It also did nothing to keep a promise.

"Of course," said Sef, knowing full well he would not hear from Nothazai again.

Knowledge was a funny thing. It could be shared. It could be given. But it could not be stolen. The archives knew to whom they belonged. If a better man than Sef Hassan became the one to properly distribute them, so be it. He already knew it would not be a worse one.

Ancient promises would not be instantaneously delivered. It was a long time yet to eventuality.

Nothazai smiled and so did Sef. A very cordial goodbye.

For a full year, Tristan had had his reflexes tested so often he implicitly understood how to recognize when a threat had entered the room. The moment the door to his father's office had flown open, his vision began its process of kaleidoscoping the room, taking on the usual modicum of self-defense at the sound of his father disabling the safety on his pistol. Tristan had been about to disarm the gun, whatever it was and however it worked—a witch had made it, so a medeian could easily unmake it—when something dismantled his own reflex for action instead. A glint of something; the metallic arm on a pair of sunglasses that dazzled him for just a moment overlong.

He knew it was Callum the same way he knew he'd recognize Callum in a dream, whatever his face might look like. The energy in the room was Callum's, the flowering effervescence, the thing that Callum himself might have called a vibe. They were Callum's shoulders, Callum's typically unhurried posture, Callum's preference for loafers, always dressed like a billionaire on holiday. Which, Tristan supposed, was what Callum was, perpetually, because he would never have nothing, would not have to try, would never even have to *work,* and that had done something to the way he entered the room. It made it so that Callum's chin was always lifted, held aloft, even when his face was swollen beyond recognition. Even when his illusion charms malfunctioned, and now anyone could see what Tristan could always see: that the blue encased in bloodshot rivulets was closer to ice than to ocean. That his hair was always more ash than it was gold.

For Tristan, Callum had not been beautiful for his optics. Actually, for Tristan, Callum had never technically been beautiful at all. He was attractive—even without the falsity of his enhancements, the elevation of his natural features, which were not necessarily bad to start—but beauty was something for Parisa to wield as a weapon, something Tristan attributed to the struggle of being near Libby. There was a tension inherent in Tristan's ideation of beauty and Callum had never been it. For Tristan, Callum wasn't beautiful. He was sleek and refined. Untroubled and cool. He was also tortured in a way that made Tristan's delusion seem palatable. Looking at Callum was like looking at a version of himself that he could punish. That was *being* punished, actively, and what seemed to be by choice.

Callum wasn't effortless. That was the crux of it. Callum tried so much and so hard that Tristan could look at him and relax for half a second, as if in recognizing his own reflection he could find a way to be less cruel to what he saw. It hadn't started that way, obviously. At first it was just a normal attraction, like being pulled into the orbit of something unimaginably fierce and overwhelmingly vast, but Callum had made the mistake of letting Tristan know him. Letting Tristan *see* him. Tristan had always understood it, the crime he'd committed, the severity of his betrayal, which was ridiculous, because Callum was not even close to a good person and therefore Tristan's morality should have been intact. But he knew, in some undeniable part of whatever soul still remained, that what he'd done to Callum was the worst thing he could have done to anyone. It might have been what Callum deserved, but it was still indefensible by Tristan.

And yet here Callum was once again.

Because time had slowed for Tristan in that moment, he was able to see things in Callum's face that Callum could not have possibly seen in his. Well, more accurately, because Tristan was Tristan, he was able to see things nobody else could see, least of all his own fucking father, who'd picked him up like a stray dog off the side of the road and hauled him back home. Not exactly kicking and screaming, because if Tristan was being honest, he'd admit he hadn't tried that hard to get away. He *wanted* his father to see him. He *longed* for his father to try him, to just fucking *have at it,* so they could both put down the pretense of paternalism and reckon with the fact that one of them was a man now and the other had never been one at all. But then Callum walked into the office and Tristan, who could see components, saw everything in sequence, though he would intuit it all at once.

Callum was never going to kill him. Callum had recently been injured and hadn't fought back. Callum was here because he thought Tristan was in trouble, because this was a game for him like everything was a game, except for when it came to the reality of Tristan's life. Callum was bleeding. Callum's shirt was stained and he'd just come from wherever Parisa was because he smelled like her, like jasmine perfume and the stain of old textbooks, and they must have just missed each other. Callum was here because he was afraid that Tristan was gone.

Callum's gaze found his immediately, a white flag of relief erected in what little whites of his eyes Tristan could see. Callum looked, frankly put, like he'd been recently run over and then spat back out again, and apparently

Callum, the vainest man Tristan had ever known, did not even seem to care. Streaks of Callum's perspiration flecked the front of his shirt, pools of it below his arms. Callum was looking at Tristan like he had witnessed a miracle somewhere in the space between opening the office door and meeting Tristan's eyes.

In the moment that Tristan should have been disarming his father's pistol, he was instead realizing something he had seen before but never adequately noticed. Hard to say exactly what it was, since this was Tristan's particularly inexplicable talent, but he observed for the first time that Callum's eyes went to all the places Tristan's mind no longer allowed him to see. The burn on his knuckle. The scar on his chest. The one on his brow. Tristan's components. The love he had been denied. The expression he'd grown into that had always been his father's. The fate he'd shrugged on like genetics itself. The muscle that had been defined by running, escaping, fleeing as far as he could, leaving behind what little home he'd ever had only to find himself back here, borne up on an inescapable tide.

What had Tristan wanted, what had he needed, what had he chosen? He saw it all when his father pulled the trigger, the realization of every mistake he'd ever made. He was supposed to have seen everything—he was supposed to have *seen,* but he was the only one who saw nothing at all. He had wanted Libby's conception of goodness because it felt righteous—her moral rigidity a gift. He had wanted Parisa's disdain because it felt untrickable, intellectual—her depression more tolerable than his. Eden, that wasn't worth thinking about, because that was a mad scramble for survival, the choice made by a man with his back to the wall—something Atlas had known. The choice Atlas had saved him from. The choice that became several choices, one of which was Callum Nova after all.

Which wasn't to say it was wholly romantic, this degree of cosmic irony. Just because it looked star-crossed didn't mean there were stars in Tristan's eyes. He hadn't wanted Callum's apathy, his selfishness, because it was Tristan's in its entirety, it was the inside of Tristan's rot: that amount of condescension, that cynicism, the foundation of shared trauma that luxuriated in its own suffering was incapable of happiness. He knew it. He had always known it. But he did not see until the end that of the two of them, only Callum had actually been brave or stupid enough to try. If Tristan had wanted to be seen, fine, Callum had seen him and Tristan had seen Callum, and by some definition that was love. A bad love. A corruptible love. Poets wouldn't write about it. But that didn't undo what had already been done.

It was forceful and inelegant, Callum's neck snapping his head backward before he hit the floor with a crumpled thud, the sunglasses falling from his hand to land somewhere beneath his unmoving fingers. Bile rose in Tristan's throat for the second time that day as time rushed back to its usual pace, a blitz of vertigo. He felt the loss cleave from him like a past life or a distant future. Like time itself had fallen away.

"There," said his father, setting the pistol down without so much as a bat of an eye for the life he'd taken. "Wyn said he might come by. Job done. You can thank me later."

"*Thank* you?" Tristan echoed with repulsion, managing to withhold a childish scowl at the impassive look on his father's face. "What about this makes you think I owe you my gratitude?"

"He came to me, didn't he? Trying to kill you. There, sorted, no more toffs out for your blood." The pistol on the desk was smoking with magical residue that Tristan read like fumes, coating the fingers of his father's filthy hands. "Like I said. Nobody threatens a Caine. And a Caine bargains with no one." Adrian tossed a look of disgust at Callum's feet. "Now." He leaned back in his chair, scrutinizing Tristan. "About that Society of yours."

Tristan said nothing.

"Told you they were no good, your little toff friends. James Wessex," Adrian scoffed, spitting a mouthful of derision over the side of his desk. "That fuckin' prick. He's out for your blood now, and for what? These cock-suckers think they rule the world, Tris, so let them have it. Give him the rope he needs to hang himself with. There's plenty to go around down here."

Adrian leaned across the desk, folding his hands beneath him. Tristan tried to avoid looking at the gun he'd set between them.

"You've got no angle here, son," Adrian said. "Pigs've got you on a watch list. You try to leave the country they'll snatch you up at the borders. Try to disappear, they'll only track you down. Course, I can help you, can't I," he said with a glint of triumph in his eye, "only it'll cost you. That kind of security detail don't come for free, not even for my son."

"This is my punishment, then, I take it." Tristan tried to recall the complexity of their relationship and came up laughably short, finding only the neat simplicity of hatred. "My choices are to work for you or take a bullet on my way out the door?"

"Tris, how many chances you think come along in life?" asked Adrian with an air of wisdom, which was of course something else entirely. A vapor of arrogance to toxify the room. "You may not be a believer in destiny, son, but destiny's shown her hand and it comes up the same as it did the day you were born. You got my blood. My name. I wrote your life onto this earth with my own fucking hands. You think the world gives a fuck what you deserve? It'll always see you the way James Wessex sees you. A roach crawling around underfoot. Begging for scraps."

Adrian locked eyes with Tristan. "That smarmy prick," he said with a flick of a glance to Callum, "was just one of many exterminators."

"He was never going to kill me. I could have taken care of him myself." A lie.

"Liar." Adrian's expression went smug. "I'm your father, Tris. I know you like the back of my hand. That," he said with a rough gesture to Callum, "is exactly your weakness. You can't resist it, the touch of a golden hand. Always ready to be subdued, to be stroked into submission. Always game to be someone's pet." A pause. "But not anymore."

Adrian's fingers drummed the desk.

"Let's say fifty-fifty split," he said. "If what the lads say about you is true."

"What the lads say about me," Tristan echoed dully. It was getting hard to concentrate. Magic was leaving Callum's body, rising up like a fume of sighs. Christ, those sunglasses were gaudy. They were so uniquely Callum's taste, and Tristan wanted absurdly to cry.

"You dodged enough of my guys. I think I've got some idea. Untapped something in that library of yours, did you?"

"You know exactly what I can do and you think it's fair to offer me *half*?" This time, Tristan's echo was tinged with disbelief.

Adrian laughed. "You can have it all when I'm dead and gone, Tris. Half for the prodigal son seems more than fair."

Fair. What was fair about any of this? Tristan had always been a cynic but he certainly no longer believed in what was *fair*. He no longer believed the world was any kind of pendulum, some wheel of fortune still to turn. Which wasn't to say that he knew better. He didn't know shit, and that was the point. Fate never promised happy endings. Not every story had to be good or even long. Maybe the scales were tipping—maybe the universe took longer than a single mortal lifespan to make things even, to make things right—but Tristan Caine didn't have that kind of time.

Adrian flicked a cautionary glance at the pistol on the desk in the same moment Tristan did, both of them lunging for it in the space of a single instant. Tristan was farther away, Adrian was quicker, but Tristan had spent a year in the archives of the Alexandrian Society, and for better or worse, matter now worked in his favor.

He closed his hand around the grip and aimed the barrel right between his father's eyes.

"Fine." Adrian's laugh was mirthful, unimpressed. "Sixty-forty."

"To do what? Bleed for your profit margin? No, thank you." Tristan's chest rose and fell and he felt a clock ticking in his chest. *Tick. Tick. Tick.*

"'Profit margin'? You spent too long in your posh little cage, son." Adrian sneered at him. *Tick. Tick. Tick.*

"I'm not working for you." *Tick.*

"If not me, Tris, then someone. That's all this world is." *Tick.* That false wisdom again. *Tick.* "You got the stones to do what I did? To put yourself here? If you did, you'd already be pulling that trigger."

Tick. Adrian's brow, so much like Tristan's own. Like looking in a mirror at the future. Time traveling in a single fucking glance.

Tick.

"Killing you won't make me a man. Killing Callum wouldn't, either. I'm not your fucking gun, Dad." *Tick.* "I'm not a weapon for your amusement."

"Fine. You made your point." A lick of dry lips. *Tick.* "What do you want, then?"

"I want—" I want your apology. *Tick.* I want you to respect me. *Tick.* I want you to love me. *Tick.* And I want you to have done it from the moment I was born. *Tick.*

Tick.

Tick.

Tick. Tick. Tick.

TickTickTickTick—

END SCENARIO 1. BEGIN SCENARIO 2.

Callum was never going to kill him. Callum had recently been injured and hadn't fought back. Callum was here because he thought Tristan was in trouble, because this was a game for him like everything was a game, except for when it came to the reality of Tristan's life. Callum was bleeding. Callum's shirt was stained and he'd just come from wherever Parisa was because he smelled like her, like jasmine perfume and the stain of old textbooks, and they must have just missed each other. Callum was here because he was afraid that Tristan was gone.

Callum's gaze found his immediately, a white flag of relief erected in what little whites of his eyes Tristan could see.

And Callum was looking at Tristan like he had witnessed a miracle somewhere in the space between the office door and Tristan's eyes.

In that moment, Tristan disassembled the blast that left his father's pistol, the shrapnel floating weightlessly, like dust. Callum sneezed, then swore, one hand rising to his broken face. Tristan's father rose to his feet for a second try and Tristan dragged time to a halt, existing in Callum's narrowly bypassed doom alongside all the moments to come, trying to decide what he really wanted, what he really needed.

It's not a gun, he heard Nico saying in his ear. *It's not a gun unless you say it's a gun.*

It's not a gun, it's a pipe bomb, Tristan thought, grabbing Callum by the shoulder and turning away from the heat of the blast, shielding himself in the knowledge that none of this was final, none of it was real.

Nothing was over unless he said so.

SCENARIO 5.

The house was a familiar sort of dark when Tristan returned, almost as if he'd time traveled to be there. He walked through the great hall, about to climb the stairs and retrieve his things and leave—to what end, he didn't yet know—when he suddenly paused, hearing something from the painted room.

He walked in to find Libby there, sitting on the floor in front of the sofa. Staring into the fire, drinking a glass of white wine. She looked up and a flicker of something passed over her features. Not surprise, exactly. Not disappointment, either.

"I'm not drinking red wine," she told him. "I'm sorry, but it tastes like Jesus."

Tristan chuckled to himself and shrugged, then sat beside her, reaching over for her glass. She handed it to him as he made himself comfortable, leaning his head back against the sofa cushions, staring blankly into the fire.

"I'm just here for the night," Libby said.

"I'm just getting my things," Tristan replied.

They nodded without looking at each other. The silence was more companionable than it had previously been, which was ironic given the state of things when they'd parted. Perhaps they'd both seen enough to realize that even the sins they'd committed with and against each other somehow paled in comparison now.

"I just want to say—"

"Rhodes, I—"

They stopped. Looked at each other.

She seemed healthier, somehow. Like maybe she'd been eating and sleeping more, a little rested, less hollow around the cheeks. She'd had another haircut and her latest fringe was long, skating her cheekbones, fashionable without changing her face. She still felt magical to him, like impossibility floating beneath his fingers, even if he understood now that magic did not mean goodness. Did not mean the timing was, or had ever been, right.

"Maybe someday," he said quietly to the silence that stretched out between them.

Libby took the glass of wine from him and set it aside. He realized he had not actually taken a sip; had simply been holding it, watching it catch the light.

"Maybe someday," she replied.

They both leaned forward to rise to their feet, him standing first, then reaching a hand down for hers. She took it, allowing him to pull her up.

"I heard about—"

"Make sure you—"

They stopped.

From the mantel, the clock ticked.

"I hate that thing," said Tristan as Libby said, "Fuck it."

Then the two of them collided in the same moment; as one.

On some level Tristan knew this was a matter of need, an itch worth scratching, no different than the other times had been. It didn't have to be different—didn't have to *mean* anything—and perhaps that's why it was different after all. A fumble up the stairs, her legs around his waist, a thundering pulse they shared like a secret. It wasn't forever and it was sweeter that way, ripe on the edge of rotten. Loss they passed back and forth between them, illuminated like a torch. Capitulation, acquiescence, rest. No longer burning just to burn.

He let her have the bed. Fate was no longer so critical, destiny unguessable but irrelevant, someone else's business to plan. He closed the door behind him quietly, leaving her to sleep.

Maybe someday. Not a promise. More like an offer, or a dream.

Maybe someday, or maybe not. Sometimes uncertainty was a blessing, knowledge a burden, foresight a fucking curse.

Maybe someday.

SCENARIO 16.

Tristan stood over the body of his father and bent down to scrutinize the trickle of blood from his hairline, traversing the map of furrowed brows and sardonic laughter on the landscape of the forehead that would inevitably become Tristan's own. He felt a sharp prickle of irritation, the knowledge of his father's expression, the way it had looked so cloddish and unrefined. As if he'd been taken by surprise, which he should not have been. For haunting Tristan's life, he ought to have known. He ought to have seen it coming, or at least had the dignity not to look so frightened by the prospect of his doom.

"Seriously?" Tristan asked, rising to his feet and looking at the weapon in Callum's hand. "Is that a Wessex logo?"

"Maybe a little," said Callum inanely.

"You look shit," added Tristan. Callum did not look cool, not even a little bit. He looked slightly green and a bit like he wanted to throw up, which was new and interesting. Tristan supposed that Callum's experience with death had always been decidedly hands-off, so this must have been unsettling.

"Yep," said Callum.

At which point Tristan rose from his father's body and the spreading pool of blood to stand before Callum, breaths away, and say, "This doesn't mean I've ruled out killing you."

He watched Callum's throat jump with a heady swallow.

"Save the pillow talk," he said. "I've got to have a shower first."

SCENARIO 17.

Tristan stood over the body of his father and bent down to scrutinize the trickle of blood from his hairline.

"I can feel your heart beating," said Callum.

Tristan rose to his feet, carefully concealing the letter opener he'd slid from his father's arsenal of hidden weapons. The one Adrian Caine had needed in the end, but hadn't quite been quick enough to reach.

"How does it feel?" asked Tristan.

Callum rested a hand over Tristan's pulse, fingers stretching out like the wings of a dove.

"Like madness," he said, tongue slipping over his lips.

Tristan's fingertips brushed the loop of Callum's trousers. Dropped to the top of his thigh.

They both felt the presence of the blade at the same moment, reaching for inevitability like a climax.

Femoral artery. "Just a nick would do it, yeah?" said Tristan, voice gravelly with effort.

Callum's laughing mouth caught Tristan's just before he fell to the ground.

SCENARIO 25.

"Get the fuck out of my office," said Tristan. "Fuck your offers. Fuck my potential. Tell my dad to fuck off, too, while you're at it. Don't think he'll care to see you, though, so mind the desk. It's where he keeps the knives."

Atlas Blakely looked disappointed, but not surprised. "Perhaps you'll change your mind."

"*Perhaps* fuck off and die," replied Tristan.

From his desk, his phone buzzed with messages from Eden. Within a week he would be promoted by James Wessex a second time. The wedding would be lovely. Tasteful. Grand. His eventual eulogy, read by a weeping Eden, would describe his scandalous death by balcony-leaping as the desperate act of a beloved husband and son. Rupesh—Tristan's *best friend* Rupesh—would become Eden's second husband after a generous mourning period of five or so years, give or take a few moon cycles. His father would toss the obituary into the kindling. Atlas Blakely would find someone else. There would always be someone else. Libby Rhodes would stab Callum Nova twenty-three times on the painted room floor.

End simulation. Begin again.

SCENARIO 71.

"What else are you willing to break, Miss Rhodes, and who will you betray to do it?"

He saw it on her face. A new expression, one that must have always lived there in secret, in hiding, or maybe it was just a secret to him, having failed for so long to see the truth. Her anguish, it was never his goodness. Her sorrow, the glint of it that he routinely took for virtue, it was always so compelling because it stood in contrast to her anger, to what had always been shadowed with fury. Lit by the presence of flame.

"I don't know," she replied dully, "and I don't—"

"Rhodes." Tristan emerged from his hiding place outside the door, too late to save Ezra, too wise in the moments since then to stand idly by. "Rhodes, it won't help. It won't save you. The path you're on, it only ends when you end it. Rhodes." The only brave thing he ever did was touch her then, dousing her pain with a clumsy, forced embrace. "Rhodes, let it stop now. Let it end with you."

SCENARIO 76.

She killed him, obviously. Don't play with matches. Don't startle physicists who've traveled here on a fucking nuclear bomb.

SCENARIO 87.

At age seventeen, Tristan Caine choked on hot soup and died.

SCENARIO 141.

"Ready the starship, Captain Blakely!" called Tristan from the ship's hull.
    "Right you are, Lieutenant Caine," Atlas jovially returned.

SCENARIO 196.

"Maybe someday," Libby said quietly to the silence that stretched out between them.

    She took the glass of wine from him and set it aside. He realized he had not actually taken a sip; had simply been holding it, watching it catch the light.

    "Then I pick today," Tristan replied.

SCENARIO 201.

There's a hairline fracture, a sliver of silence that lives in the motion of a trigger pull. Tristan heard it like a roar, an echo of consequence throughout the cavern of time and space, and the debilitating quiet was almost like a prayer. Father, forgive me; grant me the serenity to live with what I've done.

    The soundlessness that followed screamed with significance, with condemnation. Tristan felt a hand on his shoulder—the careful, calculated weight of a palm. When he didn't move, he felt the pistol eased from his hands, slipped out from the stagnation of his knuckles. From the corner of his eye, he caught the glint of a pair of sunglasses.

    "Who am I supposed to be now?" Tristan asked the room, the office that had once contained the beating heart of his father. What he meant was:

How do I go on without a reason to move forward, without something to run from, without the fate I know I'm doomed to chase?

"Whoever it is, I won't turn away," said Callum in his ear.

Elsewhere, a clock ticked.

SCENARIO 203.

"I want—" I want your apology. *Tick*. I want you to respect me. *Tick*. I want you to love me. *Tick*. And I want you to have done it from the moment I was born. *Tick*.

Tick.

Tick.

Tick. Tick. Tick.

TickTickTickTick—

"Time to quit daydreaming, son," said Adrian Caine, the letter opener glinting pointedly in his hand before he lunged.

SCENARIO 211–243.

None of it mattered because Callum died.

SCENARIO 244–269.

None of it mattered because Callum lived.

SCENARIO 312.

"I now pronounce you husband and wife," said Nico happily, tossing a handful of rice in the air as Tristan lifted the veil from Parisa's eyes and smiled the smile of the perpetually exultant.

"I'm glad it's you," he said, and she gave him a look of insouciant but undeniably compelling amusement.

"Who else would it be?" she replied with a shrug, lifting her chin for a kiss.

SCENARIO 413.

It's not a gun, it's a knife, Tristan thought, plunging it sensually into Callum's sternum.

SCENARIO 444.

"This was your grand idea?" Tristan panted, fighting the urge to vomit as he doubled over in the street. "Rob my dad *in plain sight*—and for what? It's cursed, almost definitely. More importantly, what are we supposed to do with the money?"

"Have sex on top of it," said an equally winded Callum, aviators shielding the falseness Tristan had never known of his blue eyes. He tossed a grin over at Tristan, who stood there staring at him, vacant, not nearly as filled with hatred as he should have been. He knew it was somewhere, reserves of it, huge vats of it, but it all seemed so distant. So unhelpfully less hot.

"Oh." Tristan considered that a moment before nudging Callum's arm, persuading him to keep running. "Yeah," he coughed up, leading them around the next corner. "Yeah, all right then, fine."

SCENARIO 457.

"But the damn books—"

"Kill me," Atlas said urgently. "You can have the books. All the fucking books. I don't even want to be here, I don't want any of this, just trust me, believe me." *I came all this way just to tell you, just to carry the message.* "I'm the one that needs to die."

Ezra looked at him blankly. Or what Atlas thought was blankly until he realized Ezra did not look confused, did not look angry, did not look sad. Did not look at all like the man who had once stood in his office and died for the cause of being young and reckless, and righteous.

He looked like the man Atlas Blakely had been a few seconds ago. A man who had opened a door.

"I already tried this, Atlas," Ezra said after a moment. "It doesn't work. It doesn't help."

Silence.

"Do you know what it really means to starve?" asked Ezra.

SCENARIO 499.

"Atlas," said Tristan, poking his head into the office. "Sharon from the offices is asking if you've had any problems with the new kitchen staff."

"Hm? No, none." Atlas was rubbing his temple, wearing the pair of spectacles he devotedly made sure the others did not see, as if it were critical to his personal mythology that his vision suffered no impairment. "Have you looked at this?"

"Varona's notes? Only a thousand times." Tristan stepped into the office and reached over for the diagram in Atlas's hand. "It looks right to me, not that I'd ever tell him so."

"We'll still need Mr. Ellery. And Miss Mori." Atlas's voice was its usual exhausted rumble. "Have you spoken to Miss Rhodes?"

Tristan shook his head. "She's not been back to the stone circle at Callanish. She's either on her way here now, or she's—" Something locked in his throat over the words *not coming back at all* and Atlas peered over the rim of his spectacles with something like a look of sympathy.

"And Mr. Drake?" Atlas prompted. "How are the two of you getting on?"

The house did not need an archivist. Particularly not one that Tristan felt oddly certain he'd once dreamed. At the same time, though, it was nice to have another body in the house, and Gideon's presence did mean Nico was a frequent visitor. Which was of no special interest to Tristan, of course. The last year spent with Nico's blades to his throat and Nico's hands on his chest was . . .

Of no special interest to Tristan, who coughed politely into his fist. "Fine."

Atlas's mouth twisted with wry and unforgivable amusement.

"I see," he said, turning politely back to the diagram at hand.

SCENARIO 556.

"Do you realize we've never actually talked?" said Tristan, stepping away from Nico's door to the open frame of Reina's. "Seems weird. Like maybe we have a thing or two in common but we'd never actually know." The champagne from the evening's Society gala seemed to be hitting him funny. He felt an odd, paranoid sense that he should have this conversation now. That he should have it now, right now, before it was too late.

Reina didn't seem to agree, perhaps lacking an interest in converging multiverse strands or the probability of existing in multiplicity. "I don't know who my father is, so I doubt it," she said.

"Lucky you," said Tristan. "And your mum?"

"Dead."

"So's mine."

"Siblings?"

"Half sisters. You?"

"Same." An awkward silence. "I think I might be a god," Reina commented with a stilted, armored tone, like someone testing the waters and expecting to find a pool of blood.

"Is that why you're pissed at Varona?" asked Tristan. "Because you're a god and he's too hyperactive to properly worship you?"

Reina opened her mouth. Then closed it. "Kind of, I guess," she mumbled, with a moment's afterthought. The look of a heady revelation.

"Forgive him," Tristan advised. "He knows not what he does."

Behind them, Nico's door opened, the floor vibrating with the energy of a small child traversing the high of a sugar rush. "Okay, I'm ready—"

"See?" said Tristan, gesturing to Nico, who bounced a look of joyful bewilderment between Reina and Tristan.

In response, Reina looked both repulsed and contemplative. "Try therapy," she suggested to Tristan, an apparent transaction for his sage advice. "It'll save us all a lot of time."

"Well, no problem there, we've got plenty of that," said Tristan as Nico saluted her, permitting himself to be corralled toward the stairs.

SCENARIO 615.

"Alexis." Atlas took her by the elbow and she was startled, a touch annoyed, busy with other things, with other thoughts. "We have to kill someone."

She frowned at him. "What?"

"Me," he clarified. "You have to kill me. One of you has to kill me or the rest of you will die one by one. It has to be me, Alexis, please." He put the gun in her hand, curled her fingers around it, and she stared at him.

"Why are you asking me?"

Because, because of everything we have yet to share, because of all the secrets I have yet to tell you, the ones I will never get to tell you. The ones I gave to you once that now, blessedly, you will never have to know.

"Please," he said again.

She looked at the gun. At his face. *Don't waste it.*

She looked at him again, a long look. A pitying one.

"Fine," Atlas said hysterically, snatching the pistol back from her. "Fine, then I'll do it myself."

SCENARIO 616.

"I want a divorce," Tristan panted into Eden's mouth.

"Sure you do," she replied, coquettishly slapping his arse.

SCENARIO 733.

"Oh, shit," muttered Callum, who, from what Tristan could see at this angle, appeared to be examining his undercarriage.

"Woke up dickless again?" called Tristan. (Who should not have joked about such things, as they would only be less fun for everyone involved.)

"Lucky for you, no," Callum knowingly replied, without looking up. "Just, ah." A pause. "Nothing."

Tristan sat up from the bed, observing the fragment of Callum's face that he could see from the bathroom mirror. The furrowed brow framing pale blue eyes. The set of his mouth, which was thinner now, less sneering with age. The hair that was distinctly grayer than it had been once, less gold and more silver. Which, Tristan realized, was a pigment issue likely to become a problem in other corporeal hemispheres, too.

Ah, mortality. How sad to know the nether regions also aged.

"You know," said Tristan casually, "I don't mind watching you get older."

He watched the motion of Callum's shoulders shifting firmly into place, caught between bracing and running. "Don't you?"

"No. Personally I feel I'm aging into my personality." Tristan settled himself back against the pillows with a sudden flame of fondness, an excruciating sense that his contentment in the moment was absurd and horrifically unearned. On the nightstand beside him sat Callum's sunglasses, his keys. "I wouldn't mind doing a bit more of it."

"What, aging?"

"Growing old with you," Tristan said, and closed his eyes so that he would not have to see Callum's smile, which Tristan would tell himself was a smirk and therefore something he could walk away from. If he wanted to. *When* he did.

Which was not, as it turned out, today.

SCENARIO 734–890.

Atlas Blakely opened his eyes to a throbbing head, the blurred shape of a familiar face, a pair of necromancer's hands. He heard his own voice, his mother's voices, the voice he was born with, the restless one that spoke to him inside his head. *You can't stop choosing death, Atlas Blakely, and for that, death will not reward you.*

"If you don't kill me," he croaked, "the world will end."

Ezra leaned into Atlas's line of sight, a crooked smile on his face.

"The world ends every day, Atlas Blakely," said Ezra Fowler, who would know. "That doesn't mean you can escape your fate."

SCENARIO 891.

Tristan stood by the headstone in the Nova family plot and wondered how the fuck it had ever seemed reasonable to spend this much money just to lie in the ground in a box. Surely it would be better to become useful to the world in some way. Fertilize the soil, feed the trees. Anything but this.

"Roses, really?" asked Parisa with a sigh, as if roses were not the obvious choice by every conceivable standard. Tristan glanced over his shoulder at Reina, who shrugged at him as if to say *I cannot control her, I never have.*

Tristan set the flowers down in the usual vase and straightened, his phone buzzing in his pocket. Three quick vibrations. Libby again. She'd been popping up more and more these days at random intervals. At first it was funny memes. Then the occasional *how are you*. Then the unavoidable midnight ponderings of what it looked like when he touched eternity, did he think he saw God and if so, was She pretty?

Judging by the time, she was likely sending a picture of her lunch. But there was no ruling out the possibility it was something else. Something wonderfully unguessable.

Tristan smiled to himself, feeling the world continue, slipping out from under him, a blissful freedom stretching out into the wild unknown.

"For fuck's sake, Caine, we don't have all day," said Parisa. "Are you going to help us or not?"

"Aren't you two tired of philanthropy yet?" asked Tristan, adjusting the petals in Callum's vase.

"Well, you know what we always say," said Reina, in something Tristan was coming to recognize as the tone of her voice that most closely resembled humor. "The best time to plant a tree is yesterday. Second best time is today."

Tristan fought a scoff. "That's not even close to what you two say." Not that he knew for sure, but he had a sense his guess was inaccurate. Their actual motto was probably more aligned with their initial message to him, sent several weeks ago from Parisa's new number:

Want to feel powerful today?
    How powerful?
Depends how erotic you find it to watch a white man beg.

"Eh, close enough," said Parisa, lowering her sunglasses to warm her face in the afternoon sun.

SCENARIO 1A-426.02.

Tick.
  Tick.
  Tick. Tick. Tick.
  TickTickTickTick—
"I don't want anything you can give me." Tristan realized it slowly, then all at once. Like swallowing a vat of poison, letting it flood the vessels of his brain. He lowered the gun and Adrian exhaled, tongue slipping contemptuously between his lips.

"So he's a big man, then. Noble." Adrian spat it out. "That what you learned from your bluebloods, then? Your posh prince down there on the floor teach you that? Enjoy it, Tris," Adrian sneered. "Be saintly, then. See if that puts food on the table or men in your ranks."

Tristan flexed a hand. The ticking in his chest was gone. The only thing beating in there was his heart, which was blithely unaffected by the resurgence of his father's mockery. If there was anything left for his father to give him, it was no longer of any particular use.

"You've never had it in you, Tristan. You've always been useless, always been weak. You think I couldn't see it right from the start?"

Tristan bent down, running a finger gently over Callum's brow. Fixing his hair. Reconfiguring an illusion—giving Callum back his preferred nose, which was somehow less patrician than his actual one—and obscuring the stains on his shirt, pressing the fabric back to perfection. Picking up the sunglasses with two fingers, considering himself in the frames.

"Hope you like the taste of mercy, Tris. It'll rot in your mouth the day someone makes you pay for your weakness, mark my words—"

His father ranted on while Tristan's world kaleidoscoped with possibilities, the cosmic inflation of his careful, recalcitrant pulse. Running the scenarios.

Trying to project a version of the future that came from some other version of this room. Tried, but couldn't find the happily ever after within the limits of his dull imagination. Couldn't make it. Couldn't see it.

Didn't make it not real, though, so Tristan took aim and pulled the trigger.

The end.

Reina was sitting in the dark when the lights came on around her. She heard the telltale sign of surprise, followed by a hastily guarded silence.

"Reina, isn't it?" The familiar feminine voice was pointedly calm. "No one told me you were here."

Reina rose to her feet from the impeccable white sofa, turning to face Aiya Sato where she stood in the doorway, purse in hand. Her clothes looked expensive. No doubt they were. The penthouse flat was also expensive. Tokyo real estate was nothing to scoff at. Its magical security system was very good as well, but Aiya had excellent interiors and a fondness for greenery, an apartment full of attentive plants.

Anyway, it wasn't safe for Reina to call ahead, even if it was the polite thing to do. With so many people trying to kill her, the threat to propriety was the lesser risk.

Aiya looked warily at Reina, reading her silence. In fairness, Reina wasn't trying to be menacing. She had simply not spoken to anyone in several days, not since the rally in Maryland, and was unsure where to begin the conversation.

"Is this . . . a social visit?" asked Aiya. A reasonable question.

Reina shook her head no, then cleared her throat. "I just needed to talk to you."

"Oh, I see. Yes, I heard you'd run into some problems." Aiya gestured for Reina to retake her seat on the sofa. "May I offer you some tea? Or wine?"

Reina shook her head again. "I won't be long." She sat, and Aiya moved carefully around the room, taking off her shoes and placing them with obvious sanctitude beside the door. She tied her long hair away from her face, meticulously turning on specific track lights and not others, perhaps to highlight the beauty of her Scandinavian-style furniture choices or the incomparable city view. Then she poured herself a glass of wine from a previously opened bottle, joining Reina on the sofa with an air of hospitably withheld dread.

"I was born here in Tokyo," Reina commented. "Not far from here, actually. There was a fire the day I was born. People died. My grandmother always thought it meant something that I was—" She broke off. "What I was."

"People often search for meaning where there is none," said Aiya placidly. Perhaps in a tone of sympathy, though Reina wasn't sure what to think anymore. "Just because you can see two points does not mean anything exists between them."

"In other words, fate is a lie we tell ourselves?" asked Reina drolly.

Aiya shrugged. Despite the careful curation of her lighting, she looked tired. "We tell ourselves many stories. But I don't think you came here just to tell me yours."

No. Reina did not know why she was there, not really. She had simply wanted to go home, and when she realized home was an English manor house, she had railed against the idea so hard it brought her here, to the place she'd once done everything in her power to escape.

"I want," Reina began slowly, "to do good. Not because I love the world, but because I hate it. And not because I can," she added. "But because everyone else won't."

Aiya sighed, perhaps with amusement. "The Society doesn't promise you a better world, Reina. It doesn't because it can't."

"Why not? I was promised everything I could ever dream of. I was offered power, and yet I have never felt so powerless." The words left her like a kick to the chest, a hard stomp. She hadn't realized that was the problem until now, sitting with a woman who so clearly lived alone. Who had everything, and yet at the same time, Reina did not see anything in Aiya Sato's museum of a life that she would covet for her own.

Aiya sipped her wine quietly, in a way that made Reina feel sure that Aiya saw her as a child, a lost little lamb. She was too polite to ask her to leave, of course. That wasn't the way of things and Reina ought to know it. Until then, Aiya would simply hold the thought in her head.

"So," Aiya said with an air of teacherly patience. "You are disappointed in the world. Why should the Society be any better? It is part of the same world."

"But I should be able to fix things. Change things."

"Why?"

"Because I should." Reina felt restless. "Because if the world cannot be fixed by me, then how can it be fixed at all?"

"These sound like questions for the Forum," Aiya said with a shrug. "If you want to spend your life banging down doors that will never open, try their tactics instead, see how it goes. See if the mob can learn to love you, Reina Mori, without consuming or destroying you first." Another reflective sip. "The Society is no democracy. In fact, it chose you *because* you are selfish." She looked demurely at Reina. "It promised you glory, not salvation. They never said you could save others. Only yourself."

"And that is power to you?"

Aiya's smile was so polite that Reina felt it like the edge of a weapon. "You don't like feeling powerless? Then change your definition of power. Do not fix unfixable problems. Do not devote yourself to things you cannot control. You cannot make this world respect you. You cannot make it dignify you. It will never bend to you. This world does not belong to you, Reina Mori, *you* belong to *it,* and perhaps when it is ready for a revolution it will look to you for leadership. Until then, drink expensive liquor, buy some nice shoes, and make a man stop talking by sitting comfortably on his face."

Aiya rose to her feet then, inclining her head toward Reina in something of a parting bow. "If you'll excuse me," she said. "I need a bath. The Society never said it could make anyone listen to me, but I at least have the proper security to have you removed if I ask."

Reina stood, lingering a moment more. "But you promised me once it would be worth it."

"Yes, and it is worth it. Worth it not to die in poverty. Worth it to stand in a room of men and be a threat to them instead of the other way around. It is worth it not to be lost to obscurity. To wear underwear made of silk. It does not ease the burden of being human, Reina, but life is always better with choices. Choices you now have the luxury to make."

She began walking away, down a long modern corridor, and Reina called after her.

"What is your specialty?" she asked, and when Aiya turned, she added, "I won't bother you again, I promise. But I just want to know so that I can . . . try to understand."

Aiya reached up with a sigh, removing her earrings. She dropped them both on the floor before removing her necklace, then a ring. She left them there, discarded like rose petals on the ground.

"That fire you spoke of," Aiya said. "The one on the day you were born. I could have put it out. Or I could swallow this entire country up with a single wave." She unzipped her dress, stepping out of it, and glanced over her shoulder at Reina, dismissing her with a shrug. "I am not afraid to put us underwater. The question, Reina, is for what in this life will you drown?"

Aiya slipped out of her negligee, skin bare and pebbled in the cool filtered air of her flat, before stepping out of sight, the sound of water running. Reina lingered for another long moment.

Then she opened the door and walked out, the potted orchids mewling softly in her wake.

She walked for a long time in silence. There was nothing for her here, she understood that much, but where else was there to go? She thought about the Forum, the offer from Nothazai, the implication of what Aiya Sato could do—had clearly already done. Was that the choice, then? Commit herself to a life no different from Aiya's, battling ideologies she could not change for a price she wasn't willing to pay? Six months doing a god's work and already Reina was tired, too tired to keep going, too sick with hatred to go on.

Save the inhabitants of this world, and for what? So they would go on blissfully uninhibited, destroying things just because they could?

She found herself walking the path through Aoyama Cemetery, the sounds of bustling city streets gradually transitioning to only the whispers of bloomless sakura trees. This close to winter they were a mix of red and gold, with only hints of the riotous blossoms they would eventually unveil. Perhaps because they understood the somberness of their patronage, they didn't needle Reina for attention, nor even do much to puncture the restlessness of her thoughts. They recited chants that felt like prayers and rustled enduringly on the rare and quiet breeze.

Dusk was falling. Reina stopped to feel the fading vestiges of sun, to herald the stars she knew she wouldn't see. There were always so few people here, comparably. Shibuya was nearby, Roppongi would be coming alive shortly, and yet there was a tranquility here beyond the solemn presence of the dead.

Where was Atlas Blakely now? Where was he to offer Reina the new world she felt she had been promised? To remind her of her incomparable value? All that was here in Tokyo was Reina's stepfather, a man who could see her only for her value, not her worth. A man who used all the magic the world had to offer just to destroy things; just to see whether he or James Wessex could be faster at making killing machines.

Where was Atlas Blakely to put an impossible manuscript in her hands, to show Reina that she could love something; to tell her again of all the secrets that only she was worthy enough to bear? Without him she was just a waitress in a café. Not in a past life. Not in a different version. That was all she was, with the books or without them. He had chosen her, and without him she did not see the road ahead.

Mother, interjected a sakura gently, with the weight of falling petals or softly flurrying snow. *MotherMother, sssssomeone sssseeeeeessss.*

Reina felt tiny needle pricks in the same moment, knowing without looking in that eerily atavistic way that someone nearby was watching her. She stood very still, turning her head to catch a glimpse from her periphery.

A man, maybe. Someone in a black suit, long hair tied back elegantly. Masculine shoulders, feminine features. Long lashes framing haunted eyes. The suit was impeccably cut, fine enough for a Tokyoite, though this was not one. Reina and the sakura trees both knew the intruder didn't belong.

For a moment Reina's heart beat faster, faster-faster, not fear exactly, not entirely fearless either. Not fear that she would die or be caught, not like before. More like the fear of motherhood—of knowing fear will never really leave you and still there are no other options, no other choices, because to love something is to care for it, to glimpse everything you will someday lose and still go on as if that loss will not destroy you. Because for better or worse, and so often it was worse, that love was as much a burden as a blessing. It was an anchor to all the grace and cruelty of this life.

Over Reina's head the sakura trees were shifting restlessly, disturbed by the presence of the stranger. Reina looked up and thought, for the first time without regret, and without resentment, *I will protect you. I won't desert you.*

In gratitude, the trees blossomed like spring. A slow revolution, a gradual flurry of pink that bloomed in synchronicity, in unison.

If wonder were a sight, Reina thought. If it were an action.

It would be a cherry tree in bloom.

All over the cemetery grounds Reina heard the sounds of gasps—some delighted, some awed, some rightfully bewildered. It was like a dream, this spring that she had conjured. This life that came from death. It would be, perhaps, her one true moment of godliness. Reina lifted a hand to the nearest branch and felt it soothe beneath her touch. Like a familiar song this time. *Mother.* Like nothing had changed except Reina herself.

To their credit, Reina's would-be assailant didn't move. They locked eyes and the intruder slightly bowed their head, as if to recognize they were on sacred ground. Reina thought she could read the truth in the motion, the humility. Their shared truth.

In the end we return to the earth.

The intruder shook their head once, a motion of deference or of warning, or perhaps both. Someone would be back for her, Reina read in the angle of their conciliatory gesture. Someone would be back for her, but not here, not today. Fine. She understood it. She bowed her head in return, and the stranger turned the opposite way on the path, disappearing into the thin crowd that had begun to arrive, busy city-dwellers who'd looked up from their phones, from their personal pains and their busy lives, all for a fleeting glimpse of Reina's spring.

. . .

The manor house was quiet when Reina entered, her footfalls sounding deferentially inside the walls. The fig was somewhere nearby, mourning. The last of the roses would be on their way out.

She walked through the house to the painted room, waiting for someone to appear. No one did. Atlas's office was unchanged, empty. She drew a book from the painted room bookcase, a collection of quotations, and was running a finger along the spine of a leatherbound volume of sonnets when she caught sight of a lone figure outside.

Reina took the side door, the one that could have led to the reading room and the archives if she chose them, and breathed in the heady smell of dew-laden grass instead. Someone was waiting for her, unmoving. As recognizable as an echo. Inevitable as a pulse.

And even from afar, she was beautiful.

IX

LIFE

· LIBBY ·

Belen wasn't that old, by Libby's calculations. Only in her mid-fifties. Her hair was streaked with gray and her eyes creased with laugh lines that Libby had not been there to witness, but even so, in the six months since Libby had last seen her—which were years, even decades, for her—something intangible about Belen Jiménez had decayed beyond the normal consequences of age.

Libby stepped into the hospital room and sat in the chair beside the bed. A clock ticked nearby. Doctors spoke from the hallway. Nurses. Somewhere in the building were people just beginning to live.

"I would have been here sooner," Libby said, clearing her throat. "But it took me a while to find you."

Belen turned to her with a thin smile. "Liar."

Right. "Well, it did take slightly longer than I thought." Libby paused. "You changed your name."

"Mm. It didn't fit anymore." Belen's eyes were exactly the same, still dark and discerning. Libby felt impossibly young and horrifically old at the same time.

"So, um. What—" Another throat-clearing cough. "What happened?"

Belen looked at Libby blankly for a second.

"Oh," she said after a moment. "You mean this?"

She raised a hand, which Libby realized had been handcuffed to the hospital bed.

"I'm under investigation for war crimes," Belen said.

"Oh." Libby had actually known that part, given that it was the main content of every article recently written about the woman Belen had become. "I . . . right. Well—"

"I have frontotemporal dementia," Belen told her. "Early stages. For now."

"Oh." Something in Libby's chest felt stepped on, like a creaky floorboard.

"I hear my case is unusually aggressive," Belen commented. "Things in my brain appear to have been conveniently rearranged. A favor from a friend of mine, I suppose you could say, to help speed things along." Her smile went dark, the way she used to look at her professors. The way she used to look at Mort and Fare, who felt as far away in Libby's past as the distant future she'd fought so hard to protect. "If you happen to run into Nothazai, be sure to tell him where he can stick his thoughts and prayers."

"Nothazai?" Libby echoed.

"The Forum clown. I hear he's stepping down, which can only mean he's found something more philanthropic to devote his particular skills to." Another bleak look of humor, the likes of which only Belen could conjure.

"He's . . . what, murdering you?" Libby asked, aghast. "Surely that's—"

"I suppose it could have always been the outcome waiting for me. Who knows? I doubt he's creative enough to choose this for an ending." Belen shrugged. "I'm sure he considers it merciful, honestly, like administering a tranquilizer to pipe down my theatrics. The biomancer equivalent of prescribing me a seaside convalescence, with yellow wallpaper to boot." Belen sat up, or tried to, the handcuff jingling on her wrist as she shifted on the bed and gestured to the abstract yellow painting on the wall. Libby's face must have expressed her confusion, so Belen added, "He offered to fix me— you know, my little curse of womanly hysteria. I had my choice as to his form of repair."

"And you picked dementia?" Libby asked doubtfully.

"I picked a few variations on 'fuck you and the high horse you rode in on,' so yeah, kind of," Belen replied. "The federal investigation was a nice little cherry on top."

"Oh." *Oh*. As if that could encompass all of it, or any of it. "And the, uh. War crimes?"

"Really a matter of perspective," Belen said. She was quiet again, like maybe she didn't plan to say anything else, until she did. "Power isn't something up for grabs," she remarked to herself. "You have to take it from someone. You live with the cost."

Her eyes caught Libby's then, briefly. Libby cleared her throat.

"Right." They sat in silence again, footsteps carrying from somewhere down the hall and then receding.

"Maybe I could fix it," Libby said after a moment. "I owe you at least that much."

"Fix what, my life? My death? How kind of you." It was astounding that Belen's voice had aged so much and yet remained so spitefully petty. As if thinking the same thing, Belen gave a low laugh. "Sorry. I'm old, Libby. Not wise."

"You're not old. You're just—" A shrug. "Older."

"Old enough to let go of old grudges, so they say. But you know what? I like them," Belen said. "They keep me company. Keep me warm."

It occurred to Libby that Belen likely did not want her there, and that coming here had been yet another act of selfishness. She could do very little about that now that she'd arrived. Or maybe not. She rose to her feet, thinking of leaving, but stopped.

"Did you come for absolution?" asked Belen mildly. "For forgiveness?"

To Belen's credit, she was never actively mean, or at least not mean enough that Libby felt she had to lie. "I mean, I'd take it if you had any to spare," she admitted. They exchanged a grimace that was close enough to a laugh. "But no," Libby sighed, "I think I just needed to see you. I guess for closure."

"Ah yes, closure. I love endings," said Belen.

Libby looked for bitterness. Unusual bitterness, anyway. She wasn't sure whether to gauge Belen's tone as a sign of personal enmity against Libby or some other sardonic disappointment in whatever remained of her life. "Are you sure I can't—?"

"I've chosen to see this as a gilgul type of situation," Belen replied with a shrug.

Libby frowned. "Gilgul?"

"Sort of an esoteric reincarnation thing. The soul having three chances to perfect itself." Belen paused. "I'm choosing to believe this was only my first try."

Helplessly, Libby laughed. It was always too easy to laugh with Belen, who smiled now, perennially amused with herself. "Belen, you're Catholic."

"So? You dumped me and set off a bomb. The kids call that an extreme form of ghosting now, did you know that? So this is a real pot calling the kettle fat situation."

"Black."

"I said what I said. And anyway, the point is I've got two more chances to get it right, so I'm not all that mad about it. Well," Belen amended thoughtfully. "Not *that* mad, anyway."

Libby sank back into the chair. Conversation seemed . . . not actively unwelcome. And as always, Belen's presence was an improvement on her absence. However impractical that conclusion might have been now that there was no going back. No fixing things.

"You sound very actualized," Libby noted. "Healthy, even."

"Mm yes, you know me," Belen agreed. "Self-actualized to a fault."

"What would making it right look like, exactly?" Libby couldn't help asking. "What would you do differently on your soul's second try?"

"I take it by that you mean would I still pick you if I could do it over," Belen bluntly rephrased.

"Kind of. I guess, yeah." No point denying it now. Libby had done worse, clearly, than narcissistically seek atonement.

"Well, I wish I could say I'd tell my previous self to avoid you, but I understand my anarchistic tendencies at least well enough to know I wouldn't have listened to myself." Belen looked at Libby in silence for a long time. "And as for the rest . . . I'd still try to make things better. And," she added, "some of those alleged war crimes had extremely expeditious effects, so. In terms of regrets, it's not immediately clear—which as you might guess, my public defender really isn't thrilled about. Not enough Lexapro in the world for this kind of shit."

"So . . . you wouldn't do anything differently, then?" Libby summarized.

"Not substantively, no. I guess not. I think I'd just—" A brief flutter of her hand. "Enjoy it more."

"The war crimes?" Libby asked wryly.

"And the sex." Belen's smile in return was placid, but not antagonistic.

"Right."

There was a sound behind them, a knock on the door, and Libby turned.

"Time for your afternoon medication, Dr. Araña." The nurse looked warily at Libby, then back at Belen. "Shall I come back in five minutes?"

"Yes, please."

The nurse nodded and was gone as Libby turned back to Belen. "Dr. Araña?"

"Yes. I, unlike you, am an actual professor, and I make the staff here use it because I'm also kind of a dick." Belen's smile was warmer then. "Anyway, if you're still shooting for redemption, you've got five minutes left. Might as well make them count."

"Fair enough. Well." Libby picked at her cuticles. "I guess I can continue the war crimes for you, if you like. Help you carry out your legacy."

"I'd appreciate it," Belen said, seeming to grasp the joke.

Libby smiled and continued, "But really, if you want me to try and fix this, or if you want me to come back and—"

"Nah." Belen shook her head. "Just . . . make someone deliriously happy for me and we'll call it even. Give a youngish queer her first orgasm, on me." A pause. "I meant that as something of a toast, by the way. Like, *salud.*"

"Got it." Libby couldn't fight a laugh. "That's generous of you."

"Not really," Belen said. "I kind of fucking hate you, but I've chosen to do it with grace."

Right. "Obviously." Libby rose to her feet. "Well, it's not redemption."

"And with three minutes to spare," Belen replied, miming the clink of a champagne glass.

Unexpectedly, Libby's heart hurt to say goodbye this time. She also realized she had technically not gotten what she came for, though she'd gotten a lot of something else.

"Belen, I—"

"You're young still," interjected Belen, without waiting for the remainder of the question. "You have so many years left to feel pain and regret. Try not to get all your trauma from the very first quarter."

"But I," Libby began, and faltered, because she still did not know how to put into words the thing she'd come to say. "I hurt someone," she admitted. "And now—"

She stopped.

"Was it the hot British guy?" asked Belen, and Libby bit back a pained burst of laughter.

"No. He dumped me, kind of. But as far as I know he's fine." A tiny, ragged inhale. "It was . . . someone else. Someone who was maybe my other half. If that exists."

"Could you have prevented it?" asked Belen. "Hurting them."

Libby didn't answer. In her head, though, she spun the conversation out, crucifying herself on the pain of unspoken hypotheticals. *I could have stayed and had a life with you. I could have sacrificed myself for him and let him live a life with someone else.*

Why didn't you? asked an imaginary version of Belen.

Because I wanted to know what it felt like to win, replied an imaginary Libby. *Because I chose greatness over goodness. Because doing otherwise would have felt too much like proof of everything I have ever thought about myself.*

Imaginary Belen was patient, clear-eyed, journalistic. *Which is?*

That I am not enough.

"Ah," said the real Belen, shifting on the bed to the extent that she was able. "Well. You don't have a half," she informed Libby stiffly, with an air of forgoing criticism not because it was undue, but because it was pointless. "You give yourself away to lots of people over time. You have a lot of fractures that you make and part with as life goes on. Which is not to lessen your guilt," she added, "because as far as I'm concerned, Libby Rhodes, you have the potential to hurt a lot of people over the course of what could be a very selfish, harmful lifetime."

A long pause.

"But if you're worried you'll never feel something again, then that's, you know." Another flutter of Belen's hand, dismissively. "Bullshit."

Another small knock came from behind Libby in the doorway.

The nurse again. "Miss?" she said to Libby, who took one last glance over her shoulder at Belen.

"Thank you," Libby said, figuring that to be better and less insulting than *I'm sorry.*

"You're welcome," Belen replied, which was like *I forgive you,* but also, *get out.*

· · ·

Libby stopped by LARCMA on her way out of town. The main building was the same, though its campus had spread across the landscape of downtown Los Angeles like a gentrifying rash. The dorm she'd once lived in was now luxury student housing. The old café she'd used to frequent was now a trendy vegan lemonade stand.

She stepped inside and blended immediately into the student population. They moved with the same rhythm, the same sounds, the bird's nest elevators still going up and down in ceaseless transactions like always. She bumped into someone and apologized, realizing only belatedly that it was Professor Maxwell T. Mortimer, the former boy-man known as Mort.

The slacks that had been uncomfortably tight in the nineties were the same. Still uncharitably snug around the barrel of his middle, albeit less salmon-colored. He stared at Libby for a second, trying to place her. Then he lost interest, looking away and rushing off to the faculty parking lot. To his expensive car and unfortunate wife, Libby assumed.

She watched the elevators for another few hours, the Californian sun shifting buoyantly through the skylights from one side of the building to the other like a dimpled parting wave.

Then, finally, she got to her feet and left it all behind.

· · ·

The residential street was dark and quiet by the time Libby's rental car pulled in, so she turned off the headlights and parked at the foot of the driveway, not wanting to disturb the house's occupants. She crept up to the door, which had been freshly painted, and spotted the usual hide-a-key that sat in a bed of wilting roses.

She'd let herself in with that key many times, fishing it out of the weird little frog's mouth every afternoon when her parents had been at the hospital with Katherine. Every day, the same routine. Walk home. Frog's mouth. Eat whatever snack her mom had left for her and do her homework quickly but quietly, taking the extra notes she'd been keeping for Katherine and then waiting outside for the neighbor to pick her up. Three hours a day at Katherine's bedside, where sometimes Katherine was awake, but more often she was sleeping. Some days Libby did more homework or read a book and then left with her parents for the night without exchanging a word with Katherine at all. Eventually, the days were all like that.

Libby unlocked the front door of her childhood home and crept inside, removing her shoes and tiptoeing up the carpeted stairs. The living room was unchanged from the last time she'd seen it, which wasn't much more than two years ago. Still, another lifetime now. She skipped the creaky step on the middle landing and hopped up the remainder of the stairs the way Katherine had always done. Katherine was light on her feet, a dancer. Also much more proficient than Libby at sneaking in or out of the house.

Libby's room was closer to the stairwell. Katherine's was at the end of the hall, their rooms connected by the bathroom. Libby paused beside her own bedroom door, which was open, and instead walked to Katherine's, which was shut. She turned the knob slowly and stepped inside, unsurprised to find no evidence of dust. Her mother had continued cleaning this room for as long as Libby could remember. But surprisingly, there was a small pile of trinkets on the desk, as if something new had been recently unearthed.

Oh yes, Libby remembered now. Something about the upstairs plumbing. Her mother had told her about it over a year ago while Libby had been in the middle of puzzling out wormholes with Nico, so she hadn't been paying attention. There was a fresh coat of paint on Katherine's wall, around a vent that Katherine must have secretly used to store things.

On the desk was a small journal, the cover warped with water stains. Two bottles of dried-up black nail polish, which their mother hadn't cared for until she'd stopped bothering to harangue Katherine about her nail color at all. A fake nose ring. God, of course. Libby put it on, inspecting herself in the mirror. She didn't look remotely as cool as Reina, but then again, a nose ring did not a cool girl make.

Libby took the nose ring off and picked up the journal, opening to a random page. It wasn't dated—only nerds would do that, she imagined Katherine saying—but based on the events that Katherine described, she must have been fifteen, which made Libby eleven or twelve. Katherine would have been sick already, but not as sick as she would later get.

—such a freaking tattletale I swear to god ahhhhhhhh I hate it here, seriously. I can't wait to get out of this house—

Libby stopped and slammed the book shut, exhaling.

Inhaling.

Then she picked it up again and continued reading.

—miss going to school. Can you believe that? SCHOOL.

Libby flipped some pages, skimming some things here and there about Katherine's friends who were going to parties without her, about a boy that Libby only half remembered. Josh. Did she still know a Josh? She wondered if Josh was married now, whoever he was. If he had babies with someone who wasn't Katherine. She wondered if Josh had been able to move on.

Libby paused on another page, catching her own name. She swallowed a mouthful of shame, realizing it was the last time she and Katherine had fought. Libby had found Katherine on the back porch with a bottle of beer, and a boy who must have been Josh with his hand up her sister's shirt. Libby remembered now, like a lightning bolt of clarity, that he'd had an earring and what Libby had thought was a tattoo, but he'd just drawn on his arm in Sharpie. Libby had told their mother and Katherine had screamed until she fainted and Libby had thought see, I'm just protecting you. See? I'm just trying to keep you healthy, keep you well.

—but it's like, what is the point of being alive if I can't drink ONE beer and get kissed so hard I can't see? God she's so annoying—

Libby looked up and cleared her throat, fingers poised to turn the page, skip the pain.

She must have picked up Tristan's masochism, though, and kept reading.

—love her though. She tries so hard. It's cute and it's lame and it's sad. I just wish she'd calm down and realize that I would rather die doing something amazing than spend the next however many months just lying in my stupid bed. Mom doesn't want me to talk about dying because she's afraid Libby will get scared or something but hello??? It's scary and that's GOOD. Which is apparently not a good argument for getting my tongue pierced even though I already told her it was my idea and not Josh's.

Nico would have loved Katherine. Oh god, Libby thought with repulsion, Nico would have *definitely* tried to sleep with Katherine. She swallowed a burst of something horrific and made a face, reading on, running a finger down the page, mourning her losses. Tracing the shapes of Katherine's letters as she turned the diary's final page.

I feel bad writing mean things about Libby because she's just a baby and she doesn't know anything. And Mom is too busy worrying about me so nobody is paying enough attention to whether or not Libby will grow up a narc. Oh my god can you imagine.

Only a few lines left of Katherine before the book ran out. Libby inhaled shakily, wanting to save it, to savor it somehow. To let it be goodbye, like turning a corner in a dream and just . . . coasting to a stop. Letting Katherine disappear. Letting her go.

You don't have a half, Libby told herself, allowing it to mean peace. She exhaled, ready for her sister's parting message.

Okay but seriously I do love her, she just wants everything to be good even if that's impossible. She'll get it someday. And in the meantime I'll be nice. Nicer anyway. As nice as I can be even though it makes my head hurt. Oh and also this is THE LAST MEAN THING I PROMISE but seriously.

Her bangs are so bad.

In the silence of her sister's bedroom, Libby Rhodes laughed until she cried.

· PARISA ·

After it was over, she found herself staying at the manor house. Waiting for something. She wasn't sure what. A push, she supposed. The desire to be elsewhere, or alternatively, the compulsive need to flee. She hadn't known life without one or the other but now they failed her, her usual instincts for migration. She had always been whatever version of herself came next, constantly drifting into her subsequent evolution, which was, she supposed, always just more of the same. What would she do now? Her own answers came back to her—spend money, have sex, eventually die. Depressing, and she had enough of that to contend with already. It was lucky, she supposed, that there wasn't some quota for human sadness, like a bucket that could only hold so much. If love wasn't finite then neither was pain, and neither was sorrow. She could always summon more of it, and resentment, too, for the life that had done nothing but teach her how to suffer and carry on.

She started noticing things about the house. The kitchen that needed restocking. The library that needed cleaning. The rooms that needed emptying and refreshing, the things that had been left behind that ought to be put away for whoever would come next. She knew, in part, that Nothazai would be arriving any day now, that the rooms the six of them had occupied would be replaced. That things continued, that life went on, that people would always continue bleeding for someone else's greed, that they would suffer in the name of someone else's god. Knowledge would always be coveted, power always taken and rights always robbed. The house would continue its work of draining its inhabitants for its own symbiosis, to bolster its own sentience, becoming answers that lived and breathed because the occupants inside had questions they had asked with their entire souls.

Variations on Callum's first thought when he learned Atlas Blakely had died: *That's it?*

As in: *the man to whom I attributed this much power was capable of dying without my knowledge, as if he never even existed to begin with?*

As in: *the Caretaker of the Society, a man with the key to limitless secrets about the world, is still only a man with normal limitations?*

As in: *the game is over now?*

As in: *after everything, that's all there is?*

As in: *if Atlas Blakely can disappear without a trace, what hope is there for me?*

Some very good questions. Unanswerable, as all good questions were. Parisa had given up on trying to summon the energy to reply, even for herself. She recalled the Magic 8 Ball that Gideon had dreamed up for her, the weapon he had given her in her time of need, and remembered the mix of things inside herself at holding it in her hands, this one precious thing. This one priceless seed.

Better not tell you now.

She found her sister Mehr on social media, looked at the baby pictures of her nieces, her new nephew. She thought about messaging her and then thought okay, but why? *Better not tell you now.* She checked up on her brother Amin, who was being investigated for assault. She wondered what would come of that. *Better not tell you now.* She read Nasser's obituary. Beloved son, cherished husband. It wasn't completely false, even if it wasn't entirely true. *Better not tell you now.* She looked up Atlas Blakely's mother, his father, looked at Atlas Blakely's half siblings, pulled the files for all the others in his Society cohort. They were so lovely, so vibrant, so young. What else might they have accomplished, what else might they have been? *Better not tell you now.*

She read Dalton's notes in his meticulous handwriting before it turned manic; the careful letters of a total sociopath who indiscreetly loved his craft. In Atlas's desk she found a bottle of pills, only two or three tablets remaining. Exactly how much pain had their Caretaker lived with? In Callum's room she found an empty bottle tucked behind the headboard. In Nico's, a rolled-up ball of mismatched socks. In Reina's, a children's book of fairy tales. *Better not tell you now.*

Parisa didn't ask herself what she was waiting for. She read books, rearranged rooms, walked in the gardens, had tea by herself. Many of Tristan's things were still there, and Libby's too, though Parisa didn't message either of them to ask if they were coming back because she no longer lived in a world where answers mattered.

Sharon emailed her a selfie with her daughter, the two of them on a trip to Disneyland Paris. Parisa thought about crocheting or maybe knitting.

On a whim, she finally pulled the gray hair out.

Two days crept by. Three. A week.

At night, Parisa dreamed. She woke up with no memory of where she'd been. Most of the time she had no memories to relive, no nightmares to haunt her, though she knew she was always holding something, a small weight in her right hand. Once she woke up with music in her ear, certain she'd been hearing Nico de Varona's signature laugh. Another time she woke up with a message. *I think I can teach you how to use this if you want.*

I do, she thought, I do. Not necessarily for good, though.

I don't always use it for good either, replied the dreamer in her head.

Another day or so passed before the house told her there was someone else inside it. She was in the gardens when she felt it sigh in relief, sagging around the presence of someone else. Ah, Parisa thought with a moment's irritation, an epiphany that felt more like an itch. So it hadn't been a *what* that she was staying for.

She saw Reina coming from the house and she thought okay, is this the ending I've been waiting for, really?

And in her mind, a tiny fluorescent message glittered smugly.

Better not tell you now.

· REINA ·

So Atlas Blakely would not give her meaning after all, and Nico de Varona would not give her redemption. Dalton Ellery was gone, and so was any hope of spontaneous creation.

One by one, Reina saw herself robbed of opportunities the longer Parisa spoke. Each glimpse of possibility fell away, cut from her fingers like threads of significance. Reina had let them all drop from her hands without even knowing the danger. Without even trying to hold on.

She couldn't have said exactly when Parisa stopped talking. The words had already lost their meaning before Parisa's voice had faltered, before it faded into the sound of screaming from somewhere nearby. The dogwoods rustled their condolences, individual blades of grass that wilted beneath Reina's feet. She felt tired suddenly, so tired, with a ringing in her ears.

Is it a gift or a talent? Atlas asked in her head.

A curse. Like loving and losing. To live at all was to watch something die.

Reina realized the sound in her head, the scream, was her own. Anger or anguish, misery or mourning, all of the above. She felt the softness of earth beneath her hands and realized she was kneeling prostrate, channeling her pain into the sympathy of sodden ground. She felt something lashing gently over her forearms, slithering out from her palms. Like vines; like threads of consequence.

What was the point? What was the purpose of fighting it, this thing that she was born to be? The world would always take and take and take from her. What little it gave back would also, eventually, be taken. Maybe there was no meaning. Maybe her personal meaning held no more significance than any other blade of grass. Was it always arrogance, to think she was ever assigned a destiny and not the same inevitability as everyone, as everything else? She capitulated to insignificance with a heave of energy, a burst of submission. *Take it, then, I don't need it. I don't deserve it.*

I don't know how to fix it. Just take it all.

The ground shook beneath her. The sun was swallowed up, eclipsed, dead, gone. Fresh earth was darker, blacker, like fresh wounds. She felt the crackling of roots below her kneecaps, vines that snapped under her palms.

Thorns and blossoms, blooms and needles, the ground splitting beneath her like lips parting to laugh. She bled for it, gasped for it. A thin trickle of water bubbled up below her knees.

Reina Mori, for what in this life will you drown?

It was dark now, an evening pitch of stillness, high noon swallowed up by her personal night as the crevice below her became a dribble of water, then a stream. A canopy had crowded overhead, thick with branches, impossible to see the sky or hear the pattering of rain. The ground was carpeted in moss beneath the circle of cascading oaks, roots shielding pockets of fungi; climbing the opposite sides of the freshly born riverbank were unsteady beeches, pale bark starlit by lichens. The newer growth—the silent tears—formed ripples of bluebells, lily-of-the-valley that grew in fairy rings. Ferns, curling at the tips of their tongues like tiny beckonings of fate. Reina was tied to it, to them. They would all return to earth someday. Leaves fell like snow flurries, spots of yellow drifting to the ground. Giving was easy, so easy now, once she'd started she couldn't stop. *Take it.* It numbed the pain a little, eased it. *Take it all.*

Something yanked her up by the arm and she slipped, stumbling over jagged rock and the tangles of tree roots on the banks of the stream now parting the house's grounds. Her chin met stone as she tripped out of the water, collapsing into the arms of the forest she'd grown like a cage around her, folding her in as if nothing could ever again matter outside. Another grip on her arm, two arms around her waist, pulling her backward and up. Reina lurched unsteadily sideways and in her wake, a young sapling sprouted up. An infant, a child.

Reina. Parisa's voice in her head. *Reina, you have to stop before you give it all away.*

"I don't want it." Reina spoke through the pain in her chest, tearing it open, like squeezing a drop of blood from a puncture. "I don't want it. Someone else should take it, someone else should have it, I can't—"

She stopped, the scent of jasmine surrounding her, choking her.

No, not choking her. Embracing her.

A set of cautiously enfolding arms.

The truth tore from her like a gasp. "I wasted so much of my life." Her voice was small, like the sound of the stupid potted fig, the one that loved only sunshine and gossip and Reina, inexplicably Reina. "I've wasted so much." It blistered in her chest, rupturing like a growth from her ribs. "I have to give it away, I have to—"

"You don't have to give it all away today." Parisa's voice was low and steady in her ear. "You still have tomorrow. That has to count for something." Parisa was quiet for a moment, her cheek pressed to Reina's, a cool tranquility from her touch. The smell of jasmine and salt, like Reina wasn't the only one who'd been crying. "That has to mean something."

"Haven't you heard? We're still being hunted." Reina managed a bark of a laugh, thinking of the stranger in the cemetery. Some killers were decent, but still, she didn't have forever. She barely had a now. "I might die tomorrow."

"Fine, so then your stakes are the same as everyone else's," Parisa pointed out, adding with a mutter, "So much for being a god."

Reina made a scoffing sound that was more like a hiccup.

"And anyway," Parisa continued, "you might *not* die tomorrow. So we might as well make that everyone else's problem."

At first Reina thought to argue.

Instead, though, she said, "We?"

Parisa pulled away, slowly detaching. Reina wobbled slightly, but stood on her own. In the darkness of Reina's freshly built canopy it was hard to see Parisa's face, but Reina knew it was beautiful. It had always been beautiful, but never more so than today.

"Yes," said Parisa, "we."

She didn't touch Reina's cheek. Reina didn't kiss her. A breeze whispered through the forest, like the graze of two fingers along bare skin, but softer. Less fleeting.

"Okay," said Reina.

Mothers, whispered the young sapling.

And so life gave a little back.

FIVE
James

The sitting CEO of the Wessex Corporation watched the oncoming scene from his office security monitor with a sense of prodigious ambivalence. The same could not be said for his newly promoted VP of Operations, who sat useless and frozen at the desk where they had, until two minutes ago, been having their quarterly finance review. But then, Rupesh Abkari had not been chosen for his stones.

The man on the security monitor wore an ostentatious pair of aviator sunglasses—loud, chromatic, and expensive, a sartorial statement that appeared to begin and end with *fuck you*. He kept his sunglasses on as he disabled the security alarms in the tower lobby, waltzing through the security checkpoint and flipping off the guard as he went. He parted the crowd waiting at the lift with a slight clearing of his throat (muted, but still evident) before stepping in through the doors, hitting the button for the top floor and whistling to himself as the lift rose through the Wessex Corporation's London headquarters. He appeared to note the various spells barring his entry, rearranging them as he pleased. Like balloon animals at a carnival.

You can have my debt, the mermaid's voice said through a hissing siren's smile, her parting words coming back to James Wessex as the lift on the security footage climbed the office tower floors. *Enjoy it, it comes with a price. You have your own debt now. Someday your end will make itself known, and you will not have the benefit of ignorance. You will see it coming and be powerless to stop it.*

And also, she added with a kiss, *your dick is now cursed.*

The monitor angles shifted to follow the man's progress as he stepped off the lift at the top floor. He paused the hearts of the waiting guards, freezing them on ice like a bottle of champagne to be revisited later. Wordlessly he told the retina scanner to mind its own business and pushed inside the glass doors of the office where James sat waiting, ignoring Rupesh's startled yelp.

Then, abruptly changing his mind and backtracking to where Rupesh had leapt up near the door, he handed his aviator sunglasses to Rupesh to hold.

"James," said Tristan Caine, the man who had formerly been his employee, who coincidentally would have been his son-in-law. "I see you redecorated."

James Wessex sat behind his desk with his hand on an emergency button that would summon any variety of mortal and medeian guards. He had already pushed it, obviously, but given the content he'd recently watched on the security feed, it had not worked because Tristan didn't want it to work.

"Catch," said Tristan, tossing something in James's direction, which James fumbled for and did, reflexively, catch, though he nearly dropped it in the process. "This is yours, I believe?"

James glanced down at the pistol with the tiny W inscription, hoping the dart of his eyes from the trigger to Tristan's head was not as blatant as he imagined.

"It's no longer loaded," Tristan informed him, so no such luck. "Can't be too careful these days, as I've been recently advised. Though," he added with a smile he had not possessed during his time of employment, "you're welcome to shoot me and find out what happens."

Such a pity that things between his daughter and Tristan had not worked out. A pity, really, the man he could have made of Tristan Caine. James had always had an eye for talent, a sixth sense for the right kind of ambition. Eden had thought she was getting away with some kind of rebellion against him by choosing Tristan, but really, James had been pleased. Tristan Caine was a diamond in the rough, waiting only to be polished, and James had known it. It was no wonder that Atlas Blakely had, too.

"Tristan." James's voice retained its usual quiet tone of authority. He found that the most powerful man in the room should not be made to yell. "You're aware, I imagine, that there is quite a price on your head."

"Funnily enough, I *am* aware of that," Tristan confirmed, seating himself comfortably in the chair that had moments ago been occupied by Rupesh. "I was thinking possibly you might consider lifting that silly little mark of yours."

James had had a feeling this was coming. But if Tristan Caine would not work for him, then it was better Tristan Caine did not work against him. James didn't need to understand the specifics of Tristan's magic to know that he didn't want it coming up against the empire he'd so cleanly, carefully built.

"I'm afraid I lack the power to stop what's already been set into motion," James said, leaning back in his chair. "There are a lot of pieces involved now, Tristan. The American government, the Chinese secret service—"

"Well, James, I hear you," remarked Tristan placidly, resting his elbows atop the arms of his chair while his attention drifted out of the thirty-third floor and onto the Thames below. "I can see that you're in a very delicate position, although frankly, I don't care." He turned back to James, adding without change in tone, "So. Is no your final answer?"

James knew a problem when he saw one. "If you're here to make a threat, Tristan, you might as well do it."

Tristan sighed, turning his head to the window again. "You know, this didn't have to become barbaric. It could have been perfectly simple." He flicked a smile at Rupesh before turning back to James. "But it seems some men do not care to see reason, which is a pity all around."

In an instant, the room slipped out from James Wessex's control and into Tristan's. He could not have explained how—he just knew it. Felt it. Something shifted; something that had been real but was no longer, as if the entire thing had been a private imagining. The contents of someone else's dream.

James's hands were empty. On the only plane of reality that remained, the gun sat snugly in Tristan's palm, with Tristan's finger on the trigger. James felt the sudden intangible sensation that he was nothing but a grain of sand, a speck of dust. A man whose children were a disappointment; whose legacy would deteriorate the moment he was gone. A man cursed beyond measure, a fact he'd spent his career trying to conceal, who was little more than a compact collection of matter presently held together by the will of Tristan Caine.

"Call it off," Tristan warned with his finger on the trigger of the pistol James had hand-designed, "or you will have nothing. What do you think your fortune is aside from imaginary numbers on a screen? If this is what I can do to your office, think what I can do with your money. Think what I can do to the life you so comfortably lead."

James couldn't speak, of course, being only barely a specter of existence. Whatever Tristan had done to the room, freezing it in time or placing it delicately within the void of nonexistence, it contained insufficient room for argument. With one blink from Tristan, he realized, the whole thing could come apart, and then what would it matter what James Wessex had been born into or what he had built? This was the secret, James thought, and the reason life was not a finish line, not a race. It was a very delicate conflagration of atoms and statistics, and at any moment the experiment could end.

With another blink, Tristan had returned the office to its usual configuration. James was still in his chair, Rupesh still poised to wet himself near the door. The only difference between this and their former positions in the room was that Tristan had kept the gun.

"I'm growing concerned that you'll still think yourself powerful without some evidence to the contrary," Tristan remarked in answer to James's wary glance at the barrel of the handgun. "It's very possible you might be confused enough about our respective positions of authority to incorrectly assume that my standing in this room without a weapon would be the same as me facing you unarmed."

Tristan disengaged the safety, raised the barrel. Rested a finger on the trigger.

"I thought you said it was disarmed," said James.

"I say a lot of things," Tristan replied. "I'm the son of a crook and I've always been a liar."

Yes. That was true. And James had very nearly ignored it despite the knowledge that Tristan was and would always be a pretender, a chameleon costumed cheaply in the idle trappings of the bourgeois. Even with the polish James had been willing to give Tristan over time, no amount of inheritance would have made James's life's work legitimately Tristan's. Disappointing.

The curse continued unabated, then. For now.

"Fine." Not every stand was one worth taking, even if other people would see his acquiescence as a weakness. Business was a venture of gambles, accountancy an occasional matter of loss. One red mark in his ledger wouldn't be the end.

What you want from the place with the blood wards, the mermaid's voice said again, *you will never get it. But that is not part of the curse*. A thin smile. *It is just a fact.*

James picked up his phone and dialed. It rang once, twice, before Pérez answered.

"It's James. Call off the Alexandrian marks, it's a waste of my money and time." He watched Tristan's expressionless face, adding, "The longer this goes on, the more obvious it becomes that their access isn't worth it."

There was a pause, then a quick response. Tristan leaned over to put the phone on speaker, nudging the button with the tip of the pistol in his hand.

"—zai's gone underground. Hassan's definitely out," Pérez was saying. "China's lost interest. Said a telepath took out half their operatives somehow in their sleep. Weren't even in the same country at the time." By the sounds of it, then, Tristan's visit had not accomplished much that would not have happened on its own. James felt a bit of triumph at that.

Enjoy it, the mermaid said in his head. *It comes at a price.*

"If you're out," Pérez finished conclusively, "there's no resources left."

"So we agree, then," said James, still eyeing Tristan. "We're done?"

He could hear the bureaucratic migraine in the American's voice. "Yeah, yeah. I'll purge the files. Just keep it quiet on your end." A pause. "What about the archives?"

James looked at Tristan, who shrugged.

What you want from the place with the blood wards. You will never get it.

"We'll find another way in," said James.

"Right." Pérez hung up without further sentiments in parting and James sat back in his chair, looking at Tristan. The implied question was clear enough, of course.

Do you understand now how small you really are?

He waited for Tristan to express outrage, to brave some kind of arrogant speech when it was so obvious that his coming here had been fruitless. Instead he turned around, heading for the door.

"That's it?" James called after him, amused in spite of himself. "You're not going to take over the company? Don't pretend you wouldn't enjoy that. Sitting in my place. Making phone calls that can either save a life or end it."

Tristan paused, as James had known he would.

"I know what you're made of, Tristan. I admire it, honestly. That hunger. That drive. But you would've never made it to this office without my help, you know. You're too reckless. Too short-sighted. You want everything immediately, right now. You don't have it in you, the kind of patience it takes to starve until the time is right." James had seen as much when Tristan walked away from Eden. When he accepted Atlas Blakely's offer, disrupting everything he had so cunningly compiled but not yet successfully built.

Tristan's finger tapped the trigger, still facing the door as James continued, "That's what real power is, you know. Built over time. That's how you make an empire, Tristan, not some little cutthroat kingdom like the one your father has. Oh yes," he confirmed when Tristan made the slightest motion over his shoulder. "I know who you are. *What* you are. I knew it when Eden brought you in to meet me. I knew it when I gave you your promotion, when I let you put a ring on my daughter. I liked it, the stones on you. Thought it meant you had potential. Had *foresight*."

Someday your end will make itself known, and you will not have the benefit of ignorance. James could feel the bitterness rising up, his usual calculation giving way to something else, some dismal knowledge that if Tristan left now, it was over. *You will see it coming and be powerless to stop it.*

What you want from the place with the blood wards. You will never get it.

It was over, and James would have nothing, because all the money in the world still did not feel like power in the face of James Wessex's secret. His tired heart.

"You'll never truly be powerful, Tristan Caine," said the quiet voice of James Wessex, whose four children had not a molecule of magic to split between them. Not a cell of it. Not even a spark to keep them warm. "I know you know it, and so do I," said James, who had done everything to conceal it, their inadequacies, covering them each in whatever magic he could buy and knowing it could not buy righteousness. It could not evaporate an ending.

James had spent years searching for something, anything—an animator to keep his soul alive, a traveler to lock him inside an astral plane somewhere, a library to keep his power on this plane of existence, safe from the horrors of mortality and time—but money couldn't buy him that, and so it could not buy anything. James Wessex could spin himself out into multipotency, more web than man. The Accountant, with his almighty ledger; the puppeteer, his strings of consequence expansive enough to rival fate itself. But he could not undo a curse.

Buying his daughter Eden's medeian status had not endeared her to him. Nor had it made her strong enough to carry the Wessex empire on her back.

"Someone else will always be smarter than you," James thrust at Tristan Caine like the poison it was—because that, at least, was true. "Someone else will always be stronger, someone will always be better, and someday, Tristan, when you realize you're capable of nothing more than the same charlatan's tricks, the same sycophantic sleight of hand—"

James felt it in that moment. The way Tristan took his magic from him. He broke off like he'd swallowed something, a lump in his throat, or the onslaught of a sudden headache.

(Which it was, technically. A small blockage in his brain, like rewiring a bomb. The slightest pressure on the wrong nerve. A neurosurgeon could fix it, maybe, but at what cost? Who knew if they could see that small. One shift in quanta to rewrite a man's code.)

(What was power? It looked a lot like Tristan Caine.)

"No, no, keep going," Tristan said to James's faltering silence. "Rupesh looks riveted."

Tristan shoved the gun into Rupesh's chest for emphasis, taking his sunglasses back and sliding them on as Rupesh fumbled with the pistol, smarting as if he'd been struck.

A flash of light, like the flick of a lighter, caused a moment's distraction. From the monitors through which James had watched Tristan Caine breach the building's protective wards, a glimpse of platinum blond winked before the lens.

Then, one by one, each of the Wessex security monitors disengaged, footage cutting sequentially to black like a looming, final countdown until all that remained was the imprint of an upturned chin; a self-congratulatory middle finger.

"Well," said Tristan, with faint traces of a smile. "I suppose that's done, then."

It felt just as James had imagined it would. Becoming ordinary. Becoming normal. Like dying but worse. Like dying, but emptier. Maybe it was better this way, to die while still alive. To survey the fruits of his empire without terror of the ashes to come.

"*Vene, vidi, vici,*" whispered James hoarsely. *I came, I saw, I conquered.*

Tristan barked a laugh. "Lot of good that did Caesar."

Then he walked leisurely out of the office, whistling as he went.

· GIDEON ·

With no more vials to keep him awake, Gideon was once again presented with the options of narcolepsy (familiar, annoying) or cocaine (functionally poison, slightly gauche). He had walked out of the Society's house without fulfilling the entirety of his contract—completing only six months of an intended year—and decided, *well, fuck it, I suppose,* choosing the realms over reality. Choosing dreams over life for the very first time.

He paid visits to Parisa when he felt like pushing his finger into a bruise of nostalgia, a generous and therefore defensible form of self-harm. On some occasions, Max joined him as usual. Max had a life, though, now. Perhaps because Nico and then Gideon had been so unavailable to him for over two years, Max had been forced to pick up new hobbies, which included a girlfriend who was genuinely very nice. She made dinner at their Manhattan apartment one night, which Gideon groggily attended for just long enough to personally witness the evidence that Max, at least, was happy. He was sad, obviously, but he was also fine, and in another act of masochistic generosity, Gideon realized that Max had better things to do with his life than wander around aimlessly with his saddest friend. Someday, maybe, Max would decide to organize a revolution or start a band, and then he was welcome to wake Gideon if he wanted.

Until then, Gideon was content to stay asleep.

He knew that Nico would not approve of this behavior. Or maybe he would? Nico had always wanted Gideon to be, quote, *safe,* so perhaps this was close enough. Gideon's identity seemed sufficiently secure. He no longer saw or heard from the so-called Accountant. His mother was no longer a threat. The Society didn't seem interested in pursuing him. Nothing was coming for him, nothing was chasing him, nobody was waiting for him. If he seemed depressed about it, well, so what? Lots of people were depressed. Pain didn't make Gideon special. It never had before.

He was wandering the realms as usual, pacing the shoreline of someone else's beach, watching the yawn of the tide. He'd be a blur in someone else's dream, most likely. A figment of their imagination, cobbled together by their mind's rationality and forgotten by the time they woke. It was a nice dream, soothing. Gideon had never been to the beach in real life, not like this. It had mostly been the backwater town he was raised in and the illusions of other people's consciousness. He didn't actually know what it felt like for waves to lap at his ankles, but he imagined it to be nice. Friendly. Like the dimple on a dauntless smile.

He blinked then, realizing he'd been staring so long he must have conjured a mirage. A shadow came over him in the sand, the feathered edge of a falcon's wing, and Gideon looked up, feeling his heart hammer at first with disbelief, then gradual capitulation.

Nico plopped down beside him with a sigh, kicking at the sand.

"This is very strange of you, Sandman," Nico said with a yawn, squinting at the horizon. "Where are we? Looks like my abuela's house."

There was no way Gideon could know that. He had never been to Cuba, not in real life, not even in his dreams. His heart pumped faster, too fast. It was a struggle to find his voice. *"Nicolás. Cómo estás?"*

"Ah, bien, más o menos. Ça va?"

"Oui, ça va." Gideon's mouth was dry and Nico's was curled up in expectation, like he was still waiting for the punch line, the joke. Gideon tried to gauge what version of Nico this might have been, what kind of dream he must be having. Was this young Nico, from when they'd first met? His hair was longer, the way it had been the last time Gideon had seen him in life, so maybe, possibly, was this Nico from the later few months—was it the version of Nico who had already known the cautious interior of Gideon's stupid heart?

"Tu me manques," Gideon whispered, uncertain who he was talking to or whether Nico would even react. If this was a memory, then Nico would just reply as he always had, with a carelessness that would injure Gideon as exquisitely as it would heal him. *I miss you, I miss you too,* as simple as that. Not a matter of devotion. Just simple, uncomplicated fact.

Nico's smile broadened. "I should fucking hope so," he said, which was neither expected nor wholly upsetting, and then Nico rose to his feet, holding a hand out for Gideon's. "What do you think? Should we swim?"

They had never been in the ocean together before. Not in any dream that Gideon remembered. Not in any lifetime he'd actually lived.

"Nicky." Gideon swallowed. "Is this . . . ?"

"Real?" Nico shrugged. "Dunno. I never made a talisman, did you?"

"No." *You were always my talisman.* "Could it be real, though? Dalton said—"

Gideon trailed off, wondering now. Someone had killed Dalton—Gideon had seen the body himself—so Dalton couldn't have done it, couldn't have brought Nico back to life. Unless . . .

The Society itself had said outright that they tracked the magic of their members. Dalton had said the library could re-create them, manufacture some regenerative quality of their souls. But was that ever true? Was it possible, or—

Was this just a dream?

"No way of knowing," Nico said with that shimmering quality he had. The hyperactivity that Gideon both envied and adored. That heedless necessity to move on to the next thing as rapidly as he could, like Nico had somehow always known that he was running out of time.

"Is this actually possible?" Gideon asked.

Nico made a face that meant *maybe, I don't know, I'm bored.* "Does it matter?"

A valid question. Either yes, it mattered very much, or no, it didn't matter at all, and also nothing really mattered, and who was to say what was actually real aside from the beat of his heart in his chest?

What was reality for a man who did the impossible—who was impossibility itself?

"Think big, Gideon, think infinite," Nico advised with a wink, looking smug. As if he'd made a point, which in Nico's mind he probably had.

But no, no. Having and losing. It would hurt so much more this way. It would be so much more precious, fine, but the pain would be the price for having loved.

"Infinity doesn't exist," Gideon argued hoarsely. Nico had said it once. *Infinity is false, it's a false conception.* What is reality, Sandman, compared to us? "We could count the grains of sand if we really wanted to."

"Okay, so let's do it. Unless you're busy doing something else?"

Nico's brow arched with prompting and Gideon, wretched and helpless—Gideon, little motherfuck that he was, a true idiot prince—wanted nothing more than to sink to his knees and kiss Nico's feet. He wanted to buy Nico's groceries, to write Nico poetry, to sing Nico the songs of his people in terrible Spanish and passable French. He wanted midnights in Brooklyn, golden hour in a galley kitchen, coffee with cream. He wanted to wait forever and also he wanted to do all of it now, right now, because who knew when the dream would end, or if this was actually *Gideon's* death, or if the whole thing had always been Gideon's dream, or if anything was ever real? Reality was nothing. He wanted to build Nico a statue in the sand, carve his stupid name into the trees.

He restrained himself, though, because Nico would never let him live it down, not ever. Not in this world or the next. So instead, Gideon said, "I'm hungry," and Nico said, "I'll cook," and just like that everything was perfect, or maybe it was fake, but who could tell the difference? They had no proof and it was too late to make some now. This, Gideon realized, was what came from chronic procrastination. A dumb ending for the dumbest boy in school.

But by then the carne was braising, the distant bark of a Chihuahua floating in from outside their four walls, and drowsily, Gideon thought, the sand can be counted. Which doesn't mean that you have to.

But it also doesn't mean that you can't.

SIX

Nothazai

Edwin Sanjrani was a miracle even before he was born. His parents (a diplomat and a former opera singer turned society wife) were getting on in age, and his mother had already had several miscarriages and stillbirths for which many uncomfortable procedures had had to be undergone. Eventually, Katya Kosarek-Sanjrani was diagnosed with cancer of the thyroid, at which point the Sanjranis were advised to stop. Stop attempting to procreate. Stop traveling so much. Stop living so freely and instead stay home, or at the very least stay in range of a hospital. Stop tasting food, stop growing hair, stop seeing yourself as capable or even moderately able.

But then, of course, as life occasionally has it, the seed that would be Edwin Sanjrani was already planted, and it was too late for either Katya or her husband Edwin Senior to halt the irreversible throes of fate.

Pregnancy was a strange thing. Childbirth in general. The process of a body becoming host to a slightly parasitic creature (a blessing!) meant that all functions of said body would cease to go on as they had once done. The birthing body becomes a martyr, or alternatively, a full-service studio apartment. Hormones shift. Priorities shift. Brain cell production in the mother slows to accommodate the body's new love: the growing cluster of cells that will eventually become a baby. Sometimes, of course, the birthing body decides the code is incomplete, the cluster of cells is nonviable, dragging production to a halt so that the factory may begin again, to try another time but better. In other cases, the birthing body takes a look at the malignant growth beginning to stain the factory walls and says hm, you know what? We should really get that under control, it's bad for the beloved cell-cluster.

Outside the workings of the mother-machine, Katya's cancer cells stopped multiplying. The tumor was removed and oddly, only the good cells remained. By the time the cells that would become Edwin Sanjrani and the various parts of the would-be Edwin Sanjrani equation (right-handedness, a taste for spice, dislike of the color orange, a slightly morbid sense of humor, and a tendency to over-explain) were already viewed by his mother and father as a reason to cast aside their directive to stop in favor of simply more going. Katya's burgeoning cancer was cured and did not return, and so the Sanjrani family continued their diplomatic roles until Edwin was born in New Zealand as a citizen of the United Kingdom, already beloved. Already doomed to fail up.

Which was not how Edwin saw it, of course. His last name wasn't Astley or Courtenay and his tenure at various international boarding schools was therefore not without its discomforts. It was also hard work being a miracle, because he wasn't simply *Katya's* miracle. He was born knowing how to look at a body and see its little failures, the various glitches in the factory walls. Knowing the problem wasn't the same thing as knowing the solution, but sometimes the two went hand in hand. Sometimes Edwin could see a tumor, diagnosing a headache as something worse just in time to disarm a bomb. Sometimes he could see a clot that could become an implosion or fragment of cellular shrapnel that would otherwise need removing. He could see infection, and therefore the possibility that something may soon go very wrong.

Having the answer often implied a sense of responsibility for the question, and this was burdensome, as all callings are. When Edwin was sixteen, it became his job to make his father more comfortable. When he was twenty-four, it was his mother's turn. Despite relatively early deaths, it wasn't difficult for either of the Sanjranis to believe they had fulfilled their calling on earth, because how can one be disappointed in oneself when one has created a miracle? Edwin would survive them, and Edwin would do good. This was the meaning of a legacy. This was how the body lived on.

Edwin was very obviously a medeian and he chose his father's alma mater, the London School of Magic, which had become a leading university as the world gave way to the rise of magical technologies—to a world where magic could be the solution to all of its problems, even the ones magic itself had caused. In his early days at university Edwin had trained as a diagnostic biomancer, hoping to become a practitioner, which was admittedly less flattering than other things he could have been. It was a bit like wanting to be a lawyer when one was already a duke—what would be the point? But Edwin was very serious about helping humanity, about the goodness therein. He sat at bedsides, held clasped hands. Like the miracle he'd been since birth, Edwin poured himself into the work.

Which was how Edwin became acquainted with an illness he realized he could not stop. He didn't know what to call it. Misinformation? Some toxic form of hate? Diseases without a name were difficult to diagnose—it was more a matter of knowing it when he saw it. Over time, it would manifest in several different ways. Anti-vaccination movements. Religious zealotry that meant some people staunchly went untreated. Bigotry that meant some people went untreated *specifically by him*. Edwin was already well into his studies by the time he learned of advancing biomancy techniques that meant altering a patient's genetic code, which was very like what Edwin could do, except it defused the bomb even before Edwin could see it. It defused even the *possibility* of a bomb. Obviously, there were improper uses—or *less* proper uses, anyway, wherein a medeian with sufficient means could remove a pollen sensitivity or request that his offspring not be so picky with food textures or be able to concentrate at all times.

It was slightly like guessery, statistically projecting the possibility that a thing *might* go wrong, and therefore yes, perhaps there were misuses on the horizon—Edwin's work was expensive, his patients the most privileged and most entitled, too, so that was one contributing factor to the question of ethics, which was fair enough on its own. But the conversation grew weighted against Edwin and toward some absurd state of nature; some belief in what was "natural" that began with the wealthy hypocritical and trickled down to the easily manipulated, who were coincidentally the most in need. An existential paradox, clinging to the belief that humans were good when humanity as a collective was rubbish. The more that biomancy advanced, the more people at large seemed to see Edwin Sanjrani as a devil or a terrorist. (Unclear how related this was to his identity or to his craft. It was inseverable nonetheless.)

This was all extracurricular, of course. Curricularly Edwin was a rising star, and co-curricularly he was popular among his classmates because he was—despite other little eccentricities like his name or his face—rich and sanguine and well-traveled enough to be acceptably posh. (He *was* posh, actually, but saying so defeated the purpose.) He was among the rare few to be invited to one of the London School's secret societies, the Bishops, which was where he learned of the existence of a more pressing secret: the Alexandrians. Little more than a rumor, of course, that particular Society, but Edwin had lived a comfortable enough life to know that rumors for some were usually true and accessible for others.

He did not get recruited. He passed into his thirties and the window of possibility came and went. Was it again because of his face, his name? Possibly. By then his view of humanity had grown irreversibly dim. He was starting to see less and less of it to save.

But righteous anger has a way of motivating even the most frustrated of chaps, and when the Forum came calling for a diagnostic biomancer as an expert witness in one of their Causes (the man called Nothazai would unironically use that word later in life, though at the time, Edwin could only think it with a bit of an eye roll as an asterisk) he began to see the possibilities of dismantling the system that had built him his personal ceiling; the invisible structure that only the Alexandrian Society and a handful of his aristocratic classmates could properly see. Edwin was born in a comfortable home but not the peerage. He came with a classical education and a keen eye for observation but did not intrinsically know what was or wasn't uncouth. He'd seen too much of the world before the age of five to really think it was that small—it did not begin and end with a tiny island off the coast of mainland Europe, for example—but something so conquerable should not have been such a puzzle. The problem with the world remained, for Edwin, completely elusive, its symptoms too frustratingly indecipherable to diagnose.

Eventually Edwin stopped going by Edwin. The name was too commonplace, made him feel like he was playing pretend, and he did not aspire to be common. He shrugged on Nothazai like a cloak, letting it secure him an aura of mystery, a sense that maybe he was something more than a normal human man and therefore pushing him closer to the miracle he'd been at birth. He learned of a man named Atlas Blakely, obviously weaned on a silver spoon, and the more Nothazai's heartsickness twisted—the more cases of inequity he could not solve, the more aristocratic priggery he could not unravel, the more people spoke about "their" country as if it had never been his—as if he had not been born in service to the very country "they" had done little to nothing for, coughing up phlegm from the compromised lungs he had so long tasked himself with saving—the more Nothazai buried himself in righteousness; in self-righteousness. In the knowledge that where others had failed, *he* would not. Where others were failing were merely others' failures. He, Nothazai, had an eye for corruption, and like he had once done for the body in which his cluster of potential greatness had been compiled, he, Nothazai, would be the one to suck the poison out.

In practical terms, of course, the day to day was deeply uninteresting. Legal briefs were filed. As were pages and pages of press briefings, his moniker scripted daily by the hundreds on official Forum statements, on critical website redesigns. Symposiums were given on diversity in the workplace. Staying at the forefront of evolutions in technomancy meant a lot of dull articles he read while falling asleep at his desk. Algorithms, free and transparent government, labor organizations, evidence to be presented in court. Sir, where would you like this pile awaiting your signature? Sir, Carla's on maternity leave, she's birthing some other cluster of future miracle that will surely overtake you at this glacial and thankless pace.

Nothazai had been glad, really, when Ezra Fowler dug up the thing he'd done to take part in the Bishops, the tiny bit of hazing that had gone horribly awry. (He'd known Spencer had a weak heart but how was he supposed to know how much heroin it could handle? He'd been sloshed out of his bleeding mind.) Everyone made mistakes and it wasn't like the world had lost much, just another son of a so-and-so who was a cousin of someone's Grace or Highness or some other somesuch, and anyway, Nothazai had already made his peace with it by then. He'd saved countless lives, won countless advancements in biomancer technology, and it had never been his fault to begin with—after all, Spencer's decisions weren't his.

But the library was real, and that was important. The Alexandrians were out there, and Ezra Fowler had handed it to him, the key to his personal echo chamber. To the knowledge Nothazai had always possessed, that he could and *would* remake the world—not the world that Ezra was so intent on saving, because who knew what the distant future even meant—but the world that Nothazai himself had lived in, which had been dying slowly from the start.

Who knew where the problems actually began? Institutional religion? Imperialism? The invention of the printing press or the steam engine, or was it irrigation? Why bother going that far back. The point was the library, the resources within it, which Nothazai was meant to access and to harness. He was born for this, to save humanity, and if he ever got access to the archives, he would be the savior to finally give that knowledge back.

Or.

("Not *him*," came a snarling woman's voice. "Isn't there someone else?")

Or.

("We have to take our country back!")

Or maybe it wasn't worth it, actually, putting that kind of information into the hands of capitalists like James Wessex, who had used his confirmation of the library's archives to go ahead and build some consciousness-exploding guns. It certainly did not belong in the hands of the United States government or the Chinese secret service—as if either country needed the go-ahead on further sullying the oceans and eventually destroying the sun. It belonged with the academics, of which his old friend Dr. Araña was one, but she had gone completely unhinged in recent months, and while Nothazai couldn't argue that her methodology was effective, there were certain rules about which despotic leaders you could or couldn't depose. (Again, look at the United States. Just because some things were objectively a nightmare didn't mean you were allowed to interfere.)

Nothazai understood implicitly that some people could not be saved. Some people could witness a miracle firsthand and still complain that its skin was too brown. That was the way of the world, had always been, and when he got the offer to take up the helm of the Society, he had already known the presence of opportunity. While standing in the ornate manor house, he had known it, the truth about what could be done. Written in the pulse of his chest was the knowledge that he could finally do it—he could end the secrecy, the tyranny of the chosen few, the oligarchy of academia and wealth that could change the trajectory of the world, rewrite it. He could force the Alexandrians into the light, revealing their ugly secrets, their institutional flaws. Their inherited ones. Both the real and proverbial weak chins.

But desire left him slowly, drained from him bit by bit, like the fading vestiges of light from the snakelike windows, the high slits along the hallowed halls of the sacred house. Nothazai walked by the portraits, the Victorian busts, the Neoclassical columns, and all of it faded into the cracks of a tired heart, the shadows of Nothazai's exhaustion. He knew it, deeply, like the cancer he knew he'd inherited. The ending that would find him one day. The future he could already foretell.

Humanity did not want to change. It did not deserve it.

He swallowed it down, knowing it was a door he couldn't turn back from. A truth he could never unsee.

In the moment that Nothazai turned his back on a miracle, he pushed open the doors to the reading room and found it already occupied. A young woman stood there, maybe mid-twenties, brown hair tied back in a ponytail, a simple skirt paired with unremarkable shoes. She had flat feet, something of a spine alignment problem. Nothazai didn't see doom written on her anywhere specific, but that didn't mean it wasn't there. Posture was very important.

"Oh," she said, a little startled. "Hi. Are you—?"

"The new Caretaker," Nothazai supplied for her, extending a hand politely. American accent. Ah yes, this was Elizabeth Rhodes, one of Atlas Blakely's pet physicists. He'd read her file. Very impressive, though she was exactly the problem, in Nothazai's view. All that power. All the people she could save. And instead she'd created a weapon, an unprecedented perfect fusion reaction, only to set off a fucking bomb. He could try her for treason if he were still at the head of the Forum, though it would only be a symbolic international court for violations of human rights and therefore condemnation would be more of a disapproval thing. A wag of a finger. *Not cool.*

In any case, he was not the Forum any longer. Good. He was sick of people, their lack of gratitude. Sick of people criticizing any good he tried to do. Maybe Elizabeth Rhodes was right to set it all ablaze and her only mistake had been in leaving everything mostly intact.

She shook his hand warily. "Are you the new researcher?" Nothazai asked her, because he had been told he would receive one, which was good. He did not plan to carry out his tenure attending to further tedium. Not when there was an ancient, all-knowing set of archives to explore.

"I—" She bit her lip, which struck him as an irritating tic. He hoped she did not do it often. He didn't hear the entirety of her answer, as he had not come here for small talk or the blustering of a girl half his age. She said something about waiting for a book, which, wonderful. He would set stricter parameters on who could use the archives later in the day.

Nothazai faced the pneumatic tubes with a thrill of anticipation. He had made a list, a long one, which he'd painstakingly narrowed down to a few select titles, some of which were lost to antiquity and some that were curiosities of his—Arabic medicinal texts that would supplement his theories. Hippocrates. Galen. Bogar. Shennong. Ibn Sina. Al-Zahrawi. Nothazai didn't do much biomancy these days; as a habit he routinely chose not to, because the results were always irritating. Lawsuits, several times. An almost unavoidable series of complaints, criticism that although lives had been saved and wounds had been healed, he hadn't done it quite perfectly enough. Nothing had dimmed Nothazai's opinion of mankind like healing the sick, and while he'd had to do it recently—as part of the deal that got him here, with the telepath who would likely need a mastectomy before her fortieth birthday, which would no doubt be a wound to her vanity but would save her life, a decision Nothazai did not care to take part in—he knew that good deeds never went unpunished. The young girl he'd saved, the cancer he'd removed for her, she'd be back for more someday. Maladies were endless. Life was hard. Someday she'd want his help again and he'd say no and she'd call him selfish, but what was life without a little selfishness? The only diagnosis for life was death— unless this library suggested otherwise, of course. In which case Nothazai wasn't going to waste what little time he'd ultimately have.

The tube system was simple enough. He and Elizabeth Rhodes stood beside each other in awkward but untroubled silence. There was something else in there, he realized. Some other genetic malady, some degenerative quality, unknown as yet whether it would affect her or merely her progeny over time. No use sharing that kind of information. What do you tell someone carrying around a little death? People were all vehicles for mortality, some more recklessly than others. As a matter of self-preservation, it was abjectly impractical to try.

As for Nothazai, he had gotten exactly what he wanted. The Alexandrian Society was now in his care. Perhaps he would leak some of his findings— the less critical ones, the consumable ones that humanity might like. Pictures of the hanging gardens of Babylon for someone to later claim were faked. The beauty secrets of Cleopatra, which would immediately be condemned for their crimes against feminism. Ha, Nothazai thought grimly. This was the real problem with the world. People looked at a miracle and thought wow, if only it were something else.

The man called Nothazai was right about this, of course.

Critically, though, he was also very wrong.

———

What Nothazai could not know in the moment that he and Libby Rhodes both received their respective responses from the archives was that she knew precisely who he was, and was currently battering herself with that knowledge. She had recently been a person who took it upon herself to fix the world's ills and yet there it was, another problem. Another set of unclean hands.

Libby Rhodes would, of course, *not* know that when Nothazai parted with Parisa Kamali, the telepath had already understood something important about the archives that she had not shared with anyone else, least of all him. (Parisa Kamali was not an honest person. Generally, it did not behoove her to tell the truth.)

Libby couldn't help a sidelong glance at Nothazai beside her. Specifically, at what the archives had bequeathed at his request. At the moment that Libby considered herself to be surreptitious, Nothazai would detect what he believed to be a glint of sardonic laughter in her eye, though perhaps it was merely the low light. In lieu of continuing the conversation, he would stride quickly out of the reading room, not pausing until he stood in the corridor, the paper unfurling in his hand with the softness of a petal, and Edwin Sanjrani, born a miracle, would take it like a stab of irony—the damning slam of a cosmic gavel.

Libby Rhodes knew the feeling well, because she had received the same message before. Several times, in fact. REQUEST DENIED. She would see the little slip of paper in his hands and recognize the prison Nothazai had built for himself; the same one Libby had willingly entered, and the one that had been Atlas Blakely's inescapable end. The library had a sense of humor, which Libby Rhodes knew for certain—for wretched, absolute fact.

Because this time, unlike all the other times, the archives would finally grant her wish.

Could I have saved my sister?

(How many people had she betrayed in search of an answer?)

Here, offered the archives in something of a hissing whisper, temptation coiling tighter.

Open the book and find out.

· END ·

You understand, of course, that everything out of Atlas Blakely's mouth at the time of his demise is the testimony of a dying man. The eulogizing of the person he might have been. Pardon the narcissism, but if a man can't rhapsodize himself in a moment of certain doom, when exactly can he? He poses the question of betrayal because he already knows he is a traitor. He posits that you alone can understand his story because, frankly, he already knows you can. When you were born, the world was already ending. In fact, it's already over.

It's just you and Atlas now.

· · ·

In Atlas Blakely's final moments, he doesn't see his life flash before his eyes. He doesn't see all the versions of lives unlived, the many paths he left untaken. The worlds he tasked himself with making that he will never see; the outcomes he tasked himself with seeking that he will never truly understand. It doesn't matter. If the human mind is good at anything—and Atlas does know the human mind—it is the projection of alternative realities, the thing that some people call regret and others call wonder. The thing that anyone who has ever looked at the stars has come to observe. Atlas's is a very human psyche, and so it is irreparably fragmented in some ways, regenerated more perfectly in others. If people are good or if they are bad, Atlas Blakely doesn't know. He is and has always been both.

Hard to say if Atlas is still making a desperate play at redemption. There's a lot on the line, what with the unknowable nature of consciousness and how it will feel to blink out as if he never existed at all. He does have a series of misfiring neurons and he can hear your opinion of him as plainly as if you nailed it to the door, so the circumstances for his confession are not exactly ideal. Then again, you don't get to pick your audience. You don't get to choose how you take your final bow.

Could he have done anything differently? Yes, probably, maybe. Unclear how much it matters, the alternative routes. Maybe they're left untaken for a reason. Maybe we're all just swimming around in the mind of a giant or a computer simulation after all. Maybe what we think of as humanity is just statistics in action, pattern recognition in a time loop that none of us can actually control. Maybe the archives dreamed you up for their own amusement. Maybe these aren't the questions you should be asking yourself. Maybe you should put aside the fireballs and calm the fuck down.

· · ·

Before she dies, Alexis Lai tells Atlas Blakely *don't waste it*. But before that, she says something else. Not aloud, because the things we say out loud traverse a lot of filters to get there (usually). But in her head, Alexis plants a seed that bears fruit that only Atlas can see. He fails to understand it, of course, in something of a willful stubbornness that is either his Achilles' heel or just, you know, an everyday, non-prophetic sort of problem, but he carries it around for just long enough that he can hold it here in his head—a drop of sweetness to melt fortuitously on his tongue. It's similar to what Ezra Fowler thinks in the moments before his death. At a certain point, you really have to give up on the question of existence. It all just starts to funnel inward, tighter and tighter, until the only thing you can possibly summon to wonder is hm, will it hurt?

But right before that, there's a little bubble of clarity that, for Alexis, is the sudden craving for soup dumplings. They're a street food she likes because they remind her of a perfect day spent making perfect choices, like soup dumplings and comfortable shoes and remembering to pack a raincoat, just in case. For Ezra, it's a note in a song that his mother liked to sing, something she hummed to herself while she did the dishes. Catchy pop, because life is too short to be too cool for disco. Too unpredictable not to sing along to boy band serenades.

For Atlas, the thing is the slight treacle stickiness of something mislaid among the crumbling monuments to his mother's fractured genius. He has just come from a university lecture. Well, more accurately he has just come from work, but before that it was the lecture, right after breaking up with the girlfriend whose new boyfriend will later cheat on her until she pines for the thing she once had with Atlas, which of course Atlas will never know. At the lecture, Atlas sat and listened, doing the telepath thing where he listens to the things people decide not to say and deeming them more important, even though choice is the crux of it. What leaves your tongue is what you actually control. So he's observing the thought in the professor's mind which is holy shit that lad in the back row looks just like me, how odd, I suppose I do miss what's-her-name, before dissolving into the frivolity of a man reliving tawdry desk sex with a faceless student after hours. Years will pass, the possibility of new worlds will bloom without his knowledge, and the man called Professor Blakely will never discover that the only takeaway his son will get from meeting him is that life is meaningless and people are total crap.

Until Atlas comes home to his passed-out mother, that is.

Until, specifically, he finds the Alexandrian Society's calling card waiting patiently beside the bin.

. . .

So that's where it ends. A treacle-slick of gin and hope.

You'd like to think it's more romantic, wouldn't you? Life and death, meaning and existence, purpose and power, the weight of the world. We are stardust on earth, we are impossible beings—the moral of the story shouldn't revolve so absurdly on the behaviors of a condom or the decision one man makes to buy a gun and act out his hate. And yet it does, because what else can matter?

The world as you believe it to exist is not a thing. The world is not an idea, something to be made or exalted or saved. It is an ecosystem of other people's pain, a chorus of other people's street foods, the variety of magic that people can make with the same set of chords. The world is pretty simple, in the end. People are bad. People are good. Inescapably there will be people, some who will disappoint you, some who will define you, unravel you, inspire you. These are facts. In every culture there is bread, and it is good.

There is power to be taken if you wish to seek it. Knowledge to be gained if you really want to know. You should be warned, though, whatever else you take from this, that knowledge is always carnage. Power is a siren song, bloodstained and miserly hoarded. Forgiveness is not a given. Redemption is not a right. It eats away at you, the things you know. The price you pay, and it will be costly, is yours to bear alone. For all you cast aside for glory, what prize could ever be enough?

Which is not to say stop seeking. Which is not to say stop learning. Make the next world better. Take the next right step.

Though, as a matter of professional courtesy, one last cautionary tale from a dying man: the power you have will never be enough compared to the power you'll always lack.

Do you understand? Are you listening?

. . .

Put the book away, Miss Rhodes. You won't find what you're looking for in there.

CREDITS

The book you've just read would not have been possible without the talent, dedication, and time devoted by every member of my unparalleled publishing team. It is the honor of my life to have worked with each one of them, and they all deserve proper recognition for the unique expertise and endless man-hours they spent bringing this trilogy to life. Without the following people, this book would very simply not exist.

EXECUTIVE EDITOR Lindsey Hall
AGENT Amelia Appel
ASSISTANT EDITOR Aislyn Fredsall
PUBLISHER Devi Pillai
EDITORIAL DIRECTOR Claire Eddy
EDITORIAL DIRECTOR Will Hinton
ASSOCIATE PUBLISHER Lucille Rettino
PUBLICITY MANAGER Desirae Friesen
EXECUTIVE DIRECTOR OF PUBLICITY Sarah Reidy
EXECUTIVE DIRECTOR OF MARKETING Eileen Lawrence
MARKETING DIRECTOR Emily Mlynek
ASSISTANT MARKETING MANAGER Gertrude King
SENIOR MARKETING MANAGER Rachel Taylor
ILLUSTRATOR Little Chmura
COVER DESIGNER Jamie Stafford-Hill
INTERIOR DESIGNER Heather Saunders
PRODUCTION EDITOR Dakota Griffin
MANAGING EDITOR Rafal Gibek
PRODUCTION MANAGER Jim Kapp
ASSOCIATE DIRECTOR OF PUBLISHING OPERATIONS Michelle Foytek
ASSOCIATE DIRECTOR OF PUBLISHING STRATEGY Alex Cameron
PUBLISHING STRATEGY COORDINATOR Rebecca Naimon
PUBLISHING STRATEGY ASSISTANT Lizzy Hosty
SUBRIGHTS MANAGER Chris Scheina
SENIOR DIRECTOR, TRADE SALES Christine Jaeger

MACMILLAN AUDIO PRODUCER Steve Wagner

VOICE TALENT

James Cronin

Siho Ellsmore

Munirih Grace

Daniel Henning

Andy Ingalls

Caitlin Kelly

Damian Lynch

David Monteith

Samara Naeymi

Steve West

Tor UK

PUBLISHER Bella Pagan

EDITORIAL DIRECTOR Sophie Robinson

EDITOR Georgia Summers

EDITORIAL ASSISTANT Grace Barber

COMMUNICATIONS DIRECTOR Claire Evans

HEAD OF MARKETING Jamie Forrest

SENIOR MARKETING EXECUTIVE Becky Lushey

MARKETING MANAGER Eleanor Bailey

INTERNATIONAL COMMUNICATIONS EXECUTIVE Lucy Grainger

HEAD OF DIGITAL MARKETING Andy Joannou

HEAD OF PUBLICITY Hannah Corbett

PUBLICIST Jamie-Lee Nardone

PUBLICITY ASSISTANT Stephen Haskins

PRODUCTION MANAGER Holly Sheldrake

SENIOR PRODUCTION CONTROLLER Sian Chilvers

DESK EDITOR Rebecca Needes

COVER DESIGNER (UK) Neil Lang

SALES DIRECTOR Stuart Dwyer

BOOKSHOP & WHOLESALE MANAGER Richard Green

SALES MANAGER Rory O'Brien

SALES DIRECTOR Leanne Williams

INTERNATIONAL SALES MANAGER Joanna Dawkins

SENIOR SALES EXECUTIVE Poppy Morris

INTERNATIONAL SALES AND MARKETING ASSISTANT Beth Wentworth

HEAD OF SPECIAL SALES Kadie McGinley

AUDIO PUBLISHING DIRECTOR Rebecca Lloyd
AUDIO PUBLISHING ASSISTANT Nick Griffiths
AUDIO EDITOR Molly Robinson
CONTENT MARKETING EXECUTIVE Carol-Anne Royer
VIDEO AND INFLUENCER MARKETING MANAGER Emma Oulton
POST ROOM STAFF Chris Josephs

ACKNOWLEDGMENTS

The truth is I wrote this trilogy from a place of rage. When I began working on *The Atlas Six,* the forty-fifth president was still in office and any semblance of rule of law—or human decency—seemed to have vanished completely from sight. The most common cause of death for children in the United States was then, and is now, gun violence. A recently released carbon report had suggested we had a decade or less to avoid climate scenarios best described as "dire." As I continued writing the series, *Roe v. Wade* was overturned, and for the first time, we found ourselves with fewer rights than the women of previous generations. Instead of solving world hunger, the world's richest man bought a social media site and ran it into the ground. Rather than fighting for the planet—rather than preventing the aforementioned *dire* climate scenarios—an astonishing number of my country's politicians instead mobilized the full force of their political capital against a demographic so vulnerable it makes up less than one percent of the total population.

I wanted a baby for reasons related to my deep love for my partner and some silly hormonal uprisings from my cruel, cruel corporeal cage, but how could I ever justify it—bringing a life into a world where I couldn't promise bodily autonomy, or basic safety, or even the comfortable lifespan that I myself will likely get?

What even matters, I asked myself in exasperation, if the fucking world is ending? And why should we bother to go on?

The answer, of course—the answer that took me three books to write—is that the world is not ending. *The world* will live on. We mythologize ourselves, it's what we do as humans, but ultimately we are expendable. We, and our personal comfort, are not the reason this planet makes food and water. We are not the only species that counts—at best, we are only the caretakers. What matters, then, is how we treat each other. What matters is who we are to each other, and what choices we make with the resources we are given.

So I thought: okay, I'll write a book where the whole story is just . . . six people. The relationships will be the plot, because relationships are all that matter. They're all we can ever take with us. They're the only real things we leave behind. I already knew it would require an unconventional execution, writing what was essentially a slice-of-life story against a fantastical setting, the scope of which I planned to expand with every book. I knew it would be hard to explain—the way it was not a romance and yet profoundly, entirely romantic. The way each character would be their own unreliable narrator, because as in life, the lies we tell ourselves are just as important as the truth. I knew it would require a particular audience, one that was willing to go along with a story that was part thriller, part prolonged philosophical rumination; as a reading experience, it would call for fluid, shifting sympathies and total submission to a pulpy web of ethical derelicts masquerading as magic nerds.

Impossible, I thought, and merrily self-published.

But then—the unexpected twist! You read it. In fact, *so many of you* read it that now, astoundingly, this book is in your hands bearing accolades I would never have dreamed, telling a story about anger and hopelessness as honestly and resiliently as I knew how.

(Which is to say through the mouths of six liars, because I'm not above a little camp.)

I have to once again thank my agent, Amelia Appel, and my editor, Lindsey Hall, for everything they've done to help me bring this story to life. Thanks to both of you, I get the unbelievable, hugely improbable chance to tell more stories, which even on the best of days is all I'm really fit to do. Thank you to Molly McGhee for helping me believe this one in particular was a story worth telling. And thank you Aislyn Fredsall, and/or I'm sorry, for being somewhat less willingly assigned to the glorious pipeline of ruminations to come.

Enormous thanks to the translators and editors who've brought this book to the rest of the world in the many, many languages I can't speak: thank you endlessly for living in my words and for telling my story for me.

Thank you to Dr. Uwe Stender and the rest of the team at Triada. Thank you to Katie Graves and Jen Schuster at Amazon Studios and Tanya Seghatchian and John Woodward of Brightstar for being my creative partners.

Thank you to my family—to my mom who is so supportive, my sisters who have always been such fans, my ninang who doesn't read my books because she knows it's not her thing (she's right, and it's genuinely for the best that she doesn't). Thank you to babies Andi and Eve for joining the cult, and to all the boys I love so much: Theo, Eli, Miles, Ollie, Clayton, Harry, and their parents (whom I also love). Thank you to Zac once again for lending Gideon your name. Thank you to David, my very best friend. To

Nacho, who either made all of this happen or just very powerfully knew it would, and Ana. To Stacie. To Angela. To the friends I've made along the circuit, the many talented authors who've considered me a peer even when I would've gladly kissed their feet. To Julia: you know why.

Thank you to the good citizens of social media and the bookish communities I've had the pleasure of meeting across the interwebs and IRL: I am Mr. Knightley on the floor. So many of you took the time and effort to tell someone, everyone, to *read this book,* and we are only sitting here today because you did that. I am bereft of words to tell you how grateful I am, how humbled and awkward and permanently (pleading eyes emoji) as a result of every single one of you. Genuinely, I hope the previous 170,000 will suffice because I jammed a lot of my soul in there. Do with it what you will, it's yours now.

Thank you to Garrett, my love, and Henry, my darling. You are what matters. You are my answers. I am so grateful to know beyond a shadow of a doubt.

Finally, thank you to you, Reader, for being here, for following me this far and listening to me this long. I understand that writing a book rooted in political rage hasn't technically solved any of the problems I mentioned earlier. There is something to be said, though, for inspiration and for trying to put words to the collective consciousness when we get the chance. I hope that while reading this book, you thought about something, about the nature of ethics and culpability, about the best way to honor our relationships to each other, or just about what the next step might look like, to be ready when it makes itself known. I hope you felt something, whether it was something new or just giving a name to the way the thing in your chest ticks, about what it beats for. Though, if neither of those things apply, then I hope you got a few diverting hours out of it, because living as deliciously as possible is one of the finest luxuries we're allowed.

With love and admiration, and also, betrayal and revenge,

Olivie

RELATED READING

An incomplete list, if you're interested—incomplete because I did not think anyone would be interested at the time I self-published the first book, and thus did not take appropriately detailed records—of books I read while I was contemplating subjects and themes for the Atlas series:

Helgoland: Making Sense of the Quantum Revolution by Carlo Rovelli
The Order of Time by Carlo Rovelli
The Tao of Physics by Fritjof Capra
Genesis: The Story of How Everything Began by Guido Tonelli
"Death Comes (and Comes and Comes) to the Quantum Physicist"
    by Rivka Ricky Galchen in *The Believer* (available online at
    thebeliever.net)
Under a White Sky: The Nature of the Future by Elizabeth Kolbert
Man and His Symbols by Carl G. Jung
The Blind Watchmaker by Richard Dawkins
*The Book of Immortality: The Science, Belief, and Magic Behind Living
    Forever* by Adam Leith Gollner
On Liberty by John Stuart Mill
Republic by Plato
*Zeno's Paradox: Unraveling the Ancient Mystery Behind the Science of Space
    and Time* by Joseph Mazur
The Dawn of Everything: A New History of Humanity by David Graeber
    and David Wengrow
At the Existentialist Café: Freedom, Being, and Apricot Cocktails
    by Sarah Bakewell
Myths from Mesopotamia: Creation, The Flood, Gilgamesh, and Others
    translated by Stephanie Dalley
What Does It All Mean? A Very Short Introduction to Philosophy
    by Thomas Nagel
*Greek Thought, Arabic Culture: The Graeco-Arabic Translation Movement
    in Baghdad and Early 'Abbāsid Society (2nd–4th/8th–10th Centuries)*
    by Dimitri Gutas